TREGIAN'S
GROUND

TREGIAN'S GROUND

The Life and Sometimes Secret Adventures of Francis Tregian, Gentleman and Musician

ANNE CUNEO

TRANSLATED BY

*Roland Glasser &
Louise Rogers Lalaurie*

LONDON · NEW YORK

First published in 2015 by And Other Stories
London – New York
www.andotherstories.org

First published as *Le trajet d'une rivière* in 1993 by Bernard Campiche Éditeur,
Switzerland, and in 1994 by Editions Denoël, France.
© Anne Cuneo, 1993, 2013

English-language translation © Roland Glasser and Louise Rogers Lalaurie, 2015

Manuscript page from Francis Tregian's *Virginal Book* on p 14
reprinted courtesy of the Fitzwilliam Museum, Cambridge

Document in the hand of Francis Tregian on p 246 reprinted courtesy
of the Henderson Collection, Truro, Document No HC/2/27

ISBN 9781908276544
eBook ISBN 9781908276551

A catalogue record for this book is available from the British Library.

Supported using public funding by
**ARTS COUNCIL
ENGLAND**

CONTENTS

PREFATORY NOTES

A 'recusant' was someone who refused to attend the services of the Church of England (from the Latin *recusare* – to refuse). For a long time, the term was applied, by extension, to English Catholics, who comprised the largest number of recusants.

The spelling 'Monteverdi' is a relatively recent trend. The great musician was called Claudio Monte Verde or Monteverde in his time and signed himself 'Monteverde'. Francis Tregian invariably writes the name as 'Monteverde'. In *Tregian's Ground* we choose to restore this usage.

All the epigraphs are lyrics sung to music copied out by Francis Tregian in one or other of his manuscripts.

With the exception of Horatio's speech on p 295, all Shakespeare quotations are from the First Folio of 1623, compiled by Shakespeare's and Tregian's contemporaries John Hemmings and Henry Condell.

The translators of this first English edition have made every effort to restore the original English documents and literary texts quoted from and referred to throughout. Original French extracts, including passages from Montaigne, have been given new English translations here. Texts quoted from other languages have been rendered into English from the author's own, French translations in the original novel.

A reading group guide written by Anne Cuneo is available for free download from And Other Stories' website: www.andotherstories.org.

TREGIAN'S
GROUND

The most credible thing our reason advises us is generally that everyone should obey the laws of their land . . . And what does our reason mean by this if not that our duty is ruled by none other than fortune? . . . What would philosophy have us do in such a pass? Follow the laws of our country? That is to say this heaving sea of opinions of a people or of a prince, painting justice in as many colours and reforging it with as many faces as they will have changes of passion? I cannot have so flexible a judgement. What goodness is it which I saw yesterday revered and tomorrow no more, and which a river's crossing makes a crime?

MICHEL DE MONTAIGNE
'Apology for Raymond de Sebonde'
Essays, Book II, chapter XII

BOOK I

Walsingham Way

As you came from the Holy Land of Walsingham
Met you not with my true love by the way as you came?
How should I know your true love that have met many a one.
As I came from the Holy Land, that have come, that have gone.

'WALSINGHAM'
POPULAR BALLAD

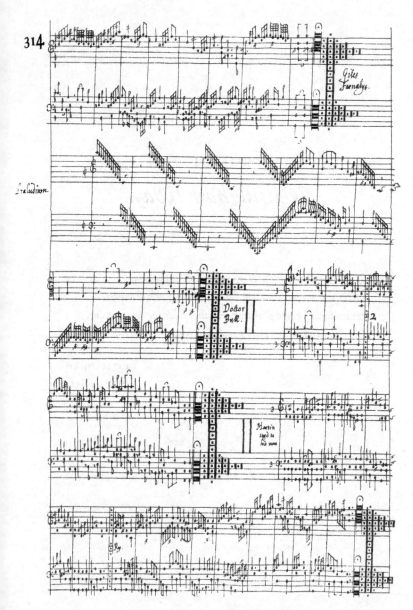

Manuscript page from Francis Tregian's *Virginal Book*

I

Cantai un tempo, e   *Once I sang, and*
Se fu dolce il canto,   *That song was sweet*
Questo mi tacerò   *But now I must cease*
Ch'altri il sentiva.   *Lest others hear.*

PIETRO BEMBO / MONTEVERDE
'SECONDO LIBRO DEI MADRIGALI'

IT IS STRANGE, but I thought of England only this morning.

Daybreak comes early this time of year, and the weather is glorious. I was awoken by an unusual flapping in the henhouse. A fox perhaps? I scurried downstairs as fast as my legs would allow and crossed the yard. Neither the maidservant nor Madame Dallinges was up yet, and there was but a single red ember glowing in the hearth.

No fox.

I was about to return to bed, when I noticed the sky. It was of a pale blue unusual in these parts, dotted with sparse, milky clouds like those that form along the coast in my own country just before dawn. They disappear over the course of the day, if the weather is fine, absorbed by the heat or scattered by the winds.

The earth exhaled a dewy scent, a nightingale sang, and the reddening dawn behind the Jura peaks heralded another radiant day.

For a moment I was transported to the countryside around Wolvedon Manor, as it was when I was a child. I could almost feel the sea-spray and hear the lapping of the waves.

I was brought back to the present by the footsteps of Jaquotte, the maid, who had entered the kitchen and was busying herself around the fire. Madame Dallinges came down next, and as usual I offered to fetch water from the well. As usual she declined.

I thought no more about Wolvedon after that. Just a faint, sweet melancholy lingered. I most certainly did not take it as a premonition.

After matins, I got on with my work, and as usual remained absorbed therein until the angelus struck at noon.

It's been nearly a quarter of a century that I've lived here now, and I still go for a walk at this time, up to the Crossing of the Ways, a crust of bread in my pocket, sometimes a book too. I sit beneath the great linden tree, on a bench I built myself. I can spend hours here, and often do, particularly at this time of year. Asked what I do up at the Crossing, I sometimes say that I go there to pray, and indeed there is a cross by the side of the road, a little way from the linden tree. But truth be told, I am content to let my thoughts wander, and if I do happen to talk with God, it's on friendly terms, man to man, so to speak. People on their way to the lake prefer the Drovers' Road, which is wider and takes the shorter, steeper route down. But going in the opposite direction, it is well known that the climb is gentler on this side. The road takes you via Morges, but the longer way is worth it, particularly if you're heavily laden. I see riders and coaches pass by from time to time, and sometimes people on foot. They come from the surrounding villages, from Lausanne or Geneva, and are generally returning to Echallens, or travelling to Yverdon or Payerne, even to Berne. Occasionally, they travel in the other direction. Some faces are unfamiliar, but most are well known to me.

I heard this morning's two wayfarers approaching from far off. They came from the direction of Yverdon at a fair pace, deep in discussion. I couldn't make out what they were saying at first, but then their words struck me like an arrow through the heart: they were speaking English.

My first reaction – after so many years! – was panic. Had they seen me? Where could I hide? I managed to reason with myself: everyone has forgotten me after such a long time. Indeed it was probable that the two men drawing closer at a brisk pace, round-faced and bright-eyed, were born after my . . . after I had departed, shall we say.

And anyway, who would recognise the Francis of old, beneath this beard, these shabby clothes?

I composed myself before they reached me. My only protection was to make sure they didn't notice that I understood English.

Everyone in Echallens is convinced that when Benoît Dallinges brought me back in his cart all those years ago, I was returning home after losing my entire family to the plague. He was the only one in these parts who knew where I really came from, and why. But I must say that on this particular morning, it was hard indeed to pretend not to understand English.

The two travellers were called Thomas and John. Thomas (the memories connected with that name!) was a Cornish sailor: I could tell by his accent and appearance. If I uttered but three words in English, he would likely know me for a fellow countryman. He and his companion were going to Genoa. I didn't quite grasp why they were travelling on foot, since they spoke only a primitive sort of French, picked up on the road, no doubt. I attempted to question them without giving myself away, and they tried to answer using their limited vocabulary. They soon returned to their debate, taking no more notice of me.

And that's when I understood – my pen can hardly form the words, the thing is so incredible: England had abolished the monarchy and Charles, the King himself, had been arrested!

John was an Anglican and Thomas a Puritan, but that didn't stop them being friends. They had agreed to travel to Genoa on behalf of an English ship-owner, and had followed the Salt Route, by way of Vallorbe. Now they were going to Lausanne, before taking the road to the Piedmont. Their opinions on the causes of the civil war differed, but they were in complete agreement regarding the facts: the King reigns no more, England is a sort of republic called the Commonwealth, power is held by the House of Commons, the Lords do their bidding and there is even talk of abolishing them. The Church of England is persecuted by the Puritans, or is it the other way round? I found it impossible to comprehend fully what they were saying, or to place all of the names. The Head of State is one Oliver Cromwell, a descendant of that other, no doubt, who was a great friend of my grandfather John. I gathered that Cromwell has repealed the laws against recusants, as those of us who remained Catholic are called. But perhaps I was mistaken and confused my desires with reality.

I would have liked to meet these compatriots again, and draw them out, so I asked them – not directly, mind you – if they were staying awhile in our part of the world. They didn't think so.

I had to make a superhuman effort not to press them with questions:

how does the Commonwealth operate? What is happening in the army? The fleet? The Church?

When I returned home, after they had gone, Madeleine Dallinges asked if I was ill.

'Just a little indisposed, it's nothing,' I replied, wishing to be left in peace.

I went upstairs, and here I sit at my table.

When Dallinges rescued me from the roadside, half-dead and consumed by fever, he heard me raving in English.

'Where are you from?' he asked, when I was fit enough to talk.

'From . . . from Venice.'

'What is your name?'

'Pietro Ricordi.'

He made no comment. But he must have seen I was not telling the truth, for I have never been a very good liar.

'Are you Catholic or Protestant?'

I was reluctant to answer. What if this stranger was a fanatic from the opposing camp? But judging by his portliness and his gentle grey eyes, I knew instinctively that this was an equable fellow.

'Catholic,' I muttered.

'Well, in that case I'll take you home with me. I live just outside Echallens. We're Catholics too. It's not like Geneva, out here in the countryside. If you are happy to attend Mass and pray quietly, nobody bothers you. Not that there aren't any fanatics here – there are. Two or three years ago there was very nearly open war between Berne and Fribourg, but things quietened down, thank the Lord. We are not so concerned with such matters. Personally, I think it absurd that people kill each other over religion when we are all good Christians, pious believers. All these endless squabbles about whether to make the altar out of stone or wood, whether it should be placed here or there. Take our priest: in the middle of conducting a Protestant funeral, he tells the grieving family that anyone following the reformed religion will be damned anyway. Or the pastor, who scurries off to Berne to complain at the drop of a hat. Like senseless children, I sometimes think. If we were heathens, I might understand.'

He glanced at me, as if suddenly realising that he shouldn't be sharing his innermost thoughts with a stranger who might be a spy. But doubtless I looked no more a spy than he did a fanatic.

'If you'd been a Protestant,' he went on, 'I'd have left you with one of my cousins, who is of the reformed faith. We discuss religion from time to time, he and I, but we never quarrel. We see each other about; our paths cross at church. . . . '

'How so?'

'Well, you see, there's just one church for all the villages in the Echallens bailiwick. On Sundays the Catholics go there first, for Mass, followed by the Protestants for the preaching.'

Hearing this calm voice talk of a single church for Catholics and Protestants as if it were the most natural thing in the world, I felt I had reached the right place. I let go, and fell into a deep sleep. I was safe.

We journeyed on for some time before he asked me another question:

'What is your profession?'

'I have been a courtier. And a merchant. I have been to war, and made music too.'

'What sort of music?'

'I play the organ and the virginal.'

'I've never heard of the virginal.'

'It's the name given in England to a certain type of keyed instrument, similar to the spinet, the muselaar or the harpsichord, but set in a case so that it may be carried easily. They're very popular. I have learned how to make them, too.'

'Would you know how to restore an organ?'

'I believe so.'

'You can read and write, I suppose?'

'Yes.'

'Well there's reason enough to take you to Echallens. I shall hire you to repair our organ. That'll set the Protestants on edge, right enough.' He chuckled. 'Can you copy music?'

For a moment, it seemed he was reading my past.

'Perfectly,' I admitted finally. 'I have always copied my favourite scores.'

'Then there's work for you in Echallens. Now, before I bring you home and take you in as a brother, under the roof I share with my wife and children, I wish to know what it is you fear, what it is you are fleeing. And I would like the truth. Your name is not Pietro Ricordi and you are not Italian.'

He sensed my hesitation.

'I swear to you before God that I will not tell a soul, not even my family.'

This man had rescued me. He had trusted me and cared for me purely out of kindness, without trying to discover who I was. I hesitated no longer.

'My name is Francis Tregian. I am English. I escaped from prison but I am not a criminal, neither a killer nor a robber. On the contrary, it is I who have been robbed. My only wrong was to be my father's son, and Catholic. I am given for dead; and if those from whom I wished to escape knew that I were alive, they might try to kill me. But I would like to live, in peace, far from wars and feuding.'

I told him everything.

He made no comment apart from clicking his tongue at the most dramatic points.

'You speak French perfectly,' he said, by way of conclusion.

'Yes, it's a gift, I believe – my musical ear. In the Low Countries nobody knows by my accent that I am not Dutch. In Reims I pass for a local. In Italy I am as Italian as the next man.'

'Perfect. We will speak no more of England; and while we're at it, you don't speak English. Take one of our local names and keep your Christian name. I know some Tréhans in Rances. You could call yourself François Tréhan.'

'No, it's too much like my real name.'

'True. Then you could be François Cousin, a distant relative who has lived in Italy. My wife's name is Cousin.'

'Cousin is an English name too.'

'Is that so? Well there are more Cousins than Dallinges in these parts, I know that for a fact. Another reason for you to take the name. Agreed?'

There was no other choice for the time being.

Things fell naturally into place. People forgot that I was ever not one of them as they saw me working in the church and at the register office, met me at the Dallinges house, came up to the Crossing to share their thoughts or cares, to seek my counsel or to have me read or write private letters. The Dallinges children called me Uncle François from the very first day, and now their own children call me Grandfather. I occupy a spacious room in the loft of the Dallinges cask workshop. It contains a writing table as well as a workbench for repairing the instruments that people bring me from far and wide; I build new ones too.

Dallinges presented me with three small, stout volumes that he had found in Lausanne, where his business sometimes took him: the *Essays* of Michel de Montaigne. It was like seeing an old friend again. I soon spoke French with the local accent, and I learned the patois. The whole region knows me as François Cousin, instrument maker and scribe, originally from the village of Corcelles. That is how I was registered by the officials of both Berne and Fribourg. It was under this name that Dallinges introduced me to the priest, the pastor and the local parishioners.

He never brought up the subject of my past again, but every now and then he would prompt me:

'François, you should write your story. Few people have had a life like yours.'

'Who would I write it for?'

'For posterity. For me. For yourself.'

I shrugged.

'It wouldn't interest anyone. And anyway, I'm no writer.'

He did not press the matter but, one day, doubtless returning from Lausanne, he brought me a ream of paper.

'For you. For your memoirs,' he said.

That was many years ago.

I have always kept this paper. Until this morning, I never dreamed of using it.

But those two Englishmen. And that clear Cornish sky.

I am ready. The tale must have been ripening within me, ever since the first time Dallinges suggested I write it down.

There are two difficulties, however. First, I have never been able to express myself: I have always relied on the words or the music of others to define me. And second, I have no idea which language to write in. It's been a good quarter of a century since I last spoke English, and even when I talk with God, it's in Italian or French.

But I feel the company of my departed friends and companions close about me, reading over my shoulder. I am writing for all of us. And for us, French, Latin, Italian, Dutch or English – what difference does it make?

II

In Peascod time when hound to horn
Gives ear till buck be killed
And little lads with pipes of corn
Sit keeping beasts afield.

'PEASCOD TIME'
POPULAR BALLAD

THE WIND RUFFLES MY HAIR, the sun dazzles my eyes. I am chewing a stray stem of wheat, so I think that the memory must fall between harvest and aftermath, the fresh growth of the new crop, towards late August or early September.

'Francis! Come here!'

Jane, my nurse, is calling to me. Jane with her autumn-red hair and lake-blue eyes. I hear her, but I cannot see her.

'Get up, lazy boy, come here.'

I roll over in the stubble, pricking my back, knees and hands. I long to walk. A blank. And then I am tottering through the furrows. The wind caresses my face and tugs at Jane's skirt. She stands, smiling with delight, arms outstretched:

'Wonderful, Francis! Come on. No, don't stop, come on, come here.'

I am amazed. I walk, propelling myself forward. I take a step, then another, and still I haven't fallen over.

'One last try, little man, one more step, and another . . . ' I end up in the safe haven of Jane's arms. She smells of bread fresh from the oven, the sky, the warm earth and the milk she feeds me.

She covers me in kisses.

'Bravo, Master Francis. Well done!'

The rooftops of Golden Mill lie silhouetted on the horizon – my horizon. Despite the name, there has been no mill there for a very long time. Golden is what everyone calls Wolvedon Manor. Everyone except my father. I know the manor is home to my mother and my sister Mary. My father is mostly absent, in London or Lanherne, two unknown places that together mean just one thing to me – 'far away'.

As far as I can tell, this is my earliest memory, there in the wheat field.

I was born – so I was told – in the fifteenth year of the reign of Elizabeth. If so, I must have come into this world in winter or early spring at the latest, for I believe a child must be at least eighteen months old to walk.

I began to talk around Christmastime of that year, and I had a new brother, Adrian. People came to fetch me for his baptism, and we went with great pomp and style to the church in Probus.

I have only vague memories of the day. My father was in London and my mother organised the ceremony as well as a reception with music and dancing. I received my first cuff on the ear for failing to recognise her, and a second immediately after for crying in front of my grandmother Anne, a great lady who lived in Lanherne. There were a great many people. The adults seated themselves at the table in the great hall, and we little ones had to leave with our nurses. To my great relief, Adrian was placed with a different nurse from me.

My mother had just turned twenty. She was small and pale with black hair and large hazel eyes. She managed the house and the estates. She oversaw the shearing, spinning, weaving and sewing, visited the sick, delivered the countrywomen's babies, went out in society and entertained at home. The ladies of the neighbouring estates all did the same. She was nervous, impatient, distant. We children were never allowed to distract her at inopportune moments. She was beset with constant worries – already the clouds were gathering on the horizon.

My father was a man of twenty-seven or twenty-eight. My memories of him are few and scattered. He only ever addressed me as Master Francis, rarely smiled, and delivered long lectures on the true faith and my responsibilities. To help me remember his lessons he had me whipped, or whipped me himself.

From as far back as I can remember, what impressed me most about him was his gaze. He had very blue eyes, deep-set and permanently grief-stricken, it seemed, but so lively and sharp, they immediately caught the attention. And curls of flaming red, like his pointed beard and moustache. To my child's eye he was very handsome, and I found out later that he had sparked more than a few passions.

Wolvedon had come to the family with the dowry of my great-grand-mother Jane Wolvedon, who married John Tregian in the reign of King Henry VIII. I am told our family name meant 'land of giants'. I believe it translates rather more prosaically as 'the estate of John' but, as a child, the other meaning had my wholehearted approval. Our size may have had something to do with it. The Tregian men were all over six feet, the women taller than average, and John's build and stature must have been great indeed because people still talked about it half a century after his death.

My images of Wolvedon from that time tend to mingle and blur. Coal-grey skies rolling with clouds swept along by furious winds. Bright intervals with sudden, dazzling sunshine. Labourers in the fields and miners returning home at dusk – the young men singing, the older men laughing among themselves. I see us coming back to Wolvedon in the dead of night, Jane clutching me close beneath her shawl, almost breaking into a run, out of breath. Where have we been? I don't remember. I see myself soaked to the skin, standing in front of the kitchen fire where Jane has set me down while she runs to fetch dry clothes.

I don't know how I came to feel constantly in danger. Maybe because in my father's house there were always people whispering in corners. I don't remember Cuthbert, the man who made my sense of danger a real-ity, as an ominous figure. He was gentle, affable, always bustling about, employed – I was told – as a steward on the estate. He often left to see to business at some far-flung property, always blessing me before setting off. And he delivered long lectures on the true faith, like my father.

I cannot be sure whether I attended Holy Mass before my third year. It seems reasonable to suppose that I did. But I have no recollection of it. Perhaps Cuthbert, with his gestures and murmured words, was reciting Mass?

My intellectual life began early. Jane often recounted the miracle: all of a sudden, I could read. And reading furnishes perhaps my richest source of memories. I am fascinated by people who write or read: Cuthbert; my father; his valet, Phillips; Jane, who often consulted her prayer book; and my grandmother, Catherine Tregian, widow of my grandfather John (my image of him is vague because he died when I was very young). My grandmother lived at the new manor house and she it was who spent an entire day patiently explaining the letters of the alphabet to me from a hornbook that had belonged to her son, my father. I can clearly remember the room, hung with fine tapestries. We must have been in Madam Catherine's private parlour. Everyone called her Madam Catherine. She was an Arundell, a scion of the richest and most powerful family in the region. I see myself now, sitting on her lap. The hornbook is a thin sheet about four or five inches by six or seven, clasped in a solid frame with a handle so that it can be held up like a mirror. The alphabet is inscribed at the top, above various combinations of letters. Finally, in the bottom half, is the paternoster.

'And what is this, madam?'

'The letter *p*, Francis. I'm tired now, be off with you.'

'Yes, madam. Just one more; this sign here.'

'It's a *t*, little one. Now that's enough. Get down.'

'Yes, madam. Just this letter here, though.'

'The boy's as stubborn as his father. I've already told you this letter. You should know it, now.'

'An *a*?'

'Yes, an *a*. And now Francis, get down from my knees and leave me be.'

I get down. Impossible to ignore the hint of a threat in her voice. I walk over to the door. But my eagerness is greater than my fear. I come back.

'Madam?'

'What now?'

'Will you teach me to write my name?'

'I said no, Francis, and no means no. Look at you; you can barely walk. And you should learn to talk properly before you think about writing.'

'Yes, Grandmother. I only wish to try.'

She gives in. She always gives in. She is forever cautioning the family not to 'spare the rod and spoil the child', but she never corrects me with the rod herself, for the simple reason, as I shall find out later, that I keep her amused.

•   •   •

THE MANOR AT GOLDEN is a vast place for a small boy like me. I am frightened of the shadows that steal over the floors in the bedchambers, which lie in darkness throughout the day. I prefer to visit the kitchens in the old manor house. There is always somebody there.

Golden consists of two manor houses. There is the new house built by my great-grandfather, where my parents lived with my grandmother Catherine and their household. It stands south of the road leading from Golden Mill to Probus, with buildings on three sides of a central courtyard. The fourth side is open to a tree-lined approach. The old manor is three or four hundred years old, I believe; it stands north of the road, diagonally opposite the new house, with its back to a raised field known to the country people as the Roman Camp. It is said locally that the old manor was once a convent. It is a tall, forbidding house with few windows, overlooking a series of outhouses arranged around an enclosed square yard, a remnant of the days when people had to protect themselves from wild animals, pirates or bands of robbers, and every lord's dwelling was fortified. The old manor is a farm, now, and a storehouse, with living quarters for a large number of servants. The old Great Hall has become the estate kitchen, a bustling, chaotic place.

Servants, housemaids, peasants, pages and ladies-in-waiting come and go all day long. It seems to me that everyone is talking or shouting at once, as they scurry in all directions.

Old Thomas is the only exception. He walks slowly, always with a stick. He has a gap-toothed smile and sparse white hair. People whisper that he is eighty years old, that he used to be my great-grandmother Jane's steward, that he was already a member of Jane Wolvedon's household when she brought it in dowry to John Tregian, before the new manor was built. It is also said, behind his back, that he had been madly in love with Jane Wolvedon. The gossips do not say whether Jane Wolvedon shared his feelings.

Old Thomas spends most of his time in the inglenook, by the fire. I am persuaded he sleeps there, too. He knows every last detail of the estates and, when seemingly intractable problems arise, he is always consulted. Even my father deigns to seek his opinion, now and again.

• • •

DESPITE HIS ADVANCED AGE, 'Old' Thomas still possesses a deep, firm voice. He knows all about the spirits that roam abroad, good and bad. And Lord knows, the Cornish countryside abounds in spirits of every shape and size. In the accents of his mother tongue, of which he has taught me the rudiments, he tells me all about Trebiggan.

'His arms were so long he had only to reach out and snatch men from the ships as they passed. And he fed on raw flesh every day. The number of children he must have devoured! No one knows how he died in the end. And hear this – they found his skeleton not so long ago.'

Once Old Thomas is set on the subject of monsters, there is no stopping him. He tells me about the legendary giant John of Gaunt, who left traces of his passing on Carn Brea hill near Redruth: the rocks you see there are known as the Giant's Coffin, Wheel, Head and Hand, even the Giant's Cradle. Cornwall is swarming with giants, if Thomas is to be believed. Our country even owes its name to them.

'They say that the name Cornwall comes from Corineus who received our land as a reward from Brutus of Trinovantum, which was the name for London at that time, after he defeated the giant Gogmagog in a bitter hand-to-hand struggle on the heights of Plymouth. Oh, what a fight it was! You should have seen it,' he declares, as if it had taken place at last year's Fair.

He looks at me, quite pleased with himself. I seize the opportunity to prompt him on one of my favourite subjects.

'Thomas, tell me about Cormoran.'

'Cormoran? He was the one who built St Michael's Mount. We call it *carreg luz en kuz* – which in our Cornish means "white rock in the forest". And halfway between the shore and the manor on its island, there is a great rock called Chapel Rock, but there's no chapel there now: it was crushed under the weight of the granite. The huge rock was dropped by Cormoran's wife. Her husband ordered her to build a manor house of white stone, but she had to travel far to find it and decided that our good greenish stone would do. Cormoran thought otherwise and, when he discovered what she had done, he gave his wife a great kick up the backside, and she was so shocked that she stumbled, and the strap of her leather apron broke and she dropped the rock she was carrying.'

'But Cormoran was beaten in the end? Killed?'

'Yes, Master Francis, by Jack, a brave boy like yourself. Jack lived near Land's End. Cormoran was running wild at the time, stealing the country folk's livestock. He slung the cows from his belt and heaved the big bulls onto his shoulders. Then he would go back to his castle on St Michael's Mount and devour the lot. That's when King Arthur offered a reward to anyone who would kill him. Jack thought hard about it, and he had an idea. He dug a great hole on dry land, just opposite St Michael's Mount, and covered it with branches and straw. Then he sounded his hunting horn and the giant hurried out to kill him – he couldn't bear anyone to come near his castle. But in his haste, Cormoran didn't see the trap, and he fell in head first. Then Jack struck him a mighty blow with his axe and filled in the hole as fast as he could, just in case the giant wasn't quite dead or had the magical power to come back to life.'

'Did he get a reward?'

'Of course. A magnificent sword and a belt embroidered with an inscription in threads of gold:

> *Behold the valiant Cornishman*
> *Who killed the Giant Cormoran.*

'Since that time, everyone has called him Jack the Giant Killer. A humble lad from Land's End! His fame extends beyond the seas.'

I hang on every word of Old Thomas's stories and dream of being a hero like Jack one day. Francis the Giant Killer – now there's a glorious title.

I LEARNED THE ALPHABET quite effortlessly and arithmetic almost without noticing. Latin and Greek, which were spoken all around me, I absorbed as naturally as Thomas's Celtic legends.

When I rejoined the household from the care of my nurse, what first baffled me were the blows that everyone felt entitled to deliver. My parents were either ignorant of the fact or, more likely, voiced no objection to it. But one day, when one of the ladies-in-waiting made ready to strike me, I found a way to stay her hand in mid-air. I looked straight at her, quite simply. She backed away, crossing herself and muttering:

'The Devil's Eyes.'

She was not the only one to think I might have been sent from Beelzebub himself, or Cormoran the Giant.

Old Thomas was ready with an explanation, of course. According to him, my eyes had come down to me in a direct line from Jane Wolvedon.

'Jane was the red-headed one. The Tregians all had black hair, and blue eyes too, but not like Jane's. I swear I was quite shaken the first time I saw you. I never thought I would see that look again – thought it was lost forever. But no, you have Jane Wolvedon's eyes.'

'And my sister Mary?'

'No, not your sister Mary, nor your little brother. Only you.'

'What was Jane like? Was she pretty?'

'She was the beauty of the whole world. Hair like copper, very white skin, small and neat, and yes, she bore four children with no apparent effort, all of them well built, and she was a tiny little thing. Though the fifth killed her, true to say. Her eyes were the first thing anyone noticed. People said she had a witch's eyes, just as some fools here say you have the Devil's eyes. But she was so kind, so bright and gay, always ready to help the poor; people soon forgot their fear of her looks. They loved her.'

For the first time in all his story-telling, I heard a tremor in Old Thomas's voice.

'Did you love her very much, Thomas?' I ventured.

'Ah, more than that.' He is talking to himself now. 'I cursed my fate that I was not born rich like John Tregian. I was a handsome young man. I had property – my father was a merchant. But Jane's father was a gentleman, and a gentleman will only give his daughter in marriage to another gentleman. I could not be her husband, so I became her steward.'

'And Jane?'

A long silence. I have overstepped the mark.

'You won't say anything?'

His voice is muted. I stare hard at him, having noticed that my gaze has the power to calm and reassure people, too.

'No, I swear by Our Lady herself.'

'We never told anyone; there would have been no point. She had been promised to John Tregian in her cradle, and they were married when she was just a little girl. Jane wished us to run away to London. Or France. We were all of the same religion in those days. I would have taken the risk. But Jane was of noble birth; we would have had her father, her husband, the King's soldiers, the whole of Cornwall on our heels. I loved her too much to impose on her a life of danger and poverty. But I was hers, body and soul. I never married; it would have felt like sacrilege. And since her death, I am a widower.'

A very long silence. Then Thomas breaks into a broad smile.

'But still, I know the secret of your looks. Your eyes are the gift of the piskies.'

'The piskies?'

'Sprites. The spirits of an extinct race that people say lived in ancient times, in the far west of Cornwall, at a place everyone believed was the edge of the world, Land's End. They're tiny and mostly well meaning. When newborn babies die, it is said they become piskies before they are transformed into Muryans.'

In Cornish legend, Muryans are tiny fairy creatures no bigger than ants. Which is why people never kill the hairy ants seen in the summer months.

'But what about Jane Wolvedon's eyes?'

'The piskies make enchanted ointments, you know. People rub them on their bodies and they confer magical powers. If you get a drop in your eye, the fairy world is revealed. One evening, Jane Wolvedon's mother, whose name was Cecilia, heard a knocking at the door. She went to open it and saw a tiny man sitting on a great horse. "My wife is about to give birth, she needs help," he said. Your ancestor saw that he was a pisky, of course, but she said nothing, climbed up behind him, and off they went. They rode fast, but the journey was long, taking unknown ways in the black of night. When they arrived, Cecilia assisted at the birth and saved the infant, a little girl. Afterwards, she washed the child with a magic soap they had given her. Some of the soap splashed into her eyes and she saw the fairy world. She was not in a thatched cottage, as she had thought when she first stepped inside, but a magnificent castle. The pisky who had come to fetch her noticed she could see the invisible world. And, as you know, if you see the pisky world by accident and the piskies find out, they will prick out your eyes.'

'And so the mother of your Jane . . . '

'No, not the mother of my Jane. She told them: "I will never tell anyone about this, I swear, but spare my eyes. I am expecting my first child; I should like to see it." And the pisky father was very grateful to Jane's mother for saving the newborn pisky. "I will make an exception for you, on one condition: that you never try to see the fairy world again." "I promise," said she. "Still, I should like to give you a gift," said the papa pisky. "You too will give birth to a daughter. Call her Jane, like our own. You'll see, she will have magical eyes with the power to persuade, soothe and save. Teach her to use them well." And he brought her home on his great horse. When she was back in front of her own door, he said to her: "If your daughter Jane grows to become a virtuous woman, like you, she will have a gift of her own: once every three generations, she will pass her eyes to one of her descendants." And that is why Jane had such remarkable eyes. I don't know why she chose you to receive the gift. We should not try to understand these things. Cherish your gift and use it well. When a person is touched by the fairies, they have a strength they must learn to use for their own good and the good of others. It's the only way to say thank you.'

III

The hunt is up, the hunt is up,
Lo! it is almost day;
For Christ our King is gone – hunting,
And brought his deer to hay . . .

'THE HUNT'S UP'
POPULAR BALLAD

I MAY TELL MYSELF that I write for no one but ghosts, but I'm lying. For while I sharpen my quill, a face appears, always the same and very real: David.

I am not of the Carpenters' Guild. But since there are no instrument builders in the region, they tolerate me, on condition that I don't also make tables, chairs, cabinets or beds. David, however, started by learning carpentry in Oron. He spent three or four years there, before the workshop where he was apprenticed burned down, the fire taking his master carpenter with it.

The Dallinges insisted I complete his training.

'He won't go anywhere else. He's learned to make furniture, but he'd rather build instruments. That's all he dreams about; and since you are partly the reason, now you must take him on.'

I did take him on, some years ago. He is presently an instrument maker and organist in Basle. I haven't seen him for a long while. I miss him.

I can count the people I have loved deeply and constantly in my life on the fingers of one hand. David is one of them.

I found him one morning, wrapped in a scrap of cloth outside the farmhouse door. He must have been born during the night. I was the first up, as usual. He looked at me with his blind blue eyes, and convulsively gripped my finger, pulling it to his mouth like a teat. I was immediately captivated. I waited beside the fire until Madeleine Dallinges got up.

'Sweet Jesus, what on earth is that?'

'You can see very well it's a child. I would like to ask a great favour: that you raise him along with your own.'

Her youngest was barely a year old then, and she still nursed him.

Meanwhile, Benoît Dallinges had entered.

'So, Cousin, you've produced a little one for us?' he said with a hearty laugh.

'Perhaps more than one, over the years, but I have decided that this child shall represent them all. He is my son, David. But if you don't wish him to live here, I . . . '.

'Room for another, Madeleine?' asked Benoît with a smile.

She shrugged:

'If we can feed six, we can feed seven, the more the merrier . . . '

The infant had not made the slightest sound until then. At that moment, he began to cry.

'Come on, give the child to me. He clearly needs to be suckled and washed, not to mention baptised. You may as well go and tell the priest, while I tend to your David, to *our* David.'

We never told him anything, and his birth remained a mystery. Neither the priest nor the pastor, both well informed of the local goings-on, knew of a young girl that had been got with child.

'Bring him up as one of your own,' the priest advised the Dallinges. 'It will be simpler for all. Cousin, you shall be godfather.'

And that's what happened. David became a Dallinges, the same as all the others, except that God in his munificence granted him the gift of music, just as he had given me Jane Wolvedon's eyes. Besides Claudio Monteverde, William Byrd and perhaps Thomas Morley, I have never known anyone with such an ear.

IT WAS FROM Old Thomas that I learned my family's history. No one paid any attention to Thomas. People consulted him for information as they would a ledger, conveniently to hand. It was tacitly understood that he could answer any question, but this earned him neither recognition nor respect. He had his own house, with servants, which I didn't know at the time and would have found hard to imagine, having seen him hulling peas, picking out stones from the grain and plucking fowl.

You had to listen carefully to Old Thomas, if you wished to grasp the nuances in the stream of his discourse. For example, I spent the whole of yesterday wondering whether he was a papist or a Protestant. I never asked him at the time, for such religious distinctions were incomprehensible to my little head; conformist, recusant, papist, Protestant and Puritan were all terms frequently repeated like incantations, yet no one dwelled on them, at least not in my presence.

It took me a good long while to understand that Thomas did not hold my father in very high esteem. At the time we left Golden, I had even made up my mind that he severely disapproved of the way things had gone.

One indication of his disapproval was the violent antipathy he held towards Cuthbert, whom my father venerated and lavished with special attention.

'Your father, who attends court and goes all over the country hereabouts on business, should know better than I that he is playing with fire. The future of us all is at stake, not to mention that while Cuthbert plays the missionary, no one is managing the estate. A master preoccupied chiefly with his own soul should have a steward with a keener sense of business.'

'What should my father know?'

'Your father left England at a time when everyone went to church as they pleased. People accommodated one another. I hardly noticed much difference myself. One day, a decree came from London that we must no longer pray in Latin. The whole region was up in arms, but people finally gave in. We had just enough time to get used to praying in English under King Edward when we had to revert to Latin under Queen Mary. And no sooner had Elizabeth acceded to the throne than we had to go back to English again. The same for Palm Sunday, the images of the Virgin and so on. We none of us knew which way to turn. But there was one advantage to all the confusion: with a little sleight of hand, we always got away with it. There was something for everyone. And that's when the new pope got mixed up in it all. He believed he was all we'd been waiting for to become Catholic again, that a proclamation would suffice.'

'What proclamation?'

'He excommunicated the Queen and forbade Catholics to obey her or to attend the Church of England. He fancied the whole country would immediately revolt. I don't know who had advised him thus. On the contrary, many loyal subjects were wary. Here they were being asked to disobey their Queen, their ruler by divine right. But your father didn't really follow these events; he was abroad when it happened.'

'Where had he gone?'

'Things being as they are, I would have preferred not to know.'

'But you do know?'

'Not officially.'

'Tell me, Master Thomas! I won't breathe a word to anyone.'

'He was in Douai, with the papists. But if you say anything, you risk putting your father in even greater danger.'

'But why does he take these risks?'

'If someone slaps you, what do you do?'

I was slapped frequently and my only right in response was to remain silent. Still, the duties of a gentleman were already being instilled in me, and I knew what answer was expected:

'I return it.'

'And by what miracle would our Elizabeth behave otherwise? She has been excommunicated, excluded from the Catholic world and declared an enemy, so she retaliates. English Catholics become *her* enemies. This reckless pope has pushed his flock to the wall, and now their only choice is between persecution and excommunication. Many sensed immediately which way the wind was blowing, and chose the Church of England. As long as you're Christian and you pray, that's all that matters, they told themselves. Others remained Catholic, but in secret. Your father, however, has inherited the arrogance of his Arundell grandfather. But then *he* could afford to be arrogant.'

'Thomas?'

'What?'

'You aren't telling me about the risk my father runs.'

'The risk your father runs has a name: Cuthbert.'

'But *why*?'

'Swear you will say nothing.'

'I swear it. On my soul.'

'Cuthbert Mayne is a papist priest sent from Flanders, which is teeming with English Catholics plotting with Spain against Elizabeth.'

'I still cannot see how that puts my father at risk.'

'It is forbidden to receive priests who have entered the kingdom illegally, or to facilitate their work.'

'What work?'

'To return the English to Catholicism and restore the power of the Pope. Oh, you should hear poor Cuthbert's fine speeches. I don't believe he himself understands the role they're making him play. He feels he is God's messenger, running around the countryside saying Mass, administering the Sacraments and converting people. Reckless indeed. Particularly since Richard Grenville is the country sheriff. A man who holds no affection for your father. He will be informed about what's going on, one day or another, of that there is no doubt.'

'And my father?'

'Your father thinks that his Catholic duty comes before his obligations to his queen, his family and his estates. Elizabeth has decreed that whoever harbours a priest entering the country in secret from abroad is a traitor, and traitors are prosecuted for praemunire. Have you already been taught what that is?'

'No.'

'It means that all your assets are seized, and that you are imprisoned for life, or banished. Or hanged.'

I am gripped with dread.

'And my father risks all that?'

'Yes, your father. And most tragic of all is that this old family steward,' he strikes his chest, 'is aware of it, while the person most affected acts as if it were no concern of his.'

Thomas was my favourite companion, but it would be wrong to surmise that I spent my days with him alone. On the contrary. Thomas was my sole source of information, but it took cunning and subterfuge of every kind to come and see him. I was supposed to stay at the new manor house, with the pages, and one of them – Robert – was charged with the particular responsibility of looking after me.

These pages and young ladies were not servants, but sons and daughters of notable families of the region, sent to other families of equal status in order to receive an education it is thought would be better imparted away from their father's house. Robert was a Courtenay, related, like us, to the Arundells by marriage. He studied fencing, Latin and Greek, decorum and duty, philosophy and music. He taught me how to conduct myself and say my prayers, and he read to me. He played the lute wonderfully well: listening to it transported me to a state of trance-like happiness. He liked me very much:

'No trouble at all with Francis. He can almost read, he can almost write, you never have to tell him anything twice and he doesn't get up to mischief.'

He used the leisure afforded him by my good behaviour to play dice with a passion. This was strictly forbidden. My father would have had him whipped if he had discovered it, but I said nothing. This was how I was able to slip away to Thomas for perhaps one hour a day. Robert knew, but said nothing either. The blackmail was mutual, though we never spoke of it; between gentlemen, it simply was not done.

Our quiet routine was soon to be broken by events that would radically change the course of my life.

My father was in London, at court. In Golden it was whispered that he was on very good terms with the Queen. Given what Thomas had said, I told myself this was a good sign. Perhaps the Queen would see that, for all he was a fervent Catholic, he was no less a friend to her.

They said he wouldn't return before summer. But we were still in the depths of winter when I was awoken by a great commotion one night. The lord of the manor had arrived from London.

The confusion in the household is such that I slip out of my bedchamber and take up one of my favourite observation posts: a small chamber built into the chimney of the Great Hall. One enters it through a concealed door in the neighbouring room. The whole family knows of the existence of this little chamber, but it is never spoken of. My sister Mary, about seven years old at the time, enters in turn, on tiptoe, a finger to her lips.

First they serve my father supper. Then my mother dismisses everyone, closes the doors and sits down. I can see her through a small opening in the chimney mantel, masked from outside by a sculpture. I cannot see my father, but I hear him perfectly.

'Well?' my mother says, in a less than agreeable voice.

'You might soften your tone, madam.'

'Sir, I would rather you not counsel me as to the tone I should take. What has happened? Did the Queen chase you out?'

'No. I left.'

My mother's face is livid.

'What do you mean, left?'

'It happened that . . . I was not expecting . . . '

'If you, sir, who generally have so much to say for yourself, are lost for words, then I fear the worst! I am listening . . . '

'I was paying court, like everyone else . . . '

'You tried to convert the Queen!'

'Madam!'

'Very well, I'm listening. Go on then, I pray. You were paying court . . . '

'I was paying court, like the others. I went to Gray's Inn as required, I played chess in the morning and cards in the afternoon. I fenced, played tennis and even went to the theatre. I attended learned gatherings. Which is as much as to say, I did nothing to draw attention to myself; I in no way attempted to convert the Queen. My religious duty I fulfilled in the poorest neighbourhoods, and I assure you that Her Majesty knew absolutely nothing about it.'

'So then?'

'Madam, have you ever heard talk of the manner in which the Queen treats gentlemen who please her?'

'They say she lavishes favours upon them and keeps them close. All within the bounds of decency.'

'Yes, they say that. And they also say that Her Majesty contents herself with intellectual intercourse. But that's what they say, and for my part, I am not so sure.'

'Whatever . . . ?'

'Well, the Queen noticed me and found me pleasing.'

'Dear Lord!'

'She bade me come to her apartments, where there were but three or four ladies-in-waiting, and she offered to confer the title of viscount upon me. And so I would have been sheriff of the county and could have made my affairs prosper.'

'And you refused?'

'My dear Mary . . .' He choked on his words. 'She wished to make me a viscount in order to keep me close to her. I would have been a favourite. How would you have taken the news that your husband, a fervent Catholic, was the intimate companion of Anne Boleyn's daughter?'

If looks could kill, my father would be dead. But my mother says nothing, and my father continues, a slight irritation in his voice.

'I told her I appreciated the honour, but the weight of nobility was too heavy for my shoulders and I could not accept it. I was not worthy, and it would be considered partiality.'

A long silence, during which I hear my father pour himself a drink. My mother is frozen in her chair, like a statue. She neither drinks nor eats.

'I thought Her Majesty would take my refusal very badly, but not at all: "Let us reason the matter," she said to me. "What concern is it of yours if people say you were made a viscount out of partiality? The title is yours all the same, and nothing else matters." "Majesty, I am not worthy of such an honour." "Well then, why are you at court, if not to advance your affairs?" "I am advancing my affairs, but they are not of a terrestrial nature." "Really? Of what nature are they, then?" "They are of a spiritual nature, Majesty." "Indeed. Explain, so that I may understand." "I am Catholic, Majesty."'

This time, my mother starts in her chair.

'What? You told her in so many words?'

'But it's true, madam!'

'It's true, it's true. . . . Of course it's true! But why must we boast of it at every street corner, as if we sought to draw misfortune upon us? Now is not the time . . .'

'Madam, firstly, the time is always right for God. And secondly, I was not on a street corner but in the apartments of the Queen of England.'

'Come, Francis. Do you know what the Pope has commanded us to think of her? That she is a bastard, a usurper, the daughter of a witch! And you refuse to be ennobled by her, giving as your reason the fact that you are a Catholic? You mortally offended her.'

'Absolutely not, madam. She accepted it with great charm and grace. She asked me what I expected of her, and I told her: "That you make it easier for us to practise our religion freely, madam." She told me she was going to think about it, and dismissed me with an amicable pat on the cheek and a big smile.'

'And you came straight back here.'

'Not at all. The incident I have just recounted occurred last month.'

'So then?'

'Something else occurred a few days ago. It was late in the evening and I was already in bed when there was a knocking at the door. Phillips opened it and on the threshold there was a lady-in-waiting with a message from the Queen: I must forthwith attend Her Majesty, who wished to converse with me on matters of urgency. And she added, for good measure, that I had won Elizabeth over and should strike while the iron was hot. Those were her very words. I could not attend the Queen at such an hour of the night, for reasons I prefer not to dwell on. I am your husband and I had no intention of engaging my affections to another, even if she be my sovereign.'

'For that, I am most grateful to you.'

The sarcasm in my mother's voice is perceptible even to a child's ear. My father goes on as if she had said nothing.

'I asked the lady-in-waiting to offer my apologies to Her Majesty: I was sick. She left, and I wished to sleep. But a few moments later the Queen herself was at my bedside, to enquire about my health. Except that instead of asking me how I was, she urgently entreated me to accept the title of viscount. So I had to reiterate all my arguments. I fell to my knees before her, I expressed all of my gratitude, I repeated to her that I was unworthy, that all I possessed was there at her feet – all except my conscience.'

This time, my mother's face turns purple with rage. She makes as if to strike him, but my father is clearly too absorbed by his tale for he continues almost immediately, and his tone is more distracted now.

'She became vexed at that, I must say. She called me an imbecile, a coward and a traitor. Who did I take myself for? She was my queen, and so on. She asked me one last time to accept the title of viscount, but I could not. It would have meant betraying my religion. She left. I lost no time but got up from my bed and gave the necessary orders for a swift departure. She is so capricious she could have had me arrested within the hour. We left at full gallop, and here I am.'

'I remember our childhood, Francis. That page who told you: "Francis, if you do not let me pass, I will cuff you so hard I'll knock you to the wall." And you did not budge. So he clouted you, which knocked you down; you got to your feet again and you placed yourself exactly where you were before.

And so he clouted you again. They had to intervene to stop him killing you, so thoroughly had you exasperated him. But in those days it was a game. Now, there is no one to come between your sovereign and you. Or *us*.'

'There is God. And I have my conscience intact.'

She shrugs and casts him a look of pity.

'Come, let us go to bed,' she says, at length.

'I have matters to attend to, I will come presently,' my father replies.

We hear the sound of his chair, then that of the door. My poor mother falls to her knees and starts to pray. We leave as silently as we have come.

'What do you think will happen now?' I ask.

'Something terrible, no doubt. I heard the maids say that Cuthbert might be arrested. If our father has displeased the Queen, he may be arrested too.'

Although I saw little of my sister Mary, I was always struck by her perspicacity. She could judge a situation with a glance. Had she been a man, she might have made a great diplomat. What she had foreseen, took place.

Not immediately. We had to wait until summer.

ONE SUNDAY AFTERNOON in June, we heard a loud banging at the door. So loud that the entire household rushed to the windows.

Between the two manor houses was an armed company, preceded by several men in stately dress: the justices of the peace. The man leading this expedition was Sir Richard Grenville, the new Sheriff of Cornwall: a big fellow with a soldierly bearing, the man Thomas had said held little love for my father. My legs threatened to give way under me.

'Open up, in the name of the Queen,' cried Grenville.

My father came out and walked forward.

'Good evening, Sir Richard. To what do I owe this visitation of force?'

'We seek a fugitive, John Bourne, and have been told he has found refuge with you.'

'You are mistaken. I do not know any Bourne. There is nobody by that name in this house.'

'I demand to see.'

'Surely you are not going to break down my door at this late hour? My word must suffice.'

'Your word! Don't make me laugh!'

'Sir Richard! You do not have the right.'

'I have a warrant to conduct a search, with justices present to prove the legality of our actions. But to hell with words,' said Grenville.

He stood up on his spurs, gave a bold signal to his company, and they forced an entrance.

There was no Bourne to be found. The man was elsewhere. He had probably already left England. I suspect that Grenville was perfectly aware of this: he was a ruthless pirate, and had taken against the Tregians and the Arundells. The soldiers dispersed throughout the house. We had been instructed to act as if nothing was the matter, but I simply had to see. They scoured the entire place, while my father protested and Grenville loudly urged them on.

'This is an outrage,' my father said.

'If you have nothing to feel guilty about, then it is a formality. The justices of the peace are here to witness that justice, and justice alone, is done.'

They finally arrived at the door to the little garden that lay somewhat secluded at the north corner of the house; there had always been something mysterious about it.

They knocked. The door opened, and Cuthbert appeared. He reddened, opened his mouth, but was seized by the collar before he could say a word.

'And who might you be?'

'I am a man.'

Everything had been quite formal until that moment. But suddenly, I understand: Sir Richard has waited for the moment when he would find Cuthbert, and he knew that he would find him.

'A man! Then what are you wearing underneath this doublet? A coat of mail?'

He rips open the doublet, and at the neckline we can all see a pendant.

'An Agnus Dei!' one of the soldiers exclaims.

The Agnus Dei is a holy image blessed by the Pope or a Catholic bishop, and strictly forbidden in England, where it is considered a relic of the superstitious practices the country has sought to rid itself of, at the same time as the Roman rite.

Thereupon, they set about ransacking the room, the garden and Cuthbert's lodge. They find his priestly garments, his devotional images and, horror of all horrors, a papal bull, possession of which has been punishable by execution since 1571.

Confusion reigns. Some servants and a handful of tenant farmers attempt to intervene. But Sir Richard orders his soldiers to shoot anyone trying to interfere with their work. They end up arresting several of our servants and two of our tenant farmers. They arrest Cuthbert. They arrest my father. They bind their hands behind their backs and take them away. Night has not yet fallen when the last cloud of dust settles at the bend on the Ridgeway, the road to Launceston. We are stupefied. A robin sings in the summer evening, and another answers. I slip away to my mother. She looks as if she has been struck dead. I would like to take her hand, but I do not dare.

'With the compliments of Her Majesty,' she finally whispers in a hoarse voice.

This brings us back to reality.

'John! Peter!' shouts Madam Catherine.

'Yes, madam.'

'Prepare some horses for me; I am going to Lanherne.'

Nobody asks her what she plans to do there: Lanherne is where her brother and family live, where she herself was brought up; she probably intends to try making some approach, to use her relations or friends to secure my father's freedom, at the very least.

I slip away to the kitchen.

Thomas is sitting there very straight, his eyes closed.

'Have they left?' he asks, without moving.

'Yes.'

He opens his eyes, which are dark and keen.

I must be very pale. My knees are shaking. I have a hundred questions to ask but nothing comes. Thomas stretches out a hand. I take a step and fall towards him, my head on his knee. I wish I could hold back my tears but it is impossible. He places a light hand on my curls.

The kitchen is strangely empty, apart from us.

'Weep,' says Thomas. 'Purge your sorrow.' And, after a long silence, he adds:

'Your father believed he was serving God, but he has only tempted the Devil.'

IV

Very lusty I was, and pleasant withall,
To sing, dance, and play at the ball . . .
And beside all this, I could then finely play
On the harp much better than now far away.

'KIND HART'S DREAM'
POPULAR BALLAD

I AM ALMOST ASHAMED to write the words: the two years that followed were among the worst of my father's life. They were among the
best of mine.

Not that I was no longer interested in his fate. On the contrary, I thought
of him constantly, and we talked about him often. Indeed, I suspect he was
at the heart of every discussion throughout the duchy.

But with the carefree innocence of childhood, there were circumstances
under which I forgot all about him. Everyone in the household was as
concerned for him as they were unconcerned for me. There was less money
now: to obtain my father's release in June, we had been forced to provide
bail of two thousand pounds, an enormous sum, enough to support a good
hundred people in comfort for some length of time. And his release was
only temporary: a mere two months, during which I hardly saw him. He
was either at prayer or receiving visitors, or out and about garnering support, I imagine. He was sombre and distracted. In September, he set off
again for the assizes in Launceston. The family never recovered the two
thousand pounds. And he never regained his freedom.

I saw nothing of what took place in the courtroom, but I heard quite
enough talk about it afterwards. Everyone in Cuthbert's immediate circle

was sentenced, fined, deprived of their liberty, and their goods and chattels were seized (under the notorious praemunire). The sanction was universal and total. My father and John Arundell were taken to London to appear before the court there. (Arundell was my grandmother Catherine's younger brother, hence my great-uncle, though he was barely eight or ten years older than my father. He had taken my other grandmother, Anne Stourton, as his second wife.)

John Arundell was sentenced to a heavy fine and released, but forbidden to return to Lanherne. To keep him in check, they detained my father, who was both his nephew and his son-in-law. At least this was the explanation given in Golden and the surrounding district.

In London, my father was imprisoned in the Marshalsea, to be held in secret and for an indefinite period. The Queen's entourage did everything in their power to seize our estates; she promised her loyal supporters the enjoyment of our properties in order to put pressure on the Tregians, the Arundells and every other Catholic remaining in the duchy.

We remained at Golden, but for how much longer, we had no idea. We lived in reduced circumstances. The pages were sent away and with them the tutors entrusted with our teaching. The schoolmaster who should have provided me with the rudiments of an education was in prison.

For several months, no one paid any real attention to me at all. My grandmother Catherine appeared from time to time, but she was often away at relatives' houses, and my mother was either absent or beset with decisions over the estate. From September onwards, she spent more time in Launceston or London than she did at Golden. She wished to be near my father. My mother was a Stourton, the granddaughter of the Earl of Derby. People said she bombarded everyone with requests and petitions, including the Queen.

And so, left to my own devices, I went exploring.

I LIVE IN SEVERAL worlds at once, each sealed off from the other. In one of these worlds are the mournful apartments of the new manor house, most often deserted. But in that world of sorrow there is a beacon: my father's library. No one goes there now he is no longer at home, and I become a frequent borrower of books, many of which are quite beyond me. Still, I dive in. I love to read.

The cosy intimacy of the kitchens is another world. More and more, I turn to Old Thomas as my private source of information, because no one else in the household takes the trouble to explain anything at all.

A kindly old man teaches me Latin, geometry, rhetoric and religion. He lives at the bottom of the hill, at Golden Mill, and I attend lessons there whenever his rheumatic pains confine him to his chair and prevent him from climbing the hill to us.

And besides this, there is the outside world, which I discover now, little by little. One day, a group of miners takes me with them to the tin mine nearby, and explains in great detail how they set about extracting the metal. They tell me that, not so long ago, people would find tin in the streams, you had only to stoop down and fish it out. But now you have to dig for it in the belly of the earth.

'Our tin,' they tell me, 'is used to make goblets that travel to the ends of the earth.'

Golden is two miles from Tregony. To look at Tregony on a map, it seems a very rural place. But nothing could be further from the truth. It's a port, far inland at the top of the Truro estuary on the banks of the River Fal, a waterway wide and deep enough to allow seafaring vessels, and even ships from across the sea, to sail inland and unload their cargoes.

In my childhood, a shallow creek led upstream from the bridge at Tregony, along which smaller boats could get as far as Golden Mill – almost to our door.

There were still large warehouses in Tregony at the time, full of merchandise waiting to be traded in or out of Cornwall.

There were warehouses at Golden Mill, too, on our own land, set in a horseshoe on the banks of the river. People came from the surrounding district with tin for export to the wide world, and to fetch goods that had come in from London or Southampton – maybe even the Americas.

It was an easy excursion from Golden to Tregony and back – no more than a day by water. I had done it several times. It was in Tregony that I made my first direct contact with music. There was playing and singing, even dancing, at home. But such entertainments were for the adults. Whenever they were held, we were taken away so as not to bother the guests.

THE AUTUMN CHILL HAS laid bare the branches of the trees. I have just left my schoolmaster's house and gone to take a closer look at an unfamiliar boat. This is not one of the regular craft plying the creek above the bridge but a skiff from a three-master doing trade with the Americas – the *Jesus*.

A tall, red-haired young man springs ashore. Unusually for a sailor he is clean-shaven, without even a moustache. We introduce ourselves on the quayside.

'Good day! With eyes like those, you must be a Tregian,' he says.

'Yes, I am Francis.'

'And I am William Courtenay. We are cousins of some sort. Is your mother at home?'

'No, but my grandmother Catherine came back yesterday.'

'Madam Catherine it is, then! I haven't seen her for a very long while. Will you come with me?'

He spends hours shut up with my grandmother, and there is no way to listen at the door. When he emerges, he looks worried. I ask if I might visit his ship, nonetheless.

'But my ship is downstream from Tregony.'

'I've been to Tregony often. Madam Catherine, please say I can go with him, I should so like to board a ship that has sailed on the high sea.'

'But . . .'

'Please, madam! I know my Aesop's fable in Latin, I can recite it to you and if I make a mistake, you can forbid me to go.'

Madam Catherine laughs.

'The boy is a little monster,' she tells William Courtenay. 'He was born knowing how to read.'

'That's not true! It was you yourself who . . .'

'I have told you before, Master Francis, grown-ups must never be interrupted. He could count, too, and speak Latin,' she goes on.

'I have to send a man this way tomorrow before dusk,' says William. 'He can bring Francis home.'

And so I leave in the little skiff, go aboard the three-master and sail with it as far as the estuary.

'If you had told Madam Catherine you weren't staying at Tregony, she would never have let me come.'

'My dear Francis, you should learn that while it is thoroughly reprehensible to tell a lie, there is often little point, when one desires something very badly, in telling the whole truth. The essential thing is never to substitute an inconvenient truth with a lie. But for that, you need a fox's cunning. You wished to see the *Jesus*, did you not?'

'Oh yes!'

'I said what was required in order to have the pleasure of receiving you aboard.'

'Thank you, Master William.'

'So tell me, this Latin text – do you really know it by heart?'

I plant my feet firmly apart, clasp my hands behind my back and reel it off all at once:

'The Lion and the Mouse, or, Why we should never forget that we often have need of someone smaller than ourselves.'

> *Frigida sopito blanditur sylva leoni;*
> *Cursitat hinc murum ludere prompta cohors.*
> *Pressus mure leo, murem rapit: ille precatur,*
> *Iste preces librat: supplicat ira preci.*
> *Haec tamen ante movet animo: Quid mure perempto*
> *Laudis emes? summum vincere parva pudet . . .*

And so on. When I have finished, William bursts out laughing.

'Well, Master Francis, you truly are a phenomenon.'

For the first time in my life, I am allowed to eat supper at the high table. My food is served to me, and William addresses me as an equal, man to man.

'Has anyone ever told you, Francis, about Golden's glorious past?'

'Yes, I was told that my grandfather, and my great-grandfather . . . '

'No, I don't mean them. I mean the people who lived long, long before them. It is said that Wolvedon may be the Roman settlement of Voliba.'

'Voliba?'

'You know the ditch that follows the road between the manor and Golden Mill?'

'Yes, the Warren, where we keep the game.'

'That's the moat of a Roman fortress that stood there a very, very long time ago.'

'Is that why the field is called the Roman Camp?'

'Yes. That's the place named Voliba on Ptolemy's maps, the place he talks about in his *Geography*: *Post quos maxime ad occasum Domnonii inquibus oppida Voliba . . .*'

'Should I know who Ptolemy is?'

He laughs at my cautious question.

'I won't tell anyone you asked. Ptolemy is the greatest sage in all Antiquity. He discovered the system of the world. But when Ptolemy was formulating his theories about the Universe, people thought the Earth was flat and the Universe revolved around it. Personally,' he lowered his voice, 'I believe, in common with many other seafaring men, that it is the Earth that revolves within a Universe that is itself moving very slowly. But the man who first wrote that – another great scholar – was challenging Rome, where people still think, like Ptolemy, that the Universe revolves around the Earth.'

'And why do you believe the Earth is turning?'

'Because when men navigate far across the sea, for a great stretch of time, it becomes obvious. Even to a good Catholic like myself. To my regret, the theory has been banned by Rome. In Spain and Italy, they'll toss you on a bonfire if you even say such a thing.'

'Can you explain how . . .'

'Not tonight. And I would advise you not to ask about it at home, either. My theories are not well thought of. Best keep them to yourself.'

'But why?'

'Because Copernicus is as much a challenge to Rome as the Reformation. As you may imagine, if someone declares you are not the centre of Creation, but a mere speck in the Universe, and not central to anything at all . . .'

'I see. It's like when we play hide-and-seek and the littlest ones think all they have to do is close their eyes for no one to see them any more.'

William laughs so hard he almost chokes.

'Ab-so-lutely!' he says, at length. And then, changing the subject, 'Do you know how to play the lute?'

'No. The pages had one when they were still with us, but my hands were too small then.'

'And the virginal?'

He points to a keyed instrument, placed on a nearby table. There was one just like it in my father's bedchamber, which he often played, though I was never allowed near it.

'No, I don't know how to play that either. But I should like to learn.'

'Come and see.'

He sits at the instrument and suggests I sit underneath the table, so that I can hear better.

I should probably have forgotten our discussion about the form of the Universe had he not repeated it to me years later. But I remember very clearly the precise moment he began to play.

C B C D E C B A G, C B C D E C F . . .

I can hear the melody of *The Short Measure of My Lady Wynkfyld's Rownde* even now, as if I were still there, sitting under the table. The music rains down upon me, envelops me, speaks to me; it is like rediscovering the warmth of Jane's body, the smell of bread and milk.

'Well, Francis? Have you fallen asleep down there?'

I look up, and William must have read my feelings in my eyes.

'Would you like to learn the round?'

I nod. I cannot speak.

'Come then.'

He holds out his hand. 'Sit here, next to me. I'll show you.'

It seems to me that we spent the entire night at the virginal. Since that day, I have played the round dedicated to the mysterious Lady Wynkfyld thousands of times. Always from memory. And each time, the ship's cabin, the lazy rocking of the three-master, William's voice, the waft of the ocean mingled with the smell of dried fish and damp wood, all come flooding back, filling me with a happiness I felt that evening for the very first time.

•   •   •

CUTHBERT'S SENTENCE was confirmed. He was to be put to death in the public square in Launceston, and the date was fixed for the Feast of St Andrew, which was also a market day – the better to impress the imaginations of the watching crowd. My father remained in prison in London, and was not condemned to die alongside him.

'If that's the case,' said Old Thomas, 'they won't kill your father. They hope that, under sustained pressure, he will be minded to conform. But he won't conform. He's as stubborn as a mule. I know him only too well. He had a page, when he was a boy . . . '

'I know: the page beat him to make him go away, but my father always came back.'

'They have freed John Arundell. Or rather, he is confined to his house, but at least he's no longer in prison – he has friends in high places, in addition to which the Queen has nothing against him personally. They're concentrating on your father. Although, thinking about it, he has plenty of supporters, too. But now that Sir George Carey has entered the fray . . . '

I had never heard the name mentioned before.

'He's a relative of the Queen. If your father persists in the Roman faith, they will confiscate all your lands, and Carey will get the enjoyment of them. Your father's stubbornness will disinherit you, wreck your future and cast your ancestors' hard work and trouble to the four winds, but he will not be told. I heard that he might have saved Cuthbert by attending the reformed church just once. But instead, he said: "I will not risk the damnation of my soul in order to delay that man's ascension to Paradise."'

It was the first time a Catholic priest had been put to death and, once the date of Cuthbert's execution had been confirmed, there was talk of nothing else.

Two of the tenant farmers insisted on travelling to see him die. The journey to Launceston took three or four hours on horseback, if the roads were dry.

'I never felt any particular liking for Cuthbert,' muttered Thomas when they returned on the evening of that dark November day, full of their adventure. 'But I wouldn't wish anyone to end their days as he did. He was an upright, honest man, the most innocent, ingenuous soul I have ever known.'

I was overwhelmed with sorrow, and an ill-defined sense of fear. I wandered out as far as the Ridgeway. In the dusk, I saw two men ride up at full gallop. One carried a sack slung crosswise behind his saddle. The other bore a black banner.

They stopped to confer for a moment at the crossroads, just a few steps from where I stood. They thought they should turn right to reach Tregony, but I knew that that road led to Probus. I stepped forward to set them straight. Just at that moment, one of the tenant farmers appeared from nowhere, lifted me off my feet and carried me all the way back to the old manor house. Before I had time to realise what was happening, we were back at the kitchens.

'Whatever's the matter?' I burst out angrily. 'What on earth do you think you're doing?'

'Do you know who those men were, Master Francis?'

'Of course I do, they were riders who had lost their way.'

'Not just any riders, though. They were the Sheriff's envoys, the executioner's assistants. You saw the sack one of them was carrying on his horse's back?'

'Yes.'

'That was one section of Cuthbert Mayne's quartered body. They were taking it to Tregony to impale it near the bridge, so that his death might serve as a lesson.'

I found myself shaking uncontrollably. That sack . . . To have seen it was almost worse than watching his execution. Or hearing the account of his death.

'He was still alive when they started cutting him up; we saw his heart beating.'

'And the blood spurted everywhere. I was so close, a few drops even fell on me. There, look there . . . '

In my child's mind, I saw my father suffering the same death – and after my father it would be my turn. I too was a Catholic. I too . . .

'And they severed his head from his trunk and put it on a spike on the castle gate where many people pass by, so that everyone would see it.'

'And one of his eyes had been put out.'

'No! No, I won't hear it! Stop!'

I shout out in spite of myself. It is unbearable. The head on the spike is mine, any time now. Tomorrow, even. I never saw Old Thomas move with such alacrity. He is beside me before I have time to run away. He places a firm hand on my shoulder.

'You two, go tell your stories somewhere else. And you, Master Francis, come here by me.'

I feel the urge to cry, but the tears will not come. I picture Cuthbert, his refined features, his gentle grey eyes, so obviously a harmless man. Where will it end? If the Queen is displeased with my father but has executed Cuthbert instead, there is no reason why it shouldn't be me next, before my poor father.

'Master Francis,' says Thomas. His voice is soft as velvet. 'Go and walk around the house, don't run, breathe deeply, and drink a cup of water. Then come back and see me here.'

I do as I am told.

'My child,' he begins, when I return. 'It may surprise you to know that what has happened is not directed against you personally, nor even against your father.'

'But . . .'

'They were looking for a scapegoat. They found one. They needed someone arrogant, rich, and not too highly placed. Your father delivered himself into their hands, quite literally. He's a fervent, staunch Catholic in the wrong place at the wrong time, and I would even say he upholds the faith in quite the wrong way.'

'But I thought there was only one way to uphold the Catholic faith.'

'A man may proclaim his faith in every place and at every opportunity, or else practise it devoutly, but with discretion and subtlety. What happened today would never have happened to your grandfather, who was on the side of the Catholics in the rebellion of 1549, but who took care not to show himself too much. And your great-grandfather was even more careful. One may be a Catholic with all one's heart and not be a prominent fanatic for all that. Look at your uncle John Arundell. He's had his share of trouble, for sure, but he's already out of prison. Your father, however, has delivered himself into the hands of his enemies. First he exasperated them . . .'

'I thought he exasperated the Queen.'

'Your father is an admirable man, Francis, and you should be proud of him. He is a man of absolute integrity. He speaks his mind whatever happens. And he believes that when right is on his side, he is entitled to proclaim the fact, loud and clear. He has exasperated a great many people as a result. There is a fine art to achieving your ends without making great concessions, while at the same time being seen to defer on matters which are in truth quite unimportant. It's an art which requires tact and discretion. Your father is wholly ignorant of it. He has been that way from childhood. He cares for nothing but Eternity and his own soul, and feels accountable only to God and his conscience. Beyond that, nothing else matters. Cuthbert was just the same.'

He goes on, half to himself:

'To die for one's faith is all very fine, and I admire men like Cuthbert who have the courage of their convictions even in the extremity of their suffering. But I cannot believe the God of Mercy would have us wish for death and not strive to live. So many toil to build His Kingdom here on Earth. To die is to flee.'

He stares into the flames, mumbling his words.

'Has anyone ever told you about William Allen?' he asks me.

'Yes, I've heard the name, but I never understood who he was. Someone important to my father and Cuthbert.'

'William Allen taught at Oxford. He was a papist priest. He fled England and settled in Douai, in Flanders, in the Spanish territories. The university in Douai was founded twelve years ago to defend the Catholic faith against the Reformation. And within that university, Allen founded an English college. I know all this from Cuthbert himself. Many English Catholics go to Douai to study. Not all of them take Holy Orders – there is a lay college too – but they do train priests, or rather missionaries who, once they are ordained, come back here in the absurd hope of converting or reconverting important people to the Catholic faith.'

'Why only important people? What about the rest?'

'They believe the rest will follow. The essential thing is to prepare the way, so that we may have a Catholic king, or rather a queen, Mary Stuart, who is Queen of Scotland. Queen Elizabeth is not opposed to Catholics simply because they are Catholics – or why would she have sought your father's friendship, if indeed that story is true? His undeniable charm is not enough to entice a woman like Elizabeth Tudor, believe me.'

'So why does she resent the Catholics?'

'Because many of them have chosen not to recognise her as queen, and are plotting to overthrow her.'

THE HIGH DRAMA OF that night is followed by an unremarkable year. The crisis continues for my father, but far away from Golden; in London, and later Launceston. The ordinary people, even those who are Protestants, say that Francis Tregian is the victim of a plot, that he is being targeted because, unlike the Cornish nobility, we are newcomers and upstarts. People say the Sheriff and the judges are corrupt, and declare, indignantly, that my father has been sentenced against the will of the court.

Thomas is hardly ever in the inglenook by the fire now, having resumed his duties as steward. He hires two younger men to patrol the estate for him, and governs from Cuthbert's old room, commanding absolute obedience – he never so much as raises his voice.

My brother Adrian returns to the household from his nurse. But he is a sickly child and, in my mother's absence, the nurse takes him back straight away. I find a book by Ptolemy in a corner of my father's library. It says nothing about geography, it is all about music. Another book, Aristotle's *Poetics*, seems to be all about music, too. Alas, I understand nothing. I ask my schoolmaster to explain but he declines.

'You are too young and I am too ignorant of the subject.'

The one important thing I have not yet mentioned was my connection to Jane. When I think of Jane, she seems unchanged from the first time I saw her to the last. Perhaps the piskies who have given me my extraordinary gaze have also given me the gift of seeing those I love through fairy eyes.

I would realise later that Jane became my nurse when she was barely more than a child herself. Her mother had married her off at the age of eleven to a sailor who got her with child straight away, then went to sea. His ship was never seen again. The child died at birth and it was I who drank its milk, I who received its mother's affection.

Little by little, I notice how closely Jane resembles my father. I mention this to Old Thomas.

'These things happen,' he replies, with a knowing smile and in the tone of a man who is keeping something back.

'What things?'

'People may look like one another, but no one knows why.'

'But you know why my father looks like Jane, I can tell.'

'Master Francis, your curiosity will be the end of you.'

'Curiosity is the wise man's virtue; you told me that yourself.'

'Absolutely. But you are too young to hear it from me.'

'I know the whole Mass in Latin. Do you mean that Jane is my . . . well, that she is a kind of sister to me?'

'My dear Francis! Your father is but twenty-eight years old. He would have been far too young . . . Wherever did you get such ideas?'

'Well then,' – I put my mouth to his ear – 'is she the daughter of my grandfather John Tregian?'

'No one knows for sure.'

'But she has almost the same pisky eyes. And red hair.'

'That's true. And your grandfather endowed her with an annuity of twenty pounds. But if Madam Catherine heard you . . . She has always behaved as if she knew nothing.'

'I don't care whose daughter she is. I love her. When I grow up I will marry her.'

Thomas roars with laughter.

'I suggest you propose nothing of the kind! You might offend her.'

'I know. I'm going to wait until I'm quite grown up.'

I visit Jane that winter, as regularly as my lessons allow – and they fill almost every day from early morning to nightfall. She bakes me cakes and walks with me in the fields, explaining the different birds and plants. It is Jane who teaches me to recognise the first signs of approaching bad weather. She is perfectly devout and remains true to the Roman rite. She knows Latin, which she has learned from her mother's brother, a priest. More than once I bring her books I cannot understand, and she explains them to me.

It is Jane, too, who teaches me any number of old songs. I have lost or forgotten the words of most of them, but I remember the melodies, and play them often on my virginal.

'You'll be leaving soon,' she tells me one day, with a sad look. 'I shall have no one left to love.'

'You could come with us.'

'Master Francis! I cannot live under the same roof as Madam Catherine. I'll tell you why one day. She was very upset that I should be your nurse, but your gra . . . your father insisted on it.'

'I know why. Because you're a kind of aunt to me, really.'

'Francis, I forbid you . . . A gentleman should never say such things.'

'All right. I won't mention it again. But I won't be little forever, remember that.'

My most beautiful, abiding image from the years at Golden is of Jane wrapped in her cloak, standing on the highest point of the Roman Camp – Ptolemy's great fortress now nothing more than a low, grassy mound with a few bits of wall sticking out – shading her eyes with her hand:

'Climb up here quick, Master Francis, quick! There's a squall coming.'

The wind swells her skirts and plasters her hair across her face. I climb up. She grips my arm, her eyes fixed on the horizon:

'Look there: the battle of the giants.'

In the distance, huge grey clouds swirl furiously above the boats clustered on the Fal, beside the warehouses at Golden Mill.

'Master Francis, you will surely have to leave Golden. There can be no hope of your father saving his estates for you. So look at your kingdom now. Look at it well. Engrave it on your heart. And if, one day, you find yourself a pilgrim without hearth or home, far from here, poor and miserable, you need only shut your eyes to see the river again and the countryside, as they were yesterday, as they are today, as they will be tomorrow. Giants fight in the sky, but the wind will sweep them away. The land will always be here. Your land. Wherever you are.'

I cling to her leg and rest my head against her hip. Her scent envelops me and, with wide-open eyes, I do exactly as she says.

V

Go from my window, love, go;
Go from my window my dear;
The wind and the rain
Will drive you back again:
You cannot be lodged here

'GO FROM MY WINDOW'
POPULAR BALLAD

THE RUPTURE CAME all at once. We had waited so long that I'm quite certain many people had ceased to believe in it. We had convinced ourselves a miracle would happen: that the sentence of praemunire would not be passed. Our many relations, even the most distant cousins, had done all they could. Sir Edmund Tremayne, a friend who had embraced the reformed faith, had attempted to reason with my father.

The only possible miracle at this stage would have been my father's recantation. But after so much humiliation, suffering and resistance, it was quite simply unthinkable.

It happened one April evening in 1579.

The sentence of praemunire had been pronounced that very morning and all our lands assigned to George Carey, Justice of the Peace for Cornwall and second cousin to the Queen.

Carey lost no time but set off straight from Launceston with a company of soldiers, reaching Golden at nightfall. He gave us an hour to leave.

My mother had made no provision. She had been at Golden for several weeks but we had hardly seen her. At some point in the preceding year, my father had been permitted to move from the Launceston dungeon (where he had been incarcerated once again, for some time) to a cell. He was still kept in isolation but my mother had been able to visit him, and they had taken the opportunity to conceive a child. The birth was imminent when the sentence was passed, and there was a large cauldron of hot water kept ready on the kitchen hearth.

It was evening, and we were already in bed. My brother Adrian had returned to the family from his nurse a few weeks earlier, and we were sleeping in the same room. I have never begrudged Carey the seizure of our assets. That was the order of things – and all's fair in love and war. But I have never been able to forgive him for driving a poor woman on the point of childbirth, and her three young children, onto the muddy roads of late winter in the middle of the night. We were permitted to take nothing with us but the clothes we stood up in.

Thomas had been preparing me for the foreseeable cruelty of our departure for months.

'It will be a surprise when it comes, even if you've been told the date and time,' he assured me. 'You must tell yourself right now: "I wish to return and I will return", and then it will hurt less because it will be farewell and not adieu.'

'And you, Thomas, what will you do?'

'I? I shall not move. I will be here, or in my own house, awaiting your return. You have been my reason for living for so many years . . . '

'I?'

'Yes, you. I hardly spoke to your father when he was a child, and not just because I was still working hard and had little time. It was a question of affinity. Indeed, I work almost as much now as I did then. But you are different. I saw it straight away. You have Jane Wolvedon's eyes, and also her intelligence and her courage. Anyway, when your departure is imminent, come and bid me farewell.'

Wrapped in my cloak, I take advantage of the general confusion to slip away to the nearly deserted kitchens. The house is filled with the sound of weeping and the kitchen of the old manor is no exception, Thomas apart. He sits staring at the door, waiting for me, dry-eyed.

'You're not weeping, Master Francis?'

'N . . . no.'

Though if the truth be told, I am somewhat misty-eyed at the idea of leaving him, of leaving my world.

'You recall our pact?'

'Yes. I am counting on you, Thomas. You'll wait for me?'

'With God's help, I will. But don't be too long. Ten years, no more....'

'Ten years!'

'Indeed. They'll send you to Douai, no doubt, and you'll be a young man by the time you return.'

'How do you know they'll send me to Douai?'

'They said as much.'

'How will I keep abreast of events, without you ...?'

'Oh, you're growing up fast, and you have a keen ear. Learn a little cunning and you'll soon have no need of me.'

'Thomas?'

'Yes, my boy?'

I am helpless to stop the tears pouring down my face. I can hardly see Thomas, but I force myself to look him straight in the eye.

'Fare ... well, Master T ... Thomas.'

'That's it, farewell, Master Francis. I will wait for you. God bless you.'

He rises, and I throw myself against him. We remain like that for a moment, in silence. Then, he releases his embrace and I take a step backwards. Our eyes meet in the soft glow of the hearth. There is nothing left to say. I turn away, and leave.

In the darkness, a woman's voice calls my name.

'I'm here.'

Someone grabs my arm roughly.

'I would whip you,' says the voice in the dark, between sobs, 'if I had time.'

A double basket, generally used for carrying stones, has been laid across the back of a pony. I am lifted up and placed in one of the baskets; Mary is in the other, with Adrian asleep in her arms. Someone holds up a small lantern and I glimpse my sister's face.

'We shall be poor and miserable, Francis.'

'No doubt. Do you know where we're going?'

'To our grandmother Anne and our great-uncle John Arundell.'

'In Lanherne?'

'No, in London. I overheard mother say we would be at risk in Cornwall, and that even we children were in danger. Our father's conviction is the result of a plot. If he were to die . . . '

'What would happen then?'

'You would be the heir. But the sentence of praemunire is not passed down from father to son. Our assets would be returned to you immediately – unless you were to die too, of course.'

'But there's Adrian, and you, and the unborn child.'

She looks at me in the flickering lamplight. I understand her silent message: they might kill us all.

Around us are moans, cries and threats. A fine drizzle completes the scene. A cart has been prepared for my mother, and a horse for Madam Catherine, who waits beneath the porch, wrapped in her cape, staring blankly, seeing no one.

My mother comes out, supported by two women. Her belly is huge. Her face is pale and drawn, but displays no emotion:

'Since we must go, let us not delay,' she says in her customary tone. 'Are the children aboard?'

'Yes, madam.'

'Madam Catherine?'

'I am ready.'

Our wretched convoy is just about to move off when light footsteps come running up to the pony, which stands a little apart. A shadow rises up out of the dark, flings an arm around my neck, and kisses my cheek. She whispers in my ear, and I recognise the quavering voice of one of the kitchen girls. With her other hand, she places a parcel between my folded knees.

'Master Thomas says to look after Jane Wolvedon's silverware and her jewels.' Her voice chokes. 'God bless you, Master Francis, we shall not forget you.'

She melts into the dark of the hedgerow; the only trace of this seemingly unreal visitation is the packet pressed closely to my stomach. I shall discover later that it contains a bowl, a cup, a spoon bearing the Wolvedon arms (Argent, a Chevron, between three Wolves' Heads, Sable), a chain with a medallion of St Crida and a ring set with a stone of bright, intense blue on which the Tregian coat of arms (Ermine, on a Chief Sable, three Jays, Or) is finely engraved. Through one vicissitude and the next, I lost everything except for the ring with its azure stone. It is now my only tangible memento of Cornwall and of my life as a gentleman.

ONCE WE REACH THE Ridgeway, a good distance from Golden, Carey's soldiers leave us to our lot. The small company comprises my grandmother and her horse; the cart carrying my mother and Bosgrave, a young cousin who serves as her lady-in-waiting; a gaunt, ageing mare ridden by Phillips, my father's valet, newly released from two years in prison; and our pony, led by Phillips.

We have two fears: that we will get stuck in the mud, and that my mother will give birth in the middle of the countryside.

'We're avoiding Launceston,' Phillips tells me, when I ask him where we are going.

Phillips is a young man, broad-shouldered and vigorous; his twinkling eyes, thick mop of blond hair and affable face give him an air of constant good humour, which I find reassuring. He speaks to me like an adult.

'It's better not to run any unnecessary risks; there might be people in Launceston who would seek to harm you. We're going to St Austell for the moment. Then we'll see.'

St Austell is barely four leagues away; two hours by horse on a dry road. But that night, the mud, our inadequate mounts, my mother's state and the high emotion we all feel, make progress slow in the extreme. We take the precaution of travelling along a sunken lane known only to the people of that part of the country. Our convoy advances at a crawl and, when dawn breaks, St Austell is still not visible through the curtain of rain.

I am chilled to the bone, but numb, so I feel nothing. My nerves are as taut as the strings of a lute. I drowse without ever truly falling asleep, clutching the parcel tight – what if we are set upon unawares, and killed right here?

I am roused from my torpor by a loud noise. St Austell bell tower is finally visible in the faint, dull light of dawn. A horseman is galloping towards us, his coat flying in the wind. When he sees us, he tugs at his reins so abruptly that his horse swerves violently to one side, nearly unseating him. Phillips, Mary and I breathe a cry of surprise as we suddenly recognise

Jane, riding astride like a man, wild and dishevelled, with her skirts hitched up. She slides to the ground in a single movement and throws herself to her knees before Madam Catherine, who looks down at her from her saddle.

'You must make a halt at St Austell, hide yourselves, wait a few days,' Jane gasps. 'I heard George Carey's men say it would have been better if they had killed you all. I stole a horse and set out to look for you. I thought I would never find you, or that I would arrive too late. Forgive me, madam, I . . . '

Tears prevent her from continuing. Madam Catherine dismounts, raises her up and embraces her.

'Thank you, Jane,' she says. 'You have been most courageous.'

'Keep me with you, madam, please. They were smashing everything at Golden when I left, and I was scared to stay in my own house. They would have reached it too, at any moment, and what's more, I took a horse from them . . . '

'Phillips!'

'Yes, madam.'

'Send the horse back, if you would. Let us not attract any more unnecessary trouble. And you, Jane, go to the children.'

A friendly slap on the hindquarters sends the horse off at a gallop, without further ado. Jane hurries over to our pony, grasps Mary's and Adrian's outstretched hands tightly to her bosom, then comes to me, cradling my head and embracing me. I stretch out my free hand and she takes it, her gaze meeting mine. There is such love in her eyes that I am no longer cold or hungry. She is here. She has defied fate.

We wait in St Austell for a few days. Nobody comes in pursuit of us. The baby, for its part, is late in coming. Anxiety and nameless danger are ever-present. Finally, my mother decides to continue the journey. An attempt to reach London by sea is a failure. We wait in vain on Black Head, at the end of the bay, for a whole night. There is a raging storm. The boat does not come – or if it comes, it cannot land. We continue by road. The weather has turned fine and the lanes are dry. Mary and I walk sometimes, to escape our uncomfortable baskets. Jane watches over us. I am so happy she is with us that all the discomforts of the journey pale into insignificance.

We leave Cornwall and enter Devon, where we travel on busier roads. We remain on the alert, but I think we all feel a certain relief: we are no longer at the mercy of the soldierly rabble of Messrs Grenville and Carey.

The sole image I retain of this part of the journey is the profusion of gorse throughout the countryside; the sides of the road are covered with its golden flowers.

We have been travelling for three days and find ourselves near Salisbury when my mother says, in a choked voice:

'I think it will be soon.'

Phillips spurs his horse and returns a while later, looking anxious:

'I have found a house where they are waiting for you, but it's a good league away.'

'Let us go, then; it is not quite yet.'

And my poor mother, her face pale and puffy, grits her teeth in the cart, while we keep on as fast as we can. Jane wipes the sweat from her face, while Bosgrave rubs her shoulders to ease the tension. When we finally reach the house – a large farm – its occupants hurry out to meet us.

My mother's face is contorted with pain.

'I can move no more,' she whispers.

They make a litter of blankets and a throng of women carries her indoors. We children remain outside, quite forgotten. We pace up and down, and little Adrian sings us an old song in a thin voice, barely more than a whisper, telling of storms, exaltations, passion and murder. Phillips finally emerges. My face must be tense, for he comes up to me and places a hand on my shoulder.

'All will be well, Master Francis, all will be well, you'll see.'

They come to fetch us. The labour was very quick and, barely an hour after our arrival, my mother gives birth to a girl, Margaret.

We wait until she has recovered from the birth. When the required time is up, we get on our way again. I am given care of the infant, for as my mother said:

'That way, you'll be two to a basket and the weight will be better spread.'

I develop a special affection for this little sister; we share a strong bond and I have always felt it was forged in this basket.

It is May when we reach London.

We go straight to the house of my grandfather Stourton in Clerkenwell, where we find Sir John Arundell and his wife, my grandmother Anne, together with their family.

I see myself arriving even now: I hand the infant to Jane, then extricate myself from the basket for the last time, with a heavy heart. What will become of us? I look up and my gaze meets that of the master of the house, the great Arundell in person. I had seen him once before, at our house, during a feast, and he had not paid me the slightest attention.

Now, he looks at me closely. Jet black hair, a Roman nose, grey eyes, the look of a professional soldier about him – his face is unchanged, as if nothing had happened since we last met. He smiles, takes a step forward and exclaims:

'So, Master Francis, have you brought us your Latin?' He extends his hand – a mark of respect I am unaccustomed to receiving from the adults of my acquaintance. I shake it with due gravity and reply:

'I hope, sir, that the journey has not crumpled it excessively.'

He breaks into a resounding laugh.

'Come and take some refreshment, we shall examine all that later.'

I trip happily into the large house: the world might not collapse after all.

In a few days, I have forgotten Golden. Thomas is all I miss. But London is a marvellous place.

The city's enchanting contrasts strike me most of all. At Golden, the silence was broken only by human voices, bellowing animals, the occasional squeal of a cart, the blacksmith's hammer or the woodcutter's axe. At times, when all was quiet in the manor garden, you could even hear the slap of water against the pier at Golden Mill or a bargeman singing. A passing bee was a distraction. London is a perpetual clamour, its echo reaching even to Clerkenwell, located, as it is, a fair distance from the city gates.

Sir John takes me under his wing. Never truly knowing him before, I had always thought him a sort of grandfather figure. But that is impossible here. This is a man in the prime of life, sprightly and alert. He becomes a second father to me.

He sits me on the back of his horse and we ride all over the huge city together. We make a tour of London's great markets: Cheapside, the largest, where it is essential to arrive early to be well served – it opens at six o'clock in the morning to the sound of a bell; Leadenhall where, according to Sir John's steward, you can find the best poultry, the softest leather, the finest cloth and the sturdiest, most expertly fashioned kitchen utensils. And the fish market, at Fish Street Hill and Billingsgate, by the river, which you can smell from half a league away, all bargemen and boats constantly coming and going, weighed down with the daily catch.

It is a vast cacophony: vendors shouting their prices and extolling their wares in stentorian voices, each trying to outdo the next above the thunder of passing carts, the lowing of cattle and the tumult of the crowd, quarrelling, laughing, singing and discussing the events of the day. Open and covered carts roll swiftly by, heedless of anyone on foot; it is every man for himself, in a constant, cheerful rush spiced with imprecations. Our little company on horseback – Sir John, his valet, his steward and myself – are often forced to flatten ourselves against the fronts of houses, and we end up covered with dust or mud from head to toe.

It is not rare for a collision to block a street, whereupon it takes hours to clear the shattered wood, tangled harnesses and twisted metal, in an attempt to save the horses. But even if no clash occurs, we often witness rows between two carters, both standing on their seats, reins in hand, each heaping insults on the other, who had the presumption not to yield a precedence to which, by definition, they are of course entitled. Their horses join in the altercation in their way: pawing the ground, neighing, snorting and tossing their manes. Meanwhile, we wait patiently to pass.

The streets are filled with stalls and shops overflowing with goods. Apprentices and servants take advantage of our forced stops to run out and contribute their own refrains to the general cacophony:

'Pins! Garters! Spanish gloves! Silk ribbons!'

'Beautiful crabs! See my fine crabs!'

'Bargains! Bargains here!'

'Would you care to buy, sir?'

'Firm pears! Buy my pears!'

'Beautiful shoes!'

'Ruffs, cuffs and farthingales!'

'See the quality, my good sir!'

'Charcoal, wood charcoal, banish the cold!'

'Ink for your inkwell! See how it flows well!'

One day, we go to the square in front of St Paul's Cathedral, where the booksellers are. To our surprise, we find none of the quiet reverence one associates with reading.

The shops are adorned with brightly coloured signs that enchant me: ships, water nymphs, Moors' faces, bishops' mitres, snarling dragons and Saracens' heads. As for the shopkeepers, they have the same stentorian voices as the vendors at Cheapside or Leadenhall. You'd think you were at the vegetable market, save for the Latin mixed in here with the English.

'What do you require, my good sir?'

'*The Mirror for Magistrates*! New illustrated edition!'

'Freshly printed! Never before published!'

'Buy my map of the New World!'

'Chronicles and homilies!'

'Come on! Come on! Take a look at my book! All you need to conjure the perils and pitfalls of the sea!'

'Read my *Book of the Courtier*! With engravings! Custom and decorum, all explained!'

It is the same at the Royal Exchange, between Cornhill and Threadneedle Street, where all the world's merchants meet to discuss their business. On the first floor there is a row of shops: apothecaries, armourers, bookshops, jewellers, mercers and haberdashers, all vaunting their wares – a fashionable garment here, a love potion there, wigs and fragrant musks; one sells beard brushes, another handbells; there are coat linings, purses, the finest Toledo blades and . . . I forget.

The place that I find most entertaining is the area around the Exchange. Here is a mosaic of fruit sellers, hawkers and chimney sweepers, apprentices dallying gaily with housemaids, and clerks scurrying hither and thither, all in a commotion, a monstrous choir of carters thundering past, their singing often audible above the racket, shouts from tavern gardens, farriers' hammers, carpenters' mallets, the din of smithies, barking dogs and the laughter of all those who, like myself, feel infinite pleasure at this monumental symphony.

In spite of all that, we always find an opportunity to talk.

'My father looked after your grandfather when he was orphaned as a little boy,' Sir John told me one day. 'So I will look after you. Let's say it's a tradition. Your father is in prison for all of us, so I will do my best to take his place here in the world outside, until he is released.'

One evening, by chance, I overhear him explaining to his wife, my grandmother Anne, who reproached him for spoiling me and failing in severity, that I have been too much neglected since the onset of the Tregians' troubles:

'Young Francis is a gentleman. He must honour the royal blood that runs in his veins and the remarkable intelligence with which he has been endowed.'

I am fairly dazzled by that. The piskies had been quite enough for me up until then; nobody had ever mentioned royal blood. But it is too late to make a royal gentleman of me now. Blue blood courses through me, of that there is no doubt – I am cousin to at least two princes and my line leads straight back to William the Conqueror – but it has been entirely wasted in my case.

It is not for want of an education.

I had read a great deal at Golden, and spoke Latin with the ease of a child at play, but had learned little else. My music was limited to *Lady Wynkfyld's Rownde*. I did not know how to handle a dagger, and, although I easily covered long distances on horseback, clinging to the mane and without a saddle, as farm children do, I knew nothing of horsemanship; the ponies and horses I had mounted were workhorses and had nothing in common with the superb beasts at the Clerkenwell stables. Our own pedigree horses had disappeared when my father was arrested.

Sir John remedied all that. In a few days, I had music and geometry teachers, instructors for riding and fencing, and a learned tutor of Latin and Greek who spent long days teaching me to master the Classics, and to write. I learned rhetoric: the eight parts of speech, subject, predicate, complement, accidents and so on. Soon I was speaking virtually nothing but Latin. Even with Sir John, Jane, Lady Anne and Madam Catherine, our conversations were hardly ever in the vernacular now. Mary and I had reached the age at which children were forbidden to speak English within the family circle.

I was interested in everything and studied from dawn till dusk, six days a week. I soon fell into a routine whose strictures afforded me a space of my own, just as at Golden.

I saw Jane only rarely, for a true miracle had occurred: Madam Catherine doted on her now. Nobody, myself apart, remembered that she had once been my nurse. She had lost her annuity of twenty pounds with the praemunire. Madam Catherine promised to reinstate this, and fought by all means possible to recover the revenues from the lands she had brought to the Tregians as her dowry, which she felt should have been excluded from the punitive seizure. Meanwhile, Jane had been promoted to lady-in-waiting, an arrangement that suited both women very well indeed. I had expected we would live a life of penury, but that was not the case. We kept our expenses to a minimum but without depriving ourselves, at least not yet.

'Your lands outside Cornwall have not been seized,' Madam Catherine explained to me, one day. 'They are not many and bring in little, but they will serve to make you a living and protect your father, maybe even to free him. Or at least to get him a more comfortable prison.'

When we arrived in London, my father was once again languishing in the depths of Launceston dungeon with the common prisoners. Once we children were safe, my mother had wished to return there. But she had suffered during the birth and on the journey, and Lady Anne had insisted she stay.

'Let us rather employ our efforts to release your husband from that terrible dungeon and have him brought to London.'

That took place in August. But although his comforts were greatly improved, my father was still being held in secret. Only my mother was permitted to see him, so she spent as much time as possible with her husband, and was with child well before Christmas.

A rumour went around that my father was planning to escape and leave for Spain; but rumour was all it remained, and I am not even certain it was well founded. I had picked it up from my new source of information: the stables.

Drawing on my experience, I had begun by approaching the oldest stable groom. But in the end it was Giuliano who became my friend, an Italian of about eighteen or nineteen, marvellously agile, exuberant and always in the best of spirits, whom Sir John had taken on in Lanherne several years before.

SIR JOHN OFFERED to disband his household in Cornwall to show his good faith, for although fiercely Catholic, he was no less a staunch supporter of Elizabeth. I had so often heard my mother refer to the Queen as a bastard and a usurper that I was amazed at this show of loyalty. I unburdened myself to Sir John in the course of one of our extended walks around the city; in Latin, naturally.

'My dear Francis,' he tells me, 'Catholic we are, and on that we shall not compromise. But still, we are not idiots. Myself, I am sufficiently patriotic and have enough good sense to understand what Elizabeth is attempting to achieve by these religious persecutions. It has not escaped me that during the reign of the late Queen Mary, we Catholics had many rights and were thus able to advance both our own affairs and those of the papacy. Yet I have always thought that as a nation, we were in error. With her religious zeal, Queen Mary pulled England down; we became a third-rate power, lagging behind Spain. During those few years when King Philip was husband to our queen, he had hoped to lay hands on the country. But if we desire to be a great nation, it is essential we escape Spain. Unfortunately, many Catholics confuse the interests of their soul with that of their country.'

He looks at me for a moment, pensive, and adds, in the vernacular:

'Make no mistake, Francis. At the moment, Elizabeth wishes to have nothing to do with me; she is wary. But I do not hold that against her. She is surrounded by sharks who take advantage of the situation to despoil us of our wealth. Despite that, I would not hesitate to lay down my life for her, were she to demand it.'

Surely there is an insinuated message in this declaration of intent? With a boldness that shocks even me, I dare to ask:

'Is my father . . . ?'

'Your father is an admirable man, Francis. Once he has taken a decision, he is immovable and can be depended upon absolutely. You owe him the greatest respect.'

His tone is final.

For the first time, I wonder what Sir John really thinks of my father.

THE CLERKENWELL HOUSE IS organised in such a way that we boys only rarely encounter the women, so I am able to exchange no more than a few words and smiles with Jane. She must be eighteen or nineteen, and is astoundingly beautiful. Through Giuliano, I know that she has suitors by the dozen and also that she ignores them all, to my great satisfaction.

Mary has set her heart on attending lessons with my rhetoric teacher and shows such persistence that she finally gets her way, accompanied by much laughter and shrugging of shoulders. She is a perfect, accomplished student. But we have no time to converse, and the lessons are barely over before she returns to her needlepoint and I to my fencing or riding.

The newcomer in my life is my brother Adrian. He is slight and pale, with huge, light-grey eyes. He often goes unnoticed because he speaks little but, when he does get around to contributing a remark, his intelligence always dazzles.

Adrian sits next to me while I revise and amend my notebooks of Latin vocabulary, expressions and exercises. I hand him the pages with the ink still wet and gravely he sprinkles them with sand that he blows out of the window. After a while, he begins searching for the words I need for my innumerable, detested Latin translations, designed to give me a greater familiarity with the language. And one fine day, he begins to construct Latin sentences of his own, to discourse in the language of Cicero.

He exudes serenity, and I find myself missing him when he isn't there. He seems to exist in a bubble inside which there is no place for doubt. It is not arrogant certitude but a quiet assurance that attracts me all the more because I myself am beset by doubts of every kind.

This relatively tranquil existence lasts for about a year.

In retrospect, I see that I mention my mother little and my father even less. But I confess that they play only small parts in my childhood. I overhear much talk about my father, couched in the most contradictory terms. He is a stranger to me: I have not seen him since I was just three or four years old. As for my mother, she is always somewhere else, returning only to give birth then leaving again; my father's situation obliges her to pursue a host of actions on his behalf. That year is no exception. She remains in confinement for some weeks, gives birth to my brother Charles and then, no sooner has she been churched than she places him with a nurse and leaves again. Most of her time is spent at the Fleet, my father's latest prison, where he was put firstly in the common gaol, and then with other recusants. Now my mother is fighting to secure him one of the apartments reserved for Catholic gentlemen, devoting even greater energies to the task than usual because my father is sick from the privations and lack of cleanliness at Launceston. In the end, she goes to speak with the Queen herself. The word is that she is likely to get her way, since both the Queen and her Secretary of State, William Cecil, are now persuaded that nothing will make Tregian flinch, that he is beyond redemption.

The change comes in the twenty-fifth or twenty-sixth year of the reign (dates have never been my strength). It turns our lives upside down.

VI

Through the Royal Exchange as I walked
Where gallants in satin did shine:
At midst of the day they parted away
at several places to dine.
The gentry went to the King's Head,
the nobles went unto the Crown:
The knights unto the Golden Fleece
and the ploughman to the Clown...

'BALLAD OF THE LONDON TAVERNS'

WE WERE TWENTY OR THIRTY living all together in Clerkenwell: adults, visitors and the Stourton, Arundell and Tregian children, not to mention the servants. Sir John had dispersed his household in Lanherne, but the man himself was unchanged and his door remained open to every Catholic in distress, even when they were not family, as we were. Clerkenwell replaced Lanherne as the bustling centre of operations. And for that reason, it could not last.

The Queen had clamped down hard on the Catholics: a confrontation with Spain was inevitable, the only question was when. Priests like Cuthbert continued to celebrate Mass, entering the country in a constant stream. When caught, they were tried and frequently put to death, but this did nothing to discourage them. I myself met one who had been arrested and imprisoned in the Marshalsea but spent his days out and about in London, saying Mass and administering the sacraments. He would return to prison to sleep, say Mass, take confession and give Communion to the prisoners, then set out into town again the following morning at dawn.

Whether he secured these favours by bribing the gaolers or because he had the good fortune to fall in with guards sympathetic to the Catholic cause, I have no idea. At the time, such subtleties were beyond my grasp and the question never crossed my mind. Still, he was finally brought before the court, sentenced, and found himself in the Tower. He was never released.

At home in Clerkenwell, Mass was said daily, even twice daily for some, though not for me.

I don't doubt for one minute that the henchmen acting for the Secretary of State William Cecil (Lord Burghley) and his chief bloodhound Lord Walsingham were fully aware of all that was said and done at Clerkenwell. Impossible to imagine that the servants' hall had not been infiltrated by at least one spy – and the experience of my later life confirms it almost beyond doubt.

The Clerkenwell spy (or spies) could report with confidence that Sir John never turned away a priest, but that Lady Anne showed rather less enthusiasm for her husband's boundless Christian charity.

'Of course,' she said, 'we must admit a priest, even two, to say Mass. But I cannot see why we should be a rallying point for every missionary newly arrived from the Continent and content to live under our roof, at our expense.'

Anyone not attending the Church of England was subject to a fine – a hefty one – which meant that many Catholics still loyal to the old religion ignored the edicts from Rome and worshipped at the new established Church. Failure to attend was a luxury beyond the reach of most: Sir John paid twenty pounds with each new moon, which made two hundred and sixty pounds a year, at a time when twenty pounds was a decent annual wage for an artisan.

The material hardships that resulted, and the persona of Sir John himself – utterly unshakeable on matters of religion, yet so open to the transformation taking place across England – had unexpected and, in many ways, unimaginable consequences for me.

In less extraordinary times, until the age of twelve or thirteen, I would have been educated at home or with another family to whom I would have been sent as a page, before going up to Oxford to complete my studies and receive my degree. That was the natural progression for a young, well-born gentleman. But there it was: in the latter half of the last century, no one from a Catholic family was well born, no matter what their lineage. And so my gentleman's education took a winding course. I congratulate myself on it today, but at the time it provoked much remonstration and gnashing of teeth, even from my father in prison.

One night, Adrian and I listen in (uninvited and undetected) on a heated discussion between Sir John and my mother. Eavesdropping is our only means of instruction on certain matters.

'I would rather the boys grow up ignorant than have them sent to such teachers,' declares my mother.

Her temper flares whenever she speaks to Sir John. He is her mother's second husband, the man who had replaced her own father, Lord Charles Stourton, himself sentenced to death and executed when she was a child. The grandfather I never knew was by all accounts a vigorous man, always active and very quarrelsome. He had fought his neighbours over a ter-ritorial dispute, and murdered them with the help of four of his men. He was hanged – with a silken rope and the honours due to a gentleman. The servants who accompanied Lady Anne and her six children into her new marriage and household say my mother had loved her father completely and wholeheartedly.

Back to the quarrel. Adrian and I listen in our nightshirts, barefoot, in a niche behind the tapestry. My mother – and above all my father, for whom she acts as spokeswoman – is concerned for the salvation of our souls, not the practicalities of our education as such. But she finds it hard to argue with Sir John.

Unlike the late Sir Charles, Sir John is a placid, measured man who considers everything with great good sense. He would never allow himself to succumb to such an excess of emotion as to actually kill a man. I know he is skilled at fencing – I saw him practise, and he taught me some for-midable thrusts. If he was ever obliged to use those skills, he would show implacable calm and perfect manners.

He has Protestant friends – religion is not his only yardstick – and this shocks my mother. In some obscure way, she sees his tolerance as a form of treason. Her irritation is evident in her voice, which suddenly turns shrill and high-pitched.

Until then, we had been taught by the tutors hired for our cousins and uncles, Edward and the younger Charles Stourton. But now Charles was about to leave for Reims, where the English College at Douai had transferred following trouble arising from the religious wars.

Sir John thinks the time is right to send us to school with other children. He has even made enquiries and found a school prepared to take us – the Merchant Taylors'. Sir John has made a generous donation and the school will turn a blind eye to our origins.

'The headmaster Richard Mulcaster is an exceptional man, the best teacher to be found in all of London, probably in all of England. His openness of mind is as great as his knowledge.'

'A Protestant. A traitor to the faith.'

'He may be a Protestant but he's a man of great good sense. We can be sure the boys will receive an excellent education if we send them to him. This is a fine opportunity for them.'

'He will make them convert. They will no longer be good Catholics.'

'He takes a number of Jewish children and none has been forced to convert. He will do the same for ours, he has given me his word.'

'A Protestant's word . . . '

'Richard Mulcaster is an honest man. I've known him for years and, despite our many disagreements, he has shown me unflinching loyalty.'

They continue in this vein for some time, until Sir John bursts out:

'My dear Mary, you talk as if your sons were imbecilic lumps of putty to shape as you wish. When they are quite exceptional boys . . . ' Adrian and I exchange a glance of mutual appreciation, eyebrows raised, in the half-light behind the tapestry. ' . . . with higher than average perceptiveness. We will explain the situation to them, and they will make the most of it. While we wait for a Catholic king or queen to ascend the throne, we live here and now. It will do them no good to remain in isolation. Know your enemy, so that you may fight him all the more effectively. Whenever a Catholic school for children of their age is established, we will send them there. But in the meantime, I shall go myself to your husband and explain what we are doing.'

And with that, he leaves the room, quickly followed by my mother, sighing heavily.

We emerge from our hiding place and bow to one another in the wavering light of the chandelier, sweeping our imaginary hats to the floor.

''Tis an honour to meet one of such higher-than-average perceptiveness, sire.'

'I assure you, the honour is all mine. Delighted to make the acquaint-ance of so unshapeable a lump of putty.'

And without further ado, we steal cautiously back to bed.

Sir John has his way. And while my poor father languishes in the Fleet, I relish two more unforgettable years of youth.

WHEN I WAS A boy, the Merchant Taylors' grammar school was undoubt-edly the best known in London, thanks to its headmaster, Richard Mul-caster. This extraordinary man was then about fifty years old and had led the school since its foundation twenty years earlier. It was one of several originally established by the London guilds for the education of poor children who were otherwise to be found loitering in the street, illiterate and unlearned. The London schools heralded the opening of many more of their kind across the whole of England.

We left for school every morning at six o'clock, usually accompanied by Giuliano. We came home again at five o'clock in the evening. We would work at our Latin and Greek until eleven in the morning, when we ate, after which class began again at one o'clock. Giuliano would collect us at five. In winter, when the days were very short, we would go to school at seven in the morning, each boy with his candle so that we could see to work later in the afternoon, when night fell.

We were two hundred and fifty pupils, all of us living at home with our families. The school's founding charter expressly stated that it would teach children from any and all walks of life, but it was not free of charge, and the modest fees were enough to exclude the children of the poorest families. The only conditions for admission were to be able to read and write perfectly, and to know the catechism in English and Latin. We were promised that, on leaving, we would be perfectly fluent in Latin, Greek and Hebrew, and schooled in literature and good manners.

At first, I feel lost and confused. Luckily, I have Adrian by my side. He looks much younger than I, being as small and slight as I am tall and well built. Yet there are no more than two years between us. When we join the Merchant Taylors' school, we have been studying the same lessons for some time already. We have become inseparable.

It is the end of summer and we arrive early, before the school bell sounds the hour. As time goes on, I grow accustomed to the short journey, but that first day it seems endless, as if we had crossed half of London. The school is housed in the Manor of the Rose, a tall, stout tower like a Norman fortress, belonging to the Duke of Buckingham. Many families have arrived early for the first day. There is a great bustle of adults and children, all as terrified as we are to find themselves in such a mass of people, far from home. The air is filled with the murmur of voices and children's sobs while, in the background, the shopkeepers of nearby Candlewick Street begin calling out their wares to the passing trade. Their cries are a counterpoint to the murmur of voices in the yard.

The bells of neighbouring St Laurence Pountney ring the hour and Richard Mulcaster emerges from the school's main doorway, surrounded by the other masters. He claps his hands and there is immediate silence, broken only by the striking of the bell.

I know now, having heard it the following year, that Master Mulcaster delivered a welcoming speech to the returning pupils and to the sixty new boys, ourselves included. But at the time I heard nothing and still remember nothing.

The schoolmasters circulate through the crowd, separating us into groups.

'New boys over here.'

'The second class here.'

'Advanced pupils, please.'

We find ourselves arranged in rows, sorted by size, so that I am the last in line. Adrian is right at the front. He hears nothing of the speech either, terrified that I am no longer there to protect him.

The family members and escorts leave and we are led indoors in silence.

The classroom is vast and lined with benches on all sides. We have been told that the classrooms have a raised platform and chair for the teacher, with benches facing it, in rows. Here, there is no platform and the benches are arranged in a square with a big open space in the centre.

Each boy is presented with a box containing paper, quills, a quill cutter, a pencil, a slate, an hourglass and a candle. Ink and glue are provided separately, to avoid accidents.

We have two schoolmasters. Robert Wyddosox begins straight away, assessing our knowledge of Latin. My brother and I owe our perfect knowledge of the language to him: he spoke it fluently. We also owe to him our perfect command of English – we have neglected the vernacular until now, all our efforts having been concentrated on our Latin.

The great Richard Mulcaster, our other teacher, is a staunch believer in the equal importance of the mother tongue alongside Latin. He teaches us Greek and Hebrew, but from time to time he tests our English too, and woe betide the boy whose style is found lacking or inelegant.

On that first day, Mulcaster tours the classrooms to deliver a short speech to each group of pupils. He keeps us till last. We are the new boys and he has more to say to us.

We are arranged by size in class, too. Thus I find myself sitting next to my brother since he is the smallest and I the biggest, and the benches are arranged in a square.

'Extremities meet,' Adrian whispers, a smile in his eyes.

The door opens and Mulcaster walks into the room.

'Stand, gentlemen,' orders Wyddosox. We stand.

Mulcaster steps into the centre of the room, then paces slowly all the way round it. He stops in front of each of us, piercing us with his stare for what seems like an eternity. It seems to me that he is trying to commit all our faces to memory. He says nothing to Adrian and me. Indeed, no one at school ever comments on our family origins, or the Catholic religion in general.

'Gentlemen,' he says in English, after his initial tour of inspection, 'you will have noticed that in this room, the seats are all on the same level, and there is no master's chair, none higher than your own. This signifies a number of things, and I wish to talk about them to you now. First, a man does not distinguish himself by sitting on a great chair two feet off the ground but by the elevation of his mind. Your teachers are learned men. Soon, thanks to their learning, you will feel their superiority in your hearts. And they will be delighted if, one day, you succeed in rising to their level. And so you see, the space where they stand, here in the middle, is vast. There is room for everyone. Your task is to find your place within it. For the end of education and training is to help nature to reach perfection, in the complete development of all your various powers. But perfection differs from one man to another. One of you will excel at Latin, another in music, perhaps. The important thing is to recognise your gifts and to work at them, to reach the highest pinnacle of attainment. That is the duty and responsibility of each and every one of you. At this school, instruction is not handed down from on high by a motionless figure seated in a chair. We believe in the Peripatetic school of learning. We move among our pupils. And our aim is for each of you to walk among us, one day, on a path of your own making.'

As if to flesh out his meaning, he paces a long, winding path through the empty space, in silence.

'I have no doubt,' he says finally, 'that your young heads are full of Latin, prayers and wisdom. Far be it from me to challenge what you have learned so far. But I speak to you this morning in the vernacular because I would like to set out some very important principles and I wish to be certain that you have understood.'

He takes a deep breath, like a man waking from sleep.

'Those who deal in the mathematical sciences are obliged to give precise demonstrations of their ineluctable results, and to reach conclusions which it is either impossible or very difficult to refute. The same is not true of the moral or political sciences. Here, we deal with Man in all his complexity, and we must take account of particular, infinitely varied characteristics. A mathematician's truth is beyond debate, but the moralist's truth must be approached with the greatest caution, never forgetting the particular circumstances in each case.'

He sweeps the motionless class with his dark eyes, then goes on, raising his voice slightly, and intoning the words in a lilting rhythm.

'It is not enough for Plato to praise a thing, for Aristotle to approve it, Cicero to recommend it and Quintilian to have had word of it, for us to adopt it. We respect them all, but we may not be able to apply what they say, because our circumstances, here in England, are different. What is to be said of those who borrow the ancient authors' authority for their own, while taking no account of the context in which our forebears expressed themselves? Harrington!'

Harrington stands.

'What did I just say?'

Silence.

'Did you understand what I said, Harrington?'

Harrington swallows, then manages to speak.

'Yes, sir.'

'So tell me what you understood. I won't ask you to repeat it verbatim.'

'You said, sir, that … that … that we should consider the circumstances in order to express truths that are not mathematical.'

'What does Stowe say to that?'

Stowe stands up.

'I say that he is right: we need to consider the context when citing an author.'

'And why should we consider the context, Arundell?' There is a pause before Adrian and I understand Mulcaster's clever subterfuge. There are Arundells on both sides of the religious divide, while the Tregians are all Catholic. We both stand up.

'Ah, true enough,' he says, with a barely detectable smile, 'we have two Arundells in our class. From now on, we will call you Adrian and Francis. Master Francis, you may sit down.'

Having found a supremely elegant solution to the problem of our identity (strictly speaking, he is forbidden by law from admitting us to the school), he now addresses my brother.

'Now, Master Adrian, why should we consider the context?'

'Because otherwise, sir, we run the risk of making an author say something different from what he intended.'

'And what lesson do we draw from this, gentlemen?' Stowe and Adrian are both on their feet now. They stare at one another. Finally, Adrian speaks:

'You have urged us, sir, to think for ourselves.'

Stowe chimes in:

'Plato is not always right, merely because he is Plato.'

'Excellent, gentlemen! You may sit down. And now, open your desks.'

We do as instructed.

'Take out the tablet you will find there. It is engraved with the prayer you will recite every morning, every day at noon and every evening before you go home. Remember that you are all equal in the eyes of God, whatever your rank or situation, and that it is your duty to honour the Lord by working hard and developing your intelligence. We shall say the prayer together now. I wish to hear everyone's voice.'

And for the first time in their lives, the Tregian brothers intone the Protestant paternoster. We are prepared. We have been warned again and again, and have been taught the practice of mental equivocation. The difference between the two religions' prayers, I notice, is not particularly striking.

MUSIC LESSONS were another revelation. The Merchant Taylors' school was unique in all London in providing daily lessons in the art of music. What is more, we were each able to follow individual lessons. We were given our freedom on Tuesday afternoons, provided that we demonstrated the requisite musical skill, and were permitted to make music daily during the midday break. The school recommended a music master who lived nearby. Some of us used to go to his house in a small group, with an escort. The man's name was Thomas Morley. After just a few days, if he asked us to dive into the Thames fully dressed, I believe those of us following his classes would have done so without hesitation.

In a tiny room, he kept a lute, a virginal and one or two viols. Morley taught us singing and, by way of that, the theory of music. He was forever indulging in wordplay; and initially, when we were about to laugh, he would stare at us so severely that we were afraid we had offended him. Until we understood that even his severe look was done in jest. But Morley never took a wrong note lightly and he became quite angry when, after a lengthy explanation, we still confused the diatonic and chromatic scales.

'One of these days,' he would say, in Latin, with heavy sarcasm, 'you will confuse *chromatica* and *grammatica*.'

I can hear his first lesson now, as if it were yesterday.

'A clef is a sign placed at the beginning of a stave; it serves to show the height or lowness of every note placed on the same stave, or in the spaces between the lines, and if we do not place a clef on each line and in each space it is so as not to complicate things, for life is quite complicated enough, is it not Master Howe? You seem a little lost if I'm not mistaken? I was saying that in order not to complicate things unnecessarily, and to spare the copyist some work, we may consider that having indicated a key, the others may be deduced from it. Do you follow me Francis?'

'Yes, sir.'

'Very good! There are seven tones in the diatonic scale A, B, C, D, E, F, G. But for singing, we use only four.'

He gives us a demonstration, with his own voice and on the lute. Little by little, he initiates us into the complexities of musical interpretation and composition.

So that we understand music, he teaches us the rudiments of mathematics, though we barely realise it at the time.

'What is proportion? In music, we do not consider numbers by themselves, but as a sign to signify the altering of notes in time. Proportion is either of equality or inequality. A proportion of equality is the comparing of two equal quantities. A proportion of inequality is when two things of unequal quantity are compared. Has everyone understood me, even you, Master Howe?'

'Perfectly, sir.'

'I am delighted to hear it. A proportion of inequality – listen carefully Master Francis, and you too Master Howe, and I advise Messrs Adrian and Harrington not to stand there gaping or I'll have them dance a pavane they won't forget in a hurry, ha! So as I was saying, a proportion of inequality, then: we have a proportion of inequality when we compare two things of unequal quantity, and the proportion is either of more or less inequality. A proportion of greater inequality is when a greater number is set over and compared to a lesser. In music, this always signifies a diminution. The inverse proportion is when the smaller is set over and compared to the greater number, which in music, Master Adrian, always signifies . . . '

'Augmentation, sir?'

'Augmentation! Excellent deduction. Naturally, in music, one may have an infinite number of proportions, but we have only five in common use: *Dupla, Tripla, Quadrupla, Sesquialtera* and *Sesquitertia.*'

Theoretical explanations like these generally left us utterly lost, but Morley gave practical demonstrations of such limpid clarity that the following day, on repeating the lesson of the day before, we were astonished that it had caused us even the slightest difficulty.

Adrian and I used our Tuesday afternoons to learn the lute and the virginal. Our master was a musician of the Chapel Royal and a great friend of Sir John: William Byrd.

William Byrd's reputation has not yet reached the bailiwick of Echallens. I often play his music, but as my English origins are a secret here, I have never mentioned his name. Besides which, the people of the Vaud share such boundless enthusiasm for the fifes and drums that there is little room for keyed instruments. This is doubtless the fault of the Reformation for having destroyed almost all the great organs. Those which I make are small and portable, and the people who come to me with orders are careful to be discreet. They are mostly Catholic. The virginal, which my clients call 'François's spinet', is more widely used, but inevitably it is the preserve of a small minority. In London or St Austell you would be quite likely to find a virginal at the barber's; not so in Echallens, or even Lausanne.

I cannot describe William Byrd in anything other than superlatives. He is, with Claudio Monteverde, the greatest musician it has ever been my privilege to meet. His music expresses the perfection of the Universe; and although he lacked the agility of John Bull, who played the organ and virginal with astonishing mastery, no one noticed because his compositions and playing were so refined that the rest is forgotten. Byrd was a Catholic and made no secret of the fact. His music protected him, and Elizabeth, a virtuoso in her own right, played his music with a passion. She would have no one touch a hair on his head.

With us boys, he was kindness itself.

'You have organists' fingers, both of you,' he told us on the first Tuesday of that memorable September, when we discovered so many marvels. 'Show me what you can do.'

We went over to the virginal, one after the other, and we played *Lady Wynkfyld's Rownde*, in great good humour. Byrd knew Thomas Morley well – he had taught him.

'The boy is an inexhaustible fount of knowledge and expertise. Theory is his speciality. He's an excellent composer and he will go far.'

Adrian and I hardly knew what to attend to first. Everything was so exciting, we worked like demons. If we took any physical recreation at all, it was because Madam Catherine and Lady Anne forced us into it, with Sir John's authority to back them up. Sir John made sure we practised our fencing and wrestling, too, with Giuliano as our instructor.

●　　　●　　　●

IT WAS DURING THESE two years that I met Giles Farnaby.

Giles's family had long been established in Truro, and his grandfather had served the Arundells and Tregians before moving to London, where the Farnabys were master joiners. They had kept in touch, and when Sir John needed a joiner in Clerkenwell, he would call on Farnaby. Giles's father, Thomas, would come to carry out the work accompanied by his son. I picture one scene in particular: Thomas Farnaby is planing a length of wood in the bedroom where Adrian and I sit talking about our music lesson. And suddenly Giles is there, talking with us. Is this the first time we have seen him? Is it before or after we have played, all three of us, before the assembled family? Is it before or after we sing at the wedding of one of our girl cousins? Before or after Giles confides in me?

'I am forced to obey my father's will and take an apprenticeship as a joiner, but I desire only one thing – to be a musician. After I have finished my apprenticeship I shall give up joinery forever.'

'You could make instruments, once you qualify as a joiner. Lucky you!'

Giles stands rooted to the spot, as if thunderstruck. He stares at me with an almost imbecilic air.

'Why didn't that brilliant idea occur to me?' he says, after a pause.

We shake hands solemnly: our friendship is sealed. Giles is a few years older than I, but that does not matter at all.

Our playing is by no means perfect but, in time, we form a consort capable of accompanying ceremonies and entertaining the household. My sister Mary sings with us at first. After a while, she is sent away to Lancashire as a lady-in-waiting, and our little group mourns the loss of her fine voice. Jane is tempted to take her place but, despite her many qualities, she has no ear and sings horribly off-key. Amid much laughter, we give up on the attempt to make a musician of her. And my sister Margaret is still too young.

My mother virtually lives at the prison. She comes back to us only once, for a few weeks, to give birth to a little girl.

We are not allowed to see my father, who becomes a distant figure to me.

People say I look astonishingly like him.

'I seem to see my son, all over again,' Madam Catherine says often. And her daughter, my aunt Elizabeth, almost collapses in shock when we pay her a visit.

'Such a likeness! Incredible!' she declares, when she has got over her surprise.

Everyone agrees that the resemblance is physical and nothing more. My father had been a turbulent child, prone to extremes and violent fits of temper. He had to be forced to apply himself to his studies, was often punished and required constant supervision, says Madam Catherine. At the age of ten, he applied the same force, the same violence, the same stubbornness to his religion that he did to everything else.

I am different. As if by instinct, I keep my passions to myself – my studies; my affection for Jane, Giles and Adrian. I have no desire to make a show of them and become vulnerable as a result.

The general zeal for correcting me with physical punishment has passed. A fixed stare is enough to dissuade my mother. Only the great Richard Mulcaster seems unaffected by my gaze. But I do little to expose myself to the risk of punishment. I pray when necessary, I am well behaved and polite, I study hard. I speak Latin at home and – without waiting to be asked – I have taken charge of my frail younger brother.

VII

The leaves be green, the nuts be brown
They hang so high they will not come down.
Browning Madame, Browning Madame,
So merrily we sing Browning Madame.
The fairest flower in a garden green
Is in my love's breast full comely seen
And with all others compare she can
Therefore now let us sing Browning Madame;

'THE LEAVES BE GREEN'
POPULAR BALLAD

IT ALMOST PAINS ME to recall these two years of plenitude. And yet, now that the floodgates of memory are open, the images pour forth in an endless flow.

The journey from Clerkenwell to Candlewick (pronounced Canning) Street:

Upon leaving the house, we pass the springs and wells on our left; Clerkenwell means 'the clerics' well', and there are others nearby. It is said that the water from these springs is the freshest in London. In days gone by, there were several monasteries and convents there, but they were dissolved by King Henry VIII. Nothing remains of the priory but the chapel, now Anglican, while all that is left of the nuns' convent is a wall against which a number of small houses has been built using stones from the demolition. The gatehouse of the Priory of St John of Jerusalem, an imposing fortification, survives intact. It has been converted and now houses the Queen's Master of the Revels. The ruins are still quite visible as we ride along St

John Street. Twenty years later, they would have practically disappeared, and today they doubtless persist only in the memories of old men such as me. Only the names remain – St John, St James, Charter House: empty raiments now.

If we take St John Street, we skirt Pardon Churchyard, which was opened during a great plague and is said to be the last resting place of fifty thousand souls. If we pass by there after sunset, Adrian and I, it is always with a touch of fear in our hearts; and returning home any later, we always take a parallel route, along Turnmill Street. The mill in question lies at the end of this thoroughfare, and during harvest time, the mule trains, voices, shouts and singing, as well as the smell of flour, which dominates all others, give Turnmill Street a festive air.

We cross Smithfield with not a second thought until, one day, one of our horses casts a shoe and we are forced to stop. An old man tells us that this is where Queen Mary the Catholic burned most of the three hundred heretics (by which he meant Protestants) condemned during her short reign:

'Young and old, men and women, children even; I saw them on the wooden pyres, praying aloud while the flames licked at their hands and faces. They died quickly, most often, suffocated by the smoke. But sometimes the flames were extinguished by the wind and the poor souls were left there, slowly dying but praying still. They had God with them.'

It fills me with horror and sadness to hear tell for the first time, and so clearly too, that 'our' Queen has also settled her affairs by means of executions. Since hearing that account, I think about the condemned every time I pass Smithfield, and at the same time I think about Cuthbert, with his pointed face and his grey eyes. Why must people die for believing in God in a different way from their neighbours?

We turn left onto Long Lane and follow it until we reach a crossway. In front of us lies the Barbican and, beyond it, Cripplegate. To our right is Aldersgate Street, leading straight to the city wall. The street is lined with shops of all kinds and is particularly busy in the morning, when a throng of carts crowds the entrance to the city. By the time we pass by, the stragglers are rushing to get to the markets, which often open before dawn. Everyone waits at the postern that has given its name to the street: Aldersgate.

Opinions differ on the name Aldersgate. As it is one of London's oldest gates, we are assured by some that it comes from the word 'elder'. Others insist that its name comes from the many alder trees that thrive there.

Beyond the postern we pass the large house of a printer on our right. Now and then we stop in for a visit, and almost forget the time as we contemplate the presses. His name is John Day. Since then, I have read many of the books printed in that large room with its low ceiling. There is a persistent odour of leather, ink and metal, a mixture found in our schoolrooms too, though much weaker, and which even today has the knack of touching me deeply. It represents a key to knowledge.

Opposite the printer's shop stands the church of St Anne and St Agnes, built against the wall itself. We ride on down St Martin's Le Grand – the continuation of Aldersgate Street, dedicated to the leather and shoe trade. The shopkeepers here all try to outdo each other by hanging up the most beautiful boot or the most gracious dancing slipper as their shop sign. One shoemaker ties a silk ribbon to an extravagant, high-heeled shoe, covered all over in gold, which he hangs above his door, low enough that everyone may admire it. Riders on horseback have to duck to avoid it or be struck in the face. One of our favourite tricks is to untie the ribbon without anyone seeing and bring it home for my younger sister Margaret, who soon amasses quite a collection of them.

We turn left again, onto West Cheap, a street so crowded full of wagons, mounted noblemen and merchants that we quickly turn off, so as not to be slowed down and risk arriving late for school. We cut through narrow back streets, Budge Row or Knightrider Street, before arriving at Candlewick Street. The story goes that it was the candle-makers who brought the cotton manufacturers to Candlewick Street, to make their wicks. It is said that the cotton manufacturers gave way to weavers and the weavers to drapers, the only occupants of the street whose existence I can guarantee, for I often saw them unpacking their goods and conferring with customers before their doors, convincing them of the freshness, durability and originality of the dyes, as well as the quality of their cloth. Here we turn right, towards the Thames, its smell reaching us on the incoming tide, and enter the covered yard overlooked by the church of St Laurence Pountney, situated just behind our school.

On occasion, we change our route and pass through a different postern: Newgate, with its prison, giving onto Snow Hill and, beyond that, the River Fleet. The Fleet had apparently once been navigable but is now just a ditch filled with refuse, at the bottom of which a murky water flows. Here there is a school as famous as ours, Christ's Hospital, which teaches poorer children.

Sometimes we ride down Old Bailey, turn onto St George's Lane and proceed, our hearts beating fast, along Fleet Lane, so making the circuit of the Fleet Prison. It is our way of paying a visit to our father. I think about him all the more for having never really known him.

At first, Giuliano comes faithfully to meet us and escort us home. Quite apart from the possible dangers along our route, his solicitude reflects our family's concern, for, with the exception of Sir John, everyone feels it is a form of sacrilege for us to attend the school of the enemy. Our grandmothers, our mother and doubtless our father fear we could succumb to what Madam Catherine calls 'the lure of Evil'.

But it is soon observed that we remain as devout, constant and well behaved as before. The differences between the two catechisms are clear, yet I still have considerable difficulty in understanding how good Christians, such as we all are, can make such a stir over so little. But I am very careful not to say so. Only Adrian is aware of my doubts. He understands them – there are few things that escape Adrian's keen intelligence and boundless generosity – but he does not share them. As he sees it, ours is not to question the Catholic faith, or our family's choices. So he attends the Anglican catechism classes at school with the aloof detachment of a caryatid.

After a time, the family breathes easily once again; prophylactic measures for the salvation of our souls are restricted to sermons pronounced by the priests and chaplains residing at Clerkenwell. Imperceptibly, the vigilance is relaxed. It happens, albeit rarely, that we go to school without Giuliano. And it happens, less rarely, that Giuliano is not there to meet us when we come out, in which case we walk home and say nothing to anyone. Only the stable hands know we have come home by our own means.

These unpremeditated walks provide unexpected glimpses of the city. On occasion we make a detour by way of the banks of the Thames, walking down to Billingsgate Quay, upstream of the Bridge, and stand looking out at the forest of masts on the river, so thick it seems that nothing is missing but the leaves. In the distance, sailing ships from far away progress upriver on the tide, the mariners singing joyously as they work, happy to have reached London:

> *There hath been great sale and utterance of Wine,*
> *Besides Beer, and Ale, and Hippocras fine,*
> *In every country, region and nation,*
> *But chiefly in Billingsgate at the Salutation;*
> *And at the Boar's Head near London Stone;*
> *The Swan at Downgate, a tavern well known;*
> *The Mitre in Cheap, and then the Bull's Head;*
> *And many like places that make noses red...*

Other times, we stop at the booksellers outside St Paul's to leaf through the chronicles and read the latest ballads, which we learn by heart, then make up for our tardiness by running straight home. We arrive for evening prayers with all due solemnity, entering at the last ring of the bell and making great efforts to ensure nobody sees we are somewhat short of breath.

Then comes a Tuesday afternoon when William Byrd forgets us. We wait dutifully, but when finally we understand that he will not be coming, we leave.

'Let's go to Southwark,' Adrian suggests.

'Southwark!'

The borough to the south of the Thames has a dubious reputation as a fiendish place of forbidden pleasures. And now Adrian is suggesting the adventure!

'Yes. I've been told about the Bear Garden.'

'Adrian!'

The Bear Garden is a ring where one of the favourite sports of Londoners takes place: bear baiting, or combat between bears and dogs; a pastime of ill repute that, seen from the drawing rooms of Clerkenwell, must remain strictly reserved for the lower orders, with whom we have nothing whatever in common. What's more, the ring is situated on Bankside, a place frequented by women of such loose reputation that they are only ever mentioned under one's breath. Such sentiments leave Adrian unmoved.

'Don't play the grandfather, Francis. I hear that one may see bears prancing, wrestlers wrestling, the baiting of bears and dogs, cockfighting too. There is music and dancing. Come on! The worst that can befall us is being whipped when we get home.'

And with his saintly little air, he starts to sing:

> *Through the Royal Exchange as I walked*
> *where gallants in satin did shine:*
> *At midst of the day they parted away*
> *at several places to dine.*
> *The gentry went to the King's Head,*
> *the nobles went unto the Crown:*
> *The knights unto the Golden Fleece*
> *and the ploughman to the Clown. . . .*
> *Thus every man to his humour,*
> *from the north unto the south:*
> *But he that hath no money in his purse,*
> *may dine at the sign of the Mouth.*
> *The cheater will dine at the Checker,*
> *the pickpocket at the Blind Ale-house:*
> *Till taken and tried, up Holborn they ride,*
> *and make their end at the gallows.*

We go down to the water's edge and ask one of the countless watermen to ferry us across the river. He looks us up and down with a circumspect gaze.

'You've got money?'

'Of course,' replies Adrian immediately and to my great surprise. 'Would we be here otherwise?'

'Well then, my young sirs, I am all yours. Where would you have me land you?'

'At Bermondsey, in front of the monastery chapel,' we say prudently.

This is downstream of the bridge, on the other side from the Bear Garden. Doubtless he is not fooled, but his work is to ferry us across the Thames, not attend to children's virtue.

We disembark, our hearts beating fast, ever watchful of the people we encounter for fear of being surprised by an acquaintance or a villain. But I am already as tall as some adults, and Giuliano has taught us to defend ourselves with a certain efficacy. This gives us a self-assurance that discourages would-be aggressors.

We walk along the riverbank to the Bear Garden. This is the first time I have seen London from across the Thames. The mass of St Paul's dominates the city, its belfries jutting between the roofs of brick and thatch like a hedgehog's bristles. The wharfs downstream of the bridge are a tangle of shifting masts and sails; they part now and then, like curtains drawn apart, to reveal Traitors' Gate and the approaches to the Tower, St Thomas's Chapel and the white facade of St Magnus the Martyr. Upstream of the bridge, one can admire a string of fine buildings along the shore: Baynard's Castle, Bridewell Palace, Greyfriars Monastery, Somerset Palace, Durham House, York House and Westminster Palace.

We enter without mishap, thanks to the small coins Adrian produces from his decidedly well-furnished purse.

Those two hours remain forever etched in my mind.

The Bear Garden was situated in an area of taverns built on a drained marsh, which may have explained why the gardens were so wonderfully green, the trees thick with leaves, and the ponds and streams so abundant.

I have no particular affection for these rings where bears are set against dogs that rip them apart with their fine teeth while the bears, made furious by the pain, try to trample them with their heavy paws. Londoners, however, adore this sort of spectacle, to which they are as devoted as to the theatre; although I should really speak in the past tense, for the word from Geneva, where they abhor such sport, is that the Puritans have closed all the theatres and bear-baiting rings in London. If that proves true, then I am convinced the Puritans' days are numbered, for the English will not stand to be deprived of such pleasures for very long.

But that afternoon I was fascinated by the novelty of it. I stared as if hypnotised at the bear's pink eyes as it growled at the advancing enemy, the dog seeking to seize the advantage, the bear dodging the attacks. The faces of the spectators were flushed with excitement. Most of the men clutched clay pipes between their teeth. Absorbed by the spectacle, they had allowed them to burn out. And when the dog succeeded in biting the bear, which in turn bit the dog to free itself, the barking, growling and howling, the shouts, encouragements and curses conjoined in a confusion, amid the dizzying, acrid scent of sweat, tobacco, sawdust and wet fur.

When we leave the ring, we come upon a little group in a garden who are playing lutes for another little group who are dancing.

'Will you come dance with us, young fellows?'

'Certainly,' replies Adrian without hesitation, 'if you play us a jig.'

'Agreed.'

And they set to playing a furious melody, which they accompany by singing and stamping their feet.

> *Tomorrow the fox will come to town*
> *Keep! Keep! Keep!*
> *Tomorrow the fox will come to town*
> *Oh! Keep you all well there!*

We join in, and would be there still, had the bell of St Paul's not struck five, swiftly echoed by chimes from the surrounding parishes.

We undertake the maddest race of our lives to get home in time, laughing happily all the way.

And that happiness is a touchstone for the delight we feel upon commencing rehearsals for the play that by tradition the school presents before the Queen.

One evening, as we leave class, Adrian and I are requested to go to the apartments of our headmaster. Being summoned to see Richard Mulcaster often means a punishment. What can we have done?

Mulcaster fixes us with a dark look.

'We are setting to work on the school's theatrical entertainment,' he says, after a long, forbidding silence. 'You, sirs, have the right to demand the principal parts in the play I have written.'

Another silence.

'Indeed, it would be unjust to give these parts to anybody else, for you both sing and recite better than anyone. Consequently, Master Adrian, you will come to school next Monday having lost your voice, and that will last for ten days. And you, Master Francis, will twist your foot on Wednesday or thereabouts. By the time you are both mended, we will unfortunately have had to replace you. Have you understood me?'

'Yes, sir.'

'There is nothing to be gained by making yourselves conspicuous in public, you hear me?'

'Yes, sir.'

I venture a question:

'Must we miss the play?'

'Francis, your logic, so often implacable, is at fault. If you absent yourselves altogether, you will be equally conspicuous. So you will sing in the back row: Francis, because you are tall, and Adrian, because you go wherever your brother goes. Are we agreed?'

'Yes, sir.'

'And now I am going to beat you, so that nobody wonders what you came here for.'

He picks up his cane. I swallow hard. Being punished by Mulcaster is as painful as it is rare.

'Master Adrian, I demand convincing groans and whimpers.'

And he sets to beating a cushion, while Adrian, mimicking pain, groans and whimpers fit to rend a man's soul. I would have laughed, had Mulcaster not been so utterly, deadly serious.

He recommences with me, after which we leave, rubbing our backsides. The school is empty and Giuliano is waiting for us in the yard.

'Can you ride?' he asks, a touch of commiseration in his voice.

'We shall grit our teeth,' we reply in pained little voices, our eyes half-closed.

We follow Mulcaster's instructions and nobody notices anything. Rehearsals are at four o'clock every day. Wyddosox conducts the choir and pays us little attention, beyond a few initial, sarcastic remarks regarding Adrian's insistence on standing next to me in the back row – 'When you go to bed, do you sleep for yourself or does your brother have to sleep for you?'

The boys with speaking parts stay until six o'clock, and we stay with them. Sitting on the floor, my left foot conspicuously bandaged, I play at being prompter.

Many a poet has poverty spurred,
By art and nature undeterred . . .

'Francis, help!'

But refrained have we . . .

'Ah yes!'

But refrained have we from presenting here
The deeds and customs of yesteryear.
We shall not court your favour with art
That scorns the virtues most dear to our heart . . .

Mulcaster is said to be a theatre fanatic, never missing a single play, and is rumoured to be a personal friend of James Burbage, proprietor of the Curtain Theatre. His great speciality is to take hold of a classic text and write a new play based on it, adapted to the requirements of his schoolboy actors.

This year we are to perform a story taken from the Round Table, with borrowings from the classics and modern plays of every kind. It is called *Ariodante and Genoveva*.

Mulcaster puts a great deal of singing, dancing and music in his plays, for he prides himself on being the only teacher in London to include these disciplines in his curriculum.

I have heard it said that in the other schools, the problem of choosing between English and Latin arises with each play. There was no such deliberation for us.

'I honour Latin, but I worship English,' Mulcaster loves to say. 'Why do we not use our language, which is both profound and exact? I can see none other so apt to express precise reasoning so clearly.'

His eyes dart fire if anyone challenges one of his two favourite battle cries – the other being that one should only chastise in moderation, and never twice for the same fault.

We rehearse in a garret at the Manor of the Rose, where the framework of a house, as dictated by the intrigue, has been built – the complete version will be constructed at Whitehall in the days preceding the performance.

The craftsman is Master Farnaby, assisted by his son Giles, who has taken to his apprenticeship with enthusiasm and is granted leave to spend two days a week with a builder of organs and virginals, learning how to make these instruments.

Forced to be a spectator for hours on end, I am able to question him at my ease – I have no idea why the construction of these instruments interests me so much. Giles, for whom this work has become his alpha and omega, explains the principles to me as he learns them. We continue to play together and exchange scores that we have each copied for our personal use.

William Byrd makes me rehearse a work by Thomas Tallis, his master, based on a liturgical theme but easy to play on the virginal, as are many organ works. From time to time, he gives us his own compositions. One day, when he wishes to explain how one might rework a theme in various ways, he asks me to hum a tune.

'The first that comes to mind. Quick! Don't think about it!'

I hum a melody that someone has been singing endlessly at school and which is stuck in my head.

'Ah! *Hugh Ashton's Ground*. Let's see what we can do with it,' says Byrd with a smile.

We work on a whole series of variations on the theme, with Byrd explaining how to proceed, and Adrian and myself taking careful note of the results. We rehearse the *Ground* until it is perfect.

'We should really call it *Tregian's Ground*,' observes Byrd with a mischievous look. 'Our excellent humour nearly transformed this work into a galliard.'

I enthusiastically recount all this to Giles.

One day, Byrd questions me closely about my knowledge of instruments. With a novice's ardour, I tell him of the hours I have spent with Giles and show him some of the scores I have copied from his album. Finally he says:

'Bring me this Giles Farnaby; he interests me.'

He sends word to Farnaby Senior. It is an honour to be summoned by a musician of the Royal Chapel, and by Byrd in particular, and Giles finds himself joining Adrian and me at Byrd's house the following Tuesday.

Besides the play itself, we are also preparing a six-person dance that we call *Merriment of the Six Mariners*. Thomas Morley has composed some lively music, to which the others dance. As for myself, my ankle is 'far too weak' for me to risk any such exertions. But I long to join in; my toes quiver. I love to dance almost as much as I love to play music. And by dint of seeing it rehearsed, I could dance the *Merriment of the Six Mariners* with my eyes closed.

With the onset of autumn and the Michaelmas term, our excitement grows, and by St Nicolas' Day we are in a state of high fever. We are going to play before the Queen during the Shrovetide festivities. Adrian and I are curious to go to court – who wouldn't be? – but our role is limited, for we are to sing in the back row of the choir, half hidden by a tapestry.

We spend most of our time reassuring the others; and little by little, they begin to approach us with their questions and concerns.

'Adrian, what do you think of these shoes?'

'Rehearse my text with me, Francis.'

'If you were me, would you say *I am asking YOU the question, Your Lordship*, or *I am asking you the question, YOUR LORDSHIP?*'

'Have you seen my mask?'

'I've lost my sword. Adrian, would you mind . . . ?'

We end up veritable stage managers, privy to everything and ready to resolve any difficulties. So when one of the six mariners does indeed dislocate his ankle, less than a month before our first performance, they turn to us.

'Francis, you are sufficiently recovered to replace me,' says the boy with the hurt ankle.

'Yes, Francis,' adds the dancing master eagerly, 'it seems to me that you're running about like a rabbit.'

I launch into a long exposition of my muscle difficulties, but they are having none of it. Finally, I ask for twenty-four hours and I go to see Mulcaster.

He listens to me with a furrowed brow.

'My dear Francis, strictly speaking, you should not even come with us to court. Nevertheless, I have no wish to spark tittle-tattle, so you will replace your schoolfellow. But your ankle will unfortunately betray you at the last minute and we will not present this particular merriment, despite having announced it already.'

He fixes me with his piercing eyes.

'God has made you the gift of music, Francis, and I hope you will be able to use His beneficence to good advantage. It is evident even in your

body, for you have that grace of movement inherent to natural perform-
ers. You would be noticed immediately, even with a mask. Rehearse the
Merriment of the Six Mariners as much as you like – I imagine that will
delight you. But your ankle must fail the day before the play. Neither you
nor I can afford that you be noticed at court.'

'Very well, sir.'

When the day comes for us to go to the court, the general excitation
reaches unprecedented heights. Adrian and I are doubtless the only boys
for whom the curiosity of seeing the Queen is mixed with fear of being
seen by her. It is impossible that her spies have not discovered our attendance at the Merchant Taylors' – I have never had proof, but am certain
of it. What if . . .

'Enough of speculating,' Adrian says, 'it is futile. Rather, let us reflect
on a way to ensure nothing bad will befall us.'

After due consideration, we go to see Giuliano.

Giuliano, as I have said, is Italian. At first glance, you would take him
for an ordinary valet: he stands out among the menservants solely by
virtue of his agility, which to my child's eyes borders on the miraculous.
He can let himself fall from the upper storey of a building without
incurring so much as a scratch; he wields a sword like a maniac; and
in hand-to-hand fighting he is as slippery as an eel. One day, I surprise
him hanging by his hands from the eaves of the roof and making a
circuit of the house.

'Why are you doing that?'

'It is good for steadiness, mental application and the wrists,' he replies,
laughing at my wide eyes. 'I'll teach you to do the same; it is not so hard,
you'll see.'

And he sets three beams in the gymnasium in a triangle, on which I
practise at length before making an attempt on the roof of the house. The
attempt is a complete success, the sole incident being caused by my mother,
who walks by, looks up, sees me hanging betwixt heaven and earth and
is so seized with horror she nearly gives birth before time. It takes all of
Giuliano's persuasion to keep me from a whipping.

After a while, I perceive that his prowess is not merely athletic. First of
all, he speaks English with ease, and not a shadow of an accent. Second,
we soon discover that he is well versed in literature and that Latin holds

no secrets for him. He makes us repeat our lessons on the way to and from school and corrects our failing memories without hesitation or apparent effort. He teaches us the rudiments of Italian in the course of our everyday conversations, and makes us read a text he greatly enjoys and which we find fascinating and exhilarating in equal measure: Torquato Tasso's *La Gerusalemme liberata*.

Little by little, Giuliano becomes a sort of elder brother to us; he is too young to be our father, being but twenty-five or so, while I am ten.

'I will consider your problem,' he tells us, when we share our concerns with him.

And two days before the play, he tells us:

'You will not see us, or hardly, but we will be there and will protect you.'

He pauses, and we sense his hesitation. He adds finally:

'Let's just say that we cannot guarantee absolute protection.'

'We understand.'

The day of the play comes. The evening before, my ankle has failed me, and Mulcaster sends the Master of the Revels a message to explain that there will be no *Merriment of the Six Mariners*.

We go early to the court that day, some in the wagon carrying our properties, the others on foot.

Master Farnaby has preceded us and, at one point, I espy Giuliano among the carpenters.

I have always found Sir John and his friends to be most elegant, particularly the Earl of Sussex, one of the Queen's generals, and the poet Sir Philip Sydney. Both are court favourites despite being Catholic. But as I roam the passageways of Whitehall I become aware that, as far as elegance is concerned, I have seen nothing yet. It is all ruffles and pleats, silks and brocades, glittering jewellery, great farthingales, and coiffures piled high. There are doubtless watchful eyes among all this rustling finery, and weapons to hand, for the Queen will be coming in a few hours. But we detect none of it that morning.

The play is a success. Stowe and Hutchinson, who have the principal roles, are quite perfect: they have worked day and night – quite literally. What's more, they are gifted. We are even entreated to return a few days later, on the evening of Shrove Tuesday, to play again. But as far as I am concerned, all that is swept away by a wholly unexpected incident.

Adrian runs and I hobble about, assisting each and every one of our fellows. Having gone off to find something, I manage to lose myself in the huge and unfamiliar palace, wandering from one passageway to another, unsure which way to turn. The worst is that, apart from a young woman who runs past and will not stop for me, I encounter no one, as in a nightmare.

At last, I open a door somewhat at random, and see ...

A lady's chamber.

I utter a startled 'Goddamn!'

From the darkest corner, a long laugh roots me to the spot. In the half-light, I see the shapes of three women. One of them steps forward.

'So, my good sir, we curse in the presence of a lady, do we?' There in the light, I see a woman such as I had never even dreamed of. Ageless, adorned with sparkling jewellery, her face painted like a picture.

I bow very low.

'Pardon, madam. I am lost and thought to find a passageway behind this door.'

'Stand up, young man, and tell me what it is you seek.'

I straighten up, look at her, open my mouth to reply and at that instant, she sees my face. She starts. Now it is her turn to be rooted to the spot. So intense is her gaze, I have but one desire: to disappear. And yet, I cannot unfix my eyes from hers.

'Ladies, go wait on me in the passage.'

The two women, who had not moved from their dark corner, walk backwards from the room, bowing.

'What are you doing here?' asks the painted lady familiarly once we are alone – as if she knows me.

I would like to answer, but nothing comes. Finally, she relaxes, and I lower my gaze.

'You are Francis Tregian.'

It is not a question but an affirmation. That's when I understand: she takes me for my father – this has already happened to me once or twice.

So much for prudence.

'Yes, madam: I am Francis Tregian, but not the one you think. I am his son.'

Another long pause.

She comes nearer, takes my hand and draws me to the window.

'Quite extraordinary!' she murmurs. 'How old are you?'

'Ten, madam.'

'You look fifteen. Your height . . . Your face . . . If you were not beard-less . . . Now that I can see you closer, I perceive that your eyes have a quality that his have not. You came with Sussex, I suppose? For the play?'

'Yes, I . . .'

'Do you see your father ever?'

'No, I have not seen him since . . . since I was very young.'

'You must surely hate your Queen for that?'

The immense astonishment she reads in my face sets her to laughter. I blush completely red, but am able to stammer:

'I cannot hate someone I know not. I have tried, but am unable to do so.'

She gives another little laugh.

'It is something one learns in the end, but you are yet too unpractised.'

She gazes into the distance. There is something very reassuring about her, a great stillness. I watch her. She looks at me again and smiles.

'With eyes like those . . . I have no justification to give, but I will offer those eyes an explanation. One day or another, you will finally meet your father, Francis, and you will tell it to him. He will not believe you, but that concerns me not. You, however, will perhaps believe me.'

She does not let me utter the words that come to my lips, but holds my wrist between two fingers in a pincer-like grip.

'When he came to court, your father attracted the enmity of power-ful figures, whom even I find hard to control. There is in him a mixture of innocence and pride that has always touched me. I desired to protect him, for at heart, I have nothing against those Catholic gentlemen, such as Sussex, who are loyal to me.'

It is the Queen! The person who grips my wrist so hard it might break, supplying me with explanations, is Queen Elizabeth. My head reels; my knees shake.

' . . . I desired to place him out of harm's way, and he failed to under-stand. He had already prepared himself for martyrdom, and the last thing he desired was to be offered an alternative. He played at Virtue taken unawares, and took off like a hunted hare. From that moment forth, I could do no more for him. Even had I not been furious, at first, that he misunderstood everything, he had missed his only chance. People such as

Sir Philip Sydney or William Byrd made no such error. I am their friend, and I shall protect William Byrd until my dying breath, in spite of his going to Mass right under my nose.'

I manage to release myself, and fall to my knees.

'Majesty . . .'

'You should not wander about the passageways, Francis; you might meet the wrong sort of people. Your face will betray you to all those who . . . Where do you wish to go?'

I tell her, and she explains the route to me. I am trembling like a leaf and listen to her instructions only with the greatest of efforts.

'Thank you, madam . . . Majesty,' I murmur finally. She gives a little laugh.

'Go, sir. Promise me you will speak to your father soon.'

I come to my senses all at once.

'No, madam, I will not promise to speak to him soon, for I would anger him and he would punish me; and he would not believe me. But I will convey your message to him when I am a man.'

She gives me her hand to kiss, and I do so with fervour.

'Go, now. They might seek you, and soon they will come to seek me too. We must not be discovered together. Farewell, Francis Tregian.'

'Farewell, Majesty.'

I follow her directions and soon find myself in the great hall with the others.

'But where have you been?' they shout impatiently at me.

'My ankle . . . I lost my way.'

'You're as pale as if you'd seen a ghost,' Giles Farnaby remarks.

'You might say that.'

I say no more, and speak of the meeting to no one, not even Adrian. I cannot bring myself to tell him that Elizabeth Tudor's proximity provoked no sense of horror in me, that I even kissed her hand. Much as he understands everything, he might not understand this.

VIII

Now, O now, I needs must part,
Parting though I absent mourn
Absence can no joy impart:
Joy once fled cannot return.

'THE FROG GALLIARD'

POPULAR BALLAD BY JOHN DOWLAND

THE UPHEAVAL WAS GRADUAL but profound, and absolute. I suppose it began with the death of the Earl of Sussex.

I have said little about Sussex until now. The reason being that, as children, we were unaware of how far we owed our relative safety to his watchful care. If the Tregian family had allowed itself to be guided by him throughout, we might not have been persecuted at all.

Sussex was an intimate friend of Sir John, who was also his brother-in-law: he had married Sir John's and Madam Catherine's elder sister, the poetess Mary Arundell. He was a Catholic. He was held in great esteem by Queen Elizabeth as a valiant soldier and an effective general. As Lord Chamberlain, he was a member of the Privy Council. Sussex was an intrepid military man, self-assured, staunchly principled and permanently opposed to the Queen's favourite, the Earl of Leicester. Their rival factions split the court in two. Sussex was straightforward and upright, lordly in manner, and he always acted on his word. Leicester was a slippery courtier and a wily politician. Sussex would dismiss him in gruff tones:

'He's an unprincipled plotter. How can anyone trust such a man?'

Coming from Sussex, the judgement was final and damning.

Their rivalry was known to all. Sussex distrusted Leicester as one who acted solely for his own advantage, never for the general good. Leicester detested Sussex as a permanent obstacle to his machinations. The animosity between them was so great that even the Queen, who loved them both, never succeeded in reconciling them.

While Sussex was alive, the Arundell clan enjoyed adequate protection and life continued much as usual. I would even go so far as to say that while Sussex lived, our persecution was relatively restrained. Any special measures were more a reaction to the activities of Catholics outside the kingdom – the Jesuits – than unprovoked molestation as such. I have heard it said more than once, that if the religious question had not also been a matter of State, Elizabeth would have been a moderate Catholic herself. Small details revealed as much. She knew that Mass was said very frequently at court, for example, but forbade anyone from intervening. This was confirmed by her words to me during our encounter. The court seethed with Catholics under her protection. It was also said that the execution of Father Campion – the most brilliant of missionaries, but unaccustomed to clandestine life, hence his capture – had come about in spite of the Queen, and that she agreed to it against her will.

After Sussex's death, Leicester was free to act as he pleased for a time, brushing aside his old rival's allies.

Among much else, he demanded that Sir John be removed from London and his household dispersed. He was deaf to every protestation of loyalty. Relations with Spain were stretched to breaking point, and Sir John's enemies decided that Clerkenwell was far too close for comfort.

He was first imprisoned in the Tower but, to our great relief, his influence and high rank ensured his quick release. He was put under house arrest in Muswell, a village north of London, where he owned a property. We were forbidden to live there with him.

WE LEAVE FOR THE Continent one hot September day in the twenty-sixth year of Elizabeth's reign.

Two days before embarking, one of the priests blessed the union of Jane and Giuliano. They have married for love. When I hear the news

I burst out crying, for Jane has betrayed me. And then Sir John tells me that Giuliano will be coming with us; if he and Jane are married, she will be coming too. My tears and jealousy vanish.

The day before we are due to leave, the Tregian children are taken to see our father in prison. He has obtained private apartments at last, and Phillips has hastened back to his service. Now, he is allowed to receive visitors. We are four: Adrian, Margaret, Charles and I. Mary is in Lancashire and two (or three) of the girls are with their nurses. We pass through the lodge and enter a vast yard. From here, we go through a small door and up a narrow staircase to the upper part of the prison, which contains the apartments of inmates who can afford them.

Seeing one another again after so many years is disconcerting for all.

'My little ones!' our father cries out in astonishment, such that I realise he must have been expecting to find us unchanged since the time of his arrest. I am not sure he has even set eyes on Adrian before.

As for us, we find ourselves looking at a very tall, thin man, his hair streaked white and his faced deeply lined, a disconcerting mixture of exhaustion and determination in his eyes.

'You are the youthful soldiers of Our Lord. When your education is complete, you will be among those who come back to restore this poor, unhappy England to its true faith. Will you not, my sons?'

I am paralysed with fear. A promise means a sacred duty.

My younger brother Charles is aged about four at the time. He smiles and declares:

'Oh yes, Father!'

'And you Francis, as the eldest boy,' my father continues, as if I too had promised myself to the cause, 'Wolvedon is your responsibility. It must be taken back from our enemies.'

He shows us around his apartments, which are as yet unfurnished, but with access to a small garden. He is full of plans and schemes: he shall learn foreign languages so that he can travel once he leaves prison, which will be soon, he is certain of that, thanks to the King of Spain.

'They tell me you are gifted at music, Francis,' he says, indicating a virginal occupying one of the otherwise empty rooms. 'Would you like to play something for me before you leave?'

I play everything that William Byrd has taught me, trying hard to concentrate on the music and forget my acute discomfort, my sense of shame: this is the first time I have seen my father in seven years and I feel no joy, only an urgent desire to get as far away from him as possible.

So many times in the years ahead, music would come to my aid. On this day, music masks my reserve, my hesitant feelings. My father kisses me effusively.

'I shall insist you make as much music as possible in France.'

'Thank you, Father.'

During the preparations for our departure (in secret, of course, because travelling abroad to study is forbidden), I spend my days with Thomas Morley and William Byrd. Byrd is working on a vast composition for the organ at the Palace of Whitehall. I follow him everywhere. From time to time, he pauses to explain things, or takes an hour to listen and offer advice while I play the virginal, or teaches me the techniques required for organ-playing. When I cannot be with Byrd, I am with Morley, who crams me with theory and makes me practise until my brain and wrists ache. I am a fast learner – he calls me his 'polyphonic greyhound'.

'You may be a gentleman, Francis,' he says, 'but if you do not become a musician I shall wring your neck with my own bare hands. And if I am already dead, I shall harry you from beyond the grave.'

My distractions make my sorrow easier to bear. It seems to me that I am losing every source of help and support at once: the Merchant Taylors' with my schoolmasters Wyddosox and Mulcaster and my classmates; Giles Farnaby; William Byrd; Thomas Morley; the Clerkenwell grooms; and my grandmother Catherine, as tenacious as ever, who has set off for Cornwall to recover her lands and income. I cannot imagine living without Sir John, whom I am accustomed to consult at every turn. I am even sorry at the thought of not seeing my mother. She has been only the vaguest of presences in my childhood and we are far from overflowing with affection for one another, but now we will be a week's journey apart, with a sea crossing and a frontier between us. Unlike all the other obstacles, these seem permanent and insurmountable.

One night, shortly before we are to leave, I see Old Thomas again in a dream. He fixes me with his penetrating eyes and says in strong voice: 'Come!' When I awake, I tell Adrian of my dream.

'I wonder where we shall board ship for the Continent?' I add.

'No one will bother to consult us on the matter.'

There is bitterness in his voice. He gives a shame-faced smile.

'There are days when I find myself wishing our lives were like everyone else's,' he says. 'I know a missionary of the true faith should not think in such terms, but I'd prefer a mess of my own making.'

I stare at him in astonishment. I had always taken it for granted that Adrian was the more devout of us two, more convinced in his faith than I.

'But there's no use moaning about it,' he continues, with characteristic common sense. 'We should try to influence events instead. You would rather we set sail from Cornwall, is that it?'

'Yes.'

'So that we could pass by Golden?'

'Yes.'

'Well then, let's try. No point in admitting defeat before we've even started.'

Naturally, we go to see Giuliano. Sir John is too busy. He is accused of harbouring priests, and of allowing my mother's brother Charles Stourton to travel to Douai, where he had remained beyond the six months permitted by law. These are mere pretexts, of course: in reality, Sir John is resented for standing firm under pressure.

A new law has decreed that anyone harbouring a priest is a traitor and punishable as such. Several of the priests who had stayed with us in Clerkenwell have already died on the scaffold. Sir John and Lady Anne live in constant fear and anxiety. They are not to be bothered with trifling concerns.

Giuliano has always been an intrepid character.

'Master Francis, you know me' he says, when I explain our request. 'What you ask is madness. But I adore a mad escapade. Say nothing to anyone, and leave it to me.'

THE CORNISH COASTLINE is long and rugged, with many parts unfamiliar even to the local people; a discreet spot can always be found to board ship for Holland, France or Spain. Many missionary priests have come to England that way. The voyage is longer, but less risky.

Our rendezvous is fixed for a September evening, in a small creek on the Truro estuary. Giuliano suggests that he and I set off on horseback, while Adrian will follow with Jane. But Jane objects. And Adrian refuses – he insists on coming with us. My coaxing and teasing are to no avail. Even my impersonation of Wyddosox – 'Adrian! Do you sleep for yourself or does your brother have to sleep for you?' – leaves him unmoved.

'You have memories of Golden,' he says. 'You even have a friend to visit there. I have nothing. I might just as well have been born in Clerkenwell. I should like to see my father's house, even if only once.'

His request is reasonable, and Giuliano gives in.

'But we'll be riding at full gallop,' he says.

'Try me. I'm not as big and strong as Francis, but I have just as much endurance.'

Finally, all four of us set out on horseback. We leave with the clothes we stand up in, not a shred more. I agree to leave everything behind except for my music. I spend my last days in England furiously copying everything William Byrd and Thomas Morley allow me to – their own music and that of others. I write on tiny, cramped staves on a narrow scroll of paper and stow it in my saddle pouch, in place of a pistol. We avoid the highways. Jane suggests tracks through the woods. At times I am scared, but we soon realise that she knows the region like the back of her hand.

'My mother's husband was a travelling merchant. When I was a little girl I often went with him, dressed in boy's clothes.'

At length, we reach the forest above Tregony. It is late afternoon. We shall set sail nearby, with the tide, on the following day.

'You cannot possibly set foot in the old manor as if nothing had happened,' Jane says sternly. 'You look too much like your father as people knew him here before, and we don't know who's in that kitchen now. Someone might run off to fetch the archers.'

And so Jane is elected to trot down the little valley to Golden Mill and up the road leading to the two manors. She returns after what seems like an eternity.

'Thomas is no longer at Golden. He lives in his own house.'

And she adds, with a small laugh and a tremor of emotion:

'Extraordinary. I might have called half of them by their first names, but no one recognised me.'

In truth, she hardly resembles the adolescent country girl of five years ago.

Jane guides us down the hill towards Golden Mill; we cross the river and continue in the direction of St Ewe and Mevagissey.

We pass through the town, ride a few leagues more and finally reach an old house approached along a short avenue of trees.

'Here.'

We knock. It is growing dark but there are no lights within. No servant comes to open the door. No one invites us in. Somewhere nearby, chickens are clucking. We circle the house and find another door. I push and it opens. I find myself in a large room. There is a fireplace, smaller than in the old manor. Faint embers glow in the hearth, and Old Thomas is sitting beside it.

'Master Thomas?'

'Come on in, Master Francis,' he says, his voice unchanged, and so naturally that I stand transfixed on the doorstep in astonishment.

Adrian is the first to step forward.

'You'll be Master Adrian, I'll warrant.'

Thomas gets to his feet. He is as tall and thin as before. Adrian holds out his hand and Thomas shakes it gravely, then pulls him close and kisses him warmly.

'Master Francis!' he exclaims, fixing me with his dark eyes. 'You are grown into a man already!'

I clasp him in my arms (I am as tall as he) and he pats me on the back with his free hand.

Once emotions have settled, we sit down together so he can tell us about Golden.

'*They* are not interested in living on the estates. They're never here. They have stewards who busy themselves lining their own pockets at their masters' expense. All they are interested in is collecting the rents. We see them once a year, twice maybe. That said, the property is well maintained, correctly but coldly, without love.'

Jane prepares us a meal from Thomas's modest stores.

'I have a housekeeper, a manservant and a family of tenant farmers,' he explains. 'But everyone is in Probus tonight. The Fair is in two days' time and they're busy with the preparations.'

Jane is surprised by the house and by Thomas's retinue.

'Were you not robbed of your income, like me?'

'Of course. The Careys took everything that used to come from the Tregians. But this is my father's house. He was a merchant, so I have property of my own. I stayed at Golden after John Tregian's death by agreement with Madam Catherine, because I believed that her son – whose character I knew – might have need of me. But your father didn't listen to me, and replaced me with poor Cuthbert, who had no experience. I stayed on out of concern, and then Master Francis was born and I saw his eyes. But once you had left, there was nothing to keep me there. A few weeks with Carey was enough. Such arrogance! Such heartlessness!'

I remember that evening as a moment of perfect happiness with Jane and Thomas – happiness compounded by the presence of Adrian and Giuliano. We talk about our sisters, our little brother, our parents, our studies. Thomas listens, fascinated. We ask for his news, but he sweeps our questions aside with a wave of his hand.

'I left the manor and came back here. There's nothing more to say.'

When it is time to leave, he gives us some advice.

'Never allow yourselves to be guided by blind prejudice,' he says urgently. 'Men are killing one another in the name of the Lord our God, but I am convinced that none of this is His will. The Lord is their excuse. Look at Carey. He has despoiled your family fortune under the guise of religion. Look at the King of Spain. He burns with frustration, having been Prince Consort to the Queen of England and almost King himself. One of these days he'll be back in force. Everyone says so around here. The Catholics are delighted at the idea, but he will send good men to be burned at the stake, as he did when he was Mary Tudor's husband. I have heard it said they plan to bring the Inquisition here. We ordinary folk must grapple with nothing but our own consciences, but for them religion is an instrument of power. And so, I say every man must keep to his own private creed, listen to his own judgement. I say that to no one but you, not even to my housekeeper, or I should risk being set on the bonfire in the market square to burn like a heretic.'

Night is falling fast. We have to leave.

Thomas hugs each of us close, and gives me his parting words:

'I have thought about you a great deal recently, Master Francis. It has done me good to see your pisky gaze. I doubt we shall ever see one another again, but don't forget: let no man dictate your conduct.'

I seem to hear an echo of my first lesson at the Merchant Taylors': 'Plato is not always right, merely because he is Plato.'

'The best way to thank the Lord for His gifts,' Thomas goes on, 'is to make good use of them. If music is your true path, don't let them make a soldier of you, or a priest. You have duties and responsibilities, but you have your own free will, too. The art of a good life is to reconcile the two, never forget one in favour of the other. Extremes are doomed to failure; they must be made to meet.'

Adrian has taken a step nearer and is listening intently.

'Promise me you'll remember that, my lad?'

Blinded by tears, I hug Thomas with all my might.

'Come now, to horse,' says Giuliano, his voice thick with emotion. He has said almost nothing all evening, no doubt out of respect for our little world, which was not his own. Miraculously, a fragment of that world had been recovered, a dying spark from the fire.

On the road, I turn to look back several times. Thomas's stooping shape is just visible, outlined in the doorway. When the house disappears from view behind a low arm of land, I know that my childhood is over.

WE BOARD SHIP at dawn.

Adrian clings to the rail, devouring the spectacle of the Cornish coastline. He has barely seen Golden. We have been bold enough to ride along the road between the two manors and returned to Tregony by Golden Mill. But the night was cloudy and moonless, and all he has seen are their massed shapes in the dark. I am glad to have been there again, nonetheless. I see myself as a small boy once more, racing down the hill to my schoolmaster's house. That was in a different life, one in which I would have been the lord of my own lands. Perhaps I would have traded with the tin and wool merchants, and taken my place among the Cornish nobility. It is a life I shall never know.

Such are my thoughts in the morning breeze. Bathed in pale sunshine, my native land dwindles inexorably on the horizon.

We spend two days at sea aboard a small ship, and the voyage offers a welcome distraction from the anguish of departure. The four of us set about learning the winds, and the names and functions of the different sails – or rather, the three of us, since Giuliano proves to be well versed and perfectly at home.

Adrian and I discuss travelling to distant lands.

'It would be a fine thing,' says my brother, 'to go to the other end of the world and start all over again in a place where our only passport would be ourselves and our skills.'

'Would you go to the Americas?'

'If the occasion arose, I would go tomorrow.'

Immediately upon our landing at a little port in Normandy, Jane reminds us: 'You have no need to hide the fact that you are Catholics here. To be Catholic is quite normal.'

This is true, but Jane's words are moderated, in the space of just two hours, by what we learn from conversations at the inn, translated for us by Giuliano: tensions are running high among the *religionnaires*, as the reformists are known here; fights have broken out, and all is far from well between the King of France (a Catholic) and the King of Navarre (a Protestant), between the Holy Catholic League and the Huguenots. We take horses, set off, and arrive in Reims under driving rain. We are directed to the English College, near the Bishop's Palace, and go straight there.

I had heard talk of this English College. It was part of the university at Douai, founded to resist the Reformation and educate English Catholics. After Douai fell to the Prince of Orange, who was a Protestant, the college moved to Reims – temporarily, it was hoped. It was chiefly devoted to training priests, but pupils not intending to take Holy Orders could study the humanities, too. A fee was charged for this, but theology was free, so that English students arriving penniless at the college all took theology, whether or not they intended to become priests. Persuaded that its 'missionaries' would advance the English Catholic cause, the college pushed its students to take Holy Orders. Indeed priests were in short supply because so many had been taken prisoner in England. At best, they were chased out of the country or fled; of those captured, many were executed.

For years the college had been run by Doctor William Allen. He was a remarkable man, a true leader, and an unparalleled administrator and organiser. It was said that without him, Catholicism in England would have been eradicated. Alas, when we arrive, he has already left Reims for

Rome, and his place has been taken *de facto* by Doctor Richard Barret, a favourite of the Jesuits. Barret worked for years with great discretion and competence under Allen's command, but since he has taken over the running of the college, his students complain that he has become harsh and erratic.

The college is overflowing with students – more than two hundred, half of whom are accommodated within its walls – so there is no room for us. The formidable Barret decides we are too young for Reims and orders us off to Eu in Normandy, where a boys' school has been established through the generosity of the very Catholic Duke of Guise.

'We shall see in a year's time whether we have space for you here, and whether you have acquired enough knowledge to join us.'

Giuliano takes us away, commenting quietly:

'I shall inform Sir John Arundell.'

I have no desire to dwell on the time we spent at Eu. We had not then heard of Michel de Montaigne, but with hindsight, his words are the perfect description of what we endured:

> *There is nothing quite as pleasing as a little French child; but the hopes we form for them are generally betrayed, and as grown men, there is no perceptible excellence in them. I have heard people of high understanding maintain that the schools to which they are sent – and there are a great many – make them the animals they are.*

My brother and I survived this brutalisation only because there were two of us, and thanks to our thoroughly Cornish tenacity. That, and Jane and Giuliano's insistence that we return home to them every evening. We were among English children and spoke Latin and English. Had we boarded at the school, we would probably never have learned French at all.

Montaigne's *Essays* paint a picture of our school teachers as if he had met them in person:

> *I know one who, when asked what he knows, will ask me for a book, in which to show me; who would not venture to tell me that he has scabs on his arse without consulting his lexicon there and then, to discover the meaning of scab and arse . . . Dionysius*

> *mocked grammarians who enquired into the ills of Ulysses but*
> *knew nothing of their own, musicians who tuned their flutes*
> *but not their manners, scholarly orators who ensured justice was*
> *mouthed, but not enacted.*

Had I been an unshakeably devout child, I would probably have accepted the inadequate studies our countrymen pursued in Normandy. But I could not share these exiles' vision of England: they imagined the entire English population ready to fall into the Pope's embrace. I had my doubts, but to say so was futile, even dangerous.

It was during these years that I mastered the fine art of leading two parallel lives: the life expected of me and the life that was truly my own.

I was a model pupil when required, and reached my twentieth year without ever having contradicted a soul. God granted me a good memory and an aptitude for learning, and I am grateful to Him – had I failed to satisfy (with ease) the expectations of all those exercising authority over me, I would surely have come to a bad end.

Thanks to Jane and Giuliano – whom we soon learned to call Jeanne and Julien, just as I was François and my brother Adrien – we quickly adapted to our new surroundings. In Clerkenwell we had spoken Latin. Here, it was French. Jane was a novice, and I'm sure Giuliano's Italian accent was as thick as butter. But he forbade us from speaking English.

'You are to come home every evening with a crop of twenty new words.'

Life with our new, adoptive parents so young and merry was indeed a great change from that which we had led until then. We had very little money and received only small, infrequent amounts from England. We lived frugally but without sacrificing good cheer.

Jane gave birth to a baby boy, anxiously awaited by us all.

'What if he dies like my first?' she would say from time to time. But he did not die. 'Julien' insisted on calling him Guillaume.

'Like his grandfather,' he explains.

'Who is his grandfather?'

'My dear François, I am the son of a priest – you will understand if I do not give you his full name.'

'What about your surname, then?'

Julien's name is Ardent.

'That's my chosen family name, inspired by my father's true name. But that's enough. I'll say no more.'

'Did you know him?'

'Yes. He was not a happy man, alas, and my mother and I were living proof of his sin. When she died, he hurried to put me into the service of the first master who would have me.'

He gives one of his hearty Italian laughs that I like so much.

'I learned the profession of arms very early on. I could defend myself and kill a man swiftly and efficiently. That's how I came to be in Cornwall, by ways I prefer not to tell. I was just fifteen years old. By a stroke of fortune, I was able to perform a service for Sir John, and he adopted me.'

He turns to his wife with a sweeping gesture.

'That was when you were nursing this tall young man at your breast.'

And he bursts out laughing again.

'But how did you come to speak so many languages?' Adrian asks.

'A mercenary's life,' says Giuliano. 'I travelled through France and Spain. I lived aboard ships like floating Towers of Babel. And I was the son of a priest – a facility for talk was in my blood, you might say.'

Adrian and I have a room on the first floor of our house, rented to us by a local merchant. Here we keep our books, a virginal we have managed to procure – our only luxury, we all play it – together with my brother's lute. Jane and Giuliano's bedroom is above the kitchen. The baby sleeps with them there, and Jane nurses him with her own milk.

'Of course, a fine lady does not do such things under normal circumstances,' she laughs, 'but I am making an exception!'

I am fascinated by our baby cousin, seeing how it must have been when I was in his place.

After two years in Eu, and thanks to Giuliano's method, we all speak perfect French. Even little Guillaume babbles his first words in French. School occupies us for twelve or fifteen hours a day, six days a week, and holidays are few. There is little time left for music or each other's company, or for exploring Eu and the countryside all around. But it is a small town, indeed, and we soon know every last corner.

One day I learn that our school's parish organist has fallen gravely ill, so I offer my services. The school takes this for an act of piety and, despite my youthfulness, my offer is eagerly accepted. From then on, I am excused from school to practise, to accompany the choir and for a host of other ceremonies. True, I have to take part in the very longest Sunday services, but time means nothing to me when I play. No one notices my clumsiness at the organ. William Byrd has taught me the basics but I am far from mastering the instrument. I rise to the challenge with sheer hard work. I am prepared to do anything for music.

I cherish the memory of those hours spent alone, for the most part, in the deserted church, deciphering John Bull's scores and William Byrd's masses and motets – newly arrived from England – by the light of a single candle. My predecessor's collection in Eu, moreover, reveals further treasures. To this man, whom I never met, I owe my discovery of the *Missa Cunctipotens Genitor* and the *Missa Kyrie fons*. I play with all my heart above the murmur of prayer, in an atmosphere of incense and religious fervour, and the music brings tears to my eyes.

IX

Fortune my foe, why dost thou frown on me?
And will thy favour never better be?
Wilt thou I say for ever breed my pain,
And wilt thou not restore my joys again?

'FORTUNE MY FOE'
POPULAR BALLAD

THE MESSAGE COMES one September day. We are returning from a short trip to Le Tréport, a place beside the sea a few hours' ride away, where Adrian and I used to go occasionally during our Eu years, to accompany Giuliano when he had business there. Having retained something of the spirit of the gentlemen we might have been, we never trouble ourselves to know Giuliano's business; we are above that.

The week-long Feast of St Michael the Archangel (our Michaelmas) provides the perfect opportunity for an escapade to the sea. For a few days, I am able to forget the burden of everyday life.

Upon our return, a messenger from Reims is waiting in the kitchen.

He bears a letter from Sir John asking the headmaster of the English College to accept me as one of his students, and a message for Giuliano instructing him to send me to Reims forthwith.

'Doctor Barret wishes me to take you back,' says the messenger, a tall, pale Englishman, dressed in black.

My blood runs cold.

'And me?' asks Adrian in his clear voice.

'I have no orders concerning you, sir. I seem to have overheard that you are still too young, and that you will not come to Reims before another year or two.'

I have already reached my full height, and look more than my thirteen years, while Adrian, at twelve years old, is a full head shorter and looks like a child.

'We need two days to get ready; I will bring him myself,' says Giuliano, after a swift glance at my face, which must be white with emotion. 'We have no wish to detain you, sir. Tell Doctor Barret that we shall be in Reims early next week.'

And with a clear gesture of finality, Giuliano bows with a great sweep of his hat. He speaks with such authority that the messenger concedes.

I weep that evening, and Giuliano and Jane make no attempt to tell me that I am a big boy for whom weeping is no longer proper.

'I can't to go to the English College without Adrian.'

'It's a matter of a year or two,' says Jane, to comfort me.

But a year or two feels like an eternity, and nothing can comfort me. Truly, my heart feels as if it will break at this separation from Adrian. Since our departure from Cornwall, we have never spent more than twenty-four hours apart.

EU WAS A SMALL, peaceful town, devoted to the Guise family and the League – the fanatical Catholic party. Our school had been founded by Henri, Duke of Guise, to educate children from Catholic families living in Protestant lands, and was closed not long after his death. 'Scarface' himself visited once, and I officiated as organist for a solemn Mass. I hardly saw him, but he did me the honour of remarking that the organ was played by a masterful hand. When he was told that the hand was that of an English adolescent, he desired to make my acquaintance.

He was a nobleman of tremendous elegance and imposing stature, one of the few people I would have been able to look straight in the eye had he lived until I reached maturity. He owed his nickname to the scar he bore on his face, but it detracted in no way from his proud, imperious gaze, replete with a natural majesty which prompted people to declare that the other nobles were mere commoners beside him.

He shook my hand with a smile that was unexpectedly soft for such a face, made the usual remarks about my age, my musical gifts and my height, and urged me not to overlook the profession of arms for all that. I promised not to, as politeness dictates. He in turn assured me that he would send me his son, the Count of Eu, who needless to say, I never saw.

This visit aside, the realities of the wide world only reached Eu in faint echoes. But set one foot outside this oasis and they crowded in. The closer we came to the heart of France, the clearer it became that war was raging here. Besides the war of religion between the papists and Huguenots, there was fighting between the King of France and the King of Navarre; civil war between members of the League, who sought to install the Duke of Guise on the throne, and partisans of the House of Valois and Henri III who sought to prevent that very same thing; as well as simmering conflict between France and Spain. Philip II aspired to dominate the whole of Europe, taking religion as his pretext, beginning with France and England. Moreover, armies of mercenaries in the service of one or other faction roamed the country, pillaging and ravaging as they went. All of this left a succession of hideous scars across the beautiful landscape through which we rode.

Giuliano had already made a fine swordsman of me. He had also taught me to shoot, and I discovered I had a gift for the pistol. Hand-to-hand combat held no secrets for me either. If I had not yet killed a man, this was because no one had yet posed a serious threat to me.

As we ride away from Eu, Giuliano explains:

'The reason I tell you not to carry your sword in plain view is because a gentleman travelling without a sizeable escort stirs keen interest.'

I have a dagger in each boot and a third in my jerkin; my sword is slung across my back, easy to lay hands on and barely concealed by my cloak; I carry a loaded pistol under my saddle – none of this apparent at first glance. I seem a harmless young theologian, dressed all in black, just like the Englishman who brought the message from Sir John.

The closer we come to our first halt, the more I feel that neither Sir John nor my father have properly gauged the consequences of their decision. Believing they were placing us in safety, they have in effect thrust us into the wolf's maw. The signs of war and pillage are everywhere. We pass by entire hamlets razed virtually to the ground, their ruins haunted by gaunt wailing creatures, barely able to drag themselves about. In a ditch, we glimpse a heap of corpses, despoiled and disfigured. We come upon people dying of starvation and small, armed bands whose countenance is far from reassuring.

For the first time in my life I am pallid with fear, true fear. I see assailants everywhere.

I am overwhelmed with relief at reaching the first post-house, but Giuliano counsels me immediately not to slacken my vigilance, so we sleep in turns that night.

At daybreak, we are back in the saddle.

After barely three leagues we come to a grove of trees, whereon several men fall upon us, quite literally.

I am no stranger to this predicament: we have rehearsed it so often that I react instinctively. The fear leaves me in an instant.

One man sweeps down on me and pinions my right arm. But Giuliano has seen to it that I am ambidextrous. In a single movement, I feign a fall to my left, seize the dagger in my boot and thrust it into his side before he can get a good grip on my saddle. A second man is already rushing at me, but I am on the ground in a flash, sword in my left hand, dagger in my right. I see us now, him seeking to trap me beneath the trees, me seeking to remain in the open. He flings himself at me, and for an instant I am on the defensive. But I quickly perceive that I am the more agile and this gives me the courage to attack. He fights furiously but my youthful ardour allows him no respite, and in the end I run him through, though I have no idea how. A few paces away, Giuliano has also laid a man low and is fighting two others. I leap to his side and we fight together, without a word.

We end up back to back, without a scratch. Our five assailants are on the ground.

'You have just undergone your baptism of blood, my young organist,' says Giuliano, who isn't even out of breath. 'You did very well, indeed, and I congratulate myself on such a fine pupil.'

But I am not proud. My whole body shakes and the fear has suddenly returned, made worse now with hindsight. My horse is dead, broached by a thrust that doubtless was meant for me. With a thriftiness of movement that I could not have managed myself, Giuliano unbuckles my saddle and places it on one of the assailants' horses.

'Let's not delay,' he says. 'They might have accomplices in the vicinity.'

We arrive in Saint-Quentin at dusk.

Sleep does not come easily.

So that is war. Him or me. In such moments, the value of a man's life is but the agility of his dagger – religion, Greek, Latin, music, count for nothing.

The next day, a convoy affords us the advantage of travelling in number, and we make halt at Laon, situated on a hill overlooking the whole of the Reims plain. The day after, we gallop full tilt through vineyards and fields, arriving before dusk.

It is 29th September 1586: one of the rare dates I recall with certainty.

Reims is entirely surrounded by ramparts, with a moat on three sides, completed by the River Vesle on the fourth side, to the south, spanned by three bridges offering the only means of access to the city.

'We shall go to the University tomorrow,' says Giuliano. 'This evening I am taking you to the inn.'

And with a confidence that suggests he has come here before, he trots straight off in the direction of a hostelry whose sign proclaims *A la Belle-Etoile*. The innkeeper welcomes 'Monsieur Julien' like a friend and prepares a meal, the like of which I have never seen. It is here that I taste my first French wine.

'You're a man, now, after what we've been through,' Giuliano declares. 'You've earned the right to drink like a man.'

There are a number of English Catholic families in Reims, whose children study at the English College. The college itself is as full as ever, so it is impossible for me to live there: it is attended by three hundred students, one hundred of whom are boarders, in buildings designed for half that number. The following morning, Giuliano takes me to the home of the More family, whose son Christopher has been my schoolmate in Eu.

The laws against Catholics of 1580 have deprived the Mores of two-thirds of their income, so they live frugally. Christopher's father is in the service of the Guise family while his mother, a charming and cultivated lady, takes in lodgers.

'You'll be better off at the Mores' than in college until we settle here,' Giuliano tells me.

And he is right, particularly because I have clearly stated from the first that I would not be a priest. Sir John is paying for my schooling, and so despite my father's insistence (he would have wished me to take Holy Orders even though I was the eldest son), I cannot be forced.

The English College is in a singular position when I arrive. It is being managed from Rome by William Allen, its founder, and on the premises by Doctor Richard Barret.

I have rarely hated anyone as much as this man.

Giuliano has scarcely departed when Barret calls me into his study and questions me as to my intentions for the future.

'I would like to be a musician, sir.'

'A musician? And you have come all the way to Reims to be a musician? Here we train soldiers of Christ, sir, not wandering minstrels.'

'One may be a soldier of Christ by playing the organ as much as by saying Mass, sir. I am here because my family is Catholic, intends to remain so and is persecuted.'

My insolence earns me a whipping such as I have never received before. I cannot sit down for two days, despite the ointment applied by the commiserative Madam More. No sooner has the pain eased than Barret sends for me again. I take my precautions this time and forewarn Madam More, who has her father-in-law, a genial old fellow, accompany me. When he sees us enter together, Barret's reddish face turns apoplectic.

'What's the meaning of this?'

'Sir, you whipped me because I stated my purpose, and since I have not changed my mind and do not wish to be whipped every time I express my intentions, I have chosen to disclose them to a mediator who will convey them to you in my stead. I consider that to be a priest demands a passion I feel only for music. I am a devout Catholic and willing to study theology, but I wish to learn music, philosophy and mathematics too. My uncle, Sir John Arundell, always told me there were several ways to serve God.'

'I hope, my dear Doctor Barret,' says the elderly gentleman smoothly, 'that you do not think to kindle a religious calling by the whip.'

Barret tries to argue, saying there is no place for 'dabblers' in the college, which is already overburdened with pupils.

We leave, and my elderly protector goes straight to Doctor Bailey who, in addition to being one of his friends, has been a theology teacher at the college, as well as its deputy headmaster and administrator for many years. Together they write to Doctor Allen. Some time later, a letter from Allen advises that I should be permitted to pursue *all the music his virtuosity requires*, calming Barret's zeal, though in no way altering the poor opinion he retains of me until the end.

I hasten to visit the many organists in Reims, and find myself once again in luck. The parish priest of the church of Saint-Jacques is Abbé de La Lobe, and his chaplain Simon Ogier; together they are responsible for the music in the parish, but they are overworked, and immediately hire me for a Mass.

'God has sent you!' exclaims the Abbé.

Having copied out the *Missa Kyrie fons*, I am able to use it that Sunday. It pleases them so much that one thing leads to another and I serve as the church's second organist for five years. I don't play every Sunday, but on request, as needed. The organs are old and in a poor state of repair. Drawing on the knowledge that Giles Farnaby has passed on to me, the guidance of an organ builder who visits from time to time and the aid of the parish warden Jehan Pussot, who is a carpenter, I manage to restore the instrument. It is not perfect, but it does not cost the parish anything and the tone is better.

During my six years in Reims, I spend many hours at the parish house, discussing music with the priests and rehearsing with them. Very occasionally, I have the opportunity of playing in other churches. I officiate several times at Saint-Rémi, at Saint-Nicaise and even once at the cathedral.

As well as my musical activities, I follow the same course of study as my schoolfellows not intended for Holy Orders: philosophy and rhetoric in Latin and French, and theology in English. I work at my studies all day long.

I will not dwell longer on this humdrum existence, which changed little during the years I spent in Reims.

But against this quiet background, events succeeded at a frenetic pace. The first was without doubt the most momentous of all as far as I am concerned.

It occured in the spring following my arrival. One evening, returning from Saint-Jacques, I found Giuliano at the Mores' house, as pale as a ghost.

I didn't even think to greet him.

'What's happened, Giuliano? Is it Jane?'

'Jane is in marvellous health, thank you. She gave birth to a boy whom we are naming Francis, and you are his godfather.'

I do not stop to rejoice.

'But then . . . ? My father? Sir John?'

'No, Francis, it's not that. It's Adrian. He's gone.'

My first, instinctive reaction is a refusal to understand.

'Gone' must mean 'dead' for Giuliano to make the journey to tell me, and Adrian simply cannot be dead. It is as if someone has told me I have lost an arm without realising it.

'Gone?' I repeat, forcing myself not to tremble. 'What do you mean by that?'

'Exactly what I say. He's gone. Vanished. We've looked for him everywhere; as far as Calais, Nantes even.'

'Giuliano, if he's dead, tell me.'

'I would rather know him to be dead than live in uncertainty. Jane has lost her beautiful complexion and Guillaume weeps day and night, bawling for his Adrian in Latin . . .' Giuliano's voice falters. 'He . . . Adrian had set to teaching him as they played: "I shall be your Mulcaster", he said. And then one day . . .'

He drops onto a stool and wipes his eyes.

'But how . . . In what circumstances . . . ?'

'Since you left, he's become friends with the apothecary on Ruelle du Guet; you know, the one who dabbles in alchemy and astrology. They spent whole nights reading Paracelsus. Recently, they had been making up dye mixtures for cloth and had achieved a quite extraordinary purple hue. They dyed their coats with it and the result was so beautiful that all of Eu clamoured for the colour. "We'll sell our purple to the weavers of Flanders," said Adrian, "and earn our fortune in spite of Carey and the Queen of England." All this to say that his cloak currently looks like no other. Last Tuesday, he went to school as usual. His schoolmasters assure me that nothing particular occurred and that Adrian was his ordinary self. Which means nothing, of course: we are talking about Adrian Tregian here. He's only thirteen but he has the maturity of a grown man. If he had decided to deceive us all, and if we, his nearest and dearest, were beguiled, it's highly unlikely that his schoolmasters or schoolfellows would have noticed anything out of the ordinary. When he left school on Tuesday, he went to the apothecary's. They experimented in his laboratory, nothing unusual in that either. At dusk, they parted and Adrian made for home.

The apothecary watched him as far as the corner of the alley. There are but three hundred paces between the shop and our house; barely an instant; two streets. Guillaume was waiting for him at the window. But he didn't come home; nobody heard anything; nobody saw anything. Two days later, I was scouring the countryside and coast in the company of a few friends, fearing at each instant to discover his butchered body in a ditch. Some fishermen told me they had found a cloak of a curious colour on the beach at Le Tréport: there is no doubt that it is his.'

'Was it washed up by the tide?'

'I think not. Rather, it had been abandoned. It was higher up the beach than the farthest limit of the rising tide.'

As he talks, he unwraps the packet he carries with him. Adrian's cloak is of the most beautiful violet purple – a colour now familiar but which at the time was the privilege of just a few flowers.

The more I listen, the more convinced I become that Adrian is not dead.

'Giuliano, you've given us the principal facts. Let's have the details. We may find something out of the ordinary there. What did he take with him from school?'

'Nothing. But when he went to the apothecary, he sometimes used to leave his satchel there.'

'And from the apothecary?'

'He took a phial of purple with him. Nothing remarkable about that. What's more, they had completed their experiments the day before and had achieved the colour, which cleaves to the cloth and never fades.'

'Had he ever taken a phial away before?'

In lieu of a reply, Giuliano stares at me as if I were mad. I am so busy unravelling my brother's thought processes that I have no time to explain. If Adrian has left of his own accord, if . . .

'He must have left a sheet of paper, a word . . .'

Giuliano's eyes grow wide. I grab him, shake him.

'What? What, Giuliano, is there a message? I beg you!'

'I am a fool,' Giuliano declares, his voice still trembling, 'but truly, it never occurred to me that Adrian might have left on purpose.'

He rummages in his doublet, pulls out a sheet of paper folded in two and hands it to me.

'This was on his desk, placed in quite prominent fashion on top of his papers.'

I understand why it held no importance for Giuliano. In the left-hand corner, Adrian has written: *Francis, my brother*, and in the centre: *extremities meet*. That is all. My heart swells. He is alive!

'Giuliano, he has left of his own free will. I cannot easily explain to you the meaning of this message, but it is perfectly clear. I am prepared to wager that Adrian has departed for the Americas to make his fortune with his dye.'

'Francis, for the love of God! I am responsible for you both. What am I going to tell Sir John? Or your parents?'

'Nothing.'

I am serene. My dread has melted away. Now, I *know*.

'How so, nothing?'

'Giuliano, do you recall the day you told me that if I was old enough to kill a man, then I was old enough to be treated like a man? On that day it was but a quip with regard to a glass of wine. Now it is serious. My father is an admirable man but it's impossible to discuss practical problems with him. He has principles that bear no relation to the reality of our lives. Perhaps he loves us, but he never concerns himself with our well-being.'

Silence. I continue:

'I was induced to become a priest, in spite of being the eldest. But I had the right to say no. A younger son, such as Adrian, would never have had the choice, Giuliano, and considering the very few private thoughts he confided in me, I would tend to think he has become quite the sceptic.'

'Francis! Sir!'

'Let's call a spade a spade. Adrian's religious life is over. His only true interests are travel, inventions and mathematics. He has discovered an unknown colour and will find wealth with it. This colour will come back to us one day; we shall follow it, and I wager we will trace it back to my brother, who, with his angel's eyes and discreet charm, will have restored the family fortune.'

'But then . . .'

'Giuliano, I am taking on something of my role as head of the family before time. I may tell Sir John everything when next I see him. But until then, it will do the family less harm to believe Adrian drowned accidentally. Death, they understand. But a life different from theirs is quite beyond them.'

I stop, surprised by my own discourse.

'If they heard you, Francis!'

'They do *not* hear me. My opinion has never been sought regarding my parents' choices, and I have never contested them, but they cannot pretend that I continue *ad aeternum* to have no opinion on the matter.'

Giuliano looks at me with a mixture of alarm and connivance.

'So, are we agreed, Giuliano? Adrian drowned accidentally. Or he was killed in mysterious circumstances. And we mention neither the coat nor the phial of purple.'

'We are agreed.'

I extend my hand.

'I swear before God to say nothing, even when the time comes to set out in search of my brother. Even if I find him.'

Giuliano places his hand on mine.

'I swear to say nothing, even if I find him,' he repeats, and smiles, for the first time since he has arrived.

'You are certain he isn't dead, aren't you?'

'Absolutely. And even if I miss him, I am not sad, nor do I blame him, since he had no choice. I would have done the same in his position, and am even tempted to do so now.'

'Ah no, not that!'

'Don't worry. I don't plan to disappear. I wish to go to Rome, and I would surely be found.'

Giuliano looks at me, shaking his head. There is no trace of the dejected air he was wearing at the beginning of our conversation. I have convinced him. I lay a hand on his shoulder.

'Giuliano, before you go to bed, let us take a walk down to the inn. I should like to raise a cup to my brother's health and to his plans.'

He does not take much persuading.

We set off. Reims is quiet at this hour but not deserted. People are at each other's homes, and the older students crowd into the taverns. The deep silence of night has yet to descend. The watch proclaims that it is eight o'clock and all quiet. We leave the Rue des Anglais and make for the

University quarter, walking past a row of arched doorways out of which burst shouts, laughter and songs.

I look up. The sky is filled with stars.

'I wonder where Adrian is.'

'If you're right, he is sailing across the wide ocean.'

I speak to him in my mind:

'Farewell, Adrian. We shall meet again. Until then, I wish you happiness.'

'Francis! We're here.'

He opens the door and we enter the Belle-Etoile.

X

ADRIAN'S DEPARTURE (officially his disappearance, but I refused to use that word) heralded a whirlwind of events that blew my life in Reims apart like a cannon volley.

History had the bit between its teeth. The confusion in the kingdom was so great that many people – and especially foreigners like us – lost track altogether.

Extraordinary events came one after another, so fast that now, years later, I cannot say for certain in what order they occurred.

The death of Mary Stuart, Queen of Scotland, for example. I am almost certain I heard the dreadful news after Adrian left.

Yet I remember exactly what we did that day. The entire college was excused from class the following morning and ordered to attend the cathedral.

Barret called me in.

'Tregian, you have a Requiem Mass to hand, no doubt.'

'There is music for one at Saint-Jacques, I think, but I've never . . .'

'You have tonight. Fetch it from the church. Learn it. Put your music to good use for once. And mind you play it properly tomorrow morning.'

'Who has died, sir?'

'You'll find out tomorrow along with everyone else. Now be off!'

I run straight to Saint-Jacques and pull hard at Abbé de La Lobe's bell, to rouse him.

He listens as I explain what I need.

'I've never read that particular Mass and I don't even know why I'm being asked to play it. . . . ' I finish, still out of breath.

Abbé de La Lobe has seen me about the place and heard me play so often that I have become a favourite, and almost one of his own household.

'The Cardinal has asked for prayer vigils and Masses, and if you promise to tell no one, I will tell you why.'

'Understood. I'll say nothing.'

'Mary Stuart is dead.'

'What? Mary Stuart . . . '

'She was executed by the heretics.'

'How so?'

'Elizabeth the Bastard Queen had her beheaded.'

'She . . . '

'Ah, here we are: a Mass for the dead and a *Miserere*. See what you can do with these!'

I sit down and decipher the music, with the Abbot's help. My performance is approximate but good enough; I keep to the melody and mostly improvise the accompaniment.

Mary Stuart dead!

For Catholics, Mary – a granddaughter of Henry VII, like Elizabeth – was the true Queen of England, while Elizabeth was the daughter of Anne Boleyn, whom Rome had never recognised as Henry VIII's wife. Elizabeth was a bastard child and a usurper. Mary had been kept a prisoner in England for years, following a series of tremendous blunders. Why execute her now?

The following morning, we are treated to a sermon by the Cardinal Archbishop of Reims himself, who is a nobleman and brother of the Duke of Guise, and another from Abbot Parsons who has made the journey especially to give us the news.

Mary's Guise uncles and her cousin the King of Spain will certainly seek to avenge her death. Her execution is the pretext for endless hate-filled speeches and warlike behaviour. Everyone present pledges a great many oaths.

Pamphlets multiply in the weeks that follow. The Protestant Henri of Navarre, legitimate heir to the French throne following the death of Henri III of Valois, is denounced as a future Elizabeth who will make France a nation of Huguenots. Catholics will be forced to choose: exile or death.

The prospect fans the flames still further. Emotions are at their height.

WE HAD SCARCELY DIGESTED the news when Reims was shaken by the Battle of Coutras, at which the Protestant Henri of Navarre inflicted a resounding defeat on the Catholics, commanded by the Duke of Joyeuse.

Praise for the King of Navarre was best avoided in Reims, but the rumours circulating about him sparked anxiety and admiration in equal measure. He was a fearsome general of astonishing courage, it was said. He had seized any number of strongholds and would risk his life like any military captain. He could go a fortnight without sleeping in his bed. His men worshipped him. He wouldn't hesitate to take up a pickaxe and help dig out a trench along with the rest of them. And when it came to the attack, he was first into the fray.

Travellers brought us news of the battle, even though it had taken place at the other end of France, near Bordeaux.

Before the battle, Henri of Navarre had encouraged his infantrymen and knights with a rousing speech:

'Companions, the glory of God, our honour and our lives are at stake. Flight or victory! The way lies open before us. Let us go forward in the name of God, for whom we fight!'

And one eyewitness added, his voice trembling with emotion:

'Upon which, the army of heretics chanted a psalm, as one man, and the field all around rang to the words:

> *This is the day which the Lord has made;*
> *we will rejoice and be glad in it.'*

It was remarkable to hear. And with that the Huguenot cannon had opened fire and felled Joyeuse's knights, who had begun a reckless charge.

The Huguenot front line collapsed in the crush, but Joyeuse's squadrons clashed with the cavalry posted in reserve behind the cannon.

'Navarre had stationed arquebusiers in among them. Each line of cavalry was covered by a line of marksmen. No one had ever seen the like before! It was a massacre.'

The battle went hand-to-hand and the Catholic infantry scattered almost without a fight. The King of Navarre, being always at the heart of combat, was almost taken. Finally, the Duke of Joyeuse and his brother were killed, with two thousand of their men. The Catholics were completely routed.

'They retreated leaving all their equipment and a host of horses without riders. And do you know what Henri did? There were a great many wounded left lying among the dead but he forbade anyone to put them to death, and threatened dire punishment if a man so much as raised a hand to the prisoners. And he showed Joyeuse's body – and his brother's body – the due honours of their rank. Unbelievable!'

The man lowered his voice, glanced over his shoulder to make sure no Jesuits were within earshot, and added:

'Some of Navarre's soldiers were not happy. When they asked him why he had shown such indulgence, he replied: "I have more room in my heart for mercy than for hatred."'

An uncomfortable silence fell around the storyteller. Could the Antichrist himself be a man of honour?

A FEW DAYS LATER, we heard news of the Guise victory over Navarre's mercenaries – his cavalry had been surprised and beaten by the Duke near the town of Auneau, on their way back from the battle of Coutras.

Guise had shown as much courage as Navarre, and left just as many corpses strewn at the scene of the attack. Innumerable Masses for the dead were spoken in Reims.

Looking back, I find it hard to conceive that in the midst of such excitement and upheaval we continued quietly with our studies: casuistry, or such thorny questions as whether or not an English Catholic could make out his last will and testament to his children if they had embraced the reformed faith, whether the Church's rules on fasting should be observed, or whether a priest could accept the presence at Mass of Catholic servants who also (for obvious reasons) accompanied their masters to Protestant services. And so on and so forth. I paid little attention.

Our casuistry classes soon became forums for heated political debate. I remember a discussion on the day we learned that the Duke of Savoy was planning to seize Geneva, inviting French Catholics to join him and raze it to the ground.

'Geneva is the fountainhead of heresy, the city feeds and legitimises the Reformation. The seizing of this hotbed of subversion, this perpetual challenge to the world's order, is a work which all Catholics have a natural duty to serve and promote. The destruction of the city of Calvin is a salutary act.'

'The King of France is against the idea,' said one pupil, in harsh tones. 'He is already half-Huguenot.'

'That's because he doesn't trust the King of Spain,' said another, 'and puts his nation before his religion. A good Catholic should never think that way.'

I should have liked a casuistry class on the question of whether a man's religion should indeed come before his loyalty to his country. And I was perplexed, too: we criticised Elizabeth for the violence she showed to Catholics, but what were we preaching if not violence and destruction ourselves?

It seems extraordinary, too, that in the midst of all this, I was able to concentrate on my music. I suppose my memory leaps over long periods of relative calm.

Echoes of the city sieges – seized by the Huguenots, taken back by the papists, taken again by the Huguenots, and so on – reached us at regular intervals, in the stories of eloquent travellers. I would do my best to stay fit and active, I decided. I was bound to find myself on the field of battle one day. My free time was divided between music and a fencing master who completed my soldier's education.

I had thought myself capable enough but, with typically French flourish, my new master-at-arms soon disabused me of that.

'You have a good grounding, young man; we can make something of you. On guard, sir!'

And he set about attacking me there and then, with great gusto.

At the same time, I spent days perfecting my Latin; my teachers praised my mastery of the language and they sometimes tried – without much conviction – to persuade me to embrace an ecclesiastical career.

'Ah, you would make a fine prelate! You have an authoritative bearing, and a preacher's eyes,' they sighed.

THE MAD YEAR OF 1588 had only just begun.

In late May, some Reims citizens came back from Paris in a state of high agitation. There had been a popular uprising; barricades had been set in the streets. The Duke of Guise, hailed by half the country as the next King of France, had made a triumphal entry into Paris. Onlookers called out as he passed: 'Now that you are here, fair Prince, we are all saved!'

We heard contradictory stories: some said that Catherine de' Medici desired Guise's death and would see to it herself, others that Guise had plans to assassinate Henri III. The devout Catholics objected that Henri III had struck too many compromises with the Huguenots, while their more reasonable co-religionists argued that this was the only way to keep the King of Spain in check. Some people even noted that after Coutras, Henri of Navarre had spared the King, by tactfully avoiding a second victory in battle (something he could have accomplished with ease); in choosing not to bring the King to his knees, he preserved the royal dignity rather than make a show of his own strength.

Not a week went by without fresh news from someone passing through, so that I paid little attention to it after a time. Everything seemed to be happening in Paris, in a narrow perimeter defined by the Louvre and the Guise mansion. The two Henris (Guise and Valois) were locked in a complex game of feints and silences, but neither actually wished to do away with the other.

Towards the end of that same month of May, word reached the English College that the King of Spain was about to set sail with a fleet of one hundred and fifty warships and the firm intention of defeating England. One hundred and fifty ships! My country was doomed. I had seen a Spanish man o' war once, on the coast near Eu – a monstrous vessel, ten times taller than an English ship. And England certainly did not have one hundred and fifty warships at her disposal. Not forgetting that half the English fleet was already at sea, heading for the Americas.

In Paris, the Catholic League was plotting against Henri III – and now the Spanish fleet was massing against the English. Could these two events be mere coincidence? Another question I was forced to keep to myself. I missed Adrian horribly; he was the only person in whom I could have confided.

More news came the very next day, it seems to me now, though it was doubtless weeks later: Drake had attacked the Armada off Calais. The news reached us in scraps and fragments, each more worrying than the last. And more difficult to believe.

Whatever had possessed Philip to anchor the Armada off Calais? Why had the fleet not sailed around by Cornwall? The Cornish coast had been fortified since the reign of Henry VIII – such was the fear of invasion by that route – but it was still the kingdom's most vulnerable stretch of coastline. It seemed impossible that the commander of such a vast fleet could have taken the decision to sail into the Channel, with its notorious, capricious weather and tides. Even a novice like myself knew it was best avoided.

In the churches of Reims, vituperative mutterings against 'the Valois' mingled with prayers for Philip of Spain's victory. I played at countless services.

Christopher More beamed with joy:

'We must pray hard for the Spanish victory, for we shall win our own country back and be free to practise our faith. God is with us, victory shall be ours.'

Reckless words. Attempts were made to disguise the scale of the Armada's defeat, but it gradually became apparent that it was absolute. As the end of the year approached, the latest news was confirmed and details of the catastrophe circulated. The numbers were vast, unimaginable: fifteen thousand killed, one hundred ships sunk. The Armada had cost millions of ducats – fifty million according to some, one hundred million according to others. Spain was ruined, in either case. None of which prevented Philip II from plotting until his dying breath to consolidate his power throughout Europe. But for all his later efforts, he never seemed so terrible as then, before the downfall of his first, thoroughly vincible Armada.

Reims was the Guise capital, and a stronghold of the Catholic League. Here, the Catholic defeats were greeted with official silence. We could usually find someone to tell us the latest news, but these were isolated voices, speaking cautiously, and we never knew which of the conflicting stories to believe. Fabrication was tempting, given the circumstances, and there was no shortage of overzealous imaginations.

ON CHRISTMAS MORNING I was seated at the organ while Abbé de La Lobe said Mass, when Giuliano poked his head through the opening at the top of the narrow wooden stairs leading to the loft. He sometimes visited me in Reims. I smiled, delighted to see him. Then I looked again and saw something was not right.

Still playing, I gestured for him to come nearer. He was covered in dust.

'I have just come from Paris,' he whispered. 'The King has had the Duke of Guise assassinated.'

My discordant wrong note must have startled the congregation below. Giuliano sat himself down on a stool and fell into an exhausted asleep.

After Mass, he explained what had happened. 'I raced here to bring you a letter from Sir John. I went to Paris first, on business, and was planning to come to you early next week. And then, two days ago, in the early hours of the morning, the King's private guard killed the Duke of Guise. His brother, the Cardinal Archbishop of Reims, is in prison. People say his days are numbered. It seemed to me that with Guise dead, the King might be minded to take Reims, as a Guise stronghold, and I was determined to get here ahead of the King's troops, if indeed the King's troops are on their way.'

The King sent no troops, but Giuliano was proved right in every other respect: less than two days later, we learned of the death of our Cardinal. There was a logic to it: had Henri let him live, this fierce young prelate would have avenged his brother's death by every possible means.

Abbot Parsons, a master of the art of disappearing and popping up like a jack-in-the-box, arrived at just the right point to give us a long sermon about holding fast to the faith against any and all assailants.

I must say a word here about Robert Parsons. He was a Jesuit of roughly my father's age. People said he had accompanied the celebrated Father Edmund – one of the very first English martyrs – on his missions, and that he had fled England *in extremis*. Now he was living in Spain or Rome.

He was a tall, sombre-looking man who had been a great friend of the Guises. Indeed, it was he who had persuaded them to open the school in Eu. If I were to sum up the general Catholic opinion of Father Parsons, I would say he was considered a necessary evil. He was a devout Jesuit – the doctrine of mental equivocation was second nature to him – and he would protest, deeply offended, whenever he was charged with meddling in politics.

'Never!' he would exclaim, with the broad, inclusive sweep of a preacher. 'God demands that we serve him through religion, setting aside the things of this world. His kingdom is my sole concern.'

And he was prepared to do anything for the kingdom of God – even to cast aside the kingdom of England. He was indefatigable, always travelling, organising, advising, writing.

At the time of the Paris uprising and the Armada, we saw more of Robert Parsons than was usual, because Doctor Allen – a Cardinal now, and permanently resident in Rome – had sent him to Flanders to 'receive' the Armada (though for a man who never dabbled in politics, it was unclear what that implied in practice).

After that he travelled to Spain, where he founded and directed the English College in Valladolid, taking with him a number of students from Reims. In one of his letters, he insisted I should be sent to Spain, too. My father would have approved of the idea, he said. My father was often cited in support of his plans. I loathed Parsons' habitual manner with me, always placing a friendly hand on my shoulder, as if to take me into his confidence. At times, it seemed he was courting me as a man courts a woman and, for that reason alone, I had no wish to see him ever again.

Barret tried to order me to Spain.

'It's out of the question,' I objected. 'I intend to complete my studies, and I intend to do so in France.'

'It is not your place to discuss the matter,' he said, in his vile voice. 'It is God's calling.'

'No. Not God's calling, nor my father's will – I know nothing of his wishes – but Father Parsons,' I answered back, at the risk of a whipping.

But I was nearly sixteen years old. I had grown to my full height and (happily) the world tended to forget my relatively young age.

'I will not leave Reims without a written order from Sir John Arundell, my guardian, who sent me here and pays my keep.'

Besides which, all other considerations being equal, I could not help but see the Spaniards as my enemies – as any proper Englishman would. I refused to have any dealings with them.

Enough of Parsons. The less I think about him now, the better.

Events continued at a frenzied pace.

We were told of the certain, imminent death of the King of Navarre, who was gravely ill, but who subsequently recovered, despite fervent prayers on the part of the English Catholics and the people of Reims for the swift dispatch of his soul (prayers which were of course offered up in a spirit of pure Christian charity).

Catherine de' Medici died of old age a few weeks after the Duke of Guise and the Cardinal Archbishop of Reims. People said she had governed the kingdom since the death of her husband Henri II and that now the time had come for her son to take over. We would see his true mettle at last.

We barely had time.

Henri III was in a difficult situation. He had killed a cardinal and, as a result, the learned doctors of the Sorbonne had released the people from their duty of obedience to their king.

'We have no king,' the people said. A bitter struggle ensued against the extremists in the League. In the spring, Henri III struck an alliance with the King of Navarre. It was the only solution, no doubt. Under Salic law, Henri of Bourbon-Navarre was the legitimate successor to Henri III of Valois. The two kings had spent part of their childhood together, and their estrangement had been dictated by reasons of State, nothing more. They soon came to an agreement despite their religious differences. Both men recognised a common cause: the nation came first. They decided to take Paris, which was held by the ultra-Catholics under the Duke of Mayenne, the younger brother of the two assassinated Guises. And then, when everything appeared settled, Henri III was stabbed by a religious fanatic.

France found itself under a Protestant king – Henri IV.

Reims stood braced for a Catholic massacre – St Bartholomew's Day in reverse. People exorcised their terror in frantic prayer. Penitents processed through the streets, clad in rough, homespun robes.

I shall not attempt to relate the history of the period that followed. But I began to take a passionate interest in the events of the day, and neglected my music for the taverns and their heated debates. Whenever I could get myself a horse, I braved the danger abroad (every traveller risked being robbed by brigands or killed by mercenaries), overcame my fear and rode south out of town to talk to the people I found there. I would make up my own mind.

Imagine my response, then, to a peremptory summons from Barret, and to the scheme he proposed:

'I'm told you're a good rider and an excellent swordsman, Tregian. Moreover, you know the countryside around Eu. Do you think you can ride as far as Eu and get there alive?'

Barret was never one to mince his words.

'I can try.'

'The Duke of Mayenne is there. We have an urgent message for him. You may have to pass behind enemy lines.'

'Enemy?'

'I mean Navarre.'

'Ah, of course – the King of France!'

'I mean the Huguenot lines. Above all, you must not get caught.'

'Again, sir, I will try. Am I to go alone?'

'We would prefer it. You'll attract less attention that way.'

He gave me a coded message – something about a trade in birds. It was meaningless to me but I learned it by heart. Wild with joy, I found myself riding out on the high road. Three years had passed since I came to Reims and my confidence was far greater now. My eagerness to travel – alone! – was such that I forgot all thought of danger.

I had travelled to Reims through a country scarred by war, but those scenes were a sunny memory compared with what I saw now. Desolation lay all around. We were in September, and the ungathered crops were plain to see, the vine stocks had not been stripped of their foliage and the grapes would most likely rot, to be trampled underfoot by passing horses or burned. I avoided the main routes, preferring even to lose my way from time to time. I was armed to the teeth, but to outward appearance I was a poor seminary student riding a gaunt nag. No one paid me the slightest heed. I reached Eu without incident in just four days.

Mayenne's army had just broken camp and left.

XI

*My fancy did I fire
in faithful form and frame:
In hope there should no blust'ring blast
have power to move the same.
And as the gods do know,
and world can witness bear:
I never served other saint,
no idol other where.*

'ALL IN A GARDEN GREEN'
POPULAR BALLAD

I WAVER FOR A MOMENT: should I hurry off in pursuit of Mayenne or devote an hour to my own affairs?

The desire to see Jane is stronger.

She is in the kitchen, holding her third child in her arms, a little girl just a few weeks old. Francis, my godson, clings to his mother's skirt. He is chubby and all smiles: his father in miniature. Guillaume is at school.

'When you were a child,' she says, after we have shared the warmest of embraces, 'you looked like your father, but now you're a man you look much more like your grandfather John. There is that same determination in your features, something your father has always lacked, religious matters aside, of course.'

Her face is so smooth, so calm, so serene, that I am seized by a sudden impulse.

'Jane, I have no idea what you and Giuliano think or practise. Caught as we all are between papists and Huguenots, there are times when I no longer know what to believe.'

She looks at me with those clear eyes of hers, that are said to mirror my own.

'My dear Francis, what are you talking about?'

'I am talking about this absurd war. Here am I, carrying a message to Mayenne, the brother of my murdered cardinal, so that he may be victorious over Henri, King of Navarre and France. Day in, day out, I listen to people heaping calumnies on the Queen of England. We prayed to God, Jane, that he may destroy her. But God has protected her. In Reims they would say "God is with us", but *we* were the ones who lost. Could it be that He was with the other side? I am honour-bound, and would die rather than fail to deliver this message. But I have no wish to see King Henri defeated.'

I say all this without pause, as if the words are spoken by somebody else. There are tears in my eyes. Carried along by a wave of emotion, I tell Jane about my encounter with Elizabeth of England.

'Master Francis, these are bad times for well-meaning men: they are persecuted even more than heretics. In this day and age, a hero is a man firmly anchored to a faction, a man who may proudly declare: "We are good, we are God's children; the others are bad, they are Satan's henchmen."' Blushing, she adds: 'We feared greatly that you had become intolerant, too, living in that nest of Jesuits.'

A long silence.

'That which your father felt to be his duty was perhaps a grave error, one from which your family will not recover,' she finally says, her voice choked.

'And Giuliano?' I ask, for want of anything else to add.

'Giuliano is Sir John's legs, mouth and eyes. He scuttles across Europe attempting to reconcile the irreconcilable and obtain religious freedoms from those in power. Persuading them would not be so hard; it's their subjects who require moral certainty. Paradise assured. They say that Henri of Navarre doesn't give a fig about religion. He's a good Christian, but broad-minded. Elizabeth is the same. They also say that his tolerance is the reason why Henri III of Valois was murdered.'

'Henri III? But he was forever doing penance.'

'You must learn, dear Francis, and this may be the last thing I'll teach you, that a man may be extremely devout and yet have no desire to put to death anyone who doesn't pray as fervently as himself. Henri III saw religion as a personal affair, beyond the realm of the State.'

Silence. She has just answered my most burning question.

'For example,' she continues, 'I maintain that your thoughts might lead you straight to Hell, yet I have no wish to see you burned at the stake, nor anyone else for that matter. I pray that God bestows an unshakeable faith upon you. Unfortunately, people tend to believe that he who is not with them is against them. We pass for the foulest fiends if we compromise.'

'And so?'

'And so, Master Francis, you must hold your tongue if you wish to live. Pray that a day will come when religion will be a private matter for each and every one of us. Until then, don't breathe a word. Take action however you can, wherever you can. Remember what Old Thomas told you: "The best way to thank the Lord for His gifts is to make good use of them. You have duties and responsibilities, but you have your own free will. The art of a good life is to reconcile the two."'

I take strength from watching her talk. She has changed little since the time she used to nurse me. I am the one who has changed; there are moments when I forget she fed me, and her beauty provokes a disquiet within me which I do not yet understand.

I take my leave, without even waiting to see Guillaume.

Giuliano is in London, or Rome, or Paris; Jane does not know where, exactly.

I have to find the Duke of Mayenne's camp.

This is not so simple. He has left to conquer Dieppe, where Henri has taken up a defensive position. Some of his rearguard still remains, but I don't have the watchword required for them to admit me.

An officer casts a belligerent eye over my mop of copper-coloured hair and declares:

'You might be an English spy.'

He approaches with such menace that I feel a shiver of unease.

'Are you English?' he thunders at me.

I reply in my most perfect French.

'Me? Dear Lord, no! I am François Tréjean of Reims, sent here under orders. And I assure you that if I am not taken to the Duke of Mayenne, he will see that you regret it.'

Eventually, they relent.

'Ride along the coast; they were going towards Neuville. But spare your mount, sir, for you will not find a single post-house supplied with fresh horses. There must be thirty thousand men on the march.'

I go on my way.

The confusion of that September day is forever imprinted in my memory. I know that I met Mayenne. I can see him now, listening attentively as I rattled off the phrases about the bird-catcher and the chirruping, wondering all the while how such a plump fellow could make a great general.

When I had finished, he thanked me profusely – the message must have made some sense to him – and asked me to return in a few hours.

'First we must thrash this heretic kinglet.'

I left the tent, got back in the saddle and rode off a little way. Suddenly, I was surrounded by four men, armed and threatening.

'So, my little priest; spying are we?'

How have I managed to cross the line between the two camps?

I make no attempt to argue: surprise has rendered me speechless, and there is simply no time. I leap from my horse and land firmly on my feet, with sword and dagger drawn. My turn to take them by surprise. The four men, officers, judging by their attire, now find themselves on the defensive. I tell myself that if I must die – at one against four, it seems inevitable – then at least I shall enjoy the fight. My master-of-arms in Reims taught me to whip plumes from hats and cut a cloak from a man's back. I swiftly demonstrate several of these spectacular moves, laughing as I do. I have no wish to kill anyone.

The man who appears to be their leader stops the skirmish.

'Halt there, fellows, I should like to know who he is, this gay sir, who pierces our hats as a prelude to running us through. And to think I took you for a priest.'

We bow to one another.

'Well, sir?'

'I am François Tréjean d'Arondelle.'

It is all I can think of, but it has the advantage of being the French translation of a truth, of stating my quality as a gentleman and not involuntarily revealing my nationality. I keep on, in similar vein.

'Might I know by whose hand I have the honour of being cut to pieces?'

'We are gentlemen, sir, and as such will not set to at four against one. Either we will hang you for a spy, or else we will fight one on one. I am Charles de Troisville. These are Monsieur d'Ardenne, Monsieur d'Aubigné the Younger and Monsieur des Archets, all in the service of the King of France.'

Elaborate bows all round.

'And now,' Troisville continues, 'we will search you to be sure you are not carrying any documents of a criminatory nature.'

I bow even lower:

'I am sorry, sir, but honour forbids I should submit to being searched alive. However, you have my word that I carry not a single sheet of paper about my person.'

We carry on this exchange, in far less jocular vein, until the arrival of a small company who take me prisoner, and even search me. There are so many of them, I have no choice but to submit and keep my honour intact. They bring me to the castle at Dieppe, where I spend a few hours, but I hardly have time to worry before Monsieur de Troisville arrives to free me.

'So, Monsieur Tréjean d'Arondelle! I have told the King about you and your japes, and he wishes to meet you.'

'The King? Which King?'

'Come now . . . The King of France. Is there another, as far as you're concerned?'

'No, assuredly, but such an honour for my humble self . . . I thought that . . .'

I am to meet Henri of Bourbon without having done a single thing to deserve it! My delight is apparent to all.

'Tréjean! Wipe that rapt smile off your face and come this way!'

I pull myself together.

'Is my attire . . . ?'

'Leave it, leave it: we're about to do battle and, besides, Henri IV is unlike other kings. He cares little for a man's attire.'

Dieppe as I saw it for the very first time was a hive of activity. Preparations were being made to defend it on several sides. The King had considered the surrounding topography and surmised that Mayenne would take the Béthune valley, following this river to its mouth, where Dieppe and its castle stood on the left bank. The suburb of Pollet lay along the right bank. Close to the town stood the castle of Arques, named after a little river that met the larger Béthune at that point. Henri had decided to make this castle an advanced defensive position, connected to the town by a system of trenches, and it was here that he had placed his artillery.

But that morning it appeared that Mayenne had changed direction, as my four gentlemen scouts had discovered, and the enemy was now going north. To avoid the danger of being encircled, Henri had fortified a fourth location, a spur of land named after the Eaulne, another river outside Dieppe, and this is where we went. Troisville led me to a dilapidated farm surrounded by a huge number of saddle horses.

Anyone who has come face to face with Henri IV once in their life says the same thing, and I am no exception: this lean, grizzled, constantly active man radiated kindliness and displayed in all circumstances a receptiveness to his interlocutor that bordered on the miraculous. There might be ten people in the room but whomever he spoke to felt as if they were quite alone with him.

On the first day of the battle of Arques, I found myself telling my story – my true story – to this king, a stranger to me, in whom I should have seen one of my worst enemies and who might have had me hanged within the hour.

But instead he asked me a thousand questions about my lineage, and closed by enquiring:

'In short, you would be related to our sister Elizabeth?'

'Yes, Majesty. One of my great-great-grandmothers was cousin to King Henry VIII. And one of my great-grandfathers was Earl of Derby. My line goes back to the Plantagenets. If it were not for the wars of religion, I would doubtless be at court, proud, cock-sure and eager for a fight.'

'Whereas today . . . ' The King had a mischievous glint in his eye.

'Today I am merely eager for a fight.' Everyone burst out laughing.

'If you swear not to breathe a word about our camp and our defences, you may return to Reims, sir.'

'I thank you, sire, but I should be delighted if you would keep me prisoner for a few days, particularly since the country around Dieppe is not without danger.'

The King gave me a hearty slap on the shoulder.

'Quite so. Troisville! Take care of Monsieur Tréjean. And make sure he doesn't do any fighting.'

Many years later, I would learn, quite by chance, that the King had had my story checked. It was war; I might have been a spy.

The siege of Dieppe must have lasted a good three weeks. Troisville, with whom I soon developed an unshakeable friendship, did his best to restrain me. But I was as if seized by a kind of madness. I had been learning to handle weapons since my earliest years. Now that I found myself in a situation where my skills might be of use, I felt a powerful urge to fight. Finally, I donned one of Troisville's tabards and a hat of his, and threw myself into one or other of the several mêlées that followed in quick succession under the collective name of the 'Battle of Arques'.

I hardly spoke to the King again, but he was rarely far from my sight, since he seemed blessed with the gift of ubiquity. He kept an eye on everything, never rested and showed an infectious ardour and optimism. His white horse seemed to appear everywhere one went.

Mayenne was confident of victory: he had 30,000 men while Henri had only 8,000. But the King had the advantage of shrewd cunning and a position consolidated by an unbroken, perfectly organised system of defence.

After four or five days of skirmishes, we incurred the first great assault. Henri took up his positions before daybreak: he placed the French infantry in the front line; his second line, at the bottom of the valley, comprised the light horse, along with the mounted knights and accompanying men-at-arms of the *compagnies d'ordonnance*; he placed the Swiss guards in reserve.

Dawn was just breaking when a patrol brought in a captured League officer. The King was on the scene immediately – where wasn't he? I moved closer, peering through the narrow gap between my ruff and Troisville's hat, pulled close over my eyes. The prisoner was laughing; he was unafraid.

'Sire, in two hours you'll have 30,000 men with 10,000 horses to contend with. I don't see sufficient forces here to resist them.'

'That's because you don't see them all, sir; I have the good Lord and right on my side.'

The battle commenced, though it was somewhat confused at first: the morning mists concealed much of the field. Mayenne had made a determined cavalry charge – at least that was what those returning from the entrenchments said. But those of us to the rear didn't see them at all, as we prepared to sell our skins dearly – I had agreed not to fight the League troops, but I wouldn't let myself be cut to pieces without putting up a show of defence.

One of King Henri's men reached us, covered in blood:

'They nearly opened a breach but the Swiss stopped them. Oh, you should have seen them. Pikes down, like a wall. They didn't lose a man, and the others were so gored and spitted, they were forced to pull back.'

Someone shouted:

'Look! Over there!'

A ray of light had just pierced the mist, which tore lazily apart, as if retreating before the sun. The valley appeared, laid bare, heaving with men, their weapons gleaming, and suddenly the great clamour, hitherto stifled by the mists, reached our ears. Mayenne's cavalry were re-forming for a fresh charge. We saw Henri ride past like a bolt of lightning, his white plume flattened across his hat:

'Aim the cannon!' he cried.

No sooner said than done. Cannonballs began to rain down on the League cavalry, gouging frightful furrows through them.

In the distance, we heard the order:

'On my command, fire!'

And from the shelter of the covered way, the arquebusiers fired on the cavalry, completing their rout.

It was not yet noon.

'Mayenne has lost at least a thousand men. And we've lost no more than a hundred,' said Troisville, who appeared suddenly at my side.

Troisville, like Henri, was from Gascony. I had not asked his age. It would not have been proper, for a man's value is not counted in years, but I am sure that he can't have been much older than I.

'If I have understood correctly, you have just experienced your baptism of fire,' he said to me with a smile.

'Barely. I was not allowed to fight.'

'Come along. I'll take you over to where the others are making merry.'

Modest merriment, it must be said: d'Aubigné had pulled a bottle of Muscadet from a saddlebag.

The siege rumbled on for a few more days. I was surprised to see quite a number of Catholics in the King's camp, including d'Ardenne and des Archets.

I mentioned my perplexity.

'One may be Catholic and a Royalist too,' replied des Archets, rather drily. 'I have no desire to find myself under the iron fist of Philip II by way of Guise. The rule of the Jesuits, and the Inquisition ... Not for me. And as good a Catholic as I am, I answer to the King and not to Rome. You can see I'm right, for Henri knows I am a Catholic and yet he treats me like a son.'

'Mayenne thought that all of us Catholics would turn our coats and open the gates of Dieppe to him,' d'Ardenne chimed in.

He must have seen the expression on my face, for he hastily added:

'So you can set your soul at ease. You are no traitor to your religion if you prefer Henri IV to Ignatius of Loyola.'

We laughed at his witticism, which I admit lifted a great weight from my mind.

One fine day, the eagerly awaited English reinforcements began to come ashore, 4,000 of them. No one recognised me or asked me any questions, but I stayed on my guard.

Reinforcements also arrived from inland. The Duke of Longueville and the Marshall of France, d'Aumont, were making a forced march in our direction.

The clashes continued for several days, mostly to the detriment of Mayenne – so much so that it seemed to me his sluggishness and corpulence had infected his troops. Time and time again they allowed themselves to be surprised and assailed by small but purposeful companies, who fell upon them quick as lightning.

I HAD BEEN THERE for eight days, living with the soldiers, learning the rudiments of German with a Swiss, dice with a Parisian, the fife with a man from Franche-Comté – in short, enjoying myself royally – when Troisville invited me to his mother's house one evening.

'How so, your mother's house? Don't you live in the Béarn?'

'We live in Bordeaux. But my mother is from Normandy. She inherited a piece of land near Eu, and had the unfortunate idea of coming here before this campaign began. She has remained stuck in Dieppe. I should tell you, though: my mother is a strong woman; compared with her, we are nothing but utter cowards.'

I was eager to meet this intrepid woman. Indeed, I was so fixed on meeting the mother that her daughter caught me quite off my guard.

Françoise de Troisville was fifteen years old, with very dark, wide eyes, olive skin and hair as black as a raven's wing. She was slim and lithe – quite the opposite of those milky-white, blue-eyed beauties who nourished our fantasies and our dreams.

Even before she smiles in my direction, I fall in love with her.

She stares at me as if I have come down from the moon, and I wonder what she should find so astonishing. My height perhaps? My clothing?

Madame de Troisville is just as her son has described, and her daughter resembles her closely. On leaving, transfixed by love and changed forever, I ask:

'How is it, Troisville, that you have never told me about your sister?'

'My dear friend, when I saw you looking at her, I myself saw her for the first time. She has always been my "little sister". Now she is a woman who enchants my friends.'

I blush and try to protest, but he stops me.

'Please, don't apologise! You're a man of honour. Love my sister to your heart's desire. I will only hold you the dearer.'

From that day forth, I often visit Madame de Troisville. Françoise is vivacious, highly intelligent and cultured. Women have barely existed for me up until now. Overnight, love is become my chief concern. Moreover, what I took for astonishment on Françoise's part is an emotion quite as strong as my own.

We discover that we share an interest in music. She plays the lute marvellously well – I have never been accomplished on that particular instrument. She even does me the honour of coming to the church of Saint-Sauveur, accompanied by her brother, where instead of playing a Mass, I fill the nave with the profane sounds of one of Master Byrd's pavanes, which suddenly takes on a whole new meaning. Where I have previously seen only science, I now see pure emotion.

It seems to me that Françoise de Troisville's dark eyes fill every note, every chord, every echo, and that the more I play, the more she becomes a part of me, the pavane tripping off the tips of my fingers in spite of myself, rising from deep within me, expressing everything I feel. Suddenly, my love has wings.

I raise my eyes from my keys and meet the twin, dark gazes of Françoise and her brother. They are stupefied.

'What is it?'

'But Tregian,' says Charles, at length, 'you're a great musician!'

'No. I'm incapable of composing a single line. I can explain everything, play everything, but I cannot write.'

'What matters who wrote the music!' says Françoise. 'When one hears you, it is as if the heavens opened before us.'

The siege of Dieppe lasts no more than a fortnight. But those days are like a diamond to me, out of time, perhaps the most perfect of my life.

I wander the streets, unaware of my surroundings, my feet never touching the ground. I am going to marry Françoise de Troisville – that much is certain, and my future life appears to me like a state of endless bliss in which nothing could be wholly awful so long as I have Françoise. Even our names are predestined.

'Hey there, Tregian! What are you doing?'

I have just entered the dwelling I share with Troisville. There is but one bed, and a narrow one at that, so we take turns sleeping on the floor. Troisville is on the rug, wrapped in a thick, broad cloak, and I have tripped over him.

'Oh I'm sorry! I didn't see you.'

He sits up and gives me a mischievous look.

'You must be in love to be so distracted. Might it be my sister who has put you in such a state?'

I am unable to hide my feelings.

'I love her. I should like to marry her.'

He shrugs off his cloak and stands up.

'We shall have to sort quite a few things out, I reckon, for the marriage to take place. We are Huguenots.'

'You're *what*?'

'You didn't know?'

'I never gave it a thought. But it makes no difference as far as I'm concerned.'

'Not for you, perhaps. Nor me. But your family will never agree to it.'

'And Françoise?'

'Oh, she is in the same state as you. She loves you. And neither my mother nor I will object. But your father . . . '

I have a brief vision of my father learning that I am to marry a heretic.

'Clearly, my father . . . We shall have to proceed as always when we are in need of something: we shall talk instead to my great-uncle, the true head of the family.'

I tell him about Sir John.

'I have no idea how to reach him,' I say, by way of conclusion. 'He is very near to London. And our trusted retainer is in Italy.'

Troisville gives a shout.

'I have it! The King was seeking a reliable messenger to go to London. You would serve very well.'

'I doubt that a pupil of the Jesuits would be his man.'

'You don't know His Majesty. When he appraises someone, he is rarely deceived. And once he has placed his trust in a man, he does not change his opinion. He asked me for news of you no later than yesterday, and I clearly saw that he holds you in regard.'

He tugs at my sleeve, ready to leave.

'Come on, let's go to him.'

The King does not hesitate. He finds it an excellent idea.

'In France you will pass for an ordinary seminary student, while in England people will not fail to recognise you as English. You are the man of the hour.'

I am exhilarated at the idea of seeing London again soon. I go along with it.

'Sire, I have two favours to ask of you. Three, even.'

'Let's hear them.'

'I should prefer it if no one, absolutely no one, knows what I am doing. There are bound to be League spies here, and if news of my mission spreads abroad, I will be massacred on arriving in Reims.'

'Quite so. Granted. And the second?'

'When I have delivered my message, there are two people I would like to see. One close to London, the other in my native lands, in Cornwall.'

'A woman?'

I smile.

'No, sire. It's . . . How can I explain? He was my great-grandmother's lover. He is very old, maybe even dead. But he is one of the people I love most in the world.'

'My message is urgent, but the reply may not be, I hope. So on that condition, granted too. With any luck, we shall be in Paris when you return.'

There is a moment of silence.

'I think,' says the King, 'that I know what you wish to ask of me. Trois-ville! What would you say of a little voyage to England?'

'*I*, sire?'

'Yes, you. Accompany your friend. Even better: if the reply is urgent, you may bring it to me while Tregian is off seeing to his filial duties.'

Troisville smiles and bows:

'At your orders, sire. There is just one problem.'

'Something tells me you wish to speak of money.'

'I am sorry, indeed, but I have none left.'

To which I add:

'And I have never had any at all.'

Henri of Bourbon, King of France and Navarre, is scarcely any wealthier than Troisville and I. But he operates at quite another level, and by the time we go to collect the message, he has procured a boat for us, a purse and a letter which will see us furnished with our first horses on landing.

I bid farewell to Françoise before we leave. It will be a fortnight at the earliest before I return. In all probability the siege of Dieppe will be lifted, and she and her mother will be in Bordeaux. As for myself, I will have to hasten back to Reims.

I am fortunate to find myself alone with my beloved for a few moments.

'You will not forget me?'

She gazes at me with an intensity that sends shivers down my spine.

'Never! Will you come to Bordeaux?'

'As soon as I am able. But I may be gone for some time.'

'I shall wait.'

She hands me a medallion, a portrait of her.

'Here, take this, as a token of my love.'

I hold out my hand, our fingers touch and suddenly we are clasping each other, lips pressed together. My body is aflame, fit to burst. Does it last an instant or an hour? I know not.

A voice approaches and we pull apart. The door opens and in comes Madame de Troisville. She looks at us each in turn, smiles and says nothing.

More than half a century has passed since that day, but the emotion is as fresh as if it were yesterday: in that embrace, we were wedded one to the other.

XII

Sing with thy mouth, sing with thy heart,
Like faithful friends sing 'Loath to Depart':
Though friends together may not always remain
Yet 'Loath to Depart' sing once again.

POPULAR BALLAD

WE CROSS THE CHANNEL aboard a small coaster, fast-moving and unremarkable. We make no attempt to land in secret – the precautions taken at the outset of our voyage are dictated solely by our fear of spies for the League. We have adopted new identities: François de Troisville, gentleman, travelling with his valet Charles.

The crossing is uneventful – an interlude during which I am haunted by the faces of Adrian and Françoise. We land in a creek west of Southampton. The captain will wait for us there. Then we hurry to London, to hand our message in person to Sir William Cecil, Lord Burghley, the Lord High Treasurer and chief adviser to the Queen.

I prefer not to think too hard about the adventure I find myself in: I, the bearer of a message to William Cecil, my family's sworn enemy, the very man who arrested my father! I, a Catholic student from the college in Reims, with a message from the Huguenot King of France for the renegade Queen of England! I should feel remorse for what I am doing, as a good Catholic, I know that. When I do consider it, the thought thrills and amuses me. Mostly though, I prefer not to think of it at all; I think of Françoise.

William Cecil is at Whitehall. To reach him, we have to cross the whole of London. Those who have never left the place of their birth, their home, become accustomed to it. Its sweetest delights fade over time, blunted by repetition. But when one has been torn away, each return is a new discovery. Of all my journeys back to England, it is this – the most foolhardy, illicit undertaking of them all – that brings me the most intense pleasure.

Troisville observes me, with a smile on his face.

'Extraordinary – in Dieppe you were so French, and now you are thoroughly English!'

We say nothing as we make our way across what had been *my* London. Troisville gazes around him, wide-eyed. I believe he has never seen such a multitude of people in all his life.

The Palace of Whitehall brings us back sharply to the realities of the moment. We have to gain admittance. After hour upon hour of formalities, we find ourselves in Lord Burghley's antechamber.

At last, I am taken in to see him.

He is an elderly man, tall but stooping, with a pointed white beard and long, slender hands, the sparkling eye of a young man and the hard stare of a merchant.

'I'm told you bring a message from King Henri of France.'

I bow, quite unable to speak, and take out Henri's letter, carefully concealed until now in a secret pocket in my breeches.

'You remind me of someone,' he remarks as I hold the paper out to him. 'Can't quite place you, though.'

I give no reply, but another deep bow.

He breaks the seal on the letter and reads its contents, glancing up in my direction once or twice.

'Will you see King Henri again, sir?'

'If you please, My Lord. At this moment, in all likelihood, he is laying siege to Paris.'

'Will you take a message to him from me?'

'Assuredly. I have agreed to do just that, if you are minded to vouchsafe me one.'

'You speak impeccable English for a Frenchman, Monsieur de Troisville.'

I am helpless to stop myself reddening to the roots of my hair.

'You are English, are you not?'

'Yes, My Lord. This masquerade is not for your sake, but to divert the attention of the League's spies in France. The real Comte de Troisville is in your antechamber, dressed as my valet. We have no desire to conceal our identities from you.'

'And your name? That a secret, too?'

'Yes, My Lord. But not from you. I am Francis Tregian.'

'Francis Tregian! I knew I'd seen you somewhere before. You're . . . '

'You have never seen me, My Lord. I am my father's first-born son.'

'Are you not a Catholic?'

'I am, My Lord. And if my father knew I was here, I think he would kill me. But truly, I desire nothing more than for our two religions to co-exist in harmony.'

Further concealment is useless now. I make a clean breast of it.

'I have no intention of becoming a Protestant, but I remain a patriot. Philip of Spain is my enemy as much as he is yours, or King Henri's. There are many Catholics in the service of the King in France. He has trusted me and I will never betray him. Just as I will never betray my faith. I feel that my beliefs are a matter for myself and Heaven above.'

'You're a strange young fellow, indeed. Courageous, too. I could have had you arrested.'

'Yes, My Lord. Which is why I preferred to reveal my identity to you myself, rather than wait for one of your informers to do so. I must travel to Golden in Cornwall, at all costs, to visit an old friend, and I must see my uncle, Sir John Arundell, on a private matter. You would have learned of my arrival.'

He bursts out laughing.

'You really are quite an original. What do you mean to do with your life?'

'If I can recover my father's estates one day, I will manage them. But my favourite activity is music.'

'Do you compose?'

'No, I play. The organ and the virginal.'

With a sweep of his arm, Burghley lifts a drape concealing the finest virginal I have ever seen. He gestures for me to sit at the instrument.

I do so, conscious that he is testing the truth of my statement; conscious, too, that if he expects something novel or exceptional he will be disappointed. The only pieces I play well are by English composers whose work is almost certainly familiar to him already.

I play. A few minutes, or an hour. As always, time dissolves. I play

Byrd, Bull and Morley – my favourites. The music rushes to the tips of my fingers. I am taut as a bowstring, having broken my family's vow of secrecy, elated at daring to say what I felt must be said, full of the memory of Françoise.

A hint of fragrance interrupts my reverie. Still playing, I turn my head – and strike a false note.

The Queen!

I stop playing immediately, jump up and sink to my knees. She takes me by the chin and forces me to look up into her face. Her fingers are dry, hot and very strong. Her eyes are light brown, streaked with yellow.

She stares at me for a long time.

Finally, she takes a step back and offers her hand to be kissed.

'I knew you were a capable actor but you concealed your skill as a musician, sir.'

Burghley is astonished.

'Your Majesty knows this young man?'

'We've met before. And Master Tregian the Younger has unforgettable eyes.'

The Queen plays a piece I don't know. I play her a piece she has never heard.

When I leave, I feel almost drunk.

Outside, in the antechamber, the sight of Troisville fairly takes me by surprise. I have all but forgotten him.

'Are you feeling unwell, sir?' he asks, with the solicitude appropriate to a servant.

'No. No . . . We have two days. Come, we must go and see Sir John Arundell.'

To reach Muswell from London, we have to leave by the Bishop's Gate. We follow the river, then turn north to Leadenhall and the Exchange.

I explain everything, translate everything, for the benefit of Troisville, who proves every inch the fascinated foreign visitor – and takes me quite by surprise with his jocular exclamation:

'Don't look behind you, whatever you do, my dear fellow; we're being followed. Brown cloak, black hat, dark moustache, beardless. Bay horse with a white fetlock to the left front foot.'

'French?'

'I don't believe so. But he could still be one of Mayenne's spies. I'm only slightly reassured that I didn't see him before we reached Whitehall, though I've been keeping a careful look-out.'

Troisville's ability to spot a man on our tail is unrivalled. Novice that I am, I would never have noticed the man in the brown cloak.

We leave London. On the Shoreditch road, the rider gives way to a vile-looking cart pulled by a thoroughbred horse and driven by an unidentifiable creature buried in the folds of a great travelling-cloak. We choose to ignore it.

'Play innocent,' Charles advises. 'It's always easier to give a spy the slip when he thinks he hasn't been noticed.'

WE TETHER OUR HORSES to the iron railing of Sir John's manor at Muswell. Troisville sits on the low limb of a tree to wait, and I slip into the house. Opening the door to the library, my first sensation is one of shock. The head bending over a quill and paper is white. I had left a man in his prime, but return to find an old man. He looks up at the slight noise. His eyes are as bright as ever and he fixes me with the clear gaze I know so well. For the first time, I notice he has Adrian's grey eyes.

We stare at one another for some time.

'You ... What are you ... How is it possible ... ? Francis?' he says, at length.

'Yes Sir John, it's me! Good day to you!'

He gets to his feet, opens his arms and I hurry to embrace him. I am taller than him by a good head now, but he holds me close like a father clasping his child.

He invites me to sit next to him in the window seat.

'Tell me everything.'

My story takes a long time but Sir John's curiosity is insatiable. He listens intently, almost motionless, watching me throughout, asking only occasional questions. Only once does he ask me to repeat what I have said and shoots a volley of questions at me: when I tell him about Adrian's disappearance, my firm conviction that he is not dead and my decision to say nothing to the rest of the family, Sir John excepted.

I keep nothing from him – not even my doubts and uncertainties on the matter of religion.

'My dear Francis,' he says softly, 'the more this goes on, the more I am persuaded that the religious fanatics will be the losers, in the long run. I know they are disliked even in the highest echelons at court. If the word "Catholic" had not become synonymous with "Spanish domination" I am not sure even the Queen would have been as stubborn and intractable as she has proved on the matter. People like Abbot Parsons are doing our cause a dreadful disservice. The end justifies the means, as far as they are concerned, and that I cannot accept. They are traitors to their country. But I must whisper such words, even here, in my own library. Rational, level-headed judgement is not well received these days, by Catholic fanatics or Protestant *religionnaires*. I am very happy to see that you are not like ... I mean, that you are a reasonable man.'

I make no comment.

'How are my parents?' I ask.

'They are living at the Fleet. You have a number of young sisters. Your brother Charles is in France.'

'My brother Charles?'

I have all but forgotten the little brother I barely know.

'He is old enough to attend school, and your father insisted he go to Saint-Ouen. He is a very pious boy.'

'Will Charles come to Reims?'

'He intends to. But he is only nine or ten, and things change so fast these days.'

'What about Mary?'

'Your older sister is married. She has two children.'

I swallow hard. I still picture Mary as a small girl.

'And Margaret?'

'I shall ask her to come here tonight, but if your mission must remain a secret, we will have to take precautions.'

'She's *here*?'

'Why, yes. She lived at the Fleet with your other sisters for some while, but she ... my wife, your grandmother Catherine, finally had her brought here. She schools her, and Margaret serves as her lady-in-waiting. We were not able to send her to another family, as we did with your sister Mary.'

In plain terms, this signifies that money is short. Sir John has supported everyone for years. And his shoulders bear the additional weight of the fines imposed on Catholics who refuse to attend the Church of England.

'If you wish to marry Mademoiselle de Troisville,' he says, 'your parents will have to be informed. Let me tell them, it will be better that way. Is the Troisville family likely to remain Huguenot for good?'

'But, Uncle . . .'

'My dear Francis, if Henri wishes to become king of all the French, he will have to convert. Only for the fourth or fifth time, at that. And his loyal supporters, in my opinion, will have to do the same.'

'You should ask her brother: he's travelling with me, disguised as my valet. We must be discreet, for if there is a League spy in your household I shall be in grave danger once I get back to Reims.'

'Bring Monsieur de Troisville to me tonight, when everyone is in bed. I must make it quite clear to him that for the moment, you are entirely without fortune.'

That evening, at nightfall, we gather in Sir John's library, where the greatest surprise of this always eventful journey is revealed – my sister Margaret. Sir John sends someone to fetch her. She is barely eleven years old but already her appearance is womanly. She is tall, with the coppery Tregian hair, very pale green eyes, a perfect oval face and a pretty smile. Troisville can barely take his eyes off her.

We do not say much. It is a furtive meeting: I am visiting my uncle in secret, and my parents and grandmother are to know nothing about it at all.

'Do you know,' says Margaret, when we have discussed the serious matters to hand and are on the point of leaving, 'I have learned to sing since the last time.'

She gives me such a mischievous look that we both laugh, but in my heart of hearts, I feel close to tears. I see her as a little girl, with her thin, reedy voice, and I feel infinite sadness at the loss of all those years when she has grown and developed and her voice has matured.

We barely have time to discuss what is on our minds.

'Monsieur de Troisville, whatever will you do if your King becomes a Catholic?' asks Sir John. 'Or rather, whatever will you do when he embraces Catholicism? He is delaying the decision for as long as possible – a wise policy. He must not be thought of as a weathervane, but apostasy is inevitable.'

Troisville gazes intently at Sir John with his dark eyes.

'I believe I shall follow his lead, Monsieur. I love the King of France too much not to do so.'

'In that case, I shall consider you a Catholic forthwith, Monsieur. And the marriage of your sister and my nephew will encounter no obstacles beyond a shortage of money.'

'A shortage that we have in common, Monsieur – so I am sure that money will be no hindrance. My mother, whom we consult on every matter – although I have been the head of the family since my father's death – has asked me to tell you that you should have no concerns in that regard.'

'Please offer my respects to Madame your mother, Monsieur. I only wish that Francis were able to command his grandfather John's fortune ...'

'If that were the case,' jokes Troisville, with a broad smile, 'I suspect your family would have nothing to do with my sister – so everything is for the best!'

We are on our way back to London, early the following morning, when Troisville speaks:

'If your sister will have me in five years' time, I shall marry her.'

'But ...'

'No buts. She is marvellous, though still a child, and I have no desire to alarm her. In five years' time, if the fact that I am ten years her senior does not trouble her.'

'She has no dowry, you know.'

'Tregian, please!' And he continues in the exact same tone. 'Don't look round, we are shadowed. We'll give him the slip. Be ready.'

The melancholy that has gripped my heart upon leaving Sir John and Margaret disappears instantly. For a while, I almost forget the purpose of my journey.

We gallop along the road for two or three miles, then Troisville signals for me to stop. He makes a great show of pointing at a stone.

'We'll wait. Our friend is sure to stop when he sees we have,' he mutters. 'Then we'll gallop into that clearing on the right. We should make it out again easily enough. Follow me and do exactly as I do; no questions.'

The cart – a different one from the day before – stops by the side of the road, and the carter even climbs down to examine one of his horse's hooves.

'Now,' said Troisville, and we tear off into the undergrowth. After a few minutes, we cross a hollow way running parallel to the road we have left. Troisville follows it but, rather than making for London, we turn back the way we have come. I admire his strategy. We are almost at Sir John's when he signals for me to stop and asks:

'Do you know another way back to London?'

'If we go west,' I say, pointing, 'we will end up on the Clerkenwell road and enter London by Aldersgate.'

Which is exactly what we do, later that afternoon, after losing and finding our way more than once.

'We won't call at Lord Burghley's front door,' says Troisville. 'Our man will be waiting for us there, that's obvious.'

We find a side entrance through which barrels of dried fish are being unloaded.

'Give me an order, quickly,' whispers Charles.

I rap out some instructions, and my 'manservant' hurries forward to roll one of the barrels. The commotion is such that no one notices us in the throng and within minutes we are inside the palace.

Fortune smiles on us and we encounter Lord Burghley's Private Secretary, who admitted us the day before. He raises an eyebrow in surprise.

'*Tiens, vous êtes là,*' he declares. 'Don't ask me why, but I thought you were lost.'

Troisville and I exchange glances, and I feel certain that, like me, he is heaving a sigh of relief. The League was not on our trail after all.

'We decided three guardian angels were probably too much of a good thing,' replies Troisville, smoothly. 'And one never knows where angels have fallen from.'

The Secretary laughs and takes us in to see Lord Burghley.

'Ah, safe and sound!' exclaims Cecil.

'We were unaware that it was you who sought to protect us, My Lord,' I venture politely.

'Tregian, you really are a most surprising young man, I am forced to admit it.'

'I hope I have not proved too disappointing, My Lord.'

'Unexpected,' he corrects me. 'Please have your servant escorted from the room; there are things I have to tell you.'

'Allow me to present Charles de Troisville, My Lord, a gentleman of Gascony in the retinue of King Henri IV. If he could speak English, this man would be the King's ambassador.'

Burghley slaps his thigh in delight and his face creases into a smile. He clasps Troisville's hands in his.

'Young gentlemen, I like you both very much. What a great shame I cannot take you into my own service.'

We bow.

'Her Majesty has prepared a reply for King Henri,' he goes on, 'and asks to see Master Tregian, in secret, of course.'

He signals to his secretary.

'Take Master Tregian to the oak chamber. Monsieur de Troisville, you will stay here with me. If Her Majesty wishes to meet you, I will have you sent in.'

Burghley speaks perfect French, albeit with a strong accent. Troisville bows once more.

I am taken to a panelled chamber and left waiting until I have lost all track of time. It was light when I came in, but it is long since dark when the Queen makes her entrance, alone, carrying her own candle-branch.

I drop to one knee.

'Cecil tells me you are a remarkable young man, and that you gave his henchmen the slip,' she says, with a little laugh.

'The merit is all my companion's, Your Majesty, he is an expert in such matters.'

'Monsieur Tregian, when I look at you, I feel fifteen years younger, and it is as if I am looking at your father. But you have about you something he has always lacked. I wish it were in my power to restore your estates.'

I fight to keep a level head.

'Ma'am, everything is within your power.'

'Wrong, my friend. My conduct is dictated by politics, and not by my own desires and fancies. It would be impossible for me, at the moment, to take back your properties from the Careys. It would provoke a crisis of State, given that your father has not recanted. My action would be taken as a sign of capitulation on the part of the Queen of England to the King of Spain. But I have decided . . . What are your plans?'

'To go to Italy and make music. In Rome, or Venice, or Ferrara. Perhaps Antwerp or Amsterdam. A place where music flourishes.'

'There will be funds for you with our Flemish bankers. They will pay you an income until such time as you choose to return to England. Take this ring. They know it. It will identify you. You shall not want, while I am alive. This is all I can do for you. I cannot return your estates, nor exempt Sir John Arundell from the fines imposed on him. Do you understand?'

'Yes, your Majesty.'

'Take this.' She holds out two folded documents. 'This is a letter for the bank. And here is my message to King Henri. When will you give it to him?'

'In ten or fifteen days, Ma'am, depending on the crossing.'

She opens the door and claps her hands. I hear a rustle of fabric.

'Go and fetch William Cecil,' she orders. Rapid footsteps fade along the gallery.

Burghley and Troisville soon appear. Troisville drops to one knee and Elizabeth presents her hand to be kissed.

'So this is the young man who shook off the guards we sent to protect him,' she says, in perfect French.

Troisville's voice trembles slightly.

'I beg your Majesty's indulgence; we thought they were spies of the League.'

'All is forgiven, Monsieur. But now that you know who they are, do not make my agents' work any more difficult than it already is.'

We take our leave, but not before the Queen – to my intense confusion and embarrassment – personally oversees the concealment of the letters in the secret pocket of my breeches.

'How many days will it take you to reach Golden?' asks Burghley, once we are alone.

'Two, from Southampton.'

'Take this.' He gives us another letter. 'Stop at the royal post-houses; you'll be sure to get the best horses and so gain precious time.'

We leave London at daybreak, riding against the stream of customers pouring into the city markets.

'I can go to Golden alone,' I suggest to Troisville, 'if you prefer to wait for me at Southampton.'

'Of course. But I should like to see the estates to which your sister can lay claim,' he says with a wink. 'And who knows when I shall see England – let alone Cornwall – again, if ever. We'll have no more talk of Southampton, please.' He grins and spurs his horse. We take just over four days to reach Old Thomas's door, hardly pausing to sleep or eat. I rein my horse sharply as the house comes into sight around a bend in the road.

'What is it?' asks Troisville. 'You're as white as a sheet.'

'I fear the true likelihood of Thomas's death had not struck me until now. If he's alive, he'll be almost a hundred years old.'

I knock. My legs feel weak. No one answers. I try pushing the door. It yields. A fire glows in the hearth but there is nobody there. I cross to the next room, then Thomas's bedroom. A candle is burning. The drapes are pulled close.

'Thomas, sir?'

I am an imbecile. How could I possibly have thought for one minute that . . .

'Master Francis!'

The voice comes from within the bed drapes. Weaker than before but still deep and firm.

I hurry to draw back the curtains. It is almost dark and I can barely see Thomas's gaunt face or his eyes, deep in shadow.

'Thomas, you're here! Oh, Thomas!'

I fall to my knees and lay my head against his hand, where it rests on top of the sheet. I find myself sobbing out loud.

'I knew you would come,' says Thomas. He extricates his hand and strokes my hair, just as he had when I was a child. 'I had to hold fast, for I so wished to see you again.' He gives a small laugh. 'I wouldn't have missed a last encounter with those pisky eyes for all the world. Have you come alone?'

'No, with a friend. The brother of the woman I love.'

'You are in love? That's good news, Master Francis. You are truly a man now. Will you marry her?'

'I hope so. She's French, and a Huguenot. A Protestant.'

'If you love her enough, she will be yours, just as Jane was mine throughout my life, and hers. Did I tell you she died in my arms?'

'No.'

'Her husband was in London. She had given birth, and the midwife told us: "She is lost." I hurried to her side. Even if Tregian had been there, even if he had killed me on the spot, I should not have cared one jot. I went in to her. She was in a delirium. I took her in my arms, I ordered everyone out of the room, her women, everyone. I placed compresses on her forehead and, as I did so, she spoke to me as she had done back in the time when we believed we might marry. At the last minute, she recovered her right mind and asked me if she had been talking nonsense. "Only that you loved me," I said. "That's all well, then, Thomas," she said. "Take care of my children. I can die in peace, knowing that you are watching over them. My last thoughts shall be of you. Go now, and send the priest in to me." When I left, her beautiful eyes, your eyes, were already blank. Everyone knew I loved Jane; no one said anything about it to her husband when he returned.'

I can hardly believe my ears. Thomas tells his story with undimmed eloquence.

'Where is your young French friend? Bring him here. You'll find candles in the dresser.'

We light two, and I get a better view of Thomas's face. I find him not so aged, in truth. He has always seemed old to me, bent over, his hair hoary, his face deeply lined. But now he seems somehow more translucent.

We help him to sit up. His eyes are as dark and bright as ever, but sunk deep in their sockets. He surprises me by addressing Troisville in French. My astonishment makes him laugh.

'As you well know, I managed your family's expanding estates for fifty years. Your great-grandparents and your grandparents were not like your father. Or rather, if they were, no one noticed it because I was there, and I was a hard taskmaster, unforgiving of idle layabouts, and unrivalled when it came to bargaining. When the French boats came upstream to Tregony, someone had to talk to the captains in their own language. I speak Spanish, too, and Italian. Even a little Arabic, for the purposes of business.' He sighs. 'When I think of the pains we took, your ancestors and I, to ensure you would inherit the estates. And in the space of a few years, all finished! Your father is an admirable man, but he understands nothing of his lands. And now it's too late. The skills of land management and business have not been handed down to you, and I would advise you not to concern yourself with your property any further. Stick to your music. And believe me, the Careys have done everything in their power to prevent your return. They have a new steward now; he'll see to it that even they are dispossessed in the end, mark my words. Ezekiel Grosse. Remember that name and avoid him like the plague. If you have any dealings with him, he'll ruin you. You might just as well flee into exile.' He gives another deep sigh. 'I should like to have had something more to leave you. But all I have is this house. It's yours, because it came to me from my father and I have no family of my own. Beyond this, all I can offer is advice, and even that is obsolete now. I am an old man.'

And with that, he orders us to tell him about our new lives, and we comply, until first light the next morning.

A fine autumn day is in prospect.

'Go before they come to take care of me,' Thomas advises. 'And if you go by Golden, wait until there are enough people about; you won't be noticed, though the river port is almost defunct these days. The Fal is a mere trickle now. There are still boats at Tregony but even there, they are few. For the smack of a sail on a tall mast, a man has to go as far as Falmouth. A journey I cannot make now. Francis!' He signals for me to come nearer. It is the first time he has ever called me by my Christian name alone, with no title.

'In front of the dresser there is a loose plank in the floor. Under it you will find a package. It contains a few mementoes and the notebook in which I recorded my daily activities as steward. Take them with you. You will learn something of your family's past. If you leave them here, all of it will be lost. And now depart. We shall meet again in Heaven. The next time you come here, I will be gone. Remember to go and see the lawyer, for this house. The tenant farmers have been told. No one else will know that my modest property has been passed to you.'

I find it even harder to take my leave of Old Thomas than I did of Sir John. But he is right. We have to leave before attracting attention.

We only just get away.

As we ride, I tell Troisville everything about the house, the old kitchens, the port and the Roman Camp.

'We'll pass between the two manors like any other travellers. I won't be able to talk to you. The Tregians are *personae non gratae* here, so much so that the Careys or their steward would have us arrested on the spot.'

We ride the length of the kitchens, the Warren and the ancient fortress of Voliba at a gentle trot, before continuing down to the landing stage at Golden and on to Tregony. Finally, we retrace our steps, and ride through St Austell once more.

Three days later we reach our ship and set sail for France.

XIII

Then sweet love disperse this cloud
That obscures, this scornful coying:
When each creature sings aloud,
Filling hearts with over joying.
As every bird doth choose her mate,
Gently billing, she is willing
Her true love to take:
With such words let us contend,
Laughing, colling, kissing, playing,
So our strife shall end

'BARAFOSTUS' DREAM'
POPULAR BALLAD

ALL IS QUIET in Echallens, save for the dulled sound of disembodied footsteps through the freshly fallen snow. Nature sleeps softly beneath. Only I am restless.

I decided to go up to the Crossing today, despite the cold. My feelings have caught me unawares. I have been writing since the summer, a little at a time, intending to recount my life coolly and without haste. I found it a pleasant exercise at first. Writing a tale seemed like a welcome distraction after having copied out so much music – *Francis, you have such a fine hand; prepare the scores of this set of pieces for us.* – *Monsieur Tregian, you know such lovely Italian poems, would you have a madrigal for us?*

I discovered a passion for writing as strong as my passion for music.

Today, I felt the need of some exercise. I have recounted that extraordinary month of September ... which year was it? The thirty-third year of the reign? Perhaps. Or maybe the year before, or the one after. It's impossible to establish with certainty. I was sixteen, I think. Or seventeen. Anyway, I recorded the events of that extraordinary September and the October that followed almost without pausing for thought. I was as stiff as I must have been after those endless journeys, my heart ever in my mouth for fear of being caught by surprise, of arriving too late, of never reaching King Henri of France and failing in my mission. London to Golden in under five days! And each of those days meant fifteen to eighteen hours on horseback, without a halt! But I was sixteen years old and had an iron constitution.

Meeting monarchs was never my ambition. I had, on occasion, dreamed of encountering Henri IV purely out of curiosity, because the whole world spoke of little else. But to actually see him . . . Yet I found myself before kings and queens, time and time again.

AMONG BENOÎT DALLINGES' GRANDCHILDREN, there is one, Elie, who shows promise of becoming as good a musician as David. Before he was even five, he would pronounce faultlessly on the sounds coming out of my workshop:

'Grandfather François is fitting the jack for the E above middle C.'

I taught all the Dallinges children Latin – a kind of second mother tongue for me. I gave these young country folk an education equal to that of any rich child's tutor, and I took great delight in doing so. They have all become notables, and today it is a real pleasure to see Benoît the Younger stand up to any gentleman from Berne or Fribourg. Thanks to their education, they have all made their affairs prosper. It was the least I could do to show my gratitude to their parents.

I have reprised my role as teacher with their own children.

'Aren't you afraid I'm too old to be a good tutor?' I responded to the younger Benoît, the first time he asked me to teach the little ones their alphabet.

'You, old, Uncle François? Surely you jest! You haven't changed one bit. If you were to shave, you'd look like a young man, no doubt about it.'

I got out the syllable and alphabet tables for the children, the same ones I had made for their parents, and I made a new hornbook displaying the Lord's Prayer with the alphabet above.

I also taught the rudiments of music to them all. It interested them in as much as I assured them it was part of the education of any respectable man or woman, for I insisted on teaching the girls together with the boys. Education had done Queen Elizabeth much good, so why not the Dallinges girls? But only two of these dozen children developed a passion for music: David first, who applied himself to it with near-religious devotion, and now Elie.

He's a short, plump lad, with a permanently runny nose, round staring eyes of palest blue and hair of an indefinable shade, somewhere between blond and chestnut. He's so quiet and diligent that he's never punished. Too quiet, I've sometimes thought. I make him run through the fields with the farm dog, and it's reassuring to see him dart about. He plays keyed instruments with ease, as if it were the most natural thing in the world. His dexterity is surprising: the fingers flying up and down the keys are thick and chubby, suggesting clumsiness rather than virtuosity.

He came to see me the other day, bright and early, and discovered me writing.

'What are you doing, Grandfather?'

'Never you mind,' I chided.

'I have a question to ask you, Grandfather.'

'You'll ask me at noon.'

'May I accompany you to the Crossing?'

'If you like.'

This wasn't the first time we'd had this kind of exchange. Generally, the question was something like:

'What does "enharmonic" mean?' or 'What's a mutation? I've forgotten.'

But this time, as we walked briskly down the path, frozen hard as granite (it had not yet snowed, but the frost was enough to cleave stone), he asked me:

'Grandfather, why is music necessary to life?'

I looked at him, taken aback.

'Really,' he insisted. 'The other day, when my mother complained because you were teaching my sister Marie the diatonic scale, you told her: "All creatures are equal before God, and music is equally necessary to all."'

The first words to rise from the depths of my memory (or rather from my forgetfulness) were those of Alessandro Piccolomini, as reported by Monteverde:

> *Non è dubbio alcuno, che secondo la sentenza di Platone e d'Aristotele, è una delle principali discipline, che dai fanciulli si debba imparare . . .*

> *(There is no doubt that, according to Plato and Aristotle, it is one of the principal disciplines children should study . . . essentially to give their adult selves the possibility of suitable entertainment, so that they do not waste their time in those idle hours they are granted when no other urgent activity presents itself. Simply listening to music will not suffice, for he who devotes himself to the delight [of playing it] derives greater pleasure than had he been content to listen to others . . .)*

Elie was not satisfied with this assertion.

'You taught me that we should not follow Plato blindly, merely because he is Plato. So if you agree with him, it must be for good reasons of your own.'

'I have a thousand reasons. Music has given me the most intense happiness, like the joy of love but more permanent. It has saved me from misfortune on more than one occasion, and it has saved my life at least once by keeping me from losing my mind.'

'It does not follow from that, that it is necessary to everyone.'

'No, of course not. But it does good wherever it may be. It is a universal language, which everyone understands equally. When I was a schoolboy at . . . no matter where it was. When I was a schoolboy, we liked to sing a song by Jean Machgielz:

> *If solemn music*
> *All immodest flame*
> *If soul is harmony*
> *Divinely enchained*
> *If the eternal dance*
> *Mimics the cadence*

If water, air and earth
Sweet war do make
Then music desirable
Your virtue so admirable
From the heart may chase far
With honour reversed
That by divine euphony
Our bodies inspire
Bestirring the heavens
With sounds harmonious
Enchained therein
With discordant chords
Who would dispute
That all must love?

Elie pressed on. 'Grandfather, when did you know for certain you wished to be a musician and make instruments?'

'You know,' I said, parrying his questions, 'the great Tasso, author of *Jerusalem Delivered*, which I will tell you about one of these days, wrote: "The purpose of music is to regale the ear with harmony, for nature delights in variety and all novelties that surprise it."'

If Elie were the adult and I the child, he would have thrashed me there and then. Francis Tregian, you answered like a dunce!

'Grandfather!' he admonished. 'I would like you to tell me your own thoughts, not those of Signor Tasso.'

'Very well. When did I know, you asked. It was … The first time, I was very young, much younger than you, even.'

I told him how (but not where) I had first heard *Lady Wynkfyld's Rownde* (a piece Elie knew already). This impressed but did not satisfy him. And, as we continued our brisk walk along the banks of the Talent (it was far too cold to linger at the Crossing), I tried to situate the exact moment. It happened in stages, in successive layers. And Queen Elizabeth cemented my decision by granting me the stipend I received up until her death.

We returned home, and Elie made me promise to tell him more of how I became a musician.

It would have been far simpler had I been able to distance myself from my caste at the time. But as grandson to the Earl of Derby and the Baron of Arundell, peers of England both, it was unthinkable that I should work for a living. It would never have occurred to my father, who learned a dozen useless languages during his decades imprisoned in the Fleet, to have no servants. He had two retainers, sometimes three, and one of the worst humiliations he suffered during his early years in prison was having not a single servant.

I was no different from my father in this regard. Manual work, even building musical instruments, was fit only for commoners. If the Francis of that time could meet the Francis of today, he would have nothing but contempt for him.

Had I not become friends with Giles Farnaby, I would have been good for nothing at all. I would probably have forgotten most of the music I'd ever played or heard, had I not had occasion to repair organs or build spinets. I would not be here today, had I not known how to make keyed instruments.

I might have become one of King Henri's companions-in-arms, as Troisville had done. But had I not been in such a hurry to reach Italy and make music, a great many interesting things would doubtless never have happened. And yet in order to get to Italy, I had to return to Reims, though I no longer recall how I managed it.

One thing is for sure. After my escapade, life at the English College was never the same again.

Reims had long been hostile to the English. Jehan Pussot, the church-warden of Saint-Jacques, had often told me:

'It was in Reims that Joan of Arc oversaw the coronation of Charles VII, and the English have always been the ancestral enemy. We in Reims have long considered you English Catholics to be a kind of Trojan Horse, so it took time to convince ourselves you were not against us.'

Their change of heart finally came when the English inhabitants came under the protection of the Cardinal Archbishop of Reims and his brother the Duke of Guise. Moreover, the English were enthusiastic contributors to the repair of the city fortifications, and helped its people in the fight against the Huguenots.

But this time it was I who felt like a stranger when I arrived in Reims.

Any clear-sighted person in France was aware that the new King was of a quite different calibre to the leaders of the League, and would eventually win the day. This exasperated every League member in Reims, which meant most of the population. The religious fervour was extreme, with endless processions, prayers and propitiatory services, in which we took part. As Catholics persecuted by a Protestant queen, our prayers were supposedly imbued with even greater power to keep the French from suffering 'our fate'.

I returned to the schoolroom as if nothing had happened: the only ways of avoiding trouble were to work and to say nothing. I hardly opened my mouth.

'That poor Tregian,' they said. 'He has been ill-disposed ever since he was a prisoner of the heretics; Lord knows what they did to him.'

Some even tried to ask me about it. I simply sighed in response, which confirmed them in their belief:

'The heretics tortured Tregian, yet he's so brave, he won't even talk about it now.'

But it was Sir John's death that silenced me utterly. I felt orphaned. Giuliano arrived, pale and sad, to tell me the news, one winter's day shortly after Christmas. He came from London by way of Saint-Ouen, where he had picked up my younger brother Charles.

I love Adrian as if he were a part of me, but I have always had difficulties with Charles. Everyone told me, time and again, that I was the perfect likeness of my father, and physically speaking that was undoubtedly true. But as far as character was concerned, we were quite the reverse of each other, and his sole true heir was Charles, this stocky, irascible cove, with inky eyes and hair, and a touch of the Spaniard about him. Charles was as arrogant and inflexible as our begetter, and a fanatical Catholic from his earliest years. I found him hard to bear, to the very end.

He was six or seven years younger than I, and I hardly knew him until he came to Reims, where he was placed under my charge. One week sufficed for me to form an unshakeable opinion of him.

The oldest children, Mary, Adrian, Margaret and I, all of us born at Wolvedon, were discreet and seldom talkative. The others, our father and mother first and foremost, always felt the need to affirm their faith with a torrent of words. They invariably took our silence for consent, interpreting it in the same light as their own declarations. It never crossed anyone's mind, at least not then, that our silence might be a sign of dissent. I know nothing of Mary, for I never saw her again, but I retain an impression of her strength, her radiance – she too could have been a queen. But Margaret, Adrian and I certainly disagreed with the rest of the family.

What distanced me most from Charles, religion aside, was his rejection of scholarship. He neglected his education to such an extent that even Reims failed to make a missionary of him. But when it came to the martial arts, he was invincible: formidable in hand-to-hand combat, fearless on horseback and a dangerous swordsman. His bravado earned more punishments than were his due, and endless trouble, while getting him nowhere. As with my father, there was little point trying to tell him that his intransigence only deepened the rifts between us, making them impassable.

Enough of the 'bonds of blood'. I will waste no more time, ink and paper on this brother.

Yet I owe him one thing, at least. Now that Sir John was dead, and his heirs no longer paid our stipend, we ought both to attend the seminary. Those were the house rules. But John Pitts, my master of rhetoric – who liked me and with whom I felt a certain affinity – pleaded my case: I had confessed to him most sincerely that I felt I lacked a priest's calling. I should mention that Pitts held a steadfast belief that a Catholic victory in England would come soon, whereupon, as he imagined, I would become a great lord; an elder son called upon to assume the family title does not take Holy Orders. My case was made even easier to plead by the fact that, at just ten years of age, Charles demonstrated a boisterous determination to put all heretics to the sword. That redressed the balance.

My last two years in Reims?

Rhetoric. Casuistry. Organ playing at Saint-Jacques, and sometimes at Saint-Nicaise or Saint-Rémi.

Regular visits from Giuliano, ever busy with his mysterious travels across Europe. For whom? When I questioned him one day, he was content to give a laconic, not entirely reassuring reply:

'If I don't tell you, you won't know, and will be unable to reveal the truth to anyone, even under torture.'

I remember my last summer. The weather was particularly fine and dry, after a decade of endless wet, which had played its part in the destruction of the region's crops, along with the armies ravaging the countryside. In the spring, Navarre (as the king was known in Reims) took Chartres, then La Fère. They were getting closer. The talk in the taverns was of nothing else.

I remember the wedding of Perrette, the daughter of Pussot the church-warden, to Nicolas de Lestre. Abbot Ogier and I arranged a superb musical accompaniment, sung by him and his choir, and played by me. The bride wore a beautiful dress, with a train carried by her young brothers. After the religious service, we all repaired to the Pussots' house near the Place du Chauldron. I spent the day dreaming of my wedding to Françoise.

And I remember the visit of the papal nuncio, the Bishop of Piacenza. I usually provided the music for such occasions. But this time, Barret insisted I give the welcoming oration, heaven knows why. In the end, I complied, delivering a succession of empty words that were just as soon forgotten. The Bishop of Parma thanked me, and I recall only that he praised my Latin – my vanity was duly flattered.

My last year in Reims was loud with the rumble of war. The Duke of Parma began it all by bringing a strong Catholic army into France to give reinforcement to the city of Rouen. League Marshal Antoine de Saint-Paul went to his assistance from Reims. It took all my energies to prevent myself being pressed into his service, and I had a narrow escape. Empowered by his alliance with Lorraine and Spain, the League Marshal had commit-ted countless acts of savagery and, in the name of religion, had amassed a substantial fortune during the civil war. I bore a dislike for him that was shared by many in Reims. Indeed I learned that the Duke of Guise, son of Scarface, eventually ran him through with his sword, a year or two later, so putting an end to his wretched ways. But to return to the siege of Rouen: Navarre finally relinquished the city, round about the time we learned of the election of the new pope, Gregory XIV.

Reims rejoiced.

The respite was short-lived. Navarre laid siege to Epernay – practically at our gates. It was late June, and my departure was imminent.

I must look further back, to recount my departure. I was concerned because I had no idea how to pay for the journey to Rome. Elizabeth's pen-sion was waiting for me in Flanders, but how could I go there to claim it?

In the end, it was a fellow countryman, Nicholas Bawden of St Mabyn in Cornwall, who smoothed the way for me.

Bawden was about forty years old and recently arrived in Reims. He was slim, beardless and nearly as tall as I. He had been leading a semi-clandestine life in London for years, and I had glimpsed him once or twice at Sir John's. The English cardinal William Allen, who had known him for a long time, had asked him to become one of his personal valets, and also to bring someone with him.

One evening, after foiling a fresh attempt on the part of Saint-Paul to enlist me, I returned to the Mores' in a particularly foul mood and slammed the door, which was quite unlike me.

'A storm's afoot,' murmurs old Master More. 'We must see what's up.'

'My turn,' said Nicholas Bawden, whom I, in my fury, hadn't even noticed. 'Do you remember me, Francis Tregian?'

'No.'

'We met at Sir John Arundell's house, in Clerkenwell. I am Nicholas Bawden.'

I smiled and shook his hand.

'Please excuse my unforgivable rudeness. Someone has just made me absolutely furious.'

I told him of my bitter row.

'I have no desire to be a soldier, but a musician,' I concluded. 'I wish to go to Italy, preferably to Rome, although I have no idea where I will find the money.'

'What if I took you?' he suggested.

'How so? To Rome?'

'The Cardinal requires two personal valets. I'll introduce you.'

'Barret will never agree.'

'Of course he won't. I've heard that he hates you. But we shan't ask him. I'll have you invited by the Cardinal himself.'

And so the Cardinal invited me.

My departure was set for early July, following the final examinations which formally instated me as a man of learning. I had a message sent to Giuliano, and he came to fetch me.

He was quite firm: 'It is out of the question that you travel to Rome alone.'

I should have left with Nicholas Bawden, but he had to depart before the appointed day, for reasons that escape me.

So one fine morning, I took leave of the English College and my brother Charles without the slightest sadness, and Reims without the least regret.

We rode out of the Vesle Gate in silence. On our right, we passed the Hospital, houses and mills, before arriving in the vineyards.

'We shall avoid the wooded hills to the south of Reims; they are ill-reputed, and we might come across Huguenots,' says Giuliano. 'We'll take the longer route by way of the plain.'

'Giuliano?'

'Yes?'

'Are we in a hurry?'

'Ask me a direct question. What is it you wish to do?'

'To travel by way of Epernay.'

'Epernay? But Navarre has it under siege!'

'Precisely.'

He fixes me with a thoughtful stare.

'So that's how you see things.'

'It is indeed.'

Another long silence.

'You were not a prisoner two years ago.'

This is not a question, but an observation.

'No.'

'If it were to become known . . .'

'But you are my alter ego, my dear Giuliano, so it will never become known. And anyway, we shall let ourselves be taken, as a precaution.'

'You know that's a huge risk.'

'True. If we chance on a rough-tempered officer, he'll put us to the sword without further ado. But I'm eager to try, nonetheless.'

'Mad to the end,' he laughs, fearless as always. 'I know I am!'

We find Troisville before anyone takes us prisoner, and so risk nothing. Troisville and I fall into each other's arms as soon as we see each other, with cries of 'My brother!' Giuliano gives a great laugh.

'I might have known you were a man of particular calibre, like your brother Adrian. And here was I fretting about you!'

I am no longer listening.

'Françoise . . . ?'

'She is in Bordeaux, waiting for you.'

'I must go to Bordeaux, but I don't know how.'

'Well, for now, come and see the King, he'll be delighted.'

As we trot down the road, I make the introductions. Giuliano keeps shaking his head.

'Francis Tregian, well I never . . . A gentleman of the Huguenot sovereign tells you: "Come and see the King, he'll be delighted." I must be dreaming.'

His stupefaction is comical. I laugh out loud.

'Life is full of surprises. There are some things a man cannot tell anyone. And if you dare talk . . . '

'My dear Francis! If I were to breathe a single word, our lives would be worth nothing. It's obvious that we are here because we were taken prisoner.'

'Obvious,' Troisville echoes gravely.

We find the King standing before a small house, virtually alone, his arm through his horse's bridle, drinking in large gulps. Upon seeing me dismount, he exclaims:

'*Ventre-saint-gris!* Unbelievable! My little priest! Back here among the people who really know how to make merry? My word, you've grown. You'll end up taller than the giant Pantagruel.'

I bow before him. He raises me up, clutches me in his arms and kisses me in great wafts of garlic. King Henri always smelled of garlic.

'Will you take Reims?' I ask Troisville.

'No. We shall seize Epernay, and the King will push right up to the walls of Reims, but he has no intention of taking the city. Just to show the people of Reims who's master.'

Troisville is of the opinion that the King will soon enter Paris.

'He'll convert. He can't reign otherwise. He knows there's really no other way.'

GIULIANO AND I set out on the road again.

'We're going by way of Bordeaux,' I declare.

'By way of Bordeaux? With all due respect, you're quite mad. You say it as if it were an idle stroll. It's not at all on our way, even if we descend the Rhône valley. We'll have to cross France!'

'If we journey along the Rhône valley, how many additional days are required?'

'I've never done it, but I'd say two weeks, depending on how fast we gallop.'

'We will go at breakneck speed.'

'We will do no such thing. We don't have the horses for it.'

'Fine, a restrained pace then. But I must go to Bordeaux.'

'You might tell me why.'

'Are you holding tight to your saddle?'

'Absolutely.'

'To get married.'

His eyes grow wide.

'Without telling anyone?' he says finally. 'Without your father's permission?'

'Firstly, I'm telling you, for you are my uncle, so to speak. Admit it, we're all old enough now to agree that Jane is the daughter of my grandfather John, and we all know as much. Secondly, my father lives cut off from the world, out of reach, and my own life cannot stop simply because he has chosen to bring his to a complete halt. The last I heard, you told me yourself he had sired another child, isn't that so? Well why shouldn't I do likewise?'

He still says nothing.

'Giuliano, I am past eighteen. King Henry of England wedded Queen Catherine of Aragon when he was just seventeen. Jane was married at eleven. My father and mother were joined when they were adolescents. My sister Mary has two children. I'm old enough to be married.'

'My dear Francis, I grant you that. But you have a duty to your family. If England . . .'

'If you are referring to England's possible return to Catholicism, I will scream! Our only remaining hope is that one day someone will invent the freedom of religion, of worship, of conscience – whatever we might call it. At that time, some Englishmen will proclaim that they are Catholic, loud and clear. But returning England to Rome . . . That was only possible through force. Spain and Rome missed the opportunity. It will not come again. And I can't wait. I must act now, while the life God has given me is mine to enjoy.'

Giuliano sighs.

'We could be dead in an hour: that much is true.'

'You see. Let us live, Giuliano. And while we are free from constraints, let us not ask ourselves too many questions.'

WE ARRIVE IN BORDEAUX in the middle of July. The Troisville ladies are not expecting us.

Françoise turns quite pale when she sees me.

Trembling like a leaf, I kiss her hand.

I am so overcome by emotion that I drop my sword without even realising, and Giuliano, watching the scene with a wry eye, picks it up without me noticing.

Troisville being the head of the family, I have formally requested his sister's hand, and he has granted it to me on condition that she be in agreement.

I introduce Giuliano as my uncle, and it is he who cautions Madame de Troisville:

'The Tregian fortune has been confiscated by the English Crown. They have virtually nothing left and there is barely any hope of recovering it.'

'The Troisvilles,' replies Françoise's mother, 'are rich in nobility and traditions only. We live on little, sir.'

We are wed in the Catholic church, with Giuliano walking me to the altar. I don't recall any Protestant service.

My only clear memory is of my first night with Françoise. I had heard tell of the thing so much that I expected it to be delightful. But we were both of us borne away on a wave of passionate folly. I was unaware that my body could experience such violent yet beautiful sensations, and I was astonished to see that I was giving my beloved sensations similar to my own. I have heard many men voice disappointment at their first amorous adventure, requiring the assistance of a proficient courtesan to attain true pleasure. This was not so as far as I was concerned. Our wedding night was not perhaps our most fulfilled – we were both of us ignorant of the mysteries of the flesh – but Françoise is the only woman with whom I have felt complete, with whom I have had the sensation of entering the gates of Paradise.

WE LEFT BORDEAUX IN the middle of October, but I recall little of the journey, beyond anguish, a hitherto unknown anguish that caught me unawares: I had always lived an independent existence, requiring nothing and no one. The closest that I had come to an essential friendship was with Adrian. But since Adrian had always been there, I saw him above all as a fragment, albeit a particularly precious one, of that mosaic called family. I didn't take his departure for a permanent disappearance. I thought of him every day – and I talked with him constantly. He never answered, but he was there.

Now suddenly, there on the road beside the Garonne river, on the way to Toulouse, I feel as if I am being pulled to pieces, quartered, that my heart is being subjected to unbearable torture: how am I to survive a single hour without Françoise?

During moments of respite, I make a second, quite disturbing discovery: I have never consciously noticed that women have a body one could touch, to which one might give pleasure, and receive it in turn. Suddenly I can see nothing else. All of them are beautiful. All of them are desirable.

I am ashamed.

Might my love for Françoise be less absolute than I had thought?

We are well past Carcassonne and already approaching the Mediterranean when I glimpse Giuliano eyeing a young peasant girl as we ride through a village. There is a glint in his gaze that seems familiar to me. Might he too . . . ?

We are travelling at a gallop, for there is no time to lose. At best, we shall reach Rome a month late, which is understandable in these troubled times. Any longer than that, and we should attract suspicion. So I have to wait until evening before venturing a cautious question, in the dark, once we have stretched out on our straw mattresses in the hostelry.

'Giuliano?'

'Yes?'

'How do you love Jane?'

'Are you asking if I love her with all my heart?'

'Yes.'

'Why?'

I seek an explanation.

'Because,' I admit after a pause, 'I have seen you looking at other women . . .'

'You love Françoise with all your heart and all your body, but I have seen you looking at other women too.'

'Exactly.'

'Aha! You're wondering if you love her as much as all that.' He stifles a laugh.

'Don't mock me, Giuliano!'

'I'm not mocking you, my dear Francis. It amuses me that geniuses too are made of the same stuff as us ordinary folk.'

'Which genius? Who?'

'You yourself. I cannot believe you still have not understood that you play the organ and the virginal like the Good Lord himself.'

I brush his words aside with a gesture of impatience.

'Don't divert the conversation. Answer me.'

'The first time I saw Jane was also the first time you and I saw each other. You had been travelling through the mud for weeks: Adrian, Mary, Margaret and yourself, all four crammed into baskets used for transporting stones. You were filthy, dishevelled and worn out. Jane said, "My little Master Francis, what pleasure to see you safely arrived," as she pulled you from the basket and hugged you close. You resembled each other so closely that I first thought she was your mother, which set me immediately to despair, for I had fallen powerfully in love with her in an instant. After that, I spent two years engaged in the most subtle machinations – with her, the Tregians and the Arundells, for our marriage to be seen not only as reasonable, but desirable for all. But I would have eloped with her and disappeared once she admitted she loved me too. More importantly, I would be prepared to do the same tomorrow.'

'And so?'

'So, once a man has tasted love, he becomes aware of the freight of love that every woman he meets carries within her. However, there are many men who do not look for it, and cannot distinguish it. They use the women they meet to satisfy themselves, but they do not see them.'

'Yes, well, and . . . ?'

'I myself see these women and the love they carry within them. I am no paragon of virtue and I admit to you that, sometimes, when I've spent months far from Jane, and when I am reasonably sure that the woman doesn't have the pox, I have had occasion to . . . But I have never done it casually. The Church considers any carnal act with a woman other than one's own to be a sin, but that's laughable: show me a priest who has never tasted the delights of the flesh. As far as I'm concerned, there is a difference. I consider it a sin to use a woman as a stallion uses a mare. But to enjoy the pleasure of the flesh with a woman whose acquaintance you have made, whom you have seduced and who has seduced you, that is quite another matter.'

'And do you have many of . . . of . . . these women friends?'

'I had a number of them before I met Jane. And I have had two or three since.'

'Does Jane know that . . . ?'

'No! What would be the point? When I am with Jane, and most of the time even when she isn't there, she's the only woman who counts for me. What would be the point of telling her about other women? Besides, I am convinced that Jane knows everything.'

'And what if she dared to do the same . . . ?'

'I have come to understand that women do not usually behave like men. But if Jane had a lover, and even if one of the Ardent children was not my own, I would tell myself that I had asked for it, with my way of living.'

A long silence.

'Are you asleep?' Giuliano finally asks.

'No, I'm thinking.'

'Chiefly, you should understand that you're no different from others; you're not fickle just because you're stirred by women other than your own. It's simply up to you to choose what you do about it. I confess that, personally, I wouldn't lose a minute's sleep over this matter. If anything were to keep me awake, it would be how you're going to tell your father that you have married an impoverished Huguenot foreigner without his permission. As for me, I'll probably get myself killed for having allowed you to commit such folly without locking you up or beating you senseless with my own hands.'

'Sir John intended to explain the thing to my father. I have no idea whether he had the time or found the proper moment to do so. If he said nothing, then neither shall we.'

'And what if your father has arranged another marriage for you in the meantime?'

'That is unlikely, but my only option would be to flee England.'

He stifles another laugh.

'Francis, if the Queen has really given you a pension that you can claim in Flanders, let us go north and try not to live within the bosom of your family any longer.'

'You would come with me?'

'With pleasure.'

'Do you think I shall have much work to do for the Cardinal?'

'I have no idea. But take this opportunity to meet as many useful people as you can, and above all understand, once and for all, that you're a player of genius. Hide behind your music, and the world of politics will not bother you. You have already succeeded in not being a priest. I gave you a helping hand, but you have held out very well on your own.'

'You gave me a helping hand? What hand?'

'Once, several years ago, I was in London, at Sir John's. Your father sent for me and instructed me to tell your headmaster Barret that as far as he was concerned there was no obstruction to your becoming a priest, even if you were the eldest.'

I burst out laughing.

'So it was true! Parsons told me, Barret too. I am very happy not to have known that, for I was able to deny it even more vehemently.'

'They didn't learn it from me, at least. I played the fool who has understood the complete opposite, and I told Barret that your father desired you not to take the cloth.'

WE GO UP the coast to Sète. The weather is splendid – a blue sky and westerly breezes.

'If we find a trusty little boat, we could make up much of the time we've lost, and be in Ostia in two days,' Giuliano says.

We wander about for a few hours, with no fixed aim it seems. But I am mistaken: eventually we find the man Giuliano has been seeking.

'Monsieur Julien' is welcomed as a friend by the inhabitants of a cluster of houses hardly worth the title of 'village'. A throng of bright, chattering people listens to our tale, many slapping their thighs and laughing loudly. Two handsome young men who have taken their time along the way – they quite understand. A trusty little boat to sail to Rome? But of course! Monsieur Julien must surely recall the time when he was at risk of missing an important meeting and Old Jehan took him as far as Genoa in less time than it took to ask?

'I was but a young lad when these people helped me for the first time,' Giuliano explains. 'In particular, it is thanks to them that I was able to escape the pirates. They hid me and found a skipper who took me to England. That's how I came to know your family. I'll tell you all about it one day.'

The boat looks decrepit and far from trusty.

'Don't be fooled,' said Giuliano. 'It's a place of sanctuary. First of all, appearances can be misleading, and designed as such; everything is kept in perfect order. Also, Old Jehan has come to an understanding with all the pirates who cross his path. We run no risk of finding ourselves slaves of the Sultan tomorrow, which is an assurance I imagine you appreciate as much as I do?'

'Oh, very much so.'

Truth be told, I feel idiotic, and amazed at Giuliano's efficiency. That is when I decide it is high time I begin to take my own affairs in hand. If not, I am bound to fall prey to misfortune of one kind or another before long. I can't count on friends, servants and luck forever. I am responsible for a woman now, and perhaps even a child.

We reach Ostia in record time. Old Jehan lands us on a secluded beach and takes us to a dilapidated post-house out in the countryside. Il Signor Giovanni and Messire Giuliano are received like old acquaintances. We are furnished with horses in no time at all, and are on our way.

I am no longer thinking of Françoise. I am dazed. It has taken no more than a few hours between sea and sky, and here I am, in a different world:

the colours of the landscape, the smells, the animals and plants, the people – everything is so different I can hardly believe my senses.

And then we reach the gates of Rome – the city whose history, language and literature I know so well, and of which I have heard tell all around me since the day I was born. It is from here that the men who built the Roman Camp at Golden set out, in the distant past.

We trot down the Via Ostiensis and along the Tiber. It is very much like the picture I had of this road in my head, from reading so much about it. Traces of its former beauty lie all around, in the form of ruined aqueducts, palaces and temples. The ground is paved with great black slabs. It is not hard to imagine the entire road lined with houses, as it had once been. When we are halfway to Rome, we dismount and Giuliano shows me the tomb of a Roman praetor, its inscription still complete and quite legible. I feel I must be dreaming.

We enter the city. The formalities take no time at all, as we carry almost nothing with us. The greatest concern of the officials guarding the gates is 'heretical' books. As we trot towards the Vatican, past the imposing mass of St Peter's (St Peter's of Rome!), it seems I am in a kind of vision. Giuliano smiles, amused by my expression and exclamations.

'Once we reach the English College, you'll find people like Father Parsons, and some very unexceptional Jesuits. Remember to stay on your guard.'

We pass Via Giulia, then enter the narrow Corte Savelli at walking pace, and stop before a yellowish-coloured house. Giuliano dismounts, seizes the heavy clapper and knocks.

We have arrived.

XIV

Quel augellin che canta	*This little bird which sweetly sings,*
Sì dolcemente, e lascivetto vola	*and wanton, flies*
Hor da l'abete al faggio	*from fir to beech,*
Ed hor dal faggio al mirto,	*and now from beech to myrtle,*
S'havess' humano spirto	*had it a human soul*
Direbb': Ardo d'amore!	*would say 'I burn with love'.*
Ma ben arde nel core,	*Indeed, it burns within its heart*
E chiam'il suo desio	*and calls its love*
Che li rispond':	*who answers back,*
Ardo d'amor anch'io!	*'My heart burns just as bright'.*

GIANBATTISTA GUARINI / MONTEVERDE
FOURTH BOOK OF MADRIGALS

CARDINAL ALLEN came as something of a surprise. I detested the men who declared themselves his friends – Barret, Parsons and others I have not mentioned but encountered daily. On the principle that birds of a feather flock together, I was prepared for a man likely to provoke my hostile dislike.

He was nothing of the kind.

Allen carried himself like a tall, powerfully built man, yet he was of average height, and slight, with a pointed face. His greatest strengths were his piercing look, his eloquence and his speaking voice. He radiated quiet confidence. His conception of Catholicism was quite as extreme as Parsons', but while Parsons quickly revealed himself to be an intolerant and unreasonable man, Allen was persuasive and captured the attention. I have been convinced since childhood that the two great Christian religions are of equal value, though I cannot say where the idea came from. Allen is the only man to have shaken that belief, even for a moment.

When Allen spoke, his listeners abandoned all thoughts of their own. He would convince them that they had come up with his ideas themselves. Had they not been saying that very thing, a moment ago? When Allen explained the superiority of the Roman religion over the Protestant religion, it became obvious, logical, immediately apparent. Allen was so intimately convinced of the fact himself that he succeeded in communicating his conviction to the listener. The moment anyone left his presence, they felt ashamed at the feebleness of their critical faculties, and their personal opinions were restored. But he had only to reappear for the phenomenon to be repeated. And I say 'anyone' because I know this happened to others as well as to me.

Unsurprisingly, then, Allen had directed the college in Douai and Reims for many years – even at a distance – with not a murmur of dissent. He had a gift for dealing with people. Everyone liked him, even people like me who did not subscribe to his views.

I remember William Allen with warmth and affection. I never thought ill of him, and when he died I was as bereft as if I'd lost a beloved father.

He welcomed Nicholas Bawden and me like old friends. I dropped to one knee and kissed his ring. I wished to speak. He gestured for me to stand up.

'Word of your virtuosity has reached us here, Master Tregian,' he said, dismissing our explanations with a wave of his hand. 'I hope you will soon delight us with music from our own country.'

I bowed. Giuliano was right, no doubt – I should concentrate on establishing my reputation as a musician, and express as few opinions as possible. This 'genius' everyone spoke of might yet prove useful.

A Mass at the church of the Trinità, a concert at the English College, another at the home of a cardinal before a great throng of prelates, and my reputation was made. I was a gentleman musician; that much was apparent every day. I should have confined myself to what is known as speculative music, a branch of mathematics, but out of regard for my father and the great sacrifices he had made for the Catholic religion, people accepted my love of music. Our family situation was known to all and was often alluded to.

Years before, Allen had translated the Bible into English. His work was known as the Douai Bible. Now, he sought to revise the translation for greater accuracy, comparing the Latin and English texts. He asked me to work on the project. There were three of us. We submitted suggestions which the Cardinal then examined, alone or in consultation with other prelates.

Soon, my days were divided into four. Mornings were devoted to work on the Bible. At midday, I went to the gymnasium, where the fencing master was a friend of Giuliano. In the early afternoon, I played music. The Cardinal had been presented with an Italian harpsichord, of the kind much admired for their intoxicating sound. I played it as often as I could. Several times a week, I had access to the organ in the church of Santa Maria sopra Minerva. Lastly, my evenings were spent either at the Cardinal's home, where we were often called upon to organise his household activities and to discuss theological matters, or with musicians I had met in a shop to which John Byas had directed me. Byas was Allen's long-serving personal valet and an accomplished lute player. The shop sold printed music, and here I discovered – moved beyond words – the madrigals of Claudio Monteverde.

I had never heard of the great musician until then. Nor had I ever paid much attention to madrigals, if the truth be known. They existed in England, too, of course. William Byrd had written some, as had Thomas Morley, who had played me several and talked to me about them.

'First came the *canzonetta*, a short air played with variations. But a *canzonetta* is essentially a simplified madrigal form. Like a madrigal, it repeats every musical phrase but the central one.'

Morley had insisted on the harmonic character of these *canzonette*. Their melodic simplicity was found in the madrigal, too, he said.

But this was a musical form unlikely to appeal to my boyish tastes at the time. The very word 'madrigal' quickly sank to the bottom of my memory.

Not so now. At times my separation from Françoise and the uncertain knowledge of when I would see her again made me half mad with pain – a pain only madrigals had the power to soothe, and then but fleetingly.

I found madrigal scores at the music shop, and there were also lutes, viols and a spinet, so that clients could play and choose which pieces to buy. I cherish bright memories of afternoons spent assembling the voices required for a madrigal by Orlando di Lasso or Luca Marenzio – often with complete strangers. Once, we even performed with the composer himself. Music masters often came in search of supplies for their noble pupils – and sometimes the noble pupils came in person. Female singers performing at the great houses would send their musicians, and sometimes visit themselves. A few cast enticing glances in my direction. My senses were awakened now, and I could no longer ignore the true nature of the disturbance they provoked. I was held back first and foremost by the simple fact that they were not Françoise. And by dread of the pox. Quite apart from the fact that any amorous adventure would have been noticed immediately and, in my situation, I could not afford to attract attention.

In this climate I discovered the music of Monteverde. My first contact came through madrigals hand-written by a musician from Mantua, where the maestro lived. There was something unique about them. For me, it was love at first sight.

> *Cor mio mentre vi miro*
> *Visibilmente mi trasformo in voi*
> *E trasformato poi*
> *In un solo sospiro l'anima spiro,*
> *O bellezza mortale*
> *O bellezza vitale,*
> *Poiché sì tosto un core*
> *Per te rinasce, e per te nato more*

> *(My love, while I gaze on you*
> *I am visibly transformed in you;*
> *And thus transformed,*
> *In a single sigh, my soul exhales.*
> *Oh, mortal beauty!*
> *Oh, life-giving beauty!*
> *For a heart is quickly*
> *reborn through you and, once reborn, must die)*

The music won me over immediately and absolutely. I grasped an expressive form corresponding precisely to my own deepest feelings.

I did not buy the scores, I copied them. Or learned them by heart, then adapted them for the harpsichord in the Cardinal's apartments, where I would play and mouth the words.

The Cardinal quickly understood that if he wished to get anything useful out of me in other ways, he would have to leave me time enough for my music. I do not know how far his interest in my virtuosity really extended, but he encouraged me to play the instrument in the evenings while he wrote private letters he did not wish to dictate. Sometimes John Byas would fetch his lute, and we would play together.

The Cardinal's private secretary was Roger Bayns, a gentleman and long-time exile. It was he who oversaw the Cardinal's correspondence and his messengers. The Cardinal sent and received a constant stream of letters to and from the four corners of the world. People came to see him from far and wide, and Bayns oversaw the entire proceedings with consummate mastery.

The prelate had great need of a man like him, for the Cardinal's days were busily occupied. He never missed the Consistory, which was called by the Pope each week to settle Church affairs. He was a member of two congregations: one overseeing German Affairs; and another responsible for the Index Librorum Prohibitorum, the Catholic Church's list of prohibited books – this involved a great deal of vitally important reading which he insisted on doing himself.

'If I give you a work to read of which the content is unknown to me, I risk your damnation, and would fail in my duty,' he used to say.

Since the death of Cardinal Antonio Carafa, Allen was also Librarian of the Vatican. And all of this in addition to his duties as director of the English Colleges – 'the missions' as he called them – and overseer of the expedition of priests to England. Tensions ran high in the colleges. One tendency I had observed earlier became common and widespread now: time and money were short, and priests were trained quickly, at low cost. Those who returned to England to preach the Good Word were not the learned theologians of old, but often ignorant, ill-prepared men armed only with their courage.

This created dreadful strife, and it was some time before I understood that the tension was crystallised in the increasingly marked disagreement between Allen and Parsons, or rather between Allen and the Jesuits.

It took Allen a long while to become aware that he was, in part at least, a toy in the Jesuits' hands. He would fly into a rage if he heard anyone state that his accession to the Sacred Purple was due to the intercession of Philip II of Spain, through Parsons, and not to his role as a figurehead for the English Catholic cause. For my part, I soon realised that this was precisely what was rumoured all over Rome. Everyone accepted it as proven fact. One day, when Roger Bayns had invited me to help him at his apartments, as he often did, I saw a remarkable document dated from before the Armada. It shocked me profoundly, while at the same time proving the sound basis of the rumours.

It was a copy of a memorandum presented to the Pope himself by Count Olivares, the Spanish ambassador to the Holy See, in 1587. The few short pages were perfectly clear: Philip of Spain saw Allen's accession as cardinal as vital to his own machinations. He had even thought ahead to a form of words for an official statement, were Allen to be killed (something along the lines of 'the purple of his Cardinal's hat is stained with a martyr's blood'). In the document, Olivares explained why the King of Spain preferred not to keep Allen in high style for the moment – Philip's politicking was better served if Allen was seen to live a frugal life; but His Majesty had given assurances that he would show far greater generosity when the time came (once he had defeated England). And Olivares continued (over several more pages) with tactical considerations as to Allen's best course of action. The state of the copy, clearly made in a hurry and apparently in secret (it was untidily written, covered in blotches and with lines overlapping), seemed to me proof that Allen had obtained it by subterfuge. I never dared tell anyone about it, and the questions I asked myself at the time have remained unanswered.

Allen, for his part, saw the alliance with Spain as a secondary matter, it seemed to me. For him, any means justified the ultimate end: the restoration of England to the Catholic faith. But the more I observed, the more I read and the more I listened, the more it seemed to me that he was blind to Philip's true intentions. He could not see that the King of Spain was animated by far lower motives than his own. And I think it took him a long time to realise that many English Catholics were not prepared to throw open the door to a Spanish invasion. Quite the opposite, indeed. It took him a long time, too, to admit the Jesuits' own, thoroughly murky role.

For Parsons, as an unconditional supporter of Philip II of Spain, the English Colleges in France, Spain and Italy were his private hunting-ground: the Jesuits freely recruited their most gifted students, training them to become skilled politicians and plotters. The only snag was that for a Jesuit, the Society of Jesus would always come first, before England. One evening I heard the Cardinal say just that, in vituperative tones, to Father Alfonso Agazzari, an Italian Jesuit then in charge of the English College in Rome. Usually so placid and measured in his speeches, Allen's voice was raised so loud that Roger Bayns and I heard him from behind the door where we were busy at our copying.

'You are running the colleges in the interests of the Jesuits and Spain,' he shouted. 'You are indifferent to the strife among the students and to the needs of our poor English Church. But we shall never win through if we do not forget our quarrels and private interests in favour of the one true cause.'

'Scurrilous rumour, all of it,' Father Agazzari replied drily.

'It is not hearsay, but fact,' retorted the Cardinal. 'Your extreme conduct is fomenting further strife.'

And they continued in that tone until finally Agazzari raised his own voice:

'How dare you doubt us? Almighty God gives constant proof of His love for our Company. And when mortal means have failed, He has intervened with His Divine Hand, to near-miraculous ends. For as long as you march faithfully at our side, God will preserve you and see that you prosper in your endeavours. But fear His wrath the day you stray from that path, lest He thwart your every plan.'

It was impossible not to hear the note of menace in his voice. As if he had said: 'Watch your step.'

'Thank you for your visit, my son, you may go now,' said the Cardinal, icily.

The next day, he began proclaiming the need to assert the independent character of the English Colleges and their seminarians as clearly as possible. In public, he never uttered a word against the Jesuits, but we noted that he had stopped receiving them at his apartments, and spoke about them very little.

Yet when one or other of the non-Jesuit English urged him to put in place a structure enabling the tensions to be addressed without the need for his personal presence and intercession, he was noticeably, and curiously, reticent. He devoted his energies to his daily tasks; there was little left for less immediate problems, perhaps. These, he preferred to set to one side. And he had such a remarkable ability to make peace in even the worst disputes – those that broke out periodically between the Welsh and English seminarians, for example – that he may have underestimated their impact. He did not realise that calm was restored thanks to his influence, not because the two sides had understood that they would do better to live together in harmony.

I was lodging with Giuliano's family at this time, in a rather fine house. Giuliano was illegitimate, but he had been received into this comfortable household with open arms, and people spoke of his mother with great affection. I spent little time there: when I was on duty – which was almost always – I slept at the Cardinal's apartments or at the house of Charles Paget, an English émigré whose palazzo was close by Allen's.

I seldom went to the English College, and I began to avoid Father Agazzari. Whenever I saw him, in the course of my work, I had the uncomfortable feeling that he was watching us, and keeping a close eye on the Cardinal in particular. My sense of unease was the greater now that Allen seemed to have lost all sense of proportion. His optimism was evident not only in his underestimation of the intensity of the disputes between individuals in Rome but also in his vision of the state of Catholicism in England. The gulf between his private vision and reality was brought home to me for the first time one December evening, in the year of my arrival in Rome. Allen wished to dictate a letter addressed to the English Catholics. Everyone was busy except me. I was playing the harpsichord.

'My son, I am so sorry to interrupt you.' I stopped playing and rose from my seat. 'Would you mind very much if I dictate a letter to you?'

'I am at your service, Your Eminence.'

I sat down to write, and he began. At first I paid little attention to the content of his words. But soon I was riveted.

'Have no doubt, my gentle and loyal coadjutors and true believers,' the Cardinal dictated, 'that in the eyes of God, the evils of our adversaries have exceeded all limits and that He will soon put an end to them, so that our brothers will no longer be persecuted for His truth and shall receive – not in the next life but here below – the reward for their pains. God is just and

merciful, and will not suffer long to see His loyal subjects cowering under
the yoke of those who would destroy them. He will end the sufferings of
His Chosen People.'

I struggled not to betray my scepticism by my expression.

'What is it, my son? Do you not believe me?'

'Oh I do, Your Eminence, of course.'

'My dear Tregian, the Queen of England will not live forever. She is
an old woman, just as I am an old man. And her successor will be James
of Scotland, son of our beloved Mary Stuart, may God rest her soul. The
days of Protestantism are numbered. England will reclaim its rightful
place in Christendom, and even if that does not come to pass, James will
institute the freedom of religion and Catholics will be tolerated, at least.
And then the truth will shine forth in the light of day. People will see that
there are innumerable Catholic nobles, and their serfs cannot but follow
the religion of their master. And in that way we shall reconquer England,
without bloodshed.'

He paused. I struggled to find something to say, anxious to conceal my
disbelief. But Allen was paying no attention to me now. He was gazing
into the distance.

'If we consider the matter from a spiritual and temporal viewpoint –
taking into account the quality of those concerned, and their properties –
reason, experience and substantive conjecture all tell us that in England,
two out of three people are favourable to the Catholic faith, and therefore
unhappy with the current state of affairs.'

I applied myself to my copying so that he would not see my disagreement.

THE INTRIGUES WITNESSED during my two years as a personal valet
would fill an entire volume. I prefer to let them lie at the very bottom of
my memory. What remains is my ready distrust, my horror of intrigue of
every kind. This was nothing new to me; rather it confirmed my natural
instincts since childhood.

In Rome, I learned to recognise the machinations and counter-mach-
inations of politics. The Italians are gifted with remarkable subtlety, and
more than once it occurred to me that, for all his intelligence, our poor

English Cardinal was not cut out for a world where conspiracy and violence were deployed without scruple, behind a superficial appearance of unctuous gentility.

I kept to my kennel and continued my revision of the Douai Bible. I submitted notebooks full of corrections. It seemed to me that Allen's translation of the texts was somewhat forced, but I took great care to formulate my remarks so as not to appear judgemental. My affection for the Cardinal, my dedication to the work, my passion for music, all helped to mask my true feelings.

My visits to Luca the printer's shop were discreet. A gentleman in the retinue of Cardinal Allen would be ill advised to show himself too openly in the company of professional musicians – mere domestic servants in the eyes of almost everyone.

'Music is fine for the young,' said a visiting prelate one day, when I was asked to play a piece for him. 'Though it tends to exacerbate lasciviousness. And any practitioner of the art is bound to find himself in such curious company . . .'

Such considerations apart, the household as a whole took a kindly interest in my music-making. The Cardinal well knew where I spent many of my afternoons, I am convinced of it – the Papal States were crammed with more spies than almost anywhere in the world, except the England of Burghley and Walsingham.

And it was doubtless to keep me from the temptations of my too-frequent contact with the city's plebeian population that Allen introduced me to the Master of the Vatican Chapel, the organist of the Cappella Giulia, the great Palestrina himself. He was a man of changeable demeanour, severe one minute, sensual the next. I had the pleasure of knowing him for an entire year, the last of his life, and I steeped myself in his *novum genus musicum*, which gave me my taste for plain expression. He brought me to it by teaching me to articulate the music in relation to the phrases of poetry. It was Palestrina who developed my sensitivity to the need for balanced cadences and the importance of counterpoint. His vocal compositions, both sacred and profane, had – have – a clarity and an elegance, a structured flow that have defined my taste ever since.

The Eternal City made a great contrast with the pace of life in London or even Reims. Here, there were no bustling commercial streets, packed with people from before dawn. Rome was, and doubtless remains, a place of courtly nobility, a city of palaces and gardens. Everyone partook of the leisurely, ecclesiastical life. There was no great difference between the feast days and ordinary working days; Roman life was a ceaseless round of elegant carriages, prelates and ladies.

More than anything, Romans love to walk. They step out from their houses and go from street to street with no precise aim. There are streets made and named for just that – the *Corsi*, the *Passeggiate*. The gentlemen walk out on the street, the ladies appear at the windows, and, seen from that distance, they are all beautiful, for they are expert in the art of disguising their flaws. If one accepts their invitation and takes the stairs to their apartments, one is often surprised, and sometimes greatly disappointed. In fine society, no one ever misses these outings. The young men ride on horseback, the older men in carriages; people make deep bows and curtseys to one another, or exchange knowing glances in passing. I found it all very strange and wonderfully entertaining.

During my two years in Rome, I never felt myself a foreigner: so many nations mingle there, one hears such a mixture of idioms that everyone feels at home. If I could have fulfilled two dreams, my happiness would have been complete: to be with Françoise again, truly as man and wife, and to meet Monteverde. His *Third Book of Madrigals* circulated among us and was sung at gatherings. Besides this, travellers brought manuscript copies of some of the airs that would later constitute his *Fourth Book*.

The madrigals offered such a variety of melody that they seemed to cleave to the sentiment, the emotion contained in the lyric, so that whoever sang or listened to them experienced the miraculous sensation that the music had been composed and written down for them alone. Monteverde felt like a true friend.

I had almost no news from Françoise. She sent letters with messengers as they passed, addressed to Giuliano, who came quite often to see me and left with packets of letters I had written and collected in a hiding-place, not daring to entrust them to a messenger – what if the man turned out to be a spy for the Cardinal, or the Jesuits? Giuliano felt responsible for my well-being and safety; he had made this known to my father and promised to watch over me until I came of age. But since the death of the only man he had ever acknowledged as his master – Sir John – he had moved to

Amsterdam with Jane and their four children, where he earned a living (a very comfortable living, to judge from his increasingly fine appearance) in the silk trade.

'But how do you manage, Giuliano?'

'It's very simple. I am the ideal silk merchant. I know the sea and maritime transport, for having sailed myself, and I know the politics and workings of Europe for having spent time in every country on the Continent. As for the textile trade, it's not much different from any other. I have a man who knows the secrets of silk manufacture as my associate. We are indispensable one to the other.'

'What about the language?'

'When you understand German and speak English, Dutch is not so very difficult. I speak it, and my Dutch clerks write it down for me.'

'And how do you find your clients?'

'My dear Francis, I have been running around Europe for fifteen years. I know everyone in authority. At first, I admit, I was afraid of what they might say. But now, whenever I meet a man whose messenger I once was, and I tell him I'm in the silk trade, he invariably says: "If your silks are as excellent as your services were before, I'll take them." I was surprised at first, but now I understand that gaining acceptance is a matter of personal style. I have clients and suppliers from China to the Americas. I hope I shall have the honour of receiving you in Amsterdam.'

'You may be sure of it.'

Giuliano brought me music, knowing I would be pleased. Thanks to him I discovered Alfonso Ferrabosco's madrigals for three voices. Ferrabosco was one of an Italian family of musicians settled in England, in the service of Queen Elizabeth. William Byrd had published a book of sacred songs for five and six voices entitled *Medius*, and Giuliano secured a copy for me.

Jane had copied out some pieces by the organist of the Oude Kerk in Amsterdam, Jan Sweelinck, who was celebrated in Holland, but unknown to me until then.

I transcribed everything into my personal book of music: pieces I was collecting for the day of my departure from Rome. A day I dreaded, in one way, though I was impatient for it in another. Life in Rome was too complicated for my taste, too centred on the Vatican, its interests and intrigues. The Counter-Reformation was watchful and assiduous, taking a close interest in what people read and what was said. The censors were ever vigilant. 'Witches' or the 'possessed' were burned at the stake with alarming ease. (In reality, they were people whose ideas had incurred the displeasure of the Curia, or who set themselves apart from the mainstream of Roman politics.)

Still, I would miss the city's wondrous beauty: at every street corner, great ruins recalled the splendour of ancient Rome and my childhood hours spent studying the texts it had produced.

In particular, I loved to walk among the fallen columns and tall grass of the Forum. I would climb the ruins of the Temple of Peace and look down at the sheep grazing peacefully between the scattered stones of this place that had once been the centre, the beating heart of the world. There was almost nothing left now but the sky under which Rome had once stood. For me, the ruins did not conjure the ancient city's life, but its death. The enemies of the Empire had begun by striking at the wondrous core of this body politic. And then, realising its disturbing power even in death, toppled and disfigured, they had interred its very ruins. When digging in Rome, people often uncovered the tops of ancient columns. The casual observer quickly understood that men had not demolished the Rome of yesteryear but had built the modern city over it. The spectacle never failed to move me. *Sic transit gloria mundi*. Philip II would pass, like the emperors and tribunes of Ancient Rome, like Elizabeth of England, like Henri of France, like Françoise and me – what would remain of us, after us? Would religious differences really matter as much to future generations?

I recall a winter dusk. I sat philosophising, as so often, gazing absently at a flock of sheep. Just then, rising from the shepherd's pipe, the languid notes of a simple, melancholy tune floated over the ancient stones, and I sensed a kind of answer to my questions.

One day our thoughts and feelings, our emotions, will cease to exist. But they will leave an indelible trace, in poetry, the expression of our innermost thoughts, and above all in music, the purest expression of the soaring emotions of its creators, and those of us – so many – who play it, or who merely listen and love it so.

And while the shepherd played his pipe, a poem by the great Tasso danced in my head:

Questa di verd'herbette
E di novelli fior tessuta hor hora
Vaga e gentil ghirlanda,
Giovin pastor ti manda
l'amata e bella Flora . . .

(Woven from sweet green grass
And budding flowers,
This pretty garland,
A shepherd boy's gift
From his beloved Flora fair . . .)

XV

Cast care away, let sorrow cease,
A fig for melancholy;
Let's laugh and sing, or, if you please,
We'll frolic with sweet Dolly.
Your paltry money-bags of gold,
What need have we to stare for;
When little or nothing soon is told,
And we have the less to care for.

'HANSKIN'
POPULAR BALLAD

1594 – A YEAR I shall never forget. It began with the death of Palestrina. This wonderful composer taught me so much during the little time I spent with him; and I had the feeling that his lessons came to an end just when he was about to teach me the secret of his greatness. No doubt I would have had the same feeling had he died ten years later.

The evening before his grand funeral, I was at the Cardinal's, on night duty. We had spent the entire day rehearsing the music that would be played and sung at the funeral ceremony the following morning. I had a head full of notes and a heavy heart.

I was brought back to reality by the sudden appearance of Giuliano, covered in the dust of a long journey, an equally dusty valet at his side.

'Are you alone?'

This in a conspiratorial whisper.

'Indeed I am. Why?'

Having ordered his valet to place himself at the end of the passage-way, Giuliano proceeds to inspect every nook and cranny, sounds the walls behind the tapestries, and finally stands close to the partially open door. I would have laughed, had he not proceeded quite so seriously. He beckons me over.

'What I have to tell you is a most dangerous secret to know,' he whispers in my ear. 'Swear to me you will tell no one. No one.'

'I swear it.'

'Who serves the Cardinal's food?'

I look at him without speaking. Has he gone mad? Seeing the doubt in my eyes, he gestures impatiently and repeats his question, in an even lower voice.

'It's John Byas, his personal valet,' I say, after a pause.

We are never much preoccupied with food in the household. Meals are frugal, and eaten in a hurry.

'A trusty man?'

'Like myself.'

'Who prepares the meals?'

'I have no idea. I fail to understand why that's of any importance.'

He comes closer and breathes right into my ear.

'Don't ask me how, but I have learned from a very reliable source that the Cardinal is being slowly poisoned, and that it's hoped he will soon be dead.'

I take a step backwards, draw breath to speak, but Giuliano swiftly claps a hand over my mouth.

'Say nothing now. I'm going to your lodgings. Try to be free tomorrow; I'll wait for you.'

'I'm playing at Palestrina's funeral.'

'Come afterwards. Don't be too long.'

He goes, and I stand there like a man who has just been dealt a cudgel blow.

Once I have come to my senses, I spend the rest of the night attempting to trace the path taken by the food. I even go down to the kitchens on the pretext of fetching a drink of water. Everyone is sleeping. Yet again, my noble upbringing puts me at a disadvantage. I know hardly any of the servants, and those I do know, it is only to nod to.

How am I to protect the Cardinal on my own? Sharing my secret with anyone is out of the question. Perhaps I should talk to John Byas? But can I trust him as much as I had supposed? Our culprit is no heretic, I am certain of that: any of the spies who have passed through the English College over the past twenty years would have had ample opportunity to plunge a knife into the Cardinal's heart or to poison his food. Agazzari's menacing words ring in my ear: '*For as long as you march faithfully at our side, God will preserve you and see that you prosper in your endeavours. But fear His wrath the day you stray from that path, lest He thwart your every plan.*' No, the danger must come from fanatics linked to the faction of the King of Spain.

There is no question of my becoming a regular visitor to the kitchens. If that is where the poisoner is at work, he will quickly suspect what it is that interests me. I am a person of no importance: I am liable to be poisoned with a single dose in my own food.

I can see us now, walking feverishly along the Tiber afterwards, Giuliano's valet watching our backs. Giuliano has insisted we talk out of doors, where no spies can hear us.

'Giuliano, I'm in despair. I don't know whom to confide in, nor how I might keep a close eye on the Cardinal's food without arousing suspicion.'

'I went to see our apothecary friend all the way up in Eu; you remember him?'

'Adrian's friend? Of course.'

'I said to myself that this man was our trustiest adviser, living as he does so far from anywhere and, above all, far from these intrigues. I asked him which poison was most likely to kill a man little by little without being noticed. He asked for a day to think on it. At the end of that day, he gave me several phials and told me: "There are two or three possibilities. Here is an antidote that will cover them all. Don't tell me anything. I would rather not know. This is what you were after, is it not? You must administer five drops a day."'

I open my mouth to ask a question, but Giuliano stops me.

'Please, Tregian, don't ask me anything. We are sitting on a powder keg. The fuse could ignite at any moment. Believe me, if I could have avoided sharing such dangerous intelligence with you, I would have. If you know nothing and are tortured, you will talk, of course, but you will be obliged to invent your story. Whereas if I tell you, you risk giving yourself away. I should not even have mentioned the apothecary.'

I am worried to death.

'I have so little experience in affairs of this nature that I don't even know how I might go about administering the five drops to the Cardinal. In eighteen months, I haven't brought him so much as a glass of water. That's not one of my duties.'

'Is there anything he takes regularly? Pay close attention, my friend, and do not tarry.'

It takes me three days to understand how the household is organised. The poisoner must be somebody from outside, I realise, not one of the Englishmen. Only now do I notice that for the last two years the Cardinal has been taking great pains progressively to push away all of the Jesuits. I learn that Nicholas Bawden and myself too have replaced members of the Society of Jesus.

Despite my efforts, no doubt too discreet, it is Giuliano who discovers the truth: the poisoning occurs outside of the palace, in the Vatican Library, where the Cardinal goes several times a week. He leaves after the morning meal and eats nothing until he returns at five in the afternoon, but he frequently quenches his thirst.

It takes me another week, and a myriad of pretexts, to persuade the Cardinal to take me along – I wish to check some texts, I need to see the originals, and so on. Once I have secured his agreement, the task is simple. When he requests a drink, I take the water vessel from the valet's hands myself, and the length and agility of my musician's fingers prove most useful. I believe I can safely say that although they finally remark that the poison is no longer working, and suspect I have something to do with it, they never catch me in the act.

The change is dramatic. In a week, the Cardinal, who has always been poorly although never truly sick, is in better condition, and in three weeks he has all but recovered his full health.

I will never know if what happened next occurred by pure chance, or whether the poisoners connected my presence at the library with the sudden improvement in their victim's health.

One morning, as we are walking to the Vatican, which we often do when the weather is fine, the Cardinal addresses me:

'I have received a letter from your dear father, Master Tregian.'

I say nothing, waiting, and dreading, to hear what is coming.

'He asks that you go to see him.'

'When?'

'Well, immediately. As soon as you can organise your departure.'

'I do not wish to leave you, Your Eminence.'

There is nothing like the truth. He smiles at me.

'You are not leaving for good. It will be a voyage of a few weeks. Your work on the Bible is too important for us to relinquish it now. I will give you one of my men, for you have reached an age at which a gentleman of your rank cannot honourably go about without a retainer.'

'I thank you, Your Eminence, but I have my own valet. I gave him leave to remain with his wife as long as I had no need of him, but he has served me faithfully ever since I was a boy, and I shall have great need of him on such a voyage. I will have him sent for, and will leave as soon as he arrives.'

'In that case, tell him to make haste.'

I am relieved that the Cardinal does not ask me for details about 'my valet': I have no desire to lie to him.

One of Giuliano's young nephews sets off to fetch him that very evening, journeying at a gallop, and soon returns with his uncle, accompanied by the retainer who never leaves his side.

'Chance plays a clumsy game,' Giuliano comments darkly when he arrives.

'My chief concern is that I trust no one in the Cardinal's entourage; I have no loyal friend to take care of him during my absence.'

I take the necessary dispositions for my departure, and Giuliano succeeds in getting his young nephew employed as a kitchen boy. Titus is actually an apprentice weaver, but I rarely saw a boy so at ease in every possible situation. In just a few hours, he has become a most authentic kitchen boy. The antidote he pours into the Cardinal's dishes does not always reach the Cardinal, but enough of it does to prevent him falling quite so seriously ill as he had the previous winter.

We leave Rome, riding north, but stop after a dozen miles, turn around and ride to Ostia along the back roads. Giuliano has organised our voyage by way of Bordeaux without my even having to discuss it with him.

Our sailor acquaintances take us to Sète without incident, despite the stormy sea. We are welcomed by our friends from the last time, and eight to ten days after leaving Rome, we are already riding down the Garonne.

My anxiety at leaving the Cardinal exposed to danger gradually gives way to joy at the prospect of seeing my wife again.

WE HAVE GIVEN OURSELVES three days in Bordeaux: three days during which Françoise and I never leave each other's side.

There is much agitation in the Troisville household, for King Henri has converted to Catholicism. Of this I was aware, the news having sparked a great deal of chatter in Rome, where the Catholics jeered, seeing nothing but a cunning move that would be as short-lived as it was insignificant. They knew Henri of Bourbon too well.

At the Troisvilles', however, opinion is quite different: Henri has converted because there is no other way for him to become king of all the French and no other way to halt the civil war that has ravaged France for two generations. He will not be changing his mind again.

My old friend Charles, who remains one of the King's confidants, has visited simply to explain that he can but follow his sovereign. Françoise, already married to a Catholic – myself – feels that the whole family should convert along with him. But Madame de Troisville, being of old Huguenot stock – her family has been Protestant since the beginnings of the Reform – tells us quite plainly, in the course of a stormy discussion, that she will not be changing her religion.

'My King,' she declares, 'is Henri of Navarre, son of Jeanne d'Albret, and that man is a Huguenot. He is submitting to blackmail, forced upon him by France, because he is a great politician.'

After continuing in the same vein for several hours, she concludes the discussion firmly by saying:

'Françoise, you must convert. It is your wifely duty. As for your Christian duty, I am convinced you may fulfil it in either religion. There is but one Christ. God does not pay such close attention. It is the fault of men who have poisoned our religions with their politics. For that very reason, I stand firm in the Church of my choice.'

Henri is crowned in Chartres with great pomp, Reims having refused to open its gates to him. One can just imagine Jehan Pussot, the churchwarden of Saint-Jacques, ruddy faced, wagging a vengeful finger:

'That damned Huguenot? Never! A heretic on the French throne? Reims will have nothing to do with it, converted or not!'

Now that it is done, Henri will have to find a way to win over the people of Reims, and the rest of France too.

Madame de Troisville wishes to know my plans.

'You really should live with my daughter as husband and wife,' she remarks with a smile.

'I will talk to my father, since he wishes to meet with me. Then as soon as I can leave Cardinal Allen, it will be Bordeaux, Amsterdam or Antwerp, with Françoise. On that you have my word.'

WE DEPART, TRAVELLING LIGHT. I bring along Michel de Montaigne's *Essays* that my wife has given me. I am so affected by leaving her that I bring the books without even looking at them.

As before, my senses are heightened. Colours, sounds and smells are sharper, more penetrating. Françoise has acquired a beauty and a radiance that make her even more desirable. My only wish is never to leave her again. For that, I have no need of my mother-in-law's exhortations. Throughout the entire journey, I think only of my beloved.

We ride north through France, and it seems to me as if the countryside through which we travel is a little less desolate than in the past. At the very least, people are working the land.

We reach Le Tréport without incident. Giuliano still has a number of trusty friends here, and we board a coaster disguised as a half-wrecked old craft. When we land close to Plymouth, a day's travel from Grampound and Golden, I waver. What if Thomas . . .

I confide in Giuliano, who shakes his head.

'I stopped by there a while ago and made some enquiries. He passed away after your last visit. You know that his house belongs to you? You are his sole heir.'

'I?'

'He told you so.'

'True, but I didn't believe it.'

You can count on Giuliano to find out such things. He has a roguish smile.

'With those pisky eyes of yours, you'll be rich. A pension here, a bequest there ... '

I blush deeply and he bursts out laughing.

'Sometimes, I still see in you the boy you once were. Let's go to London. We shall hope to call on the notary on the way back. After all, we'll be sailing from here.'

'And what if my father won't let me leave?'

'Tell him about the Cardinal's health and your work on the Bible and he'll let you go. Be as determined as he is.'

'And what to tell him about Françoise?'

'I am at a loss for advice, but, if I were you, I would refer to your marriage as a future intention rather than a past action. You can always tell your family in a few years, when even they will be forced to see you as an adult.'

I have thought little of Thomas since my last voyage to England, but he is constantly in my mind as we gallop towards London. I fear it will not be quite so easy to stand up to my father. He *is* my father, even though I hardly know him, and his power over me is still absolute. I try to draw on the advice Thomas has given me over the years for the determination I know I will need.

We arrive in London.

THOSE FIVE OR SIX weeks spent in the capital give me an entirely new perspective on my place in life.

This is only my second visit to London, since leaving childhood behind. But the first time hardly counts. I had been in such haste, so fixed on my goal, so busy, too, with showing Charles de Troisville the city, that, paradoxically, I had paid no attention to anything, seen nothing. On returning now, one of the first things that strikes me is how much smaller everything seems than in my memory. The houses have shrunk.

We go to Muswell, where my grandmother Anne Arundell still lives when she is not in Dorset. On the way, we agree that Giuliano will be my steward for as long as necessary. He will look after my affairs while I visit my family.

Baroness Arundell's welcome is somewhat reserved. I have no time to wonder why. No sooner have I set down my baggage than she sends for me.

She receives me at her fireside, sitting bolt upright with the grandeur of a queen. She is an old lady but she hardly looks it: few wrinkles, an alabaster complexion and 'Titian-red' hair, as they would say in Rome, after the painter. This is the first time I have dealt with her directly. It is also my first opportunity truly to pay attention to the woman herself – truly to see her.

She smiles at me, her white teeth glinting.

'I recall how I used to say to you: "Come here, my little one." Now you might almost call me *your* little one.'

'Madam, I would not be so bold.'

'No, of course not. For you are not only grown-up, but a gentleman too.' Her delicate voice is jocular, her amusement barely disguised.

'Promise me, Francis, to answer me frankly.'

'Ask me any question you like, madam.'

'Have you been ordained a priest, yes or no?'

She reads the surprise in my eyes. Doesn't she see my mother every day? Don't they keep each other informed? Her smile broadens:

'I know, I know . . . But your mother is an inveterate prattler. One never knows quite what to believe, for her stories vary as often as her humours. When my dear husband was alive, he steadfastly refused any of the Jesuits' requests. But ever since . . . I have heard at least three tall tales of your exploits. The latest would have you employed as Cardinal Allen's secretary, and a familiar of the Pope.'

I smile at the thought.

'That does me too much honour, madam. I am one of the Cardinal's many personal valets. As for His Holiness, he once paid me a compliment on my organ playing. That hardly makes me his familiar.'

'And *are* you a priest?'

'No, madam. I went to Italy for music and not for religion. I have great esteem and affection for Cardinal Allen. But he knows that I am not drawn to the priesthood, and has never pushed me in that direction. Rather it was Father Parsons, the English College and my father, apparently, who sought to make an ecclesiastic of me, and no doubt a Jesuit, if possible.'

'And how are your relations with the Jesuits?'

'Distant. As are the Cardinal's, I might add.'

'Excellent. I am quite relieved, for I have not changed my views and wish to see no more Jesuits under this roof. You are perhaps aware that they tried to persuade my great-nephew, the Earl of Derby, to become engaged with a plot, the result of which would have seen him reign instead of Her Majesty. To that end, it was suggested he should convert to Catholicism. Being an honest man and lacking an appetite for such mad ventures, he denounced them. Now, eighteen months later, he has just died of an inexplicable malady. Such terrible things are said of the Jesuits, even among our own folk. I wish to see no more of them here. The only priest I will have is the one who comes to say Mass. I am no heroine. I see no reason to endanger our safety. We are English and we condemn those who have kept their allegiance to Spain. I must tell you they have just discovered the Queen's physician was secretly working for Spain. I do not believe he wished to poison Her Majesty, as has been claimed. And he was not Catholic but Jewish. But we must be prudent nevertheless. As long as we do not meddle in politics, we shall be left alone. Do not engage yourself in politics, is that clear? Needless to say, your mother considers me practically a heretic.'

'That is perfectly clear, madam. I will not meddle in politics. But I must go to see my parents, who do meddle in it, if I am not deceived.'

'If you give me your word that you will keep quite clear of their intrigues, I will see to it that the rumour goes about that you are merely performing your filial duty. You will be left in peace. Otherwise, you risk arrest for studying in foreign parts without the Queen's permission. At Southampton House, young Henry Wriothesley is keen to make your acquaintance; he is the same age as you. He is eager to show you what London has to offer in the way of entertainments and culture. Let him be your guide and do not engage in dubious machinations.'

I bow. She stands up, stretches her hand towards my cheek and I bend forward so that she can touch it: a gesture of unexpected gentleness. I am surprised to see she has tears in her eyes.

'Sir John loved you dearly, you know,' she says in a choked voice. 'You were his favourite.'

She makes an abrupt exit, leaving me quite affected.

I have no wish to recount my first visit to my father. It fades into insignificance alongside the rest of those few weeks. White-haired and bitter, my begetter saw me purely as his successor, and the only reason he had sent for me was to tell me that. It was obvious that I would carry the torch of *his* religion, or so he told everyone. When I made him understand that I intended to wed a Frenchwoman, he opposed it most vigorously, for it was equally obvious to him that if I was to marry at all, it would be to a young English Catholic girl, robbed of all her means by praemunire. Or, better yet, a Spanish one from a good family. He had several in mind. A Tregian does not wed a Frenchwoman about whom one knows nothing.

'But, Father, we know everything about her: she is a Troisville from Bordeaux. Her brother is the right-hand man and confidant of the King of France.'

'Has she means?'

'Not yet. But now that Henri has been crowned King, the family will assuredly become rich.'

'Is she Catholic?'

'Yes, Father.'

'So how is it that her brother serves a heretic?'

And so on and so forth. I shall omit the details. Even now, decades later, it irks me to think about it.

My father would have liked me to live in his apartments at the Fleet, which were of considerable size, and where my mother and sisters also lived, along with two valets and several maids, but I refused. The only sister I desired to see was Margaret but she was not there, so I made the acquaintance of the younger ones: Catherine, Sibyl and Elizabeth, the littlest, who was barely five years old. I also met a man who, I was told, would probably marry Margaret. His name was Benjamin Tichborne and he had a deceptively open look, thanks to which I took an instant dislike to him. He was plainly a machinator. I tried to tell my mother, when I finally met her: she spent her time dashing about London, busy with obscure tasks. She showed me a small vial of holy water.

'It took me a good while to find it, but we celebrated Easter as good Christians,' she said proudly.

She was outraged at my remarks concerning Margaret's suitor.

'He's a charming boy. Always obliging and most considerate. A good Catholic. And anyway, we cannot allow ourselves to be too particular. We have nothing, and if a man desires to wed one of your sisters without a dowry, we should not be difficult about it.'

There was an innocence about my mother which cut short the slightest urge to anger. She was even quite touching. Slight, very lively, with black hair and a beautiful face that was still young, she was carrying a child – her eighteenth, so she said. She was not far off giving birth, but that did not slow her one jot. She was wonderfully garrulous. Her world was her husband and her religion, nothing more. Her initial disapproval, the memory of which is etched into my mind, had disappeared. The word of law was now 'Whatever your father wishes', as she said, and no further argument was possible. He had chosen to defy authority and was right to do so. I was tempted to believe that if he had converted to the Church of England, she, the devoted spouse, would have found good reasons for him to do so.

I left them as soon as possible.

Over the next few days, I roam the London of my childhood, eyes and ears wide open this time. I plunge back into the symphony of noise, and the capital's characteristic odour: a mixture of burned wood, old fish, salt tang and dust. The season is particularly stormy and I return from some of these expeditions soaked to the skin, my horse plodding slowly through the driving rain.

I go to see Richard Mulcaster. He is no longer headmaster of Merchant Taylors' but lives by private tutoring and a small pension from the Queen, who loves him dearly.

'Ah, Francis!' he says, recognising me instantly. 'I am told you speak Latin to perfection.'

'I am very pleased to see you, sir,' I reply, caught unawares.

'But that goes without saying, my dear Tregian, that goes without saying. Otherwise, you wouldn't be here. Let us not waste time with manners. What of your brother?'

I tell him of Adrian's disappearance. He laughs.

'You don't seriously believe he's dead,' he comments, when I have finished. It is not a question.

'No.'

'Neither do I. I have rarely seen a man beguile everyone as much as that little boy. He'll surprise us one of these days. What do you intend for your London sojourn?'

'My dearest wish would be to see the Queen again. I have with me some scores that I copied just for her. Italian pieces only recently composed.'

'You didn't tell me that you knew the Queen.'

'Err – well . . .'

'Do you know the right people to ask?'

'I'm not really sure . . .'

'I have to see her tomorrow, as it happens. There is talk of giving me a new school. I will let her know of your presence. It will be quicker that way. Come back on Monday.'

And the following Monday:

'It's all set. Her Majesty says for you to attend Lord William Burghley's audience tomorrow. Have you already been to the theatre?'

'To the theatre? No.'

'Go there. The theatre is one of the best schools there is for a young gentleman. Don't listen to those who claim that actors are all cut-throats. The theatre is an incomparable school of deportment, wit, memory and courage, not to mention that the plays currently presented do full justice to the rhetorical richness of our wonderful English language.'

Lord Burghley greets me brusquely on finding me waiting in his ante-chamber the next day:

'Come, young man, you are expected.'

Once we are alone, he fixes me with his habitual, stony stare:

'The Queen trusts you,' he says.

Coming from him, it sounds like a reproach.

'I am highly honoured.'

'We have just foiled a plot to poison her and the earth is still fresh on the conspirators' graves.'

We are on dangerous ground. I keep my eyes lowered and say nothing.

'You have everything to commend you, even if you are His Eminence Cardinal Allen's personal valet . . .'

I look at him, surprised. Lord Burghley is smiling.

'We know that. We also know that you prefer to keep clear of intrigues.' His stiffness suddenly disappears. 'I would like to hear one of your pieces, before taking you to Her Majesty.'

I sit down at his virginal and play *Vestiva i colli*, one of Palestrina's madrigals adapted for the instrument. As I play, one of Burghley's men searches my coat, the inside of my hat and my roll of scores. I see him reflected in the varnished cabinet. It makes me smile. The honourable Lord Treasurer is taking no risks.

I finally find myself with the Queen. Ours is a discreet meeting, for the time has not yet come when the Queen of England can openly meet with a Tregian. My father is still an enemy of the State. Consequently, there is but a single lady-in-waiting and Robert Cecil, Lord William Burghley's son.

'Why, you still have no beard, sir!'

This is how the Queen greets me.

'No, Majesty. Nature has not desired it thus far.'

'So much the better. It suits you. And have you brought me some Italian music?'

She extends her hand, which I kiss, and into which I then place my roll of scores.

'Majesty, I have brought you some freshly written pieces.'

She bids me sit at her instrument and commands me to play. I do so.

When I have finished, Sir Robert and the lady-in-waiting applaud, but not the Queen. My heart is in my mouth. Have I displeased her?

'Sir,' she says, after a pause, 'your performance exceeds anything I have yet heard. You are an angel.'

She rises, approaches and obliges me to remain seated at the virginal – she herself doubtless plays standing up.

'Continue!' she commands.

I play. Everything I can think of. The reworkings of Italian madrigals I found in Luca's shop. My own versions of certain Masses. The English pieces that are regularly sent to me. I lose all sense of place; I forget the Queen. The instrument is quite marvellous, its keys seem to play my fingers, rather than the other way around. Rarely have I experienced that sense of communion with God himself, despite the many hours I spend each day at the virginal or at the organ.

Until this moment, I have never played *for* other people, but solely for my own pleasure. When finally I turn around, nobody applauds, but all stand looking at me in silence. I am just becoming aware that my performances tend to strike people dumb with emotion. Clearly it is an idea I will have to get used to.

'Before leaving, would you play *The Car-man's Whistle* for me?'

'I am sorry, Your Majesty, I do not know the piece. But if Your Majesty would do me the honour . . . ?' I indicate that she might play it herself.

'No, not now. But we shall get you a score.' And one of the ladies-in-waiting duly brings it.

'These variations were written by our mutual friend, William Byrd.'

This is my first opportunity to see one of those adaptations of popular melodies that are all the rage in London but quite unknown in Italy. I am conquered immediately. The refrain – the one the carters, or car-men, whistle to drive on their horses – is familiar to everyone, and many bawdy songs are sung to its tune, yet here it is rendered into a little melodic marvel, by the grace of William Byrd.

XVI

What is love? 'tis not hereafter;
Present mirth hath present laughter;
What's to come is still unsure:
In delay there lies no plenty;
Then come kiss me sweet and twenty,
Youth's a stuff will not endure.

'O MISTRESS MINE'
SONG FROM *TWELFTH NIGHT*
WILLIAM SHAKESPEARE / THOMAS MORLEY

I LEAVE THE PALACE and go to Southampton House in Holborn, near the Inns of Court, on the corner of Chancery Lane. The lawyers' district is a very lively place, full of inns and entertainments. Henry Wriothesley, Earl of Southampton, is waiting for me there. I have heard him spoken of as a cultivated man, generous to the point of extravagance. I am eager to meet him.

I discover a youth of my own age, with very pale grey eyes and a razor-sharp, incisive look. He has long blond hair which he wears swept around the nape of his neck and hanging forward over one shoulder. He is shorter than I (if the truth be known, almost everyone is shorter than I), with a girlish beauty. Like me, he is still beardless.

'Master Tregian, I have heard a great deal about you.'

'Not about me, sir, I think. You must have heard talk of my father.'

'And you are not to be confused?'

'Not really.'

He smiles at me for the first time.

'I'm told you play music – the lute?'

'No, sir. I play the virginal and the organ.'

'I have a virginal here. Be so good as to play me something. So that we may get to know one another. Please, go ahead.'

The order is given with such grace that I comply. But I am ill at ease. Playing is like breathing for me: a vital act. To think that others appreciate it as a mere pleasing entertainment!

Opening my eyes between two pieces, I see Southampton start up out of his armchair, his eyes wide, seized with evident delight. I stop and rise to my feet in turn.

Southampton rushes to embrace me.

'Extraordinary. You have the virtuosity of Bull and the sentiment of Byrd.'

'Byrd was my first master on the virginal and organ. I was but a small boy at the time.'

'You simply must meet Shakespeare. This very day!'

'Is he a musician, too?'

Wriothesley laughs.

'Clearly you have come from abroad. William Shakespeare is currently our most fashionable playwright. So much so that Lord Chamberlain Carey has adopted his troupe of players, and they are known officially as the Lord Chamberlain's Men.'

'And we shall see them today?'

'No, today we shall see the Earl of Pembroke's Men, but Shakespeare and his friends have all come from their ranks. I think they are playing *The Taming of the Shrew*. We have had no theatre for eighteen months, because of the plague. Now that the danger of contamination is passed, I will not miss a play at any price, and especially not a play of Shakespeare's. I've already seen this one, truth be told, but I should like you to see it too. And most of all I would like Will to hear you: he's a true connoisseur of fine playing.'

'I'd be interested to see the Lord Chamberlain's Men. After all, my family's money is keeping them, too.'

He stares at me for a moment, perplexed. Then he understands. It is well known, especially among Catholics, that the Tregians' property and estates have been seized and annexed by the Careys. Southampton laughs until he chokes.

'Indeed!' he says at length. 'Behold their true patrons, right here. We two!'

'Why, your family's . . . ?'

'No, I have undertaken to sponsor William Shakespeare, and he alone. He is a very great poet and a true gentleman. I feel the deepest affection for him. I envy his talent and his spontaneity. He is a kind of father to me, a friend too, the ideal companion, in short. One is never bored in his company. He has extraordinary energy and zest. The king of wordplay, whether he is about town or on the stage. And nothing escapes him.' He smiles, half mocking, half affectionate. 'Well, almost nothing.'

Only later shall I learn, from scraps of gossip, that Shakespeare – a married man and the father of three children – has fallen madly in love with a lady musician at court, a member of the Bassano family. The young woman had been Lord Chamberlain Carey's mistress (truly, the Careys are everywhere). Having got her with child, Carey married her off, as is the custom, to another musician at court, Alfonso Lanier. Her notoriety has done nothing to deter men from falling wildly in love with her, even fighting over her. And rumour has it that Southampton snatched her away from Shakespeare. The poet has taken their rivalry, it seems, as the subject matter for several of his plays.

But I'm getting ahead of myself. On that day, I had no knowledge of this, nor of Shakespeare the man. I watched his version of the classical story of Xanthippe with glee. I had read dozens of plays in Latin and Greek, and had seen one or two performed. But I had never attended a spectacle like this: such a delight to the eye and ear that every other sense is drawn in too. Southampton had described Shakespeare's verve and energy, but his talent is far beyond mere skill at wordplay. He crafts language like music, in a completely new way. Byrd's setting of *The Car-man's Whistle* played over and over in my mind as I watched. He had transformed the simple tale of a scold into a work of art. And he had done the same with our English vernacular.

Everyone present agreed that he is a great artist. Mulcaster, for one, was a devoted admirer, heaping praise on his name.

'He is the pride and honour of our native tongue. Greene, Marlowe and Watson did as much, but alas they are all dead now. The plague has carried off many great talents, these last two years. Long live Shakespeare, say I!'

I met the man himself after the performance. He had played the part of Gremio, one of the older, ousted suitors.

'He adores playing character parts,' Southampton had whispered, while a small ensemble played the prelude, a fantasia by Thomas Morley.

Once he has got himself out of his costume, wig and paint, I see that William Shakespeare is still a young man, though his already receding hair accentuates his high, domed forehead. His clear grey eyes are bright and quick with laughter, and his lips are full and well drawn. That he is such a convincing actor is doubtless due to his strikingly mobile and expressive features.

Southampton insists I play the virginal for Shakespeare, and my performance moves the poet beyond all reason. Only later, when I have been informed of the gossip, do I understand: my playing provokes thoughts of Emilia Lanier-Bassano, herself a virtuoso on the virginal.

The Southamptons are Catholics, and Henry's father has experienced the usual difficulties. But he died when his son was still a child. Wriothesley has had the good fortune to be made a ward and pupil of Lord Burghley, who has not – it seems – forced him to convert.

Henry attends Mass (I accompany him) but, despite the orders from Rome, he also attends the Church of England from time to time (I accompany him, too). Religion is the least of his concerns.

'I agree with the late lamented Marlowe,' he says:

> *I count religion but a childish toy,*
> *and hold there is no sin but ignorance.*

'He actually dared to write that, in *The Jew of Malta*.'

It is rumoured that Southampton House sheltered two Catholic priests, who lived there for eight years. The Dowager Countess tells me she is a friend of my mother, who visits often. A discreet reference to the many Masses spoken at the house, no doubt. Now, the Countess of Southampton is about to marry her second husband, the Queen's vice-chamberlain Sir Thomas Heneage, an Anglican.

'A timely move,' the whisperers comment. 'The Southamptons need protection now that the young Earl has gone against his guardian's wishes and refused to marry the young lady chosen for him.'

It was said, too, that the Queen was greatly displeased with Sir Thomas for marrying a Catholic. But I admit that with all this hearsay ringing in my ears, I was unable to distinguish between what was true and what was false. I had never heard so much gossip in all my life. Rome was hardly free of it, but among the prelates and their entourage it tended to be polite and discreet. Not so in London. Utter strangers would take you aside in a window-seat and cheerfully review the entire assembled company, and much of the rest of society, too.

I prefer not to imagine what was said about me.

'People are surprised you do not take a closer interest in women,' says Henry (being of the same age and rank, we now call one another by our Christian names). 'They wonder whether you prefer men. Fine and handsome as you are, with such extraordinary eyes, it's inconceivable that you should love no one, and there are many who would love you.'

I had heard rumours to the effect that the young Earl might prefer men himself. I had seen him retire with a young woman, and with a young man, too. I did not know what to think. From the way Henry framed his question, I understood: he was testing the terrain, with great delicacy. His personal beauty was indeed troubling. Even I felt it, who have never had a taste for men. And his openness and generosity in every gesture, every smile, his apparent purity of heart, despite the occasional flash of cunning, his ready accessibility to all, conferred on him an irresistible charm. Even Shakespeare, that indefatigable ladies' man, had succumbed to it.

This angelic youth invited confidences, an innocent smile playing at his lips, and I fought hard not to tell him everything. But I had to cut short the gossip and supposition.

'I do love a woman, indeed, with all my heart,' I told him. 'And I beg you not to ask me her name. I cannot tell you, for my own honour and hers. I should appreciate it, too, if the news did not reach my family.'

'You can depend on me,' he said, with a bow. I'm not sure he believed me.

'And you?' I asked, as if to return Wriothesley's polite interest.

'Oh, I . . . My family would like me to marry Lady Elizabeth Vere, the daughter of the late Earl of Oxford, and Lord Burghley's granddaughter. He is my guardian and has even managed to secure the promise of marriage. I know it would be an advantageous match. She is charming. But – how shall I say this, Francis – I am not ready to live with a woman. All around me, everyone marries according to their family's wishes, and then the husband goes his way and the wife hers. My mother tells me this is quite normal in married life. But I . . . I see the power of love. I see that it can lead to appalling tragedy, that the wisest men have lost their minds for love. Look at Shakespeare – Emilia Lanier has led him a fine dance: when it comes to her, he is like a child. I know all that, I see it, but I dream of a marriage of true minds, a woman who will fill my life with long years of happiness. Compared to that, all my wanton nights are mere lust in action. Nothing more.'

He confided in me quite spontaneously, with warmth and honesty. He expressed what we all dream of, but seldom put into words. I understood how Shakespeare had found inspiration in this young man. He was a stimulant, a revealer of truths.

IN THE ONRUSH of events, I have forgotten some important moments. I sent a letter to William Byrd, informing him of my presence in London and suggesting we meet: I wished to thank him in person for the many pieces of music he had sent me. Did we see each other during those weeks? I cannot remember now.

I do remember Thomas Morley, however.

As part of her marriage festivities, the Countess of Southampton attended the first performance of a play written especially for the occasion by Will Shakespeare, to be performed in the central courtyard at Southampton House. For days beforehand, the great space had been cluttered with strange objects and structures. Master Shakespeare appeared at regular intervals – bright and alert one minute, organising everything, firing off orders, then wandering and hesitant the next, staring about him absently.

'He's writing in his head,' said Henry, when we came across him one day, and he failed to acknowledge our presence.

Southampton House was a fine mansion, always full of people, but in the days preceding the Countess's marriage, it became a veritable fairground. Staff hired for the festivities swelled the house's already sizeable retinue of servants, and the guests – myself included – were without number. I was graciously invited to stay and avoid the constant journeying back and forth from Muswell.

Accustomed as I was to a spartan life, I had only one servant and one groom. Even these had been forced upon me by Lady Anne Arundell, who would have had me surrounded by a good half-dozen domestics if she had had her way:

'You are out in fine society: you must assume your rank. You cannot be taking care of your own wardrobe, for goodness' sake.'

'I have always done so.'

'In Rome, such behaviour may pass for virtue. Here, it will be taken as a sign of baseness.'

And true to say, with my two valets, I cut a modest figure. The bridegroom's sister had arrived with a retinue of forty attendants.

Henry, for his part, was waited upon constantly: there were his butler, his gentleman of the wardrobe, his chief groom, his bailiff, his barber, his falconer, his steward, and more besides; and each of these men had one or several servants under his command.

In the midst of such extreme agitation, Shakespeare worked as if he were entirely alone, never once losing his train of thought, even for a minute.

And so, one day, emerging from my apartment, which opened off the long gallery, I saw him in the courtyard below, deep in conversation with Thomas Morley, whom I recognised immediately. I ran downstairs and positioned myself nearby, waiting for them to finish their discussion. William Shakespeare was explaining what he required, gesturing vehemently:

'When Puck makes his entrance, there must be music to introduce a different dimension, another world, do you understand? Not the Christian afterlife, the realm of the dead, but an earthly paradise of pleasures and dreams. Do you see?'

'I see. You desire profane music that evokes the idea of paradise, but in no way refers to church-going. This borders on sacrilege . . . '

'Oh, Master Morley!'

'Very well, very well,' Morley wore his usual, somewhat wicked expression: 'I will say no more, my dear Master Shakespeare. We may only hope that the gentleman listening to us over there – long and lean like a day without music – does not give us away.'

He turned towards me and suddenly his expression was hard and ungracious. I stepped forward, profoundly embarrassed.

'Please excuse me, I had no intention of . . . '

Shakespeare had shot a worried glance in my direction. But he softened just as quickly.

'Master Tregian, our virtuoso!'

We all bowed to one another.

'Tregian?' Morley searched his memory. 'You remind me, sir . . . No . . . But yes! Impossible!'

'It is possible, sir. Francis and Adrian. Pupils of the Merchant Taylors'. I am Francis.'

He stared at me, saying nothing. I went on:

'We have not seen one another for ten years. You haven't changed a jot.' This was both true and false, for his face was much paler now.

'My "polyphonic greyhound"!' he declared at last. 'Well, goodness me!'

Shakespeare had other business to attend to, and made to leave.

'So, Master Morley, you've understood what I require?'

'Earthly paradise. Dum dum dum, de dum. Leave it to me. Or rather, bring me the poems you wish me to set to music.'

'Until tomorrow, gentlemen.'

Shakespeare bowed and hurriedly took his leave.

'Did I hear the word "virtuoso", or was he describing your virtuous nature?'

'Master Shakespeare is generous in his estimation . . .'

'Do you still play the organ?'

'Yes.'

'The lute?'

'Badly. I play the virginal.'

'Ah, perfect! Come along, there's one here. You can help me.'

We install ourselves at the instrument, and I play, brimming with apprehension. I may be a virtuoso player, but Morley is a true master. It is a relief when, far from going into raptures, he interrupts me:

'Your technique is extremely slovenly; you have acquired bad habits. Reposition your left hand, there.'

For what seems like an eternity, rather than helping him, I find myself on the receiving end of an exhaustive music lesson.

'Not bad,' he concedes at length. 'You have a decent grounding. It's not perfect yet, but you have done the instrument justice. When I have finished with *A Midsummer Night's Dream*, we shall go over this again.'

'Do you still teach?'

'In truth, I do not. I have been a Gentleman of the Chapel Royal for the past two years. It demands an extraordinary amount of time, but it is a lucrative substitute for teaching. And I am a publisher now, you know. At the moment, I am writing a treatise – a plain and easy introduction to practical music, for boys such as you and your brother once were. But enough of that. Here is the first of the poems to be set to music. How might we express it? "Dum! Da-da-da-dum! Dum dum dum, dum-dum."'

He seems to be waiting for me to play the music. I try it. He listens, leaning forward over the keys, his head cocked to one side.

'No,' he says at length. 'You have the fingers of an elf, I admit. But you do not have a composer's temperament. What you suggest is too . . . It's too mannered, yet too plain, all at once.'

He plays his own version standing up at the instrument. Straight away I understand what he means. I hear the difference: the melody is barely accompanied, but it emerges with a richness and purity I am for now incapable of creating.

'The overture and the intervals between the Acts are nothing. The most complicated things are the songs. Shakespeare never writes them until the very last minute. It's a miracle I have one here already. Let's get to work.'

And he sings, in a slightly rasping voice:

> *Over hill, over dale,*
> *Over park, over pale*
> *Through flood, through fire*
> *I do wander every where,*
> *Swifter than the moon's sphere*
> *And I serve the fairy queen,*
> *To dew her orbs upon the green.*
> *The cowslips tall her pensioners be:*
> *In their gold coats spots you see;*
> *Those be rubies, fairy favours,*
> *In those freckles live their savours.*

As he sings, he plays an accompaniment in canon, first with one, then two, and finally four parts. It is astonishingly beautiful. He pauses, takes out a pencil and a sheet of paper, makes notes.

'I must go,' he says finally. 'You may come, if you wish. Do you know Giles Farnaby?'

'Giles Farnaby?' I hadn't thought of my old friend for years. 'Of course! He often came to Clerkenwell.'

'Well he's coming to see me now, or rather my virginal. The instrument is in need of some attention, it hasn't been playing properly for days. Easier to restore it to the vigour of youth than its master, eh? Come along then.'

Giles Farnaby has grown to a solidly built man with broad shoulders, a shock of hair and a deep, booming voice. His smile is unchanged. We take up just where we had left off, as if uninterrupted by the intervening years.

'Master Francis, the man to whom I owe my present happiness,' he exclaims without hesitation, as soon as I enter the room. 'Without this man, I should never have had the idea of becoming an instrument maker.'

'I feel sure it would have occurred to you, Master Giles.'

'Perhaps, but allow me to credit you as my good fairy nonetheless!'

He lifts the lid of the virginal.

'Master Morley, each time I am amazed at how a great musician like yourself can treat the quills of your instrument so badly. They must be cut and trimmed with immense care!'

'Ah, Master Giles, you know I have no patience with such things. I have my valet cut them for me.'

'And he goes at it with a billhook.' Giles's voice is muffled by the instrument's case, into which he has poked his head; cutter in hand, he removes the jacks one by one in order to clean the quills.

He chats to us as he trims the tips.

I tell him my life's story and he tells me his. He is married and the father of two children. His daughter's name is Philadelphia, and he has a new baby son, called Richard. Like every industrious joiner, he makes tables and chairs, but his true passion lies elsewhere.

'Do you know I am a bachelor of music? I write psalms and sing them. And I belong to the Worshipful Company of Joiners and Ceilers. I make harpsichords and spinets, and virginals, which are my favourite.'

Thomas Morley and Giles Farnaby are both keenly interested in Italian music. I tell them about Palestrina, Orlando di Lasso, Luca Marenzio, Monteverde. They have heard of them all, except Monteverde.

'Yet he is by far the greatest, I assure you.'

'Here, sir, hold this. There's the last quill all properly cleaned and cut. Will you play us a piece by this Monteverde, then?'

I sit at the instrument and try to make up for the missing voices with my fingers. I play and sing a setting of a poem by Tasso, a piece that often moves me to tears:

> *Non si levava ancor l'alba novella,*
> *Nè spiegavan le piume*
> *Gl'augelli al novo lume,*
> *Ma fiammeggiava l'amorosa stella;*
> *Quand'i due vaghi*
> *E leggiadri amanti,*
> *Ch'una felice notte aggiunse insieme*
> *Com'acanto si volge in vari giri,*
> *Divise il nuovo raggio:*
> *E i dolci pianti*
> *Nell'accoglienz'estreme*
> *Mescolavan con baci e con sospiri.*

> *(The dawn was unbroken,*
> *And in the growing light the birds*
> *Had yet to spread their wings.*
> *But the loving star burned bright until,*
> *Betwixt the beauteous lovers,*
> *The new day entwined*
> *Like an enveloping vine,*
> *Mingling with their last embrace,*
> *Their soft sighs,*
> *Their tears and kisses.)*

They ask me for another, and another. They admire the music. They note it down.

Morley is a great admirer of Alfonso Ferrabosco the Elder, to whom he more or less attributes the invention of the madrigal form itself.

'The essential thing is for the music to have a life of its own, do you see? If you sing, there is no need to illustrate each word with a note. With musical notes, you can say things you cannot say with speech. This is exactly what Master Byrd and Master Alfonso do. They are so great that their memory will live as long as there is music. Byrd's variations and Ferrabosco's are the finest in the world, and we should count ourselves happy and fortunate to have been Master Byrd's pupils.'

Giles Farnaby settles himself at the instrument after me. Thomas Morley takes hold of a lute and we begin to play pieces for one another – *canzonette*, dances, madrigals. We barely notice the fading light, and then we have no desire to take our leave.

The Morleys' lackey runs to fetch Jack, my valet, who is waiting for me at The Bear nearby, and he takes our excuses to the Southamptons and Farnabys.

We part at first light, having sung and played all the night through. I note down the pieces written by my two friends and those by their best-loved composers – Bull, Dowland, Ferrabosco and others – and leave with my pockets stuffed full of music.

I reach the courtyard of Southampton House at dawn, cheerful and dishevelled, dragging my valet behind me like a man walking in his sleep. I find Henry awake.

'Ah, I knew you would succumb to the charms of an English lady, sooner or later!' he says, laughing out loud. 'Or was it an English man?' he adds quietly, with a wink.

'Two English ladies by the name of Euterpe and Terpsichore,' I inform him. And without waiting for a reply, I climb the two flights of stairs to bed, with my valet at my heels.

'Are you content, sir?'

'Very. Why?'

'Because you have the look of a man who has just won himself a piece of gold.'

IT MAY SEEM ODD that I should have discovered Messire de Montaigne's *Essays* in London, after so many years in France, but there it is.

One morning, as I sit alone in one of Southampton House's great rooms, reflecting that I will soon have to think about returning to Rome, I am approached by Henry's tutor, John Florio. Florio is Italian by birth and speaks French, Italian and English, all without the shadow of an accent.

He no longer teaches the young Earl but has remained in his retinue. He is older than us, though he hardly seems it, being so bright and energetic.

I had been thinking, with many a sigh, about the distance between Françoise and me. I would never have betrayed her, but though I have seldom mentioned it, I encounter ravishing beauties everywhere I go, and am often courted with enticing looks. More than once, I have been forced to call myself to order.

My reverie is disturbed by Florio, who is sitting in the armchair opposite mine. He is deep in thought, too. For a time, neither of us pays much attention to the other, but then he sighs in a low voice:

'How I should love to be in Bordeaux.'

Imagine my astonishment. My own thoughts are fixed on Bordeaux, at that very moment.

'And why is that?'

'Because it is the city of Messire de Montaigne. I should love to see the places where he has lived. Have you read his remarkable work?'

'No, to my shame. But I have the book with me here. I was given three brand-new volumes just as I was leaving France.'

'And when did you leave France?'

'Two or three weeks ago.'

He sits up straight in his chair.

'With a brand new copy?'

'Yes.'

'Published in what year?'

'Well . . . This year, I believe. Would you like to see it?'

'If I may be so bold . . . I should be delighted.'

I turn to Jack. My valet accompanies me everywhere, like my own shadow.

'Madam Catherine told me to stay with you even if you beat me,' he told me once, after I had tried several times to send him away, in the sharpest terms. 'She even gave me half a crown so that I would put up with your beatings patiently. Now sir, whatever you may do to me, I will not leave you.'

I have no desire to upset my grandmother and so say nothing about it. On the rare occasions when I call on Jack's services, he invariably comes running, his face breaking into a broad smile.

'Sir?'

'There are three books among my things, bearing the word . . . Can you read?'

'Oh, sir!'

'Three volumes bearing the word *Essays*. Bring them here.'

Jack fetches the books, and Florio seizes them straight away, eagerly turning the pages, reading the frontispiece aloud in perfect French:

> *Essais de messire Michel, seigneur de Montaigne! A Paris chez Abel Langelier, imprimeur ordinaire du roi. Edition augmentée d'un troisième livre et de six cents additions! Quinze cent quatre-vingt-huit!*

His voice rises in pitch with each new exclamation. The King's printer! A third volume, with six hundred new additions! In the year 1588!

'Oh, my dear Tregian, sir. My very dearest Tregian! Permit me to compare your copy with my own. I have an old edition, and I have heard, and now see, that Messire de Montaigne has made numerous corrections.'

He leafs through the pages delicately, carefully, as if handling a precious work of art.

> *C'est ici un livre de bonne foi, lecteur. Il t'avertit dès l'entrée . . .*
> Reader, you hold a book written in good faith, warning you here, on the threshold, that I have set myself no purpose beyond the domestic and private . . . In it, I wish to be seen in my own simple, natural, ordinary way, without controversy or artifice: because it is my own portrait that I paint, from the life. My faults will be read in it . . . had I been born to one of those nations said to be living still under the sweet liberty of the first laws of Nature, I assure you that I should happily have painted myself at full length, and stark naked.

'So beautifully put. Is it not?'

I have yet to open the book, but I am touched by its opening lines. Reluctantly, I leave him my three volumes. I think about them several times over the days that follow. And finally, not having seen Florio again, I send Jack to his lodgings to fetch them back.

I began my reading of the *Essays* one day in May, in the thirty-sixth year of the reign of Elizabeth, shortly after the wedding of the Countess of Southampton and following the enchanting performance of *A Midsummer Night's Dream*, which set its seal on those unforgettable days. I have never put them down since. Now, I know entire chapters off by heart. Others read the Bible; I read the *Essays* of Messire de Montaigne. They speak directly to my heart. No other book has done this, with the possible exception of a play Master Shakespeare was to write some years later. I am struck by the resemblance between Montaigne and Mulcaster. On education, on language, on religion, their utterances are the same. One is French, the other English. One is Catholic, the other Protestant, yet they speak in unison.

I read some of the most striking passages to Mulcaster:

> *We study only to fill up our memory, leaving our conscience and understanding empty . . . If our judgement be no more agile as a result, I had much rather the schoolboy spent his time playing tennis, for at least his body would be leaner and in better health. Do but observe him when he comes back from school, after fifteen or sixteen years of study; there is nothing so unfitted for useful work; all he may be seen to have acquired is greater self-love and swagger than when he left home, thanks to his Latin and Greek. He should return with a soul filled with good things, but instead, it is merely puffed up, engorged but not enlarged.*

Master Mulcaster listened, rubbing his hands in glee, a smile on his lips.

'Wonderful. The work is a great success, I hope?'

'I believe so. This is already the third or fourth edition.'

'And Messire de Montaigne himself?'

'Dead, two or three years ago.'

'The great thing, when a man becomes a teacher and acquits himself well at his task, is that he never truly dies. A good master will always live on in his pupils.'

'You may count on me for that, so long as I live, sir.'

'You and all the others. You are my passport to immortality.'

XVII

As I went to Walsingham,
To the Shrine with speed
Met with a jolly palmer
In a pilgrim's weed.
Now God save you jolly palmer!
Welcome lady gay,
Oft have I sued to thee for love,
Oft have I said you nay.

'WALSINGHAM'
POPULAR BALLAD

FROM TIME TO TIME I would visit the Fleet. It was another world, where the only talk was of the Catholic faith and its re-establishment by the King of Spain.

I understood now how Cardinal Allen could so firmly believe that two-thirds of the English were crypto-Catholics, for the Queen was surrounded by a surprising number of 'papists', out of all proportion to the number of Catholics in the land. It may not have been two-thirds, but my mother was right to claim that as many Masses were said at the English court as at the royal court of any country on the Continent.

It must be said that Catholics were nowhere so safe as at court. This I observed with my own eyes. In consorting with the Earl of Southampton, I enjoyed the same protection as he. And I saw that the way to stay out of trouble was to avoid politics. Provided a man kept his beliefs to himself and refrained from voicing a desire to see a Catholic King on the throne, nobody interfered. My father had not understood this, which was why he found himself with his back to the wall.

There was a bowling green in the Fleet gardens, where the Catholics met and debated vigorously as they played. They made my head ache with their litany of cruelties committed against Catholics by the 'heretics'. One does not excuse the other, but the Inquisition tortured heretics too, and burned them alive, Protestants first and foremost.

My twenty-year-old head span with all this, but I said nothing, for I bestrode two worlds. Deep down, I shared Marlowe's and Southampton's view: there is no sin but ignorance.

My father was most troubled because Abbot Cornelius had been arrested just when I was preparing to leave. He turned pale every time Phillips brought him a message.

I saw Benjamin Tichborne again, the fellow who was to marry my sister Margaret, and was told that he was a good boy whose cousin had wed my sister Mary – but what did I know if my sister Mary had made a successful marriage? Decidedly, there was something about this Tichborne that offended me. And then there was Charles de Troisville, who might still love my sister; I would have to warn him. To my great regret, I never saw Margaret herself, for she was staying with Mary.

Phillips was as busy as ever, coming and going from the Fleet, where there were about thirty Catholic families and which, paradoxically, drew many Jesuits, come to confer with my father.

They were all a little wary of me and never discussed their business in my presence, restricting themselves to very general declarations when I was there. This was a relief, and it proved the absurdity of the situation, for even among Catholics we were split into two camps, the Jesuits (including my father) and the non-Jesuits, the so-called secular priests, who were less arrogant and less conspicuous. Increasingly, voices were heard from both this latter camp and the wider Catholic laity, demanding that Rome be less inflexible. They would have liked to swear allegiance to the English Crown while also adhering to their faith. In truth, that was all anyone demanded of them, and Southampton was the living example of it. But Rome wouldn't budge, chiefly because of the pressure applied by Spain and the Jesuits. Elizabeth was a usurper and therefore unworthy of fealty. Consequently, attitudes in London hardened.

'My son,' said my father solemnly, 'you will soon reach your majority. I would like to give you enjoyment of all our family's means, which are considerable, but circumstances have wished otherwise. God has demanded a great sacrifice of us, and in order not to profane His house, we have had to abandon our terrestrial goods. Our enemies enjoy our revenues without scruple. Be proud to be poor: it is for the good cause, and never forget that you are a Tregian, a Catholic, one of Christ's soldiers. Come, let me bless you.'

I knelt. He placed a hand on my head and appealed to the Lord.

'Amen,' I concluded, between gritted teeth.

'I would like you to go to Spain, my son, and take a message to His Most Catholic Majesty, whom we all revere and who will show you his gratitude.'

'My father, I am truly sorry, but I promised Cardinal Allen to return as quickly as possible and I have tarried for too long already. Several of us are busy with a complete revision of the Douai Bible, and the Cardinal insisted I return soon to continue my work on it. There is also his failing health; he needs his entire retinue.'

I persuaded my father, in the end, and he found somebody else to go to Spain.

During my stay, I hardly saw Giuliano, who had taken his role of steward most seriously and had set off to enquire after my various interests. Jack informed me that he had returned to Muswell several days before, and there I went after seeing my father. It seemed to me that the sun failed to shine a single day that year, and it was raining again as I rode slowly up Crouch Hill thinking about what my father had just told me:

'You shall be heir to all of the estates one day. If it were to cost you your soul, then better to lose everything. But it is your duty to yourself, your sisters and brothers, and to your descendants, to make every attempt to recover them. Promise me – promise your ancestors – that when the time is ripe, you will do all you can to reclaim the title of Lord of Wolvedon and the lands of your forebears.'

In a flash I fancied I saw Jane Wolvedon's eyes.

'I promise you, father.'

At Muswell, my grandmother addressed me in a peremptory tone:

'There is no question of your departing by yourself. Jack will accompany you, along with the groom Joseph.'

'That's impossible, madam. I'm living off charity in Rome.'

'I am not asking you to pay them; I will cover that.'

'But their board and lodging, I wouldn't know how to . . . '

'Don't be as stubborn as your father. I am not your mother and will not yield to a Tregian's whimsy. I have said that you shall not depart like a ragamuffin, and I will not be argued with.'

'Madam, if I really must, then I agree to take Jack, but I have no need of a groom. In Rome, I don't even have my own horse.'

'That is nothing for a grandson of the Baron of Arundell and the Earl of Derby to boast about.'

We reached a compromise: she kept the groom and I took Jack, who needed no encouragement. Naturally, he would also take care of my horse as required. Naturally, he would be devoted to me, body and soul. Naturally, I would be served like a king. Jack had such clownish qualities, I should have handed him straight to Master Shakespeare, but if I were to have a valet at all, I had rather it were him. Lady Anne had not chosen him by chance. This peasant lad from Muswell was as alert and trusty as he was droll.

We were not out of London yet when Giuliano and I placed ourselves either side of Jack and spoke to him:

'Jack, you now serve Master Tregian.'

'Assuredly, sir.'

'My happiness is your own.'

'Assuredly, sir!'

'So your loyalty is to him, and you report to nobody but him.'

'But, that goes without saying, sir.' He was worried now.

'How would I know that you aren't a spy?'

'A spy? Me? And for whom?'

'Oh, there are a thousand possibilities. Lord Burghley. Sir Topcliffe. Father Parsons. And so forth.'

He gave a nervous laugh.

'Sir, I know none of those gentlemen, and I swear on my soul that from this day forth I shall have no master but you. I will report to you alone, and as far as all those who might question me are concerned, I know nothing of your affairs. I can play the idiot as well as any man.'

I left London with a heavy heart. It had not been possible for me to take leave of the Queen. Lord Burghley was unwell and so had me received, albeit discreetly, by his son Robert, a charming man – short and hunchbacked, with an intelligent glint in his eye.

'Master Tregian, Her Majesty holds you in affection.'

'I thank you, sir.'

'Yours is an unstable, dangerous life.'

'Yes, sir.'

'May I offer you my support?'

'I prefer your affection, sir. I do not wish to feel I have been bought.'

He laughed.

'You already have my affection, Master Tregian. Return whenever you wish. I shall not forget you.'

I tore myself away from Southampton House and its merry company, from Thomas Morley and Giles Farnaby too, with whom I had spent so many long nights making music. Where would I find such entertainment and glad company now? Thomas Morley was a great believer in writing things down and he advised me to keep a 'common book', a personal collection of scores.

'You'll lose that humble-jumble of papers and little notebooks you carry around with you.'

I adopted his idea, procured myself the necessary materials and began immediately, copying only the pieces I could play on the organ and the virginal, and for which I needed no accompaniment. I must say that Morley and Farnaby had filled my head with so many melodies that I would not have remembered them all had I not set them down.

I began my collection with some of Bull's superb reworkings of *Walsingham*, a ballad we had sung when we were children:

> As ye came from the Holy Land of Walsingham
> Met you not with my true love by the way as you came?
> How should I know your true love that have met many a one,
> As I came from the Holy Land, that have come, that have gone.

OUR LITTLE COMPANY SPENT the first night of our journey at the Mermaid Inn in Salisbury. Jack and Kees, Giuliano's valet, ate and drank in a corner of the main room. Giuliano and I sat in a private room and were served what I have always considered a quintessentially

English meal. There were meats in abundance, sauces of every kind, pancakes and baked apples, washed down with the Mermaid's delicious ale: everything to appal an Italian. I pushed the food around my bowl, lost in thought.

'You should eat, instead of sifting all those gloomy thoughts in your head.'

Giuliano was thirty-five, still had a head of black curls and only the merest glint of silver in his short beard. His agility and good humour were intact, and the few wrinkles round his eyes only served to strengthen the feeling he had always conveyed: that when he was there, no trouble would befall me, and all problems would be solved by his capable hands. I had grown so used to consulting him about everything from boyhood on that he had become a brother, father and companion to me, all at once. Strictly speaking, he was my servant, as was Jane, who had been my nurse, but I never grew accustomed to seeing them in that light. They were both children of great lords, and you could see it in their bearing.

'So you're fasting, are you?'

Giuliano's words tug me back to reality.

'No, no. I was wondering what I would do without you.'

'You would live. A little less comfortably, perhaps. Talking of which, I have undertaken some enquiries. You know that your father is not quite as impoverished as people say.'

'My father? How so?'

'Firstly, praemunire orders the seizure of two-thirds of your estates, not the entirety.'

'Right, and ... ?'

'Everything your family owned in Cornwall has been sequestered.' He left a dramatic pause. 'Except that the Tregians also have estates in Devon and Dorset.'

'Ah? A third?'

'Not quite, more like a quarter or a fifth, according to my information. It would be possible to bring a case against George Carey to force him to return the excess seizures. But given your father's fervently papist attitude, in which he is quite resolute, it would be a waste of time in my view. I must say, poor devil that I am, it is strange to see how much your father has lost interest in his affairs. Your grandmother Catherine fought tooth and nail until her dying breath to recover her pension of sixty pounds. Your father, however, lets hundreds of pounds a year be stolen from him without batting an eye.'

'He has no head for business.'

'To say the least. Just imagine: your grandfather John not only doubled the family fortune but succeeded in living peacefully under Henry VIII, his Protestant son Edward VI, Mary the Catholic and finally Elizabeth, a period of nearly twenty years. He not only had a head for business, but also a subtle way in his dealings with others. Then he died, his son took over, and disaster followed shortly thereafter.'

We look at one another, sigh and shrug in unison. My bed is made; now I must lie in it.

Two days later, the notary solemnly hands me the title to the property Thomas had left me. It has been drawn up in such a way that it would be practically impossible to dispossess me of it. The estate is called Tregellas, like Thomas himself.

We spend one night in the house which holds so many memories for me. Two servants and the family of the tenant farmer maintain the place as if I might return to live there any day. They call me Master Francis as if they had known me for years, and they speak of me as 'Master Tregellas the Younger'. The beds are made up, the rooms are aired and scrupulously clean. The temptation to stay makes me dizzy.

Still, we bid farewell to England the following day, on the dawn tide.

I have never regretted leaving so much as I did that morning. Over those last few weeks, I lived in a world that was my own. I was no visitor but felt at home for the first time in a very long while.

THE FIRST THING THAT strikes me when I see the Cardinal is his cadaverous face.

Nicholas Fitzherbert, Roger Bayns, William Warmington and Nicholas Bawden are there too. We are soon engrossed in one of those discussions of which the Cardinal is particularly fond.

I hardly pay attention to his words, so fixed am I on his sunken eyes, deep as wells. He is close to death.

The next day, I take up my work on the Bible again. Titus, Giuliano's nephew, remains in the kitchens, just in case.

'I've done my best, but I reckon they've changed the poison, or the method.'

Titus has told no one, of course, but to my great amazement, rumour is rife that an attempt has been made to poison the Cardinal. At first I think this might help us – surely it will protect Allen if everybody suspects something. Finally, though, I understand the talk must be a stratagem: a connection has been observed between my presence and Allen's state of health, and fearing I might say something, the plotters have preferred to spread a controlled rumour. If things now take a bad turn, I can always be accused of being the poisoner myself.

Meanwhile, whether by poison or by sickness, the Cardinal's health grows visibly worse.

I am on duty one evening. It is very hot and I have opened my doublet to breathe easier. Suddenly, the Cardinal is standing before me – I hadn't even heard him approach.

I stand, bow, mutter an apology and button up.

'Call for some men to accompany us; I would like to take a walk with you.'

Once outside, he speaks to me first about King Henri IV, whom he calls 'that Navarre'. He has done all he could to persuade Pope Clement to refuse the French king's conversion. He has written, pleaded, made speeches; he is convinced 'that Navarre' will do as Henry VIII of England had done, and that France will follow England's fall into heresy. Allen feels that the French throne would be better with any other prince on it than a Bourbon.

I do not reply and succeed in holding back a certain irritation. After all, he is talking of a man who has been a friend to me. I try to think about something else.

A change in his tone of voice pulls me back to the present moment.

'You know, the work you're undertaking on the Bible is most precious. You are extremely able, and your mastery of Latin and rhetoric is exceptional.'

I bow in silence. In the half-light of dusk, his eyes bore into me.

'I have always wondered why you never assented to your father's wish that you take Holy Orders.'

Now I am on the alert. It is rare for the Cardinal to ask such a direct, personal question.

'But, Your Eminence ... How to put it ... When the idea was proposed, I had already chosen another path. And I still hope to manage my family's estates one day.'

'Let me be plain, Master Tregian: what do you think of the Catholic religion?'

Alarm bells ring in my head. This man can send me to the Inquisition at any time. Perhaps he has drawn me out of the house just to have me arrested discreetly.

'Your Eminence!'

'Oh, I can see very well how devoted you are to me, and that you watch over me with filial care. They tried to get me to believe you were poisoning me, little by little, but I know that's impossible.'

'Your Eminence!'

This time, I fall to my knees before him, my cheeks wet with the tears that come pouring now, unchecked.

'Your Eminence, I love you like a father!'

He bids me stand up.

'My son, you don't waste time with excuses; I like that. I sometimes worry about your piety, for you are most discreet in all matters except when you sit down to play music. But I have never doubted your loyalty. And I have noticed your concern for me.'

I struggle to remain silent.

'You know, don't you, that attempts have been made to poison me?'

'Your Eminence, I assure you ... '

A silence.

'So, you will tell me nothing; that is most politic of you. Byas thinks that if I am being poisoned, then it is with the water I drink at the Vatican Library. So he always pours it for me after fetching it himself. That has not prevented me from falling sick. But perhaps I owe my ill health to God's will rather than to poison.'

'I wish you long life, Your Eminence, and I beg you to use me as you see fit.'

'As long as I don't wish to make a priest of you, isn't that so? No, no, protest not. But I regret it. You are a gifted orator. What a preacher you would have made!'

We walk home through the dark.

Now that I know John Byas is aware of the poisoning, I am able to share the duty of protecting the Cardinal with him. Titus continues to watch over the kitchens. None of it is any use.

The Cardinal is soon confined to bed. In October 1594, he dies.

All of us are around his bed. We hear the churches of Rome ringing Matins. The Jesuits, led by Alfonso Agazzari, have attempted to block our admittance to his chamber, but the Cardinal has interceded with unsuspected energy. Once he has perceived that he is doomed, and in spite of his terrible pain, he sets about dictating letters to the great and good of this world. He writes to the Pope to warn him against false friends, to the King of Spain to request forgiveness for the errors committed in his service. Father Champion and Father Ingram, whom he knows well, have been hanged in England over the summer. He prays for them to intercede so that God might welcome him to Heaven.

'My greatest sorrow is to have been responsible for sending so many to prison, to persecution and death. May God have mercy!'

We approach him one by one, and he gives us his blessing.

When I kneel by his bed, he takes my chin and pulls my head towards him.

'Leave immediately, you are in danger,' he whispers to me. Then he kisses my forehead. 'They know that you endeavoured to save me. *'Ego te benedico . . . '* – and he traces a cross on my forehead.

Father Warmington says Mass at the foot of the bed. The Cardinal expires shortly after the Communion, his face serene and free of pain.

I WOULD HAVE LEFT within the hour, had the decision been mine. But the repercussions of Allen's death echoed throughout Rome and would soon reach Spain and England. Allen had been in conflict with the Jesuits, but, apart from a few among them, everyone loved the Cardinal, whose greatest gift was perhaps that he knew how to kindle devotion.

He was barely cold, and still lying in the chapel of the English College, as he had requested, yet the fight to succeed him was already under way.

The new Cardinal must be English. There was no written law to that effect, but the King of Spain wished it. All that was lacking was a man capable of filling the position.

Nobody desired to give the funeral oration. For two days I watched the deliberations, distanced from them like a spectator at a play. It had nothing to do with me, and I was already wondering whether to halt my journey at Mantua to attempt to meet the great Monteverde, when Gabriel Allen, the Cardinal's elder brother, came to find me. He lived in Rome, along with other members of the Allen family, but I had rarely seen him and only ever from afar: we didn't really know each other.

'Master Tregian,' said Gabriel, 'the Cardinal loved you dearly and held your mastery of Latin in special admiration. I think he would have wished you to give the funeral oration.'

'Me?'

Nobody wished to accept the task – a single word out of place could prove highly dangerous in these fickle times.

'Not only do you speak Latin as if it were a living tongue but you are an excellent orator.'

'I thank you, sir, but it is too weighty an honour. And since the funeral is tomorrow, how would I . . . ?'

'I shall assist you. Nicholas Fitzherbert has said he is also ready to work with us. We would not wish to leave this oration to the Jesuits of the English College.'

There was a steely determination in his usually kind face. Given the position I was in, there was no more risk in delivering the speech than there was in keeping quiet.

'I accept. But let's set to work immediately.' I sent Jack to fetch Nicholas and some writing supplies.

'And something to eat and drink while you're at it. We'll be working all night.'

'Very well, sir.'

Jack had settled so happily in Rome you would think it was but three leagues from Muswell. In just a few months, he spoke the language quite intelligibly and was perfectly at home. He soon returned with quills, paper, penknives, sand, ink, wine, bread and cheese; and was followed closely by Nicholas Fitzherbert.

'Don't you wish to give this funeral oration yourself? You attended the Cardinal for nearly ten years and knew him better than anyone.'

'I am an execrable orator. But I write well. I see you have everything we need.'

We sat down, discussed the matter and, after several failed attempts, we finally began to compose the *Oratio funebris*.

> *Utinam intra unius aulae provatos parietes se contineret causa doloris!* ...

We recounted the life of William Allen. I agreed with what I was to say, despite my reservations: the Cardinal had been a kind man, incapable of meanness, one who never served his own interests. Even when he was ready to deliver England to Philip II of Spain, it had been for the greater glory of God, and he had never understood how he might be accused of treason. He never doubted for a moment that, once the country had returned to Catholicism, the King of Spain would withdraw and leave it to the English. Eloquent, subtle in his dealings with others, replete with knowledge and generous too, I had tears in my eyes as I listed his qualities. I am sure that God welcomed him with open arms.

We finish as dawn is breaking. I just have time to change my clothes.

'What are your plans, Master Tregian?' asks Gabriel.

'To leave, sir.'

'That's good. It was the Cardinal's wish. Here's a pass so you may leave Rome without hindrance. Don't tarry. We shall cover your departure as long as we can.'

Jack has spent all night trimming quills and dipping them in ink, but is as alert as ever.

'Jack, do you have the strength to prepare our baggage?'

'Our baggage, sir? To go where?'

'To leave Rome before I am poisoned, or someone picks a quarrel with me, or my horse makes a lethal stumble, or I don't know what ... '

'Ah, I see, sir. As soon as you get out of the church?'

'Yes, as soon as I get out of the church. We have a pass. And let's not take too much baggage, so we aren't noticed. Leave whatever you like except my music.'

'Very well, sir.'

The church of the Trinità, adjoining the English College, is full of cardinals, ambassadors – the Spanish ambassador has pride of place – and priests, as well as many lay-people. It is a solemn ceremony.

I try to construct my pronouncement of the *Oratio funebris* as one would compose a song in three voices, with one voice questioning, a second answering and a third commenting.

' . . . *Quid multa? Haec suprema vox – oportet meliora tempora non expectare, sed facere – ita alte in Cardinalium . . .* ' and so on. *Ours is not to wait for better times, but to provoke them.* This notion of the Cardinal's, told me by Nicholas, and which I share with the audience, seems to be dictating my course of action. I must take my life into my own hands.

That very evening, Jack and I go to sleep in an inn beside Lake Trasimeno, on the way to Mantua.

BOOK II

Between Earth and Heaven

Heaven and earth and all that hear me plain
Do well perceive what care doth cause me cry,
Save you alone to whom I cry in vain,
'Mercy, madam, alas, I die, I die!'
. . .
A better proof I see that ye would have
How I am dead. Therefore when ye hear tell,
Believe it not although ye see my grave,
Cruel, unkind! I say, 'Farewell, farewell!'

'HEAVEN AND EARTH'
THOMAS WYATT / FRANCIS TREGIAN
'SONGS' XCVII

Notwithstanding the time of two yeares mensioned in
the deede within writen of the cutting of... wood
granted by me unto Thomas Tregian and his assignes
... I doe now hearby give him and
his assignes the same libertie... of
the saide... and carying away the same...
times, limet... the... yeares... of
shall be in the yeare... one thousand
six hundreth and fourteene.

Francis Tregian

Document in the hand of Francis Tregian
(agreement of sale for a plot of forest, 18th March 1610)

I

Come up to my window, love, come, come, come,
Come to my window, my dear;
The wind nor the rain
Shall trouble thee again,
But thou shalt be lodged here.

'GO FROM MY WINDOW'
POPULAR BALLAD
THOMAS MORLEY

THE FIRST SIGNS OF SPRING are here; the first buds peeking out.

I interrupted the story of my life some time ago, beset by a deep crisis of faith in my undertaking.

What does it matter, I suddenly told myself, if I went to Mantua and met Monteverde? If I went to Amsterdam, to Brussels, if I went to Antwerp? Simply put, what does it matter how I lived once I attained my majority? In the grey damp of February, I resolved to write nothing more, and then the unexpected happened.

I fell ill.

This is a rare occurrence for us Tregians. My father survived the worst treatment in prison and my mother gave birth to some twenty children – the last when she was over forty – and yet no one would have thought it, to look at her. As for me, I can't have spent more than twenty days ill in bed in all my life, and any fevers I suffered were the result of wounds. I lived through several plague epidemics unscathed. But sickness laid me low this time.

They told me I'd caught a cold, but I scoff at that. I have always been impervious to bad weather. Sometimes I think it was the idea of reliving through my pen the next chapters in my Tregian life that unbalanced my humours and provoked the fever.

Unaccustomed as I was to illness, I did everything contrary to what sick men usually do and, just as when I was wounded, this helped me recover very quickly. By the third Thursday in Lent, I was back on my feet.

My feverish deliriums and dreams were full of the faces I have evoked thus far, in describing a life I originally thought to recount in a few pages, a few days. Yet by the time I rose from my sickbed, I had all but forgotten about my writing.

Imperceptibly, though, it returned to haunt me, nagging at my conscience. I began to feel remorse. And so, after a walk of several hours on that suddenly mild Sunday, I saw I had no choice: if I failed to complete my story, my life would end without that final chord the echo of which prolongs a melody's enjoyment for listener and musician alike.

WE ARRIVED IN HOLLAND one cold evening in late November. The last few days of our journey we had spent struggling against a violent wind that shook houses, bent over trees and made our horses snort.

We had stayed in Mantua just long enough to meet Monteverde, with whom I struck up an immediate friendship. He was six or seven years older than me, almost as tall, quite as thin and quite as passionate about music. I felt him to be a kindred spirit as soon as we met, and I believe the feeling was mutual. Our meeting was a precursor to one of the great revelations of my life.

Over the previous two or three years, I'd been told I was an exceptionally skilled musician. People saw it as my calling. Music took up a large part of my time and, even when travelling, I never missed an opportunity to stretch my fingers over the keys if I found myself in front of an instrument. I took scores everywhere with me, and if I couldn't play, I would read them to myself. I was even criticised for my diligence:

'A gentleman should not make a show of his musical abilities, except in private and when he is at leisure, nor should he neglect more important occupations,' I was told.

But I remained unaffected by such comments. They may as well have been directed at somebody else, for I pursued all of my musical activities heedless to the chorus of objections. I needed music to survive, as a man needs his daily bread. Catholic gentleman that I was, I saw myself as a failure for my inability to perform the preaching expected of me, preferring music to a life of idle religious fervour. According to the general use of the term, I understood a musician to be above all a composer. But I considered most of my compositions to be so bad – or worse, so ordinary – that I regularly threw them on the fire. In short, I thought I was a good-for-nothing.

So what revelations did I draw from those few days with Monteverde? That music was the centre of my life and that nothing else truly interested me. All the energy I might have poured into the administration of my Cornish estates was diverted into my music. This happened quite unawares: I remained deaf to the comments of my companions, only noticing them once I was in Mantua.

To my great surprise, Claudio Monteverde was not accorded the reverence due to a master. He played the viol most excellently and sang to perfection. But his compositions were sublime and remain so today. The second edition of his *Third Book of Madrigals* had just been published. A musician whose name escapes me spent an infinite amount of time attempting to prove to me the 'faults' of composition contained therein. When he finally saw that I considered these 'faults' to be bold flourishes of incomparable beauty, true proof of Monteverde's talent, he declared drily:

'This is what happens when one attempts to make music without having the necessary theoretical foundations. Neither yourself nor Signor Monteverde has the slightest idea of the most elementary rules of this art.'

I would have liked to point out that it was the beauty of the result that counted, but his purplish complexion made me fearful for his health: I decided not to add blasphemy to sacrilege and find myself with a death by apoplexy on my conscience.

Mantua was home to several other interesting musicians, such as Giaches De Wert, the *maestro di cappella*, whom Monteverde introduced to me as his master, or Benedetto Pallavicino who, like De Wert and Monteverde, wrote the most marvellous madrigals.

I had the opportunity of hearing all three of them during one of the Friday concerts they gave at the palace of Duke Vincenzo Gonzaga. It took place in the Hall of Mirrors, in the afternoon, after the card games. Once the music began, it seemed to go on forever. They sang madrigals and played melodies, and the trills, cadences and *passaggi* filled me with delight. Adriana Basile and Caterinuccia Martinelli, famous singers at the court, displayed quite astonishing skill. I recall one particular madrigal of Monteverde's, in four voices, that began with *S'andasse amor a caccia*, constructed very much like a canon and to an almost military rhythm. The feeling of the hunt, with all its excitement, was marvellously conveyed; I had only to close my eyes as I listened to imagine myself and Sir John hunting with falcons or to feel I was galloping off to see Françoise.

When I returned to my senses after such moments of happiness, I saw that the effect had been achieved by a cunning mixture of declamatory passages, chromatic modulation and dissonance; 'faults' according to that shortsighted theorist whose name I still don't recall. I saw the mastery with which Monteverde stimulated a whole range of emotions that coalesced and commingled, transforming both themselves and the listener in just a few lines, a few moments. In the same concert, we also heard some madrigals by De Wert that were as accomplished in emotion as Monteverde's. Yet you could tell the difference between their two musical styles. De Wert was more 'literary', Monteverde more 'musical'. De Wert's chief concern was the words. The insistent emphasis of the recitative mattered more to him than the shape of his music. Monteverde took quite the opposite approach, crafting his music to express the words, seeking literary equivalence through the notes; the words were only important in so far as they inspired him to find musical textures and forms. As for Pallavicino, he was yet to compose the madrigals that so overwhelmed me when I heard them years later. His works were beautiful but followed a traditional style. The decisive moment for me occurred after the second and last of these concerts that I attended.

I had made an appointment to see Monteverde and play him some pieces by English composers he didn't know, including Byrd and Morley, but whose music he was curious to hear. He did me the honour of declaring himself 'transported' as much by my skill as by the pieces I played him.

'I would so love,' I replied, 'to be able to express my own feelings more palpably . . .'

'But your soul was there in your fingers.'

'I am flattered but still, I regret that I lack your talent for composition.'

'My dear friend, a skilled musician is as necessary to a composer as water is to a plant, and indeed as a composer is to a musician. Without composers, you would be nothing. But what would we be without you? What use would there be in my producing these chromatic, dissonant pieces you love so much, if nobody knew how to sing them? Without anyone to play them, they would sink into obscurity. You are the candle that illuminates the night. Without you, nobody would see anything in the darkness. You consume yourself and disappear, it's true, for music cannot be retained. Play a note – and already it is fading into the past. But time is the stuff music is made of, and it is through you that the Creator gives us a crystallised measure of it.'

From that day forth, I no longer considered music my passion but my profession, one which those wise words imbued with a sense of dignity, necessity and urgency that has never left me.

I didn't linger at the Court of Mantua, for I was eager to see Françoise again, Jane and Giuliano too, not forgetting the Queen's banker. In short, I was eager to be in Amsterdam.

I could write an entire discourse on the musical aspects of my brief stay. It was in Mantua that I became aware of what I dare to call my vocation. Monteverde conversed with me as a musical equal, treating me to a zealous explanation of his *seconda pratica*, an entirely new and original way of seeing music freed of its traditional constraints. In the course of our long discussions, I understood that my inability to compose mattered not the least.

I was a musician.

I left Mantua in a state of great exaltation. We were unencumbered by baggage, for all my gear was packed in my saddlebags and in a portmanteau that Jack insisted on placing on top of his own, despite my protests:

'You are absurdly laden, while I have practically nothing.'

'I am your servant, Master, and care of your baggage falls to me. You are ill-acquainted with your prerogatives as master, if I may be so bold.'

'All right, all right. Tell me, is that a viol you're carrying over your shoulder?'

'It is, Master.'

'I have never seen you play the viol.'

'I only play a little, Master. Unfortunately, I don't know how to read the notes and so I have to pick up melodies by ear as best I can. But I told myself that as valet to a gentleman musician, well . . . '

'You've never played an instrument?'

'Not really. Everyone sings where I come from, although one of my brothers plays the lute. I used to work for a spice merchant who never gave me leisure for anything. But I have begun to like music since being in your service. After hearing you practise the same piece a hundred times, I finally said to myself . . . That's why I accepted this gift of a viol. If you permit me, I will practise my viol when you practise your virginal.'

'Indeed. I shall even teach you to read music.'

I came to appreciate Jack during this journey. It is true that, as he said, I was so unused to being served that I often forgot he was at my disposition. He was entirely uneducated, but absorbed knowledge at astonishing speed, and I liked that about him. In a matter of days, he had understood how a score was organised.

This blond young man, barely fifteen years old, was remarkably skilled. Nothing was impossible for him, nor did anything surprise or scandalise him. He was happy to converse on any matter. I couldn't share with him all the worries that assailed me but, even when we talked of trifles, it was comforting to have him at my side.

Besides, I had to tell him something of my story. The first time I took him into my confidence was the morning we left Milan.

We took the north road, passing the castle fortifications. Once we were in open country, I brought my horse to a halt.

'Where are we going, sir?'

'That is precisely the question. Jack, if you had a wife ten or fifteen days ride to the south, but you wished to go and live ten or fifteen days to the north, what would you do? Would you first go fetch your wife from the south, or would you begin by venturing northwards?'

'I should go north, sir,' he replied without hesitation, 'make preparations to receive her and have a message sent that she should come join me. Are you asking me a theoretical question or a practical one, sir?'

'A practical one.'

'Ah, because Master is . . . Madam the Baroness never mentioned a wife.'

'Madam the Baroness doesn't know. I got married in secret. Nobody knows except my friends in Amsterdam and my wife's family.'

'Ah! I see. And will you inform your family?'

'One day, no doubt. For the moment they know only that the lady exists but not that we are wed. And you don't know either.'

'That goes without saying, sir. And ... excuse me for asking the question, sir: do you have children?'

'No, Jack, not yet.'

'Ah! With all due respect, sir, I didn't see you as a father.'

'That will happen soon enough, once we're living an ordered life.'

'No doubt it will, sir. But what shall we do, practically speaking?'

'Well, as you said, we shall go to Amsterdam.'

We crossed the Alps, joined a convoy, continued up the Rhône valley, then on to Basle. We followed the Drovers' Road for part of the way and, although we didn't go as far as Echallens, that was the first time I told myself, as I gazed out over the landscape, under a chilly November sun, that the Gros-de-Vaud looked a little like the country around St Austell.

From Basle, we headed north, avoiding the lands occupied by Spain, for I had no wish to be pressed into service in a Catholic army.

I had ample time to reflect on my situation during this long journey. There was nowhere in the world I could call home. London was the only place I never felt like a visitor. But as my father's son, London, or rather England, was forbidden to me. I knew exactly what it would take to change that: simply conform and embrace the Protestant religion. But that was impossible. My father had sacrificed his comfort and his fortune to the Catholic cause. Whatever I thought of his actions, and whatever my relative indifference to either religion, out of respect for my family, I would never convert, on pain of dishonour in my own eyes.

There was something else. I may not have been as heroic as my begetter, but there was one thing in which I believed deeply, a faith born of my whole life's experience: my religion was my own and could not be bartered for convenience or advancement. I answered to God alone. Michel de Montaigne expressed this admirably:

> *The most credible thing our reason advises us is generally that everyone should obey the laws of their land, as suggested by Socrates, inspired, so it is said, by divine counsel. And what does our reason mean by this if not that our duty is ruled by none other than fortune? Truth must have a single and universal visage.... Nothing is so subject to such continual dispute as law. Since I was born, I*

have seen our English neighbours change their laws three or four
times, with regard not only to politics, which we would wish to be
free of constancy, but to the most important subject that may be,
namely religion. This causes me shame and misery, particularly
since it is a nation with which those of my region were once so
privately acquainted that there remain traces of our former kin-
ship in my own family . . . What would philosophy have us do in
such a pass? Follow the laws of our country? That is to say this
heaving sea of opinions of a people or of a prince, painting justice
in as many colours and reforging it with as many faces as they will
have changes of passion? I cannot have so flexible a judgement.
What goodness is it which I saw yesterday revered and tomorrow
no more, and which a river's crossing makes a crime? What truth
is it that stops at the mountains and becomes a lie for those who
live on the other side?

I SHALL DRAW A veil over our long journey and the vexations we encountered at each border. I resolved to say that I had been sent to Amsterdam by
the Queen of England, and I often had to show her ring, making sure that
it was neither confiscated nor stolen. Jack and I also watched our backs,
to be certain we weren't being followed by the malevolent henchmen of
some sinister authority. We saw no one.

Finally, we reached Holland. It was early December, the days were short
and the relentless sleet chilled us to the bone. To avoid crossing Spanish
territory, we had to travel as far north as Bremen and enter Holland from
there, through the province of Groningen.

We were told that Amsterdam was a five- or six-day ride away. And so
began the most surprising part of our journey. Those first impressions of
Holland were different from all the rest.

The region of Groningen had few inhabitants and few houses, but
was clearly well cultivated. Small villages were hard to find in this vast
expanse and we even spent one night out of doors, shivering in the shelter
of our horses. Here and there, traces remained of the battles between the
Dutch and the Spanish, who had recently been driven from the province.

Imperceptibly, the landscape changed and we entered a region of oak forests, as thinly inhabited as Groningen but apparently much poorer. We crossed several rivers: since entering the Low Countries, water had become integral to the landscape, but here the earth really seemed to dissolve. The only truly convenient way to travel between the scattered villages was by boat. On several occasions we were offered passage along the canals, so in this way we crossed the vast plains, carried by the wind that filled the sails of these flat boats, steered with great skill by peasant children.

The Dutch countryside was monotonous, though quite charming. The water that lay all around, in the form of canals, rivers, lakes and marshes, and the windmills that poked over the horizon in every direction, all combined to create incomparable variety amid the uniformity. I was delighted and soon forgot the extreme discomfort of our journey. Furthermore, everywhere we went, preparations for the Feast of St Nicholas were afoot. Sweetmeats were baking in kitchens and gifts were being crafted in workshops, while children scoured the clogs they would place around the hearth for the good saint to fill, in accordance with tradition. All this, accompanied by charmingly old-fashioned songs and enchanting children's rhymes.

I would have preferred that we arrive for the Feast but bad weather forced delays upon us, and so on St Nicholas' Eve we were only as far as Muiden, barely two or three hours from Amsterdam, though it was too dark to consider going further. In none of our previous halts had we experienced anything like the bustle we encountered in this little village. The few Dutch phrases we picked up along the way served to procure lodgings.

Following one pointed finger, then another, we find ourselves in front of a house with children running in and out in great excitement. The door lies open, wide and tempting. I pass my bridle to Jack and venture inside. It smells like a bakehouse. Children dash about in all directions. Two little devils engaged in a vigorous squabble use my legs to shelter from each other's blows, and each time they miss, it is I who take a battering. I am trying to extricate myself and beat a retreat when a door flies open and a comely matron surges forth, wiping her hands. She unleashes a torrent of words at the two little imps, deals several clouts and they finally let go.

She addresses me with a smile and I answer with a gesture of powerlessness.

'Ah, ah! Do you speak French by any chance?'

'Yes, madame.'

'Please excuse us, it's a madhouse tonight. But that's St Nicholas! Are you in search of lodgings?'

'Indeed, for myself and my valet, and a stable for our horses. I was given to believe that you . . . But I must be mistaken, not speaking the language.'

'No, no, you are not mistaken. The inn faces the street parallel to this; you'll find my husband there. This side is my brother's bakehouse, but it's all the same building.' She looks me up and down. 'I don't know if we have a bed to fit a man of your height, sir.'

'That is often a problem, I find. My usual solution is to place two mattresses end to end on the ground and sleep on those.'

'In that case,' she says with a laugh, 'come round to the other side of the house and I'll let my husband know.'

One hour later we are nicely ensconced, I with a pitcher of ale in front of me. I attempt to question the innkeeper about this swarm of children but he does not speak French so goes to fetch his wife.

'Ah!' she exclaims in a fit of laughter, when she finally enters. 'It's because of St Nicholas, the children's feast. Come see.'

Without ceremony, she seizes my hand, pulls me from my seat and takes me through into the bakehouse.

Children are standing in two rows, shoulder to shoulder, either side of the long kneading table. They are cutting out shapes from thin sheets of dough and sticking them with egg white onto the gingerbreads that cover the table. Two little boys are fighting in a corner and the baker's wife smartly pulls them apart.

The unintelligible hubbub, the eyes twinkling with excitement in the candlelight, the fragrant smell of aniseed and cinnamon; I am transported back to my childhood.

'You could do with a bit of music,' I say, almost in spite of myself.

'Would Monsieur like to sing us something?'

'Do you have a lute?'

She disappears into the depths of the house, to return with an instrument not entirely like the lute I know, but sufficiently similar that I can play it.

In an instant, I find myself standing there with one foot on a stool, singing to this pack of suddenly silent children:

A flea have I in my ear, my dear!
Buzzing and biting me night and day
Mad doth it drive me
No remedy for me
Hither and thither I scurry about.
Take it from me, relieve me, I pray,
Oh my beauty, do help if you may.

I continue with *Francus Came the Other Day*, then *Beauty Who Enchants My Life in Her Eyes*, *My Heart Commends Itself To You*, *Maiden by the Fountain*, *A Young Monk Came Out of the Convent*, *Spring Is on Its Way*. In short, my entire French songbook.

Then the children sing me a timely song, translated for me by the baker:

St Nicholas, good holy man,
Wear your best coat if you can
And ride for Amsterdam.
Oranges you'll find there,
Pomegranates too.
Rich gents and lovely ladies stroll
Their double sleeves on view.
Come my darling let's be wed
And start the year anew.

Everyone dances wildly to the sound of my ungainly twanging on the lute. I play galliards by Bull, Byrd and Morley – Morley's are the gayest, and the room resounds to the rhythmic clatter of clogs. For greater ease, we spill out into the street and candles are placed on the window ledges. Indifferent to the cold, people come out from the neighbouring houses to join the dance.

A young man arrives with a flute, another with a viol; Jack joins him, and soon the entire street is singing and dancing, lit only by a few flames flickering in the wind. Even the watchmen, who would usually send everyone home, stop to see, and end up clapping their hands to the rhythm with the other spectators.

A few people sit around eating gingerbread. All is merriment and I am filled with such peace that this moment is engraved on my heart forever. No other Feast of St Nicholas would better it.

When we leave the next day, the innkeeper refuses my money.

'Sir, you brought such cheer to the gathering; it would not have been the success it was, without you. My wife enjoyed your French songs so much. She was transported back to the Brabant, her country, which she had to flee before the Inquisition had a chance to burn her alive. You've earned your lodging, your meal and your horse's oats. Return for Twelfth Night. You're hired!'

I barely argue with him – it amuses me to think that I have earned my keep with my music for the first time in my life. Most unworthy of a gentleman, that!

The weather is ghastly, with strong wind driving the rain sideways.

'Take the wherry to Amsterdam,' the innkeeper suggests. 'With this wind, you'll be there in no time. You'll wear yourselves out if you go by road, you and your horses too.'

We take his advice. With the wind filling the sails, the landscape rushes by, green despite the grip of winter and the great grey clouds louring over the horizon. The boatman explains, in a mishmash of bad Latin and execrable French, that he makes the journey every day, leaving Amsterdam around six o'clock in the morning and Muiden around noon.

It is already dusk when we reach the port. Our boat makes its way through a dense mass of ships, their forest of masts reminding me of Billingsgate, before slipping into a canal. The boatman leaves us close to Dam Square, site of the Town Hall.

'God bless you, gentlemen. And if you wish to return to Muiden, you know where to find me.'

Night is falling fast and I am eager to reach Giuliano's house before dark. All I know is that it looks onto the Stromarkt, the straw market. The few passers-by are all in a great hurry, but someone points it out to me at last.

Finally, we have arrived.

The house looks vast in the twilight, at least five or six storeys.

We knock at the door of what must be the trade counter. A young man comes and opens up. He looks like Guillaume but I cannot be sure. I address him in French:

'Is your father in?'

'Yes, sir. I'll call him.'

If it is Guillaume, he hasn't recognised me either, but he goes off with a glint of curiosity in his eye. Giuliano soon appears.

'Well, I say! What a pleasure it is to see you at last; we were beginning to worry. We feared you had changed your minds, or something had befallen you. Welcome! You are most impatiently expected.'

We exchange a firm embrace.

What with the halts, the foul weather and the indirect route, the journey has taken nearly two months.

We ARE INVITED UPSTAIRS to the Ardent family's apartments. The rooms are laid with black and white paving-tiles, the walls panelled with dark wood, and the chests and cupboards so polished that they gleam like black gold. Candles are burning on the chimney-mantle and the whole house smells of vegetable soup and gingerbread.

Jane enters the room, an anxious look on her face.

'Was it . . . ?' Then she sees me and breaks into a smile:

'Francis, my Francis!' she cries, rushing to me.

Any pretence at decorum is soon forgotten as we hug each other and I kiss her hair. She smells of the sky and warm bread, of milk and love – she bears the fragrance of my childhood.

Jane has not changed. Despite giving birth to five children, her confinements have left no trace. Her beauty remains intact.

'You will stay, Master Francis, won't you?'

'Assuredly, at least for a while. It would have been unwise for me to tarry in Rome, I cannot return to England and I have no wish to travel to Spain. I have no idea where to go.'

'Well then, you shall stay with us. Come, sit with me while they prepare an apartment for you. You may wash, and tomorrow you shall get settled. Do you still play much music?'

I tell her of my activities, of the visit I made to Monteverde and the illumination that accompanied it.

Giuliano soon returns, his eyes twinkling. I know that smile. It generally means he has played a trick on someone.

'Your room is prepared; I shall have some water brought up to you. Go and wash, then we'll dine, and afterwards I'll present the household to you.'

'Very well. Do you live alone in this large house?'

'No, not really. Our business occupies the ground floor and the first floor. If you look closely, you'll see that it is actually two houses, one adjoining the other. We occupy the part on the corner and my associate occupies the other.'

He urges me towards my room.

It is lit by two tall candles. Jack has unpacked my meagre possessions: my musical scores, my Montaigne and my few clothes.

I undress and wash, after a fashion. I put on a clean doublet and collar and smooth back my hair. I can hardly do more.

I peer through the windowpane. The inky black of night is broken here and there by the dull gleam of lamps carried by occasional passers-by. A man wrapped in a large coat hurries across the Stromarkt. In the glow from his lantern, I am able to follow his path until he disappears, as if our house had gobbled him up.

I hear Giuliano call for Jack from the ground floor.

'May I, sir?'

'Jack, Master Giuliano and Madam Jane are as much your masters as I. Tell them I shall be down shortly.'

'Very well, sir.' He leaves.

I remain there, standing at the window, musing that my future resembles this dark void in which I can distinguish no clear shapes, having never seen it by light of day.

A breath, a creak, something, draws me from the depths of my reverie. I turn around.

And freeze in surprise – and terror. I have never believed tales of apparitions from the hereafter. But this ... My knees buckle. The ghost of Sir John stands at the threshold. Not the aged Sir John of our last meeting, no: this apparition – for I have no doubt that it is such – is young, with black hair, twinkling eyes, round and rosy cheeks; an altogether fine figure of a man.

What to do in such circumstances?

It is the phantom who takes the matter in hand. He walks forward several steps, the creaking floor lending him a weighty reality, stretches out his hand and smiles.

'Francis!'

The creaking floor, the sound of this voice and the sight of that smile bring me back to my senses and I let out a cry.

We remain there, face to face. It might be a minute or an hour. Then I open my arms, he throws himself into my embrace and we hug as if the world will never end. Tears and emotions stop our mouths and we can but hold each other and weep.

The phantom is Adrian.

O mistress mine, where are you roaming?
O stay and hear, your true love's coming,
That can sing both high and low:
Trip no further, pretty sweeting;
Journeys end in lovers meeting,
Every wise man doth know.

'O MISTRESS MINE'
WILLIAM SHAKESPEARE / THOMAS MORLEY

MY LIFE IN RECENT MONTHS had been quite agitated, but finding my brother turns everything upside down. The heady euphoria of that unique moment of recognition passes and, even as Adrian and I cling tight in each other's arms, my mind races ahead: *they've led you a fine dance, and Giuliano knew it, but no, impossible, Giuliano was devastated. I've found my brother and nothing else matters. It had to be. He's here, he's here, found at last!* My thoughts crowd in and are immediately overwhelmed by a sensation of delight beyond words. I am speechless, Adrian the same.

The door creaks on its hinges. Jane steps into the room and closes it behind her, one finger pressed to her lips.

'My dear boys,' she whispers, 'watch your words.' She raises her voice a notch or two.

'My dear Francis, allow me to introduce Jan van Gouden, our family's associate and joint proprietor of the house of Ardent and van Gouden.'

I cannot suppress a grin.

'Van Gouden, you say?'

'Indeed.'

'A most intriguing name. Have I not met this gentleman before?'

'Impossible: he is Dutch and this is your first visit to Holland. But I am delighted to see such warmth and promise of friendship.'

I lower my voice.

'Anyone who knows Sir John is bound to recognise *Mijnheer* van Gouden as his relative, the resemblance is astonishing. If I've been followed . . . '

'Have you been careful?'

'We've taken every precaution, but there's no guarantee . . . '

'I wish I could hurry up and sprout a beard,' says Adrian, 'but Mother Nature seems intent on withholding that particular gift.'

'I know. Same here! Have you travelled much, sir?'

'A great deal, indeed.'

'Surely we may have met somewhere before?'

'I don't believe so. And we shall speak in French, until you have learned Dutch.'

'Agreed.'

Jane listens at the door, then hurries towards us, her arms wide. We rush to her and she hugs us both, great hulking men that we are, just as if we were little boys again.

'This is one of the happiest days of my life,' she whispers in our ears, in English, with the Cornish accent of our childhood. 'To see my two boys grown tall and strong and handsome; together again, safe and sound. And now, with God's grace, we shall be happy.'

UNLIKE MY BROTHER – whom I now call nothing but Jan (I shall do the same in writing here, and abandon the name he used in his first life) – I find that I cannot break clean away from my family. I am the oldest and I feel the burden of duty – I have no right to disappear. I owe my father little enough, but I have a duty before God and He will hold me to account, I am certain of that, should I fail.

To better please the Tregians I should live in Antwerp – and I would have gone there, were it not for Françoise. We are still unsure exactly how the Roman Church would welcome Henri IV's supporters and their families – especially if they are Huguenots or have converted recently.

We all know well enough that if the French King were to turn Protestant again tomorrow, his companions in arms would follow suit, or remain suspicious in the eyes of Rome, to say the least. I dread the prospect of a closely curtailed life with a daughter of the Troisville family, in a fiefdom of the Inquisition.

I decide to send a message to Charles de Troisville, requesting an interview. Also reminding him of my previous letter, written from London, on the subject of my sister and the man my parents had chosen for her.

Giuliano places his manservant Kees – who speaks French – at my disposal. He sets off with the message.

Meanwhile, I look for lodgings, and find what we need a stone's throw from the premises of Ardent and van Gouden, on the corner of Brouwersgracht – a comfortably appointed house with a narrow frontage but extending back a long way from the street, with no more than two rooms on each floor. It belongs to a squire whom I am never required to meet. He has built himself a fine house in the country and rents his townhouse to lodgers, finding himself unable to part with it for sentimental reasons. It was in these narrow quarters, opening onto a small garden to one side and the newly dug canal on the other, that his family had made its fortune.

The hardest thing in those first weeks is to keep myself from showing an exaggerated interest in Jan van Gouden.

Finally, one afternoon, we ride out separately and meet 'by chance' along the Amstel. The cold has kept everyone but us indoors.

We trot along the icy path and Adrian sketches the bold outline of his story:

'For years I had been telling anyone who asked that I would become a clergyman. And then one day the desire left me. I cannot tell you why or how, but a refusal to take that path had been growing inside me, and once it made its presence felt, it was absolute and irrevocable. I would have talked to you about it had you been with me, but you were in Reims.'

'What about Giuliano and Jane? We can tell them anything.'

'I tried. But I wasn't sure of myself. Two things happened while I pondered how to break free of my destiny. Pierre the apothecary and I perfected a new shade of purple; the colour was strong and fast, and for months my cloak showed no sign of fading. Everyone in Eu praised it – success was guaranteed, it seemed. Shortly after, one Sunday, I travelled as far as the coast and encountered a Dutch ship that had run aground in a creek. The hold was filled with unfinished silk, taken aboard in Gibraltar. Besides the crew, there was a representative of the trading house to which the silks were being sent. All were Calvinists, terrified at having landed in Catholic territory. I suggested a pact: I would help them set sail again in complete secrecy, and they would take me with them and secure an introduction to the silk merchant. Once they had agreed, I swiftly made the necessary preparations for my disappearance.'

'How did you . . . ?'

'There was an empty building. I waited there until Pierre had retreated indoors from his look-out on the doorstep and Guillaume had left his vigil at the window.' His eyes take on a faraway look, and when he speaks again, his voice is strained. 'I bitterly regretted abandoning the family but I had no choice. I cannot tell you how I suffered for the sorrow I inflicted on you all.'

'You should have told Giuliano. He can keep a secret.'

'True. But I didn't know if he would feel able to lie to Sir John. They were so close, so trusting of one another. I couldn't take the risk. But I left a message I knew you would understand.'

'*Extremities meet* . . . Yes, I understood. I told Giuliano you weren't dead, and I told Sir John, too.'

'It wasn't quite the same as letting you in on the secret, of course. You might have come to the wrong conclusion. I wasn't even thirteen years old at the time. If I had told anyone of my plans in plain terms, they would have dissuaded me, or set off in my pursuit.'

'Not necessarily: we knew you were alive, but we imagined you were in the New World. What did you do next?'

'After that, it was simple. I sold my expertise. Pierre and I were the only two alive who knew the secret of Ardent purple – the name we gave to the new colour, the name that suited it best.'

'Did you tell Pierre what you were doing?'

'No. I sent money later, by messenger. But Pierre is a recluse, a contemplative. The world of atoms is all that interests him, not money. He told the messenger not to bother coming back again. Before that, he thought I was in the Americas, as you all did.'

He anticipates my next question.

'Had I attempted to contact you, I would have been discovered, and I was determined to reach my majority before our father could find me. I had no desire for him to dictate what I should do. I must be extremely cautious, even now, for at least another two years.'

'How did you find Giuliano?'

'He found me. He became a silk merchant by chance when one of his debtors, a Venetian nobleman, paid him in bales of unfinished silk. He decided to dye and sell them. And while he was looking around for colours, he found our purple. Giuliano has a tremendous hunter's instinct. When he sets out on the trail of a thing, he is certain to find it, and he followed the trail to my door. We took a risk when we became associates but, at that point in time, it was the only sure way for me to reap the benefits of the purple. I'd had enough of merchants earning riches on the back of my discovery, making my exclusive colour available to them and getting no thanks for it. Giuliano had some capital but he knew nothing of the art of silk, whereas I had spent several years learning its secrets. But I knew no one in the business and had not a penny to my name. I spoke Dutch like a native. Hardly anyone remembered that I had sprung suddenly out of nowhere, and if people did remember, they thought I was fleeing persecution in the Brabant. I am unrivalled as a supplier of fine cloth and sumptuous colours. Giuliano is unrivalled as a salesman. Our business prospered. Of course, I worked hard. Nothing could be further from the refined leisure befitting a gentleman of my rank.'

This last is spoken in the suave tones of a prelate and we both burst out laughing.

'Giuliano was against travelling to Rome to tell you about me, and then he learned from one his agents that your cardinal had been poisoned because he dared to assert that since the defeat of the Armada, there was little hope of returning England to the papist fold.'

'On the contrary, I never heard him say anything of the kind.'

'Oh, these were not things Cardinal Allen would ever say in public. Nor to his catechumens. But he said as much to the plenipotentiary of the King of Spain, who hastened to repeat it to his master. Giuliano heard it from an acquaintance – an Anglican historian visiting Rome in the guise of a devout Catholic, who had sought out the English cardinal, as was customary. Allen talked about a change of policy. Philip II's henchmen had orders to rid the King of a pawn who had become a thorn in his side. You were the only person in the Cardinal's entourage whom Giuliano knew he could trust absolutely. So it was best not to distract you: the important thing was to keep Allen alive for as long as possible.'

'So while we all had you off discovering the New World, you had scarcely left your own back yard.'

'I left our caste, and that is the longest journey any man can make. The safest too, for me. I might have taken a job in Lady Anne's kitchens, or our father's: I swear no one would have recognised me.'

I smile at the thought.

'You would have been recognised, for sure. You are the very image of Sir John, and probably of his father, too, our great-grandfather.'

'I swear to you now, with my hair all undone and rather filthy, under a knitted cap, they wouldn't have given me a second glance.'

'I envy you for having found an occupation to your liking. I am a product of the same caste, and good for nothing.'

'If I understand rightly, you have one flaw: you devote yourself to music-making with greater zeal than most gentlemen.'

'True. And if pressed, I know how to build an instrument and repair an organ. But . . .'

'You have a clear, elegant hand. You could even keep our accounts.'

'That's true, too.'

'But I'm not suggesting that. Only never again let me hear that a gentle-man must do nothing but wage war and politics.'

'Our schooling was turbulent.'

'We learned the basic principles but we have never had leisure to put them into practice.'

I am reminded of the time Lady Anne tried to equip me with a retinue of six servants; I tell Adrian about it, and we shake with laughter. Our old understanding has been restored. We ride back the way we came. For a long time, neither of us speaks. I am preoccupied.

'I, the eldest son, have not broken away from the family, and I must send news of myself to our father sooner or later. He cannot impose a wife on me now, and at last I can tell him about the wife I have chosen. I have a sense of duty, I can't simply disappear. But I know the Catholics have a network of spies every bit as efficient as Lord Burghley's; my presence must not lead to your discovery.'

'No one remembers me but you. Our father saw me once when I was six years old and our mother hasn't set eyes on me since we left for France. I am but a vague memory in her long line of children. And Sir John is dead. No one will suspect a silk merchant calling on the services of a musician; no one will guess I am your long-lost brother. Concentrate on your music, lead the life expected of you. Giuliano has long been your devoted servant and is still your steward, and his wife was your nurse – the English will think it perfectly natural that you should visit them. We will become friends, little by little. Not forgetting that Giuliano is himself a Catholic spy, which is protection in itself.'

'Are you certain?'

'Absolutely. He doesn't work for Spain but for the moderate Catholic faction – the ones the French call *les politiques* and the English call *secularists*. Europe's very own Sir Johns – people who desire to live in peace without fear of the Inquisition or the Habsburgs, without having to change their religion. Why do you think he has travelled so widely, so frequently, ever since we've known him? He offers his services, as he puts it. Judging by the clients he brings us, he moves in very high circles.'

'I never truly understood who he . . . '

'Don't even try. He protects us – that's all that matters. You know he has managed your English properties wisely and well. You're an investor in our silk workshops. Made quite a bit of money out of them, too.'

'Me?'

'Of course. Giuliano has decided to make a rich man of you. So make music, dear brother. Play, read, listen and travel for music! Take an interest in your business affairs if you like, but from a distance. No one coming to see you will be interested enough in my side of things to identify me as Adrian Tregian. And if anyone can be bothered to poke their noses into the annals of the van Goudens, they will find a direct line of descent dating back more than a century. There are multitudes of van Goudens here. My birth and that of my parents, my grandparents and their parents before them, and all their marriages and deaths, are recorded in the parish registers.'

•   •   •

CURIOUSLY, MUSIC, ONCE A flourishing art in Holland, had become a wholly private affair; the patrician classes practised it with zeal and brilliance but neither Jan nor I went anywhere near the Dutch nobility, except to sell them our cloth. There was no association in Amsterdam resembling the Italian academies. Here, as in London, it was impossible to spend more than a few minutes in a tavern without a small group singing you a ballad or striking up an air, but the music was quite unlike the pavanes and galliards of Byrd, Bull, Morley, Weelkes or Wilbye. Small groups of travelling musicians roamed the country, often very ragged or dressed in motley, playing in villages, at fairs and weddings, or for lovers seeking a serenade. I was enchanted by their popular tunes and simple accompaniments, and the strange instruments they often played alongside the customary lute and tin whistle. There was the *bomba*, a kind of upright, one-stringed fiddle, with a pig's bladder forming the soundbox; and the *draailier*, a portable hurdy-gurdy. Their tunes and songs could be heard on every street corner, but music was not a respected art. Rather, it was an indulgence, like painting, and it was viewed with suspicion by the Calvinist clergy.

At first, I practised mostly at Giuliano's. I played the virginal, Jan played the lute, Guillaume and Francis the viol, while their sister Mary sang in a still reedy but promising voice. Later, I gave up my place at the virginal to Mary and instead organised performances of the madrigals I had brought back from Italy with a widening circle of acquaintances and friends eager for new musical forms from southern Europe. The virginal underscored the voices of the novice male and female singers. Monteverde, Pallavicino and Marenzio had made no allowance for it, but we were making music for our own pleasure, and our addition was, I decided, a pardonable offence.

One day, Kees returned with a message from Charles de Troisville.

> *My dear brother,*
>
> *I never received the letter you speak of. I am going to London and I shall marry your sister if she is still free. On our return, we shall fetch my sister and bring her to you. I have sent her a messenger, so that she may prepare to leave with us. I have very little time. Make preparations to receive us. Until then, God bless you, I am delighted at the prospect of seeing you again.*
>
> *Your devoted brother, Charles.*

'I left Paris four days ago,' Kees told me, 'at the same time as the messenger to Bordeaux and Monsieur de Troisville himself, on his way to London. He expected to return to France within a fortnight, and thought he would be here in three or four weeks.'

With Jane's help, I organised my house and hired retainers, though not such an extensive retinue as I would have had in England – Holland has few such great households overflowing with servants.

Every day, I spent a few hours at the Ardent and van Gouden silk counter: I wished to understand the workings of the silk trade. I discovered that I was quite as fascinated by how things were made as I was by the things themselves, sometimes even more so. I asked for explanations of the mechanics of the entire process, from spooling to throwing, from weaving to baling, and from the weaver's bench to the warp beam. Soon I could tell taffeta from serge and seven-heddle satin from the eight-, nine- or ten-heddle varieties, and identify the weaves obtained by drawing-in or raising the warp – the proper terms rise obediently to the surface, as I think back.

I did not forget my gentleman's rank, and practised daily at the fencing-strip to maintain my skills with a sword. Besides this, I occupied what little time remained with music-making. During those first weeks in Holland, I was content to play through the great mass of copies I had made over the preceding months. My new life was too engrossing for me to embark on fresh musical discoveries. That would come later. I needed time to digest everything I had learned in Mantua.

Added to which, I lived in a fever of expectation. As the days went by, I regretted more and more not having gone to fetch Françoise myself, though I knew that I would have provided an inadequate escort – only her brother had the means to organise one worthy of the name.

The first signs of spring had made their timid appearance when I was awoken one morning by Jack, calling out:

'Master! There are a gentleman and a lady below, they wish to see you and will not give their names.'

I leaped out of bed. Françoise!

'Show them in and prepare some refreshment.'

'Yes, sir.'

The large front room is still in darkness when I enter. They stand with their backs turned, warming their hands at the fire. At the sound of my footsteps, they turn: Charles de Troisville and my sister Margaret.

I cry out in delight and disappointment. To see Margaret is a wonderful surprise. But not to see Françoise . . .

Charles leaves me no time to speak.

'Don't worry, we left Françoise at Weesp. She's very tired. We thought you might prefer to fetch her from there yourself.'

I look from one to the other. They make a radiant couple. I throw my arms wide and we share a long embrace.

'Did you leave with our family's consent, Margaret, or was Charles forced to steal you away?'

'We are married. I narrowly escaped the dreadful Benjamin Tichborne; he was revealed as a spy just days before the wedding. Which is why we received our father's blessing: he graciously pointed out that it was given because I have no dowry and that when a man is poor and has so many daughters, he can hardly pick and choose.'

Seeing Margaret's green eyes, shot through with flecks of gold like an August meadow, I think again of Old Thomas, and I wonder to what lineage he might ascribe them. For her eyes are unlike mine. She doubtless owes them to quite another fairy family.

'Now, you will excuse me. I must go and fetch Françoise. You must be tired; please make yourselves comfortable. Jack!'

'Sir, I have taken the liberty of saddling the horses.'

'Then let's go.'

'Francis?'

I am gripped by sudden alarm at Charles's uncomfortable look.

'What is it? Françoise is in good health, I hope?'

'Quite. She is very well indeed. And so is your son.'

'My . . . What?'

'Your son Francis is in fine health, too.'

I know I should be jumping for joy. But the news takes me so much by surprise that I feel nothing but a kind of cold rage that obliterates my delight.

'This is too much. Why does everyone feel it necessary to keep the truth from me?'

'Not to hide it from you but from the spies clustering around you in

Rome. We concealed your fatherhood on your wife's orders. For as long as you remained in Rome, you were to be told nothing.'

What can I say? Remembering those days when my every sinew was tensed for action, when I lay half-awake, night after night, when death seemed to stalk me at every turn, ready to overwhelm the Cardinal and me, I feel almost grateful that no one told me I would see my brother again, that I would have a son. Had I known, I would never have lingered in Mantua. I would have gone to Bordeaux. But I would not have directed my full attention to outwitting death and watching my back. My anger subsides in an instant.

'Then I am all the more eager to set off. Show me the way.'

'Sir?' Jack ventures a suggestion. 'I have spoken to this gentleman's valet. I know where your family are. Their Lordships can rest here and take some refreshment.'

'Thank you Jack. Come, then. As for you, dear friends, my home is yours, rest at your leisure.' I lower my voice. 'Be discreet. The servants are new, I don't know them well enough yet.'

I am about to leave when a thought strikes me.

'Were you followed?'

'In England, we were. But my visit was known. I was there to fetch my betrothed. We lost them in Calais and, if they are still after us, they'll be in or around Paris, perhaps even Bordeaux. Trust me, I took all the necessary steps to ensure we came alone.'

With that, I rush down the stairs, spring into the saddle and we gallop off at full tilt.

HOW CAN I FORGET the sight of those two faces turned to mine, framed by the wooden beams of the inn at Weesp, like a painted portrait. How can I forget my beloved's deep, dark gaze, her gentle light touching the beholder like a kiss?

Françoise's beauty stops me in my tracks. And when I see the infant she is holding in her arms, I understand for the first time what people have always told me about my own eyes. Young Francis has Françoise's complexion, but his eyes are periwinkle blue, and my first thought is that the piskies have made me a gift.

My son does me the honour of bawling with terrific energy when I take him in my arms.

But why report what was said at that meeting? Our words were unremarkable compared to the powerful emotions that gripped us. We set off for Amsterdam in silence. Françoise had only to offer young Francis her breast (she had not wished to provide him with a nurse) for him to fall silent and break into smiles of delight.

I have only a confused memory of the grand evening organised by the house of Ardent and van Gouden to celebrate the arrival of the King of France's envoy, officially on a silk-buying trip to Holland on behalf of the court.

I had been convinced that Jan's likeness to Sir John was blindingly obvious, but I saw now that my brother was right. Imagining him lost forever and not expecting to see him, Margaret failed to recognise her own brother. I was on my guard, ready to intervene, but her perplexity extended to nothing more than a 'Have we not met before, sir? Your face is familiar, yet I cannot place you.'

'If we had already met, madame, I could not possibly have forgotten you,' replied Jan, with a bow.

Margaret accepted the compliment with a smile and passed along, to my immense relief. The fewer people who were in on the secret, the better. We presented Charles with a bale of the finest Ardent purple silk to give to His Majesty King Henri, and the house was granted the right, following Charles's return to Paris, to the legend: 'Suppliers to the King of France'.

Françoise told me, with some amusement, how everyone in Bordeaux referred to her family as Tréville, combining our two names.

'They have even adopted the name in Paris, and almost everyone refers to Charles by it, too!'

And then . . . The fog of memory retains scarcely any precise recollection of those quiet days.

Scattered images surface.

Each day at around five or six o'clock, returning from the trading house or the fencing strip, or a music rehearsal, I do as every other householder and sit – if it is not too cold – on the bench in front of the house, beneath the overhang. Françoise comes out with little Francis, whom she rarely leaves behind. She nurses the babe herself and has grown deeply attached to him. Some of our neighbours have tried to tell her that so close an attachment is not good for his upbringing, but she simply shrugs and carries on taking care of little Frans (we both call him this, in Dutch), with as much solicitude as ever. At first she would bring him out in his cradle, but soon he is running down the stairs and playing in the street with the other children.

Outside the neighbouring houses, other little groups like ours form. We exchange gazettes, comment on the news, discuss the politics of the day and set the world to rights, nodding sagely at any particularly edifying phrases. We assure each other, with some conviction, that the Spanish will never take back the United Provinces (what we called the seven Protestant provinces in northern Holland). We complain about the heavy taxes levied for the war and console ourselves that such is the price of independence and tranquillity.

My right-hand neighbour, a portly goldsmith aged about fifty, has taken a liking to me since the evening when, rapier in hand, I saw off two individuals seeking to rob him in the street. He would often tell me: *Kaart, keurs en kan dederven menig man*, meaning that many a young fellow has been lost to cards, petticoats and the bottle. 'You keep a close eye on him, madame,' he would add, addressing Françoise. 'As we say here, *De gelegenheid maakt de dief* – it's opportunity makes a man a thief!'

'Rest assured, sir,' Françoise quips back. 'I've got my eye on the scoundrel!' And everyone laughs.

In winter we gather indoors. Françoise sits at the table, working at her sewing or her embroidery, and if we have visitors, their wives do the same. From the kitchen, we can hear the serving-women at their spinning Everyone expects me to read from the Bible, or a history book. I comply, though with little enough enthusiasm. In a short time, we had all mastered Dutch – as in so many other circumstances, I made sure not to stand out from the crowd. I seek – I need – to lead a life like any other; nothing is more hateful than the idea of setting myself apart. People admire my virtuosity and my knowledge of Italian music, but this is hailed as a gift, like my neighbour's prodigious skill and expertise in fine metalwork, or our great family friend and constant visitor Jan van Gouden's passion for sumptuous fabrics, or the business acumen of Mijnheer Ardent, another frequent guest. On winter evenings, a passer-by might hear the muffled sound of the virginal, flutes, lutes and viols coming from within, for when everyone takes to their instruments we make a fine consort, and our neighbours come knocking at the door and sit in corners or warm themselves at the hearth.

The Trévilles, as we too come to be known, quite unintentionally on our part, are gaining a reputation throughout the neighbourhood as fine musicians and generous hosts. People come readily to sing, or to listen, while sipping a glass of mulled wine or beer. Sometimes they bring collections of popular songs – love songs, pastorals, songs of adventure or journeys to distant lands. There must be hundreds of these collections in circulation.

We improvise an accompaniment and everyone sings. I love the fresh naivety, the spontaneity and jollity, even the ribald nature of the refrains. They are the opposite of our madrigals, or of other pieces in my collection of English and Italian composers, but no one objects to a musical evening in two halves, and these are played, too.

Sometimes the gathering ends with draughts or cards or Nine Men's Morris, which everyone greatly enjoys.

WITH SOME RELIEF, I quickly realised, from our acquaintances, that while the Dutch are a deeply religious people, and while religion is omnipresent in everyday life, and although Holland is officially a Protestant country, Catholics are generally accepted at all levels of society. Discretion is all that is required.

When I first arrived, the Jesuits were the only Catholics excluded from holding positions of public service. Catholics could not be schoolmasters either, because anyone holding that position had to profess the reformed faith. We were free, however, to attend the universities, especially Leyden, where students were not required to take an oath of allegiance to the Calvinist religion.

I know that nowadays in Holland, the Mass may only be said in private. Catholic churches are not clandestine but they are concealed within private houses and nothing hints at their presence. In my day, there were still Catholic churches on some streets, and no one was bothered by our habits of prayer, provided we refrained from noisy, public manifestations of piety. We Catholics paid slightly higher taxes than the Protestants, but the country was entirely tolerant, on both sides: the Catholic curates were civil when the bailiffs visited to collect their taxes. I always offered our bailiff something to drink, and he always dandled young Francis on his knee, for he loved children.

There were Catholics in almost every profession and they were especially numerous in some regions – the textile workers in Leyden, for example, as I had occasion to notice, or near the southern border, where some would send their children to study in Brussels (in the Spanish territories) despite the ban on this. But in all my time in Holland, no one was ever punished or arrested for it.

The important thing was to respect the forms and rites of one's own religion. The ecclesiastical authorities of all faiths would strike unhesitatingly at what they saw as lost sheep: people who did not conform to religious rule, who proclaimed their lack of faith or abstained from the observances of their church. In such cases, the Church – any Church – meted out harsh punishment, under the approving gaze of the followers of other faiths. But conform to the rules, and you were allowed complete freedom.

The Catholic curates reproached the Calvinists under their breath, and the devout Puritan pastors railed aloud against the idolatry of the papists, thundering accusations against the exorcists, whom they saw as the disguised agents of the most backward Catholic propaganda. People would wait outside each other's churches to mock the practices of the other faith. Even I was ridiculed in this way by one of my neighbours, but when I asked him why, he replied jovially, pouring me a drink:

'It's done in good jest. Your servants do the same with mine – and sticks and stones may break my bones, as the saying goes, but words will never hurt me.'

The Protestant sermons criticised Rome freely and openly (I went to listen, for, provided it was not taken as a sign of political allegiance, one might as well hear what the other side had to say) and the authorities declared they would tolerate no act of force on the part of the Catholics. But compared to the intolerance shown by the Catholics of Reims, or Rome, or that of the English Puritans, these practices were inconsequential indeed. It should be noted that no one, in any community, followed their preachers blindly.

Despite our priests' instructions, we Catholics had Protestant friends whom we made no attempt to convert. We went to their weddings and baptisms and burial services, and to their religious festivities, when we were invited. We read their philosophers.

The Calvinists did the same. And they danced, too.

Dutch women are tireless dancers. They can dance for two days at a stretch, and their partners and musicians are worn out long before they. The Dutch dance on every occasion – even during our regular musical evenings, men and women would tap their feet, then rise and throw themselves into a wild dance to the rhythm of any music, even a madrigal.

The Catholic Church views such frolics with suspicion but has never formally opposed them, while the Protestant Church strictly forbids dancing, as well as theatrical performances. Their preachers condemn them in the roundest terms: dance is harmful to both physical and spiritual well-being, they say.

Young girls are warned endlessly about this shocking pastime: they are risking their reputations, and their souls. But the preachers have no real means of carrying out their threats. People go on attending each other's ceremonies, and everyone dances on regardless.

Ultimately, and despite the unstinting efforts of the clergy, tolerance prevails. The Dutch are, at heart, an open-minded, peace-loving people. I have always regretted that when I was forced to disappear, circumstances did not allow me to settle in Holland, where it would have been too easy to track me down.

III

AFTER A WHILE I began to travel. We had been so careful that nobody recognised me as Francis Tregian, son of a notorious English recusant. Monsieur Tréville was my name. And thanks to that divine gift our family had received, the ability to learn languages perfectly and with ease, I passed for neither French nor English as far as most people were concerned, since I took great pains never to speak my mother tongue. I was a Fleming who had learned both Dutch and French from birth; a cloth merchant with a taste for music, which I cultivated with special diligence. Eyebrows were raised when I was first seen fencing like a gentleman, but once my neighbour had zealously put about the highly embellished story of how I'd plucked him from the jaws of a very certain death, my skill with a blade was seen as yet another virtue. The Brouwersgracht could sleep sound in its bed, for Master Tréville was keeping watch. I was even asked to join the Civic Guard, an inestimable honour. There was further surprise at my leaving the trade counter early on occasion, to go and play music. But the astonishment ceased the day I made the acquaintance of one of the city's most popular musicians, Jan Sweelinck, organist at the Oude Kerk. And it was quite forgotten when he attended one of our madrigal evenings for the first time. If no less a man than Master Sweelinck recognised Monsieur Tréville as a kindred spirit, then that was enough for the neighbours. And besides, Ardent and van Gouden prospered despite my occasional absences, which was all that mattered.

My first meeting with Jan Sweelinck did not proceed altogether smoothly. His reputation as a teacher and highly skilled musician had gradually spread across Europe, and he was greatly sought-after. I went along one day and asked, in my still rather faulty Dutch, if he might allow me to play the organ now and again, when he was away, in order to maintain my own small skills. He cut me short:

'No room! I have quite enough pupils now. And I haven't the time.'

'But, sir . . . '

'Where are you from?'

'I am arrived from Italy.'

I would later learn that Sweelinck never travelled abroad and that he was greedy for any music that might be brought him from the four corners of the world.

'Did you bring back any scores?'

'Yes, sir.'

'Do you have them with you?'

'I have some of them.'

'Do you know how to play?'

'Yes, sir.'

'Very well then, but I will tell you now: I'll not give you a single lesson.'

'Very well, sir.'

I sat down and played him a Morley fantasy and a Byrd rondeau.

'There is little more I could teach you,' he asserted, looking solemn.

'I would be most honoured to have you correct my playing,' I said, 'but I did not come for that.' And finally, I was able to present my request.

I cannot say that we shared an immediate affection, for Jan Sweelinck was an extremely reserved fellow and difficult to approach. But we remained in contact ever after, even when I returned to England, much later. He was the only person in Amsterdam outside the family circle in whom I confided the secret of my true motherland. We began with a mutual esteem that transformed imperceptibly into friendship. Along with John

Bull and Master Claudio da Correggio, Jan Sweelinck was undoubtedly the most accomplished organ player it has ever been my good fortune to meet. His improvisations, in particular, were astonishing. And I was even happier the first time he knocked at the door to attend one of our musical evenings. Upon leaving, he shook my hand with unaccustomed cordiality:

'The evening was quite delightful. Truly.'

'We were overjoyed to receive your visit, sir, and hope you will return.'

Return he did, sometimes alone, sometimes with his young sons and his wife.

The family business afforded me the opportunity to combine commerce with the pleasure of travel. Jan was too busy in the workshop to journey far. He was intensely occupied with perfecting a new colour and a new kind of silk velvet; he worked day and night. Giuliano had lost some of his relish for the endless journeys on horseback. As for myself, I enjoyed good health, I had leisure and I was capable of riding long distances in very short time – we discovered quite how fast one day, when an urgent delivery of cloth was required for an important ceremony.

I was the ideal negotiator – thanks to my height, my phlegmatic air and my inscrutable countenance, according to Jan. Whenever someone made me a proposition, I took a moment to reflect, smiling all the while, to soothe any impatience in the other party. This was because I often had difficulty making up my mind. But I soon came to understand that my interlocutor interpreted this as an invitation to alter the terms of the bargain to my advantage. My smile became my secret weapon.

I travelled the length and breadth of Europe, from Bremen to Prague and from Copenhagen to Paris. But Italy was my passion, and I took any pretext to go there. I visited Venice with special delight: the printing of music flourished there. Having extolled my cloth and sold it, I would hurry to the Houses of Amadino (Monteverde's publisher), Gardano and others to savour their delights. Their shops were the haunt of many fascinating musicians. After a while, I was as familiar with the organs and music printers of Europe as I was with the Continent's lovers of fine silk. I knew musicians, composers and players everywhere. I could count off an entire rosary of them.

The first to come to mind is Claudio Merulo da Correggio, who lived in Parma and had been recommended to me for his faultless playing of the organ:

'He's the Good Lord in person, you'll see. He plays so fast he'll make you giddy. And he makes the organ speak. One moment it whispers, the next it growls ...'

You may imagine my curiosity. I went to Parma. Several times. Thanks to Claudio da Correggio, I acquired a quite different, highly effective style. Correggio made you play with fingers curled, paying special attention to the thumb, which he kept for the lower notes, and the little finger, which he used only for the top of the scale. When using the other fingers, one should take into account the expressive force of the *forte* and *piano* passages. If one desires a very loud note, one uses the forefinger and the ring finger, with the middle finger serving only for the quietest notes. I still apply these rules and I teach them to my young pupils. Even though the virginal does not allow such shades of expression, the method has wonderful uses for that instrument too.

I met other musicians in the course of my travels, such as Ippolito Baccusi in Verona, Ludovico Balbi in Treviso and Melchior Borchgrevink in Copenhagen. In Milan, I came across a former schoolfellow from the Merchant Taylors', John Cooper, now calling himself Giovanni Coperario. He didn't recognise me. In Paris, I made the acquaintance of Claude Le Jeune. Moreover, my sister Margaret entertained Eustache du Caurroy, who loved to spend hours holding forth on the mathematics of counterpoint. I travelled regularly to Mantua to see Pallavicino and also Monteverde, at whose house I met musicians from all over Europe, drawn by the controversy surrounding the *seconda pratica*, of which there was much talk in music salons across Italy. It would be futile to list them all, but I was introduced into musical circles everywhere I went.

The only region where I feared to tread was the Papal States. But as I gained assurance in my musical merchant's role, I took my courage in both hands and ventured into Spanish territory. This was no simple task, for it was impossible to travel directly from the north to the south of the Low Countries, which were at daggers drawn. Spain retained a firm grasp over the south and considered the north a rebel to its authority, as it still does today! As for the north, she considered herself to be a state in her own right, a view held by most civilised countries, and saw Spain and its

Flemish limb as an oppressor from which she must take back the provinces
that had been seized by force, and against which she stood ready to fight
at any moment.

I particularly liked Antwerp where, in addition to the musicians I frequented, I discovered other people of interest, such as the Ruckers family.
Hans the father and his two sons, Jan and Andreas, owned a workshop where
they built some of the most beautiful virginals I have ever seen or heard.

I was fascinated by the place and loved to visit it. On one occasion I
asked so many questions that Ruckers the Elder fixed me with a sudden,
hostile gaze and enquired:

'You haven't come to steal our secrets, while pretending to admire our
instruments?'

'No, no! Far from it. Or rather yes, I should like to know how you
proceed, but not to steal your craft. Simple curiosity, that's all. I have
no intention of becoming a builder of virginals.' I never imagined, at
the time, that this was exactly what I would do much later in life. Their
father remained mistrustful but I got to know the sons, both young men
of my age, and also one of their friends, who often painted the inside of
the lids with those landscapes that inspire the player, seated at his open
virginal. I mention him because he later came to glory and his name is
known even here in Echallens: Peter Paul Rubens. Back then he was just
like us, a young and undoubtedly talented man, but green and without
pretension.

We spent merry evenings together in the tavern. I recall once, after a
great deal of drinking, we returned to the workshop: the two brothers had
an instrument they had promised to finish for the next day. Rubens put the
last touches to his lid painting, while I sat at another virginal and played
for them. We were in great high spirits, and sang a number of Orlando di
Lasso's ribald songs.

> *A young monk came out of the convent,*
> *Met a nun with a body most pleasant.*
> *Dost thou wish, asked he,*
> *To jig with me,*
> *Or dance the two-step sprightly?*
> *Oh monk, what mean'st thou by jig, I pray?*

> *Why, kissing and hugging, my sweet;*
> *Jig's what we call in our liturgy,*
> *Bare body to body betwixt two sheets.*

And so on and so forth.

My mercantile duties accomplished, I loved to visit Pierre Phalèse, an Antwerp music printer, publisher and seller. On my second visit, I brought along some scores by musicians I had met in the course of my travels, and we exchanged opinions and pieces. He published – and I eagerly bought – excellent compilations of contemporary composers from all over Europe. We became friends.

It was at Phalèse's shop that I met Peter Philips. Philips had left England ten years before, not only because he was a Catholic but also to forge a successful career as an international composer. He was living in Antwerp at the time I made his acquaintance, and there was keen competition for his lessons. I never told him I was English and we always conversed in French.

I especially favoured his compositions and arrangements for keyed instruments or consorts. At this, he was a genius, and I still play his transcriptions of Lasso, Marenzio and Striggio: *The Nightingale*, *Margott Laborez*, *Chi farà fede al cielo*, *Tirsi*, *Così morirò*, and others.

As for my own compositions, the plain truth is that the only ones I could ever bear to play are those that Peter Philips agreed to arrange for me.

One day, we had a very lively discussion about Monteverde's *seconda pratica*, one of my favourite subjects of conversation at the time. I have no recollection of whatever summary arguments I presented, but Phalèse and Philips both cast an incredulous eye on me.

'Is there a virginal to hand?' I asked, to cut short what I considered a superfluous discussion.

Phalèse led us behind the arras that divided the room, and I sat down at the instrument and gave my demonstration.

I have no idea whether they paid any attention to my arguments: this was the first time either had heard me play, and all the talk after that was of my skill and technique.

After a moment, Philips took a scroll out of his pocket, placed it on the lectern and said to me:

'Take a look at these.'

The scroll contained his *Pavane* and his *Galliard Dolorosa*, both of which I still play often.

'Quite marvellous,' I said, after scrutinising them. This was music imbued with a rare strength of feeling, expressed through chromatic modulation and low notes of a quite remarkable beauty.

'How magnificent they would sound played in consort.'

'You think so?'

'I'm certain of it.'

We discussed the matter briefly.

'I'll see what I can do.'

And when I next returned, he had arranged the pieces for viols, lutes and organ.

'I wrote this pavane while I was in prison,' said Philips. 'I was unwise enough to make companions of some English fellows, Catholics like me, who were fomenting plans to return to England and kill the Queen. It took me some time to prove that I knew nothing about the plot and that music was my sole interest.'

I swallowed nervously but did not flinch, although privately I wondered whether he was being followed and if I might be discovered. It seemed not, although Antwerp was crawling with spies, both English and Spanish. It was a disquieting place, where double-dealing and treachery held sway, and everyone had their price. If it had been a simple matter of Catholics attempting to unearth Protestant secrets and Protestants doing the same in response, then – deplorable as the practice might be – one could understand why some thought it necessary. Unfortunately, things were never that simple in reality. Each party comprised several factions, the ones closely watching the others. Burghley's men spied upon Essex's fellows, who returned the favour; the Pope's scouts observed their Spanish counterparts, and vice versa; the Jesuits watched the political plotters; the plotters watched the Jesuits; and the Inquisition kept their eye on everyone.

If Jack and I escaped recognition, it was because we never spoke English and took care to keep our distance from our compatriots. People approached us from time to time. I would grin like a fool, pretending not to understand, while Jack played the idiot – he had translated his name into Dutch and called himself Jaap. Nobody ever insisted. Certainly, nobody ever made the connection between François (or Frans) Tréville and Francis Tregian. Giuliano gave us extensive instructions: which inns to avoid at all costs, the traps to watch out for. We were constantly alert, and had perfected a series of masquerades that we rehearsed diligently at home before setting off, and which proved highly effective on the few occasions we had recourse to their use.

I think I can say that I succeeded in properly disappearing during my Amsterdam years. Discretion was less important once Jan reached his majority, but old habits die hard, and anyway, what was the use of informing our parents of a state of affairs that would have pained them? I have always firmly believed that a discreet life is a happy one.

I found a means of getting news to my father without breaking cover, by sending messages from towns through which I travelled. I journeyed frequently to Paris to see my sister, who had become a true Frenchwoman. She kept a small household but one renowned for its fine food and music, as much as for its chatelaine's *esprit*, as they say in Paris. She and Charles had two delightful children.

His own sister having failed to recognise him, I never mentioned Adrian to her. I simply explained that if Spain had in fact arranged the poisoning of Cardinal Allen, they might see me as an awkward witness: better they not discover my whereabouts. Who knows? Perhaps it was true.

I liked visiting the Troisvilles, and used these occasions to write to my father. Margaret would add a word or two to my letters, or else I would add a word or two to hers; it allowed one to suppose I was living in Paris, or at least in France. In this way my family discovered that I was married, and a father myself. Sometimes I was sent messages through Margaret, who had them conveyed to me with all the usual precautions. And if none of that was possible, for whatever reason, Jack would travel to London on my behalf.

Once or twice a year, he went to Dieppe or Nantes and boarded a ship for England, carrying my letter to Lady Anne, who conveyed it to the Fleet. Meanwhile, Jack would go to see his family. When my parents had provided their reply, he would return to France. From there, he did his best to throw off any pursuers, and returned to Amsterdam by a roundabout route.

News from England reached me attenuated and muffled.

I learned that my brother Charles was in Rome, at the English College, I believe. My father suggested that I take care of him, but I gave no response to the suggestion, and he didn't repeat it.

Along with the whole of Christendom, we learned of the taking of Cádiz by the English fleet.

There was fighting along the coast of the Low Countries and northern France for control of the Channel.

Lord Burghley died. The news saddened me for, despite the many bad things I had heard about him, I had always found him a pleasant and likeable man. His son Robert succeeded him.

I also learned of the passing of my Grandmother Tregian, Madam Catherine, born Arundell, in the little house close to Lanherne to which she had retired. A flood of potent memories overwhelmed me: Madam Catherine teaching me the alphabet; Madam Catherine riding through the Cornish mud, sitting as straight as a post; Madam Catherine threatening me with the whip if I didn't take my exercise 'immediately, and briskly too, if you please, my little gentleman!' The images streamed before my mind's eye, and the accompanying tide of pain and regret kept me from sleep.

According to Jack, the Queen was not ageing well and her moods were increasingly capricious. She had still not named an heir to the throne. Bets were laid, with the favourite being James VI of Scotland, son of Mary Stuart. Jack claimed he'd picked up the news from sources close to the palaces, which is to say his opinions were in fact founded in the royal kitchens.

I must admit that although I was aware at the time that these events might affect my future, the news from England was of only relative interest to me. I was much more concerned with the present. I travelled widely and my life was full to the brim.

For the second time, I was to become a father. For no discernible reason, we had not had a child for three or four years, and this second birth was eagerly awaited. Everything proceeded according to Dutch custom, which meant that the entire neighbourhood would take part in the event.

In the days preceding the birth, the house was taken over by women. Sometimes I was allowed to sit with my wife, but I had become an intruder.

As soon as the first pains commence, I am shown the door with no further ceremony. One of the women runs to fetch the midwife, another rushes to the Ardents', where young Francis has been placed until after the event. Jane comes running with her eldest daughter, Mary, who is ten. The door gapes open and I glimpse Françoise upon the birthing chair. Then Jane closes the door, firmly and with a friendly smile. I am obliged to wait in the kitchen, where Jack serves aqua-vitae to my neighbour, who is delivering a lengthy discourse to which I pay no attention.

Suddenly a woman runs out, a blood-soaked cloth in her hands. My heart skips a beat. She rushes past us into the yard without a glance and throws the bundle into a hole that has been prepared beforehand: she is burying the afterbirth. She dashes straight back into the bedchamber, giving us no time for questions. Soon the door opens a second time, slowly and with great ceremony. As godmother, Mary comes out first, her contemplative face bent over the baby she is cradling in her arms. Mary is wearing a ceremonial dress that Françoise has spent weeks sewing and embroidering. My neighbour walks forward and crowns me with the traditional cap of fatherhood decorated with feathers, identifying me as the husband of the woman in confinement. Ardent and van Gouden make a special taffeta for this cap, and every family has one. It is customary to hang a *kraam kloppertje* over the doorway to the house; this is a doll made of paper and lace indicating the child's gender.

Mary looks at me with her large grey eyes, gives a little curtsy, lifts up the little baby and solemnly declares:

'Here is your daughter Adrienne, cousin Francis. Through her, may Our Lord give you days of joy, or may He recall her if such is His will.'

These are the ritual words with which a newly born infant is presented to its father. They signify that the feasting may begin.

Trembling, I scrutinise the little face, its eyes closed; my first contact with this fragile being who, God willing, will become my daughter. Out on the doorstep, the neighbours are calling for their husbands. It has been a beautiful day and the men, with Jan and Giuliano at their head, have been waiting on the bench in front of the house. They enter noisily. The child is taken back from me and I am at some difficulty disentangling myself from the embraces, for I wish to speak to Françoise.

She smiles on seeing me enter, while eagerly devouring a slice of bread and honey.

'So, Master Tréville?'

'Your daughter is a very beautiful young lady, Madam Tréville; my compliments.'

Tradition dictates that I provide some merriment for the children, who have gathered, restless with excitement, outside the house. We lay out heaps of sugared almonds and a large bowl of warming posset that we ladle out to young and old alike. It is late afternoon; neighbours and passers-by stop on their way home to drink a cup of posset, share the laughter, bombard me with advice and maxims, admire the baby and pay their respects to the mother.

Guillaume Ardent, who goes by the diminutive Wim for Willem, the Dutch version of Guillaume, brings out his lute and bursts into song:

> *Sweet wine but freshly press'd*
> *From the sagely planted vine*
> *I drink as from the breast*
> *Suckling your nectar fine*
> *Sweet wine but freshly press'd*
> *From the sagely planted vine.*

This is one of the tunes from our musical evenings, so everybody sings along with him. Other instruments appear, and soon there is quite a serenade beneath Françoise's windows.

Feet tap under skirts and, if we do not dance, it is out of consideration for the mother, and so as not to upset Pastor Claas. He lives two houses down and has come to sit with us and smoke his pipe, despite knowing we are all Catholics.

THIS QUIET, ORDINARY LIFE seemed so unusual it might have belonged to somebody else. Seven or eight years it lasted.

The first sign of change, unrecognised by me at the time, came when I got the news that my father had been released from the Fleet. He had settled in Chelsea, which was where Jack found him – a tall, stooped figure of a man, he said.

'He lives in splendid style, sir, with many servants and a beautiful house.'

'So he has been freed?'

'Yes and no. He is more keenly watched than a chest full of gold. But Her Majesty has permitted him to enjoy fresh air and to live outside of the Fleet. He has quite a court around him, a household considerably larger than Lady Anne's. You have an endless number of sisters, sir; the youngest can't be more than six or seven. Dorothy's her name and she looks just like you.'

My father wished to see me, and I had a thousand questions for him.

But by the same occasion I also learned that the Earl of Essex, one of the members of the Privy Council, had sought to force the Queen to change her rule; he had intended to take her hostage until she agreed, and some said he would have killed her had she refused. Sheer madness.

Much as the Queen loved Essex, he received no pardon from her this time. I had met the man and thought him quite crack-brained even then. He was convinced he would succeed Elizabeth and saw himself as King of England already; but he took his desires for reality and tumbled into the trap of his own arrogance. He perished on the scaffold. Southampton had been imprisoned with Essex for having faithfully followed him in this lunacy. Condemned to die, his sentence was stayed, but he now resided in the Tower.

This did not seem like an opportune moment to go and see my father who, Giuliano assured me, still maintained close links with Spain and the Jesuits. But he was so insistent that I finally gave in, after careful consultation with the Tregians in Amsterdam and the Trévilles in Paris.

We were in the forty-third year of the reign and, as on my previous visit, it was spring.

AT THE LAST MINUTE, Giuliano decides to come with me. It has been so long since he has accompanied me on one of my journeys that I feel like an adolescent again. I am quite moved.

We cross the Channel in plain sight. There are fewer spies about, now that Philip II of Spain and old Lord Burghley have passed on. Indeed I hope Robert Cecil, Burghley's son, will understand that I am neither a rebel nor a plotter, despite his having neither seen nor heard from me for so many years. Plotters always end up ensnared by a spy, sooner or later. I have not forgotten his declaration of affection and I hope he remembers too, for I intend to go and see him. Jan has given me permission to reveal his identity, should that prove absolutely necessary.

We land and go straight to Lady Anne's. Having harboured priests from France, she has been forced to leave Muswell and return to Chideock, one of the Arundell estates in Dorset, but then having encountered serious trouble there, too, she is now back in Muswell for the time being. My mother is in Chelsea. In Muswell I make the acquaintance of Elizabeth and Dorothy, my two youngest sisters, who are around the same age as my son Francis, and quite lovely. There are three other sisters, but they are ladies-in-waiting in other families.

'How is it you're not in Chelsea too, young ladies?'

'Well, dear brother,' says Dorothy calmly, with all the graveness of a stately lady, 'our esteemed father is of a nervous disposition, and we sometimes forget to not laugh or not run about; thus, after several incidents, we preferred to avoid unnecessary whipping and asked Lady Anne if she would have us here.'

'And what did our esteemed father say?'

'Oh! Our esteemed father said nothing. He was so caught up in his affairs on the day we left that we were unable to bid him farewell. No doubt he was relieved to hear us no longer; he prays a great deal and has little time for us.'

This worries me; I seek further information from Lady Anne.

'Your father spent so long in the Fleet that he has lost all sense of reality. He was scarcely out of prison when he accepted a pension from the King of Spain. I ask you!'

'Does he receive it here?'

'No, of course not. The Queen forbade it.' She sighs. 'Why must he always indulge in such futile provocation? He has enough money.'

'Doe he live off Catholic charity?'

'Not at all. He lives as he has always done, off the revenues of his estates outside Cornwall. But officially he now owns nothing, having disposed of his affairs in such a way as to place some of his means beyond harm's reach. Or rather, my late husband did that for him – his own mind being devoted to higher things.'

'Allow me to ask you a question, Lady Anne: you have no love for my father, and never had. Why did you let your eldest daughter marry him?'

This is not the kind of question it is customary to ask in our family and I expect Lady Anne to rebuff me. But no, she looks at me thoughtfully. Her face is lined, but there is a sparkle in her eye and vigour in her limbs. And she has lost not a single tooth; her smile is as bright as a young lady's.

'Mary and Francis met when I took Sir John as my second husband and went to live in Lanherne with the children from my first marriage. They fell in love with each other when they were adolescents; it was a profitable marriage for everyone. Why would I oppose it? None of the other Tregians were like Francis. They were obstinate, but their obstinacy did not constrain them to the point of making them lose sight of their interests and those of their family. And although Francis was a stubborn lad, he remained delightful and discreet as long as his father was alive. It was Douai that changed him.' Her gaze blurs with the memories. 'I remember that they were asked to arbitrate a quarrel over a rich shipwreck. Your father was barely twenty and he accompanied Sir John to the courthouse. It was the first time for a long while that my husband had spent a whole day alone with his nephew. When he came home he told me: "This boy will bring us trouble: he is quite reckless. We were there to resolve a disagreement, yet he publicly derided as thieves all those who laid claim to part of the wreck. 'A wreck is no honest way to get rich', said he. One cannot say such things to the men whose right it was to empty the ship. Even the Queen demands her share of the booty in such cases. We were not there to moralise but to make sure that the division was fair. Tregian undoubtedly made himself some dreadful enemies." He was very alarmed. And trouble soon arose that had nothing to do with bad luck; it was to be expected.'

'But you too received Cuthbert Mayne at Lanherne.'

'My dear Francis! Everyone received priests! If what was done to your father was visited on all those who harboured a priest, there would be few of the great Cornish families remaining, believe me. When Sir Richard Grenville was named sheriff, we all kept our heads down until the storm passed.'

'All except my father?'

'As soon as his father was dead, he began to conduct himself as if everything was owed him. When a scapegoat was required, the people he'd offended pointed at him. The priests who came from Douai were persecuted furiously, particularly if they were Jesuits, but the Catholic nobility were left alone, provided they had not been plotting. Your father's case is still unique, because of its magnitude. He even offended the Queen!'

I make as if to speak, but she bids me keep silent.

'Yes, I know the story. She resented his virtue because she herself is not an honest woman. It makes for a great story, but unfortunately the reality is much more commonplace: in order to protect this second cousin once removed, she decided to make him sheriff, which he refused, and was good enough to leave the post vacant for Sir Richard Grenville, a man whom he had made an enemy and who used his new position to heap misfortune upon the Tregians and the Arundells. They seized the estates of the two richest families in Cornwall and sent us packing with a harshness they seldom displayed elsewhere, believe me.'

Her face is hard.

'To answer your question: when your father's true character became apparent, Mary and he were already married. Nobody ever imagined that the son of that old fox Francis Tregian the Elder would throw himself headlong into a trap that was as conspicuous as it was deadly. And Mary was in love. All the women fell in love with your father, back then; handsome, young, rich and delightful as he was. A profitable marriage that was also blessed with love – what more could one ask?'

I have no idea what to say, but she continues as if I am not there: 'Our life would have been much simpler without him.'

She gives me a piercing look, to see if I am angry. I merely smile and kiss her hand.

'Have you made me a great-grandmother, too?' she pursues.

'Yes. Francis and Adrienne. They are too young to travel.'

'I shall never know them. But when I'm in heaven, God willing, I shall ask Him for a well-placed window. Fourteen great-grandchildren have I, with more to come. I'll be kept busy watching over them all!'

•   •   •

ALL THIS RUNS THROUGH my mind as I sit before my parents. My father is a dour old man with a long beard; my mother's frame is small and neat as always, though her figure is fuller than before.

'My son, the time has come to succeed me.'

'But father, you still have a long life ahead of you.'

'I aspire to peace. Before I die, I should like to see our family recover its estates.'

'You know very well, father, that they'll be subject to praemunire as long as you live, and that Sir George Carey will not give them up as long as he lives. Or are you telling me I must convert? For if I were to become a Protestant, our troubles would be . . . '

I am provoking him, I know. Still, his reaction astounds me. Old my father might be, but weak he is not. This is the first time I have ever challenged him to his face. On hearing these words, he cuts me off bluntly, and heaps curses and imprecations on my head. I am ungrateful, unfaithful, inept, insolent, intolerable . . . The torrent is endless. Ah! If he could only whip me still!

I feel like a spectator at a play, content to let my famously inscrutable gaze rest on the action taking place upon the stage. My mother, sitting a little back from my father, gestures her reproof. The days when she displayed her disagreement with her husband openly are decidedly long gone: Francis Tregian the Elder is not a man to be confronted head-on. I have transgressed this fundamental family credo. My begetter perceives nothing but further provocation in my calm composure, and his rage towers higher still.

'Father,' I say at length, when I have had enough; 'Father, I shall return tomorrow and in the meantime we shall both reflect on the matter.'

I ride back to London. Recover the estates? Absurd. But the next day, and the day after that – every day, in fact – my father makes fresh attempts to convince me.

Cooler heads, such as Old Thomas or Sir John, had warned me ever since childhood: the sentence of praemunire is not passed down from father to son, but I would be asked to change my religion upon my father's death, and only then might our estates be returned. Yet this was one point on which I had always been as stubborn as he: I would never recant. I would, however, swear loyalty and obedience to the English Crown, place my sword at its service and be prepared to spill my last drop of blood fighting my country's enemies, whatever their faith. If it be possible in Holland, why not in England?

Arguing in these terms with my father is futile – he who continually declares, loud and clear to anyone who would listen, that in his view, the throne should pass to the Spanish Infanta upon Elizabeth's death – and publicly rejoices at the prospect of England's certain, ensuing return to Catholicism.

'And you would deliver your country into the hands of the Inquisition? They are as inflexible in their own way as the forces of the Crown, you know.'

'Deliver my country? Your impiety terrifies me, my son. The Inquisition is a necessity, particularly in a country subjected to heresy for so long; heresy that must be hunted down in the very souls of all who dwell here. A few burnings will not go amiss to restore the natural order of things.'

'The English people will never stand for it.'

'The English people will do what they're told and obey the divine bidding.'

Ours is a dialogue of the deaf – utterly futile. I decide to keep silent. Or rather, before deciding on a course of action, I choose to await Giuliano's return from Cornwall, where I have sent him incognito, to get an idea of the situation.

My father repeats the litany of my obligations, again and again, and after a few days, I simply stop visiting him. It has become more and more difficult to keep my exasperation in check, and I have no desire to quarrel with him.

IV

How should I your true love know
'From another one?
'By his cockle hat and staff,
And his sandal shoon.
He is dead and gone, lady,
He is dead and gone.

OPHELIA, IN *HAMLET*

WILLIAM SHAKESPEARE

POPULAR BALLAD, TO THE TUNE 'WALSINGHAM'

'IN THE MOST HIGH AND *palmy state of Rome,*
A little ere the mightiest Julius fell,
The graves stood tenantless and the sheeted dead
Did squeak and gibber in the Roman streets:
As stars with trains of fire and dews of blood,
Disasters in the sun; and the moist star
Upon whose influence Neptune's empire stands
Was sick almost to doomsday with eclipse:
And even the like precurse of fierce events,
As harbingers preceding still the fates
And prologue to the omen coming on,
Have heaven and earth together demonstrated
Unto our climatures and countrymen –
But soft, behold! . . .

'Master William, what are you doing there?'

'I'm going on stage. That's my cue.'

'Not a bit of it. I have at least ten lines before you enter.'

'Absolutely not, Master Thomas! We revised the text, remember?'

'Revised the text? Again?'

'Yes, again. A thought occurred to me just now, when I was talking, and I told you . . . '

'You told me the ghost was no longer a mere spectre, but Hamlet's father. I thought it an excellent idea. But that's no reason to cut my speech.'

'My dear Thomas, I have cut nothing, merely revised the text, and I shall continue to do so as long as we rehearse. Now, you are to say: "Behold, lo! Where it comes again, I'll cross it, though it blast me."'

'Is that new?'

'Yes, it's new. You were quite in favour of the idea, but a minute ago.'

'Good, then. But I wonder how we can get any proper work done in these conditions. One never knows which text to keep to.'

'Are you two done with your idle chit-chat? I'm the one who should complain. Transforming the ghost into my deceased father changes all my most important scenes in the first act, not to mention all the rest.'

'Yes, but you, Master Richard, have a fine memory, whereas I . . . '

He stops short, pointing an accusing finger.

'Who goes there? Gentlemen, we have been quarrelling before strangers! Have I not always insisted, there must be no one else present at rehearsals, for God's sake!'

All eyes turn to the gallery, where I stand gazing down at the stage.

'Strangers?' Master Shakespeare is astounded. Then he sees me. 'No! This is no stranger. He's Master Morley's Polyph . . . I mean, this gentleman brings us Ophelia's music, since poor Master Morley cannot bring it himself, in his suffering. Do not consider him a stranger, gentlemen, but rather as an authority. This is Master Francis Tregian, cousin of the late Lord Ferdinando Stanley who was such a help to us in our earliest days; allow me to present Masters William Kemp, Richard Burbage, Thomas Pope, Augustine Phillips. And down there you see Masters George Bryan and John Hemminges, furiously correcting the text so that our revisions are not lost.'

We all bow, and they go back to their business.

The text they are rehearsing is a fine summary of the emotions I have experienced since returning to London: the mood is apocalyptic indeed. It seems Master Shakespeare is as affected by it as I. Sorrow lurks behind every smile and the people's dismay is apparent, especially to me, coming from abroad. Barely three months have passed since Essex was sent to the scaffold; Southampton's future is uncertain and, though his own execution has been stayed, it has not been discounted altogether. People speak in hushed voices of the Queen's imminent death, or rather the question of her succession, for she has no direct heir. James VI of Scotland, the current Lord Derby and Madam Arabella Stuart – all great-grandchildren of the sisters of Henry VIII – have an equal claim to the throne. It falls to the Queen to choose from among them, as custom dictates. But she does nothing, and her silence is loud indeed, omnipresent and suffocating.

The only heir people know anything about is James VI and his reputation is execrable: proud, self-regarding and a poor statesman. I hear this (and worse) ten times over. As for the Infanta of Spain, I believe the island would rise up as one man if her candidacy were taken seriously.

I have left my card at Sir Robert Cecil's office – he is now Secretary of State – and requested an interview. Jack, an expert these days in matters of surveillance, assures me that I have been followed for no more than two or three days, after which Cecil's men lost interest in my comings and goings.

In Amsterdam, I was very far from all this. But upon arriving in London, I felt caught as if in quicksand, sinking slowly, unable to extricate myself. I needed to find a purpose.

The day before my visit to the theatre, I had been to see Thomas Morley, for whom I had copied out the parts of a great many recent Italian madrigals, knowing his passion for them. He has published several books of madrigals and *canzonette* – Italian airs in four parts, adapted into English, copies of which I have seen at Pierre Phalèse's shop.

Morley greeted me with his usual enthusiasm, but I was alarmed at his appearance: emaciated and pale as a shroud.

'So, you're a father now?' he exclaimed. 'Children born to the strains of music, I hope?'

'I was not present for the birth of my first child, but my young daughter heard her first music before she felt the holy water on her brow.'

I asked if he had written his book on the theory of music for young people.

'Yes indeed, my dear Greyhound. And I have given it a clear, ringing title: *A Plain and Easy Introduction to Practical Music*.'

'I shall acquire a copy for my son, though if the truth be told he doesn't know a word of English. He speaks only French and Flemish, both perfectly. And Latin, of course.'

'Here, give him this from me.'

He invited me to take a copy out of a nearby chest, opened it, dipped his quill and inscribed a dedication: *To Francis Tregian, child of the seconda pratica, with the author's profound respects. Thomas Morley.*

We spent the evening reading, deciphering, commenting and singing the scores I had brought, with the help of Madam Morley and one of the Misses Morley. We pushed the invalid's chair up to the virginal; his playing was finer than ever. When we parted – or rather, when I left, for Morley remained in his seat the entire evening – his eyes shone so brightly that I quite forgot his pallor.

'Thank you for these splendid scores, sir. You could not have given me any finer gift. Have you seen Giles Farnaby since you've been here?'

'Not yet. Do you have news of him?'

'He comes regularly to take care of my plectrums and play me his compositions. The boy will go far, you know. He has a thoroughly original mastery of counterpoint. But with his father now passed on, and mired as we are in the gloom that cloaks these last years of our Elizabeth's reign, he talks of leaving London to find fresh vigour somewhere in Lincolnshire, where he has been offered an advantageous post as a musician.'

'Has he stopped building instruments?'

'Not at all, thank the Lord! But he would prefer to concentrate solely on his music. I will send word to him that you're in London, and invite him to meet you here. My legs have been playing me up lately and I would prefer it if my Polyph . . . But no, I really must find a better term. You shall be my Contrapuntal Greyhounds from now on.'

'Thank you.'

'My Contrapuntal Greyhounds had better come to me, than me to them. Which reminds me, would you be so kind as to do me a service?'

'If I am able, with all my heart.'

'Will you go to the Globe tomorrow, early, and take an arrangement of Walsingham I have done – to Master Shakespeare's words – for their new play?'

'With great pleasure.'

He explained to me how the air should be performed.

'You'll be sure to have them rehearse it for you?'

'You may count on me, sir.'

'Otherwise, he will massacre it, which would be a shame. Will you have time for that?'

'I will have time. Would you like me to send my valet to invite Giles Farnaby here tomorrow night? Then I can tell you about the rehearsal and we can enjoy an evening with Master Farnaby too. How does that sound?'

'Wonderful. You can see yourself out; you'll forgive me if I don't get up.'

Outside, Madam Morley took my arm, her eyes brimming with tears. 'How do you find him, sir?'

Such questions are only asked in the hope of an encouraging answer.

'I find him quite his usual self.'

Which was true, too.

'He will surely die, sir. The doctor has given him from three weeks to a year.'

I was touched by her distress, and the news – which I had guessed – tugs at my heart. I am become very attached to Thomas Morley.

'Madam Morley, I know this will be of no consolation to you, but when God has taken Master Thomas's stricken body unto him, his music will continue to make many people happy, and even in four or five hundred years, he will live on when we have disappeared without trace. He is a great man.'

'Thank you, sir.' She wiped her eyes and I left, full of a sense of my own futility. She would rather have her husband here and now, than his posthumous glory.

And so, this morning at daybreak, after the customary Mass at Clerkenwell, I have journeyed to Bankside by water – the first time I have set foot there since that glorious day when Adrian and I crossed the river for our illicit trip to the Bear Garden, when we were still schoolboys.

The Lord Chamberlain's Men (the troupe belongs to George Carey now, who has succeeded his father) have built their new theatre with timber brought from Shoreditch, where James Burbage's father has his own theatre. The story amused the whole of London two or three years earlier: with Burbage the Elder dead, the authorities took advantage of a dispute between the Privy Council and the actors at the Swan Theatre to close all the theatres in London. The Burbages' landlord seized his opportunity, in turn, to throw them out. But the theatre's timber frame was not his; in his absence, Cuthbert and Richard Burbage – helped by the actors and a handful of carpenters – took the whole thing down. When the proprietor returned, he found nothing but a patch of bare ground. He was furiously angry and tried, in vain, to take them to court.

As for the Lord Chamberlain's Men, they rebuilt their theatre, even finer than before, not far from the Bear Garden and slightly nearer the river, on Maiden Lane in St Saviour's parish, more or less opposite Baynard's Castle and St Paul's Wharf. The Rose Theatre is nearby, as is the church of St Mary Overie. The area has filled up in the space of fifteen years. But we are outside the City walls (theatres are still banned within) and despite the many cheap hovels and the rows of whorehouses, it remains a rustic scene, with small streams and gardens and orchards. Almost all the houses are reached by wooden bridges over the watercourses, as are the theatres. I look for the great door of the Globe, surmounted by a wooden pediment carved with a torso of Hercules carrying the world on his shoulders, and the troupe's device: *Totus mundus agit histrionem* ('all the world inspires the player'). From without, the building resembles a tower topped with a roof of thatch and a tall mast from which a flag is flown whenever a performance is in progress.

I arrive early in the morning. No one is there but William Shakespeare himself. The weather is fine and he is sitting at the very front of the stage, in the open air, his legs dangling over the edge. He is reading Montaigne's *Essays*, and so concentrated on his book that I hesitate to disturb him. Eventually, he senses my presence and looks up. 'What can I do for you, Sir?' he says, jumping down from the stage.

'My profound respects, Master Shakespeare. You cannot place me; but…'

'Wait, yes I can. Master Tregian! I had to think for a moment, please excuse me. We haven't seen each other in a long while.'

'The first performance of *A Midsummer Night's Dream*.'

He sighs. 'Carefree days. But let's not dwell on all that. To what do I owe the pleasure?'

'Alas, Master Morley's illness. His legs can no longer carry him. He asked me to bring you his arrangement for the young princess's songs. He explained everything to me, and said he would like me to rehearse the young man playing the role of . . . er . . . '

'Ophelia.'

'Yes, Ophelia. That's it. He asked me to rehearse the young man playing Ophelia, according to his instructions, which are very precise.'

'But Henry Condell won't be here until this afternoon.'

'I'll come back in that case.' I replace my hat.

'Have you eaten?'

'No, as a matter of fact I haven't.'

'Do me the honour of accompanying me to the Pig and Whistle. The hostess keeps a splendid table and a passable ale.'

We exchange our stories, seated before a handsome feast in a corner of the almost deserted inn. Master Shakespeare tells me about Essex's rebellion. The events took place some months before, but they are still the substance of every conversation.

'I didn't know Essex well,' says Shakespeare. 'I hardly ever saw him except at the theatre. He was always devilishly excitable. My instinct told me to be wary of him. Which left me looking an idiot at times, for he was irresistibly charming. My poor Southampton let himself get caught like a fly in birdlime.'

'Do you think he will be hanged, too? Beheaded?'

'No. They would have done it already. But he has lost his dearest friends. Sir Charles Danvers has been executed.' He sighs. 'On the eve of the rebellion, which of course we knew nothing about, he came here in a quite dangerous state of excitement. I had never seen him thus. And he asked us to play *Richard II*.

'"Why in hell's name *Richard II*?" we asked. "Most of us can't even remember the lines, it's been so long since we did it."

'"You will read it through," he said.

'"We no longer have the costumes, or the painted hangings for the scene," we objected.

'"My dear Will," he said, "that is of no importance. What matters is that you perform that very play and no other." He was accompanied by six or seven gentlemen: Sir Charles Percy, Lord Monteagle and others I have forgotten. We told them, too, that the play was so old it would attract scarcely any audience.

'"No matter – we will be there. Here are forty shillings for your pains. We must see the overthrow and death of Richard II."

'We ought to have suspected something, when they said that. But how could we imagine . . . ? Essex was the Queen's favourite. I know now that he had fallen from grace, but I was ignorant of it then. Looking back, I can see that giving him his freedom was a very great risk. But things weren't so simple at the time. Essex was much adored by the mass of the populace: he dazzled them, and they forgot all reason. Had he succeeded, we would probably have had a civil war, a national disaster. But on the day of his execution, all London was in mourning.'

'What about you, his accomplice's protégé?'

'We had witnesses who had heard us object to playing *Richard II*. For a moment, I truly thought we would be implicated in the disgrace. But not at all. On the eve of the execution, the Queen even summoned us to court to play *The Comedy of Errors*. One of the hardest things we have ever done. Indeed, it may have been a way of punishing us. The whole city held its breath, waiting for dawn the next day, and we still had no idea, yea or nay, whether Southampton would be executed too. He's a hothead, but I've come to feel a strong affection for him. We danced the final ballet, but our feet felt as if they were in irons.'

'My own life seems dull indeed, by comparison.'

Perhaps because Shakespeare has opened his heart to me, perhaps because my own heart is near breaking – I have been subjected to sermons and tirades from my family for days, but must hold my tongue – whatever the reason, this polite question from Will as to the state of my own affairs unleashes a torrent in reply.

'In Amsterdam I am a respectable burgher, an associate of a silk-trading house noted for its fine quality. I have a wife and children, who speak not a word of English; the Tregian family's preoccupations do not touch them in any way. I have my music, which fills my many leisure hours. My life is perfectly arranged. I seem to be another person, living in another world. And yet, when I come here, I lose all my mirth. I grow weary and my life seems stale, flat and unprofitable. My father looms like some terrible spectre. He has only to say, "Remember, my son . . . " and I am lost.

The trivial record of my life and business, all my wisdom, knowledge and reason, are wiped from the tables of my memory, and I hear nothing but the voice of a duty alien to me. I tell myself: the time itself is out of joint, and I was not born to set it right. And yet I am caught like a mouse in a trap.'

I feel the blood rise to my face. Shakespeare is staring at me so intently that I shudder.

'What is it Master William?'

'You consider yourself a man caught between two worlds, sir?'

'A man caught between two worlds? Indeed I am. I envy a man who can still find excitement and exaltation, and throw himself into acts of folly, even unto death. We, who are not fanatics, are caught between two camps, two ways of life. We are omniscient, god-like in our apprehension. And so we cannot embrace one or the other. In musical terms, there's the *prima pratica* and the *seconda pratica*: but the one does not exclude the other, they merely express different sentiments. They say music is the highest expression of the divine. Why then, is it so impossible for two different practices to co-exist in our spiritual life?'

'Keep your voice down if you are placing music above religion, Master Tregian.'

'I didn't say that.' I stop short. 'Well, I implied it. It will go no further, I trust.'

'We are gentlemen, sir. The secrets we confide and receive are not ours to divulge. How will you resolve your dilemma?'

'I don't know yet. Doubtless I shall have to do as . . . as a gentleman of my acquaintance has done. He made his family believe he is dead and rebuilt his life in the New World.'

'The New World is full of people who thought themselves unable to bear the ills they suffered here, only to flee to others they knew nothing of. I have heard it said by returning travellers that in the end, they would rather not have crossed the ocean at all.'

I sigh. 'I am caught in a duel with my own self. And I don't know if I am up to the fight.'

'Do you not have brothers?'

'Yes, one. But I am the eldest son.'

'You might renounce your right of primogeniture. Pass the torch to him.'

'That's true. I should give it some thought.'

'Avoid thinking too much, or the trap will close around you.'

'If it hasn't already.'

'Master Tregian, do you know the play for which you have brought me Master Morley's arrangement?'

'No. I don't believe he told me the title.'

'The music is for *Hamlet*.'

I look at him and raise an eyebrow. What of it?

'You don't know the play? Did you not see it at Newington Butts some seven or eight years ago: the story of the prince whose throne is usurped? And a ghost comes to encourage him to take it back, and he pretends to be mad, to secure his revenge . . .'

'There's a tale like that in Belleforest's *Histoires Tragiques*, I believe. But I haven't seen the play.'

'Southampton and Essex are reckless men of action. But you and I are men of reason and thought.'

'I'm sorry?'

'Sir, I should like to ask you a great favour. No one must ever know that they came from you, but I should like to put some of your reflections this morning into Hamlet's mouth.'

'What manner of man is he, your Hamlet?'

'A prince, caught between the modern world of Europe and the backward-looking court of Denmark.'

'Yet the Danish court is very modern. Quite refined, in fact.'

'You know it?'

'Yes indeed.'

'Well, then we shall have it torn between modernity and a vision of the world as it was a century ago. Hamlet is torn, too, between love and the demands of State, between his scholarly urge to explore the majesty of the firmament and his paralysis at the prospect of breaking free of earthly bonds, between his desire for freedom and the voice of his father, calling him to order and to remember his duty.'

'Ah!'

'You see – it is your story. And mine. You look quite thunderstruck.'

He is right. He speaks as if he has read my very soul.

'I have a proposition. Come to the theatre at noon. I'll make a few changes to the text before then. We'll rehearse a few scenes – not in their proper order, sadly, for it depends on which actors are present. You will rehearse Ophelia. And this evening, you can try to read the manuscript. It's full of corrections and revisions, for the moment; I must have it copied to make a clean book for the prompter.'

'What if I were to copy it out for you, as I read?'

'My dear sir, you demean yourself.'

'I demean myself by peddling silks, by copying madrigals and having people sing them, by playing the organ and the virginal, even by knowing how to build instruments. None of these things befits a gentleman. But allow me, this once, to demean myself out of sheer curiosity.'

And so I find myself sitting in the main gallery, watching a rehearsal of various scenes of *Hamlet*.

I send Jack home.

'Tell Lady Anne, and come back later with a very sharp penknife and some fine quills; you know how I like them. I'll need your help. Get some decent rest this afternoon: it may take the better part of the night.'

'Very good, sir.'

Jack is in the habit of seconding me when I copy music. Sometimes, when the original scores are available to us for no more than a few hours, we have to work at great speed. He has learned to imitate my writing to perfection and, on occasion – if we are in a great hurry and my hand is cramped – he copies in my stead. We also use the services of expert copyists, who can imitate our hand in all points.

I admire Master Shakespeare's skill. A few hours later, my story is already incorporated into the text.

I have of late, but wherefore I know not, lost all my mirth, forgone all custom of exercise; and indeed, it goes so heavenly with my disposition, that this goodly frame the Earth, seems to me a sterile promontory; this most excellent canopy the air, look you, this brave o'er-hanging, this majestical roof, fretted with golden fire: why, it appears no other thing to me, than a foul and pestilent congregation of vapours.

What a piece of work is a man! How noble in reason? How infinite in faculty? In form and moving how express and admirable? In action, how like an Angel? In apprehension, how like a God? The beauty of the world, the paragon of animals; and yet to me, what is this quintessence of dust?

My own sentiment, expressed that very morning. Or his – I can no longer tell. I am astounded by the speed with which Shakespeare has blended my words and feelings into the text of his play.

In passing, Shakespeare mentioned the problem of the Children of the Chapel, a highly fashionable troupe of actors at the time.

'Your relative, William Stanley, is their patron. And Ben Jonson writes for them; he's a young playwright – rich, turbulent stuff. We know him well; he has worked for us in the past. Jonson has them speak ill of our public theatres, as if those children will never grow up and become professional actors themselves. They'll have need of us then, all right. They're cutting the very branch on which they – and their author – sit. Tragedy is poorly conveyed by child actors.'

By five o'clock this afternoon, this is in Hamlet, too:

. . . an eyrie of children, little eyases, that cry out on the top of question and are most tyrannically clapped for't. These are now the fashion, and so berattle the common stages (so they call them) that many wearing rapiers are afraid of goose-quills and dare scarce come thither.

Jack makes his timely entrance just as I have finished teaching Henry Condell the airs he is to sing, which he does very prettily indeed.

> *How should I your true love know*
> *From another one,*
> *By his cockle hat and staff,*
> *And his sandal shoon.*
> *He is dead and gone, lady,*
> *He is dead and gone.*
> *At his head a grass-green turf,*
> *At his heels a stone.*
> *White his shroud as the mountain snow –*
> *Larded all with sweet flowers*
> *Which bewept to the grave did not go*
> *With true-love showers.*

The four of us set about making the clean copy for the prompter's book. Shakespeare dictates, Jack cuts the quills, I write and Condell reads it all back. We stop for a while to take refreshment at the Pig and Whistle.

There is much merriment at our table:

'You'll be back tomorrow, Master Tregian? We'll have revised the whole thing all over again, and we'll need a complete new text for the prompter.'

'You are admirably perceptive, dear friends. As soon as I fall asleep, the ideas flow free and the Ghost comes to dictate his own lines.'

'Pinch yourself, Master Shakespeare, so you don't fall asleep between now and the first performance!'

'Truly, though, I feel sure we have it this time. The Ghost was bothering me. Why just any ghost, coming to speak to Hamlet? But if it's his father's ghost, it makes sense. No more revisions, I promise you. Which is not to say we won't retouch the text a little, here and there.'

'But ... we might discover at the last minute that Hamlet has a brother, unbeknown to all, a bastard child fathered by Claudius, long before.'

'Or that Old Hamlet had been tupping Polonius' wife. Quite plausible. What does our Ghost here say to that?'

Everyone chuckles.

We return to our task. I am quite transported with delight. With the exception of a few details, the story dictated to me by the great poet is my own, and Hamlet's many questions are the very same ones I ask myself. Golden is my Elsinore and I am no more attracted by the 'rotten state' of England than Hamlet by his Denmark. There are innumerable parallels.

Hamlet seems the finest of all Shakespeare's plays, and I come to know it almost by heart. I revere it as much as the *Essays* of Messire de Montaigne.

A FEW DAYS LATER, Giuliano returns from Cornwall.

'So? What news?'

'Master Francis, I do not know what to say. Golden is rented to an efficacious tenant farmer and the property is well kept. But I met the Careys' steward, one Ezekiel Grosse.'

'The man Old Thomas told us about years ago?'

'The very same. And if you take my advice, you'll keep well away from that man. I don't trust him.'

'He's dishonest?'

'Not really dishonest, but he has his eye on Golden. It's a lordly manor of long standing and he believes it will enhance his prestige. I have never understood why people like him think that by taking possession of some property or other, their reputation will rise; in reality, they merely tarnish it. No one's fooled in the country round about. Even now, so many years later, people still say your family were the victims of a plot. Everyone remarks that your father lacked diplomacy – the old refrain – but now they also say that he didn't deserve such harsh punishment. Your property at Tregarrick – Old Thomas's house and farm – is flourishing, and perfectly maintained. People would love to see you installed there. And to show you how little regard anyone pays to your being a Catholic, no one, not even the lawyer, who is a strict Puritan, has ever told Carey or Grosse that you are the heir to it. People know, but you would have to commit some truly dreadful act before they would breathe a word.'

'Could we return by way of Cornwall?'

'Yes. I have taken a passage back to Holland from Falmouth; I hope you are in agreement.'

'Oh, perfectly. I am growing tired of London and, once I've seen *Hamlet*, I suggest we leave. Which means in three days, as far as I am concerned.'

I revisit my father. He has not shifted his position one jot.

'Father, I will see what I can do when the time comes. I can promise nothing, and make no commitment now. I can give my word but once, and I cannot give it lightly.'

My father's blessing is not easy to obtain after that, but I force it out of him at the last moment.

Two days before leaving, I go to see Richard Mulcaster. For four or five years now, he has been Rector of St Paul's School, which is of comparable reputation to the Merchant Taylors' but a much bigger establishment. Under his leadership it has become, like his previous school, one of the finest in the country. The man who has taught thousands of schoolboys recognises me immediately, as if we had parted only the day before. People tell me he recognises every one of his former pupils thus. He has less time for me than on my previous visit, but greets me nonetheless, brandishing the first volume of Montaigne's *Essays*.

'The reading matter of every honest and decent man, now that John Florio has translated these admirable volumes,' he declares. 'London is mad for Messire de Montaigne.'

I tell him I found Master Shakespeare reading it.

'That doesn't surprise me. People say he has reworked Thomas Kyd's *Hamlet*.'

'He hasn't reworked it. I didn't see the other play, but I know the story. He has created it afresh. I'm going to see it performed tomorrow. That's one thing I simply can't miss before I leave.'

I tell him of my discussions with Will Shakespeare.

'I'll go and see it next week, when I get a free afternoon. Everyone is talking about it and people are impatient to see it on stage at last.'

'From the scraps I have seen and from reading the text, I believe it will be a truly great work.'

'Tregian, I am happy indeed that you have not forgotten your old schoolmaster. Tell me, do you know your brother's whereabouts?'

I hesitate. He smiles.

'So you've found him but you prefer not to give him away to me.'

'I will happily tell you, sir, if it stays between ourselves.'

'You have my word, Master Tregian.'

I tell him everything. He does nothing but smile, nod and ask the occasional question.

'I always said that boy would go far.'

'That boy, always such a puny child, is now almost as tall as me and twice as broad.'

'Has he started a family?'

'I believe he has considered it recently. But it has not yet come about.'

'Tell him his old schoolmaster never doubted his abilities.'

Before leaving, I keep two further appointments, with Robert Cecil in the morning and *Hamlet* in the afternoon.

'I am greatly discomfited by your family,' says Cecil, after the usual exchange of greetings and formalities.

'As am I, sir. I am a loyal and constant servant of Her Majesty, ready to lay down my life for her, though I am still a Catholic; but my loyalty counts for nothing while my father dreams of installing Spain on the English throne.'

'Precisely, Master Tregian. And as a result, your situation is such that I cannot do anything for you, unless you agree to conform to the Anglican faith. I know you are a loyal subject, that you have fled the Jesuits and our

Anglican authority alike. But as for the rest of Her Majesty's Privy Council, your conversion is the only thing that would give a sufficient guarantee.'

'And that cannot be, sir. I am a man of peace, but no weathervane. My sword is Her Majesty's but my conscience remains my own.'

The conversation continues in much the same manner, with a great deal of repetition.

'My affection for you endures,' says Robert Cecil, finally. 'And I understand your refusal to convert. But things are difficult, very difficult.'

I try to hide it but my anguish must be visible in my face.

'Believe me, Master Tregian, if I could change the current state of affairs, I would do so. I promise you that should the occasion present itself . . . Come and see me whenever you wish. And if you seek a place at court, I will take you into my service tomorrow.'

'Thank you, sir, but I prefer to be my own master, for as long as that is still possible.'

He bows, smiling, with genuine goodwill.

A few hours later, I go to see the performance of *Hamlet*. I have reserved a private box, and bring Giuliano, Jack and my young sisters. The Globe is full to bursting.

> . . . *will you see the players well bestowed? Do you hear, let them be well used, for they are the abstract and brief chronicles of the time; after your death you were better have a bad epitaph than their ill report while you lived.*

The lines capture what I feel as I leave the theatre. I seem to have seen my whole life, the essence of our time, condensed. Impossible not to see Mary Stuart in Gertrude; the late Lord Burghley in Polonius; Essex's wise and cautious friend, Lord Francis Bacon, in Horatio; and my father in Old Hamlet; as for the 'mad' prince, he might have been Essex or Southampton, or myself – or even Will Shakespeare. I am not the only one to see so much in it. The audience treats the players to prolonged and hearty applause, and the Globe is full for the days I remain in London.

In the early evening I return to Thomas Morley's house, where Giles Farnaby is waiting, very much his usual self. I describe the performance in detail. Thomas Morley says:

'The idea of making the Ghost the young prince's father gives the play a universal aspect: everyone will have forgotten the earlier version in a matter of weeks.'

'Did you see Kyd's version?'

'Yes. But it was concentrated on Hamlet's madness as a ruse through which to wreak his vengeance. It was an adventure story, not the political and philosophical treatise you describe.'

'Should you not like to see it, Master Morley?'

'And how might I do that?'

'On a litter. You can take Jack tomorrow, then, between him and your manservant, they can carry you there.'

The idea puts Morley in an excellent mood, and we spend a memorable evening. I find Giles Farnaby's compositions enchanting. He does not have Morley's perfect technique or Byrd's fluency, but his originality and imagination are plain to hear.

'Thank you for liking my compositions,' Giles breathes.

His voice is full of humble gratitude. I am quite taken by surprise.

'Are they not appreciated otherwise?'

'They are not much heard, apart from the psalms and one or two of my *canzonette*. I spend more time building virginals than I do playing them.'

'Would you allow me to copy down some of your pieces?'

'It would be an honour, sir.'

I leave with his scores under my arm and spend half the night copying them. The task helps me overcome the profound sadness I feel, certain that I shall never see Thomas Morley again.

WE REACH ST EWE after a journey of five or six days. Our tenant farmers greet us with delight. The house is as scrupulously maintained as on my previous visit; time seems to have stood still. We stay for just two nights, but it seems to me I am drinking from the very source of life. My energies are restored. But the reminder of my deep attachment to Cornwall does nothing to clarify my thoughts.

I visit Golden. The road between the two houses, leading to Golden Mill, is quite well used, and I attach myself to a group of travellers both there and back. The properties are in good order: the Warren is laden with game, wheat is growing on the Roman Camp, the animals look well fed, and the people seem serene and content.

Giuliano suggests we go to the King's Arms in Probus, a hostelry that Ezekiel Grosse likes to frequent. And so I see him for the first time, though he is unaware of my presence. He is a man of about forty, stockily built, with a loud voice, stout fingers and small, round, darting eyes. There is no refinement about him, and I immediately dislike his swaggering, disdainful air. I see straight away that I can be no match for him when it comes to striking a bargain. I am utterly defenceless against men of his kind.

'Shall we make ourselves known to him?'

'Sir, your reticence is written all over your face. You had better leave it to me, but another time, when you are not here. You will spoil everything.'

'No doubt you are right. We shall leave it for now.'

And we leave. Questioned on the matter, the notary confirms that it would be almost impossible to take back the lands seized under the praemunire, until my father's death.

'Your family is a rather special case. The original aim was to dismantle the hegemony they feared would arise from a permanent alliance between the Tregian and Arundell families.'

'My mother is not an Arundell.'

'But her mother married old Arundell himself. Your grandfather John Tregian was married to Catherine Arundell. Two consecutive marriages united the two greatest fortunes in the region. Understandably, that worried some people. The fact that the two families were Catholic was the perfect pretext for their persecution. There is an element in the current hostile climate that goes beyond religion, and you will find it very difficult to reinstate the property as it was before your grandfather's death. I would even venture that every precaution has been taken to make it impossible. In your place, I would content myself with the small property and farm that have come down to you as a personal legacy. I have mentioned it to no one, and it brings you an adequate rent by which to live.'

I find myself so undecided that I postpone any major resolutions on the matter.

We board ship at Falmouth that very evening, on the high tide.

V

How now shepherd what means that,
Why wearest willow in thine hat?
Are thy scarves of red and yellow
Changed to branches of green willow?
They are changed and so am I.
Sorrow lives but joy must die
'Tis my Phillis only she
Makes me wear this willow tree.

'TELL ME DAPHNE'
POPULAR BALLAD

WHEN I LOOK BACK on the period that followed, I am put in mind of a late-autumn rose that miraculously opens and blooms as winter beckons, unfurling its poignant beauty without a care for the louring frost.

I was well aware that I was living through the end of an epoch, but I still felt the future was all mine. When I left England, my mind was almost set against making any attempt to recover Golden: I would write to my father – which would be easier than talking to him directly – and suggest he hand the task to his son Charles, with whom he seemed to have closer affinities than with me.

Once in France, Giuliano and I go our separate ways, for he is in a hurry to return to Amsterdam. I travel to Paris, where I spend an evening with Margaret and Charles de Tréville and recount my journey.

'What if you were to redeem your lands by buying back your entitlement to the revenues the estates bring in?' asks Charles. 'What would that cost?'

'Three thousand pounds a year was the figure commonly mentioned in our family,' Margaret replies.

'That's not an accurate figure,' I say. 'There might have been one or two years when that sum was achieved, in our grandfather John's day, but then the estates were all administered together, under the authority of a particularly honest and competent steward. According to the papers he left me, it was closer to one thousand pounds a year recently, and even that is more than any of us will ever have. And that steward knew what he was talking about: he returned to his former duties after our father's arrest.'

'You could borrow that sum and pay back your father's debt with the revenues from the states,' Charles says. 'You don't need the income. Your Dutch capital will earn you sufficient to live. Your cloth has become a vital commodity. Even Their Majesties' wedding was a riot of Amsterdam Ardent silks, as they are called here.'

'I think that the parcelling out of the estates has brought the yield down: we shall get five or six hundred at the very most.'

'Even so, in seven or eight years you'll have recovered everything. We'll help you, if necessary. But still, they won't demand a fortune for something that belongs to you.'

I have a hundred further objections to their idea, but I need time to reflect. And I would talk to Jan before deciding.

'The King has asked me for news of you on several occasions,' says Charles. 'I told him that you had become a father, and just a few days ago he asked me:

'"Do you think he's about to have a son?"

'"I do not know whether he is expecting a third child, sire."

'"If he has a son at the same time as we do, have him send the boy to us; we shall make him a companion for the Dauphin."'

This surprises me.

'Has the Queen given birth to a Dauphin?'

'No. But you know the King. A true son of Gascony. The Queen is with child – what else would it be but a boy?'

'My own Queen, Françoise, is indeed with child, and if she gives me a son, I shall take His Majesty at his word, as long as my wife agrees.'

'We could take in Francis here to give him a gentleman's education, while we await the sons who may or may not be born.'

Francis is seven and has already had two or three tutors: harmless, mediocre fellows. I have taken charge of much of his education myself. None of them have been capable teachers, in my view. I have recently heard tell of a Swiss from Lucerne, a most learned man who has made true scholars of the children of one of my Dutch acquaintances. I am not keen on the idea – I should not like to hear my son speak Latin with a German accent.

The thought of sending him to a large household, as is done in England, and my sister's household at that, enchants me. It only remains to be seen if Françoise . . . She will no doubt agree. Of course, sending my son to Paris would not be such a separation for me: I travel that way often enough. The same cannot be said for Françoise, who travels rarely and unwillingly.

But when I discuss the idea with her, she agrees immediately.

God gives us our little Catherine in early summer, and just as soon takes her back.

Once she has been churched, Françoise urges Francis to leave for Paris, as if driven by some sense of foreboding, and I bring him with me on my next visit, around Michaelmas, the traditional start of the school year in England, which we take as a good omen.

Francis is a passable rider but he cannot gallop as fast as I, so our journey to Paris is long, and made longer because the boy is blessed with an insatiable curiosity. Every step of the way brings new questions; he is not content until he has seen and understood everything.

With our journey in mind, I have taught him some rudiments of combat, and he shows astonishing skill with a foil, as if he has been waiting all his life for someone to place a sword in his hand and teach him the flourish, the guard position, the stop, the traverse, the lunge and the *imbroccata*.

'You'll make an accomplished gentleman, my son. You speak Latin, and you wield that sword like an old soldier.'

'Why? Must one speak Latin when fencing?'

'That would doubtless be an additional weapon in combat with certain opponents, if only to unsettle them.'

Sometimes I wonder what he thinks of our journey. But this lively lad is also a quiet one. He observes everything with his wide, bright-blue eyes, taking everything in and storing it away, but once he has asked all his questions, he barely utters another word.

Margaret welcomes him with great affection:

'How you've grown, my darling child! You'll be in fine company with your cousins, I'll warrant.'

Margaret's boys are six and four.

'Do they fence and speak Latin, madam?'

'They're just beginning their Latin. As for fencing, it's a little soon. They're not as old as you.'

'Ah! I'll wait then. Fencing is the only thing I enjoy.'

'A budding solider!' Margaret declares. I present him to His Majesty King Henri the next day.

'I feel as if I saw you last only yesterday, dear sir,' says the King cordially. 'And your son looks just like you. We shall have him at court.'

'You do us too much honour, sire.'

'Not at all, not at all. Tréville!' Charles bows in reply.

'I imagine that young Tregian will reside in your household?'

'Yes, sire.'

'When my son is born, I wish him to have such a companion. You shall bring us your nephew and son.'

'As you command, sire.'

When we are alone together, Charles remarks:

'If he says no more about it, then mere courtesy was all it was. But if he repeats this invitation, then he means it and shall not renounce it ever. In that case, the fortunes of Arnaud and Francis will be made. We must wait.'

My son loses no time in replying:

'I shall wait, and in the meantime I shall study.'

Charles and I exchange a look over the top of young Francis's mop of auburn curls. Such wisdom combined with such warlike ambition in this little boy: it is an explosive mixture. The stuff of great men. Of great rogues, too.

JAN'S WEDDING WAS THE last petal of that radiant autumn rose, a shivering memento.

We prepared a glorious ceremony. Never have I organised the playing of so much music for a single occasion.

Jan was marrying a neighbour, Antje; she had a childlike face and was the young widow of a cloth merchant. She had long been a frequent visitor to our household, and Françoise had taken her under her wing since the night her husband fell into the canal dead drunk and was drowned.

First Giuliano, then Jan gave her some help with her business. Jan fell in love in an instant, and I believe it was reciprocal. But they said nothing about it to each other for a long while, since it wasn't done for an honourable woman to give her heart to another, nor for a man of worth to declare his love, before the mourning period was over.

It was two years before he asked for her hand.

The betrothal was announced. It should have been done by the suitor's parents, but since Jan was an 'orphan', the announcement was made by the widow's parents instead. The banns were published thrice, as was the custom, but at the City Hall rather than the Protestant church, since the bride and groom were both Catholic. The date was chosen following long discussions: Sunday was impossible, not being a very propitious day for festivities; Friday was a day overcast by the evil eye; and the month of May brought misfortune, at least in Holland.

The house on the Stromarkt seethed with the coming and going of friends, known as 'playfellows' – friends of the betrothed who helped them prepare for the wedding. I was in charge of the music, while Françoise oversaw the decoration of the nuptial bedchamber. An entire room on the ground floor was set aside for the purpose of making Antje's dress. Once completed, the dress and its crown were displayed for all to see in a richly decorated basket. The groom's clothes were prepared elsewhere, as was the pipe, decorated with leaves, which he would smoke on the wedding day.

Catholic weddings were not recognised by law in the Low Countries. Consequently, we had to hold both a civil ceremony and a religious one. Giuliano paid the deputy burgomaster handsomely to perform the wedding at our house, after which the priest performed the religious ceremony in the hall where guests were customarily received.

The front of the Ardent and van Gouden house was laden with flowers. Splendid rugs, woven for the occasion in the unique colours that had made the company's fortune, were hung at all the windows. Up on the roof, a consort played William Byrd throughout the ceremony and could be heard as far as the other side of the harbour. And as all this took place in the middle of the afternoon, a considerable crowd of neighbours, friends, customers and passers-by gathered round the house.

'I do', said the one betrothed to the other, and the bride took her gold engagement ring from her left hand and placed it on her right, according to custom.

The feast was held in the shop, which we had emptied of its cloth and everyday furniture. We stretched garlands of flowers across the room and, as was the custom in Holland, brought in every mirror in the house, each one decorated with riddles and aphorisms. I also set up a harpsichord I'd brought back from Antwerp as a gift for the bride, who played it delightfully. The elder of the Sweelinck boys, Dirk, agreed to come and play it during the feast. Out in the garden, we erected a temple of green branches, with a statue of Venus set between branched candle-holders.

Once the ceremony was over, we placed the married couple's chairs in the guest-hall, and the guests came in one after another to present their gifts and to admire Antje's dress, which was truly a masterpiece. It was made of a specially woven taffeta: white with fine stripes of the famous Ardent purple, interwoven with a gold thread that made it shimmer like a starry sky.

I had always found Antje pretty, but in that dress, on the day she wedded a man whom she plainly loved, she was resplendent, eclipsing even her sparkling gown. The hues of the cloth accented her copper locks and milky skin; her eyes, surprisingly black for such a complexion, enhanced her beauty even more. As for my brother, I had never seen him look so magnificent. He called to mind one of those gods of Antiquity who, gazing out across the ruins of the Roman Forum, are rendered more superb still by the toppled figures of those around them, suggesting a majesty quite out of reach. Jan was all that, with the addition of warm flesh and feeling.

During the presenting of gifts, a choir stood just behind the wedded couple's seats, singing Italian madrigals I had rehearsed with them for some weeks.

We sat down to eat as night fell. It was a gargantuan wedding banquet: at least thirty dishes. We thought it excessive, but Antje's parents were intractable. Any respectable family was obliged to serve their neighbours a feast they would never forget.

The banquet was also accompanied by a consort and madrigals.

At the close of festivities, we upheld the last Dutch wedding custom, according to which the bride and groom must try to leave without the guests knowing, while the guests, expecting this, would try to prevent their departure.

To peals of laughter, Antje was seized by her female friends, who went off to hide her.

Jan looked for her throughout the house, but she was nowhere to be found.

The young women made a circle with him at the centre.

'We shall return her, gracious host, once you have sworn to give us a banquet in a week's time,' they sang.

'I shall promise once you've returned my wife! I won't be quailed!' Jan protested.

'Well then, your marriage is already over before it's even begun,' the choir answered.

He promised in the end, and they brought him back his wife amid great peals of laughter.

The guests then made another circle around the bride's crown and danced merrily around it to the sound of the viol, the lute and the psaltery.

After which they bowed and took their leave, singly or in pairs, taking with them as mementoes the garlands that adorned the house inside and out.

'It's not over, sir, you'll see,' said Jack, as he helped me off with my shoes.

'Yes, I know full well: there'll be baptisms, and Jan had to swear that in a week's time . . . '

'A week? Is that what you think? They'll all be back tomorrow to eat up what's left, so the kitchens assure me.'

'But I've dismissed the musicians.'

'Yes, but when I learned of this, I asked them to return. I paid them a little more and almost all of them have agreed to come back. They expected to be asked. The second day of a wedding is usually a musical affair. You owe me eight florins, sir.'

'Sometimes I wonder what I'd do without you, Jack. You make up for my many flaws.'

'Without you, sir, I would never have the opportunity to display these qualities you esteem so kindly. Consequently, I often wonder myself what I would have done had you not retained my service.'

We laughed, albeit wearily.

It is true we'd become inseparable.

And so the next day was indeed spent dancing, music-making and feasting, with great good humour.

Throughout these two days, the heavens in turn consented to put on a fine show: a bright blue sky, without a single cloud.

I STRUGGLED LONG AND hard to blot out the momentous events that followed, so that to write about them now requires an enormous effort.

I departed, as I had so often before, travelling to Venice, or Milan or Padua or perhaps Prague. A journey not unlike any other, or so I assume, since I have no recollection of it whatever; music took precedence over secondary matters such as negotiations for the sale of Ardent cloth or the purchase of China silks.

A single image remains with me, burning bright these many years. It is the day of my departure and I am about to ride off, having bid my farewells, when Adrienne comes running out of the house:

'Father, father!' she cries in her little, piping voice. She sounds so sorrowful that I take her in my arms.

'What is it, little lady?'

'Father, what if I never see you again?'

'But Adrienne, I shall be back soon, God willing.'

'Promise you'll return?'

'I promise, my little lamb.'

'And you'll greet me before anyone else?'

The adults around us laugh. What a queer little thing!

I mount, ask Jack to hand Adrienne up to me and we trot along the *gracht* together.

'You see, it's just as though you were coming with me. And we'll go on another little ride, as far as the port, when I return.'

'You won't forget me, Father?'

A pang grips my heart. Perhaps it is a fleeting premonition of misfortune.

'I shall never forget you, Adrienne. You'll be my little darling until my dying breath.'

We trot back to the house, I drop the girl into her mother's arms, and our convoy sets off.

I look back when we reach the corner of the *gracht*.

Françoise's smile shines in the sunlight which dapples Adrienne's mahogany locks.

This is the last image I have of them.

WE COMMENCED OUR RETURN journey in early summer. As often, to avoid crossing Germany loaded with silk, we boarded a barge in Basle. On many an occasion I had left Jack with the merchandise and continued alone by road to see the Ruckers or Peter Philips in Antwerp, or my family in Paris. This time, I chose to return by barge too.

The captain looked so troubled, I could not help but ask him what was the matter.

'I have heard worrying rumours,' he admitted in a low voice, after a pause.

'What sort of rumours?'

'I have been told several times that Holland has been ravaged by the plague these last three or four weeks.' And, giving me no time to respond, 'But I beg you, sir: say nothing, otherwise everyone will lose their heads. That will happen soon enough once we reach Holland herself.'

'Where did you get this information?'

'A group of Basle travellers returning from Amsterdam and who determined to place themselves in quarantine of their own free will so as not to risk infecting Basle. One of them told me that he himself had remained in fine health, while everyone in the house where he usually stayed was dead.'

'*Father, what if I never see you again?*' The memory pierces me like a sword-thrust. Adrienne's question haunts my thoughts as I stare blindly at the landscape of graceful vine-covered hills going by. '*Father, what if I never see you again?*' The little voice echoes in my head day and night. What if she had known? Children can be strangely prescient at times. The river voyage seems endless. At one point, I am tempted to leap out onto dry land and gallop all the way to Amsterdam. But I would only be giving myself the illusion of speed, for I would be forced to halt at twilight, and then there are all the hazards of the road. On this barge, we progress at a steady pace, day and night; were I in full command of my faculties, I would have recalled the several times we have seen our merchandise arrive before us, even though we have ridden hard for home. But the inactivity is driving me mad.

In Rotterdam, we dispatch our bales of cloth to Amsterdam. They will wend their devious way, from one canal to another, and I have not the patience to wait. I dread setting foot on land, but the epidemic has not reached the great port, at least not yet. So many diseases have journeyed inland from here, brought by sailors from afar, that I dare to hope.

But in the countryside, people speak of nothing but the plague at every halt. We reach the first infected town, Gouda. The streets are deserted.

We pass a cart covered by a sheet, with several pairs of feet sticking out from under it. I bring my horse to a sharp halt and Jack lets out a cry of woe:

'Where are you going?' he asks in a choked voice.

'There's no more room in the cemetery,' dolefully replies the pale, dishevelled woman pulling the cart. 'My husband is dead, so I make myself useful for as long as God gives me life,' she adds, before plodding on.

Jack and I exchange a look of horror.

We reach Amsterdam just as the sun is setting, in a perfectly tranquil sky. The city is a ghost of its former self. There is no movement in the harbour, nor in the canals or streets, except for the occasional 'plague doctors', conspicuous by their special garments and the handbell they ring to make their passing known. Nearly every door bears a white cross announcing the presence of one stricken with the plague. A distant tocsin sounds with incessant alarm. All else is sullen silence. Every window is closed and dark. It is the hour when families usually take the air outside their house after work. This evening, the doorsteps are deserted.

No cries can be heard, no voices of any kind; just the tocsin, the frantic pulse of a city in its death-throes.

We arrive at the Brouwersgracht. There is a white cross on every house, including our own.

I jump down from my horse and bolt up the steps, Jack at my heels. The door opens to my touch. Silence.

The house is in almost perfect order.

I hasten to the bedchamber. The bed is uncovered, the imprint of Françoise's and Adrienne's bodies still visible on the straw mattress. '*Father, what if I never see you again?*'

Jack enters, so pale one could no longer discern the line of his lips.

'Sir . . . ' he says in a choked voice. 'Sir . . . ' He closes his eyes.

'Tell me, Jack. You have some information.' He nods.

'Tell me.'

He suddenly looks up, his eyes full of tears.

'All, sir.'

'All?'

'Yes, all. Madam, Mistress Adrienne, the maidservants, the groom, the drudge. All.'

Among the maidservants was one he had been preparing to wed. How long we stand there, I do not know, our eyes fixed on the impression in the bed, weeping heavily. I wish to lie down and contaminate myself with the disease that has killed my wife and daughter. Why go on living? '*You'll think of me, sir?*' The voice of my son, alive and well in Paris, God willing, holds me back.

'We'll go to the Ardents,' I say at last.

Have I also lost my brother, and Jane, who has been like a mother to me?

The door of the trade counter is marked with a white cross.

I knock, and have to knock several times more before a distant voice calls out hoarsely:

'Keep away!'

The door stays shut.

'Open, I pray, it's Master Tréville.'

The door flies open. Pieter, the chief clerk, stands on the threshold, his face weary and worn.

'Master Tréville, you'll contaminate all those among us who are not yet dead.'

'Master van Gouden?'

'Master van Gouden, Master Ardent and Master Wim departed for Scotland just before the epidemic. We have no tidings of them. Maybe they died on the road. Maybe they already had the plague when they left.'

'And madam? And the other children? And the clerks?' The tears stream down his wrinkled cheeks.

'Young Master Frans Ardent, Mistress Mary, the little ones, Madam Antje too. They are all dead. Nearly all the clerks have been cut down. Madam and I were obliged to close the weaving workshop. Nearly all the weavers . . . ' He breaks off.

'And madam?'

'A miracle: madam is cured.'

'Where is she?'

'In her chamber. Come through this way. There is no one to open her front door.'

I hasten through the house, rush up the stairs and enter the chamber, the door of which stands wide open.

In an armchair sits a figure of wax: Jane. Her hair tumbles out of her bonnet, her skin is chalky white, her face sunken. She stares at the floor and does not get up.

I kneel before her and speak to her in English.

'Jane! My beloved Jane, it's me, your Francis.'

'God did not wish to take me, my little Francis. I tried everything, but they died in my arms, one after another. To have to meet your gaze, or Adrian's, or Giuliano's, I could not do it. When the disease laid me low, I gave thanks. But God would not take me. I offered him my life in exchange for the children ...' She finally raises her eyes to mine. They are deep and blue as lakes. Almost Jane's eyes. Almost, for in that moment they are swimming with madness. She cannot see me. The Francis she addresses so familiarly is the little boy she nursed.

I take her in my arms.

'We must take care of you, Jane. God has granted you your life; you must live.'

As for myself, I banish all thoughts. Later. Now it is better to act.

'Jack!'

He comes running.

'Are there any servants left?'

'A few, sir.'

'A maidservant to care for madam?'

'I doubt it, sir.'

'Say ... Jack? Have they told you where the others are buried?'

'Nobody knows, sir. The cemeteries filled up immediately. They had to bury everyone together in huge pits. They ... They say a quarter of the population is dead.'

The tears return. Not knowing where my beloved lies is like losing her twice over.

'I will seek some information.'

'I shall stay with madam, if you permit it, sir.'

'I very much wish it, Jack. As long as you don't fear infection.'

He smiles sadly:

'If we must be contaminated, then we already are.'

Nearly all the servants have fled, in the hope of saving themselves, or to die in the bosom of their family. In the kitchens there are but two very young girls, Truns and Saskija, orphans of around ten years old whom Jane has taken in.

'Were you sick?'

'Saskija a little, me not at all. I believe that God spared us. Everyone was dying these last few days, but now that's stopped. Whatever may be, I am unafraid, sir.'

'Good. Then you shall scrub the whole house with soft soap and plenty of water. We shall endeavour to save ourselves, as well as the gentlemen when they return.'

'And the nursling, sir.'

'The nursling? What nursling?'

'When the plague doctor came, Madam Antje had just died. But she was close to childbirth. The plague doctor opened her stomach, sir, and removed the baby. It was horrible.'

She raises the heap of rags she has been holding on her lap.

'It's a little boy. Madam told me that Master and she had decided to call him Thomas, so we had him baptised Thomas.'

'He's alive?'

'Yes, sir. We were terrified to fetch a nurse in case her milk had been contaminated. We nursed him with milk from the neighbours' goat, which we mixed with water. It's been two weeks already and he is still alive.'

'Truns, Saskija, you are quite marvellous.'

I hold the little body in my hands, blinded with tears. This tiny creature seems like a message from God: 'Do not despair, for I am the Lord your Father and will never abandon you.' The plague has fallen upon us to expiate our sins. But little Thomas, who would not die, is proof of Heaven's forgiveness.

The babe opens his wide grey eyes – eyes that swirl with the swell of a stormy Cornish sea. He gives a wail. Life is returned amid this destruction, and in his weak cry I seem to hear echo the voices of Françoise and Adrienne.

THERE IS A GREAT void in my breast. *Françoise. Adrienne. Françoise. Françoise!* Each name falls like a drop of blood to the floor. If I pause for even a minute I shall die; not struck down by the plague, for the disease takes no interest in either me or Jack, but by grief. And so I never pause. After sending Jack to lock up our house, I set about getting things in order in the double-fronted house on the Stromarkt.

Nobody recalls how it was that Giuliano and Jan left together, for that happened only rarely. They would return one day, if they were not dead. Better to waste no time and do what I can to enable life and business to carry on once the epidemic has passed. If they are dead, the onus of administering Ardent and van Gouden will fall to me. There are at least two heirs, Francis and little Thomas. I believe I can rightly claim that Adrian's son and my own keep me going in these direful days. Without them, I would not wish to cling on.

Amsterdam comes back to life, little by little. Doors are inched open, then flung wide. Walls, floors and paving stones are scrubbed with soft soap. Clothes are boiled in large cauldrons, for everyone knows the Devil detests water, especially when it's hot. And the plague could only be the work of the Devil.

With the assistance of the sole remaining clerk, I answer orders, give explanations, request delays.

Jane keeps to her bedchamber for several days, in a state of senseless lethargy. Now it is I who nurse her. I put her to bed, get her up, wash her, feed her. I sense she would let herself die of grief. As much as I talk to her, she hears nothing, and utters not a word in reply. Then, one fine morning, she comes down to the kitchen. Upon seeing the little baby, she returns to life.

'Whose is he?'

'He is Antje's and Jan's son.'

'Their son . . . Why didn't you tell me?'

Her former radiance is almost fully restored. She takes matters in hand.

'What is he nursed with?'

'Goat's milk, madam.'

'Is it you who've been feeding him, Saskija?'

'Yes, madam, mixed with water like you did for . . . '

'Very good. Has the house been scrubbed with plenty of water?'

'Yes, madam; Master Frans instructed us to do so last week.'

'Very good. How many are we . . . ' her voice trembles slightly, 'in all?'

'Six, and the little one, madam.'

'Right. We shall prepare dinner.'

Standing in the shadows, Jack and I exchange a look of relief.

When Giuliano, Jan and Wim come home from their long journey, the city has all but returned to its usual pace, and the house to its usual appearance.

When we hear their voices – we have been listening out for days and days – Jack comes running.

'Send Kees to me,' I tell him.

And when he enters, I ask:

'Have you heard the news, Kees?'

'What news, sir?'

'Where have you been?'

'We went to Scotland. Master Jan was seeking a particular kind of wool for a new cloth. What is it, sir?'

'You have heard no news from Holland?'

'We're freshly landed from a Scottish ship, sir.'

'Kees, the plague has been raging here for weeks.'

'What are you saying, sir!'

'Madam Antje, four of the Ardent children, Madam Françoise and my daughter Adrienne, and I know not how many housemaids and servants . . . a quarter of the city, so they say, are . . . '

'Oh dear Lord, sir! My family too, perhaps?'

Kees's family come from around Rotterdam.

'I believe not; we came from there and the plague hadn't struck at all. These gentlemen must be told the news. Bring them to me and make sure that nobody tells them anything beforehand.'

'Yes, sir.'

They come in, full of life and energy. Their smiles vanish as soon as they see me, sitting at the empty trade counter, Pieter alone at my side.

Ordinarily, I would come there only briefly, for that part of the business was not my realm.

'What is it?'

'Sit down.'

'Francis! Why did Kees make me come here instead of letting me go up to greet Antje?'

Giuliano sees the tears running down the old clerk's face.

'Francis – for the love of God – what is it?'

I know then that no form of words will spare their pain. There is nothing for it.

'Between your departure and just now, Amsterdam has fallen prey to the worst plague the city has ever known.'

'And so?' asks Jan, his voice faltering.

'I have lost Françoise and Adrienne; you, Giuliano, have lost four of your children, and you, Jan . . . your wife.'

They look at me, aghast.

'I do not know exactly how many clerks have been cut down, nor how many weavers. We had to close the workshops. The province is in utter disarray.'

Still they say nothing. Neither of them moves.

'Jane was taken ill with the plague but recovered; Saskija too, one of the orphan girls. Truns, the other orphan girl, and Pieter here were spared. And the plague doctor succeeded in saving your child, Jan. You have a son.'

I am counting on this last news stirring them as it did me, and am not disappointed.

They set to weeping, in silence.

'Pieter . . .'

He smiles at me, nods and goes out, to return shortly, followed by the orphans carrying the baby.

Saskija holds out the infant to Jan with a bow:

'Here is your son Thomas, sir. Through him, may Our Lord give you days of joy, or may He recall him if such is His will.'

And she adds bashfully:

'We were unable to await your return for the baptism, and we had no one else, so I agreed to be the godmother, and Pieter the godfather, but we can change that if . . .'

Jan's face is so pale that for an instant I fear he would be taken ill. He stares motionless at the newborn infant, who looks back at him, babbling quietly.

'He is your son, Jan.'

Suddenly the colour returns to his cheeks.

'He didn't get the plague?'

'No. And the goat's milk hasn't killed him either.'

'Where's Jane?' asks Giuliano.

'In the kitchen, or in her bedchamber.'

He goes out.

I take the baby from Saskija's arms.

'If you would leave us now, young ladies, we'll bring the little one back to you in a while.'

We are alone. Jan continues to stare at the child without touching it.

'Did you lose yours, too?' he asks me in English.

'It's as if God were telling us our Dutch life is a sin, don't you think? He has left you a son. He has left me a son. But now we must walk the straight and narrow path.'

He looks at me with a wan smile.

'Easy to lay the fault with God. But it's our own ignorance that has brought this calamity on us. I went to Eu during this voyage, to see Pierre the apothecary. The Duke of Guise spent several weeks in Eu, and he had in his retinue an Indian from the Americas, whom he dragged around with him like a curiosity. This man spoke perfect French. He revealed a host of secrets to Pierre. For example, a man may cure himself of many contagious diseases and fevers by swallowing a certain mushroom that can be cultivated on a certain type of moss. This American, a great priest of his people, knows how. Yet nobody would think to ask him anything. We're only interested in the Americas for their gold, not for their peoples and their wisdom. We have exterminated them in their millions, without listening to them. Rather than a punishment, the plague might be a warning: there exist, perhaps, other conquests to be made than those of war.'

What can I say to that? I hand him the child.

'Here, take him. God has allowed him to survive.'

He takes the boy with trembling hands.

'They called him Thomas?'

'Yes. And they saved him, first by staying when everyone fled, and then by knowing how to care for him.'

'These two little girls ... I shall adopt them so Thomas may have a family.'

'That is good.'

'And you, brother, what will you do?'

'My son is in Paris, at the court of the French King. Perhaps I shall go there. I cannot say.'

At that moment, little Thomas gives a faint wail, then bawls at the top of his lungs. His voice is a sign to me. Whatever my decision, and in spite of the pain that crushes me, death has retreated and life blooms anew.

VI

Aim not too high in things above thy reach;
Be not too foolish in thy own conceit;
As thou hast wit and worldly wealth and will.
So give Him thanks that shall increase it still.

'FORTUNE MY FOE'
POPULAR BALLAD

I HAVE STRUGGLED IN VAIN to wipe clean my memory of life at that time. Disjointed images remain, but each is the clearer for that.

I tried to help Jan and Giuliano, and to restore the house of Ardent and van Gouden. I see myself at work on the ledgers, taking over the duties of the clerks dead from the plague, until such time as they could be replaced. My limbs felt heavy as lead.

I see the large house on the Stromarkt. We had shut up my house on the Brouwersgracht. Jane was inconsolable after the death of her four children, unable to speak of them without breaking down in tears. But she recovered her health and strength, and often seemed lively and bright. It took a pisky's sensibility to read the infinite grief in her eyes.

Giuliano said nothing. He kept his sparkling demeanour and energetic carriage, but his beard and hair were turning swiftly grey.

Ardent and van Gouden incorporated the Pierson weaving workshops, inherited from Antje's first husband. We tackled the new challenge of fine woollen cloth. Jan threw himself into the work, body and soul. Leaving ordinary woollen cloth to the countless textile merchants already established in Holland, he set out to create very fine, luxurious fabrics in exclusive colours obtained from dyes he had developed himself. He left his workshop only to take care of his son Thomas, and this he did with devoted, zealous attention.

The house was greatly changed. At times, we found ourselves listening out for the quick patter of young feet, youthful voices, laughter breaking the silence. Wim was the only survivor, and at sixteen or seventeen, he was a man himself. Thomas was still too small to make much noise. We awaited the return of a little girl, Jana, aged two or three, who had escaped the plague because she had been sent to a nurse in the country, Jane having found herself with no milk for the first time in her life.

Thinking to fill the empty house, I briefly formed a plan to fetch young Francis from Paris, but quickly abandoned the idea: I had not recovered sufficient zest for life. The idea of taking a new wife, as many around me were doing, filled me with horror. I have never found myself able to remarry. Whenever the occasion presented itself, I felt that by taking fresh vows before God, I was obliterating Françoise, our happiness, our passion. I would remain her husband forever.

I went to Paris.

It must have been after the death of Queen Elizabeth: I see myself lamenting her passing during an interview at the court of Henri IV, with one of my cousins, William Stanley, the young Lord Derby, younger brother of Ferdinando who had very probably been poisoned by his former supporters for betraying their attempt to establish him as the Catholic pretender to the throne. I no longer cared who knew my identity. I had nothing left to protect. My 'heretic' wife was dead.

My brother was so thoroughly cloaked in the identity of Jan van Gouden that it was doubtful even he remembered being Adrian Tregian. And when his former self came to mind, he was firmly rejected:

'Just remember that Adrian Tregian would have scorned silk- and cloth-trading – the only activity that interests me – as beneath him. Unthinkable! No, Adrian Tregian is dead, God rest his soul. Long live Jan van Gouden!'

Together with his cousin Arnaud, my son was a gentleman of the chamber to the Dauphin Louis. He spoke French like a Parisian, but had not forgotten his Dutch, in which he often discoursed with a fellow Amsterdammer – a learned scholar in Paris. He distinguished himself not by his height (at ten years old he was, like his father before him, as tall as many adults), but by his skill at arms, and in this he earned quite a reputation. He devoted himself to it with the same passion I had poured into my music. On horseback or foot, with a sword, foil or pistol, he was a fanatical practitioner and of invincible skill. No one suspected he was but a child.

I'm a decent swordsman myself, having never received more than a scratch in the skirmishes I have fought over the course of my life (and there have been many). But by the grace of God, I never had to fight my own son: at the strip, he almost always got the better of me. And Arnaud was as formidable an opponent as he. It was partly thanks to them that the Dauphin, who shared their passion for the martial arts, became such a fine swordsman himself.

All of which is to say that young Francis had secured himself an excellent place at court, and had no need of me. Adrienne and Françoise's deaths plunged the Troisville household into deep sorrow. Charles had been greatly attached to his sister, and my son to his mother. But Francis found consolation with his aunt Margaret who showed him as much love as her own children. Indeed, at court everyone believed François de Tréville (as he was known), was Charles's own son.

I heard news of the death my grandmother, Lady Anne Arundell. Another sorrow to add to the rest.

Was it in Paris, where I often stayed, that I received a letter from Robert Cecil, now Earl of Salisbury? Be that as it may, Robert Cecil wrote to me:

> It is rumoured that an attempt is planned on the life of King James I. Such rumours are not uncommon, and are merely that – rumours. But we cannot ignore them. And unlike so many other occasions, this time my agents have no information on how the attempt might be made. I am all the more concerned, having learned from extremely reliable sources of a determination to kill not only the King but all his entourage with him; whether his family or his political allies also remains unclear. Has this come from the Catholics? And if so, from whom? Some clues point to the Jesuits. And so I thought of you. Since the peace with Spain, relations between our two countries have eased. To the point that His Majesty has even, as a gesture of goodwill, allowed Archduke Albert to raise a regiment of English Catholics in Flanders, in

> *the service of the Spanish Crown. The English captain charged with their command is your relative, Thomas Arundell, whom His Majesty has made 1st Baron of Wardour. I am told that the conspirators are to be found among the recruits to the new regiment. I should like you to enlist.*
>
> *You told me once that while your conscience would answer to no one but God, your sword was forever in the service of the Crown. I have nothing to offer you beyond a commitment: if you wish to return to England, I will work to facilitate it and do what I can to help you recover your estates at minimal cost. If you accept my offer, the bearer of this message will explain what you must do. If not, forget this letter, I will not hold it against you.*

I accepted. A suicide mission was exactly what I needed.

Robert Cecil required of me that I travel to Antwerp or Brussels and spend time among the entourage of Archduke Albert, who ruled with an iron hand in the name of His Most Catholic Majesty. I was also to spend time among the Jesuits and ally myself to a certain Captain Hugh Owen and a number of other unrepentant English Catholics. Cecil asked me to keep my ears and eyes open, or better still, to encourage talk on the part of men likely to know something. I was, of course, sworn to the utmost secrecy.

'My two servants are no fools,' I told Cecil's envoy. 'They have known me too well, for too long – they know that I would never enlist with the Archduke without very good reason. After all, he is fighting against a country I hold in the deepest affection.'

'Tell them as little as possible, but be sure they remain on their guard: the King's arm is long, and the Inquisition is a monster with many tentacles.'

I went to Antwerp, took lodgings, and then, before embarking on my new life, I took a turn out into the countryside with Jack. We reached the middle of a field and reined in our horses. I explained to him what was afoot. His eyes shone. He was an adventurer at heart.

'So we shall be soldiers and spies, sir?'

'That's not how I see it. We shall simply be spending a little while in the service of our King. Using unorthodox methods, true enough. And if the Jesuits discover our true intent, we risk our lives. You must show the utmost care.'

'That goes without saying, sir.'

'I'm telling you this because you'll have your part to play too. Get to know the valets, the common soldiers.'

'Understood, sir. You can count on me.'

I sent a message to Giuliano, who arrived quickly from Amsterdam with Kees. He shook his head when I told him the plan.

'It may be a mistake to get mixed up in this. To my mind, Robert Cecil is not a man to trust blindly. He tends to use men in his service as instruments of his own glory. I had sworn never to get caught up in it again, but I will make an exception for you: I'll give you three days of my time, for I'm much needed in Amsterdam. But I'll leave Kees with you; he's a master of such matters.'

Kees merely smiled.

'In any case,' Giuliano was pensive now, 'if the rumours are already so specific, we shall have to act fast.'

I became a soldier overnight: I was admitted into the regiment without the slightest hesitation. My father was a fervent papist celebrated throughout the whole of Catholic Europe. I was his son. Of course I would follow in his footsteps. My loyalty was never questioned, it seemed.

The vice-prefect of the English mission in Antwerp was a fellow Cornishman – William Bawden, a relative of Nicholas Bawden, who had served Cardinal Allen with me in Rome. I cultivated his good favour assiduously, but remained cautious in the extreme: this Jesuit was a true Machiavellian, and the highest English religious authority in Flanders, despite his modest title. Nothing happened without his knowledge. Giuliano advised me to pay court, and so I did, with some repugnance. He engaged me in long discussions whose only purpose, it seemed, was to reach the same inevitable conclusion:

'You have neglected your theology since leaving Rome, Master Tregian. You are a better musician than you were then, but music will not afford you entry to the kingdom of heaven.'

I was tempted to ask whether he thought to ensure his own place hereafter through plotting and intrigue.

Most alarming of all was his way of fixing me with his sly yellow eyes and asking:

'Why have you chosen this precise moment to join the fight?'

Was this his way of asking whether I was involved in a plot? Was he a plotter himself?

'My conscience determined this course of action a long time ago, but circumstances . . . '

'Your father is a model for us all, Master Tregian. Is it he who has sent you?'

Now his question, tone and look were heavy with insinuation. I answered like any man under oath who has no wish to show his hand:

'He has urged me to join your cause for a very long time.'

As a Catholic gentleman in the service of the Archduke, I spent endless hours at the fencing strip and inspecting the troops under my command. I had no idea what I would do if I were dispatched to conquer Holland, but the Lord spared me that particular ordeal. I was indifferent to all the rest. Our captain, Thomas Arundell, was the youngest brother of my grandmother Catherine and of Sir John, but I had never met him before, though his warrior exploits had been much talked about in Clerkenwell when I was a child. I knew he was a Catholic, and not afraid to show it. Our relations were distant – all we shared was our hostility to the Jesuits.

I met Owen, and drank with him often, but our conversation remained trivial. He was of mature years, overtly pro-Spanish, and explained his position with implacable logic. There was nothing of the conspirator about him, it seemed to me. We disagreed on everything, but I couldn't help liking him.

From time to time I encountered my brother Charles, who had also enlisted in the regiment. We made frequent promises to spend an evening together, but we both knew we were much too different and had nothing to say to each other. The planned evening never took place.

Peter Paul Rubens was in Rome and I regretted his absence. I often went to Pierre Phalèse's house to see the scores he published with Ruckers, from whom I had bought a virginal for my lodgings. And to the Golden Compasses, the sign of the printer, publisher and bookseller Jan Moretus-Plantin, whose premises on the Vrijdagmarkt overflowed with fascinating volumes – behind the Jesuit literature filling the front of the shop, for this was also the official printer of the Society of Jesus. And it was here, at the Golden Compasses one afternoon, leafing through a promising tome, that I collected my first useful scrap of information.

By the end of his three days, Giuliano had managed to discover that something was indeed afoot among the English Catholics, who were not only unhappy that Mary Stuart's son remained obstinately Protestant, but were pushed almost beyond endurance by an unexpected surge in acts of persecution, not to mention fines even heavier than those imposed under Elizabeth. Giuliano heard it said that such extremities of misery demand desperate solutions. But neither he nor we were able to discover just what these 'desperate solutions' might be.

While leafing through a Dutch book, I overhear two men talking in English, in very low voices, on the other side of the shop. The premises are very small and my hearing is sharp. One man in particular attracts my attention. I have seen him talking to Captain Owen.

'It won't be long now.'

'How will we be alerted?'

'You'll know: we'll hear it from here.'

They both laugh.

'That's what I keep telling myself. I try to be patient, but I long to be home.'

'So many statesmen will need replacing, we'll each get our seat.'

'Quiet!' They pause.

'A word, sir . . . ' The Englishman I do not recognise is addressing me in his own language.

A thoroughly clumsy trap. I neither look up nor acknowledge him. The man walks over and addresses me again. I raise my head from my book. 'Yes, sir?'

'Ah! So you are English after all!'

'At your service.'

'May I know your name, sir?'

'But it was you who spoke first; so you should introduce yourself to me.'

I place a hand on the pommel of my sword.

The two men exchange a glance; one is armed and he puts his hand to his own sword. But on a mutual signal, they simply shrug and walk away, muttering to one another.

'I feared for my books,' says Jan Moretus, quietly.

'I feared for my patience, and even more for my person. Do you have a back door?'

'At your service, sir. This way.'

We cross the yard, enter the type room and leave the building by a small door used for delivering the lead. Moretus goes ahead of me down a narrow alley which opens onto a busy thoroughfare. He glances around quickly.

'If they're waiting for you anywhere, they'll be in front of the shop, or at the door to the print workshop. There's no one here.'

'Do you know those two men, Mijnheer Moretus?'

'One is a Jesuit Father, a Master Green. The other is an English gentleman whom I have heard addressed as Lord Winter.'

'Thank you, my friend.'

By one of those strokes of luck in which we are apt to see the hand of God, Jack and Kees come home that very evening, bringing with them an exchange overheard between two English gentlemen: '"The fire of God will consume the heretics," said one. "It'll be hot, for sure", said the other, "but the flames will bring purification."'

Putting all this together, we reach a thoroughly improbable conclusion: someone is plotting to explode a powder-chest in the midst of a celebration given by the King – a banquet or reception of some kind. But would that lead to the deaths of 'so many statesmen'? Not necessarily. What, then? Surely there can be no possibility of blasting Parliament itself? Could there?

My suppositions seem absurd. But the Englishman's other phrase haunts me: *It won't be long now.* Better to be mistaken and ridiculed than to arrive too late. My contact misses two of our prearranged meetings. I decide to send Jack to London with a concise message: 'Sir, my envoy will discuss the spectacle I can arrange for you.' This is the phrase we agreed on beforehand. I order Jack to mention no names, only the facts, for, while I am committed to preserving His Majesty's life, I would have no part in any arrests, torture or executions.

When he returns two weeks later, Jack tells me everything:

'The reality was even madder than we had supposed. You remember Lord Winter, the gentleman you came close to running through with your sword at the Golden Compasses?'

'I remember him. If we had come to arms, it might very well have been me that was run through. What of him?'

'He was one of the conspirators. He's in the Tower now. He had come to Antwerp to consult Captain Owen and the papal nuncio. I had to pay a fortune to secure all the details.'

'You did well. I will repay you.'

'Indeed you shall not, sir!' he laughs aloud. 'I've been paid back, and handsomely. I gave Lord Salisbury my bill, for I reasoned it was at his charge.'

'Tell me about the plot. The rumours are contradictory. Bawden looks as grim as the grave but I can get no information from him whatsoever. Was there a plot to assassinate the King?'

'Yes sir, but those concerned had laid bigger plans than that. Much bigger. They had filled the cellars of the Palace of Westminster with gunpowder. They intended to blow the King up, and with him the whole of Parliament, the Privy Council, the Lords and Commons. And the whole neighbourhood, I don't doubt. When I reached Lord Salisbury – and I swear, it was no easy task – he had only just heard rumours of the Gunpowder Plot (all London is calling it that) from another source, and he found the idea so incredible that he refused to take it seriously. But then he heard my message. "What? You come from overseas to tell me the same mad idea?" His voice trembled, I swear. "Sir, we feel ridiculous even for entertaining it, it seems unthinkable, but . . ." He cut us short: "Oh, if the information I have received from elsewhere is accurate, it's not ridiculous at all. It's the absolute truth."'

Jack sighs.

'And it is indeed the absolute truth. It's said they had packed enough powder beneath Parliament to blow up half of London. It was discovered at the last minute. The day I left London, the chief conspirators were already dead or under arrest. But it was whispered that other Catholics were in for a hard time. Viscount Montagu, Lord Mordaunt and your uncle Lord Stourton were not in London on the day the Palace was set to blow, and since they are Catholics, they are suspected. Lord Salisbury has promised to facilitate your return to England, sir, but with a plot like that, you'll still be viewed with suspicion. Your father is on the Jesuit side. He wasn't aware of the exact details of the plot, but he knew something was afoot. His servants told me he'd had Masses said for the success of the undertaking. And if I am informed of it, then Salisbury's spies are too.'

•   •   •

ONE MORNING in late November, I am awoken by Giuliano bursting into my bedchamber.

'Giuliano, whatever are you doing here? I thought you were in a hurry to return to Amsterdam?'

He brushes my question aside. I have seldom seen him so agitated.

'What did you promise Robert Cecil?'

'To stay for at least a year. Why?'

'Because I have just learned from a source who has never been mistaken, ever, that the Gunpowder Plot was a great contrivance orchestrated by Salisbury himself to justify the persecution of Catholics and destroy the peace with Spain.'

'The same was said about Essex's rebellion. And Watson's plot. I even heard William Cecil say the same thing when they executed Doctor Lopez ten years ago. I find it hard to believe.'

'And yet . . .' Giuliano unfolds a paper and reads:

> *The fire which was said to have burnt our King and Council, which has been so hot these two days past in every man's mouth, is but* ignis fatuus *or a flash of some foolish fellow's brain to abuse the world. For it is now as confidently reported that there was no such matter, nor anything near it beyond more than a barrel of powder found near the court.*

'This is a letter written by Dudley Carleton to John Chamberlain on 13th November, just a week after the discovery of the plot. I know Dudley Carleton. He's no rumour spreader – certainly not rumour as dangerous as this. That's just one of the things I've heard.'

'But how could you, from Amsterdam . . . ?'

He smiles more calmly.

'My bloodhound instinct. Something wasn't right. The three days I spent here were enough for me to sense it. I returned to Amsterdam, but I was restless. So I set off again.'

We stare at one another for a long time in silence.

'Have you done anything to arouse suspicion?'

'Suspicion? Whatever do you mean?'

'Did Guido Fawkes share any secrets with you when he was in the English regiment?'

'I don't know who that would be. No one presented themselves to me under that name.'

'Or Lord Winter?'

'It seems he's a gentleman I came within a hair's breadth of fighting. If what you say is true, then what I heard that day was part of the contrivance.'

'And Hugh Owen? Did you tell Cecil about him?'

'He would have been delighted if I had, but I had nothing to say about him, so never mentioned him. Indeed I mentioned no names, on principle.'

He gives a great sigh of relief.

'If this story is true, they hired you – and others – to give credence to the appearance of a plot, or to undermine you and prove that all Catholics are capable of becoming conspirators. But I think above all it was to provide honourable external witnesses. To cover their rear, in tactical terms. Of course, if you show the slightest doubt as to the official version, Cecil will find a way to prove you were involved. With a name as politically charged as yours, that wouldn't be difficult. I even think the Catholic pseudo-regiment was created as an accessory to Cecil's plot. If it's disbanded six or seven months from now, my suspicions will be proved right. And here's another interesting thing I discovered: when Thomas Arundell negotiated his departure to Flanders, he asked – among other things – for a guaranteed halt to the persecution of the Arundells and Tregians in England. Robert Cecil gave him his word, but refused to confirm it in writing.'

'And my father?'

'According to my informers, they gave thought to implicating him because of his great friendship with the Jesuits. But in the end, they decided he was too old and, above all, too upright a man. And then the minute he was included in the bargain struck by Thomas Arundell, they gave up on him completely.' He gives a small, bitter laugh. 'They still haven't managed to implicate any Jesuit directly. For Robert Cecil, that must be a disaster. Because I'm convinced this whole elaborate device was put in place to destroy the reputation of the Catholics, especially the Jesuits, and also to persuade the King that Cecil is indispensable.'

'Giuliano, I really find it hard to believe all that.'

'So do I, Francis. But my source has never been wrong before. He's ideally placed to know everything. For example, they say that Ambrose Rookwood and Sir Everard Digby never knew there was a plan to blow up Parliament. They thought they were preparing their departure to serve in the English regiment in Flanders.'

'But what of these great traitors we hear so much about: Catesby, Percy, Winter, and that Guido Fawkes you mention?'

'Cecil's agents.'

'No. That's not possible.'

If all this be true, Machiavelli was an innocent babe compared to Cecil. I see him, that little man with bright, intelligent eyes, in his world of luxury and refinement. But I know, too, that my incredulity is rooted in my own incapacity to conceive of such a plan.

'In any event,' says Giuliano, 'whether it's true or not, the end result is the same. The crime hurts Catholics, which is what prompts me to see it as a clever machination – infinitely profitable to Salisbury, not to say alarming to the King, whose father Lord Darnley died precisely because a large quantity of gunpowder was placed in the cellar beneath his house.'

'The more I hear, the more I think you're right. So what should I do now?'

'Nothing. Forewarned is forearmed. You are on your guard. Under no circumstances should you travel to England, until the mood has calmed. And you must behave as if you knew nothing but the official version of the Plot. Whatever the truth of it, never forget that Cecil is a man without scruples, whose personal status is his sole concern.'

'Might we not take back Golden?'

'Perhaps. But, in spite of everything, I fear Ezekiel Grosse. I can never trust that man.'

AFTER THAT, MY TIME in the Brabant was uneventful in the extreme. I remember drilling my men in the early morning:

'On the command "Have a Care!" you will stand to attention, take the pike in your right hand and place it outside your right foot, thumb outward, looking straight ahead, with your left arm held straight down at your side.'

And to the musketeers, every morning, day in, day out: 'Blow off your loose powder!' And so they would. At times, the loose powder caused a small explosion that would singe their eyebrows and moustaches, but that was all part of barracks life and its regulations.

Looking back, I seem to have seen very little combat for a soldier. Rather, I made a great deal of music and I travelled widely. From time to time, I would cross my more warlike brother Charles. He persisted in his disagreeable habit of parading his convictions at every opportunity, but his bellicose nature ensured he was not obliged to take the cloth. We spoke little, thereby avoiding coming to blows.

I continued to visit Paris and my son, and travelled often to Amsterdam, too, not in secret, but without announcing my presence any more than necessary. I did my best to advance the affairs of the house of Ardent and van Gouden, but if I was to keep up the appearance of an English gentleman, my business activities had to be kept discreet. A gentleman has no hand in commerce.

From time to time I fell in love, but never for long. Inevitably, the moment would come when the image of Françoise eclipsed the lovely young women who attracted me but could never keep me. I earned a reputation as an inconstant lover, a heart-breaker, so far removed from my true nature that the very idea is laughable.

This quiet existence came to an abrupt end in the fourth year of King James's English reign. As Giuliano had predicted, the English regiment was unravelling fast, and it seemed to me that by autumn there would be nothing and no one left. We were even encouraged to leave, in veiled terms. Thomas Arundell returned to England, as if none of this was his concern any longer. I went to Brussels and took lodgings there.

One July day, I was astonished to receive a visit from Phillips, my father's manservant. I had always liked Phillips – it was often thanks to his efforts, in childhood, that I succeeded in avoiding the whip.

'I am very glad to see you in such good health, sir.'

'And I am glad to see that you're still as strong as an oak, Phillips. What of my father? How is he?'

'Alas, not so strong as an oak, sir. He suffers greatly with his sciatica, and stays up too late far too often. He takes little care of himself. But you will be the judge of that, sir, for he is on his way. He has stopped at the English College in Douai and will be here in a few days. He sent me ahead to tell you.'

'My father, here? Why?'

'His arrest was sought after the Gunpowder Plot, but his friends did their utmost to prove he had nothing whatever to do with it. Finally, the Privy Council agreed to his continued freedom, provided he leave the country. He is on his way to Spain.'

My astonishment is unconfined.

'Whatever does this mean? Why Spain?'

'Because the King of Spain has granted him a stipend.'

I am overwhelmed by the shock. My father is incorrigible.

'And my mother?'

'Your mother is not going with him.'

Were I not sitting in my chair, I would have fallen over backwards. My mother, leave her husband!

'Phillips, this must be some jest.'

'No, sir. I was surprised, myself. But it appears that my Mistress does not wish to leave England, and my Master cannot remain there. So they have agreed to part. Perhaps, one day . . . '

'Will she ever join him, do you think?'

'If you ask my opinion, sir, I would be so bold as to say no, I do not believe she will. Madam resides at the house of her brother, Lord Stourton, and has taken your young sisters with her.'

'And my father?'

'Your father will be here in three or four days. I am to prepare lodgings for him, and he begs you await his leisure. He has a matter of great importance to communicate.'

'I am at his command, of course.'

No doubt Phillips detects the bitterness in my voice. He gazes at me with his kindly grey eyes but says nothing.

My father arrives, and I go to visit him.

'Listen at the door, for I may wish to discuss this interview with you later,' I tell Jack.

'Sir, I would steal for you if such were your command. So when you ask nothing more than the execution of my normal duties, I am only too ready to oblige.'

My father's tall frame is bent and stooping now. His eyes have lost their gleam, he no longer smiles, his face is deeply lined, and his sparse hair and beard are a yellowish white. He wears a pinched expression, and his mouth is a thin, lipless line. He has the pallor of a dying man.

'My son,' says this aged man, solemnly. 'You must take up the flame in my stead. I have long hoped that a great uprising would restore a Catholic monarch to the throne, and that you might return home with your head held high. God has not granted my wish.'

He pauses, as if inviting me to speak, but I prefer to say nothing. He goes on:

'None of which absolves you of your duty, my son. I am leaving England so that I may end my life in devout prayer and sanctity. I have a thousand sins to expiate, and must secure my place in the company of Heaven. You must buy back your ancestral estates. George Carey is dead, so your dealings are now with his widow. And Lord Salisbury has agreed to facilitate matters. I leave you Phillips. He knows everyone and will help you.'

'Did you not receive the letter in which I begged you to entrust the task to my brother, your son Charles?'

'I received it, yes. But I attributed it to a moment's aberration. A Tregian never shirks his duty, and you are a true Tregian.'

Hamlet's words echo in my head:

> *His greatness weighed, his will is not his own,*
> *For he himself is subject to his birth.*
> *He may not, as unvalued persons do,*
> *Carve for himself . . .*

'I am a musician first and foremost, and a merchant.'

My father's parchment complexion purples with rage and his voice rings out with unexpected force.

'Cease this blasphemy, sir! You will not abandon your family, your brother, your sisters. The quality of "gentleman" is not some discarded cloak to pick up or throw down at leisure. It is a duty before Heaven, and we are born to it. You are to return to England, to fight for the true faith and your ancestors' rightful estates. You have no choice.'

Let not thy mother lose her prayers, Hamlet; I pray thee stay with us, go not to Wittenberg.

I shall in all my best obey you, madam.

I think of Adrian. Here am I, caught in a dilemma from which he managed to extricate himself when but a child. I must act.

If it be not now, yet it will come. The readiness is all.

I give in.

'I shall do my best to obey, sir. But I need your help. To buy back the land, I will need money. And I have none.'

'Neither have I.'

'How have you lived in such fine style, all these years?'

'With our incomes from Devonshire and Dorset. The Crown never touched those.'

I am relieved he would not have me swallow the lie circulating throughout Europe: that he has lived solely on the charity of his friends.

'Then I shall use those to buy back Golden.'

'No. They are not enough, and you will need money to live. You, your brother, your mother and your sisters.'

'In which case, Father, I cannot see . . .'

'You will borrow against your Cornish income for a while. And I shall send you the greater part of the income granted me by the King of Spain.'

We continue in this vein for some time, and finally I agree – the arrangement does not seem unreasonable, after all. With the money from Spain and the income available to me from Paris, as well as the income from our estates outside Cornwall, not to mention the borrowings against part of my revenues there, it seems possible I could buy back the estates within a few years, especially if I could also count on Lord Salisbury's benevolent support.

'Mark my words, he'll send you nothing from Spain. I wouldn't count on his money if I were you,' says Jack, once my father has gone. 'He seeks your consent, and for that he was prepared to promise anything. But he'll forget. My own father has always done so with us.'

Alas for me, I pay his wise counsel none of the attention it deserves.

I TELL NO ONE I am leaving – I would not be gone for good, merely to see to the business of my English estates.

After my father's departure, I call Jack and Phillips.

'Phillips, in the many years since you last saw me, I have grown to a man. Jack and I have been together for more than ten years, and are perfectly familiar with one another. He invariably knows what I would do in any circumstance, and I always know how he would react, what I need to tell him and what may easily be left unsaid. We no longer even irritate one another. You, on the other hand – well, I love you dearly, and I've known you since I was born, but not at all in the same way. Quite apart from the fact that Jack and I are used to living at a tremendous pace, travelling for months at a time, which may not appeal to you. That said, I hold you in great affection.'

Phillips smiles.

'Sir, it is true I know almost nothing about you, at least not since your departure for France at the age of ten. But rumours have reached my ears.'

I raise an eyebrow, and he smiles more broadly still. Phillips has a distinguished air, and could easily pass for a gentleman in his own right. He must be only a few years younger than my father. But he is not tormented by sciatica, his thick blond hair is untainted with white and there are few lines around his eyes. He is of taller than average height and, although he has spent more than twenty years serving a man in prison, his strong build suggests he is accustomed to physical exercise – a Herculean worker, no doubt.

'I heard you had children, and that your wife fell victim to the plague, for which I am most infinitely sorry. I know too that you assist Giuliano Ardent in his silk-trading business. Don't look so alarmed, sir. I have never told your father, nor anyone else for that matter. For years, I lost sight of you altogether. People said you were living in Rome, or in Paris – at Madam Margaret's house. Then, more recently, I had occasion to read a report sent to your father by the Jesuits, in which . . . '

'What – a report from the Jesuits?'

'Sir, when you reappeared from out of nowhere and enlisted with the Archduke, the Jesuits were as suspicious of you as they were of everyone, and they set their spies on you. William Bawden had you followed, and the henchmen of the Inquisition discovered you were living with the Ardents in Amsterdam and frequented Master Jan Sweelinck, a Huguenot, that your silks were to be found everywhere, in the homes of Catholics and heretics who seemed to know you personally. From the report, your life resembled that of a respectable burgher, rather than a gentleman. And indeed, you were living among the burghers of Amsterdam. Yet when you travelled to Paris, you lived in fine style and were a friend of His Majesty Henri IV, whom the zealots still view as a heretic.'

'I'm quite horrified, Phillips! My father . . . ?'

Phillips looks as contrite as any Pulcinella in a Venetian farce.

'No sir, your Father never read the report. I was lucky enough to see it first – for it had become unsealed – and somehow it stayed in my pocket. But it made me believe you were not, perhaps, the man your father depicted.'

'In essence, my dear Phillips, there is nothing to suggest that you are not yourself a Jesuit spy.'

'Nothing indeed, sir.' He maintains his impassive expression. 'Except the passage of time – spies invariably give themselves away in the end. But I would venture to point out, sir, that one may be the devoted servant of a gentleman whose extreme views one does not share.'

'True. And so, dear Jack, I ask you to get to know Phillips, and mistrust him until I give you notice to the contrary. He may be an enemy.'

Jack understands. And I don't doubt that Phillips too receives the message loud and clear. But it takes just a few days for Jack to be sure of his man.

'Sir, fervent Catholic that he is, Phillips shows such great devotion to your family that even were you to go and live among the heathen Moors and become the Grand Mufti himself, he would follow you without question. He has a wife and children, but his only true family is yours.'

We quickly observe that he is as fit as a young man for any task, and capable of riding for days at a time with no sign of fatigue. He tells us his family is in Kent, where he goes from time to time. For my own peace of mind, I send for Kees in secret, since Phillips does not know him, and instruct him to follow the latter's movements. Phillips does exactly as he has said: he goes to visit his family in Kent.

Finally, one day, I risk taking him with me to Amsterdam. I have only temporary lodgings in Brussels and Antwerp, and I like to go to Amsterdam from time to time to see Jane, my brother, Giuliano and young Thomas – a miracle child, in everyone's eyes. He seems to embody every dear soul we have lost. I delight in Jan Sweelinck's company, too. His eldest son and he were spared by the plague and, though we never speak of it, we are united in that bond. I take him as many scores as I can lay hands on and, while sorrow keeps me from attending to my music (something I would never have thought possible), I maintain my connection to it nonetheless, out of love for Sweelinck.

We arrive in Amsterdam one evening. I send Jack on ahead: Jan should be forewarned that Phillips is with me. But Jan is away and so, on his return, finds himself face to face with Phillips, utterly without warning. I am the helpless witness to their meeting.

Jan pushes open the door, sees Phillips and recognises him, stares at him for a moment, then looks at me. I make a sign behind the old servant's back, then step forward and present them to one another.

A week goes by before Phillips observes:

'At times, one might almost believe Master van Gouden were your relative. He has something of Sir John about him.'

'I've noticed the same thing. But the resemblance is pure chance – like his name. There are thousands of van Goudens in Holland.'

Phillips chooses to believe me, and smiles broadly.

We are all amused at his horrified look when I lend a hand in the silk workshops or receive customers at the trading counter. I take him on a brief visit to Germany, where I strike a hard bargain: woollen fabrics are less readily placed than silk, and the competition is all the harsher.

'Sir, you astonish me. Happily, your family cannot see you!'

'We stand on the threshold of a new age, Phillips. The way ahead is perhaps more difficult to discern from our great island home than it is here, on the Continent. I am persuaded that the time will come when there will be many more of us engaged in business. Princes of finance, people will call us. Or dukes of commerce.'

'You have Plantagenet blood in your veins, sir. But when you sell wool, you become a citizen like myself, with all due respect.'

'No, my dear Phillips; I don't become anything at all. I have always been a citizen like you, even if my ancestry includes one or two kings of England. Do you know the old Tregian smallholding?'

'I don't believe so, sir.'

'It's a small Cornish domain, in the parish of St Ewe. That's where my ancestor Thomas Tregian came from. He was a peasant, the youngest son of a poor family who chose to go to sea and was fortunate in his adventures. He went to London, finally, where he met the King, earned his friendship and married Lady Mary Grey of Wilton. My noble blood is hers. Thomas Tregian was a man of strong character, to achieve all that before he reached the age of thirty. But originally he was just an urchin living under the thatch of a miserable hovel, whose parents laboured from dawn till dusk so as not to starve. He earned his nobility through intelligence and hard work. I am merely following in his footsteps – and far less ably at that.'

'Allow me to say that I admire your talents, sir. You are one of the finest musicians I ever heard, and, thanks to your father, it has been my privilege to hear some excellent players indeed. And you live by your work. That deserves respect. The same cannot be said of my lord your father, even less so your mother, who never forgets her noble origins and is at pains to ensure that no one else does either.'

'Which is why I have chosen to remain in Holland, my dear Phillips. Amsterdammers have broader minds. Religions co-exist here, and I am not the only gentleman who earns his living.'

Nevertheless, Phillips is at pains to take me aside one day, checking first that no one is within earshot.

'Sir, you know you can trust me.'

'I was not convinced of it at first, Phillips, but as time goes by, I am increasingly persuaded.'

'I have devoted my life to your family. I cannot conceive of loyal service to anyone other than a Tregian.'

'I'm delighted to hear it.'

'And so, sir, be so kind as to settle a matter that has rankled with me to the point of obsession.'

'I shall, if I am able.'

'Master van Gouden . . . '

'Yes?'

'I recall Master Adrian's wide grey eyes as if it were yesterday. And his striking resemblance to Sir John Arundell, father of the current Sir John, who, by a strange caprice of divine will, looks nothing at all like his own father.'

'What of it, Phillips?'

'I see it all in your . . . your associate, sir. It is he, is it not? Master Adrian? He was so young when I saw him last. I was undecided at first, but with time I am more and more convinced, in spite of the beard, in spite of his build. Those eyes, that smile, the pragmatic line of thought, so straight and direct. Everything puts me in mind of Master Adrian.'

'You ask me to reveal a secret that is not mine to disclose, Phillips. I suggest you ask Jan himself.'

'Thank you sir, I believe I shall.'

Doubtless he and Jan speak together, for Phillips never mentions the matter again.

I gather my courage for the return to England, but find it no easy task.

'Phillips?'

'Sir?'

'I shall rely on your help, in England, to try and take back Golden and the surrounding estates.'

'I will do my best, sir. You can count on me absolutely, whether I can be of any use or not.'

Reassured, in part, by his support, I launch myself upon the great adventure of reconquering the Tregian estates.

The undertaking seems so impossible, it draws me out of my apathy. I step back into the current of the time. I stop surviving and begin to live again.

VII

This dance is now in prime,
And chiefly used this time,
And lately put in rhyme.
Let no man grieve
To hear this merry jesting tale,
The which is called Watkin's Ale:
It is not long since it was made;
The finest flower will soon fade.

'WATKIN'S ALE'

POPULAR BALLAD

'GRANDFATHER FRANÇOIS?'

'Yes, Elie?'

'I know that a gentleman doesn't ask personal questions, but ...'

'But you'd like to ask me one. Dear Elie, you proceed so delicately that I've already forgiven you. Ask your question.'

We are riding along the Talent at a leisurely pace. For a little while now, I have been giving Elie fencing lessons in an unfrequented grove of trees. This exercise has transformed him. Gone is the young whelp whose attitude and bearing amused me so, not that long ago. He is tall and muscled for his thirteen years, his face has lengthened and his eyes are deeper set. There is an air of distinction about him, like that of a young lord. One wouldn't recognise him.

'Well, sir, this question?'

'Grandfather François, how is it you've changed so much this past year?'

This boy would surprise me always. He is saying of me what I was just thinking of him.

'What mean you by *changed*, my young friend?'

'You've shaved off your beard, you've begun exercising again, you have an eye to your garments. People were saying after church that you'd fallen in love, for your appearance has returned to that you had as a young man.'

At this I smile.

'The parishioners of Echallens never knew me as a young man, for I was over forty when I arrived here. It's true that I've never looked my age. At ten I appeared twenty, and at fifty I appeared thirty.'

We ride on in silence. I recall a line from Montaigne: *In painting myself for others, I have painted truer colours within myself.*

'It's not easy to answer your question, Elie. I believe the act of writing my life's story has transformed me. When I began it, little was I aware that I would be forced to revisit all of my actions, and that this would oblige me to revalue and reconsider them. The great Montaigne wrote: *I hunger to make myself known, but I care not to what extent, so long as I am known for my true self.* I made this maxim my own, although I'm incapable of writing like him. I find myself wondering why I have continued to guard the secret of my origins so closely – not that it's anyone's business. And I am sure I was right to have said nothing to those English travellers who came this way last year and whose passage spurred me to write. But you are different.'

'You have my word, Grandfather: I will never tell.'

'Thank you, Elie. You see, a year ago, if you had asked me to teach you to fence, I would never have revealed to you that I'm quite skilled with a sword, and that I have practised fencing my whole life, openly or in secret. I was careful not to teach fencing to your uncle David, my most diligent pupil before you. Twenty years ago I decided that I would cease to be the man I once was. I've used any number of false identities and that seemed to be the solution yet again when I arrived here. Indeed, it may even have saved my life at the time. But now . . . '

'You're no longer in danger, sir?'

'If the man who desired my death had found me, he might very well have killed me. But he got what he sought in the meantime, and, anyway, he has no doubt passed on. I've had a very full life; suddenly I no longer feel the need to hide. That's why I've recovered my old self, why I shaved and why I had a new tabard made for me.'

'But Grandfather, if I may be allowed one further question, how do you practise in secret? I have seen how formidable you are with a sword. But I only ever knew you pacing slowly about like some great sage, wrapped in those long coats of yours.'

'Well you see, Elie, dissemblance has become second nature to me. You would never imagine that I consort with brigands, would you?'

'You, Grandfather?'

'And yet . . .'

'Tell me, Grandfather. I swear that . . . mum's the word.'

So I tell him about my dealings with the brigands.

I was new to the region when they set upon me – I was travelling to Lausanne one day on behalf of Benoît Dallinges. They made a misreckoning. Had they known I was local, they would never have approached me. They enjoy a certain impunity by sparing us and only attacking passing strangers. Four of them attacked me, the poor devils. I was quite the warrior at the time, young and lusty. And Giuliano, the best master of arms I had in my youth, had taught me how not to be taken unawares. With a weapon in each hand, I wounded two of them and stunned the other two in hand-to-hand. I tied them to a tree and cuffed them back to their senses. They were astounded. These scoundrels were used to meeting with little resistance. As a rule, they would knock a traveller out before he had time to react.

I laugh, recalling the expressions on their faces. Elie listens open-mouthed, which makes me merrier still.

'I told them: "I could kill all four of you, could I not? It's what you would do if you were me. I could also hand you over to the bailiff." They stared at me in silence. "But I won't, for it is not my pleasure. When you see your chief, tell him it's better to have François Cousin with you than against you. I am but a poor instrument builder, with no money. But I know how to defend myself. Extort one penny or harm one hair on the head of anybody in my family, and I swear you'll live to regret it, if you live long enough."'

We halt in a grove of trees and dismount.

'And then?' asks Elie, agog with excitement.

'A few days later, a man came to see me at the Crossing of the Ways. I had only recently taken to going there, and not regularly. He must have been watching out for me . . .'

He was stocky, dark and hairy, with a scarlet kerchief around his neck, such as you sometimes see worn by Italian masons at work on the churches around here.

'Are you François Cousin?'

'At your service.' Deep in my pocket, I clutched the dagger I always kept about me.

'Were you a mercenary?'

'How is that any of your business?'

'You put four of my best men out of action. I received your message. What is it you desire?'

'Me? Nothing. Or rather, yes, one thing. I desire to be left in peace. I desire that my family and I may travel freely without fear of being despoiled. Rob the rich as much as you like or are able. But if I have four pennies, it's to buy wood, tin or strings for my instruments. Or paper for my writing.'

He was of quite ordinary appearance, just a few extravagant touches in his clothing: the red kerchief; a silk belt, old and worn but embroidered; an earring. He had a smouldering gaze, eyes ever darting about.

'Will you make us one of your instruments?'

'Why not, if you pay me for it?'

And believe it or not, I did make them one of 'François's spinets', as everyone calls them round here. As they had no desire to make trouble with the people of Echallens, they did me the honour of taking me to their den in the woods. Their chief, Aristide, is a remarkable man, more civilised than ordinary robbers and very quick-witted. He asked me to teach him first the principles of music, then how to play the spinet. I got so caught up in telling him about major thirds and perfect fourths, counterpoint, *prima* and *seconda pratica*, that the idea of betraying his band to the law never crossed my mind. There are intelligent men among them, hotheads who may once have committed the sort of foolish act that would earn them a hanging if they did not go into hiding, but who were not genuinely ill-intentioned. There are some bands here in the Jorat region where men are brigands from father to son, but they tend to exercise their terror over towards Chalet-à-Gobet or Moudon. Aristide's band is a little different. Still. I've often said to myself that Thomas Morley must be laughing aloud from up on high to see these killers, robbers and outlaws listening piously to an *In Nomine* by John Bull, or else delicately tripping over the bone keys of a spinet to play *Now, O Now I Needs Must Part*.

'And you see,' I conclude, 'this was a good thing, for nothing ever happened to me, nor to any of the Dallinges.'

'But did you see them again?'

'My dear Elie, it is thanks to them that I have been able to keep in shape. I have some old companions-in-arms among them. I will take you to meet Petit-Claude one of these days. He stands over six feet tall, fast and slippery as an eel. If you're able to cross swords with him for two minutes without receiving a single hit, you may esteem yourself a fine fencer. It's true that most of them use the quarterstaff. Gentlemanly duels are of no interest to them.'

'Do my father and mother know all this?'

'No, my dear lad, neither your father nor your mother, nor your uncles and aunts. Your grandfather Benoît knew and I am sure that your grandmother Madeleine is well aware, but we have never spoken of it.'

A look of surprise that turns to disapproval passes across his face. I smile.

'Come, Elie, you must quit thinking *how could my darling grandfather have . . .*'

'But indeed, Grandfather, how *could* you . . . ?'

'Firstly, I conceitedly fancy that some of these wretches have softened their ways thanks to me. I know from experience what it is to pay for a momentary error one's whole life long. Our justice seeks to fight wrong with wrong, that is to say by punishment. He who has acted wrongly is forever wrong: such is God's will, and punishment must serve as a lesson to others. I thought I might see whether certain kinds of wrong might be overcome with intelligence. This simple idea is blasphemy to most theologians of whatever creed. Keep this to yourself, I pray. But God is also forgiveness, after all. I have even had some success with my method. It is unlawful to have dealings with the Jorat brigands, so I have told no one. But think a moment: did I not tell you that the men I fled from in England would have killed me had they found me?'

'Yes.' His face lights up. 'Oh! I understand!'

'You see. You'd have done the same. Not forgetting that, at first, I lived in fear of being tracked down and murdered by certain cut-throats whose clutches I escaped, not far from here. I was a witness to their savage deeds, and might have identified them. Once I was Aristide's friend, I explained my situation to him and he assured me that I could sleep soundly. Which is what I did. At worst, I had my sword.'

'I take it all back, Grandfather. You are very shrewd.'

'I may have become so, at last. But I needed protection because I was originally an arrant fool.'

AT SEVENTY-FIVE IT IS easy, of course, to judge the things I did at thirty-five. It is easy to decide now that what I did then was indefensible. At the time, things were not so clear.

I was gripped, quite literally, by Hamlet's madness.

Hamlet would never admit it, but he knew very well that he should not have given in to his mother's blandishments. Just as I knew I should never have obeyed my father. Like Hamlet, I knew in my heart of hearts that I should never have trusted Salisbury (Laertes!). I sensed some kind of underhand trick in progress. I should never have had dealings with such people.

As for King James I, that ridiculous, dangerous Fortinbras, how could England ever have imagined he would bring prosperity? Or felicity? We knew everything about him before he became our king. We knew he cared for nothing and no one but himself. Yet I threw myself into that wolf's maw – with some apprehension, it's true, but also with hope, though everything that befell me was quite foreseeable.

It was not as if I had rushed to England on the news of our great monarch Elizabeth's death. Three years had passed, by which time everyone understood that James had promised what was asked of him in order to win the succession. He gathered up the English throne without so much as a pause to stoop; and, once he was certain of his preference over Arabella or one of the three daughters of the late Ferdinando Stanley, he acted with complete disregard for the promises he had made. An ordinary gentleman must stand by his word. A king need not.

I had but one excuse: my innocence of the affairs of men. For too long I had been part of a system that operated chiefly on the initiative of others: Sir John, Giuliano, Jan. True, I was a peerless salesman for Jan and Giuliano, worth thousands of florins a year, as they frequently told me. But it is not true to say that I was of any value on my own, for it was Jan and Giuliano who impelled me. If I was effective, it was thanks solely to them.

Cornwall was my country, the land of my ancestors, but these were fond, foolish thoughts and the reality was otherwise. I had left Cornwall when I was five years old. I was a stranger there, I knew no one, and my influence was curtailed further still by my Catholic faith – and my reappearance shortly after the Gunpowder Plot.

But enough of regrets. As an Italian proverb says: the ditches abound with wisdom in retrospect.

I returned to Cornwall.

IT SEEMED, AT THIS time in my life, as though there were two men within me, each acting without taking counsel from the other.

There was Francis Tregian, eldest son of a recusant, subject to his duties of birthright, seeking, with little conviction, to redeem his family estates. And I had my Horatios, begging me to desist. But theirs were distant voices.

Jack told me repeatedly:

'This is madness, sir. We would be much better off in Amsterdam. Why subject us to such an ordeal?'

Phillips also ventured, in his own discreet way, to suggest the obstacles were perhaps too great.

Yet there was a weakness in me, incapable of remaining indifferent to my father's voice, swelled by the chorus of my mother, my brother Charles, my sisters and their respective families. I hardly saw them, but they made certain I heard their message. My mother made her position quite clear, in shrill tones, punctuated by sighs of despair, during a discussion in London. She and my younger sisters still lived at my uncle Lord Stourton's house in Clerkenwell, where I had spent part of my childhood. I made the acquaintance of a sister, Philippa, whose existence had always passed me by. She was married to one James Plunkett, an Irishman, who waylaid me one fine day and delivered a homily on my duty to protect the family estates, not only for myself but also for my sisters. Mary's husband, Thomas Yates, came – the first time I had ever laid eyes on him. Citing my sister's lack of a dowry, he insisted it was only fair that he get his share. One might have supposed that after fifteen years of marriage, other considerations would have taken precedence. But no. Poor Mary!

And then, I imagined myself the victim of a plot. The offer made by Lady Carey, George Carey's widow, was perhaps a lure to be rid of me. It was a sound notion: the Careys' steward, Ezekiel Grosse, had urged Lady Elizabeth to rid herself of Golden. He would then be master of it, while I, as a Catholic, would not dare show my face. This was undoubtedly the calculation he had made. By the time I understood his intentions, it was too late: having come from nothing, he wished to buy himself some importance by acquiring Golden, and he would stop at nothing to be rid of me.

The objections of those around me seemed of secondary importance at the time, for I was too busy rediscovering Cornwall, its customs, its people and its music. If I had not declared my interest in the family estates, nobody would have paid me any attention. The tenant farmers and even the parish notables showed unfailing discretion. It must be said that George Carey proved to be a harsh, capricious and rapacious lord, served by a wily steward who inspired fear rather than affection. But the people were quite well disposed towards me: the youngest among them because they were heedless of the past and the oldest because they retained fond memories of my grandfather John.

'He could be harsh. But he was a fair and kind man,' I was told on several occasions.

Giuliano and Jan exhorted me constantly to return to Amsterdam. It had been five years since the plague, but they had not recovered their former prosperity. Still, they remained hopeful. Kees arrived with urgent messages: 'You have no need of Golden. Cloth has a promising future, particularly our own, which is highly prized. A little patience is all. Soon, we will have finished paying back all the loans we secured to start the business afresh.'

I turned a deaf ear. In my inexperience of matters of land and property, I turned to a local man whose family had remained openly friendly with my own, though they were Protestants. So, at first, George Spry represented my interests. For far too long, I was completely unaware that this man was, perhaps quite unwittingly, a puppet in Grosse's hands.

Lady Carey returned the use of our lands to me – for six thousand, five hundred pounds. I was paying to recover estates that belonged to me by right: strange, but such was the practice. At the time, I was not even shocked.

I had two thousand pounds. My father assured me he would send another two thousand pounds from Lisbon, where he now lived. Charles and Margaret thought they could give me another thousand. There remained just one thousand, five hundred pounds to be found. I sold some land in Devon. George Spry lent me a thousand pounds, which I thought I'd easily pay back with the revenues, and he advanced me the three thousand pounds I was to receive from my father and my sister.

Phillips offered to keep an eye on the estates; his family lived in his wife's house in Kent, but he was of old Cornish stock like us: his father had been one of the Arundells' stewards. He would no doubt have left the Tregians' service long before, had it not been for the arrest of my father as well as his own. His family was well known in the region. I accepted gratefully.

To the best of my knowledge, my affairs were perfectly in order. I could devote myself to the activities I truly loved.

ALONGSIDE THE OBEDIENT SON, there was another Francis Tregian – the only one who counted for me at the time. His days were filled with discoveries, music, pleasant dalliances, and comings and goings between St Ewe and London.

The discovery of Cornwall held a particular charm for me: all around I saw things that evoked the echo of old memories, buried deep within me and apparently forgotten. Apparently, for my heart trembled constantly, as when reunited with a dear friend.

I had no desire to live in Golden, the house where I was born. I felt as if it had lost its soul; my family had no home there now. I walked through the buildings, but the distant voices of my first years had gone. They rang out no more, either there or at the old manor. The kitchen was a sad place, compared to my memories of it; without Old Thomas the charm was broken.

What's more, the manor was rented and the tenant had no desire to leave: I reassured him.

When I was in Cornwall, I preferred to lie low at my house in Tregarrick, near St Ewe. I believe I passed unnoticed for so long due to the great number of names in the region beginning with 'Tre' – the word means 'homestead' in Cornish. The locals called me Tregarrick quicker than I'd been called Tréville. And those who sensed the truth kept quiet.

In the eyes of the Tregarrick tenant farmers, I was the spiritual son of Old Thomas, whom they had revered. I enjoyed the same esteem in which he had been held, and they were all the more devoted to me for my never having been a particularly demanding master. I had no need for that: they never stole from me and the property was kept in perfect order. My initial esteem reflected that still held for my grandfather John (in the case of some) and his steward Thomas Tregarrick (in the case of others); later, I earned their trust by helping with work on the estate and by taking an interest in local customs and ceremonies. My interest was chiefly dictated by my curiosity on technical matters and by my love for music; the tenant farmers, however, read into this a concern for individuals that I perhaps didn't truly feel, at least not at first.

It began with the harvest. It is customary in many countries to celebrate its conclusion, and I had been a more or less attentive witness to harvest festivities in France, Italy and Holland.

The end of the harvest in Cornwall is marked by a ceremony called 'Crying the neck'. To explain it, I must recount the entire ceremony.

The 'neck' is the name given in Cornwall and Devon to the last sheaf of the harvest. In appearance, it is no different to the others – a clutch of ears of wheat bound together for ease of transport. The last sheaf acquires a sacred character, and Geneva and Rome together would quake at the veneration of it by Protestants and Catholics alike, echoing the rites of their forefathers in ancient times, no doubt. For the last sheaf is the very spirit of the grain made flesh; it becomes the neck of a mythical creature whose favour must be courted so that the coming year's harvest will be as good as, or better than, the previous one – just as we pray to God to keep us safe and protect us.

I was struck by the form of the prayer uttered at this ceremony, held in the tranquil calm of a summer's evening. A group of men would gather on one side, a group of women on the other. 'The neck!' they cry in unison, as the last sheaf is cut.

'We hav'et! We hav'et! We hav'et!' the men chant.

'What hav'ee? What hav'ee? What hav'ee?' the women answer.

'A neck! A neck! A neck!' The closest group chants in the key of C; a little further off, another group in another field echoes them in the key of F. And further away another, and another and another still. There may be as many as ten or twenty choirs chanting the canon to each other in the twilight without a single false note, around and around, in waves. Nature is quiet at this time of evening, so they may be heard from very far off, two or three leagues away, even. For a moment they strike a chord, in four, six or eight parts. Then silence. Suddenly, the chanting starts over again and, as if by chance, invisible in the twilit fields, voices call out, responding, entreating, each in their own way: counterpoint in its most natural and perfect form. The essential chant is everywhere the same, dictated by age-old custom. But the variations are infinite, like Master Byrd's *The Bells*, which I have recently copied: the voices converse, call out, overlay and reprise one another. The tune also reminds me of Byrd. He gathered it with an infallible ear in his *Peascod Time*, and I know now why I plucked the piece eagerly from among my scores: it evoked this forgotten melody of my childhood.

Until then, I had always shared Messire de Montaigne's opinion: *I am no glutton for the sweet delights of the country of my birth. Acquaintance and knowledge that are wholly new, and wholly mine, seem to me quite as a worthy as the common acquaintance and knowledge that come with accidental, neighbourly proximity.* But Montaigne did not foresee my own situation: my 'wholly new' acquaintance and knowledge, here in Cornwall, were also the deepest roots of my person. Later, I saw the truth of his opinion once more, but for the time being, I was bound to the land of my birth.

All together, the harvesters would lift their sickles. One of them – the oldest man, as custom dictates – brings his down, a last glint of metal in the encroaching dark. He cuts the sheaf and raises it in the half-light. Immediately, the melodious chant breaks into confused cries of joy, the sheaf is unbound and each person takes two, three or four ears of wheat, wrapping them with garlands and calling out: 'A neck! A neck! A neck! We yen! We yen! We yen!' – the latter meaning 'We've finished!' Whereupon everyone bursts into shouts and laughter; headgear is thrown into the air; boys take advantage of the confusion to kiss the girls. Miniature corn-ricks are fashioned and decorated with flowers and ribbons.

A procession then forms for the return home. The 'neck' is solemnly suspended from a kitchen beam, where it shall remain until the next harvest. Hugh and Mary, my tenant farmers, prepare the traditional meal for the harvesters. This is called *Gol Deis* in Cornish, meaning 'the Feast of the Ricks'. Everyone sits down to eat and a huge pot of boiled pork and turnips is brought out, followed by an apple pie covered in very thick cream. I have never eaten this 'clouted' cream, made by a process of scalding, anywhere other than in the land of my childhood. All this is washed down with quantities of cider, beer and aqua-vitae in a great clamour of laughter, jests and bawdy insinuations that might ordinarily cause offence, but which on this occasion nobody minds at all.

That evening binds me closer to the land of my birth than all my father's preaching. I feel as if in communion with heaven, consorting with the whole wide world: this is one day when the universal prayer for 'our daily bread' – uttered by Protestants and Catholics alike – can take on its full significance.

A few days later, I even go and lie down in the *arrish*, the stubble field, to rekindle the sense of my first steps as a little child, the music of Jane's voice and the plenitude of a time when my life was full of certitude and intent.

IN THESE FIRST DAYS of innocent happiness, my mind turns to practical matters and it suddenly occurs to me that I could combine the agreeable with the useful: what if we were to raise the sheep whose wool Jan coveted?

I discuss it with some of the country people and immediately they are interested. Armed with all that my brother has taught me, I explain to the interested breeders what the necessary qualities are. We need sheep similar to those of Shetland to obtain the incredibly fine wool of which Jan has become a specialist. One of the tenant farmers from Creed whose land runs along the banks of the Fal, on the Golden estate, asks me one day if he might create the necessary pasture by clearing silt from the riverbank to improve the flow and so drain his fields. I willingly give him permission to do so.

The better to know how to proceed, I go back to Amsterdam, where Jan gives me precise instructions accompanied by drawings showing me how the wool should be shorn, carded, spun and woven.

'Tell them that if they achieve the quality I seek, I will pay well,' he assures me with a wide smile. 'I shall derive even greater pleasure from working a wool that comes from the lands of my forefathers.'

I discover that there are ancient tin workings on the outskirts of our lands, too, especially towards St Austell. I think to look for them the same day I fall to wondering what it was the Romans had sought to defend with the fort of Voliba. I go to find the Reverend James Hitch, the vicar of Creed.

'Here's our great heretic,' he says cheerfully by way of a greeting. 'Have you thought better of it?'

'Better of what, sir?'

'I mean: have you come to conform?'

I look at him without replying. I don't know what he reads in my eyes, but he blushes and lays a hand on my arm:

'Forgive me; the jest was unseemly. What can I do for you?'

'I was wondering if you had a history of the region. I'd like to know why the Romans built a fort here.'

'To protect the tin route,' he replies without hesitation or looking in a single book. 'The rivers and streams were full of it at the time.'

'And today?'

'It is less accessible now. But there is still some around St Austell. And quite a few people are busy looking for it.'

'Who?'

He gives me a litany of unfamiliar names.

'First see if any of your land is rich in tin, then, if it is, you must apply to the Stannary Court for a licence to mine.'

The pastor has very pale grey eyes, a slim pointed face and milky white skin. I find his stare quite frightening. A vague feeling of unease prompts me to declare:

'I ask but one thing: to be allowed to live my life in peace. I shall not convert, despite my very great disagreement with my father, and even if the Jesuits are, in my opinion, quite wrong.' I am startled by my own audacity.

There is a silence.

'I have heard that you are an excellent musician,' he says.

I have no desire to discuss music, but I force myself. We exchange several remarks. He has learned the viol – and mastered it, judging by the tune I hear him play. In the corner is a virginal, which his wife once played.

'I lost her nearly two years ago,' he explains in a sad voice. 'Since then, the virginal has stood quiet.'

I bend over the poor instrument, too long abandoned, and set to work with the penknife I always carry on me for such a purpose, together with the tools I find in the instrument's drawer. First I trim the plectrums – the quills are in a very poor state. Then I tighten the strings. I feel as if the souls of Mistress Hitch and Françoise are floating about us. Having restored the instrument's melodious voice, I play a tune by Morley that Françoise particularly liked.

The Reverend brightens when I tell him I was one of Master Morley's pupils. The ice is thawed, the discussion springs to life, and our polite affability turns to warm affection when I casually tell him that I attended the Merchant Taylors' and am on good terms with Richard Mulcaster, who is still headmaster of St Paul's School in London. It is in this friendly mood that he decides finally to make the observation that he has doubtless been impatient to make since the beginning of our meeting.

'Master Tregian, I fear that you may offend the interests of people who would use your religion to malign you, thwart your schemes, even banish you.'

'What do you advise?'

'I hardly know what to advise you: your only safe refuge is the Church of England. Do not protest – I know that you will not conform out of expedience, which is all to your honour. Unfortunately, I have no other counsel on the matter.'

It is my turn to stare at him in silence.

'I think you have need of a guardian angel,' he says. We are already on the doorstep.

I gesture to Jack, who holds the bridle of my horse.

'I have an excellent one.'

'No doubt, but you require an angel of another kind, too. I will see what I can do for you.'

I am in the saddle now, and feel apt to dismount and embrace him, but his strange gaze dissuades me.

•   •   •

I GATHERED A FEW tenant farmers and some miners who had come up from around Penzance. We set out and found some tin near St Ewe. I learned to begin by studying the ground, the colour of the soil and the nature of the stones. Often, pebbles of tin ore look quite unremarkable; they must be picked up and weighed in the hand to determine whether they contain any metal. Next you must see where they lie and follow the trail, climbing to the higher ground from where they have been washed down; you dig, and if there's a vein of tin, it will lie six or seven feet deep. We found a promising site, at last, and I petitioned the mining authorities to obtain a licence.

'In what capacity have you come here?' the judge asked me.

'I own the land. I intend to invest in the mining gear. I have a right to a fee for the land, as well as a share of its revenues.'

'Quite so. Or rather it would be so if you were really the owner of the land.'

'I can show you the titles to the property. I redeemed my usage of it.'

'Your lands have been subjected to praemunire and your father still lives. You have no right to redeem them.'

He leaned forward. He had an affable face with greying hair and red cheeks.

'Master Tregian, I have no desire to prevent you from going about your business. It has always been my view that your family was treated with disproportionate severity. I am simply a judge of the Stannary Court. I mean you no harm. I merely point out a fact – and I wonder if someone has not tricked you, in the basest possible way. Anyone who wished you harm could take back your lands tomorrow. Only your father himself can redeem them. After his death, however, they will be returned to you by law, and you will have nothing to pay. Then, you can only be stripped of them by praemunire, and the sentence of praemunire cannot be passed without concrete proof. Do you harbour priests?'

'No, sir.'

'Is Mass said at your house?'

'No, sir. Indeed, I travel quite far to attend it.'

'Are you a partisan of the Jesuits?'

'I am a loyal subject of His Majesty, sir. My sword and my life are at his disposition.'

'Do you pay your Catholic fines?'

'Absolutely.'

A silence.

'I have studied the law and tell you this with full knowledge of the facts; seeing the look on your face, I am surprised to find nobody warned you sooner.'

'I am grateful for your counsel, sir.' I was startled to hear my voice shaking; for the first time, I was aware of how unsafe my situation was.

'Is there a man you can trust?'

'There may be.'

'Sell him the land where you wish to dig, if it is not in mortgage. And do it quickly. As for your estates, I wouldn't count on them. Unfortunately, I can do nothing for you. My jurisdiction only extends to mines.'

I returned to St Ewe in a sorry state.

I pursued my plans for the sheep breeding and the tin mine, over the weeks that followed. I 'sold' my share in the mine to Jack. But I had woken from a beautiful dream. I felt as if a barrel of gunpowder had been placed beneath my bed and someone might light the match at any moment. That *someone* was surely Ezekiel Grosse, though nobody uttered his name. Phillips went to request the estate accounts from him and was not satisfied:

'He's been lining his own pocket, stealing as much as he can from Sir George Carey; that's my view. He knows I suspect him. There are but two possibilities. Either he'll step aside, or he has something unpleasant in store for you. But he's not the type of man to step aside. The rumours I hear are alarming.'

'What rumours?'

'Of a deal between Lord Robert Cecil, Lady Elizabeth Carey and Grosse. It seems Cecil forced them to restore your lands in return for payment of a sum of money on your part, but this is not entirely lawful as long as your father lives.'

'And so?'

'Cecil might just as well have signed, or got the King to sign, a decree of restitution. It's true that you bear a discreditable name, but you are also a grandson and nephew of several Catholic peers of England who sit in the House of Lords.'

'What are you trying to tell me, my dear Phillips?'

'I am trying to tell you that rather than ensure the restitution of your properties as promised, the Lord Treasurer has handed Carey and Grosse an opportunity to carry on stealing from you. It will cost Grosse dearly in bribes, but he'll get what he desires in the end, as far as I can see. He is wily while you are not, in the slightest.'

Phillips had thoroughly alarmed me. I reflected that I was in mortal danger, that Grosse might be contemplating having me killed. Rarely has an intuition of mine been so exact, though I dismissed the thought at the time. What would be the point? I argued. I had a son, though Grosse was ignorant of his existence, and besides him, I had a brother, a bevy of sisters and a dozen nephews. No, Grosse had nothing to gain by ridding himself of me that way.

I could not foresee that he might create a situation whereby my death would guarantee his uncontested ownership of my lands. And when I did, it was too late.

VIII

Fain I would wake you, sweet, but fear
I should invite you to worse cheer;
. . .
I'd wish my life no better play,
Your dream by night, your thought by day:
Wake, gently wake,
Part softly from your dreams!

'THE HUNT'S UP'
POPULAR BALLAD

AUTUMN 1608. I cannot forget the date, nor the circumstances.

I had taken advantage of the fine weather and travelled to London, where I was in the habit of spending at least as much time as at St Ewe. Once Phillips had taken control of my affairs, I no longer felt, as I had at first, that my presence in Cornwall was constantly required. I had no desire to live at Clerkenwell, so Phillips found me comfortable, discreet lodgings elsewhere. He had spent much of his life in London and knew where to go. He found me a house on Chancery Lane near the Inns of Court, a neighbourhood peopled with lawyers and students. The ground floor was occupied by a widow, while I had the first floor, which comprised a spacious apartment for entertaining and music-making, together with various smaller rooms where we slept.

A gentleman of my rank required a sizeable household as a mark of status, but my situation was precarious, and I deemed my debts too great for me to keep a large retinue. I might certainly have employed a consort of three or four musicians, but for now I made do with Jack and his viol,

of which he had become a more than passable player. My only other servant was Jack's younger brother, Mark, who had come to us at the age of
thirteen or fourteen.

'A good-for-nothing,' said his mother, her voice tinged with tears.

A short introductory speech was required, I felt:

'Mark, it seems to me that you have no interest in the things asked of
you thus far. But I can offer you travel and instruction in how to defend
yourself, so that you come to no harm. You will be entrusted with precious
merchandise and confidential messages. If you wish to learn music, you
will be able to do that, too.'

Offer a very young man a daredevil life and he will seldom fail to reveal
his true qualities. Mark's faults became his greatest virtues, overnight. He
began by spending a year in Paris, in the service of my son, whose enjoyment of a good fight was undimmed. He made sure to chase young Mark
from pillar to post, and set upon him at every opportunity. To defend
himself, Mark learned to become as quick and slippery as an eel. Giuliano
and Guillaume taught him hand-to-hand combat, Phillips instructed him
in the alphabet and arithmetic, his brother in music, until, although still
not twenty, he was travelling with me wherever I went, proving himself
to be highly efficient, and proudly sporting a livery of sorts, cut from fine
Dutch woollen drape in one of the subtle hues that are the glory of my
brother's trading house.

Barely three or four years after the death of Elizabeth, London was
undergoing a perceptible change.

When I arrived, all the talk was of the trial of Father Garnett, the Jesuit
leader who had known of the Gunpowder Plot but had chosen to say nothing. My co-religionists were divided on the subject – the rift extended to the
Stourton and Arundell households. Was Garnett a criminal or a hero? For
the Jesuits, the downfall of the Protestant monarchy justified any means.
They owed loyalty to no one but the Pope. But the secular Catholics (as
the more moderate papists were known) were eager to be recognised as
loyal subjects of His Majesty, despite their faith. The very thought of the
Plot filled them with horror, and they took every opportunity to prove
their loyalty to their country. They were outraged at the very idea that
Catholics were behind the Gunpowder Plot and even refused to believe it
for a time. The rumour was a vile calumny, they were certain of it. Hence

my cautious response to Giuliano's account – his version of the Plot was perhaps born of a gut refusal of the possibility of such violence.

Public opinion made no distinction between the Catholic moderates and the extremists. The body of the Protestant clergy did nothing to urge conciliation. A new vein of Puritanism emerged, every bit as fanatical as the Jesuits on the Catholic side, so that even moderate Protestants were urged to greater extremes of intolerance. The Puritans were much heeded – ordinary people like a strong, clear argument; it reassures them. But in private conversation, the tone swung from one extreme to the other.

'I'm a good Anglican,' I was told by a merchant with whom I went to dine in Candlewick Street. He had bought quantities of silk from me over the years. 'I'm a good Anglican, but the way some Catholics are being treated by the highest in the land is worrying. I could never see you as an enemy.'

'I know plenty of Jewish merchants who wouldn't hurt a fly, fanatical patriots all, but there are places where they are so distrusted, they are put to death. In Spain, for example. Men will always paint their fears larger than life and twice as bloody.'

'Exactly so. And the State is doing nicely out of you, is it not? Collecting your fines, seizing your estates . . . There are those who pray every day that you never convert, mark my words. This way, they can do with you as they please.'

My astonishment was plain. He laughed to see it.

'Not everyone supports the hue and cry against the Catholics, you know.'

'I'm glad to hear it. I have never relished extremes.'

'Nor I neither, my dear sir. Let us drink, then, to moderation in all things. And I would be honoured if you would play me one of your marvellous Italian pieces. I cherish the memory of that evening when you delighted us all at Master Ardent's in Amsterdam.'

Giles Farnaby was in Lincolnshire, and devoted solely to his music. He taught the children of a local gentleman whose name escapes me. I was happy for him, but I missed him greatly, and the more so since Thomas Morley's death – entirely foreseen – shortly after my last visit.

Southampton had saved his own neck thanks to Robert Cecil, and converted to Protestantism shortly after his mother's death. He was released from prison on the accession of James I. His property – seized after the Essex rebellion – had been restored to him.

We met from time to time but we had little to say to each other. He thought me a fool for my stubborn determination:

'Your father ruined himself and your entire family. You are not obliged to copy him.'

I tried to explain that my own motives were quite different. He shrugged.

'Your principles count for nothing while we remain bound by the custom that the monarch's faith must be that of the country. A man of your ancestry who wishes to show loyalty to his sovereign has no option but to adopt the royal religion.'

What would Messire de Montaigne have said in my place?

> *What would philosophy have us do in such a pass? Follow the laws*
> *of our country? That is to say this heaving sea of opinions of a people*
> *or of a prince, painting justice in as many colours and reforging it*
> *with as many faces as they will have changes of passion? I cannot*
> *have so flexible a judgement.*

I FREQUENTED THE GLOBE and saw many plays by Master Shakespeare. I was especially moved by a performance of *King Lear*.

It seemed impossible to me that the public would not see the character of the king as a strident denunciation of royalty, with its prejudices, caprices and partiality, and all their dark consequences. Although it's true that, in *Macbeth*, James I's ancestor Banquo emerges as a hero, an innocent victim. Some whispered that the murderous queen was a portrait of Mary Stuart herself.

One day I sought out Master Shakespeare after the performance.

He was quite bald now and his hair very grey. His cheeks were a little fuller. But his grace and easy manner were unchanged. His smile, too.

We arrange to meet the following day at the Mermaid, an inn where all the playwrights gather, as he tells me. On the day of our visit, we are almost alone.

'Master Tregian, what a joy to see you again! You are the very breath of sea air.'

'Truth be told, I have promised myself to travel less. I have settled in Cornwall.'

He frowns. He knows my situation and disapproves as strongly as Southampton. But, unlike others, he would make no comment.

'I know what I'm doing is reckless,' I say hurriedly, 'but I've had enough of running away.'

'I hope they won't track you to your last hiding-place,' he mutters, prophetically.

'You, sir, are in no position to preach against recklessness. I saw *Macbeth* a few nights ago. And *King Lear* yesterday. You're stirring things up, and no mistake.'

He glances around in alarm.

'Whatever do you mean?'

'The bastard Edmund seizing power . . . '

'He is punished for it,' Shakespeare retorts, rather too quickly. 'As is Banquo.'

'Master Shakespeare, I accuse you of nothing. *Lear* is a masterpiece in my view. But the play says what it says, and clearly, too.'

'If it was as clear as all that, we would not be here talking about it.'

'Surely I cannot be the only one to . . . '

'No, but His Majesty laughed when that particular interpretation was put to him. He summoned me and demanded to know if there was any foundation to it. I told him there was not, and we left it at that. So please, I beg you . . . '

'My dear Master Shakespeare, I have no contact with the gossips at court. We shall do just as you did with His Majesty, and leave it at that. Tell me, what of your future projects?'

'In truth, I am hoping for a quieter life. I should like to go back to Stratford and stay there. But business keeps me in London.'

'You have a thousand more stories to tell.'

'Sad stories, and high tragedies, Master Tregian. The time for revels is ended now. Gone forever. I may tell one, or two, or three more stories. I'll do what I must for the King's Men to prosper. But it would be just as wise to hand over to Ben Jonson, Fletcher and others like them. They are very great playwrights.'

I took a close interest in the life of the theatre in the years that followed. The Puritans gave it a very bad name, but the London theatre showed more originality and diversity than I had seen anywhere else, and it touched me

to the core. London was to the theatre, in those years, what Mantua was
to the madrigal.

I saw Master Shakespeare regularly. He loved to hear me talk about
Italy, France and Holland. For a while, he toyed with an idea for a play
about William of Orange, 'William the Silent' as he was known – the
Dutch monarch murdered by the Pope's henchmen some thirty years
earlier. He bombarded me with questions about the Netherlands, forgetting his habitual melancholy, laughing loudly and slapping his thigh when
I supplied some piquant detail – such as the Dutch custom, on the eve
of a wedding, whereby the groom would spend the night at his bride's
house, trying by every means to get into her bedchamber and thwarted at
every turn by her family, only to gain admittance and find her thoroughly
guarded. Innocent entertainment indeed! Shakespeare's ribald wordplay
on the matter was dazzling.

Italy was of great interest to the English as a whole, it seemed. My Italian madrigals were always immensely well received, earning me invitations
to houses where a Tregian would normally have been shunned for fear of
compromising the master's patriotic loyalties.

Thanks to my younger sisters, I conceived the idea of our forming a
consort. There were four of them, aged between fourteen and twenty:
Catherine, Sibyll, Elizabeth and Dorothy, the youngest and my favourite,
doubtless because in some indefinable way she reminded me of Adrienne.
I copied out the scores of the pieces I had brought back from Italy. They
all had fine, well-trained voices and we did not need much rehearsal to
form a presentable ensemble. All four were passable virginal players, and
Catherine also played the lute a little. We performed at Clerkenwell and
were soon invited hither and thither. We were much talked about, or
rather, our repertoire was.

Even before setting foot in England again, I knew I would be under the
protection of Lord Salisbury, Robert Cecil. So when I reached London, I
went to pay my respects and remind him of his promise.

'You should convert. Then I could be of some use to you.'

'There are other Catholic gentlemen at court.'

'True, but they are not your father's sons.'

Sometimes I questioned whether my stubbornness was at all reasonable.
Does Our Lord, the omnipotent Good Shepherd, truly concern himself

with the livery we adopt to worship him? If I converted, I would certainly recover all my properties, and no one would be in a position to deprive me of them again. My sisters would have dowries and they would be able to make good marriages – our poor mother's constant concern.

I went to see my cousin William Stanley, Earl of Derby. He often invited me to his evening gatherings and showed me much affection. One day, he suggested I bring my sisters to sing Monteverde's madrigals for his guests. In Holland this would have been perfectly natural, but in England, no gentleman would exhibit his sisters 'like travelling minstrels'. I explained to the assembled guests that Monteverde's music required a very particular timbre of voice which I had discovered quite by chance in my own family. The explanation was accepted. My sisters were in seventh heaven. Their hitherto rather dull lives became far more adventurous.

I was surprised by our audience's fervent enthusiasm. We were bombarded with compliments and questions. With the exception of a few drab souls, everyone present hurried to embrace my sisters and heap praise on their performance. The voices of Catherine and Sibyll were moving, indeed. We were encouraged. And so I began to compile a systematic collection of all the madrigals I had noted down, or of which I had an exact memory, classifying them by the number of voices: three, four, five, six and eight. Over time the collection absorbed more and more of my energies. I would make long journeys in pursuit of printed or manuscript copies of certain pieces. Marenzio, Pallavicino, Agazzari, Alfonso Ferrabosco (father and son), the composers I had met by chance on my travels, such as Antonio Orlandini, Giovanni Maria Nanino, Ippolito Baccuso, and of course Monteverde himself – I copied them all. Their melodies filled my memory so delightfully. There are thousands of them, by hundreds of composers.

My collection became well known in musical circles. Until my last day in London, I was receiving musicians eager to 'borrow' (which is to say, copy) some air or other.

I FIND MYSELF DWELLING on that happy time – a moment's grace, when it seemed a new life was taking shape. Again, my pen balks at the prospect of describing the twists of fate that followed those two quiet years.

The clouds were gathering yet the sky remained bright and clear. No one heard the distant growl of thunder.

The first serious blow came one grey day in late autumn 1608. Plague had emptied the streets of London, but I was quite indifferent. To suffer the same death as my dearly beloved would have been a deliverance. Yet the plague remained stubbornly uninterested in me.

A few weeks earlier, I had sent Jack to Lisbon, as arranged, where my father was to give him the two thousand pounds now required to repay my debts.

One look at Jack's face on the morning of his return tells me all is not well.

'Sir, I should like to bring you better news . . .'

'Don't keep me in suspense.'

'First, sir, may I say that it is with the deepest sorrow that I have to tell you that my lord your father has passed to a better place.'

'Whatever are you saying? My father's dead?'

'Yes, sir. And my sorrow would be untainted if he had been content merely to die. I could have forgiven him for leaving us, and prayed for the salvation of his soul.'

'Jack, I beg you, what worse news could you bring than my father's death?'

'The news, sir, that before dying, he lost all reason – in a manner of speaking, begging your pardon – and distributed the money that should have restored your family's former glory, to the poor. Apart from that, all is well.'

Jack's voice shakes with tears.

'There is nothing left?'

'Nothing, sir. I did everything within my powers, and more besides. I went to the Court and obtained an audience with the First Minister – having borrowed fine clothes and attendants. I explained to him that if, as all Lisbon was whispering, your father was truly a saint, and enjoyed the King's favour, then the King would find it in his heart to help his family. I told him about the two thousand pounds. I . . .'

Jack crumples into a chair and bursts out sobbing.

I feel I could do the same.

'I take it from your tears, Jack, that you obtained nothing.'

'No sir.' He is half-choked. 'My lord your father had been to see the same nobleman shortly beforehand, to tell him of his great despair because – these were his very words, it seems – he had learned from reliable sources that you had converted, you and your brother Charles, together with your sister Philippa Plunkett. All my protests, all my assurances to the contrary were in vain. Truly I have failed. I am a wretched man indeed.'

I am cut to the quick. My father has betrayed me!

'Who could have told him such madness, do you think?'

'No one sir. I spoke at length with his Portuguese manservant, who speaks French. My lord your father got it into his head shortly after reaching Lisbon. At first he only spoke about it occasionally, but then more and more frequently, and finally he was convinced he had heard the news from a whole host of different messengers. Felipe, the manservant, read all his letters and was present at every meeting. It was Master Tregian who spoke about your conversion to everyone, not the reverse.'

'Where's Mark?'

'He is below, sir. He dared not come up. He says we should have attacked a convoy on the highway or boarded a pirate vessel: anything to return with the money.'

'Go and fetch him.'

Mark enters the room, hanging his head.

'Mark, I am infinitely grateful for your devoted service. Now, take the best horse you can find, go to Cornwall and see Phillips. Take him into the middle of a large field and tell him everything. Ask him for his opinion on the matter. But don't breathe a word to anyone else. No one must know that we don't have the money.'

I would have to go to Paris and Amsterdam.

But first I go to Clerkenwell to break the news to the rest of the family.

My mother remains dry-eyed. My sisters affect a suitable show of sorrow. No man is a prophet in his own land. In Lisbon, Francis Tregian the Elder might well have been hailed as a saint, but his wife and daughters had suffered his capricious, authoritarian nature; in his own drawing-room, the news of his death is greeted with measured grief.

When I have told them, my voice trembling with indignation, that he has spread news of our conversion, Elizabeth murmurs:

'That doesn't surprise me.'

My mother shoots her a furious look, then shrugs.

'So many people speak ill of others.'

'But he might have trusted us!'

'My darling boy, your father had a difficult life. He compensated for his own misdeeds with flights of fancy. Perhaps he truly believed he was the last of the Catholic resistance. Grant him that satisfaction!'

What can I say? I keep my gnawing anxiety to myself. Dorothy sees something in my expression. She leaves the room along with me.

'There's more to tell, isn't there Francis?'

'Will you keep it to yourself?'

'A woman's word!'

I smile. The oath is spoken by a delicate young girl, but I bow in acquiescence. I could not resist that pretty little face, so like my own departed daughter.

We ride at a trot to Islington and I tell her everything. I even shed the tears that have choked me since that morning. What have I done to deserve such a betrayal by my own father?

Dorothy does not try to console me. She clenches her fist against her horse's neck.

'Why was I not born a man?'

'You would have found yourself, like me, with three solutions, all of them bad.'

'And what are they?'

'To convert, which would cut me off from the whole of the family. I would have money, but you would refuse to take it. To go back to my trade as a silk merchant, but I would earn the sums required far too slowly. Or to disappear. And there is no shortage of will in that regard, but it will resolve none of your problems. Where is our brother Charles?'

'In Brussels.'

'He always speaks such fine words. Let him come and resolve the difficulties we face.'

'You know full well he will serve no purpose whatsoever. My poor brother. What will you do?'

'As soon as Mark returns from Cornwall, I shall go to Paris and Amsterdam, and take advice from our sister Margaret and my friends the Ardents.'

Dorothy wears the shadow of a smile.

'Something amuses you?'

'Me? No, nothing at all.' And she spurs her horse on.

Mark returns a fortnight later with a letter from Phillips. He has been able to borrow the two thousand pounds at a very favourable rate of interest, and confidentially, from George Spry:

> *But this is a temporary solution only. We must quickly find the means to pay it back, as Master Spry currently wants for cash. My lord your father's death strikes me doubly, and I reproach myself for not insisting I accompany him to Portugal. I could have prevented him from committing such folly.*

We leave for the Continent immediately. The night before, Mark comes to ask if he might bring one of his cousins. I consent, then promptly forget all about him.

I see the stranger, a slight figure wrapped in a travelling cloak, just as we are about to mount. I frown.

'Mark!'

'Sir?'

'You didn't tell me your cousin was a child.'

'He's not a child, sir. Don't be fooled by his stature. You should see him fight – the Devil himself would be hard put to resist. He's a little shy and dares not approach you himself, but at the first occasion, you'll see.'

It is cold and dark, and I am half asleep. I do not object. We leave London by the Aldgate, riding through the usual morning crowds.

We gallop in silence to the Golden Fleece in Faversham, where we are known and expected. After eating in the yard, we take fresh horses and continue on our way. There is no time to lose, for we must embark before nightfall in a bay near Ramsgate – we know a ship's captain there, and he will be eager to sail on the ebb tide.

We arrive at four o'clock. The captain welcomes us aboard and sends us to eat before leaving. I have almost finished my meal, served by Jack, when I notice his expression.

'What is it, Jack? Has someone upset you?'

'Yes sir, I am wild with rage.'

'What about?'

'About Mark. You have not seen our cousin face-to-face yet, have you, sir?'

'Ah! Did Mark not tell you about him beforehand?'

'Indeed he did not. Moreover, I don't like the idea of taking him along.'

'Go and fetch him here.'

'No, not I, sir. If I go anywhere near my brother, I'll kill him.'

'You think it would be wiser to leave your cousin in England? Is he not of good character?'

'No – no. We must take him with us. I would have preferred Mark to present him to you, sir – and to me – before we left.'

Jack has sparked my curiosity. As soon as we are on board, I go over to them. Mark and the stranger are sitting in a dark corner.

'So, this cousin of yours. What is his name and what does he desire of us?'

The cousin speaks, in a quiet murmur that has me frozen to the spot.

'Brother, do not move or make a sound. This "cousin" wishes to come with you. He could find no official way, so he sought an ally. Do not protest. A letter from you, stating that you will take me with you and watch over me, is already in the hands of madam our mother.'

It is my sister Dorothy.

'But my darling girl . . .'

'If I were a woman, you would have to dance attendance on me, but like this, it's no matter. Mark will take care of me; I can defend myself come what may! Don't worry about a thing. I've never had such fun in all my life.'

And she shrinks back into the dark behind the coils of rope, without further ado.

'What do you say to such presumptuousness, sir?'

'I say, Jack, that I would not have wished it so, but knowing the young lady in question, I absolve Mark of all blame.' I cannot help smiling. 'And I confess that the idea of taking Dorothy to Paris and Amsterdam is not displeasing to me. She's right, of course: madam our mother would never have agreed to it. It's far simpler this way.'

Jack rolls his eyes

'Very well, sir. If you say so. But you're too kind-hearted. Be careful not to give yourself away.'

'I shall. On which subject – what is your cousin's name?'

'Dorian, sir. Known to all as Dot.'

I laugh aloud at this and Jack smiles, too, after a moment. Dot would do very well for Dorothy, of course, but it was also a nickname often given to men of small stature.

I HAD ACCEPTED ONE unforgettable surprise, but I could not have imagined what was to come. On disembarking in France, I take Dot to one side and deliver my speech:

'My dear Dot, things being as they are, we must take a few precautions. You must never allow yourself to lag behind us, so that we may all protect you.'

Dressed in boy's clothes, my sister resembles an awkward adolescent youth. She even manages to move like a boy. She stares at me, unsmiling.

'Protect *me*? And what about you?'

'But my dear . . . Dot!'

'What if a bandit were to drop from a tree? A venerable old fellow such as yourself – you're at least thirty, aren't you? You need youngsters like us to defend you.'

And in a trice she dashes to the mule bearing our packs, draws one of my swords from its sheath and starts flashing it back and forth under my nose, thrusting the blade to either side of me.

'On guard, sir! On guard!'

I take a while to pull out my sword, I admit.

'Try him out, sir; you'll understand better,' says Jack, in gloomy tones.

So finally I do. Had we been locked in a serious duel, I would have been killed out of sheer stupefaction. She is unmatched. She parries and lunges, anticipates everything, darts about and foils my best thrusts. She is tiny but gifted with prodigious energy. Her lace gowns conceal the body of a true athlete. Conceal? But not to all. Someone must have instructed her.

'Fine!' I say, at length. 'I never heard tell of a woman warrior besides Joan of Arc. You have no need of me. I assume you owe your martial skills to Mark.'

Both of them stare up at me, struggling to suppress their smiles.

'And Dirk, your uncle Lord Stourton's equerry, in Clerkenwell. The shame of it!' declares Jack.

'Enough of all that! Where's the shame? What if I enjoy it? What if I have a gift for such things? Not everyone can be a musical genius or spend their days cross-stitching samplers. Dirk taught me because he saw I had an aptitude for arms. And for no other reason! Enough of your objections! While we are travelling, I am Dot, one of your men.' Her eyes blaze. She whirls her weapon one last time, then puts it up in its place. 'If one of you dare say anything about my honour, or my marriage prospects, I'll run you through.'

Jack and I exchange glances. He looks so utterly downcast that I burst out laughing.

'Go on, Jack, smile! If a woman may rule, she may also wield a sword!'

'If my Lady Tregian knew about this . . . '

'But she doesn't know, and her daughter has hidden her skills for a good ten years at least. Now let's be on our way.'

WE REACH AMSTERDAM on the eve of the Feast of St Nicholas. When the serving girl opens the door, we are enveloped in the warm aroma of gingerbread.

'Mijnheer Frans! Oh, everyone will be so happy!'

And she runs off to announce us.

'Mevrouw! Mijnheer! It's Mijnheer Frans, Mijnheer Frans!'

Jane and Jan are the first to appear.

'Francis! What a surprise!' We embrace.

'You are the very two I must see, alone.' I catch Dot by the arm as she tries to slip past, and hold her firmly, almost roughly.

'Come along with us, dear boy.' And I push her into Jan's little office. Jan follows, his curiosity aroused. When we are all four inside and the door closed, I begin:

'My dear Dot, allow me to present my nurse, Jane Ardent. And may I also present Jan van Gouden, a man I love as my own brother. It is my honour, dear friends, to present Mistress Dorothy Tregian, eighteenth and last child of the late Francis Tregian and his wife Mary.'

Jane and Jan make as if to speak, but I cut them short.

'Yes, our father is dead. We'll talk about that later. Now, my chief concern is that this young lady should resume her rightful place, and for no one to breathe a word about this. She disguised herself to force my consent, left our mother on a false pretext and sent her a letter, imitating my hand, stating that I agreed to take her with me. Nothing to worry about there, then.'

Neither Jane nor Jan seem at all put out by the story.

'I have just finished a gown in an entirely new colour,' says Jan. 'We shall have it fitted for you; it will be perfect.'

He stares at her in amusement.

'Not once since I was a young woman have I thought to disguise myself as a man when travelling,' says Jane quietly. 'It would make things much easier, no doubt.'

The ladies leave the room.

'She's quite mad,' I tell Jan. 'Mad. But of all our extraordinary family, she's the only one I trust absolutely.'

'She's . . . very surprising. Quite unlike Mary or Margaret.'

'Quite unlike the others, too. You can tell her anything. No, our real difficulties lie elsewhere.'

I tell him about our father's death. He listens, turning pale as I speak but unflinching, until I have finished.

'I have always thought that man was a danger to us.' He spits the words out.

'Adrian!'

'You always came to his defence, I've no idea why. I respect that. But he has been our downfall. From my earliest childhood, I felt the need to get away from him.' He places a hand on my shoulder. 'He played you false until the very end, my poor brother.'

We remain silent a moment.

'Come, time to eat. We'll see about the rest after.'

Seated around the family table are Wim, a strong, decent young man of twenty, his sister Jana, almost nine, little Thomas, aged seven, and the two orphan girls, now young ladies in their own right. Jan has not remarried either. Giuliano's hair has turned whiter and he is paler but his vigour is undimmed. Jane's extraordinary periwinkle eyes have lost none of their intensity.

Dorothy makes her entrance. She is wearing the gown in Jan's 'quite new colour' – an indefinable shade of blue that seems to turn pink at times. She pauses in the doorway, abashed. In the silence, her hazel eyes scan the room and alight on Wim, who gazes intently at her in turn, his cheeks unusually flushed. Time stands still. Jane glances at me. She has noticed it, too. Then everyone begins talking at once and the moment is past.

I WILL NOT REHEARSE the many different solutions we entertain. One thing is certain, Ardent and van Gouden are not in a position to supply the two thousand pounds I need: it would leave the company too short of capital.

'My dear Francis,' says Jan. 'Why did you obey your father? You have no need of Golden. You've a house of your own here, do you not?'

I don't know what say. *To be, or not to be, that is the question.* By shouldering the burden of my family's past, I have sought to destroy myself.

'Had it not been for the plague, I might have had the strength . . . Perhaps.'

I lean against the stove. Jan gets to his feet and puts his arms around me.

'My brother, I know you so well. Without my son Thomas, I too would have let myself sink into the abyss.'

He looks at Dorothy.

'Wim and Dorothy, I must tell you a secret already known to Jane, Giuliano and Francis. Swear you will keep it.'

They swear, and he tells them his true identity.

'I always knew it,' says Wim, calmly. 'I was just a boy, but when my father brought you back to Amsterdam, I recognised you. No one said anything. So I didn't say anything either.'

'And I,' says Dorothy, kissing him, 'I think I felt it too. It seemed as though I'd always known you.'

After three days of discussions, I promise to try to make the best of the various businesses I have established in Cornwall – the wool farming, the mining, the tenant farms – but that if I have to I will give up the effort. Everyone accepts my desire to make one last attempt to succeed.

Dorothy insists on accompanying me to Paris, dressed as a young man. I give in, and it makes the journey a great deal easier.

To my relief, Margaret has enough French mettle, by now, to take the whole adventure as a tremendous joke. When young Francis hears about our duel, he leaps to his feet with all the fire and vigour of his fifteen years.

'Oh *Madame*, my . . . my . . . Are you my cousin, *Madame*?'

'I am your aunt, dear boy,' says Dorothy, smoothly. She is barely a year older than he and stands as tall as his chest.

'*Madame* my aunt, I have never duelled with a woman.'

'I should hope not, dear nephew.'

She accepts his invitation and they go together to the fencing room. Dorothy spends half her time in Paris fencing with Francis and Arnaud, Charles and Margaret's son, while Mark keeps watch, making sure no one surprises them. Charles listens to my story, one eyebrow raised.

'I will help you. But next year, things may be quite different.'

He prefers not to explain how he will find the money, but find it he will and I leave with greater peace of mind. My son remains a great friend of the Dauphin, as is his cousin Arnaud. Henri IV is preparing to wage war against Spain. Charles will go to fight, and Francis and Arnaud with him. The two boys speak of nothing else. Their warrior aunt, whom they have not yet beaten, is a mere passing distraction. The death of the distant, unknown lord their grandfather leaves them completely indifferent.

We set off again for Amsterdam, but not before I have paid my respects to the King, who greets me as warmly as ever. And from Amsterdam, I set sail for England. Without Dorothy.

'My brother, I am going to stay here. You should stay here too.'

'My dear girl!' She infuriates me, but I expected this.

'I wish to marry Guillaume, who is only my half-cousin. Jane has explained everything.'

I make a show of contesting the idea. I know she will never give in.

'When will you marry?'

'We shall be betrothed, as custom befits. In a year, perhaps.'

'I shall see what our mother has to say.'

'Try telling her I'll be marrying your nurse's son. I, the descendant of any number of kings.' She bursts out laughing. 'And please, bring the family to the wedding.'

We set sail on a windy day in January. Naive as ever, I truly believe the crisis has passed.

IX

Kind-hearted Christmas, now adieu,
For I with thee must part;
But oh! to take my leave of thee
Doth grieve me at the heart.
Thou wert an ancient housekeeper,
And mirth with meat didst keep;
But thou art going out of town,
Which causes me to weep.

'PEASCOD TIME'
POPULAR BALLAD

THE EVENTS OCCURRED over several years, but in my memory they rain down upon me in a continuous stream. I feel as if I had no life at all in the intervals between each stroke of misfortune. When I think about myself as I was then, I see a swimmer drawing close to shore, knocked back by a wave each time he reaches it. I forget the order in which the blows struck. I'm not even sure I remember them all.

I will start with the most painful.

One morning in London, Phillips bursts into the apartment where I am rehearsing some villanelles with my sisters.

'I must speak with you, sir, without delay.' The three young girls leave without a word.

'Sir, you are to receive a most disagreeable visit. From Master Ezekiel Grosse. I might have a day's advance on him, perhaps only an hour.'

'And what makes it so disagreeable?'

'It is no longer Master Spry to whom you owe three thousand pounds, but Master Grosse; Master Spry has transferred all his debts to him. He was forced into it by his own situation. Master Grosse came to demand that I pay him the sum by next week. This is his right, and he would not discuss the matter. He then demanded an annuity for his work, claiming that he was your administrator. He even wishes this annuity to be paid in retroactive fashion from the day Lady Elizabeth Carey stopped paying it. He'll do all he can to ensure that no matter what you pay him, you will still owe him money. He hopes to prevent you farming sheep. He hopes you to find no tin. He hopes to dispossess you of your lands and your mansions as cheaply as possible. And he's had twenty years to familiarise himself with the region. He lends upon usury. Nobody likes him, but he maintains a grip on many people through money.'

I don't know who is paler, Phillips or I.

I saddle my horse and ride to see Robert Cecil, though I am certain he will be too busy to receive me. He isn't.

'Your Excellency, you made an undertaking that I would recover my estates.'

Forcing myself to remain calm, I tell him what is happening. He listens stony-faced, while one of his secretaries takes notes.

'I shall see what I can do, Master Tregian. Master Grosse has backing at court, for which he pays a great deal. And he is also under the Careys' patronage. Send him to me, should you meet him.'

Grosse arrives that very day. I refuse to admit him, but have him sent to see Cecil. He returns on the morrow. Lady Carey's obliging steward has changed into an arrogant and stiff-necked fellow.

He has prepared an account of what I owe him, and my debts to George Spry are now swollen by exorbitant interest. He is accompanied by a bailiff. Either I am to sign the paper he presents or I shall be arrested and thrown into the Fleet at once.

'But I offer the best of terms,' he adds, with outrageous presumption. 'Here, read this.'

I read it.

> *And whereas the said Francis Tregian the Younger did grant to the said Ezekiel Grosse an annuity of £30 for life, to be paid at the house of the said Ezekiel, at Rosewarne, in the parish of Camborne, at the two usual feasts; and whereas the said Francis hath acknowledged to*

> *be bound to the said Ezekiel in £3,000, it is now agreed that if Ezekiel*
> *and his heirs shall peaceably enjoy the Manor of Rosmondres, and*
> *all the premises, without hindrance from Francis Tregian, or Charles*
> *Tregian, brother of the said Francis the Younger, or Mary Tregian,*
> *mother of the said Francis, the said bond will be null and void.*

It is signed *Ezekiel Grosse.*

He is telling me, in tortuous legal language, that he is ready to buy one of our finest family properties for three thousand pounds. Cecil has hardly gone out of his way for me. I would lose Rosmondres, but gain my freedom.

I refuse to sign in the presence of the bailiff, knowing that Grosse is trying to beguile me. I send everyone away; I would think about it. I go downstairs to see my widow.

This widow, Mistress May Hutchinson, is a young woman of twenty-seven or twenty-eight; very affable, and if I were ever to remarry, she would doubtless be my choice. I have spent many nights in her bed. This simple woman is most comely, noble and kind, but also has a head for business. She has been a widow for five years but sternly manages her late husband's tailor's shop, which produces quite elegant garments. When we made our acquaintance, she began to use Jan's cloth, which earned her a fine reputation. The shop employed three apprentices and five master tailors. She is gifted with rare good sense and has been of sound counsel to me.

I find her comforting my three weeping sisters. They have been listening at the door and told her the bailiff had arrested me.

'But you can see very well he's here! Innocent people aren't arrested just like that.'

Elizabeth throws her arms around my neck.

'Oh, my brother, what will you do?'

'Well . . . I think I'll let him have Rosmondres. I never go there, and that way I'll be rid of my debt. Grosse is right, it's a fair bargain for me. But I will think some more. Mistress Hutchinson?'

'Sir?'

'I believe we should take counsel from Master Treswell.'

This is a lawyer at the Inns of Court who lives close by. We have spent numerous evenings talking or making music, and I have had occasion to appreciate his talents.

'I share your view, sir. He must be sent to find out what's what.'

'I'll take these young ladies home, then I'll go to see him.'

Master Treswell comes straight to the point.

'If you have no particular affection for the manor and its land, then forget about it. Have me read everything you're asked to sign before you do so. I would also like to give you another piece of advice.'

'Please do.'

'Firstly, before accepting, go for a long walk and make sure that your conscience is settled and that you will truly never change your mind, nor ever convert. I know your reasoning, which is why I am emboldened to say: think closely on it one last time. If you are certain that you will stay a Catholic always, then sell. Sell all that you can. A law was passed in 1606 giving the Crown the right to seize at its pleasure two-thirds of the estates confiscated under praemunire. Grosse is an excellent lawyer.'

'Grosse, a lawyer?'

'You weren't aware of that? I know him well. He was completing his studies at Lyons Inn when I began my own, and had already acquired a fearsome reputation for cunning. He is certain to think to apply the law of 1606. Sell Golden too, if you can. Forget these dreams of becoming a sheep farmer or a mine owner. This man wishes to supplant you. Sell quickly, while it all still belongs to you, and invest your money. I will help you. Do this for your sisters.'

I leave Treswell, pensive. Rather than take a long solitary walk, I go to request another audience with Robert Cecil. He has been unwell for some time, and at each of my visits his body seems to have shrunk a little more. Only his face remains unchanged, and his lively expression. He gives me precisely the same advice as Master Treswell, but out of different considerations:

'I may not always be here to support you, and Grosse knows this, otherwise he would not have dared offer you such a bargain. I quailed him, but I am powerless to stop him. You'll be undone in that Cornwall of yours. You are too alone, too unprotected, and I cannot help you. Sell, Master Tregian, truly. If I were you, I would leave for Holland. If something were to happen to me, you would be in immediate danger.'

I heed some of his counsel.

I begin to sell my estates, some openly, some in secret, through Master Treswell, friends or cousins. I share the money between my brothers and sisters, investing it in their names without telling them, for fear they will refuse. My own share, I invest in Holland. I make but one mistake – my weakness: I do not sell Golden, even though it is Golden, the lordly manor, that Grosse desires at any cost.

I shall not list all of these transactions. The fact is that by the time the next catastrophe happened, I had got rid of a considerable portion of my estates and, with some regret, sold the mine. The only businesses I still controlled, through one of my Arundell cousins who had bought them to humour me, were the sheep farming and wool weaving, which were quite prosperous.

THE NEXT CATASTROPHE AFFECTED me personally, but it was universal in scope. Good King Henri of France was murdered. I learned this at the Royal Exchange one day in May. A moment of silence was decreed. People fell to their knees and prayed, and many faces ran wet with tears. The whole of Europe was in mourning. Few kings have been as loved as he.

I was caught up in my various transactions and hesitated between leaving myself and sending Mark for news. Before I could take a decision, young Francis surprised me by arriving one morning with Denis de Montmartin, right-hand man to Charles de Troisville, from whom they bore a message:

> *My brother, we are leaving the court. Queen Marie de' Medici has been appointed Regent and, alas, I am not to her liking. Her favourites are vipers with velvet tongues such as Monsieur Concini, from whom she cannot bear to be parted. I, as you know, am one for plain speaking. That is why His Majesty extended me the honour of his affection. The Regent is ill-tempered, fickle, cold and harsh, superstitious and incapable of taking an overview. She lacks the essential quality of a good ruler: consistency in all affairs. Her opinions change with her moods, and she is obstinate in her decisions to the point of idiocy. She has no other concern but herself, and any love for her children is no more than lip-service. I dread to think what lies in store for France. She informed me that I and my two sons must leave the service of the young king, and when I told her that I would do so if such was His Majesty's pleasure, she replied*

with disdain: 'His Majesty will do as I decide. I no longer wish to
see the two young Trévilles in his apartments, and I would be glad
if you were to return to Aquitaine.' I acquiesced without protest.
Discuss it with Francis. If you decide to keep him in England, we
will understand. King Louis told us when he bid us farewell: 'Don't
go too far, Messieurs de Tréville, I shall not always be a child,' and
for that reason I think we shall stay, in Bordeaux or Tarbes, living
off our tiny means, but at His Majesty's disposition, on whom we
are incumbent in both affection and devotion.

'I know the content of this letter,' Francis tells me. 'I should like to return
to the Trévilles, if you permit it, sir. I don't speak English and I know
nobody here, except you.'

'I'm quite glad for you to do so, my dear child; and even if you wished
to stay, I would force you to leave, given the current situation. I myself am
hunted. I see no reason to expose us both to deadly danger.'

'Are you able to tell me about recent events?'

Francis Marie Tregian de Troisville, or de Tréville as he is called at the
French court, is sixteen years old but already a man. He is as tall as I and
shows a gravity equal to the impulsive fury with which he wields a sword.
It is impossible for me consider him as a son. He is a companion, a younger
brother. At no time do I reserve myself the strict role of his father. I tell
him everything.

'I hope that once we are no longer burdened by these vast possessions,
once the uncertainties have melted away, we might live in peace. God has
been merciful in not taking everything from us; we remain privileged.'

'That's how I see things, sir. Show me London. This will perhaps be the
only time I'll see it in your company. And then I'll return to Bordeaux.'

I banish the pain which the reminder of Bordeaux always evokes in me.
We spend a few days exploring London.

He leaves, and it is with a heavy heart that I watch his horse disappear
into the countryside beyond Aldgate. Shall I ever see him again?

The London of 1611 was quite different from that of my childhood. The
court was no longer the crucible of philosophy it had once been; now any
culture practised there was quite fawningly frivolous in nature. It was one
entertainment after another. The only great composer to follow on from

the likes of Morley, Bull and Byrd was Orlando Gibbons, whom I did not know but whose melodies I admired.

It was as if the King's character suffused the entire city. London was at once less harsh and more hostile. I find it hard to express what I felt. So many steps had been taken to eradicate poverty that certain spectacles of destitution, so common when I was a child they weren't even mentioned, had vanished. But poverty was still rife. Spain was no longer feared and, while recusants were pursued, they were not persecuted as they had been when they were seen as the enemy within. Also, the court, encouraged by Queen Anne, showed greater clemency to Catholics than it did to Puritans. The parliament of the gutter, that most independent of institutions, was not slow to make its opinions known. The more the King crushed the Puritans and the more he deprived their preachers of a pulpit, the more the population of London, indeed the whole of England, embraced their views. And their views regarding Catholics were inflexible in the extreme. Consequently I found myself more alone than ever. Many turned their backs on me. I had few staunch friends left.

One of them was Richard Mulcaster, whom I visited regularly; he had left London a year or two before, and was now living in Stanford Rivers, in Essex, where he was quite lonely since the death of his wife. I liked to listen as he described how he had gradually revised his ideas on education. We frequently discussed Montaigne.

The master must have been nearly eighty-four – and his age showed. His tall body stooped, his sight was dim and, as time passed, he increasingly preferred me to read aloud to him. But his comments had lost none of their acuity.

'You are a new kind of man, Master Francis, you know that,' he told me warmly.

'Me, sir? I am a very ordinary man.'

'Not at all. I cannot approve your religion, but your notion that each man is alone with his conscience, and that the sovereign cannot impose a religion upon his subject ...'

'That is not my idea, sir, but Messire de Montaigne's. And what is more, Kings Henri III and Henri IV of France held a firm belief in it, too.'

'It was also expressed by Monsieur de La Boétie, who disliked tyrants as much as he disliked the inconstancies of religious devotion. You people don't read Monsieur de La Boétie, for it was the Calvinists who got hold of his work and printed it. Nevertheless, there's a sentence in his *Discourse of Voluntary Servitude* with which you, in your obstinacy not to surrender to the King's religion, would doubtless agree: *Let us raise our eyes to Heaven, to Almighty God, the assured witness to our deeds and true judge of our faults, for the sake of our honour or for the love of virtue. As for me, I quite believe I am right in stating that there is nothing so contrary to our tolerant and generous God as tyranny, and that he reserves a special punishment for tyrants and their accomplices.'*

'I know, sir,' and I continued: '*How does he who controls you have any power over you except through you? You could free yourself from it if you tried, not by delivering yourself, but by simply wishing to do so. Resolve to serve no longer, and you shall be free.* Such freedom costs dear.'

'Aha! I have you! You read La Boétie, even though he is on the index of prohibited books. You see, he takes the opposite approach to Machiavelli, whom everyone rails against but has never read, whereas I have studied him. Do not cast that unfavourable eye upon me.'

'It is not an unfavourable eye, sir, but a surprised one. I have always admired your boldness. *Our* boldness, I should say, since I too have read Monsieur de La Boétie. But you were speaking of Machiavelli . . .'

'La Boétie and Machiavelli both consider that if tyrants have any authority, it is because their subjects agree to it. Except that Machiavelli teaches the ruler to force their assent, while La Boétie shows the people the power of their refusal. And you, my dear boy, you and your admirable brother I should say, are the incarnation of the principle of this freedom.'

'I thank you, sir, but you do to us too much honour.'

He cut short my objections with a wave of the hand.

'Hence all your difficulties. It is always difficult to be a forerunner, as the ashes of Signor Giordano Bruno could tell you. I met him: a remarkable man. Far ahead of his time. Things were simpler under our great Elizabeth, true enough. She too was remarkable. Ever wavering and circumspect in politics, but never concerning the arts and sciences. She always supported the boldest pursuits in these fields.'

I lost this peerless master in that sad year of 1611. Having thought I would come and read to him one day, I arrived just in time for his funeral.

Robert Cecil was also at the end of his life. He grew thinner and thinner, and ever paler. Apparently a tumour was gnawing away at him, causing considerable pain. He never spoke of it. But he was so often indisposed that the King began to push him aside. The royal favourite, Lord Howard, had an eye on his office and titles.

I called on him one day and was received by one of his sisters, in tears: Cecil was gravely ill. I saw him one last time. There were few people around him now. That power, for which he had plotted so long, was already ebbing away from him. In a weak voice, he repeated his earlier counsel.

'And do it quickly, before the monster devours you.'

He expired in early summer and, almost at the same time, England lost Henry, Prince of Wales, a young man whose weight was already felt in government and who promised to be as wise a monarch as Elizabeth. He died in just a few days and was succeeded by his brother Charles, who (alas!) was not like him at all.

James I now had nobody to hold him in check. His rule was erratic and arbitrary. Justice went to the highest bidder, and I was the greater fool for not plying my wares at that particular stall.

I soon saw how right Cecil had been, for the order to arrest me was not long in coming.

ONCE AGAIN IT IS Phillips who rushes to London, where I have stayed longer than usual, quite by chance. I have been intending to go to Cornwall for the past month, but have kept delaying my departure because of the rainy weather, which has turned the roads into rivers of mud.

He enters, all mucky in his boots, and I marvel at how this man, at close to sixty, shows not the slightest sign of weariness.

'You must leave, sir. Quickly . . . '

I have already understood.

'*He* has found a means to get rid of me.'

'He no longer desires Rosmondres Manor, sir. Nor does he feel bound by the promise made to Lord Salisbury. It's money he's after. As simple as that. And since you cannot pay . . . '

He hands me a parchment.

*James, by the Grace of God, etc, etc, to the Sheriff of Cornwall –
whereas Francis Tregian Esq on 14th Nov Ad 6 King James acknowledged that he owed Ezekiel Grosse of Trelodevas in Buryan Esq
£3,000 and has not paid the sum as yet, we order you to arrest the
said Francis Tregian and keep him in prison till the debt be satisfied.
His lands to be put under an extent for this purpose.*

Peter Edgecombe, the Sheriff, has endorsed the document and added:
*Francis Tregian is not found in his bailiwick, but his lands have been seized
upon.*

By sequestering my remaining estates, they have deprived me of my
revenues. Without the revenues, I lost my most important means of
repaying my debts.

Consummatum est. The mousetrap has snapped shut.

'How much time do I have?'

'None at all, sir. The bailiffs might be at the corner of the street. In order
to act you must evade capture. Go, before Grosse persuades the sheriff to
send your description to the ports.'

While Phillips talks, I gather my most precious scores. Jack and Mark
pack our portmanteaux. My book of pieces for the virginal is with my
sister Elizabeth, who has thrown herself body and soul into learning the
instrument. I would have to do without it. I cannot even take leave of
my family.

'Let's take the underground passage,' I suggest.

This runs beneath houses, streets and gardens, linking the Hutchinsons'
house to their shop, two streets away. Almost no one knows of its existence. It dates from time immemorial and Mistress Hutchinson often used
it when she stayed late at the workshop, to avoid exposing herself to the
dangers of the street at night.

Jack and Mark go first with the baggage. By the time we come out in
the workshop, Mistress Hutchinson has already been informed.

'I wish I could . . . '

She puts a finger to my lips.

'Say nothing, my friend. I hope to see you again one day. Be careful,
and may God protect you.'

'If anyone questions you . . . '

'I know what I have to say. I am merely your landlady. Have you ever disclosed any of your intentions to me? It goes without saying that I am ignorant of everything.'

I think we are all teary-eyed.

We leave by the shop entrance without the workers seeing us, and are galloping through the countryside towards the coast before the city gates close for the night.

The late July sky is filled with stars. We make swift progress but the dawn tide has ebbed by the time we draw near to Folkestone. We have changed our horses only once and they are tired out.

Jack goes to see a fishing captain we know who has given us secret passage across the water in the past.

'I'll take you to Holland, but we must wait for this evening, when the boats go out to fish. We'll be questioned otherwise.'

'What? A whole day?'

He makes a good-natured gesture with his pipe.

'You'll look no different from my mariners. Stow your baggage at the bottom of the hold, out of sight, then put on a cap and a jerkin. Nobody will think of looking for you here.'

'I didn't say anyone was looking for me.'

'No, but that much is obvious. Get on board and grab that line over there. It'll make you look the part. Rest assured; you'll leave.'

And leave we do. Better still, we land safe and sound on a beach not far from Rotterdam.

Phillips stays in England, as he is in no personal danger. Loyal to the end, he and Master Treswell would help me settle my affairs.

During the crossing, I have ample leisure to reflect upon the injustice that has befallen me. Treswell had warned me:

'We would be less exposed if the laws on recusants were applied in a rigorous and uniform manner. We could rely on the practice of law. Unfortunately, the laws are applied inconstantly, dictated more by the zeal and cupidity of neighbours than by the Crown's desire to eradicate Catholics. You came across such a neighbour, who prepared his case most carefully and laid a trap for you. When the King's attention is drawn to a case like yours he takes firm action. Grosse no doubt paid someone to convince His Majesty that the sequestration of your estates would earn him a great deal of money. In such cases, the King has been known to sign decrees that are the height of capriciousness while giving the impression of being fair. And once it's done, he sticks to it.'

With anger in his voice, Treswell had told me something else:

'Your peculiar friend Robert Cecil could have introduced you at court and presented you to His Majesty – had he truly been your friend. I have never met anyone who was not won over by your music, once they'd heard you play. The King is very keen on such things and would probably have succumbed to the charm. He becomes exceedingly munificent in such cases. His benevolence would have protected you.'

Giuliano has made similar remarks. But in truth, Robert Cecil had no desire to put himself at risk and a Catholic Tregian was not presentable at court; that much the Lord High Treasurer has told me time and again.

When we knock at the door of the trade counter on the Stromarkt, I am feeling crushed by a ghastly sense of defeat. It seems that my life has lost all meaning. Nothing and no one can justify my existence any more.

'On the contrary,' says Jan forcefully when I confide my sorrow to him. 'You are rid of this burden of inheritance at last.'

'I am not rid of the thought that my mother and sisters have nothing to live on.'

'*Little* to live on, brother dear. What with the revenues from their remaining properties in Devon and Dorset, and the Stourtons' help, those ladies are better off than we are. How many servants do they have?'

'I couldn't say. Six, seven, eight.'

'And we have three domestic servants for two families.'

'I know. But our mother's notion of nobility . . . '

' . . . is such that if she's not in a manor with forty retainers, she declares herself a pauper. Dorothy told me that. If our sisters agreed to marry commoners, they would have the finest dowries. But of course, only an earl or a duke is worthy of their attention. Such folly is not your responsibility. I forbid you ever to set foot in England again.'

I FOLLOWED THIS ADVICE for two or three years. I returned to my life as a musician and occasional merchant. I travelled to Antwerp and sometimes Brussels. I loved Italy as much as ever and went there as often as I could, making long stays in Mantua, where Monteverde was constantly refashioning his genius into new forms: works such as *La Favola di Orfeo* or *Arianna* delighted the eye as much as the ear, not forgetting his *Scherzi musicali* and the new madrigals of course. Monteverde had been the Duke's *maestro della musica* for some years. Then he became *maestro di cappella* at St Mark's Basilica in Venice, which I began to visit much more frequently. I avoided Jesuit circles, believing they would be spied on by the English, but nevertheless I did approach old acquaintances such as Peter Philips or the Ruckers sons. I met Peter Paul Rubens again, too. His fame spread far and wide now. He welcomed me warmly to his splendid workshop, the only completed room of his new house on De Wapper, where every possible trade was engaged in enlarging and beautifying the place. Here he worked, entertained and argued in an unbelievable racket of hammers, saws, shouts and rushing footsteps, which he seemed not to hear.

Through Rubens, I made the acquaintance of Jan Brueghel, as sublime a painter as the Master of De Wapper, and we immediately became friends. We held long conversations, one of which I recall quite clearly – about his scheme for an allegorical painting on the subject of hearing. How might one depict hearing in paint?

And through Peter Philips, I met John Bull.

I had only seen him from afar until then, and on just a few occasions. We didn't move in the same circles and I confess that I was surprised to hear that he'd taken refuge in Antwerp to flee religious persecutions. I had never heard it said that he was Catholic. The rumours spread about him in London, at music printers' shops for the most part, were quite different in tone, portraying him as a violent man of dissolute morals. In the shadow of a stall at the front of St Paul's, I heard that he was accustomed to share his wife's bed with the housemaids. I listened, unmoved, for we had never met and I could but observe that his morals in no way affected the quality of his music.

The man I met was of middling height, with black hair and an olive complexion, a longwise face and a piercing, almost demoniacal gaze. He looked about thirty-five, but I was told he was nearly fifty. He lacked the corpulence one might expect to find in someone of his age and supposed excesses.

It was said that he could fly into terrible rages and that he was capable of anything when in one of these bouts.

'Even killing a man,' declared Philips.

I saw nothing of that. My memory is of a bright companion and an absolutely peerless musician.

I owe him a huge debt: we sometimes played highly intricate pieces together, wagering that I would not play them as quickly as he. It was a long while before I was able to catch him up. Speed of execution was less important to me – and it sometimes made Bull's playing appear superficially dazzling: to proceed as quickly as him, I had to review my entire technique, forcing me to put aside my habits and reconsider everything I knew. I had not received such a salutary musical shock since Claudio da Correggio.

The pieces we played together were ones that John Bull brought along and that I copied. I was familiar with some of them already; others I knew well, but Bull had recomposed them, incorporating some fresh difficulty he hoped would be insurmountable.

We laughed a great deal, and our occasional listeners did too.

Bull lived in Brussels most of the time. He was protected by Archduke Albert of Austria, who ruled the Catholic Low Countries.

'I am even at the centre of a squabble between the two princes,' he said smugly. 'James I would like to throw me in gaol to punish me for having left. He does me the honour of nursing a fury out of all proportion to our relations.'

James I finally prevailed – or nearly. Archduke Albert dismissed Bull so as not to aggrieve the King of England, but continued to pay him, then helped find him a position as organist at Antwerp cathedral. It was not an office he earned by plotting but rather through his enormous talent as a musician.

Doubtless he had understood the need to settle down quietly. For all that he was much talked about in England, he passed unnoticed in Antwerp, except for his music. Having forsworn all mischiefs, his fiery temperament poured forth in his playing. More often than not, the cathedral was packed with music-lovers who had flocked to hear Bull play, and who quite outnumbered the handful of pious souls come to praise the Lord.

His reputation was such that Master Jan Sweelinck asked me one day if I knew him, then beseeched me to arrange an introduction.

This was how I came to have the great honour of witnessing the meeting of these two giants. It was one of the brighter moments in that black period of my life.

I owe Bull yet another thing: my knowledge of organ-building.

Over time, I had finally come to understand how a virginal is built. On more than one occasion, circumstances obliged me to undertake repairs or instruct others to do so. Giles Farnaby had recently returned to London at the very moment I was forced to flee the country, but I had been determined to visit his workshop and devote myself seriously, once and for all, to the process of building the instrument. In Antwerp, I was always welcome at the Ruckers', though they still retained a shadow of unwillingness to show me everything, despite our old friendship – good craftsmen are like that.

I had been told I played the organ well. A single day in the Oude Kerk, listening to the two masters demonstrate their skills, sufficed to reduce my confidence to naught.

One such day, Bull said:

'Do you hear that odd noise?' Neither Sweelinck nor I have noticed it.

'Yes, indeed, I even think I know what it is. The Fifteenth.'

He disappears, as if swallowed by the instrument, and begins to take it apart, under Sweelinck's worried gaze. The noise attracts the beadle but Bull does not give him a second to speak:

'Fetch me a hammer, my good man. I must dismantle the Twelfth to reach the Fifteenth pipe, which is certainly cracked.'

The beadle does as instructed, with a look that combines perplexity and suspicion, while Bull tinkers with the organ, whistling to himself. The pipe, which is one of the most high-pitched and most inessential, is indeed cracked.

'I'll be back in a moment.' Bull hastens away.

'Leaving me the organ all in pieces like that! And what if he doesn't come back?' grumbles the beadle.

'We shall run after him. Let us dine in the meantime.'

Bull returns a few hours later. The crack in the Fifteenth is fixed, and the beadle's sullen humour turns to respect as he watches the musician deftly put the pipe and everything else back into place, then play a series of dazzling variations to make sure that the operation had been successful.

Later, as we quench our thirst at the inn, I remark:

'You seem to be quite an expert organ-builder.'

'Why, yes; it's part of my profession. My teacher, John Blitheman, always said that in order to master an instrument, one should also know how to build it, down to the tiniest detail. Twice he made me dismantle the organ on which he taught me. And he compelled me to make frequent visits to an instrument maker's workshop.'

In my mind's eye, I dimly recall the churchwarden of Saint-Jacques in Reims letting me repair his organ. Would I still know how?

'Master Tregian, the longing is written all over your face,' says John Bull with a roguish twinkle.

'I took an organ apart once; I must have been fifteen. I am trying to remember . . .'

'I will shortly be supervising the building of an instrument, if that would help you refresh your memory. You can come along.'

'I take you at your word.' And so John Bull taught me to build an organ. I buried my nose in manuals, conferred with craftsmen, and followed Bull and others about. I would never be a master, but I learned the principles; John Bull also taught me a few tricks and some of his own little secrets, which I still apply today.

THE RESPITE WAS SHORT-LIVED.

One day, I received bad news from England. Bad for me, and for countless English people, too.

The monopolies were one of England's open sores. Originally designed to encourage the growth of a particular trade, the monopoly had long since become a purchasable privilege. They cost the country's economy dearly, enriching only those individuals to whom they afforded the opportunity for wild trading ventures, while bringing the national Treasury virtually no benefit.

So when a certain Lord Cockayne went to the King with a suggestion that the profits from the monopoly on the overseas trade of English cloth, one of the foundations of English commerce, should be diverted to the Crown, his idea was immediately adopted.

England had been weaving cloth for centuries. Although the cloth produced in towns and cities for the English themselves was traditionally dyed and finished locally, the cloth from rural areas, which had long accounted for the great bulk of production, was exported raw, to the Low Countries, where it was dyed and finished by companies such as Ardent and van Gouden, then exported again to Germany and the Baltic. Most of the shipping was handled by one company: the Merchant Adventurers. I knew them well, having struck agreements with them for the conveyance of fine wools. They had trade counters in all the ports and were highly organised, exceedingly efficacious and reasonably honest.

Dyeing and finishing were undoubtedly the most lucrative operations in cloth production. Lord Cockayne's suggestion was that from now on, all English cloth should be dyed and finished in England before export, thus promising handsome profits. The King didn't hesitate for a second. The Merchant Adventurers' privileges were revoked, and a new company, the King's Merchant Adventurers, was formed; they alone were authorised to export finished cloth.

We learned all this from a letter sent by Phillips.

> They say that Lord Cockayne has promised the King three hundred thousand pounds a year, and that he himself, who controls everything, counts on making at least as much profit. Alum and dyes are now easier to come by than in the past, thanks to the indigo imported from the East Indies. When considered from that point of view, it might seem like a good idea. But although there is much talk of profit, nobody seems to be concerned with how this wonderful project would work in practice. There are insufficient dyeing and finishing workshops. The former Merchant Adventurers are taking a stand by refusing to carry anything. I fear the worst for our weavers.

'The whole profession will be under the control of this bungler of a king,' Giuliano indignantly pronounces. 'It's a terrible blow for the country folk. Even with sufficient workshops, there will never be enough dyers.'

We attend a meeting of the Amsterdam Drapers' Guild, and events move very swiftly. In just a few days, Holland unanimously forbids the importation of English cloth, whether dyed or raw.

All four of us – Jan, Giuliano, Wim and myself – support the step, but it is a difficult decision. After all, we know the country whence our cloth used to come, and I personally know each of the weavers who had produced our wool.

I cannot sleep. In those Cornish lands for which I feel responsible, poverty is never far away. I have promised these people work and prosperity. They placed their trust in me.

'Oh my brother, you look like a dead man walking,' Dorothy says to me one morning. She and Wim have married, and she is with child – her belly so big she must be very close to giving birth.

I confide my worries. She sighs.

'It is our destiny, particularly yours, always to be living between two worlds. Why did you support the ban on cloth imports, if it causes you so much hurt?'

'Because it is fair. England is governed by a dolt. He must be told, and the prohibition was a means to tell him. But it opens the floodgates to a torrent of penury that will sweep away people we know. I do not regret giving my assent to the Guild's reprisals, but I fear the consequences.'

'The English fleet has been left to rot these last ten years,' says Jan. 'The Royal Navy has virtually ceased to exist, and the Merchant Adventurers have been obliged to organise their own protection. For some time now, Turkish pirates have ventured as far as the Channel without any risk to themselves. The King's traders will never succeed in exporting their cloth to the Baltic. The Merchant Adventurers have made it clear to anyone who'll listen that they wish to have nothing to do with them, and the new company has neither the necessary strength, nor means, nor experience.'

'Do you see what this means? The country folk won't be able to sell anything at all and many families will die of hunger. All these people whom I encouraged to build their own looms – I have ruined them.'

'No, my brother! You are not the harbinger of all the world's ills! King James is the author of this foolishness.'

It was true, and yet I could not resolve myself to see things that way. I sent Jack to Cornwall.

The picture he painted upon his return exceeded my worst fears. He told me of insurrections and suicides. Some families who could not afford to pay their rents, because they no longer earned a penny, had been ejected from their cottages. Ezekiel Grosse distinguished himself by his harsh judgements.

The notion slowly formed within me to go and see for myself. No need to tell me now, as I sit peaceably on the bench at the Echallens cross, that this was suicide. For it was quite the apotheosis of my suicide. I see that now. But my concerns were otherwise at the time.

> *Whether 'tis nobler in the mind to suffer*
> *The slings and arrows of outrageous fortune,*
> *Or to take arms against a sea of troubles,*
> *And by opposing end them?*
> *... Thus conscience does make cowards of us all;*

The answer to Hamlet's question seemed self-evident to me. I must take arms, and risk death. I left at dawn one day, carrying nothing but the money I had at my disposition, having told no one, accompanied only by Jack and Mark, who had no idea where we were going. I left Jan a short message. We journeyed for several days, as far as France, for I retained some sense of caution, and preferred to arrive in England by a roundabout route used by many Catholics to enter the country in secret.

When Jack learned of my plan, he begged me to think again, but in vain.

'If you wish to stay behind, then stay,' I told him finally, in annoyance.

'Me, sir? You affront me! This is not about me. I risk nothing. This is about you. There's a price on your head. Grosse has promised fifty pounds to any man who betrays you to the sheriff. You should not set foot in England as long as this situation lasts. You will be walking into the jaws of catastrophe, and this is not the moment for us to forsake you. We must go with you.'

I was deaf to his arguments.

We landed in a creek close to Falmouth one spring morning.

X

I see a mouse catch the cat,
'Fie, man, fie:
I see a mouse catch the cat,
And the cheese to eat the rat,
Thou hast well drunken, man,
Who's the fool now?

'MARTIN SAID TO HIS MAN'
POPULAR BALLAD

AS SOON AS WE REACH Tregarrick, I send Mark to see the Reverend Hitch.

'Tell him the man in need of a guardian angel wishes to see him.'

Hitch's greeting is succinct: 'Leave immediately. Grosse tells anyone who'll listen that England's ills are all the fault of the Catholics. Did you know he accuses you of having ruined the weavers? And of being hand-in-glove with Lord Cockayne? You have friends, while Grosse has hardly any. But too many people are on the brink of ruin, and the first man to recognise you will have you arrested to get his hands on the fifty-pound reward. Everything is in place for your dispatch. Guardian angels have their limits; I can't see to everything. Your best course would be to leave England just as you came.'

'But . . .'

'I was talking about you to a gentleman of the region. Someone who has no particular affection for you, but who nonetheless is of the opinion that you have been shamefully robbed. He believes a gentleman has a duty to defend himself always. So get away quickly, now, before you are set upon and clubbed to death – Grosse's life will be all the easier once yours is at an end. Can you trust your people?'

My tenant Hugh is listening to our interview, and starts at this.

'Good Lord, Reverend! No one will betray Master Tregian. We could have no better master. Grosse doesn't even know this property belongs to "Master Tregarrick", as we call him here.'

I sweep Hitch's question aside with a wave of my hand.

'Tell me what is happening with the weavers?'

'Nothing that isn't happening elsewhere in England. The sheep are sheared, the wool is spun, cloth is woven and it stops there. No one will buy the stuff – it is forbidden to buy it unfinished, and the skills to dye it properly are lacking. The region is ruined.'

'I've heard Master Grosse myself,' says Hugh. 'He says the weavers have no work because you led them astray.'

'They had no work anyway, when I first convinced them to take up weaving.'

'That's what one of them said in reply. Master Grosse is greatly disliked in Grampound. People refuse him the slightest service. One of his men ventured to object in harsh terms, recently, and was promptly thrown into the criminals' dungeon. But alas, Grosse has the Sheriff in his pocket.'

I can hear no more.

'I should like you to compensate those weavers who paid for their looms out of their own pockets,' I tell Hitch.

I hold my purse out to him. All the coin I possess.

'No one expects you to do that, sir!'

'I've heard a great deal from people about honour, my whole life long. And about the sanctity of my word as a gentleman, which remains sacred even when it pains me to keep it. I promised these people a prosperous living, and look what has happened.'

'It's not your fault.'

'Perhaps. But try explaining that to Little John in his thatched hovel. I gave him my word. It's up to me to do something to make amends for this vile business.'

Reverend Hitch takes the purse, fixing me all the while with his limpid gaze.

'I have often heard talk of your family from my older parishioners.

People respected your grandfather; his only fault is generally held to be the raising of a fine young squire who paid heed to his soul rather than his properties, and left his tenant farmers at the mercy of Carey and Grosse. Lately, people have been saying you are your grandfather's worthy successor, and that perhaps you are quite unlike your father.'

'I make a point of being as unlike him as possible, and I'm honoured that people here compare me to my grandfather.'

'I will do my best to distribute your money, Master Tregian. I fear it will come too late for many people. And I will keep the rest for you. You will have need of it soon enough.'

BELIEVING I STILL HAD time, I lingered. But I was being watched. And I was arrested. A Cornishman in desperate straits recognised me and alerted the authorities. But I was not seized in Cornwall.

Before leaving England, I determined to go to London one last time. I would be harder to find there, I thought. I even agreed to take the precautions I had been advised. Reverend Hitch 'lent' me his housekeeper's son: the lad knew every pannier-lane in the region – deep, hollow trails most often taken by foot-travellers with an occasional pack mule, to move from one village to the next. Being very little used by the heavier carts, they remain grassy and are far less muddy than the main highway. It was unlikely I would be looked for on them, whereas the bridle-paths were riskier, being laid out for travellers on horseback. And so we left Cornwall, taking a circuitous route northward to throw off any potential pursuers.

It took us a good ten days to reach Clerkenwell. I had come to warn my family and consult with Treswell, but I was unprepared for what I found on my arrival.

My brother Charles had returned from Belgium, decided that it was time for him to take charge of our family's affairs: I was irresponsible, unreliable, a virtual criminal. He had won over our mother, doubtless because he expressed himself in terms similar to those used habitually by our father.

'Have you never heard of the Cornish law forbidding the eldest son to sell family property without the consent of his younger brother?'

'It is a custom, not the law. Besides, you were not here to consult.'

'How could you relinquish Rosmondres to escape prison?' He had lost none of his hollow bombast. '"Death, not surrender!" That's what our officers told us when we were cadets, and what we told our cadets when we became officers.'

'But we're not in barracks here, dear brother, and things are rather more complicated.'

Objection was useless. Only my sister Elizabeth supported me. My mother, my sisters Catherine and Sibyll, and above all the Stourtons – of whom there were many – all agreed with Charles. The Arundells were consulted and showed polite interest but refused to become involved – they had more than enough on their hands; the more distant branches of the family, such as the Chandoses, merely assured the Tregians of their warm regard and affection.

I shall never know whether I was betrayed by one of my own, or caught by the long arm of Grosse and his men.

It has even occurred to me at times that my brother and mother viewed me as any other debtor, and had me seized in order to recover 'their' property. I never had occasion to talk the business over calmly with either one of them.

MY FIRST MEMORIES OF prison life are fragmented shards. As fate would have it, I was alone in the house in Holborn when they came for me. I was taken by surprise and offered no resistance. My arrest attracted no attention.

I had not a farthing on me and was thrown into the common gaol as a result – but even this was a better fate than being fed to the poor wretches in the beggars' hall, akin to the sixth circle of Hell, or clapped in irons and thrown into the dungeon.

It took my friends several days to locate me. Days that turned my vision of the world, and life, on its head.

Until then, I had taken scant account of my noble origins, and felt no guilt engaging in activities that might have been deemed beneath me. I had led a frugal, not to say Spartan life, owning only the bare essentials – simple lodgings, and as many horses as were needed, no more. I had two swords and two pistols, as a precaution. But I had always eaten adequately, and been served.

In those few days, I was deprived of everything. You might say that a few days is nothing. But at the time, it felt like an eternity: I lived through each day with no knowledge of when it would all end. I felt I was cut off from the world forever. I didn't know that only the Warden of the Fleet was authorised to receive prisoners and allocate them a lodging. In his absence, I was kept where I could be most easily watched (with the exception of the dungeon).

English debtors were less well provided-for than their Roman counterparts. In ancient Rome, the debtor became his creditor's slave: he had a duty to work for him, but was protected against violent or abusive behaviour, and was fed and housed by his master. Nowadays, in our own country, a debtor locked up in the Fleet is a lost soul, to be released only once his debt is acquitted. His continued presence in gaol is often, then, his creditor's only hope, albeit a vain, not to say absurd hope, in most cases. Because once in prison, most debtors have no means of acquiring money. Declaring a man an insolvent debtor and placing him under arrest is an excellent way to be rid of him without the bother of executing him.

Once under the Warden's authority, I became the living token of my debt, and the Warden was responsible for my fate. If I managed to escape, or went missing, he was personally liable for the amount I owed. He was obliged to produce me on demand, and to ensure I answered every summons to court.

For the truly destitute shut up in the beggars' hall (often for a debt of two or three shillings), the conditions were so appalling that they often paid with their lives, dropping like flies from hunger, cold and the lack of air, collapsing one on top of the other in the filth. Things were a little better in the common gaol, but at a price: our lodgings cost us eight pence a day.

Prisoners of means – like my father – could pay more to enjoy their own apartment and receive their families.

My arresting officers hurl me into the common gaol and leave.

I am well dressed, with no appearance of poverty. Though my sword is taken from me, I still have my daggers, which I clutch in my pockets as I enter, while a pack of murderous-looking men move slowly towards me, forming a circle. Fortunately, I have been careful to maintain my skill at arms.

'Sire,' croaks one, stepping forward and removing an imaginary hat
with a sweep of his arm.

'Leave me in peace!'

'You pays for your peace in here, my little Lord.'

'Let's have that purse,' says another.

'Is it forthcoming or must we fetch it ourselves?' says a third.

It has been a while since I have found myself in such company – once
or twice, on my travels. My height, agility and skill at arms have always
ensured I kept the upper hand. For a moment I am tempted to let them
have their way. They would strip me of all I have, kill me, and so make
an end of it.

To die to sleep. To sleep, perchance to dream; aye, there's the rub . . .

'I'll have the guts of the first man who comes within reach.' I speak the
words calmly, not moving a muscle, staring the apparent ringleader in the
eye. I am confident of my effect. They freeze.

'Well now, an arrogant little lord is it? Looking to be taught a lesson,
is it?' brays someone behind me. Finding myself near a pillar, I fling my
back against it, still clutching the daggers in my pockets.

'Arrogant, says who? I'll show you a lesson all right.'

A curious silence follows my declaration, stated evenly, without boast-
fulness, as a matter of fact.

A phrase of Archduke Albert's runs in my head:

'Master Tregian, you are a born leader of men. You have a rare authority over others, when you choose to exercise it. Indeed, you can dissuade
an adversary with a single look.' Go to it, Francis Tregian. No sleep, nor
dreams for you.

'Better my friend than my enemy, believe me. When I strike, I hit home.'

'Ha! All the fine gentlemen say that! Proving it's another matter.'

'Approach if you dare.'

The man takes a step forward. I aim a kick at his gut, not too hard – I
do not intend to injure him. One sharp, precise kick is the ideal; with skill,
the assailant won't see it coming, and may even feel he's been knocked
backward without being touched. The crowd is duly impressed. One man
takes out a knife.

I draw one of mine.

'Will you have the measure of me?'

I step forward, still within protective reach of the pillar, keeping my eye on him all the while.

They all step back, in complete silence. I have won. They would never leave me in absolute peace, but I have instilled fear, and they will think twice before approaching me now.

Towards evening, people begin pouring into the gaol: prisoners who have been allowed out for the day. Among them is a priest arrested for entering the country under cover. He has spent the day out and about in London, officiating at Mass. He has done the same for several years, he assures me.

'One day, they'll drag me to Tower Hill or Holborn, and I will be hanged. Meanwhile, I'm making myself useful. I see you have gained acceptance already. That's a rare thing.'

He shares a crust of bread with me, and a gourd of water, and offers to share his straw mat, which I refuse. It is too small – and I have no intention of sleeping.

The din continues with nightfall. If anything, it grows louder still. For all that it is difficult to get free of the Fleet once incarcerated, visitors to the prison enter and leave as through an open barn door. In one corner, a group plays at cards and dice; a fight breaks out, to a round of blasphemous oaths. Elsewhere, whores at every stage of decline and drunkenness strive to earn a coin or two from the unfortunate inmates. Vile couplings end in shouts and curses. I even see people creeping into the Fleet to hide – the ultimate paradox. I am approached and defied once or twice. I stare them down, and then another inmate will pull the reckless challenger's sleeve, whispering something in his ear, until he backs off and goes on his way.

I feel sure that if I should sleep, I shall wake stripped bare as the day as I was born. But even in monastic silence, I would have found it hard to sleep. I must escape my predicament. But how? I spend hours making calculations. The Tregarrick income is meagre; enough for me, but no more. In any event, I cannot return to Cornwall. I am too tall to pass unnoticed or disguise myself. My Dutch monies are substantial, but everything is invested. And my Cornish properties have been sequestered. There is the Devon property . . . A wave of nausea overwhelms me. Have I still not understood? I am here because someone wishes to be rid of me. Selling more property, paying more money, would serve no purpose at all. The irony of it! I, who have found it so hard to accept my father, have suffered exactly the same fate. But my father had the benefit of his devout faith, the absolute certainty that his sufferings would earn him a choice corner of Paradise. I have no such powerful antidote.

'You're not asleep?' It is the priest.

'No. I'm contemplating the scale of the disaster.'

'May I be of some help?'

I need help, but have no desire to confide in him.

'You might perhaps go to a woman of my acquaintance, and tell her that her harpsichord player is here.'

I give him Miss Hutchinson's address, and hope I am not making a terrible mistake.

He leaves early the next morning. I spend the day without food or drink: meals have to be paid for, water, too. No one knows me well enough to grant me credit. No one challenges me. No one pays any attention to me at all. The Warden's Men – known to all as 'bastons' – make their rounds among us. I say nothing, and no one asks anything of me.

At length, I make out a quiet group of men next to a barred window. I approach them. Their corner is cleaner and better kept than the rest of the vast hall. Here I find a handful of tradesmen and one or two recusants; they have joined forces above and beyond any religious differences to try to preserve some dignity. One man lies on a straw mat, staring empty-eyed at the roof. I sit beside him.

'Are you taken ill?'

'No. I was imagining . . . The detail is unimportant. A life without debt, at any rate.'

'Do you owe a large sum?'

'Fourteen pounds.'

'You're here for fourteen pounds?'

'You're a gentleman. Fourteen pounds is nothing to you. But I'm a poor cloth finisher. It would take me a year to earn as much – assuming I can get work. I hope I die soon, so that my wife may remarry and my two sons will have enough to eat, perhaps to purchase an apprenticeship. They will bless poor Peter Osborne who had the good sense to leave quietly. And you, what do you owe?'

I feel almost ashamed.

'Three thousand pounds.'

He stares at me, and manages a faint, pale smile.

'Ten shillings, fourteen pounds, three thousand pounds. It's all one. In here, you're a mere token of debt, like me. Die, and your debt dies with you.'

THE PRIEST RETURNS LATE. I am anxious and restless.

'What news?'

'I have seen Mistress Hutchinson. She says to be patient.'

He unfolds a square cloth and I cannot help but smile. It is a strip of woollen drape from the house of Ardent.

'She has sent your supper.'

'For us to share, Father.'

'For us to share, Master Tregian.'

'She told you my name.'

'No, I discovered it elsewhere. I am an admirer of your family, Master Tregian.'

I make no reply. What can I say to people who think, inevitably, that my ideas are my father's, that I would have behaved as he had and be suffering the same consequences as him, for the same reasons?

Over the days that follow, I make some semblance of existence for myself in the recusants' corner, with the priest's help. To stave off my anxiety and dread, I teach them some Italian madrigals, and we arrange them for our own voices. The result is by no means perfect, but it makes a welcome distraction from our troubles.

Mistress Hutchinson comes at last, early one morning. I have lost count of the passing days. I have been wearing the same clothes since I arrived, I am unshaven and have hardly eaten, despite the entreaties of my companions in misfortune. Mistress Hutchinson's expression of horror, when she recognises me, comes as no surprise. She hurries to where I stand.

'Come no nearer, I beg you. I'm covered in lice.'

She sweeps my protest aside with a brusque wave of her hand, rushes toward me and holds me tight in her arms.

'What harm is that? You're alive; the rest can be remedied.'

'My children,' the priest interrupts. 'Step behind that pillar – you'll be more comfortable.'

The priest's attentive concern and Mistress Hutchinson's presence overwhelm me. Out of sight behind the pillar, I weep like a child.

Mistress Hutchinson and I have maintained a somewhat distant relationship, even in our private moments. Now, for the first time, she abandons her reserve, covering with me kisses and caresses, whispering sweet words. I have need of these even more than food. She knows it. I have never called her May until this moment. Thenceforth, I would call her nothing else.

'Why did you say "You are alive; the rest can be remedied"?'

'Jack came tearing back from Cornwall this morning at dawn. Reverend Hitch had heard there was a plot to assassinate you. The plan was to have you arrested, shut you up in the Fleet, then have you killed in a fight provoked by a man in Grosse's pay.'

'But why?'

'Because Grosse is persuaded the King is a friend to the Catholics. And he's afraid your properties will be returned to you before he can secure possession of them for good.'

'And where are Jack and Mark?'

'Jack is at my house, or rather in your lodgings, packing your things. Mark is bringing Phillips – who begs you not to bargain with the Warden. He knows the Fleet and thinks he can obtain better quarters for you himself.'

'He's surely right. I will wait.'

Phillips arrived shortly after, and I was taken out of the common gaol. I met the hateful Alexander Harris – the Warden, back from his travels – but made no attempt to parley with him. Phillips took charge of everything. When I stepped into the apartment he had secured for me, I felt as if I were walking into my own study: Jack had done a fine job. Some of my books were there, with my furniture, my harpsichord and my lute. The windows looked onto the courtyard garden, far from the bowls and rackets yard, which I scarcely heard. There was a separate apartment for my servants.

'I preferred to place you in the section reserved for Catholics,' said Phillips. 'The apartments are more comfortable and there are fewer fights.'

'My dear Phillips, can we truly be here once more, fifteen years on?'

'Times have changed, sir, and one way or another, you will not be here for long. You'll see. But we decided that if you must be here, you might as well live in comfort.'

Still, Phillips had reckoned without the extreme vexation caused me by Sir John Whitbrooke, my immediate neighbour, a recusant thrown into prison for his own stubbornness (he had decided he had no need to pay an admittedly exorbitant fine). He had not come alone, but was accompanied by a whole string of servants, every bit as loud and turbulent as the man himself. Sir John found fault with everything, out of principle.

'We cannot let Master Harris think we are housed here in palatial comfort. If we show the slightest satisfaction, even indifference to our conditions, he will raise the prices. We must protest day and night.'

And he did just that, supported by his indefatigable valets and friends. Some of the other prisoners did the same – Nicholas Rookwood, for example, who was the son of an old friend of my father. I allied myself to him; prison is no place to forge friendships, but our relations were cordial at least. We discussed music, literature, theology and the law. I found him all the more interesting because he was the only non-Catholic member of a family that was traditionally loyal to Rome. He showed an unshakeable faith in the freedom of each individual to choose his own religion, and he stated his creed unambiguously:

'Civil power does not and never will have authority over a man's conscience. Our misfortunes have come about because the ecclesiastical powers have allowed themselves to be drawn into politics and made our consciences the field for battles that have nothing whatever to do with spiritual matters. I have quit my family's religion for the same reason you have clung to yours: to show my independence of mind.'

Nicholas Rookwood was a skilled swordsman; I spent endless hours fencing with him, between discussions. Music and fencing are the two activities that have always restored my spirits. The guards didn't like it but we convinced them, with the finely minted coin of our argument, that this was a mere pastime between bored gentlemen.

Phillips suggested that Jack return to Cornwall.

'I think I can be of more use to you here at the Fleet, sir,' said Phillips. 'But I believe you need someone reliable to see to your interests there, too.'

'I'm willing to go but not for long,' said Jack. 'I feel I'm in exile, sir, when I am far from you.'

'Far from me and far from – what is that charming young woman's name? Marianne?'

'Yes, sir.'

He set off. Phillips and Mark divided their time between prison and my London lodgings. My mother visited once or twice, generally escorted by Lord Stourton. They delivered lengthy sermons which I tried hard not to hear.

Elizabeth came almost daily to play music, and sometimes she succeeded in persuading her sisters to come too, though they maintained their habitual reserve. I had them sing villanelles in three voices. After the arrival at the Fleet of Lady Amy Blunt – who had a magnificent voice – we sang four-part madrigals.

I prefer to remember these moments rather than the everyday routine of our lives as prisoners. I tried not to be drawn into the quarrels provoked at every opportunity by Alexander Harris, the bursar Robert Holmes, the porter Henry Cooke (a particularly detestable individual), and the bastons and their inferiors. Truly, Mark was my guard-dog. Phillips had given sufficient guarantees on my behalf, it seemed: a considerable length of time elapsed before anyone demanded money.

I had to bide my time. Justice would not be done. Treswell was viewed with suspicion merely for defending my interests – and not because I was a Catholic. At court, matters of religion had dwindled in importance. Catholics were only of interest there because their religion left them prey to greedy courtiers whose Protestantism was based on shakier foundations than faith alone. Grosse was doubtless sharing my spoils with one such, who made it his business to ensure I was punished with continuing severity. But Treswell was tenacious, and gave me his word that he would defend my family's interests to the end.

'Sir,' said Phillips one evening. 'Why do you not try to attract the attention of His Excellency Count Gondomar, the Spanish ambassador to the court? Your father is wreathed in the odour of sanctity in Lisbon. They say King James refuses Spain nothing at the moment. He would surely allow you to leave for Madrid.'

'I am too different from my father, Phillips. Music is my religion; I wouldn't know how to give proof of a fervent piety I've never felt. If I feign religious sentiment, I will fall into another trap, worse than this. At least here I am free to think as I please.'

'You are too honest, sir, in a world that is not. I'm suggesting an honourable expedient to get you out of here.'

'But then I should have to play the role expected of me. A proper courtier. I don't have the strength to live a lie. The end cannot justify the use of all means.'

To my surprise, Phillips's eyes gleamed with tears.

'I give thanks to God that you are what you are, sir. Forgive me for saying something that may be disagreeable to you, but, in your unflinching rectitude, you are a worthy son to your father.'

He saw the expression on my face.

'Oh to be sure, in his place you would have moderated your stance, made amends and small concessions to save the core of the estates; you would have taken your family's material interests into account, where he made not the slightest provision and thought only of himself. But where you do stand firm, you are quite as intransigent as he. Allow me to give you a piece of advice, sir.'

'Go on, my dear Phillips.'

'Devote yourself to an occupation, while you wait for something to happen. Your father learned seventeen languages. Do anything, but do not become listless. In prison, those who break are those incapable of occupying themselves.'

'Thank you Phillips. Tell me, despite our financial difficulties, do we have fourteen pounds at our disposal?'

'Easily, sir. We are only paupers when it comes to dealing with the Warden. You are not rich, sir, but you have enough to live comfortably.'

'Well then, by whatever means you may, see to it that the debt of a certain Peter Osborne is paid – a cloth finisher in the common gaol. Once he has been released, give him another twenty pounds to set him off on the right foot.'

Phillips was doubtful, I could read it in his eyes, but he did as instructed, without comment. Osborne was released, never knowing that it was I who had secured his freedom. Only afterwards did Phillips tell him about my 'extreme kindness'.

'The men of his trade were very pleased to see him again,' he said. 'He is esteemed as a hard-working artisan. A shame that the cloth trade is in such dire straits, and that the lack of finishing workshops prevents him from exercising his skill.'

'There's still no one setting them up?'

'No, sir. People talk of reverting to the old system. No one will invest in activities under His Majesty's direct control. Millions have been sunk into such schemes – and lost, sir. The experience has left many feeling very bitter. And the King's new Merchant Adventurers are incapable of organising exports as their predecessors did.'

'Even if they do revert to the old system, it will take more than good intentions to persuade the Dutch drapers to lift their ban on the purchase of English cloth.'

In fact, thanks to my communications with Holland, I knew that alternative solutions had been found. More cloth was being woven there and also imported from northern Europe. Like so many others, Ardent and van Gouden ceased trading with England.

I THROW MYSELF INTO my music. I begin by getting my scores into a sort of order, with a system of classification. I add the occasional new piece to my collection, having hired a skilled music copier to help me in my task. But – alas! – it is difficult to keep up to date without travelling. I am sure that Monteverde has written new madrigals, for example.

One day, a side panel splits on my virginal. I send Mark to find a joiner. He is already out in the passageway when an idea occurs to me:

'Mark!'

'Yes, sir?'

'Try and find Master Giles Farnaby, if you can. The Guild of Virginal Makers, or the Joiners and Ceilers, will have his address.'

He returns with a fine, tall young man of about twenty.

'My respects to you, Master Tregian. I am Richard Farnaby. My father regrets he is unable to come straight away. Meantime, he has sent me to inspect the damage.'

From that day forward, the Farnaby family adopt me as one of their own. Giles spends innumerable evenings at the Fleet and brings astonishing music with him. I know some of the pieces from earlier versions, but he has made great progress. His technique is sometimes limited but he has turned the handicap of a life spent making furniture and instruments rather than studying music (as Bull or Byrd had been able to do) to his advantage: he achieves his greatest heights when he disregards every rule of musical composition. Strangely, his music puts me in mind of Monteverde. The pieces he brings are the product of a mastery of melody I have seldom seen, before or since. His is a bold, spontaneous genius, with an enviable, palpable ability and generosity of spirit. He attends one of our madrigal gatherings and, a few days later, brings me a remarkable fantasia inspired by that same evening. Effects of echo, melodic sequences, experiments in rhythm, delightfully graduated figures, a finale in the style of a toccata and a magnificent cadenza to finish, with a double flourish I would never have dared contemplate. A masterpiece, which I copy straight down and include in my repertory of scores. Giles had the art of transforming an invariably exquisite melody into a free-moving counterpoint, that passes almost insensibly from the left hand to the right, and so fills the whole piece. When I play it now, my fingers fly from one end of the keyboard to the other and my soul rises to unexplored regions, far from the travails of this life.

I found Giles's pieces more appealing than Gibbons's, and at times more daring than Master Byrd's. Richard composed, too. I especially liked his way of treating counterpoint. He was less inspired than his father but he was young, and Giles had not been so accomplished at his age.

The Farnabys were the last musical discovery of my first life, and one of the finest I ever made.

PHILLIPS WATCHED OVER ME with paternal care. His blond hair had paled while not turning completely white, and deep lines furrowed his temples and brow; but like all those who are lucky enough to keep their teeth, he had a youthful look, accentuated by his upright, lean figure. It touched me to think that he had taken care of me forty years before. I saw him as he was then, on our flight from Cornwall, helping me as a small boy out of the basket in which I had made the journey. I remembered his strong, protecting arm, somewhere in Devon or Dorset, while my mother gave birth to my sister Margaret. And I thought of the devotion he had showed my father. Now he was watching over me, displaying not the least sign of weariness. On the contrary, he was full of energy and useful ideas, endlessly coming and going. I had always declared that I couldn't live without Jack by my side, and it was true that I missed him at times. But in my current situation, Phillips was indispensable. I felt a truly filial affection towards him.

He bargained with Harris for an exit pass – a right as old as the Fleet itself, allowing a prisoner to leave the building with a guard specially appointed for the purpose. Some prisoners were even allowed out alone, provided they left an adequate deposit with the Warden.

Phillips arranged just such a thing, furnishing Harris with a paper of no value whatsoever, but cleverly drafted so that the poor man was convinced it entitled him to the equivalent of three thousand pounds.

'Do you not think Master Harris will see it's quite worthless?'

'I do not, sir. I have made sure that he if makes enquiries, he will be amply satisfied. I hope we shan't be forced to disappear without the necessary preparations. But I would advise you all the same to leave nothing you value at the Fleet – we may be forced to leave suddenly. The opportunity may present itself at any moment ...'

'What opportunity, my dear Phillips?'

'I hope sir will forgive me for saying no more at the moment. I have an idea but it needs time and the conjunction of a certain number of conditions. No sir, I beg you, ask me no more questions.'

I acquiesced. I had placed my blind trust in this man.

And so I was able to absent myself from the Fleet, almost at will, provided I paid the exit fee and remained in London.

I went frequently to the Farnabys', where I learned the art of virginal-making. Sometimes, when Giles had to take long journeys in search of the wood needed for his instruments, I would go with him, dressed as his valet – otherwise my name would have been demanded at the city gates and I would have been arrested. I left for weeks at a time, working patiently day after day to make the registers, then the jacks for the registers and the plectrums for the jacks. I learned how to cut the keys and cover them in bone. I watched the artisan making the strings on a kind of spinning wheel. It was intricate work: the metal had to be 'spun' to a precise gauge.

Giles and Richard taught me how to build not only virginals – both the version known as a spinet (with the keyboard to the left and the strings plucked as for a harpsichord, a quarter of the way along their length) and the muselaar (with the keyboard to the right and the strings plucked in the middle) – but also harpsichords, which were less widely used but demanded a great deal more work and complex operations in their assembly. I drew on my memories of the long hours spent watching the instrument makers at the Ruckers', consulted a treatise on the subject and devoted myself to studying the instruments' architecture. When I wasn't working with the Farnabys or singing with my sisters and the ladies of the Fleet, I busied myself with setting my madrigals in order. I no longer had Jack to help – he imitated my hand to perfection – and so copied everything out myself. What with one thing and another, I often worked for eighteen, even twenty hours in a day.

I had a horse, as did Mark, and often stayed with May, only returning for a few nights at the Fleet, intermittently.

I stopped thinking constantly about myself, my problems and miseries. I thought only of music, playing music and musical instruments. I visited the shops of music publishers and printers, who sold the pieces I had collected sometimes fifteen or twenty years earlier. And I added to my own collection with extracts from some of their pieces, too.

On occasion, I took my sisters to sing at gatherings in Catholic homes. We were much talked about; our performances, too.

A musician borrowed some Monteverde scores from me, then informed me eight days later that they were un-singable. I offered to conduct his singers and explained the particular technique of *seconda pratica*. The madrigals were sung and the musician declared it a miracle. News spread and people came seeking my advice, inviting me to conduct their consorts. Through music, I re-established a contact of sorts with the world. Thanks to music, I forgot my troubles. Cornwall faded from my thoughts. Such is the human mind: we wipe the slate of memory clean, almost at will.

It was then that word reached me of my sister Mary's death. The news left me almost indifferent at the time. Only little by little did I feel a sense of sorrow, steeped in memories of our childhood.

I took little part in the turbulent life of the Fleet, but I agreed to join an action I thought just and which involved a number of prominent prisoners, both Protestant and Catholic, at the suggestion of one of the most active Catholic inmates, Edmund Chamberlayne. Chamberlayne was a gentleman who declared to anyone who would listen that he was indeed a Catholic but that this was not the reason for his incarceration: he was at the Fleet because his brother had accumulated debts of fifteen thousand pounds. To enable his family to continue going about their business despite this terrible handicap, one of the brothers had to agree to shoulder the debt, and go to the Fleet. It had fallen to Edmund to do so.

He had not gone quietly to this sacrifice but had brought with him his wife, children and servants. He was gifted with remarkable charm, and quickly succeeded in persuading Harris – God alone knows how – to vacate his own apartments and make way for the household. After a while, the Warden sought to recover his lodgings. Chamberlayne wouldn't hear of it, and held out in Harris's apartments for at least a year. The enraged shouts of one and the other irritated and amused us in equal measure, becoming the butt of many jokes.

'Harris is venting his spleen on Chamberlayne, again,' we commented. Or 'Chamberlayne's in fine voice today – Harris is in for it now.'

We totted up the score, like gamblers at a cockfight.

It was Chamberlayne who first hatched the idea:

'Why pay Harris for our meat and drink? We should stop. He'll be ruined.'

A new arrival, Sir Francis Englefield, declared immediately that he would take charge of ordering food from a nearby inn, and invited us all to dine at his table.

I was out and about often enough to eat my fill of good food, and had no complaints about the meals at the Fleet. I confess that I've never paid much attention to what I eat. If it's good and tasty, so much the better; if mediocre, I don't give it a second thought. But the services and board at the Fleet were costly, and other privileges were dealt with a mean hand indeed. Nothing was free of charge. Harris had sub-contracted a number of functions to the bastons, who hoped to make their fortunes at our expense.

Chamberlayne made it known, loud and clear, that he was no longer paying. Others among us went about it a different way. Quietly and calmly, we stated that we would pay – tomorrow. Or next month. Our debts to the Warden mounted up. Finally, I was eighteen months in arrears. Two hundred pounds. Harris threatened to stop my exit passes, and I retorted that, in that case, I would stand little chance of ever getting the money to pay him. Phillips sighed heavily in confirmation of the fact, and on it went.

Harris was especially infuriated by Sir Francis Englefield's dinner club, and maintained that Sir Francis was robbing him by choosing not to eat meals from the Fleet's admittedly questionable kitchens. The Warden and his inmates played cat-and-mouse with the steaming dishes of food. We all joined in, and often ate (cold) after hours of to-ing and fro-ing. I found it all greatly entertaining, but the games drove hungry diners to wild exasperation. At such times, they talked of murdering Harris, and he took their threats quite seriously: his had always been a very poor sense of humour.

Sir Francis Englefield was just as loud and vociferous as Chamberlayne, Sir John Witbrooke and others I no longer care to remember. Had I not been able to go out, I believe I would never have slept. The noise was constant, night and day – the breaking-down of doors, the blowing of horns and the beating of drums; shouts and quarrelling without end.

Let no one imagine for an instant that it was possible to accustom oneself to life at the Fleet, even with the freedom to come and go from time to time. The mean-mindedness, coercion, mediocrity and pettiness of the inmates and their factions (we had our Puritans and our Protestants, our Jesuits and our secular Catholics, just as outside in the city), the gossip and promiscuity all made the prison a particular form of torture, gentle but nonetheless real. The Fleet clung to my clothes, insinuated itself into the creases of my skin; and galloping out into the countryside did nothing to rid me of it.

I owe my salvation to Phillips, May Hutchinson's goodness, the Farnabys and my sister Elizabeth, who worked at her playing like a slave, most often at the Fleet, and to whom I taught everything I knew. Without my many distractions, I hardly dare think what would have become of me. I would have gone mad.

On the few occasions when I stepped outside my world of music and plunged back into the reality of my life's troubles, such as when my brother Charles came to demand payment for some transaction or other, or when I had to travel to Cornwall to procure funds by selling some small parcel of my remaining land, I sank straight away into the deepest melancholy. No music could reach me then. I felt ready to give up everything, to lie down, turn to the wall, as I had seen so many prisoners do, and let death take me. But it never came to that.

Without hope, one cannot find the unhoped-for: it cannot, by definition, be tracked, and no path leads to it, said Heraclitus. I continued to hope, but for what? I did not know.

And so two, perhaps three years passed – an eternity I prefer to leave under the cloak of silence. Until, at long last, the day came when the opportunity Phillips had been looking for presented itself.

XI

A better proof I see that ye would have
How I am dead. Therefore when ye hear tell,
Believe it not although ye see my grave,
Cruel, unkind! I say, 'Farewell, farewell!'

'HEAVEN AND EARTH'
THOMAS WYATT / FRANCIS TREGIAN

WRITING HELD LITTLE INTEREST for me before I began this memoir; I always found its melody too linear. In music, the composer can make several voices speak at once. Beneath the upper register that sets the tone, there may be a concurrence of other melodies, signifying sadness or reflection, gaiety or religious devotion, like those dazzling *In Nomine* pieces by Bull or Sweelinck: in these, the solemn plainsong, played in the lowest register with the left hand, may be heard beneath the variations, fantasies, trills and flights of fancy expressed by the right hand. With writing, it is difficult to make several voices heard at the same time; perfect chords in literature are the work of rare geniuses, and even they cannot be relied upon: Master Shakespeare achieved it in *Hamlet* or *Lear*, Messire de Montaigne on a few of his pages, Francesco Petrarca, Torquato Tasso and Thomas Wyatt in some of their poems. But one rarely finds such complex melodies on the written page.

Now that I myself have begun to write, I understand much better how hard it is.

Every time I put a thought, a conversation or an event down on paper, I seem to betray another through omission. However long my story may be, it remains fragmentary and incomplete.

I have given the main points of this pavane. But a thousand other things happened at the same time. Beneath the melody that I have copied here as best I can lie other notes, both high and low, that would perfect its meaning.

I did not recount my infinite sadness upon learning of the death of Master Shakespeare, which occurred a few months after my imprisonment, at a time when I was quite taken up with obtaining permission to leave the Fleet without an escort.

While Chamberlayne carped on about his lodgings and whether he would have to move or not, and as I learned how to build a spinet register, it was with unbridled joy that I discovered *The History of Don Quixote of The Mancha*, which had just been translated into English.

Back in the days when I used to present musical evenings for Catholic gatherings, the King made Sir Walter Raleigh the agent of his shameful moves towards reconciliation with Spain. I should have seen this great man as my enemy – oh, how he railed against Catholics! – but he drew my compassion. The King had sent him to the other side of the world to secure control over Spain's gold. As soon as Raleigh set sail (in dreadful weather), our sovereign lost no time in informing Spain, giving Philip III every detail of the expedition. The Spanish lay in wait for Raleigh at key locations, wiped out his army, killed his son and, of course, protected their gold. Raleigh returned to England empty-handed, and, in order to prove his goodwill to Spain, the King had him executed for high treason. This disgraceful act was the cause of much indignation.

'His Majesty's powers will not last,' May Hutchinson remarked drily.

'I take it as a portent of England's possible return to the bosom of Rome.'

May was Protestant; we rarely spoke of religion. But that day, she replied.

'You misjudge the English soul, my friend. It may well be that out in the countryside there are entire villages of Catholics. At least, that's what they say. But in the towns – *all* the towns, from the biggest to the smallest – the Reform is very firmly rooted. Based on what they've seen, people believe that only the Protestant Church can assure the growth of the human spirit and intelligence, and . . . '

'My dear May, are you not going too far?'

'Yes, I know; you've described the beautiful monuments in Rome. But a building is not an idea; it poses no threat to anyone's life, as long as it's properly built. Have you ever seen Protestants send a man to the stake because he maintained that the Earth turns on its axis, that blood flows around the body or that the Universe might not fit Aristotle's system? Don't look so astonished. You've brought hundreds of books into this house, of which I've read a few, and they've allowed me to understand the discussions my customers have among themselves while I adjust their garments for stitching. I don't say much when they're here, but I thought I could speak more freely with you.'

I might have mentioned Geneva and the merciless severity of the Calvinists. To what purpose? I was content to raise my hand to shield myself from the flow of words.

'Forgive me. Ever since the day I saw my sister fence with the skill of a professional swashbuckler, I should know that women are capable of anything, even of becoming great philosophers.'

'Mock away, but you'll see – one day!'

'I mock not. I hail the pleasure of discussing philosophy with a lady – something I have never done.'

'To return to Sir Walter Raleigh, I hope that his ghost will harry the King – and his son even more – unto the grave.'

These are some of the things I might have recounted as a musical medley, making five, six or eight voices speak at once. As a writer, I must be satisfied with an imperfect account.

I am aware that I have made no mention of either my Dutch family or my son. Yet I was in constant communication with them during that time. Either Mark or Jack – and once even Phillips – would go to Amsterdam and to Tarbes. They brought back letters, accounts, money and warm encouragements.

When King Louis of France was about eighteen years old, he resolved to reign. He had his mother's favourite, Marshal Concini, murdered, drove Marie de' Medici from power and sought the support of the nobility. He summoned back to him those he called the 'Tréville Brothers', together with their father. But Charles preferred to remain in Tarbes. His Catholicism was not rooted in deep conviction. He feared an imminent persecution of Protestants, which was something he could not have stood to be involved in, and so chose to remain on his estates. Arnaud had joined the Musketeers, a choice company under orders from the King himself. Francis joined alongside him. But one day, he declared that he spoke Dutch fluently and wished to be sent to The Hague. An opportunity soon arose. When he was not quartered with the French ambassador, he lived at the family house in Amsterdam.

'Is it known that you have a son?' Phillips whispered to me one day, near the beginning of my imprisonment.

'I rarely talk about it. My mother seems to think that he died of the plague with the others. The Tregians don't speak of it and I have never pressed the matter. Why this question?'

'Because there are those who would cause him harm, out of fear that he might seek to replace you, and demand the return of your estates more vehemently and effectively than you.'

'For that very reason, I have never flaunted him in England. I have no wish to bequeath him the burden under which I stagger. The duty to take care of it fell to me, but I shall be the last of the line.'

'The last will be your brother Charles. He proclaims rather too loudly that one day he'll become as rich and powerful as his ancestors, all over again. He seethes with impatience, for he believes he'll succeed where you have not. But he has no subtlety and will find himself ensnared.'

I could but sigh. Phillips was right. I tried to tell my family all these things. They chose not to hear me.

I BEGAN TO TELL myself that the time had come for me to depart. I have no idea if the time between idea and action was long or short. I recall the day when I gathered together Jack, who had come especially for the purpose, Mark and Phillips. We met in the depths of the countryside, as was our wont when we wished to avoid eavesdroppers.

'I remember what Peter Osborne told me the day I arrived at the Fleet: "Die, and your debt dies with you." I believe that the time has come for me to do away with my debt. If someone were to persuade my brother not to demand the return of our estates, the Tregians would be freed, and Charles, my sisters and my mother could live, modestly perhaps, but in peace.'

A look passes between Jack and Phillips.

'What? You don't agree?'

'We agree with you so much, sir, that we have been preparing the thing for a long while.'

'Is that so? Without telling me?'

'We hoped to avoid any indiscretion or imprudence.'

They amuse me.

'Were you scared I would betray you?'

'No, but it took time for us to perfect a plan.' Philips looks pensive. 'It will be difficult, sir. It will be impossible to do things by halves. You must truly disappear, and you will never be able to return to England to see your family. Your son, at a push, if his existence is not known. Antwerp and Brussels will be out of bounds to you, and the stay you'll have to make in Amsterdam must be short and discreet. Then you'll need to find a place where nobody has ever heard of you. But cities like Bordeaux, Rome or Venice are out of the question. Unfortunately, your unusual height and distinctive eyes will give you away wherever you are known. In ten years perhaps, if God grants you life, but not now.'

'I see. Indeed, the idea had crossed my mind. But how am I to die? This is more complex than an escape.'

'Permit us to tell you nothing, sir, and promise to follow our counsel.'

'Your orders, you mean.'

'Sir, I would not permit myself . . . '

'Please, Jack. Not with me. And you? What will you do when I'm no longer here?'

'I shall go with you, sir,' says Mark without pause. 'How, I know not yet, but I shall go with you.'

'As for you, Jack, I shall ask you to look after Tregarrick. "Master Tregarrick" might live on, might he not? As long as he remain abroad?'

'Certainly, sir. But I would rather abide with you, be it at the far side of the world.'

'I should like that too, Jack, but I cannot say where, or how, I shall live, nor even if I may keep Mark. Watch over Tregarrick; it will be useful, no doubt. If I see the means to fetch you one day, I promise to let you know. And now, explain your plan to me.'

The plan is at once so simple and so intricate that it has every chance of succeeding, if the utmost secrecy be maintained. At least, that's what I prefer to think, for if the enterprise should fail, I will be clapped in irons, and not at the Fleet but in the Clink, the Marshalsea or the Tower. If, however, it succeeds, nobody will ever think of pursuing me, for I shall be dead.

ONE DAY, A CERTAIN Long John appears at the Fleet – lean, bearded and hirsute, of indeterminate age and with an idiot's grin. His associate is shrill of voice and ill-defined of figure, and goes by the name of Rosy Bottom – professional fools love to burden themselves with such names. Long John utters not a word; Rosy Bottom talks without cease, recounting the most ordinary things with astonishing eloquence, making them droll with a single gesture or a look. A quite extraordinary clown. As for silent Long John, he is as dextrous as the Devil himself. Cards, coins, objects large or small, appear then vanish betwixt his fingers, all in complete silence.

Some days these two individuals are accompanied by a certain Spike, a broad-shouldered figure with a deep voice, the equal in length and breadth to the bear he holds on a leash. According to this fellow's rhetorical flourish, which I can hear even in my apartments, the beast is blessed with an implacable hatred of dogs and great agility as a dancer.

They keep out of doors by the racket-yard and the tennis court, or else in the common gaol. They entertain everyone, and even the bastons often stop to laugh at their antics.

The trio soon becomes part of the Fleet. Everybody knows them; some throw a few halfpennies into the hat they pass around. I am sure they do not earn much, but they do not seem to care. They become familiar figures; nobody pays them the slightest attention as they come and go. Sometimes they spend the night in a corner of the common gaol, or in the yard, if the weather is fine, huddled up against each other.

I am told of them, and see them from afar, but it is weeks before one of them approaches me. Nor do I make any effort to get to know them. One morning, Spike is playing with his bear directly under my window, which is open, for it is hot. I am at the virginal. Suddenly, the ball that the bear tamer is wont to throw to his charge lands on my floor.

I get to my feet, pick it up and go over to the window. There is something strange about this ball, as if I have seen it before. But where? Suddenly, it comes to me. It looks exactly like one I made for Guillaume Ardent when he was a boy, using the skin of a small creature taken while hunting. I look at it for a moment and am filled with a rare swell of regret: I recall that free-hearted time when I had all but forgotten I was a Tregian. And then I see the letters I myself branded on the ball with an iron: a G and an A entwined. I rush to the window, look out – and find myself gazing straight into the eyes of Giuliano:

'My good sir, be not vexed if my ball was unable to resist your music,' he says, giving me no time to react. 'If you would be so kind as to play a pavane, my bear will make the most perfect dance to it.'

'Ha! Is there a piece he especially prefers?' My voice doesn't even shake.

'He loves *The Hunt's Up*.'

'Is that so – *The Hunt's Up*?'

'Yes, sir, if you would.'

'I shall play it.'

I draw the virginal close to the window, and begin to play the *intavolatura* of this popular song.

There are few people in the yard at this hour. Long John, Rosy Bottom and a few standers-by gather round and help the poor bear keep time by clapping their hands.

'Ho, there! I shall sing a tune to which I defy the bear to cut a caper!' declares Rosy Bottom, before making a deep, extravagant bow to the spectators, leaning too far forward and falling flat on his face.

Everybody laughs.

'Oh yes, Rosy Bottom, sing us something.'

'What takes your fancy? Tragedy, comedy, history, pastoral, pastoral-comical, historical-pastoral, tragic-historical, tragical-comical-historical-pastoral . . .'

'By Jove, young man, give us a pathetical-pastoral.'

'So be it. Silence! I give you *Love Will Find Out the Way*.'

And he begins to sing:

> *Over the mountains,*
> *And over the waves,*
> *Under the fountains*
> *And under the graves;*
> *Under floods that are deepest,*

Which Neptune obey,
Over the rocks that are steepest
Love will find out the way.
Where there is no place
For the glow-worm to lie,
Where there is no space
For receipt of a fly,
Where the midge dare not venture
Lest herself fast she lay
If Love come, he will enter,
And soon find out his way.

The song conjures a whole retinue of memories. I close my eyes to avoid looking at the curious master-mistress of a creature singing the tune I have rehearsed so often in another life, with another person . . . Another person? Francis! Francis, you who vaunt your perfect ear . . . I keep my eyes closed and listen. Beneath the clown's rasping voice I sense, now and again, the pure voice of . . . But yes, who else? I open my eyes and recognise her in a flash: Rosy Bottom is none other than my fearless sister Dorothy. But that means her lean, wretched companion can only be . . . And then I see it as plain as day: Long John can only be my son.

I know the three clowns will be the accessories to my escape. But Jack and Phillips have kept their identity a strict secret – fearing that I would put a stop to it.

They must have seen from my expression that I have recognised them. They set to performing a dazzling bit of foolery which keeps everyone's eyes fixed on them. Rosy Bottom sings at the top of her voice, heinously out of tune:

Come live with me and be my love
Thou, in whose groves, by Dis above,
Shall live with me and be my love.

I cannot help but laugh. Why did the Creator not bless me with the levity, eloquence and talents that he lavished so plentifully upon this small, spirited woman? Mother of two children she may be, but she is as much at home playing the fool as she was playing the gracious host to an Amsterdam worthy, a customer or neighbour at the Stromarkt. She is an astonishingly talented actor. Master Shakespeare – and Master Mulcaster – would have disapproved but admired her talents nonetheless.

On the evening of this revelation, which of course we do not discuss, Phillips observes, before a dozen prisoners and nearly as many bastons:

'You don't look well, sir. Are you indisposed?'

'I cannot say, Phillips. I don't feel at all my usual self.'

And little by little, I fall ill. The only person I wish I need not deceive in this way is my sister Elizabeth, bound to me by our close affection and our shared passion for music. But I am forced to lie to her. She would not know how to keep the secret, being a person devoid of artifice, righteous and pure.

Everything that I hold dear is taken to Phillips's house: my collection of madrigals, my Montaigne, my few Shakespeare plays, my volumes of Gibbons, Dowland, Byrd and Morley, to name but a few. I keep only my collection of pieces for virginal, which I intend to imprint on my memory before entrusting it to Elizabeth.

My 'sickness' lingers for weeks on end: I am obliged to abide at the Fleet permanently, spending considerable time in bed. I take exercise in secret, for it is essential that I not stiffen up, quite apart from the fact that inactivity is more than I can bear. But going without tennis, riding or fencing is not easy.

Summer is drawing to a close when Phillips lets slip one day that he thinks he has 'found the remedy'. This is our watchword.

About the same time, Rosy Bottom and Long John, who have never been ones for sitting still, commence a frenzy of comings and goings to and from the Fleet, with and without the bear tamer, at all hours. They never come to see me.

But one day, when they are absent, I receive a visit from my sister Dorothy.

She wears a magnificent dress of pale purple silk, under a white velvet cloak. Her sleeves are of prized Flanders lace, her collar is exquisite with embroideries and she makes such an impression on Harris that he comes to announce her himself, having taken the opportunity to inform her, as Dorothy would tell me later, that I owe him nearly two hundred pounds in board and lodging.

She does not stay long, weeps abundantly and hugs me tight despite my exhortations for her to keep her distance – I am a very sick man, after all.

'My dear, dear brother, what is death to me? There is no one dearer to me than you in the whole world, after my husband and my children.' She leans close to kiss me. 'The man we were waiting for is here at last. Exceedingly indisposed. He will doubtless die. It is only a matter of hours now, possibly days. Be at your sickest. The next time your sister Dorothy comes to call, you will no longer be here.'

She straightens herself and sets to weeping loudly again. Phillips and Jack, who escorted her, hold her upright as she leaves. She has them give Harris ten pounds.

'That's all I have, but be assured that I shall do my utmost to see you receive the rest as quickly as possible.'

She proffers her hand to be kissed. Harris is astonished and beguiled in equal measure. It would have taken a feat of imagination to recognise her two hours later, japing about with Long John. Every shred of femininity is gone and nobody, myself included, would ever imagine that Rosy Bottom be a woman.

My mother comes to see me, too. She weeps copiously.

'My poor son, I never thought I'd live to see you mouldering on the same poor pallet as your father. I am proud to see the suffering you endure for your faith.'

The rumour spreads, ably fanned by Phillips, that my sickness might be contagious. Visits to my apartment become fewer and fewer. To my great regret, Phillips bars the door to May Hutchinson. I would not see her again. Sir Francis Englefield and Nicholas Rookwood sometimes come as far as the threshold to exchange a few words. But nobody draws close to my bed, save for my servants and my dearest Elizabeth. I should have known she would insist on staying despite the danger.

Elizabeth has found a husband, a rich spice merchant by the name of Robert Johnson, who has fallen deeply in love with her and of whom she speaks with true affection. She cares not a jot that the entire family, Tregians, Arundells and Stourtons combined, are opposed to her wedding a commoner. The only thing that gives her pause is her lack of a dowry.

'I do not wish him to wed me out of charity. And also, it would not be right. It is the custom for a woman to furnish a dowry.'

I could have pointed out that her grace and beauty were dowry enough, but I know very well that she reckoned them for naught in the balance. I resolve that it is up to me to help her.

'Phillips, we must find Elizabeth a dowry, otherwise she'll die an old maid.'

'I am of the same mind as you, sir. You still have one estate in Dorset; it doesn't bring in much, and never will, unless waterways are dug. But it's quite large and well situated, and it seems to me that it's quite suited to the building of a merchant's residence, for example.'

'Fetch me a quill and paper.'

I write out the necessary conveyance document, and Master Treswell visits to have me sign it before witnesses and to record it. Seacombe, a property lying on the Devon border, to which I attach the document with which she could obtain the money I'd invested for her, becomes Elizabeth's dowry. I make out no will for the remainder. If I were to bequeath Golden to my brother, he would be imprisoned in the Fleet no sooner said than done. Grosse would see to that. Golden is lost; to persist is futile.

THE DAY COMES FOR the long-prepared plan to be executed.

It begins, truth be told, in the middle of the night, in those few brief hours when the Fleet is quiet. Richard Farnaby enters, carrying a lifeless fellow over his shoulder, head down, arms dangling, wrapped in a cloak.

'He's a little smaller than you, but that will not be seen, for the poor devil was very tall, all the same.'

'He wasn't killed on my account, at least?'

'Rest easy: we have been attending to him for weeks. He really could not be healed.'

He lays the body on the bed and a shiver runs through me. This dead man will assume my identity. By tomorrow, he will be me. I am overwhelmed by the strange sensation of being both alive and dead.

'I shall leave you, sir; have patience. If all goes well, you will be gone by noon.'

'Have you taken the necessary steps, so that Elizabeth will not insist on coming to see the body?

'Yes, sir. Her betrothed is to take her to see their new house, where she will find the harpsichord you made for her. That will take the whole day, and by the day after tomorrow the burial will be a done deed.'

He goes. It comes as no surprise to me that Farnaby, too, has a part to play in Phillips's plan. I spend a few grim hours one-to-one with my second self. The wheels are in motion and I can do nothing to stop them now. I am still surrounded by familiar objects, but Francis Tregian is no more. I open the cloak; the corpse has already been undressed, as agreed.

I clothe him in my well-worn garments. Having taken great pains to whiten my hair over the past few weeks, I hope that I bear a sufficient resemblance to the poor wretch lying there. Once I am done, I carefully draw the curtains round the bed. I trim my beard to give it a different shape and brush my hair to remove a little of the talc. Then I sit down and I wait.

The sky grows pale, the church bells chime peal after peal. My last London dawn, perhaps. A tide of images, in spite of myself: our arrival at Merchant Taylors'; Master Francis and Master Adrian; 'extremities meet'; Master Morley and his lute; 'Are you following me, Master Harrington?'; the Queen grasping my wrist so hard it might break; 'You will tell your father . . .'

When the door opens, I start out of my chair.

It is Rosy Bottom, carrying a packet. Without a word, I put on Long John's rags and his hat, and smudge my face. I have spent hours rehearsing his simplest tricks in recent weeks. I hope I can pass muster, if necessary.

We slip out in silence. Just in time. The bastons are beginning their rounds. The solitary night guard is easy to avoid, but soon there will be half a dozen making their way around the prison, going past my room. Nobody will think to open my door, for it is well known that Master Tregian is sick and sleeps late.

We squat in a corner of the yard, joining Spike, who is already in position with his bear. He does nothing to acknowledge us, and if I didn't know him by heart, I would have thought him asleep. Only the bear grunts, but is quickly soothed.

Lady Amy Blunt comes out for her morning walk. She has brought the clowns some cake, as she often does. Rosy Bottom takes it and hands it round. Lady Amy hardly looks at us. She sees nothing out of the ordinary in our little group.

The thorniest moments of the operation are still to come, beginning with my exit.

The bear tamer and the clowns have become such a familiar sight that we are able to exit without Henry Cooke, the gatekeeper, so much as lifting his head. The moment has been chosen with care. Cooke has just come on duty and is still puffy-eyed with beer and sleep. Rosy Bottom gives the ritual line:

'There are three of us and we request permission to exit, Master Cooke.'

He nods his assent and sticks out his hand, into which Dorothy places the customary shilling. Exits have to be paid for. Even if Cooke had bothered to look us over, it would take a keener eye than his to recognise me beneath Long John's rags. What with our having the same height, same nose, same beard and same filth, my son and I easily pass the one for the other. Once outside, we make towards Blackfriars Steps, where Richard Farnaby is waiting with a skiff. I change clothes in the boat and become an honest merchant, crooked with age beneath his brown tunic and black cloak. The other two turn back. My heart is tight in my chest. My son is in the Fleet, and my darling sister and Giuliano are exposed to every danger.

We make our way up the river towards Richmond and land at Twickenham Park. The bank is deserted. Our prayers are answered: the sky darkens and it begins to rain.

We wait for a long while in an empty cottage, the property of Mistress Farnaby.

'How is it you got mixed up in all this, Master Richard?'

'Master Phillips was able to convince my father. He had need of a joiner for the day when a coffin would have to be made. A trusty man was essential. Our families have known each other for a long time. Master Phillips knew my grandfather Thomas, and you are one of the most ardent lovers of my father's compositions.'

'And of yours, Master Richard.'

'You are most kind, but I know my own mediocrity. Still, my father didn't hesitate. He is entirely devoted to you. I was charged with taking care of . . . of the person who would replace you, because I was little known at the Fleet.'

'Who was he?'

'A Lancashire weaver. He lost everything in the crisis and came to London in the hope of rebuilding his life. He lived on credit at an inn

until the day he fell ill and the innkeeper had him arrested to be rid
of him.'

A long silence.

'He told me something of his life over his last days. I felt I was losing
a friend. And frankly, sir, even knowing that you were waiting, if I could
have restored him to health, I would have done so.'

'I would have done as you did. I would not wish to be free again for
the price of a murder.'

Night is falling when the others arrive. The bear is gone. Giuliano is
resplendent as a wealthy Dutch merchant; Francis is dressed as a French
gentleman, and Dorothy as a cadet, a sword at her side and hat set at a
jaunty angle. They are served by Jack and Mark. Only Phillips remains
exposed to danger.

We look at one another in the grey dusk. Francis throws himself forward and hugs me close. Nobody can summon so much as a word, so
affected are we.

'Well?' I venture, at last, in a choked voice. Dorothy finds the means
to reply, albeit softly.

'I returned to the Fleet with Giuliano. I went into Cooke's lodge and
asked him:

'"What have you done with Long John?"

'"How's that? What have I done with Long John? He exited with you."

'"Assuredly not! You must have stopped him, for he was there, at my
elbow, when I gave you good day, and there no longer when I turned the
corner of the street."

'"Come now. I am not the keeper of every clown who resolves to
spend the night in the Fleet, I have better things to do. The bear must
have eaten him."

'"My bear eats no one!" says Giuliano. "Master Long John might have
changed his mind at the last moment."

'"*Master* Long John, as you say, is doubtless loitering in some corner
or other. Clear out of this entrance, now! Can't you see people wish to
pass? Go and look for your idiot yourselves, and pester me no further."

'As simple as that. We went and found Francis and passed by the lodge
again a few moments later. Cooke gave us his: "Try not to lose each other
this time!" and there we were, safe and sound.'

'Do we know if . . .'

'We do. Giuliano stayed with his bear. Nothing happened. I returned one or two hours later in my finery, accompanied by Phillips. We were coming to take leave of my brother before I returned to my husband. We entered and discovered you dead, my poor fellow.'

She giggles, but I cannot share her levity. I know the plan and have prepared for it, but events assume a far greater force in the deed than in our imaginations: what Dorothy had found there was truly a part of me, that I had abandoned forever. I even find myself wondering: to what end? What do I expect from a new life? I am forty years old. Many who were born at the same time as me are long dead already. Yet I feel an unknown hand, firm and strong, on the nape of my neck, urging me to hope, to live. But there it is. *Without hope, one cannot find the unhoped-for: it cannot, by definition, be tracked, and no path leads to it.*

'Forgive me, brother,' says Dorothy, her voice softening immediately. 'I understand how difficult this is for you.'

'Well, instead, tell me what happened. You entered and you found me . . .'

'We roused the whole place. I wept every tear in my body. Harris was away, but that was no surprise. We knew he wouldn't be there. He always spends his Wednesday evenings in the company of certain ladies of his acquaintance, and rarely returns before Thursday noon. There was quite a crowd gathered. Only Phillips drew near, but he warned that nobody should follow suit. The dreaded contagion . . . He wrapped the body in a sheet and we were forced to buy it back from Robert Holmes, the bursar – your body belongs to Harris, didn't you know? Your very flesh and blood was not yours while you were at the Fleet!'

'Did everything go smoothly?'

'Without hindrance. The only mishap was when I suddenly saw your collection of virginal pieces sitting on top of your instrument.'

'*Ventre-saint-gris*! We forgot that!'

'I demanded it. Robert Holmes refused to let me have it without Harris's agreement. I seized it and clutched it to my breast. Holmes made to take it back but Phillips told him:

'"Fie, sir, you would lay your hand on a lady in the presence of the dead! Heaven would not forgive you."

'Sir Francis Englefield declared that this book belonged to me, that it

was a memento of my brother, and that there were sufficient other chattels
left behind for Holmes and Harris to take their pick.

'"But Master Tregian owes more than two hundred pounds in board
and lodging."

'"You shall pay yourself with what remains," said I. "One book will
make no difference to you."

'You know how peremptory Sir Francis can be. Holmes did not press
the matter. I paid ten pounds to buy back the body, and Master Farnaby
was sent for. He came with two labourers; they measured up for the coffin
and Francis Tregian left the Fleet shortly after.'

'Nobody checked that it contained a corpse, or that the corpse was me?'

'On the contrary. Holmes is a circumspect fellow. Phillips let him proceed after he had wrapped the body in the winding-sheet. But he merely
cast a swift eye over it, to be sure it was indeed a body. The notion that
it could be anyone other than you didn't occur to him. It didn't occur to
anyone, at first glance.'

'Has anyone informed the Tregians?'

'Yes, sir, I did.' It is Jack who speaks. 'I went to Clerkenwell once everything was finished. I advised madam your mother not to go to the Fleet for
fear of possible contagion. The ladies all wept there and then, and Master
Charles wished to know if you had left a will. "I must make one straight
away," he said. Mistress Elizabeth was not returned.'

'What amazes me, Giuliano, is that you were able to be away from
Amsterdam for so long.'

'My dear Francis, when Phillips came to explain his plan, with which
he trusted nobody but us, it was all I could do to keep Wim and Jan from
departing that very instant. A fierce discussion then ensued as to which
of us would be the most efficacious. They yielded to my arguments: Wim
doesn't know England, and Jan has forgotten it. So they let me go, but told
me very clearly not to return unless it was with you. My wife will throw
me out into the street and my associates will slit my throat on the spot if I
don't bring you back. At first, I had no desire to see Dorothy involved in
all this, and I feared for Francis, who doesn't speak enough English . . . '

'But we devised this masquerade at the suggestion of Master Phillips.'

'I must say that, although I commanded the company in the field,'
Giuliano observes, 'the overall contrivance was his. The clowns, the bear,

the weeks of painstaking preparation, the organising of the substitution, the idea of making use of the perfect resemblance between your son and yourself, all of that came from Phillips. And nobody outside the family was party to the secret, except Giles and Richard Farnaby.'

'But the body of my ... my twin didn't leave the Fleet. Nobody remarked that?'

'Who would have troubled themselves to care? He was a beggar. Master Richard paid the repurchase fee and left the premises, and no one would have noticed that the body remained in the prison, barring the very unlikely event of the baston who received the two pounds repurchase fee questioning the gatekeeper. Two pounds is a tidy little sum; we wagered that the baston would have no intention of sharing it with anyone. As of now, the whole thing is over. Phillips made sure it was all done quickly. We were watching out for such a man for months: tall, thin and sickly.'

'And what if the clowns are never seen again?'

'No one would make the connection between them and you. There's no reason to. People die at the Fleet every day.'

'It's true that Master Harris would be wise to keep quiet, even if he guessed the truth. If I were a living fugitive, my debt would be at his charge.'

BUT FRANCIS TREGIAN was buried without comment. His death was accepted by everyone. My family had Masses said; only Elizabeth displayed any real sorrow. At my request, Phillips gave her my pieces of music:

'I will cherish them as I do the harpsichord he made for me; I will play them my whole life and it will be as if my brother's voice echoes in my ears.'

She didn't trouble to return to the Fleet; she alone could, in her innocence, have exposed one of our lies – by showing surprise at my sister's presence, for example. Her wedding day was set.

Alas, my brother Charles drew up the will to which he attached such great importance. I hoped for his sake that my gloomy predictions would not come to pass.

Once I had been informed of all these things, I felt I was free.

Now to quit London.

It was with a heavy heart that I took my leave of the Farnabys. As artists,

I admired them; as craftsmen, I owed them everything; they were devoted friends. I knew I would not see them again.

We travelled to Kent and stayed in the Phillips family house, where nobody knew or recognised me. I met Mistress Phillips for the first time; she was an old lady, for the years had been less clement with her than with her husband. I quickly learned that she was, however, his equal in generosity, for she bestowed a lavish reception on Monsieur de Troisville, a French gentleman come with his retinue to pay a visit on Master Tregian and arrived too late.

All that remained was to get out of England. But Giuliano and I were quite proficient in that particular undertaking.

I took my leave of Phillips, doubtless for the last time.

'My two sons died at sea,' he told me, his voice trembling. 'You replaced them, sir, and have given me considerable happiness these dozen years I've spent in your service.'

I was taken aback and even felt a little ashamed at my ignorance of Phillips's family life. I would have liked to thank him for his fatherly kindnesses and for having organised my escape in such expert fashion. But nothing came. I hugged him tightly. Francis Tregian's voice had run dry; my new voice had yet to flow.

Jack returned to Tregarrick. Before he left, we agreed a means of communication. I still had the medallion of St Crida that I'd carried with me since that distant evening in my childhood when I was driven out of Golden. I gave it to him.

'I shall keep the ring. If, one day, someone brings you a message sealed with this ring, you will know you can trust them, and I will trust anyone who comes bearing the medallion. I shall let you know where I am, if I can.'

'Sir, I . . . ' His voice broke. 'Sir, with you . . . '

'Without me, you will live the peaceful life of a Cornish countryman, you'll see.'

Autumn was upon us and with it the usual storms at sea, but we made the crossing nonetheless, one overcast November day, and landed in Brittany, close to Concarneau.

Here began a new life – one of my own invention.

XII

Beauty who holds captive
My life in your eyes,
Who ravished my soul
With your radiant smile;
Come and save me;
Or perforce I must die.

Why must you flee, sweet love,
If I am close to you,
When I look in your eyes,
There I do lose myself:
Such is your perfection,
I must alter my action.

'THE FRENCH CORANTO'
THOINOT ARBEAU / WILLIAM BYRD

PRISON LAYS SIEGE TO a man's spirit, even when he is as free to come and go as I was at the Fleet. The greater part of his energies are mobilised in the effort to escape the petty chicanery and endless discussion of matters to which, prior to arrest, no ordinary individual would give a passing thought. In this way, I encountered a number of officers whose harassment of their soldiers exercised the latter to such an extent that the men forgot everything but the battle in hand. Harris was a master of the art, the more so because he had studied law and always had some hefty clause or other with which to belabour his petitioners.

Good my lord, vouchsafe me a word with you . . .

Hamlet's rejoinder might have been Harris's personal device: *Sir, a whole history*.

This scheming and chicanery muffled the rumour of the outside world. I had quickly shown the door – politely but firmly – to the Jesuit sent by my mother early in my captivity. Instead, I took a secular Catholic as my confessor. My choice cut me off from what would doubtless have been a thoroughly partisan but nonetheless rich source of information. I knew a little of what was happening in London, while the rest of the world had all but disappeared.

Amsterdam was a rude awakening.

I saw that the whole of Europe echoed to the clash of arms. That the United Provinces were in uproar. To a Dutchman, Spain had always been a Damoclean sword, and the skirmishing, outright battles, territorial conquests and counter-conquests had always been a part of our lives – so everyday an occurrence that we hardly spoke of them. I knew that Frederick, the Elector Palatine, had been invited to become King of Bohemia, as Frederick V. This had caused a great stir in London for the very good reason that he was married to 'our' Princess Elizabeth, daughter of King James I.

But as soon as I reached the Continent, I discovered that concern was far more widespread this time. The interests of the King of Spain, the Holy Roman Emperor, the German princes, Sweden and the Danish king further complicated, not to say distorted the inter-religious conflict. And the great religions themselves were far from monolithic: the Protestants comprised the Lutherans (in Holland they were known as the 'Remonstrants'), who were relatively moderate, and the Calvinists (known as the 'Gomarists'), who were mostly fanatics; among the Catholics there were those of the 'political' persuasion (myself included), who placed State above religion, and the Jesuits, who placed religion above all else. They fought among themselves just as much as they did against the followers of the opposing religion. As for the Pope, his interests as sovereign of the Church often conflicted with the realities of his role as a temporal ruler.

Holland – the whole of the Protestant United Provinces – was directly affected by the upheavals. The twelve-year peace signed with Spain was coming to an end and Spinola – Philip II's man – was making preparation to recapture what everyone in Madrid was already referring to as 'our Provinces'. In Antwerp and, more recently, in Prague – from where a few escapees had fled with their king to Amsterdam or The Hague – the Dutch had seen all too clearly the extent of the cruelty exercised by Spain to re-establish the Catholic religion. Throughout the country, all the talk was of defence. The Rhine must hold.

Life lost some of its earlier spontaneity. Debate raged between the supporters of the Land's Advocate of Holland – Oldenbarnevelt, a Remonstrant who pleaded for lasting peace with Spain – and Prince Maurits of Orange (on the Gomarist side) who sought to resume hostilities after the twelve-year peace treaty had elapsed. The debate was further complicated by the fact that political discussion of the Spanish question was fast becoming tainted with religious conflict. Rather than talk in terms of war and peace, people fought over who was right – the Remonstrants, who called into question the doctrine of predestination, or the Gomarists, who believed it with all their characteristic Calvinist fervour.

The Catholics were drawn into the dispute in spite of themselves: a work attacking predestination, by Cardinal Bellarmine, was published in Holland just as Prince Maurits was gaining the upper hand. The powder was lit. Oldenbarnevelt was arrested and later executed. Prince Maurits ordered a purge. Remonstrants were to be removed from all positions of authority (devout public servants assimilated them with the Catholics, because they contested the doctrine of predestination). But the Dutch naturally eschew intolerance. The purge barely touched Ardent and van Gouden, though neither had made any secret of their religion: friends, neighbours, clients and suppliers flocked to encourage them to stand firm but keep a low profile, to wait for the storm to pass. Never since the Reformation, and never before Prince Maurits, had the Catholics been persecuted, provided they steered clear of conspiracy. This could only be a passing caprice.

At first, I lay low in the house on the Stromarkt. My time there was a kind of convalescence: I was gathering my strength, moral and physical, before venturing forth.

But the risk of discovery was too great; that would bring to nothing all my efforts to solve the Tregian family's troubles with my death. Faced with the prospect of my imminent departure, Jane showered me with kindly attention and Dorothy scarcely left my side. We talked for hours at a time while the children gambolled around us. We played a great deal of music. I made a final scrutiny of the business, which Giuliano was continuing to run with his usual success. Ardent and van Gouden were now so prosperous that they could face any blow without fear of ruin (a dread that haunted them before – at times of plague, for example). We were wealthy people. In any other circumstances, I should have been able to lead a quiet, respectable life.

Sometimes we would go down to the cellar, where Wim had installed a fencing room for his wife. The whole family, from Giuliano – still a formidable opponent – to young Wim (Dorothy's eldest son) practised their skills here.

Young Thomas, the miracle child, was studying at university in Leyden; he was a brilliant rhetorician, they told me, and fascinated by the natural sciences.

'He will be a cloth merchant, and a learned scholar to boot,' people said proudly, on the Stromarkt.

I never saw him again.

I accompany Jan on a journey to the weavers in the north.

Despite the failure of Cockayne's 'King's Merchant Adventurers' – the former Merchant Adventurers had now recovered their privileges – the United Provinces were in no hurry to lift their ban on the import of unfinished English cloth. Four or five years passed – an eternity for a merchant or weaver with no work. The Dutch found other sources of supply and other markets. The English cloth trade was ruined.

On this last shared journey of ours, Jan and I talk a great deal, as if to steal a march on our inevitable separation. For the first time we speak of our childhood and of the deep-seated motives that pushed us to act as we did.

I retain a vivid image of an evening we spent at an inn in Groningen. Outside, gusts of wind are battering the windowpanes. Seated at a table, Jan is busy writing. He puts down his quill, takes the sand-shaker, scatters sand over his sheet of paper and blows on it. Suddenly, in this solidly built, greying merchant, I see my puny younger brother Adrian, in Clerkenwell, solemnly drying the sheets of my Latin prose exercises.

He looks up.

'Francis, what is it? You're crying!'

'I was thinking that there are few I have loved so much as you.'

He doesn't move, but gazes intently at me.

'Even if we never see one another again, that sentiment is indestructible,' he says, his voice raw with emotion.

I LEAVE THE STROMARKT but remain in Amsterdam. I cannot set off into the unknown. I need a purpose.

Amsterdam has become a dense hive of activity. A scheme talked about for years has been put into action and the place has doubled in size. Beyond the old defensive wall, three broad new canals – the Herengracht, the Keizersgracht and the Prinsengracht – now encircle the city. The Brouwersgracht, which ended in the open countryside when I last lived here, is now in the very heart of town. New neighbourhoods are springing up along the canals. I settle in one such, still very much under construction, known as 'Le Jardin' to the Huguenots, many of whom live there – and more are pouring in daily, for they fear that the new French king will revoke the Edict of Nantes. French is spoken in the street and in the shops. We might be in Brabant or Poitiers. There is much activity and confusion, controls are slack and, in the hubbub, I pass unnoticed.

I adopt the first name that presents itself: Roqueville. It is bequeathed to me, in a manner of speaking, by an old Huguenot come to Amsterdam to join a family who never arrived. He had looked for them in vain. We stayed in two adjoining rooms and reminisced together: he had been at the battle of Arques. One morning, suddenly, he was unable to catch his breath, and there he died.

'You won't forget me. You'll tell them . . . Roqueville . . . ' These were his last words.

I take this as a sign I should bear his name, and add a Christian name with which I seek to mark my openness to both religions. Perhaps my dream of tolerance is just that – a fantastical dream. But I cannot relinquish it. I know I am not alone: the Farnabys (very pious Puritans), May Hutchinson, Master Treswell, even Reverend Hitch have honoured me with their affection, and help me with no thought for my religion, just as I would help them now – tomorrow, if I could. We are all Christians. Religion's standard flutters on high, justifying massacres and abuses of every sort. But I am convinced that things will change – tomorrow or a hundred years from now, it matters little – and, since life has given me the opportunity to do so, I choose a new forename as my battle-standard: I will be Christian Roqueville.

Outside the family home, only two people know my secret: the Sweelincks, father and son. I happened to meet Dirk Sweelinck in a narrow street in the Jordaan (as the Dutch call the French Huguenots' *Jardin*), and affected my usual astonishment when confronted with someone who thought they recognised me.

'You must be mistaken, sir.'

I had shaved, and now wore a moustache and a small pointed beard in the French manner. I had cut my hair differently and was dressed as an officer. In short, my appearance was passably transformed – enough to convince my less intimate acquaintances. But Dirk Sweelinck would not be deflected.

'Mistaken? I do not think so, sir. There cannot be two men with an organist's hands, like yours.'

'Are you an organist yourself, sir?'

He was plainly amused at this, but genially decided to play along.

'Absolutely, sir. Aren't you?'

'The Lord knows, I try my hand at it, but very clumsily.'

'Would you like to come and play the organ at the Oude Kerk?'

The offer indicated he was standing by his initial identification. The Sweelincks guarded their instruments with their lives; I was one of very few exceptions to that rule.

'I'd be delighted, dear sir.'

We set off.

'Master Dirk?'

'Master . . . ?'

'Christian Roqueville, at your service.'

'Master Roqueville! Well, I am all ears.'

'In Amsterdam, sir, you and your father are the only people outside my immediate family to know what I have become. But I will tell you nothing and admit nothing if you do not swear absolute secrecy before God.'

'On my honour and my soul, sir.'

We reached their house on the esplanade and disappeared inside. Sweelinck the Elder, that great master, was whiter and stooping now. Only his fingers retained the agility of youth. He left his harpsichord, listened benevolently and thanked me for my confidence in him.

'What will you do now?'

'If the United Provinces really are in danger, I shall enlist to defend them.'

This encounter proves to me the fragility of my situation. I seek a decent opportunity to slip away.

I also throw myself into the martial arts, with all the ardour of one long deprived of practice. As I hoped, one of the Dutch officers at the fencing hall offers to enlist me.

'The United Provinces need swordsmen like yourself.'

I promise him I will be ready whenever it is time to leave. And the day comes soon enough.

News reaches us that the Protestant King of Bohemia, Frederick V, has been defeated by the devoutly Catholic Emperor Ferdinand of Habsburg at the Battle of White Mountain, near Prague.

Until that moment, war has been confined to far-off Bohemia. But Frederick is king of the Rhine Palatinate, too, and it is widely rumoured the Emperor would take advantage of his victory to despoil its wealth. The war draws nearer to the United Provinces, which cannot stand by and watch the Emperor install himself on their doorstep. A troop is formed, of which I am part.

I am admitted as Christian Roqueville, and so, since I come from the Jordaan, people suppose I am a Huguenot. The commander, with whom I have crossed swords at the fencing hall, recognises me as a gentleman despite my protests, which he sweeps aside, and commissions me as lieutenant straight away. As in any army, religious distinctions are blurred and there are more than a few Catholics among my men. Mercenaries don't enlist for high ideals, as a rule, but to earn a keep for their nearest and dearest. As a current saying has it – hard to swallow for a man of principle like myself – *Serve any master, but serve him honestly.* The Dutch enlist readily: if they are maimed in action they secure a pension for life; if they are killed, the pension is paid to their family. Between draining the polders, driving piles into the sand for the foundations of new city neighbourhoods, or setting off on a military adventure, the choice is quickly made.

For the first few weeks, we train and make ready to leave. The danger becomes increasingly imminent and finally the Prince of Orange sends our troop to the Palatinate to join a contingent recently arrived from England, under the command of Sir Horace Vere.

Before departing, I take leave of my family. Mark has gone to The Hague to alert my son, who arrives as quickly as he is able. He has been singled out at the Louvre Palace as a man with a foot in France and the Low Countries alike, capable of valuable service, and has thrown himself into a life of diplomacy.

'France will defend King Frederick of Bohemia,' he assures me. 'Louis is profoundly Catholic and so he hesitates. But we will convince him soon enough that he has no interest in allowing the Emperor to seize an excess of territory. If Germany becomes too strong, France is lost.'

'I am astonished that King Frederick's defeat is accepted, nonetheless. I know the Protestant nobles believed that if they sacrificed him, they would put an end to the war. But the Emperor's ambition is boundless. He will not stop there.'

'We know that. If Frederick was Catholic, France would have flown to his aid. Unfortunately, he's a Protestant, and the King of France has his scruples. We are working to convince him, but I know him well: he must persuade himself that it's the right thing to do. I am hopeful, because even the Pope balks at the idea of an excess of German power.'

'And so I may cherish the hope of next meeting you in battle some day, my son.'

'Yes, father. Though I would rather it be in a drawing-room.'

'So would I, believe me. I can wage war as capably as any man, but I prefer the spinet to the musket.'

Before boarding ship, I spend a last night at the Stromarkt. No one goes to bed. Every eye is dry, every heart heavy, every mouth silent. Only Jane sighs, from time to time.

I leave the house at first light, accompanied only by Mark. We make our way along the dyke to the landing-stage. I turn to take a last look, but the house, and the faces pressed to its windows, have disappeared into the morning mist.

•   •   •

WE JOURNEY up the Rhine to Worms, where Sir Horace Vere has established a garrison with the English contingent – barely two thousand men, well trained and well armed. But what can they do against Spinola's army of twenty-four thousand?

True to form, the English king is full of fine words, but these are not compounded by action. Sir Horace Vere, a true soldier, declares as much, loud and clear. I often wonder whether the English would remain there in such conditions, facing almost certain death, with any leader but Sir Horace, who is adored by the whole troop and respected for his distinguished battle record. People say he can strike fear into the heart of any man, even Spinola.

Our predicament is such that I forget my fear of being recognised. I am made a messenger for Vere, whom I have never met, which is fortunate, though he has spent much time in Holland. I pass for a native of Lorraine who has lived in Plymouth for many years – the accent is close enough to that of Cornwall. Vere accepts my story without question. He has no reason to disbelieve me. Once, in a discussion about religion, he cites the example of my own father as an illustration of religious obstinacy. I listen, careful to make no reaction at all; he suspects nothing.

The news is disturbing. The Protestant Union is on the verge of breaking up and it is rumoured, too, that the United Provinces are asking to withdraw from the conflict. In Heidelberg, where we are billeted, we are aware that Spinola's army is advancing on us. We make ready for battle.

The Emperor intends to take the Palatinate – and the Palatinate has only meagre defences at its disposal. Our only hope is Ernst van Mansfeld, a career general and the one man capable of providing effective opposition to the Imperial armies. His powerful force is camped at Heilbronn. But he is late arriving. We wait for several weeks, in a state of growing alarm, and begin to prepare for a siege.

Sir Horace Vere has divided his troops into three, to occupy the Palatinate's vital strongholds: Heidelberg, Mannheim and Frankenthal, on the opposite bank of the Rhine. With enough forces we might hold both banks. But we are weak in number and quickly lose contact with our English allies, which makes our task all the more complicated. We are wearing ourselves out in skirmishes, sallies and hand-to-hand fighting. Whoever takes fright first will lose the day.

The Palatinate is overrun with soldiers. The populace can see no distinction between friend and foe: everyone behaves like a conqueror. Mansfeld's (friendly) army is especially greedy. Vast in number, it satisfies its needs through pillaging, thieving, murder and arson, giving no quarter. When I first arrive, it is rare to come upon burned-out villages along the river. A few months later, the charred ruins have multiplied, as I see when the Dutch general decides to consult Commander John Burroughs, who holds the Frankenthal. Eight men are dispatched with me. We cross the Rhine by rowing-boat.

My small troop lands not far from Speyer, then rides a good league. No one speaks. We are all on our guard.

'Lieutenant!'

The speaker is a countryman from southern Holland, a fellow whose keen powers of observation I have already had cause to approve. He jumps down from his horse and presses his ear to the ground.

'What is it?'

'Riders approaching from the west.'

'How many?'

'Between thirty and fifty.' We are nine.

'Take cover. There, and . . .'

Too late. A good thirty horsemen come into view, wearing the red rosette of Spain. We are quickly spied and surrounded.

I fight like a man possessed, first on horseback, then on foot. One by one, I see my men fall. They perform miracles but, faced with an overwhelming number of experienced fighters, they cannot hold out. I fell one adversary after another, but the Spanish keep coming. At length I hear a distant clamour and think help must be at hand. Before I can be certain, a great blow strikes my head, and I sink into a black void.

MY SOUL LIES CRADLED on a soft cloud. I must be in Paradise. The Lord has shown mercy. He has spared me the torments of Purgatory. My years in the Fleet have been judged sufficient. I lie for a long while entertaining thoughts such as these. Then I move and feel my body. Am I flesh and blood still?

I open my eyes. The sky passes overhead. Or am I passing beneath the sky? I try to sit up.

'*Ruhe, Ruhe!*'

With difficulty, I turn to see where the voice is coming from.

A countrywoman. A boat, loaded to the brim. A man at the prow, two adolescent boys taking care of the sail, and a third leading two horses on the towpath.

I try to speak, but we cannot understand one another.

Later, the father of the family tells me in a mixture of French and German that he had obtained the barge in order to flee the fighting with his goods and chattels, and that when the time came to leave, he had returned to fetch one last item. In the meantime, my companions and I had been set upon by the Spaniards, close to his house, and I had been left for dead. When he reached the scene, the ground was strewn with corpses. I had uttered a groan. The clamour I'd heard must have been that of friendly soldiers who had put the Spaniards to flight and given chase; otherwise I would have been killed on the spot and all my belongings taken.

'As you weren't wounded, I told myself that once you'd revived, you'd be useful to us. Do you fight for the Catholic or the Protestant religion, sir?'

'I was fighting to hold the Rhine, for the freedom of the United Provinces.'

'Thank you sir. If you wish, you can stay with us. God willing, we are on our way to Rheinfelden, to my brother's house.'

'Had I been robbed when you found me?'

'No. Your skirmish was soon over, it seems. We hadn't been gone long. When I came back, the beasts' slashed stomachs were still steaming. Had I not been on horseback, we would have left you, so as not to lose time: robbers are never far behind.'

'You carried me?'

'No sir, first you walked, then you rode with me. But I had to stop you from falling out of the saddle.'

'I rode? I fell out of the saddle?'

He laughs heartily.

'You were half senseless. You didn't know your own name. You gave us a whole list to choose from. I don't know whether you are Franz or

Christian, or if your family's name is Tréville, Troisjean or Roqueville ... or something else, come to that.'

'My name is Christian. Christian Roqueville. I've forgotten what happened.'

'That's what I said to my son. I'm Hans Schulz. This is my wife Frieda, and our sons Hans, Karl and Joseph.' He holds out my tunic and scabbard. 'Here is your clothing. As for the sword, I took the nearest to hand. I can't be sure it's yours.'

I put out an arm and try to sit up, but everything spins around me and I feel violently sick. The woman utters a stream of words.

'My wife says you have had a bad blow to the head and must lie down for seven days and not move, or the Devil will take possession of you and never leave.'

'Are you sure he hasn't taken up residence already? My skull is splitting with the pain.'

'He is trying to gain admittance. The Devil is cunning indeed. Don't move, or he'll find the way in.'

I see no reason to object to their wise theological counsel.

'Have I any money?'

'Yes sir. Six silver thalers. Thanks to which we can eat and pay the tolls. They are speeding us on our way. We are sorry, sir. We are not thieves, but we thought ... '

'Please! You're paying my passage too. I should be heading north, not south, but that's no matter.'

I am exhausted. I sink into a deep sleep, or perhaps I faint. I would have found it hard to get to my feet during the requisite seven days, in any event. The Devil dances a jig on my skull, and it takes the full force of my faith to believe that he has not broken his way in already. The mother helps me by binding my eyes. Daylight provokes shooting pains, right down to my feet.

Pain is like prison: it lays siege to its victim. From time to time my thoughts turn – sluggishly – to Mark, who I know will be looking for me, at some risk to his own life. By now, he has doubtless given me up for dead. We agreed that if I disappear, and my body is not found, he should go and wait for me at the Stromarkt, and from there, if he prefers, at his brother's house in Tregarrick. All being well, I shall know where to find him. But 'all' was heavy with uncertainty. The Dutch and English contingents may well have been slain, and Mark with them.

I am astonished that no one pesters or tries to rob us. In Basle, I realise why. Terrified at the prospect of invasion, the United Provinces have made a separate peace with the Emperor, on condition that both sides recognise their neutrality. For their part, the German nobles have ceded the Palatinate, for the time being at least. We pass through during a lull in hostilities. Then we head south while the armies mass to the north: we have escaped the Spaniards and Mansfeld's men alike.

In the region of Strasbourg, the Devil admits defeat. I fall into a deep sleep one evening while he stamps gleefully across my scalp – and awake of a morning, refreshed, revived and free of pain.

'You have slept for almost two days,' says Karl, in the sing-song language I am beginning to understand, for it is not so unlike Dutch.

'You can try to get up a little, but be careful. Do not tempt him!'

I take a few faltering steps. It is several more days before I regain my strength.

'You say you took me along so that I could help you. Without you, I would surely be dead!'

'Your money has helped us a great deal already. We took you along in case we ran into soldiers. But Providence has watched over us. You have saved us just as much as we have saved you.'

'I'm delighted to hear it.'

While recovering over the following days, I consider my position. Here I am, entirely alone, torn away from what remains of my world. It would be too risky to return down the Rhine now – we are told as much wherever we stop. I have no money left, and will surely have to sell my fine sword, either by putting myself and it at someone's service, or by trading it for a sum of money. I know how to fight, certainly, yet I am no hardened warrior. I am a musician – but who cares about music in these troubled times?

As a distraction, and to exercise my memory, I mentally review the pieces for virginal and harpsichord that I collected, having numbered them all (at great length) according to my own system, taking care to trace the numbers in thick characters. To think of a piece, I have simply to recall its number. I tap my fingers on the boat's rail, humming as I 'play', under the intrigued gaze of the two adolescent boys. At last, their curiosity overcomes them.

'Whatever are you doing, Master Christian?'

'I am practising my playing. I'm a musician.'

'A musician? So you are not a gentleman? An officer?'

'Indeed I am, or rather I was, a lieutenant, but before that I was a musician.'

'We have a hurdy-gurdy. And a spinet.'

'A spinet! Here?' I am incredulous.

In response, Hans disappears into the depths of the barge and soon re-emerges dragging an oblong wooden box measuring one foot by two. I have no need to open it to know what it contains: a portable spinet, the smallest of all the virginals.

'Can you play it?' I ask.

'A little. Our father plays mostly, to accompany our hymns.'

The instrument has suffered from being bundled hastily into the barge, and from the damp. It takes me a good day's work to restore its voice. But then I play for the last hours of our voyage. The Schulzes watch and listen, saying nothing.

The miracle of the spinet helps set me to rights once more. By the time we reach Basle, I have recovered my spirits and, to a large extent, my health.

WE ARE PENNILESS. At least two more tolls lie ahead of us, and we have no money to pay them. Nothing to buy food with, either. I hesitate to sell my sword. It might yet prove useful.

I wander along the river's shore. What to do?

An idea rises above the mist of uncertainty. Tentatively at first, then clearer and brighter. I am indebted to the Schulzes, of course. But it is a duty I could choose to forget. All I need do is turn a corner, not return to the port. My father's stern ghost, my mother's strident voice, my brother's reproachful looks, my sisters' sighs, these hold me back no longer.

It occurs to me suddenly that, by arranging for my death, Phillips has brought a new man into the world, has presented me with the freedom I dreamed of without realising it, and which I expressed – only a little – in music.

My uncertainties lift.

First things first.

I return to the barge and ask Frau Schulz to make my clothes decent. Accompanied by young Joseph, I go to knock at the cathedral presbytery door.

'I am a Dutch organist passing through. I wonder if you should like to hear the music of Master Jan Sweelinck of Amsterdam, Master Bull of Antwerp, and others?'

The minister looks at me with bulging grey eyes that give him an air of persistent astonishment.

'Dear Lord! Truly you have been brought here by Providence, sir. Our organist is suffering with a fever, and we have sent to enquire with the organist of the Poor Clares convent, but he will raise objections, knowing him.'

He asks to hear me play. Twenty bars are enough.

'Perfect, perfect! Here is the music.'

I play for several days and earn what we need to continue our journey.

In Rheinfelden, the Schulz family welcomes their own without effusion. A brother in distress cannot be turned away.

I do not stay. The Schulzes invite me, making much of my music. *An organist such as you . . . Rheinfelden would be honoured . . .* But I know I must leave.

Frau Schulz has managed to collect the six thalers that I provided at the outset, not wishing to see me out of pocket. I set off, intending to reach the Atlantic coast, from where I would set sail for the New World. Having reached the Americas, I would send for my share of the Dutch capital and settle in one of the colonies – Massachusetts or Hudson Bay – with no questions asked.

In Basle, to where I return with the aim of reaching Rotterdam, I am advised against journeying back down the Rhine. The city is in a state of high alarm. For some time now, the citizens have struggled to prevent the opposing armies from crossing their territory. Basle is under pressure from all sides; it is a miracle no one has seized it yet. The sole reason, it seems to me, is the city's status as part of the Confederation of thirteen Swiss cantons, from which both sides hope to enlist mercenaries as reinforcements.

The news has just broken – brought by a mass of Protestants fleeing the fighting elsewhere – that the Catholic General Tilly has taken Heidelberg, and a Spanish garrison is holding Frankenthal. The exiles tell horrifying tales of torture, brutality, rape, appalling mutilations: enough to make a man despair of Christianity itself.

'There's nothing left. People are eating nettles and wild herbs boiled in broth. They have it without salt or fat, or even bread; merely something to fill their bellies, so they do not feel their hunger.'

No one seems to know what has happened to the English and Dutch soldiers. I have no doubt that, unless they have fled, they have been massacred.

No convoy will agree to cross the Palatinate, either by water or on land.

'There are convoys of merchandise travelling into France on the Salt Road by way of the Jura, and from there, one way or another, they reach the coast. They often take travellers with them.' My informant glances at my sword. 'Especially if they know how to fight.'

I find such a convoy.

'I am making for Nantes,' its leader says, 'but I shall not be travelling there directly. I have merchandise to deliver in Cossonay, in the country of Vaud. If you wish to join us, and know how to defend yourself, you would be very welcome.'

'My sword is at your service.'

We set off: twenty mules, a handful of wagons, four escorts on horseback, and I.

We reach Cossonay. The escorts deliver their goods and we continue on to Vallorbe.

I would never complete that journey.

Our last stop before the toll at Jougne is an inn, the Relais des Trois-Chasseurs, set on high ground. In the middle of the night, the place is attacked. Doubtless the brigands assume the chief escort has been paid in silver for his merchandise, and they plan to rob him. His throat is cut where he lies in bed, but he cries out so loudly that none of us is taken by surprise. Sword in hand, I fight my way downstairs. Though still weak from the blow I received in Speyer, I know that if I fail to fight, I am a dead man. Some of our assailants carry sabres, others knives, still others cudgels – these are the most difficult to disarm.

I find myself outside without really knowing how. I am in my shirt-sleeves, but thank God I pulled on my boots. In the dark and confusion

I thrust my sword into several adversaries, impossible to know whom or how. The night is loud with panting, groaning and pleading all around. Then a cry goes up:

'Fire!'

A great sheet of flame springs over the roof, illuminating the scene.

A few men have mounted our horses and are driving the mules ahead of them. They are making slow progress. I seem to recognise one of them. My astonishment has me off-guard for a moment and my adversary seizes his chance, striking me a blow with his sword. I sway and let myself fall, concealing my weapon, then wait for him to come nearer. If he tries to deliver the fatal blow, I will run him right through. It is a trick I learned as a very young man, but have never used until now. But my assailant knows the feint, it seems, or is determined not to be left behind by his companions, who are already some way off. He scurries away, as fast as his legs can carry him. I stagger to my feet.

I try to approach the inn, but it is burning like a torch. The flames are devouring everything. Even the screams have ceased. The shoulder of land around the building is deserted but littered with corpses: the innkeeper's wife, the scullery maid, a few of the attackers, one of the escorts . . . all are dead.

If I am found there, the only man alive in the midst of such carnage, who will believe the crime is not mine? I have to get away. Without thinking, I reach for my sword. It came from Toledo and I paid dearly for it in a shop at the Exchange, in London.

No. I will leave with nothing. As I am. I have a dagger in my pocket, another tucked tight in my belt, and a third in my boot. That will have to do. I toss the sword aside.

I plunge into the woods and walk blindly until dawn. I have no idea where I am. My wound is painful, and it seems a hand is clutching ever more tightly at my throat, choking my breath. My head hurts just as badly as when the Devil tried his best to break in. How long do I wander for? I am dazzled by a thousand suns, shaken by a thousand tremors. I cannot go on . . . But still I walk. Hours? Days? I make out a stream in the midday heat, and drink until I am gasping for breath, then I vomit. I cannot go on. Harris comes at me, threatening, brandishing my Toledo sword. You tried to escape but Death stalks his prey to the end. Françoise! Jane! My

Jane, with autumn-red hair and lake-blue eyes. I cannot go on. God of mercy – save me . . .

'COME ON NOW, TAKE some water! Drink, I say! No point in spitting it out. Try again.'

A man's voice, firm and full. A strong hand holding my head. The pain shoots through me, I cannot stop shaking, I cannot stop the pain.

'Here, take my cloak.'

I struggle to open my eyes. An immense effort. A man in his thirties, with kind, grey eyes.

'My poor friend, someone has given you a thorough seeing-to. What happened?'

'I . . . I was escorting a convoy of merchandise. At the Relais des Trois-Chasseurs . . .'

'Quietly now. Take it slowly. Where have you come from?'

'From Basle. We delivered some goods to Cossonay. I think one of our escorts arranged the attack. They thought to steal the money. I tried . . .' My eyes filled with tears at the thought of the serving-girl, her throat slit, lying in the grass.

'If they knew I was still alive and could recognise them, they would follow, and kill me . . . They would . . .'

'Don't upset yourself. We're a long way from the Trois-Chasseurs here. I know everyone here and everyone knows me.'

I can hardly hear him. The Devil holds me in his clutches: my head, and my whole body, too. I am unable to answer. The candle burning inside my skull is snuffed out.

I am brought back to my senses by the rattling of the cart.

'Ho, friend! Where are you taking me?'

'Ah! You've woken up. Woah, Mignonne, Woah, girl.'

He pulls on the reins, and I hear him block the brake. Then he jumps down from the driving seat and settles himself next to me, holding out a gourd.

'Drink, but take small sips. Slowly. There. All right now?'

'All right.'

'So, tell me where are you from, exactly?'

'From Venice.'

'What is your name?'

I give the first name that comes into my head.

'Pietro Ricordi.'

He makes no comment. But he must have seen I was not telling the truth. I have never been a very good liar.

'Are you Catholic or Protestant?'

I am reluctant to answer. What if this stranger were a fanatic from the opposing camp? But judging by his portliness and his gentle grey eyes, I know instinctively that this is an equable fellow.

'Catholic,' I mutter.

'Well, in that case I'll take you home with me. We're Catholics too. It's not like Geneva, out here in the countryside. If you are happy to attend Mass and pray quietly, nobody bothers you. Not that there aren't any fanatics here – there are. Two or three years ago there was very nearly open war between Berne and Fribourg, but things quietened down, thank the Lord. We are not so concerned with such matters. Personally, I think it absurd that people kill each other over religion when we are all good Christians, pious believers. All these endless squabbles about whether to make the altar table out of stone or wood, whether it should be placed here or there. Take our priest: in the middle of conducting a Protestant funeral, he tells the grieving family that anyone following the reformed religion will be damned anyway. Or the pastor, who scurries off to Berne to complain at the drop of a hat. Like senseless children, I sometimes think. If we were heathens, I might understand.'

He glances at me, as if suddenly realising that he shouldn't be sharing his innermost thoughts with a stranger who might be a spy. But doubtless I look no more a spy than he does a fanatic.

'If you'd been a Protestant,' he goes on, 'I'd have left you with one of my cousins, who is of the reformed faith. We discuss religion from time to time, he and I, but we never quarrel. We see each other about; our paths cross at church. . . . '

'How so?'

'Well, you see, there's just one church for all the villages in the Echallens bailiwick. On Sundays the Catholics go there first, for Mass, followed by the Protestants for the preaching.'

Hearing this calm voice talk of a single church for Catholics and Protestants as if it were the most natural thing in the world, I feel I have reached the right place. I let go, and fall into a deep sleep. I am safe.

We journey on for some time before he asks me another question.

'What is your profession?'

'I have been a courtier. And a merchant. I have been to war, and made music too.'

'What sort of music?'

'I play the organ and the virginal.'

'I've never heard of the virginal.'

'It's the name given in England to a certain type of keyed instrument, similar to the spinet, the muselaar or the harpsichord, but set in a case so that it may be carried easily. They're very popular. I have learned how to make them, too.'

'Would you know how to restore an organ?'

'I believe so.'

'You can read and write, I suppose?'

'Yes.'

'Well, there's reason enough to take you to Echallens. I shall hire you to repair our organ. That'll set the Protestants on edge, right enough.' He chuckles at this. 'Can you copy music?'

For a moment, it seems he is reading my past.

'Perfectly,' I admit, finally. 'I have always copied my favourite scores.'

'Then there's work for you in Echallens. Now, before I bring you home, and take you in as a brother, under the roof I share with my wife and children, I wish to know what it is you fear, what it is you are fleeing. And I would like the truth. Your name is not Pietro Ricordi and you are not Italian.'

He senses my hesitation.

'I swear to you before God that I will not tell a soul, not even my family.'

This man has rescued me. He has trusted me and cared for me purely out of kindness, without trying to discover who I am. I hesitate no longer.

I tell him everything.

He makes no comment, apart from clicking his tongue at the most dramatic points.

He offers me his hospitality.

'Take one of our local names and keep your Christian name. I know some Tréhans in Rances. You could call yourself François Tréhan.'

'No, it's too much like my real name.'

'True. Then you could be François Cousin, a distant relative who has lived in Italy. My wife's name is Cousin.'

There is no other choice for the time being.

'And I am Benoît Dallinges, of Echallens. I have a wife, Madeleine, and three lovely children. I grow produce, and I am a cask-maker.'

'My name is Francis Cousin. If God restores my health, I shall try to make myself useful.'

I have no wish to journey on, to keep fleeing, to fight again. And I am seized with the sudden conviction that it is not by chance I have come to this country, so very like the landscapes of Truro, St Austell and Golden. If God restores my health, then here I shall stay. Here I shall try to make a living for myself, not through my family or from others, but by and for myself. I am burning with fever, and shot through with stabbing pains, but I feel the same lightness as in Basle: I have laid aside my Toledo sword at last; I am no longer a gentleman ruled by a code of honour imposed on me from without. I am free.

Twice, I have found myself in the arms of My Lady Death, a fair mistress who would not have me. Her message is clear: this is my time. I will seize my chance and make good use of it while awaiting her return.

XIII

Yonder thou seest the sun
Shine in the sky so bright,
And when this day is done,
And cometh the dark night,
No sooner night is not
But he returns always,
And shines as bright and hot
As on this gladsome day.
He is no older now
Than when he first was born;
Age cannot make him bow,
He laughs old time to scorn.

'ALL IN A GARDEN GREEN'
POPULAR BALLAD

ONCE MY HEALTH was better, things fell naturally into place.

But it took me a long while to recover entirely. My body healed fast, my scar was soon but a red streak across my skin, and the Dallinges took such great care of me that I could not fail to recover. It was my mind that needed time.

I was a reasonable man, on the whole, of measured speech and action. It seemed I was in control of my faculties. But the tissue of my memory was holed.

It nearly always began with a dream: I am in front of the Schulz house near Spire, when along comes Ezekiel Grosse dressed as a river bargeman. He gives me such a clout with his club that my head splits open. I collect my blood in my hands and go down to the riverbank to offer it to a veiled woman who stands there. She rebuffs me, my hands open and my blood disappears down a bottomless well. Then I awake, not knowing who I am but conscious of my terrible ignorance.

All music escaped me on such days. I no longer knew a single note or piece, my fingers were paralysed and I felt as though I were floating on air. I would wander the fields and go to sit under the linden tree up at the Crossing, where I had yet to build a bench. I was told that I talked to myself out loud and gesticulated.

'Your kinsman is possessed; you should lock him up.'

'No need,' Benoît and Madeleine Dallinges replied patiently. 'He was wounded in the war. We just need to give him time. It will pass.'

And pass it did. The dream occurred less and less often, then ceased altogether. My music returned to its old lodgings in my brain, while my fingers recovered their skill and agility at playing and building instruments. One fine day, I went to borrow some tools from Benoît Dallinges' cask workshop and set about building my first virginal, patiently, with many wrong turns. I had never worked on an instrument entirely without help. Later on, I procured from Basle, Lausanne and Geneva the more specialised tools that are essential to the builder of key instruments: a bow drill, a tongue punch, a cutting gauge, a slip gauge, a jack broach, a mortise chisel, a set of bits, a tuning hammer.

I repaired the simple, modest organ in Echallens church – and nearly caused another war of religion, for the Protestants were quite opposed to this sacrilege, and I was obliged to go to the castle and explain myself to the sheriff – the office was held that year by a man from Berne, Jacques Bickardt.

'They tell me you're mad,' he barks when I enter.

'In Basle, where they are quite as Calvinist as here, Protestant churches have their own organs and organists. Why not in Echallens? I am happy to play for everyone.'

'Aha! A libertine! One who cares nothing for religion!'

This is a more serious accusation even than heresy.

'No. I am Catholic, and have endured much for my faith. However, in this town there is but one church for all, so all should be able to enjoy it. That's only fair.'

'What conceit, sir, this pretension of yours to resolve religious conflicts with a little music!'

I look at him and say nothing. This pacifies him. And since he is rather small, he invites me to sit, so that he may appear less so.

'You've got to be out of your mind to start fiddling with organs,' he says rather less severely. 'That church is the source of enough conflicts as it is. Don't you know that we came within a hair's breadth of a war between Confederates over the Echallens church?'

'Your lordship, my madness, as you call it, is love of music. I cannot bear to see an instrument fall into neglect.' He is so surprised that I seize the opportunity to continue: 'Look at that spinet over there. You've probably not laid hands on it for a good while; I should like to give it some care and attention, if you would permit me.'

I hoped he would be caught off guard, and I am not disappointed. Finally he gives a laugh. It is the start of a reserved but sincere friendship which would endure after he left office. He even has me come as far as Berne to build him a harpsichord. This episode marks my true beginnings as an instrument builder: the whole region knows that I restored the Echallens organ which, in truth, nobody plays except me, and then only on very rare occasions and after protracted negotiations. Above all, everyone whispers that I have turned the old spinet up at the castle into a brand-new instrument.

Dallinges tells Bickardt about my proficiency as a scribe, and soon I am employed at the register office one or two days a week. The rest of my time I spend teaching the Dallinges children, and, more and more, building spinets, sometimes muselaars and occasionally harpsichords, or repairing the instruments that people bring me from far and wide. It is around then that I move into a spacious room in the loft of the Dallinges' cask workshop, a short way from their house. I set up a stove there for the winter, along with my writing table, workbench, instruments and my straw mattress.

I learned to speak the patois quite quickly, and French with the local accent. The whole region knows me as François Cousin, instrument builder and scribe, originally from the village of Corcelles. That is how I was registered by the officials of both Berne and Fribourg. It was under this name that Dallinges introduced me to the priest, the pastor and the local parishioners. The Dallinges children called me Uncle François from the very first day, and we shared an immediate affinity. The eldest, Benoît, was about ten years old when I arrived; the second, Marguerite, seven or eight; Claude was just a little baby; and Germain and Marie were not yet born. Once my faculties were fully restored, I took advantage of their natural curiosity to teach them everything I knew. Children in this rural region receive only mediocre education. I began with Latin, then scoured the recesses of my mind for everything that Mulcaster had instilled in us, and all that Morley, Byrd and everyone else had taught me.

In my mind's eye, I see those winter days, when Benoît and Marguerite sat in my workshop, blue fingers poking out of their mittens, finishing the jacks, applying the leather to them, trimming the plectrum, setting the strings and sniffing while repeating after me:

> Sweetheart, let us see if the rose
> That this morning did disclose
> Her purple gown to the sun,
> Has now, at dusk, mislaid
> The folds of her purpled train;
> Her complexion, as yours, the same . . .

Or:

'A muselaar is a virginal where the keys are placed to the right and the strings are plucked in the middle, while a spinet has the keys placed on the left, and the strings are plucked at the quarter of their length.'

'How many accidents are there?'

'There are twelve accidents in music, that is to say: letter, song, key, *ut*, voice, tone, nuance, note, measure, pause, the sign and the point.'

'Tell me about . . . let me see . . . the nuance!'

'The nuance is double, perfect and imperfect. The perfect is when you take the *re* of the nuance to ascend and the *la* to descend in the same place; the imperfect is when you take the *re* of the nuance to ascend and the *la* to descend in several places . . .'

Truth be told, I have to wait until David comes along to see one of the Dallinges children throw themselves into music, body and soul; from that point of view, David, an otherwise quite ordinary little boy, is extraordinary from the first. He can read a score at four years old, he plays beautifully at eight and when he is seventeen he abandons his joinery apprenticeship to devote himself to instruments, building them to perfection almost immediately. He imitates me so readily in all things that he even comes to resemble me. But as soon as he steps away from his workbench or his keyed instruments, he becomes a man with two left hands, quite incapable of holding a sword properly, and there is no one to match him for slurping his drink, or spilling food on his clothes. He will always remain my favourite, much as I try not to show it – and I suspect I hold a special affection for Elie simply because he reminds me of David.

I applied the principles of my old teacher, Mulcaster, in my role as schoolmaster, and devoted as much effort to teaching Latin and Greek as I did the vernacular. I made no distinction between boys and girls, which earned me a number of pointed remarks from Madeleine Dallinges. But it was perhaps partly thanks to this that Marguerite drew the attentions, and the love, of the Fribourg noble she later married, though I am not convinced her life with him has been as fulfilling as she deserves.

Throughout all these years, my life has been as calm as a pond. Initially, I dreaded coming face to face with the bandits from the Trois-Chasseurs: what if they had determined to rid themselves of an inconvenient witness? But the sheriff had them sought in vain. What's more, the secret of my English death was not impenetrable. I attempted to establish a line of defence against an unlikely but not impossible emissary from Grosse. For those reasons, I fell in with Aristide's band; I cultivated these dubious, but friendly and useful relations, which ensured that I, as well as the Dallinges and the whole of Echallens, was able to travel throughout the region alone, and in complete safety.

People forgot that I was ever not one of them, as they saw me at work in the church and at the register office, passed me on the road and met me at the Dallinges house.

As time went by, I took up the habit of going up to the Crossing every day at noon to stretch my legs. The Crossing is on high ground, marked by a centuries-old linden tree with strong, hoary branches. From the village, one need only glance up the hill to see if I am there. After a year or so I built a bench, and since then, weather permitting, I have gone there daily to read or to reflect. I couldn't say how it happened, but people began to come to the Crossing to share their thoughts or cares, to seek my counsel, and to have me read or write their private letters. They talk to me as if I were above religions and controversies, and ask me to arbitrate disputes that are often over my head, between landowners, between husbands and wives, between Catholics and Protestants, as if I had an answer for everything. And there are sometimes people who come from as far away as Poliez-le-Grand, Goumoens-le-Jux or Villars-le-Terroir. It is perhaps because people still dimly remember that I came from elsewhere, or sense how I am at peace with myself, that they unburden themselves so easily. I often seek the answers to their questions in Montaigne, who gives better counsel than I. I might have run into trouble with the ecclesiastical authorities, but I always take care to avoid jealousies by encouraging the supplicants to go in search of the priest or the pastor, whichever is appropriate, or by going to see them myself on their behalf.

We are now at our second priest since I came here, one Father Bécherra, with whom I enjoy as excellent relations as I did with François Clavin, his predecessor. I know the pastors less well: they are appointed from Berne, come to this mixed region much against their will and therefore don't stay so long. It's an awkward thing to be continually confronted with those of the other religion and to have to live alongside them in harmony. In addition, the officials in Berne frown upon friendly relations between pastors and priests. On the pretext of avoiding discord, young pastors are exhorted not to frequent the priests at all, in order to remove opportunities for argument. In reality, the pastors fear that too much friendship between rival preachers will cause the Protestants to lose some of their flock.

The Protestant Church no doubt secretly dreams of holding a second 'Plus', a ballot of parishioners to determine whether Echallens should become officially Protestant or not. The most recent Plus was the one that nearly caused a war and set the whole of Switzerland ablaze: the two religions were neck and neck, but since the Protestants had a one-vote majority, Berne wished to take advantage of this to outlaw the Catholic rite in Echallens. It took two years, the intervention of the Diet of Baden and even some petitioning on the part of the King of France, so I am assured, to reach a compromise. Since then, the main concern has been not to let the Catholics become the majority. Even now, thirty years after the last Plus, people still tell how Fribourg sent two Jesuit preachers to try to establish a Catholic majority: they didn't last long, not only because of the grumbles from Berne, but because the populace didn't like them. Whether in this bailiwick of Berne or in England, Jesuits often lack subtlety when dealing with the common people.

Things calmed down thanks to Father Clavin, a man whom parishioners of all confessions recognised as one of their own. Great indignation and general agitation arose when Their Excellencies fined Pastor Samuel Thorel for having attempted to bridge the gap by sharing a meal with the Father. Poor Thorel, a quite affable fellow, was sternly upbraided and had to pay a fine of twenty-five *batzen* into the poor box.

These local skirmishes are the faint echoes of the great war that has shaken the world in the name of religion. The clash of arms, which has been deafening the Continent for nigh on thirty years, reaches us only in vague ripples. All sides had need of Swiss men for their armies, so they all kept the promise not to cross the Thirteen Cantons and were zealous in their efforts to oblige them to remain neutral.

After three or four years, I journeyed as far as Basle, where I hoped to find metal strings for my virginals. Everything else I make myself, but strings are just too complicated. They must be of precise diameter and regular form, which requires craftsmanship and a complete workshop, with a forge and a furnace, all taking up nearly as much room as Dallinges' cask workshop. I was a little worried, but the journey passed without incident, for I undertook it as part of a convoy that was armed to the teeth – the business at the Trois-Chasseurs had caused quite a stir and, ever since then, travellers were wont to double their precautions.

I met a Dutchman in Basle, at the inn where I lodged for the night, and he disclosed a concern that was gnawing at him: he must go to Amsterdam, but the fighting had broken out again, fiercer than ever, thanks to the Danish king's meddling, and he feared what might befall him on the road. The fellow was in negotiation with the English king's ambassador, who was in Basle and must go to The Hague, and who might agree to take him along in his retinue. On the same occasion, I learned that James I was dead, that his son Charles had succeeded him and, by all accounts, nothing had changed in England.

'I say,' I put to him after many a flagon, 'if you go to Amsterdam, might I entrust you with a message?'

'What kind of message?'

'A sheet of paper bearing a few words that you are free to read, but which I would like you to deliver to an address I shall give you.'

'It's not a plot, I hope?'

I laughed lustily.

'No, it's an affair of the heart.'

I gave him my sheet, sealed with Jane Wolvedon's ring to confirm its origin, as one might consign a corked bottle to the sea. On it, I had written a single phrase: 'Jan, my brother, extremities meet.'

I still do not know if the message reached him, but I felt a weight had been lifted from my shoulders. Holland was very far away now, but I simply had to seize this opportunity, perhaps unique, to make it known that I was still living, so as not to cause my son, Jane, Dorothy, Jan, Giuliano and everyone else, more pain than was necessary.

'And what am I to say if I'm asked where I got this letter?' the Dutchman enquired.

'Firstly, you simply have to hand it to whoever opens the door, and then leave, that's all. But if they push you, simply tell them the truth: you met Master Chrétien on your way and he asked you to take this message.'

He had the face of an honest man, and he swore to me on his soul that he would accomplish the undertaking.

One might be surprised that I wasn't tempted to make the journey myself. Of course, it would have been quite a risky venture to journey to Amsterdam with war raging all around. In truth, the idea never even crossed my mind at the time. It was in Echallens that I had, for the first time in my life, carved out that nook of independence to which I had always aspired, and it was in Echallens that I would remain. If such had been possible at Golden, if I had been able to avoid all the vicissitudes of my existence, then so much the better. But God did not wish it, and I bent to His will. To leave the place which I felt He had chosen for me would have seemed like an unforgivable sin.

I have few regrets: sometimes I miss my son, the van Goudens and the Ardents intensely. But in agreeing to disappear from the Fleet, I also agreed to this separation from them, and I often tell myself that even from afar, even without knowing where I am, they will feel my affection as I feel theirs. Still, I very nearly made the journey the day a group of travellers told me that the Spanish army had taken 's-Hertogenbosch, then Amersfoort, ten leagues from Amsterdam. I cannot say what I would have done had Amsterdam been attacked. It is a deep-rooted instinct that if my family be in danger, then I would wish to die nearby, close to them. Before I could set off, another group of travellers told me that the United Provinces had driven out the Imperial armies, retaken 's-Hertogenbosch and repulsed the threat. I returned to my instruments.

In the meantime I have become a citizen of Echallens, although it took several years. Both sides fear an influx of newcomers from the other confession. Only very few candidates are approved, according to a strict principle of alternation: a Catholic for a Protestant, a Protestant for a Catholic.

Music may well be the reason why people come to talk to me as a friend, and why it was accepted that I, a Catholic, might just as well frequent the pastor as the priest, and encourage children of both confessions to sing at church. Before I came here, people played the fife a little, or sang a few psalms in wavering voices. Nowadays, many people have taken up – or returned to – the spinet, the harpsichord, the lute and the viol. I have had to give up being a scribe in order to make more time for music. I am just about able to build two instruments a year, for I work alone, apart from the strings, and have no assistants, except for the children from time to time. I had David for three or four years. But he wished to leave and I did not stop him. Still, as things are, I could build at least four instruments a year if I wished.

Such is the miracle of music. A few notes was all it took for the people who dwell on this verdant plateau to subscribe to the views expressed by Master Shakespeare in *The Merchant of Venice*:

> *Their savage eyes turn'd to a modest gaze*
> *By the sweet power of music:*
> *... Since nought so stockish, hard and full of rage,*
> *But music for the time doth change his nature.*
> *The man that hath no music in himself,*
> *Nor is not moved with concord of sweet sounds,*
> *Is fit for treasons, stratagems and spoils;*
> *The motions of his spirit are dull as night*
> *And his affections dark as Erebus:*
> *Let no such man be trusted. Mark the music!*

The more inflexible Calvinists would consider such an opinion almost sacrilegious. Fortunately, nobody of any consequence has ever taken a close interest in my activities: so long as I don't play the church organ without permission, I have always been left to get on with my life. Some sheriffs have been friendlier than others. One of them, Gaspard Gady from Fribourg, once entreated me to organise a dance up at the castle for Shrove Tuesday, but the pastor grumbled so excessively that things might have ended badly. I got Gady to see sense, and we finally made do with a concert, during which a choir, whom I'd spent a good while rehearsing, sang, more or less perfectly, some psalms by Clément Marot, several madrigals by Monteverde and a few songs by Lassus, among other delights.

I REALISE THAT I find it difficult to speak about these twenty-five years. In that time I've lived the same life as everybody else. I have had no serious dispute with anyone; all sorts of people have done me the honour of their friendship and their trust. I have been able to be myself, standing for no one but myself, my only duty that of being a good Christian and an honest man.

I have become friends with the musicians hereabouts, notably Jacques Yssauraud, the Lausanne cantor, and François Simon and Jean de Billaud, cantors in Yverdon. I made spinets for some of them. About fifteen years ago, when Jacques Yssauraud died, I was even asked, at his widow's urging, if I would replace him while they found another cantor. I did so for a year or two, amused to watch how everybody pretended not to know that I wasn't Protestant. After a century of anathema, it wasn't easy to reinstate music and musicians.

The study of musical principles had been reduced to its most basic form in the region. This was a far cry from England, where everyone down to my barber and my valet played an instrument, read scores with ease and knew the major principles of the art of music. There are very few publications here, and those there are generally contain nothing but psalms. Secular music is passed around from person to person, from copyist to copyist, but it would be most frowned upon to print it. I spent a great deal of time looking for a musical treatise, and finally laid my hands on a pamphlet published in Morges, the *Brief Instruction of Music*, written by a certain Colony, a Frenchman, and I used it to instil the rudiments of the art in the students of the Collège de l'Académie. *Music and the Science of Good Singing*, announces this little book, before continuing thus: *Music is both theory and practice. Theory is the art of proportioning various sounds by an instrument and by the reason. Practice is how we sing true.* Morley must have been turning over in his grave to see such outrageous simplification of the principles he had expressed with such clarity and completeness.

The only thing that reconciled me to Monsieur Colony was the conclusion of his book:

> ... *at first, I set out the musical scale using eleven lines and twelve spaces representing the twenty-three letters of the alphabet, but fearing that this was not generally acceptable, I used the first seven letters to make the said scale, with the recommendation to water it using the fourth musical key, which is that of the cellar where we keep fine wine:*
> *For the key to the well-stocked cellar*
> *Makes the voice smooth and mellow.*

That said, I thanked the Lord yet again for my memory and I drew on everything that Byrd, Morley, Palestrina, Monteverde and so many others had taught me.

Ever since Jacques Yssauraud, the position of cantor in Lausanne has been filled only infrequently. I myself left the position, since I had no wish to live in Lausanne permanently; sooner or later, attempts would doubtless have been made to force me to convert. It would also have been expected that I maintain a certain rank in Lausanne society. I missed Echallens, and Lausanne is too far away for anyone to visit me. It need only rain for more than two or three days for the roads to become thick with mud, and impracticable, after which Echallens is as inaccessible as London.

The thing that most distressed me, three or four years ago, was the death of Benoît Dallinges, whom I had come to consider as a brother. A fever took him in just a few days.

•   •   •

I AM NOW SEVENTY-FIVE or seventy-six years old. God has granted me a very full life, which I know is almost at an end. Ever since I fell ill last winter, I have often thought that it was a sign, that the Reaper was letting me know he'd not forgotten me. It was as if he were telling me:

'I gave you a second life, and now that is over.'

I have wondered recently if I should not attempt, before I die, to commingle these two lives, which together have fulfilled my being. If I had been born here, never would I have experienced the untold happiness of music, never would I have met Françoise, Jan, Jane, Giuliano, to name but them, never would I have known the wide world. But if I had remained in England, I would never have known the happiness of being completely myself, without all imposed obligations. I have been very lucky.

I look at the mountain of pages on my table, and I am amazed to have written so much in a year. I have journeyed the long way from Golden to Echallens, with the fragile vessel of my goose-quill pen. More and more, I ask myself whether I shouldn't take advantage of the strength and life God has vouchsafed me even now, to make the journey in the opposite direction, as a sort of pilgrimage.

I will have finished a harpsichord in a few days' time. The weather is lovely; summer looks to be dry. Perhaps the time has come to leave, and make my way back up the river of life to its source.

From Elie Dallinges,
currently in Amsterdam,
to Madame Madeleine Dallinges
in Echallens, in the country of Vaud

I AM KEEPING the promise I made to you, madam, my beloved grand-mother, and write to you now with fresh details of my journey. There is a great deal to tell. I do not know if my last letter reached you with its sad news, because I sent it from Paris via a gentleman who promised to give it to another gentleman who was intending to travel to Geneva.

We left Echallens, as you will remember, on 3rd June last, with a passing convoy that was returning to France after a delivery of wine to Bern.

In Echandens, we were joined by the person known as Petit-Claude, whom Grandfather François told you about. The man was (or had become) a brigand, because in an access of rage he had killed his commanding officer. But rest assured, such fits of temper are behind him now. In Geneva, Grandfather took Petit-Claude to a tailor and then a barber, and it was a fine horseman and knight, 'Claudius des Fontaines', who accompanied us for the rest of our journey. We were attacked on several occasions, and Master Claudius responded with lightning speed.

I will say nothing of the journey from Morges to Geneva, because there is nothing much to tell. The places we passed differed from our own village in two ways only: first, there are fewer cattle and ploughed fields to be seen, and more vines, and then, they have no Catholic church. But on Sunday, Grandfather took us to a family who received us with much kindness. We heard Mass. Grandfather played marvellously on their small portable organ, an instrument he had made himself.

In Geneva, we stayed only as long as it took to turn Petit-Claude into Monsieur des Fontaines. We set off for Dijon; from Dijon to Paris, we travelled with a group of merchants. We could choose to ride in their wagons or on horseback. Personally, after a day or two of riding, I experienced great discomfort in the saddle area and in my back, and I often took advantage of the wagons. But Grandfather François always rode; he called it 'an old habit'.

On the journey, Grandfather François slept even less than usual. As for Monsieur des Fontaines, he said he always slept on a knife-edge and the slightest sound woke him at night. At first I was frightened in the inns, because in the straw we were pressed up close against people we did not know. But after a few nights, I slept as soundly as if we had been in our own barn, because no one could have taken Messieurs Claudius and François by surprise. French inns have very little room for travellers. The horses were better provided for than we were. We were often above them, in windowless lofts. Sometimes there were women. They would go to bed before us, and we would wait until they had made themselves comfortable before taking our places. In certain inns, we were given excellent meals. In others, there was nothing, and I remember one night when we shared an apple between the three of us.

At last we reached Paris after crossing a region covered with vineyards, and another all of fields. 'When I think of how I came this way half a century ago,' said Grandfather, 'I would never have imagined this verdant landscape; everything was so desolate then.' Our travelling companions laughed at Grandfather's way of saying: 'I did this or that, forty, fifty, sixty years ago.' They thought he was lying, or touched in the head. But no one laughed to his face. As you know, he has always commanded respect in his own way.

When we reached Paris, we went first to a tavern-keeper on the Rue Saint-Denis, a person known to Monsieur Claudius, at the sign of Notre-Dame. He gave us an apartment for the night. Grandfather François was up even earlier than usual, and went to take a steam bath before putting on his finest clothes. He asked us to go with him. We went to the guard's hut at the entrance to the Louvre Palace, where a Swiss soldier was stationed. We could tell by his uniform that he was from Bern; he spoke French like them at any rate.

'I should like to speak to Monsieur de Tréville,' Grandfather said.

'Monsieur de Trrreffill is not at the Looffrrre. I know not whether he be in Parrrisss even. Go see at his mansion, they will know better than I.'

Grandfather François was visibly moved. Monsieur Claudius had the man tell us the way. We went first to the banks of the Seine, where there are many fine mansions belonging to princes and other nobles. We asked a porter to show us the Tréville mansion. Just before we reached the door, Grandfather sent me on ahead. His voice was shaking – I had never seen him like that. He gave me his ring – you know, the one he has never taken off – and told me to ask for Master Francis Tregian of Tréville or, in his absence, for Arnaud. I have never seen Grandfather François prey to such emotion as on that morning.

After lengthy negotiations which I will spare you here, I was admitted to the private office of a plainly dressed gentleman. Now it was my turn to stammer: he resembled my lord François like two flecks of spittle in the dust. He told me rather gruffly that he had just returned from travelling, and been late to bed and would thank me to be brief. I held out the ring and said that the gentleman who owned it had asked to see him. He stared at the ring, said nothing, then looked at me, then back at the ring, and he was so pale that I was afraid he had taken ill.

'Where is he? Quick, sir, where is he?'

'My lord, he is waiting outside on the quay by the Seine.'

He dashed outside, shouting orders as he ran down the staircase. I ran behind because he had taken with him the ring Grandfather loved so much. Outside on the quay, he stopped in his tracks, and when Grandfather saw the gentleman, he stood rooted to the spot, too. Then Monsieur de Tréville cried out 'Father!' Grandfather opened his arms and the younger man rushed to embrace him. We always said we had never seen anyone as tall as Grandfather, but his son's stature is every bit as imposing, he is thin like him and with red hair. In truth, they did not look like father and son, but like brothers. They went off together and I cannot tell you what was said between them.

For my part, I made the acquaintance of an Englishman, Master Mark, who was Monsieur de Tréville's chief manservant. He told me that he had been manservant to 'Master Francis', too – Francis is Grandfather's real name – that he had lost him at the battle of Speyer in the Palatinate, and that everyone had thought him dead, but that he, Master Mark, had searched far and wide without finding his body, and had chosen not to believe he was dead. He went to Amsterdam where Grandfather had family, then to The Hague, where Monsieur de Tréville was ambassador at the time. Since then, he has waited.

A few years later, the family received a message. Everyone was sceptical except Master Jan, Grandfather's younger brother, who said: 'He should have done so a long time ago. If he was dead, I would know.' Master Mark explained that they therefore waited, begging the Lord in their prayers not to call them to him before Master Francis had come back.

There was a reception that evening, at which there were many fine gentlemen. His Majesty King Louis XIII died a few years ago. His son, Louis XIV, is but a child, so his mother is Regent, and in conversation people said: 'The government is in the hands of a miserable stranger.' The name of that person is Cardinal Mazarin, who's Italian. I only saw him at a distance.

Monsieur de Tréville sent a message to Tarbes, where his cousin Arnaud de Tréville lives – he was a captain in Louis XIII's musketeers; and to Madam Margaret de Tréville, his aunt, who is a sister to . . . well, I no longer know what to call our Grandfather, but Grandfather Benoît was right to say that he is a nobleman. Seeing him in Paris it was hard to remember that not so long before, he used to insist on going to draw water for the livestock.

Paris is so vast that when one is in Echallens, or even Lausanne or Geneva, it is hard to imagine that a city could grow to such a size. Master Mark took me walking in the Cité, and out to the Faubourgs, which are like separate towns all around Paris, making it look even bigger by comparison. I have never seen so many shops and taverns and carriages and people. The streets are so thronged you might think the entire population was out and about. But the taverns, too, were full to bursting, and people poured in and out of the houses.

I was assured that Paris consumed three thousand bulls, two thousand sheep and over a thousand calves daily, and almost one hundred thousand chickens and pigeons, though I do not know if this is to be believed. On fast days, uncountable numbers of salt- and fresh-water fish are eaten. I was told that over five hundred thousand pots of wine are drunk, not to mention the beer and cider. There are thousands of street sellers who take their merchandise from door to door. But there are markets, too, for wood and skins and cloth. These are on the banks of the Seine. People go there to choose, then errand boys deliver everything to your house. There are over five thousand porters, too, some of whom achieve great wealth. They have organised themselves so that none may damage another's business.

And there are water-carriers, because there are few freshwater wells, and people who prefer a clean house ask one of these men to bring them sufficient quantities of drinking-water every day at an appointed time, so that at every hour of the day and night, there are porters drawing water from the fountains. Great care is taken to ensure that everyone gets the quantity of water they need. I could tell you a thousand more things about Paris, but I shall keep them for when I see you again.

For the moment, I shall return to Grandfather François, because I know that is what interests you most.

Master Mark told me that Monsieur de Tréville was the only one of Grandfather's children to survive the plague, in which his mother died, too (Grandfather's wife).

Monsieur de Tréville has two sons and two daughters. His wife died a year ago. The daughters are married; we went to visit them. One of the sons was in Münster, where he was negotiating an end to what everyone in Paris calls the 'Thirty Years War'. The other was in garrison, I do not know where.

We left Paris with Monsieur de Tréville, who returned to Münster himself, as he was taking part in the negotiations, too. He gave us passports, to allow for greater ease of travel – until then, the fact that Monsieur Claudius had no such papers had slowed our progress considerably. We travelled with Monsieur de Tréville to Wesel, first overland and then along the river Rhine. On the way, Grandfather pointed out the place where he had been struck so hard he was left for dead, as he has often told us. In Wesel, Monsieur de Tréville and Grandfather said their farewells. They found it very hard to part.

Journeying along the rivers of the different German principalities, I saw unimagined scenes of destruction. All the houses were burned; only sections of their walls remained standing. There were no ploughed fields or pruned vines. We saw many hungry people on the riverbanks, begging us for something to eat. I did not understand their language, but their gestures were more than eloquent. 'To think I escaped all that,' said Grandfather François. 'Thank the Lord, down on your knees, Elie, for allowing you to be born in a country that managed to keep out of the conflict. Pray for His mercy on these people, who have suffered so much that they no longer believe in Him.'

When we reached the United Provinces, which people call the Low Countries, the contrast was striking. Everything was green, there were plentiful cattle, the windmills turned gaily. Grandfather was in great good humour; he said several times that he had never realised how much he missed this country. Everywhere we went, Grandfather had been there before. He always took us to very good inns, and he began to tell us parts of the story of his life.

We entered Amsterdam by boat; and, as in Paris, Grandfather sent me ahead with his ring, so as not to take people too much by surprise, as he said. I found myself face-to-face with an elderly white-haired man, almost as tall as Grandfather, and I saw straight away that he was another of the family. He smiled when he saw the ring.

'Do you bring me news of him?'

'Sir, Master François Cousin of Echallens has sent me to ask you the favour of an interview.'

The man was dressed in clothes as fine as any nobleman's; I had never seen such cloth. But what struck me most was his smile. He was an old gentleman. He was missing a few teeth on the side, but his smile was so kind, he put me in mind of an angel. I learned afterwards that this man, Jan, or Adrian, as Grandfather called him, was his brother, though he went under a different family name.

In this large house, I saw a shop with the finest cloth imaginable. I will have occasion to tell you about all that again, and about the city of Amsterdam, too, where almost all the streets run alongside canals.

Grandfather François was very happy to see his brother again, but later he wept when Mijnheer Jan (this is the common title) told him that Master Giuliano and Madam Jane were dead. It was explained to me that Jane had been Grandfather's nurse, and Giuliano, her husband, had been his master-at-arms. I owe my most formidable fencing thrusts to him, it seems. 'I knew very well that they would be dead,' said Grandfather. 'But to see again the places where we were all so happy together, it makes me feel as if it were only yesterday. They were like parents to me, and I am as sad as you would be if you learned of the death of your father.' These people left a son, called Wim, which means Guillaume, and a daughter, Jane, who is married and lives nearby. All their other children were killed by the same plague that wiped out Grandfather's family. Master Wim is married to a very small woman who is always cheerful and bright, and I was astonished to discover that she is Grandfather's and Master Jan's sister. She looks more like their daughter. She is the eighteenth child of their same mother, and Grandfather and Master Jan were the first.

Madam Dorothy, which is her name, has five children – three sons and two daughters. One of the sons and one of the daughters are of my age; the others are older. They are all in the cloth business in one way or another. The older son, named Adrian, studied the science of colours in Leyden, so as to invent new shades. 'Our house made its fortune in dyed cloth, but our Uncle Jan says that we mustn't rest on our laurels,' he told me. Master Jan constantly asks questions of everyone. He says it develops one's curiosity. 'We must keep our minds agile, not let them become paunch-bellied.' Master Jan has a son, Thomas, who is a professor at the university in Leyden. He is a famous scholar, apparently. I like Master Jan quite as much as Grandfather François.

The family urged Grandfather to stay in Amsterdam, but he said: 'You know very well that is not to be my fate.'

He promised they would have news of him soon, and Master Wim agreed to take me on, when the journey was over, to complete my education. I shall perfect my playing with Master Dirk Sweelinck. He's a friend of Grandfather. We went to hear him at church; he plays divinely. If I can play the organ one day half as well as Master Sweelinck or Grandfather (I heard him play too in the same church, quite different from in Echallens), I should count myself very happy.

We left Amsterdam and went to the coast; we crossed the Channel – the English also call it the Narrow Sea – and landed in England. I never imagined the sea would be like that. I saw a storm on the lake when we were travelling from Morges to Geneva, but it was nothing by comparison. When we arrived at the beach where we were due to embark, the waves were as high as the houses. I was half-dead with fright, and my lord des Fontaines showed none of his usual composure. But Grandfather laughed, his eyes truly sparkled. 'If you were not here, my friends, I would make the crossing nonetheless.' The storm eased a little, and we went aboard a broad, low Dutch ship known as a *fluyt*. The sea was still quite rough. Our journey took seven or eight hours, during which I was continually sick, and des Fontaines too, while Grandfather chatted with the captain just as if he had been sitting under the linden tree at the Crossing.

It was on this voyage that I saw the first white hairs on his head, and it seemed to me that I saw more and more after that, each time I looked.

We avoided London. Grandfather said there was never any sense in tempting the Devil, he had done so once and it had cost him too dearly. We travelled for ten days, I believe, or perhaps twelve. We crossed beautiful countryside in the regions called Kent, Middlesex, Dorset and Devon.

Grandfather told me we were going back to the place where he was born. I admit he was starting to worry me. He was in excellent spirits: 'When a Cornishman comes home, Cornwall has her own way of reaching out to take him in her arms.' He told us wonderful stories – sometimes adventures of his own, sometimes legends. As you advised, I noted everything down from day to day.

What worried me was that Grandfather seemed hardly to sleep at all now, and ate nothing. He was getting thinner and thinner by the day, and soon his hair was almost completely white. He urged us to hurry along as fast as possible; he was already up and to horse at six o'clock in the morning, goading us to follow his example. Monsieur Claudius said nothing, but I could see he was worried too, the more so because Grandfather was no longer taking the time even for his morning fencing bout.

Besides this, I should say that I was suffering some considerable discomfort, because the saddles in England are small, covered only with leather or cloth, and very hard as a result – truly, they wear a man out.

Sadly, I could not understand that country's language, so I could not follow what Grandfather was told each evening at the inns. There were very lively discussions. Grandfather recounted them to us, but I am not sure I can render them faithfully here: the Parliament and one part of the country refused to recognise the authority of the Stuart King, Charles I, whom they considered 'incapable of steering the ship of State', in Grandfather's words. What's more, they accused him of depriving the English of their traditional liberties. But the King had his partisans, too, and they had been at war for years.

'And do you know what?' Grandfather continued. 'After all the Tudors and Stuarts had said about the Catholics, after all the persecutions we suffered, the most loyal subjects of this unfortunate King were of our religion, and His Majesty, in thanking them, found the very words that should have been pronounced fifty years ago.' You should have seen Grandfather when he told us that: his voice was terrible with rage, and his expression . . . It was quite frightening. 'You see, my boy, Messire de Montaigne is right. We cannot entrust our souls to noble princes, they use them and toss them aside like balls in a game of tennis.'

We arrived in a region where the marks of war were very visible. Grandfather kept us to hidden track-ways. 'We'll be safer here,' he said, 'because only the local people take them. Strangers don't even know they exist.' And so despite the 'Civil War', as everyone calls it, we made swift progress. On the last night, we avoided any inhabited place. In any case, the inns in Cornwall are hardly deserving of the name. Grandfather told us we would do better to sleep under our horses, so as not to attract attention. Fortunately, the weather was fine.

At last, the next day, we reached a village which Grandfather told me was called Grampound, which is a poor pronunciation of our Grand Pont, because the place's true name is French.

I saw the bridge, but it isn't so very big, and under it, the river is a mere trickle of water. 'No matter,' said Grandfather. 'Once upon a time, when the world was a narrower place, this bridge and river seemed vast.' We were in the land where Arthur and his knights had lived, the place where all the wonderful stories took place, that Grandfather told us so often when we were children. It's a country quite like our own. We did not stop in Grampound but continued on our way for a few hours more, towards the sea. At length, we reached a house hidden in a copse, at the end of a tree-lined track.

Once again I was sent ahead to knock and present Grandfather's ring. I was reluctant to do it, because of the language, but he said: 'If the person who can understand you is no longer to be found there, I'll go myself, for it will not matter any more.' So I went up and knocked and asked for Master Jack in my poor English. This Master Jack is a man of about seventy, all white-haired and pale, small and wiry, straight as a rod, and very affable.

'A French traveller?' he asked in our language, which he speaks very well.

'Not really, I am Swiss. Vaudois.'

'No matter, you are welcome. What may I do for you?'

'You may extend your welcome to my friends, who are outside.'

'What? You have left your companions outside? What manners! Bring them in, bring them in.'

'Well . . . They asked that you look at this ring first.'

He sank to his knees as if thunderstruck.

'Sir – Master Francis!'

I was quite embarrassed.

'Where did you get this ring?'

'From the gentleman who sent me ahead to greet you, and who is waiting outside.'

He leaped to his feet with the agility of a young man.

'The gentleman is outside and you have said nothing?'

'But I . . .'

He was no longer listening. He put the ring on the table and shot outside like an arrow. I followed hard on his heels. When the door opened, Grandfather stepped forward. Monsieur Claudius was holding our horses.

'My very dear Jack!'

'Oh, sir!'

After that neither of them said anything, but they wept as they shook one another's hands.

The house belongs to Grandfather, and Master Jack has looked after it with a few country people since Grandfather left. Master Jack said he had decided that, as long as he lived, he would keep his master's bedchamber ready for him, and indeed the room was fresh and polished, and the bed smelt of newly laundered linen.

'But I never expected you would come back one day, sir, all the same.'

'Did you not hear that I had a message carried to my brother?'

'Why, yes. Master Jan and Master Francis sent Mark once or twice, to see how things were, and Mark told me. But he has such an imagination . . .'

Later, they fell to speaking in English and forgot all about us. Monsieur Claudius asked how it was possible that a man in possession of such a fine property could willingly hide away at a barrel-maker's in Echallens. Grandfather replied that at that time his life had not been worth so much as a farthing, and if he had been found, he would have been killed or clapped in irons at the very least.

Grandfather took us for a long ride to show us from a distance the house where he was born; he took us up to the top of a hill. 'Everything you see, right to the horizon, belonged to my grandfather. My father lost it all for the sake of religion, and I, who tried to take back what was rightfully mine, lost everything for clinging faithfully to an idea. My brother and mother were determined to make one last attempt, poor things; they hadn't learned their lesson. They ended up in the same prison as me, and died there. For my father, restoring Golden to the family was like a quest for the Grail. Not for nothing was King Mark's forest part of his domain! I discovered that my sister's children managed to reclaim part of our vast estates. Good for them!'

I should say that the property still in Grandfather's possession must bring in about ten times the income of our cask-making workshop. Grandfather said on several occasions that the property belonged to Master Jack now, to his wife, Madam Marianne, and their son Jonathan, whom we met a few days later. Master Jack was Grandfather's valet for thirty years. In Tregarrick he did everything for him, and Grandfather barely had time to break a sweat before Jack passed him a handkerchief to wipe his brow.

The whole region was in a state of feverish tension because people in London were talking of having the King hanged like a common criminal and of doing away with the monarchy forever. Jonathan was barely any older than I, but he had been fighting in the Civil War for two years already. He told me all about his exploits over an entire evening, but unfortunately Monsieur Claudius and I understood little, and didn't like to offend them all by asking for explanations. The war had passed close by the house in which we were staying, and it was a miracle it had not been occupied or sacked by one army or the other.

I was more and more concerned for Grandfather. He joined in every discussion, went visiting, walked alone in the countryside and was bursting with energy; but he grew even paler, even thinner than before, and his skull and bones began to show beneath his skin. A doctor came to see him and shook his head. Master Jack said he wished to obtain a second opinion, but Grandfather refused. Little by little, his energy waned, almost imperceptibly. He talked less and less, and spent whole days at his spinet, which he played better than ever. 'Perhaps the soul of this instrument is my Holy Grail,' he said. 'I even learned how to build it, so that I might capture its heart, but still I feel as if it lies waiting to be discovered at the end of each bar.'

Sometimes, he spent whole days in bed.

One morning – it was 14th October – he asked me to come and help him dress. His window was wide open, and he gazed out at the countryside and the sea.

'I had a visitor at dawn. A robin came in.'

'Robins are very pretty.'

'Yes, very pretty. Here in Cornwall, people firmly believe they herald the coming of the Lady in Black. The great appointment is perhaps for today.'

After lunch he had the horses saddled. He asked me to go with him. We trotted through the countryside and he took me to the house where he was born. The sun shone thinly between the clouds. There was a stiff wind. I think I shall never forget a single detail of that day.

In passing, Grandfather told me some stories of his childhood. We stopped beside a hedgerow, for example, and he told me how he had seen his first fox point his muzzle there, and disappear just as quickly; later, his father had returned from the hunt with friends, and they brought back a fox they had killed. Grandfather was convinced it was his fox, and cried for so long, his father had him whipped. 'And all for a fox that may not even have been my friend from the hedgerow.' He told how he hated hunting with falcons, but he did not say why. I won't tell you the other stories, but I will set them down in my book. We wandered like that all morning. In this country, the roads are some of the worst I have ever seen, but fortunately it had not rained for several days.

We went to a church on the banks of a river. It was called Creed and was built of great grey stones. Grandfather said it had been there since time immemorial. We went inside. You could see it was a very ancient church, but it was Protestant. I remarked on this to Grandfather.

'You see that stained glass window, my boy?'

'Yes, Grandfather.'

'You see the arms? This one, with the ermine on a sable and the three jays or?'

'Yes, Grandfather.'

'Those are the arms of my family. They were placed there by my grand-father John, who paid for the restoration of the church and endowed its bells. One day, men decided that the Protestant faith would be preached here, and Mass would no longer be said. Do you believe the Lord troubles himself over the way we choose to thank Him for His gifts? The important thing is to thank Him.'

Grandfather had said that once before, in Echallens, and again in Amsterdam when he played at the Oude Kerk, which is Calvinist. We prayed, and Grandfather gave a long speech, in English. Then we mounted again, but I could see that Grandfather was riding with great difficulty. I suggested we stop at a house along the way, but he said: 'No, I must carry on, so as not to be late for my appointment.'

We trotted the short distance along the river to the bridge by Golden Mill, and crossed over. The river was a mere trickle. Grandfather said once again how extraordinary it was. 'When I was a child, this was a river port.' There was not even the smallest boat there now. 'Truly I have done my time,' said Grandfather. We rode up along what he called the Warren. We reached a flat expanse of ground from where we could see, between the trees, the two houses that Grandfather called the Old Manor and the New Manor. He was so pale that again I suggested we stop.

'We're here. We'll take the turning to the right.'

To the right there was nothing but an almost perfectly round field, bordered here and there by low, ruined walls. We went up to its highest point. Grandfather reined in his horse. I did the same. From up there we could see far out across the hills on all sides. The fields were green and yellow, and the trees were green, yellow and red. The sky was blue, with great, scattered clouds.

'I think I shall need your help to dismount, my dear Elie.'

I helped him and found he was as heavy as lead. Then I started to feel truly afraid. I had never seen him like that. His face was smooth, his periwinkle eyes took on that intense look he sometimes wore when he was playing a piece of music he loved very much. His white hair, still streaked with red, formed a kind of halo, like the sun's rays.

He was like an apparition from the world beyond.

'Can you hear, dear boy?'

We heard the cries of birds.

'Yes, Grandfather.'

'Can you hear the singing?'

'Singing? Grandfather?'

'Yes. We hav'et, we hav'et, we hav'et. What hav'ee, what hav'ee, what hav'ee. A neck, a neck, a neck.'

And he sang in his fine, ample voice.

'You hear, they're answering: We yen! We yen! We yen!'

Even the birds had fallen silent now.

'Do you hear, my boy?' He gripped my hand fit to crush it.

'It's Jane, my beloved Jane. Look at your kingdom now. Engrave it on your heart. Giants are fighting in the sky, but the wind will sweep them away. The land will always be here. Your land. Wherever you are. I did as she said. I have always loved Jane more than all the rest, perhaps even more than Françoise. My land, wherever I am.'

He opened his arms and stood there, saying nothing, for how long I do not know. Then a tiny bird, a robin I think, flew up from its hiding place in the grass and fluttered around us, then landed and began to sing. Grandfather gazed at it. 'You have come for me, at last,' he said. Then he fell down backwards, straight as a rod.

'Elie!'

His voice was a whisper.

'Yes . . . Grandfather.'

'Elie, give me your hands.'

He slipped his ring onto my finger, then entwined my fingers in his.

'Elie, I am about to leave, and this is a journey I must make alone. Do not be afraid. I shall only take a moment to slip away. I am not leaving you. I shall be back at your side straight away.' And he gripped my fingers with unimaginable strength. 'All the skill of my fingers is yours and David's now; I am giving it to you. I shall always be with you, there, in your fingers.'

And he stiffened, released my hand, stared up at the sky and cried out in his strongest voice:

'Lord, forgive me for doubting and open your arms unto me. I am Your servant!' He paused. 'My brother, extremities meet. Extremities . . . '

The stiffness eased and he lay still. I did not understand straight away that he was dead. He was staring up at the sky and he looked like that handsome man of whom all the Echallens gossips said that he must have been in love.

Dusk was falling and I knew I had to tell the others, but I couldn't leave him. Only when I feared getting lost in the dark did I decide to go. I kissed his hands and his brow, and closed his eyes, and then I confess I was unable to hold back my tears. I covered him with my mantle to protect him from the wild animals, leapt into the saddle and galloped hard back to the house. We returned as soon as we were able, with torches. Master Jack wept, Monsieur Claudius' voice was gruff, Hugh the countryman was white as a sheet.

We fashioned a litter and carried Grandfather back to Tregarrick. The women washed him and dressed him in his finest clothes. I took his muselaar, a splendid Flemish instrument, into the bedchamber where he lay at rest, and played to him for the rest of the night.

Hugh went to fetch a priest, but the priests all live in hiding hereabouts and he was only able to bring one the following morning. He gave the absolution *post mortem*. The next day, we buried him as he had wished, beside one Thomas Tregarrick who was, I think, his own grandfather.

Grandfather left a letter to say that the house passed to Jack and then to his son. Monsieur Claudius was asked to take me back to Amsterdam so I could perfect my playing with Master Dirk Sweelinck. We set off for Dover the next day. The port officers asked us a thousand questions and we had to explain the reason for our departure ten times over. Grave events were taking place in London. I learned later that King Charles I had been beheaded. They asked if we were papists and we were forced to deny it, and to say that we had come from Bern (which is what was written in our passports), and since it was stated that I was a musician, I had to play to prove it was true. At last, we boarded an English ship bound for Calais. This was not our destination but we felt lucky to have been able to get away, and in France, everything would be simpler because we had Monsieur de Tréville's seal on our passports.

We went to Paris. Monsieur de Tréville was not there, but I told Master Mark everything. Then we joined a group of travellers heading north and in a few days we reached Amsterdam. Master Jan came to open the door himself, as if we were expected. 'He's dead, isn't he? I sensed it.' I tried to give him the ring, but he would not accept it.

Now I am living at Master Jan's. My days are very full. In the morning I go to Master Sweelinck's and in the afternoons I sometimes go to Master Willem's. I have found a harpsichord-maker who has agreed to take me on for a while, so that I can learn how to make a passable jack and register. Master Jan gives me books to study, and I fence with the Ardent boys. I have the beginnings of an understanding of the cloth trade. I speak a little English and a little Dutch. Master Jan says he'll make a well-rounded man of me yet.

Monsieur Claudius has been hired, as Grandfather requested, to provide a safe escort for the convoys of cloth. 'Nothing like a brigand to see off the brigands,' he always says. He goes off for weeks at a time and, when he comes back, he always has a thousand stories to tell. He takes a close interest in my playing, on the organ and most of all on the harpsichord. 'Master François left his voice in your fingertips. See it continues to sing and express the beauty of his soul.' There are a great many scores here in Grandfather's hand, and I play them often.

There, madam. This is everything I wished to tell you. I beg you to assure my parents of my filial love. Do not feel too sorrowful. Grandfather has gone, but I am working hard to express his beautiful voice.

I embrace you, with profound respect,

Your grandson,

Elie Dallinges
Amsterdam, Easter 1649

MY BELOVED SON,

Writing is not my strength. But I wished for no one else to bring you the news of the death of Monsieur François, the circumstances of which you will read in Elie's letter, which I have copied for you.

I am also sending a packet of scores that Monsieur François Cousin asked me to give to you, should any misfortune befall him. With it, I include a long personal memoir which occupied most of Monsieur François's time over his last year living with us. We have left his instrument-making workshop untouched, and at your disposition.

I believe that all this is rightfully yours now, for reasons which I will explain. I am not your true mother, and my husband was not your true father. You are the son of Jeanne du Moulin and Monsieur François Cousin. You did not know your mother: she died when you were six months old. Strange to say, but your father François never knew you were his own flesh and blood, though he treated you as such.

When my late husband took Monsieur François into our household, he told me: 'I have brought a noble prince back in our cart, my love. He is wounded and his mind is not his own just now, but I have never come across anyone who so put me in mind of a king. I should like us to take care of him, for he is very badly hurt.'

My mother was still alive at the time and she looked after him, watching at his bedside for weeks. His body recovered slowly, and then he was quite well. But his soul was stricken. We all grew very fond of him. He was so gentle, so attentive to everyone, so conciliatory. He was always ready to offer a solution, and took everything seriously, from the children's knocks and scratches to the older ones' crises of conscience. The whole village loved him – Protestants and Catholics alike. Half of Echallens went into mourning on the news of his death, and there is always a flower laid at the Crossing, or a piece of fruit, and a candle kept burning in his memory. When he first came, for about a year, there were times when he seemed to lose his reason completely: it was due to the terrible blow he had received to the head, which took a very long time to heal. During those seizures, which would last for anything from a few moments to several weeks, he would recognise no one and he disappeared for days at a time. Once he was gone so long that we thought him dead. But it was then, when he came back, that he asked to install himself above the cask-making workshop, began building his first instrument, and had no more attacks. He was healed.

One morning, when he rose, he discovered you on the doorstep. You were new-born and he decided to adopt you straight away. To avoid any difficulties, our curate Father Clavin – to whom we explained everything – suggested we raise you as our own child. So I was your nurse. You resemble your father, and some of the gossips insinuated that I had been unfaithful to my husband, but no one truly believed it. Monsieur François and Monsieur Benoît were both such upright men, and my own honesty was well known.

That time when we thought him dead, your father was found by Jeanne du Moulin, your mother. Jeanne was the daughter of Perret, the miller. Her entire family had died of the plague when she was fourteen years old. She had kept the mill working all alone, and made a good job of it, too. She was a tall red-head, a beautiful girl, and many men desired her. But a gipsy had told her she would be the wife of a prince, and she refused everyone. She must have been thirty years old when she met Monsieur François wandering in the fields, his memory quite blank. He no longer knew who he was, but she knew straight away – he was her prince. She took him in and cared for him. One day he disappeared. He must have come to his senses somewhere out walking in the countryside. I witnessed some of those moments: he never remembered anything that had happened while he was taken ill. He came back to live with us. He did not remember the mill, nor Jeanne, and he did not remember having got her with child.

Jeanne was a simple girl. She was quite strange enough herself not to have noticed that Monsieur François was not entirely in his right mind. He called her Jeanne, 'as if he had known me for a long time', she told me. When he left without a word, she was too proud to chase after him.

She did not know where to find him, and he had told her his name was Christian. She only found out who he was shortly before the birth. She had managed to conceal that she was with child and delivered you alone. She worked up until the very last day. She couldn't have kept you: it would have dishonoured her. She brought you to our door. She thought that Monsieur François would know. And though he had clean forgotten Jeanne, something in you conquered him straight away. Later, Jeanne came to see me, and I learned the whole story. I suggested we speak to Monsieur François, but she forbade me.

'I will not force him. He must come of his own will.'

'But he was sick! How can he come to you if he remembers nothing?'

'Then it is the Lord's will; we cannot force his hand.' It hurt me all the more that I could not tell anyone about Jeanne, not even the curate. He was pitiless with regard to young women who had sinned and I dreaded to think what would have become of poor Jeanne, had he known. I decided to confide in Monsieur François, despite Jeanne's instruction against it. He was a man of honour and I had never seen him do a wrong deed. He would have married her forthwith. But Jeanne was struck by fever and died. And then there was no point in talking to him. Why would I? It would only have complicated everyone's lives. I held my tongue and did not confess it, even to my husband. But I do not wish to take this secret with me, when it is yours. You have a right to know that you are not just the pupil but also the son of a noble prince.

Be proud of your parents, my son, and – with Elie – cultivate the voice your father has left you and which, thanks to you both, will be lifted up pure and true, like François himself, beyond time and death.

Vouchsafe the affection of her who has loved you twice over: as a son entrusted to my care by Jeanne du Moulin and as the child I helped to raise. May God bless you.

I remain,

  Your Mother,

          Madeleine Dallinges
          Echallens, Pentecost 1649

LOOKING FOR FRANCIS TREGIAN

I first met Francis Tregian[1] on Sunday 25th May 1986, at an Elizabethan garden party in Zurich, held at the Rietberg Museum. It was the first day of Zurich's summer cultural festival, which that year was devoted to music from the Fitzwilliam Museum in Cambridge, a collection comprising handwritten scores by Purcell, Haydn, Mozart, Brahms and many other composers, and including the *Virginal Book* of pieces copied out by Francis Tregian in the early seventeenth century. Throughout that sunny May Sunday in 1986, soloists and ensembles sang, played and danced pieces drawn from the *Fitzwilliam Virginal Book*. I had never heard of the *Virginal Book*[2] before a quiet word spoken in my ear following one of the performances.

I was left with one burning question after this unforgettable day: who was the genius collector who had gathered so much beautiful music, who had assembled such a perfect collage? Simple to answer, I thought, for I was sure that my curiosity would be satisfied by a simple visit to a music shop the following day. I never imagined that by framing the question in those terms, I was embarking on a journey that would last seven years.

The ease with which I was able to procure the *Fitzwilliam Virginal Book* itself only served to bolster my illusions. This manuscript, a compilation of keyboard music composed between the approximate dates of 1550 and 1620, was first printed at the end of the nineteenth century, to great acclaim. Its publication undoubtedly did much to ensure that the music of the English Renaissance, by composers such as Byrd, Bull, Morley, Farnaby and others, burst into the twentieth-century musical consciousness of Britain, at first, then Europe.[3]

In the years following its publication, the *Virginal Book* was thoroughly studied on only two occasions. The first was in 1905, when English organist and composer Edward W Naylor made it the subject of his *An Elizabethan Virginal Book*. The second came in 1912, courtesy of Charles van den

Borren, a musicologist at the University of Brussels. The original French
edition of his book, *Les Origines de la Musique de Clavier en Angleterre*,
has been practically forgotten in favour of the English translation, *The
Sources of Keyboard Music in England*, which contains a little additional
material and was published in 1913. This English version is generally cited
as the original and remains one of the authoritative studies on the subject.
Van den Borren goes further, making an almost exhaustive analysis of the
Fitzwilliam Virginal Book among other works, for he considered it to be
the cornerstone of Elizabethan music, a view shared by Edward W Naylor:

> It is not going too far to say that if all other remains of the period
> were destroyed, it would be possible to rewrite the history of
> music from 1550 to 1620 on the material which we have in the
> *Fitzwilliam Virginal Book* alone ... Thus the collection is more
> correctly regarded as a library than as a mere book, for it contains
> more direct evidence of the musical practice of Tudor times than
> most of us have of the music of our own century ... [4]

Neither of these two studies attempted to understand the character of
the man behind such a remarkable collection. The era in which they
were written was not conducive to such an approach. In that time before
widespread recording, a virtuosity propped up by the choice of scores and
not by the compositions themselves hardly interested anyone. For a long
time, nobody looked any further.

William Chappell was the first to suggest, sometime between 1840 and
1850, the hypothesis that the hand which had copied out the 297 pieces in
the *Fitzwilliam Virginal Book* was that of a Tregian: the name appears at
several points in the manuscript, either abbreviated or written in full. As
far as Chappell was concerned, it was clear that, whoever it was, they had
lived in the Low Countries for a long time. He based this theory primar-
ily on the inclusion of pieces by Peter Philips (Flanders, the Spanish Low
Countries) and by Jan Sweelinck (northern Low Countries), which are
found only in the *Fitzwilliam Virginal Book*. [5]

Yet the name 'Tregian' (a great Cornish Catholic family) holds almost no
musical connotations in England but rather is linked to the major political

and religious conflicts of the Elizabethan age; if anyone has already heard of 'Francis Tregian', he tends to be the musician's father, a man who had the sad privilege of defying the English sovereign's power at a time when Catholic Spain and the papacy wished to have done with Protestant England. Rome had excommunicated Queen Elizabeth and relieved her Catholic subjects of any duty of obedience. The English Crown and government felt they had to react to survive. An example had to be made and a suitably exacting punishment meted out that would discourage anyone else with similar thoughts. Their choice fell upon Francis Tregian the Elder (1548?–1608), who was seen as an ally of the enemy; he was imprisoned and a significant proportion of his assets was confiscated. He spent thirty years in gaol, twenty of them in London's Fleet prison. Francis Tregian the Elder and his wife Mary had eighteen children. Their eldest son was called Francis (1574?–1618?).

The first people to publish the *Fitzwilliam Virginal Book* (in 1899)[6] also undertook what was exhaustive research for the time on Francis Tregian the Younger. They concluded that although the details were rather obscure, 'It seems likely that Francis Tregian was convicted in 1608–1609 of recusancy and was imprisoned in the Fleet, where he remained until his death, about 1619. It may be conjectured with some plausibility that the present collection of music was written by the younger Tregian to wile away his time in prison.'[7]

In 1986, I had decided to stop writing prose. Instead, I would write dramatic texts, as long as I found suitable themes. In Fuller-Maitland and Squire's introduction to the *Fitzwilliam Virginal Book*, a phrase caught my eye in which I glimpsed the ingredients for a dramatic work: ' . . . the present collection of music was written by the younger Tregian to wile away his time in prison'.

I imagined this man shut up in a dungeon, remembering, in spite of everything and everyone, all these forbidden pieces of music, forbidden because they were Catholic, and writing them down, saving them from oblivion: an Elizabethan *Fahrenheit 451* in effect. I had only one question: how did an Elizabethan prison function, and the Fleet in particular?

I set to researching the few documents pertaining to the prisons of the era, and that is how, without realising it, I began work on a narrative text: *Tregian's Ground* (original title: *Le trajet d'une rivière*).

I told myself that if I wanted to provide a proper description of this
character in his prison, then I needed to know something of his past.

The British Library in London holds two books devoted entirely to his
father. The first, written around 1934, barely mentions the son.[8] The other
contains a dozen pages about him, but they left me sceptical. This book
about Francis Tregian the Elder[9] was written by diehard Catholics for
whom the Elizabethan wars of religion were still being fought. It was not
an historical account but a self-serving appeal promoting a single theory:
the persecution of the Tregians was an abomination, for all Elizabethan
Catholics were righteous and true, and all Elizabethan Protestants were
killers and thieves – in short, bad by definition.

The 1950s saw new facts come to light, facts which changed perceptions
somewhat. It was noticed that a manuscript[10] recently acquired by the
British Library and containing over 2,200 musical scores (madrigals,
villanelles, fantasias, motets) was by the same hand as the *Fitzwilliam
Virginal Book*, and that a collection of some 350 similar scores[11] was held
by the New York Public Library. At the time, authorship of these was
attributed to Francis Tregian the Younger, thanks to a second major event:
the discovery of the Tregian family papers, which had been collated by the
Cornish historian Charles Henderson before 1933 (the year of his death)
and had remained in a trunk until someone thought to take them out and
sort through them. As far as the experts were concerned, the identity of
the man who copied out the pieces in the *Fitzwilliam Virginal Book* was
now established, for the handwriting shared many characteristics with
that of Francis Tregian the Younger.

It is striking to note that, for a long time after they came to light, historians and musicologists cited these documents without changing their
view of either Francis Tregian or the collections attributed to him. Yet
their discovery changes many things. What was simply a compilation of
scores indicating an interest in (mainly English) keyboard music becomes
a collection of international importance, given the range of authors, genres
and kinds of work contained therein.

Further research confirmed this impression of a collection displaying a
sense of taste and thorough knowledge of the most advanced modern music
of the era. We can no longer talk of a mere copyist (the theory advanced by

Pamela Willetts,[12] according to which Francis Tregian might have copied out music to earn his living, seem absurd to me): the reality is that we are now able to contemplate the passion and dedication of a life's work.

I didn't write a single line for a long time. But I did decipher the 297 pieces in the *Fitzwilliam Virginal Book*, constantly asking myself why such-and-such a piece was placed before or after another, and what the music, the type of piece, the title might be expressing. I even looked into the mistakes pointed out by the editors, but the (very few) explanations I came across tended to suggest criteria other than errors, although there are clear copying mistakes. I listened to all the madrigals that interested Francis Tregian and for which I could find recordings.

The day I decided to tackle a preliminary biography, with the intention of writing a play, I seemed to glimpse a silhouette.

I started from the supposition (now become near certainty) that the *Fitzwilliam Virginal Book* and *Tregian's Anthology*[13] were collections compiled by an individual for their personal use. They are the equivalent of a modern-day music collection. The pieces are not placed in chronological order or by author, despite a clear intention to systematise – pieces by certain authors are numbered independently from the rest, for example. Even where there are sections devoted to a single author such as Farnaby, there are also pieces by this composer scattered elsewhere in the collection. Here and there, a score is attributed to two different musicians, fifty or sixty pages apart. I therefore considered that the author's intended system had sometimes been disturbed by life's ups and downs as the days passed. I felt I could conclude that, from a certain point of view, I possessed the collector's private diary. I also decided that if the pieces were there, it meant he was able to play them or have others sing them. Yet Burney writes: ' . . . some of the pieces are so difficult that it would be hardly possible to find a master in Europe who would undertake to play one of them at the end of a month's practice'.[14] Thus we have a virtuoso Francis Tregian with a romantic attachment to his country, au fait with the contemporary musical scene there, yet fully immersed in the most modern Italian music.

Finally, I arrived at the conviction, against the current of all interpretations, that in music – and doubtless in life – religion (which in those days meant politics) was not the overriding preoccupation of these collections.

It is specious to attempt to prove that the musical selection was a 'Catholic' one. Anyone could find as much proof of 'Protestant' choices, should they so wish.

It's true that these collections contain a certain number of Catholic composers. But we find Byrd or Ferrabosco (for example) in all collections of the period, whether Catholic or Protestant. Their importance is such that it transcends religious barriers. It is difficult to follow Elizabeth Cole[15] when she states, for example, that the piece entitled *Tower Hill* (composed by Giles Farnaby, a Puritan) is a homage to hanged Catholics or an allusion to Lord Lumley, a Catholic who lived close by. The slopes of Tower Hill were also inhabited by Anglicans. And the gallows which stood there dispensed death without religious discrimination.[16]

However, one notices that the closer one gets to the end of the *Fitzwilliam Virginal Book*, the more pieces there are by Farnaby, that these pieces are found only in the *Fitzwilliam Virginal Book* and that it is quite possible the compiler was on friendly terms with Farnaby. Peter Philips was Catholic, and several of his pieces are dated, which encourages some to suppose a friendship between the two men.[17] But Jan Sweelinck (at least one piece of his is also dated) was the organist of the Protestant Oude Kerk in Amsterdam. One can find many such examples pointing to sympathies in both camps.

As for the choice of pieces, the 134 dances and forty-six arrangements of popular songs in the *Fitzwilliam Virginal Book* (more than half the collection) suggest a person with a capacity for gaiety. The writing suggests a meticulous, responsible, dedicated, cultured man, a secretive yet passionate character, strong and calm. A graphologist assured me that the writing was that of a tall man. And all that is corroborated by the only appraisal of Francis Tregian the Younger that history has left us: *Molto nobile . . . di ingegno felicissimo, dotto in filosofia, in musica, et nella lingua latina.*[18]

I spent several days leafing through the manuscript of *Tregian's Anthology*, with its extremely meticulous comments in the margin neatly written in Italian, French and English. After completing this exercise, I felt as if I had shared a tête-à-tête with its author. He even let me glimpse his weaknesses: this man was undoubtedly a great musicologist and great virtuoso, but he was not a great composer. His *Dolcemente piangendo*,[19] a musical setting for a poem about unhappy love, is mediocre. That said, it formed one of the most touching moments of my reading. You see him making corrections, changes; the page still bears traces of drops, which I like to imagine were tears.

After these readings I became convinced that, although it was just possible for a man shut up in prison for ten years to compile a *Fitzwilliam Virginal Book*, it was impossible for him to have collected such a mass of madrigals and pieces for consort (some 1,550 compositions) over the same period. The discovery of scores by the same hand scattered throughout other music collections bolstered my opinion.[20] It seemed to me that only a man who had a certain freedom of movement could have found these pieces, even if some of the scores were taken from anthologies that had reached England.

I wanted to experience something of the Francis Tregian I was beginning to imagine, so I travelled to Cornwall, to Golden where he was born and from where his family had been driven out. I saw the house of his birth and the landscape of his childhood. I walked down to the banks of the River Fal at Golden Mill, where the buildings used as warehouses at the time of grandfather John Tregian still stand. I followed the river as far as Tregony, then retraced my steps as far as Creed. There, in one of the windowpanes of the little church (among the most charming in Cornwall), I discovered, intact, the last fragment of a stained-glass design showing one of the 'Jays Or' of the Tregian coat of arms. I then continued as far as Probus (on foot, as always, so I could 'feel' the countryside), where I admired the tallest church tower in Cornwall, entirely funded by great-grandfather John Tregian. Inside Probus church, I found, beneath a rug that had slipped out of place, the memorial slab of John Wolvedon and his wife Cecily, the great-grandparents whose daughter Jane would marry the first John Tregian, bringing him the estate of Wolvedon (or Golden) as a dowry.

In Truro, I discovered the Courtney Library and the collection amassed by Charles Henderson, who had roamed the countryside, combing through dusty garrets and trunks, eventually finding, among other things, a number of documents concerning the Tregian family that nobody knew existed. There are still some missing, for sure, and gaps remain, but between the Charles Henderson Collection and the Cornwall Record Office, there is much to shed new light on the doings of Francis Tregian the Younger, from his return to England in about 1606 to his disappearance in 1618.

These documents confirm what had merely been an intuition, until I read them: Francis Tregian the Younger did not spend ten years in prison, copying musical scores out of idleness. First, he had not been in prison since 1608, as had been stated. The arrest warrant, dated 27th July 1611, reads:

> James, by the grace of God, etc., etc., to the Sheriff of Cornwall – whereas Francis Tregian Esq. on 14th Nov Ad 6 King James [1608] acknowledged that he owed Ezechiell Grosse of Trelodevas in Buryan Esq £3,000 and has not paid the sum as yet, we order you to arrest the said Francis Tregian and keep him in prison till the debt be satisfied. His lands to be put under an extent for this purpose.

The document is then endorsed by Peter Edgecombe, the Sheriff, who adds: 'Francis Tregian was not found in his bailiwick, but his lands have been seized.'[21]

In Truro there are a number of business papers and contracts signed by Francis Tregian the Younger which attest to his frequent presence, even while he was theoretically in the Fleet: in 1613, 1614 and 1616. Finally, there is a will dated 12th October 1618 made out by Charles Tregian, the younger brother, as head of the family.[22] This can only mean one thing: his brother had died.

The image I'd adopted of the prisoner copying out his music by the light of a cellar window collapsed. Francis Tregian had lived in prison, with interruptions, for five or six years, maybe less. During the few days I spent at the Courtney Library, the conservators, Angela Broome and H Les Douch, suggested I read a pile of manuscripts and publications they brought to me, and that's how I learned everything we now know about Wolvedon and the Tregians, including elements of family oral tradition recorded in writing about a century after the event:

> This persecuted family suffered in his person [Francis Tregian the Younger] a further and second loss of their estates . . . Mr

> Tregian, resolving to do the best that he could, received some
> money by compounding with various parties to confirm their
> titles and thus embarked for Spain, where, as it is said, he was
> very well received on account of his own and his father's suffer-
> ings for religion, and he was made a grandee of that Kingdom.
> His posterity still flourish there with the title of Marquis of St
> Angelo. Whether this be true or not I cannot affirm, having it
> only by tradition.[23]

This tradition would have it too that he was still alive in 1630.

Upon returning to London, I was fortunate to find what must be the only
text recounting life in the Fleet between 1615 and 1620 (and recounting it
down to the last detail), the very period when Francis Tregian the Younger
was there.[24] From this I learned that, with the exception of Catholics
considered dangerous (Francis Tregian the Elder had been one of them),
the Fleet was an open prison, as long as one paid an exit fee. Between 1570
and 1666 the Catholic prisoners lived alongside insolvent debtors of all
religions and the two categories got along decently enough. According to
AL Rowse, 'If you had a little money, living at the Fleet was like being on
probation with an apartment in town.'[25] There were no limits on visiting
rights (some prisoners received up to sixty people in a day[26]), and the 'cells'
of those who could afford to pay a rent were real apartments, where rich
debtors lived with spouse, children and domestic staff.

Francis Tregian the Younger certainly spent time in prison – the afore-
mentioned document proves it – but for debts and not for religion, even
if he lived among his co-religionists once in prison.

As proof of his destitution, biographers have used a statement from
memory of the warden, Alexander Harris, according to which Francis
Tregian the Younger died while owing more than £200 for food, drink
and rent.[27] But punitive confiscation of assets did not exceed two-thirds
of a person's fortune (something that Catholic historians regularly forget
to mention), and there were a number of prisoners who lived quite lavishly
on the 'third third'. Moreover, upon reading *The Œconomy of the Fleet*
(beyond the two pages specifically devoted to Francis Tregian the Younger),
one notices that Harris complains bitterly and on several occasions about

prisoners refusing *en masse* to pay their rent for months on end, by way of protest against the bad food and other humiliations. They were effectively going on strike. One Edmond Chamberlayne owed between £1,300 and £1,400![28] Francis Tregian's debt is consequently not an indication of the state of his finances.

As one reads further in descriptions of the Fleet around 1615–1620, a key question arises: shouldn't the hypotheses be reversed? Was it possible to devote oneself to such a vast work of erudition amid the havoc that the prison seems to have been? And would not most of the collector's work have been conducted outside the Fleet? We have no concrete proof either way. But all hypotheses must be envisaged.

The final touches to the canvas I owe to a strange text, a rambling apologia for Francis Tregian the Elder, written in 1655 by Francis Plunkett, the son of Philippa Plunkett, née Tregian. This ecclesiastic, a grandson of Francis Tregian the Elder, set down in writing what was said in his family. Behind the ultra-Catholic excess of the remarks, one glimpses certain probabilities.

I believe that Francis Tregian the Elder was, from the start, a man lacking a sense of practical realities. John Tregian, his father, survived three changes of king and religion while making his affairs prosper. He died in late 1575, perhaps early 1576. Eighteen months later, his son had already committed all of the foolish actions that destined him for royal condemnation and punishment. Francis Plunkett recounts a story of 'sexual advances' that Queen Elizabeth supposedly made to Francis the Elder: since these advances were accompanied by a suggestion that he be promoted to viscount, we may wonder (assuming that the story contains a grain of truth) if the Queen hadn't instead been attempting to protect him from the persecutions she knew to be imminent by granting him a noble title. After all, the Tregians were her distant relations and Elizabeth knew how to look out for her family.[29] Also, historians generally concede that, politics aside, religion was not her primary concern: she protected Catholics (William Byrd, for example, or Lord Sussex, one of her most illustrious generals and an avowed Catholic) as much as she did Protestants. The court abounded with Catholics.

Francis Plunkett records another surprising fact which appears incongruous in the context of his account: '[In Lisbon,[30] Francis Tregian the

Elder] ... was particularly preoccupied by the persecutions in Ireland, and feared that his sons and his grandchildren were infected by the poison of heresy.'[31]

For Tregian the Elder to entertain such a fear, the faith of the sons must not have been quite as unshakeable as some would wish to describe it.

And finally, Plunkett complacently relates how the father handed out considerable sums at the very moment he had dispatched his eldest son to indebt himself up to the neck in an attempt to recover the family estates.[32] While the father uttered fine words in prison and made grand gestures in Spain, his wife and children grappled with the realities of a hostile world. What does a son do in such circumstances?

From examining the known deeds and actions of Tregian the Younger, one discerns an identification with his father (or at least with his family), combined with a desire to live an independent life.

Converting to Anglicanism (the easy solution, as his assets would have been restored to him almost automatically) seems to have been out of the question, and as for disappearing, he may have thought about it, as the family legend and the choice of the poem *Heaven and Earth* by Thomas Wyatt (the title of which he used for one of the few compositions generally attributed to him) might suggest:

> *A better proof I see that ye would have*
> *How I am dead. Therefore when ye hear tell,*
> *Believe it not although ye see my grave.*
> *Cruel, unkind! I say, 'Farewell, farewell!'*[33]

What is certain is that when he was about forty-five years old, Tregian the Younger had had enough: whether he died or whether he escaped, he disappeared. I should note in passing that his death is recorded nowhere and that, at a time when Interpol and the electronic transmission of data did not exist, it was relatively easy to disappear into thin air: we find more than one example of that in the histories of the time.

In 2001, long after this book was first published, I read a study by the musicologist Ruby Reid Thompson, based upon a microscopic examination of all the manuscripts attributed to Francis Tregian (paper, watermarks, handwriting, inks, margin notes, crossings-out, etc), which attempts to show that he could not have been the author of the collections. They would then be the work of several copyists.[34]

Of course this cannot be ruled out. But it seems to me that Thompson has been a bit hasty and turns on its head the assumptions which have sustained such research up until now. For a century, it has been said that the collector had to be the only copyist. She now declares that once she can prove (and doubtless it is possible) that he was not the sole copyist, it goes without saying that he cannot be the collector. It seems to me that this requires some justification.

The handwriting of the titles, of the few notes in the margin of the *Fitzwilliam Virginal Book* and of the words to the madrigals is similar to that in the texts which were certainly written by Tregian himself.[35] But even if we suppose it took several people to complete the copying of all the pieces in these voluminous collections, there remain the historical factors. Whatever the handwriting, the cultural and musical links between the collections, as well as the unity of the ensemble, hint that behind all this was an erudite man, a connoisseur, who was passionate about music and quite au fait with what was happening not only in England but also in Europe, someone who had spent a long time in Italy and the Low Countries, and no later than from 1606 to 1612 approximately – in short, someone corresponding to Francis Tregian, whose surname and initials are found on several occasions in the volumes.

Thompson would like to replace him with 'someone well connected and of high status who would have had access to the considerable resources necessary to assemble these four anthologies'. She considers that he cannot be the collector, as 'it seems likely that the instigator of the project came from the ranks of the English aristocracy'.[36] We are entitled to ask: why does Thompson dismiss Francis Tregian ipso facto? His ancestors bore such names as Arundell, Stanley and Grey; his mother's brother, Lord Stourton, sat in the House of Lords. His poverty was quite relative, and blown up out of all proportion by Catholic interpretations that wanted to make him a martyr at any price. In reality, Francis Tregian would have been perfectly able to commission, supervise and pay for his collections. He lacks not a single one of the characteristics ascribed to a hypothetical alternative author.

None of that excludes there being two, or even several copyists. Almost immediately, Dr David J Smith, a professor at the University of Aberdeen, contradicted Thompson, showing that her interpretations could mostly be reversed.[37] It so happens that the historical backbone of this novel coincides with Dr Smith's analysis.

To the extent of our current knowledge, there is no absolute certainty regarding the identity of the collector. But the common characteristics of the writing and, above all, the numerous historical and cultural consistencies, mean we cannot dismiss Francis Tregian. At any rate, they were enough in my eyes to make the collector this Francis who history tells us was 'of great nobility ... exceptional intelligence, learned in philosophy, in music ... '[38]

I constructed the life of Francis Tregian the Younger around these facts and these documents, starting from the premise that the active collector of the anthologies was he – the hand doing the copying seemed of secondary importance to me. I placed him in a carefully reconstructed setting, according to the known chronology, as well as that of English and European history. It is not always certain whether Tregian experienced this or that event, but the events described did take place. Some examples: Richard Mulcaster actually expounded the theories on education that I have him say; Thomas Morley really did talk about music in the way I have him do; the circumstances of the Battle of Arques were quite as I describe them. And so on. I always sought to be logical in my reconstructions, and I was inspired by memoirs from the Tregians' own time.

One should not imagine, for example, that I made Tregian a precocious child to render him even more exceptional. Childhood, in the modern sense, did not exist in the sixteenth century, and the academic education of a child of the upper classes began in the cradle. There are diverse accounts of four- and five-year-old children discussing, in Latin, their reading of texts that today's high-school students would find tough going. It was common to work from the age of fourteen (poor children from six, seven or eight), or to go off to war. Life was short for most people, so it had to be lived fast.

One might also be tempted to believe that I have given my character far too adventurous a life, or that I made him meet too many people who are now famous. While it is true that he meets some historic figures, there are many more whom he does not meet: he never sees his great-uncle by marriage, Francis Drake, despite his fame as a general, or Leicester, the Queen's favourite; and he meets neither the Careys, nor Ben Jonson, nor John Donne, nor Orlando Gibbons, nor so many others.

If he knows Monteverde, then it is because he shows an exceptional interest in him, as proven by his manuscripts. The Italian musician was twenty-seven or twenty-eight then, and not yet an important man. He was little known outside his region, and was a controversial figure for the musical authorities of the time: yet Tregian (with that intuition he so often shows in his choice of music) copied out Monteverde's first four books of madrigals.

If I imagine that Francis Tregian met Shakespeare, it is because nearly all of the music referred to in the great playwright's works can be found in the *Fitzwilliam Virginal Book*. This makes such a meeting even more probable, for the theatre was a popular pastime of all the social classes in Tudor London. One should not forget that Tregian lived during an exceptional period of European and English history: never again would England produce so many celebrated figures at once. If the reader turns to the memoirs of Robert Cary, for example, a contemporary of Tregian the Younger in both age and education,[39] they will see that Tregian's life was rather dull in comparison.

Nor should we forget that the royal court of this period was not a restricted place, the preserve of a select few. Thomas Platter, an obscure medical student from Basle visiting England for pleasure, saw Queen Elizabeth during a stay in London lasting two to three weeks.[40] Everybody went to speak to the Queen about their problems. And the Queen and her entourage received everyone: even Mary Tregian, at a point when Francis the Elder was being most cruelly persecuted. Ever the fine politician, Elizabeth would never have insulted the very noble Earls of Derby by not receiving their relations, the Tregians. A man such as Francis the Younger would have had privileged access virtually everywhere, should he have so wished.

And finally, Tudor London had barely two hundred thousand inhabitants (slightly fewer at the start of the book, slightly more at the end), living in an area a tiny fraction the size of modern London. People knew each other. The capital of the late sixteenth century was comparable to a town such as Oxford or York today.

•   •   •

Until now, Francis Tregian the Younger was only of interest to musicologists and, to a certain extent, a few Catholic historians. Nobody was sufficiently interested in the man to conduct the type of research that would see the documents concerning him examined from every angle: musical, religious, but also historical, intellectual, psychological, emotional. The theory propounded about him during the nineteenth century was not changed following the discovery of what must be considered the product of the collector's chief activity, whether or not that collector be Francis Tregian: his collections of madrigals. Nobody took the trouble to correct the dates of his imprisonment, despite there being at least two documents which suggest the earliest and latest dates.[41]

I have taken liberties in *Tregian's Ground*,[42] but my tale is based on historical research that was as thorough as possible, even though it was not exhaustive. I investigated the facts, like all the commentators who came before me. Working at a distance of four centuries, there are certainly points where I have made errors of perspective, but unlike the authors of most of the previous studies, I have never attempted to place the documents at the service of either a Catholic or a Protestant 'truth'.

And above all, I affirm that mine is a free interpretation based on the information reported here. Such frankness is sorely lacking in Helen Trudgian, Boyan and Lamb, and Elizabeth Cole, who freely let their imaginations run wild according to their personal convictions, while claiming to establish historical truths.

By being sensitive to his preferences and choices, taking into account the available historical information as much as I could, and trying to evoke a Francis Tregian of flesh and blood, I attempted (subjectively, that goes without saying) to give him back a voice, to reconstruct this man caught between two sensibilities, two cultures, two religions, two worlds, just as one reconstructs an ancient monument based on its layout and its ruins.

The author of what we might one day call *The Tregian Virginal Book* (one of the most important music collections of its era), the passionate collector, the enlightened connoisseur of these anthologies deserves to be plucked from oblivion after four centuries, even if it is only to make a literary character of him.

ANNE CUNEO, ZURICH, 1994

NOTES TO

'LOOKING FOR FRANCIS TREGIAN'

A reading group guide written by Anne Cuneo is available for free download from And Other Stories' website: www.andotherstories.org.

1   Opinions differ as to the correct pronunciation, but the most common are 'TRADJ-an' or 'TREDJ-an'.

2   The term 'virginal' refers to either of two rectangular keyboard instruments: the 'muselaar', where the keyboard is placed to the right and the strings are plucked in the middle, and the 'spinet', where the keyboard is placed to the left and the strings are plucked a quarter of the way down their length. Any music for virginal can also be played on the harpsichord, which was a luxury instrument, whereas the spinet and muselaar were the more affordable instruments of the people, before they were supplanted by the piano. Virginals were to be found all over Europe.

3   The *Fitzwilliam Virginal Book*, two volumes, Leipzig and London, 1894–1899. A paperback reprint appeared in New York in 1979 and is still in print. The manuscript is in the Fitzwilliam Museum, Cambridge, shelf number 32.9.29 Mus MS 168.

4   Edward W Naylor, *An Elizabethan Virginal Book,* pp 4 and 112.

5   William Chappell, *The Ballad Literature and Popular Music of the Olden Time*, London, 1859.

6   John Alexander Fuller-Maitland and William Barclay Squire.

7   Fuller-Maitland and Squire, vol i, p viii. Their conclusion regarding Tregian is cautiously worded.

8   Helen Trudgian, *Histoire d'une famille anglaise au XVIe siècle: les Tregian*, Paris, 1934. This very casually researched doctoral thesis mentions some studies of the Gregorian music of Francis Tregian. It would appear that Helen Trudgian never saw the *Fitzwilliam Virginal Book*. She also confuses Francis Tregian with his younger brother Charles on several occasions.

9   PA Boyan and GR Lamb, *Francis Tregian: Cornish recusant*, London, 1955.

10   MS Egerton 3665, called *Tregian's Anthology*.

11   New York Public Library, coll. Drexel, No 4302 (*The Sambrooke MS*).

12   Pamela Willetts, 'Tregian's Part-Books', in *The Musical Times*, 1963.

13   See notes 3, 11 and 12.

14 Charles Burney, *A General History of Music*, vol iii, p 14, quoted by Fuller-Maitland and Squire, p V.

15 In 'Seven Problems of the Fitzwilliam Virginal Book', in *Proceedings of the Royal Musical Association*, vol lxxix, 1952–1953, pp 51–63.

16 John Stow describes the place in detail on several occasions in his *A Survey of London*, 1603.

17 Charles van den Borren, *Les origines de la musique de clavier en Angleterre*, 1912, p 21, note 1.

18 'Of great nobility . . . exceptional intelligence, learned in philosophy, in music and in the Latin language' (in *Letters and Memorials of William, Cardinal Allen*, 1882, p 374, transcription of a list of people in the service of Cardinal Allen in 1594).

19 Nos 435 and 436 of *Tregian's Anthology,* pp 401–402, signed 'FT', may be consulted in the facsimile published in New York in 1988 (ed Frank D'Accone).

20 Willetts describes them in her article 'Tregian's Part-Books', in *The Musical Times* (see note 13), and even states: 'The surviving section of Tregian's work is, alas, only pages 97–140 (with a blank leaf numbered 141) of more extensive volumes.' It is therefore quite probable that we are not yet aware of all the scores attributed to Tregian, although the current total is around two thousand.

21 Henderson Collection, Truro, No HC/2/498.

22 Henderson Collection, Truro, No HC/2/142.

23 Davies Gilbert and Thomas Tonkin, *The Parochial History of Cornwall*, 1838, p 361. Tonkin, who wrote these lines in the 1730s, was a descendant of the Tregians: ' . . . being myself descended from this gentleman's [Francis Tregian the Elder] sister, Jane Tregian, married to Thomas Tonkin of Trevaunance . . . ' (ibid, p 358).

24 *The Œconomy of the Fleet*, the memoir of Alexander Harris, Warden, written around 1620, published with an introduction and notes by Reverend Augustus Jessopp, London 1879.

25 Interview with the author, 28th May 1991.

26 *The Œconomy of the Fleet*, p 62.

27 *The Œconomy of the Fleet*, pp 140–141.

28 *The Œconomy of the Fleet*, pp 120–121.

29 Even if the Tregians were in disgrace, nobody forgot that Mrs Tregian (Francis the Younger's mother) was niece and cousin to the Derbys, who were among Elizabeth's potential legitimate heirs. The Derbys and the Stuarts shared a (great-) grandfather with the queen: King Henry VII Tudor.

30 The city was held by Spain at the time. Francis Tregian the Elder settled here in 1606 after being freed, and died here in September 1608. His wife and the rest of his family did not accompany him to Lisbon.

31 Francis Plunkett, *Heroum Speculum*, 1655, in *Catholic Record Society*, vol xxxii, 1952, pp 30–31.

3 2 'He was most generous to the poor, and aided them in their needs with steadfast charity.' In *Heroum Speculum*, pp 30–31.

3 3 Thomas Wyatt, *Poems, 1557–1578*, 1978 (ed RA Rebholz), and *Fitzwilliam Virginal Book*, No CV, *Heaven and Earth*, vol i, p 405.

3 4 Ruby Reid Thompson, 'Francis Tregian the Younger as Music Copyist: A Legend and an Alternative View', *Music and Letters*, vol lxxxii, No 1. (Feb 2001), pp. 1–31.

3 5 See p 246 for a facsimile of one of the documents (No HC/2/27, dated 18th March 1610, Henderson Collection, Truro) which was used to identify Francis Tregian in 1952. Unlike his practice in other contracts, Tregian was not content simply to sign this one: it is entirely in his hand.

3 6 Ruby Reid Thompson, 'The "Tregian" Manuscripts: a study of their compilation', in *British Library Journal*, vol xviii, 1992, p 203.

3 7 David J Smith, 'A legend? Francis Tregian the Younger as music copyist', *Musical Times* 143 (2002).

3 8 See note 20.

3 9 *Memoirs of Robert Cary, Earl of Monmouth*, London, 1903.

4 0 *Thomas Platter's Travels in England, 1599*, London, 1937, pp 228–229.

4 1 The arrest warrant (Henderson Collection, Truro, No HC/2/498), and the will of the younger brother, Charles, (Henderson Collection, Truro, No HC/2/142).

4 2 Any knowledgeable inhabitant of Switzerland's Vaud region will have remarked, for example, that the church in Echallens did not have an organ. My major twisting of history is having sent Francis Tregian to the Gros-de-Vaud. But my choice of Echallens was not an arbitrary one: at the time, it had one of the few churches in Europe officially attended by both Catholics and Protestants.

SOURCES

WRITTEN SOURCES

Anonymous

> *Brief . . . against Francis Tregian* (the Elder), undated (late sixteenth century), British Library, London

Anonymous

> *The great and long sufferings for the Catholic Faith of Mr Francis Tregian* (the Elder), 1593, St Mary's College, Oscott

Douch, H Les

> *The Grosse Family in Norfolk and Cornwall*, undated, Courtney Library (Henderson Collection); County Record Office, Truro

Salisbury's Manuscripts

> Documents from the archives of Robert Cecil, Hatfield House

Stanley, Jane

> *The Glory of Golden*, manuscript, circa 1954, Courtney Library, Truro

State papers

> *Domestic Series, Elizabeth, James I*, Public Record Office, London

Tregian, Francis

> *The Fitzwilliam Virginal Book*, original manuscript, Fitzwilliam Museum, Cambridge
>
> *Tregian's Anthology*, original manuscript, British Library, London
>
> *The Sambrooke MS*, original manuscript, New York Public Library, New York
>
> *Tregian's Part Books*, original manuscripts, isolated scores, Christ Church, Oxford

Tregian and Wolvedon families

> *Papers, contracts of sale, court rulings, valuations, wills* (fifteenth to seventeenth centuries), Courtney Library, Truro

PRINTED WORKS

The following lists only the principal and most pertinent works that I consulted.

A date after a solidus signifies a reprint of the original edition.

Ackermann, R

> *The History of the Colleges of Winchester, Eton and Westminster: With the Charter House, the Schools of St Paul's, Merchant Taylors', Harrow and Rugby, and the Free-school of Christ's Hospital*, 1816

Allen, William
  The Letters and Memorials of William, Cardinal Allen, 1882
Arbeau, Thoinot
  Orchesography, 1948/1967 (in English; the original French *Orchésographie* (Langres,
    1589) was republished in Geneva in 1979)
Arnold, Denis
  Monteverdi, 1975
Ariès, Philippe
  L'enfant et la vie familiale sous l'Ancien Régime, 1960
Babaiantz, Christophe
  L'organisation bernoise des transports en pays romand, 1961
Bates, ES
  Touring in 1600, 1911/1987
Besant, Walter
  Besant's History of London (vol i: *The Tudors*, vol ii: *The Stuarts*) 1903/1990
Boussinesq, Georges, and Laurent, Gustave
  Histoire de Reims depuis les origines jusqu'à nos jours, 1933
Boyan, PA, and Lamb, GR
  Francis Tregian: Cornish recusant, 1955
Boyce, Charles
  Shakespeare A to Z, 1990
Braudel, Fernand
  Les structures du quotidien: le possible et l'impossible, 1979
Burdet, Jacques
  La Musique dans le Pays de Vaud sous le régime bernois, 1963
Carew, Richard
  The Survey of Cornwall, 1602
Carey (or Cary), Robert
  Memoirs of Robert Cary, Earl of Monmouth, 1759/1903
Colony (Jean-François de Cecier)
  Briève instruction de musique, 1617
Cecil, David
  The Cecils of Hatfield House, 1973
Chappell, William
  The Ballad Literature and Popular Music of the Olden Time, 1859/1961
Clancy, Thomas
  *Papist Pamphleteers: the Allen-Persons party and the political thought of the Counter-
    Reformation in England*, 1964
Cole, Elizabeth
  'In Search of Francis Tregian' (in *Music and Letters*, vol xxxiii), 1952

Cole, Elizabeth
> 'Seven Problems of the Fitzwilliam Virginal Book' (in *Proceedings of the Royal Musical Association*, vol lxxix), 1952–1953
>
> 'L'anthologie de madrigaux et de musique instrumentale pour ensembles de Francis Tregian' (in *Musique et poésie au XVIe siècle*, study by the CNRS), 1955

Collective
> *Echallens et ses églises*, 1965

Constant, J-M
> *Les Guise*, 1987

Cunningham, Walker
> *The Keyboard Music of John Bull*, 1984

Dricot, Michel
> *Deux artisans rémois de la musique et du chant religieux: Jehan Pussot et Gérard de La Lobe* (in *Mélanges d'histoire rémoise*), 1979

Dumas, Alexandre
> *Les Trois Mousquetaires* (Schopp annotated edition), 1991

Dupraz, E
> *Introduction de la réforme par le 'Plus' dans le bailliage d'Orbe-Echallens*, 1915–1916

Edwards, Francis
> *Guy Fawkes: the real story of the Gunpowder Plot?*, 1969

Einstein, Alfred
> *The Italian Madrigal*, 1949

Erlanger, Philippe
> *La vie quotidienne sous Henri IV*, 1958

Farnaby, Giles
> 'Keyboard Music' (in *Musica Britannica*, vol xxiv), 1965 (ed Richard Marlow)

Febvre, Lucien
> *Le problème de l'incroyance au XVIe siècle*, 1942

Fellowes, Edmund H
> *William Byrd*, 1948
>
> *The English Madrigal Composers*, 1948

Finlay, Roger
> *Population and Metropolis: the demography of London 1580–1650*, 1981

Fleay, Frederick Gard
> *A Chronicle History of the London Stage 1559–1642*, 1890

Gilbert, CS
> *An Historical Survey of Cornwall*, 1817/1820

Gilbert, Davies, and Tonkin, Thomas
> *The Parochial History of Cornwall*, 1838

Graham, Winston
> *The Spanish Armadas*, 1972

518 ANNE CUNEO

Hamilton Jenkin, AK
  Cornwall and Its People, 1945/numerous reprints
Harrison, GB
  The Elizabethan Journals, 1933
  The Jacobean Journals, 1934
Hauser, Henri
  La prépondérance espagnole (1559–1660), 1933/1973
Hawkins, Sir John
  A General History of the Science and Practice of Music, 1776
Haynes, Alan
  Robert Cecil, First Earl of Salisbury, 1989
  Invisible Power: the Elizabethan secret services, 1992
Henderson, Charles
  A Survey of Cornwall, 1930
  Essays in Cornish History, 1935
Hill, Christopher
  The Century of Revolution 1603–1714, 1961
Hugger, Paul
  Rebelles et hors-la-loi en Suisse, 1977
Jaquemard, André
  'Le régime des deux Etats souverains à Echallens' (in *Revue d'histoire vaudoise*), 1936
Jessopp, Augustus, ed
  The Œconomy of the Fleet: an apologeticall answeare of Alexander Harris (late Warden there), 1879
Killiam, Tim, and Tulleners, Hans
  Amsterdam Canal Guide, 1978
Knox, Thomas Francis
  Records of the English Catholics under the Penal Laws, 1878–1882
Kratochvil, Milos
  Hollar's Journey on the Rhine (1636), 1965
La Boétie, Etienne de
  Œuvres politiques, 1578/1963
Le Huray, Peter
  Music and the Reformation in England (1549–1660), 1978
MacElroy, RA
  Blessed Cuthbert Mayne, 1929
Marlot, Guillaume
  Histoire de la ville, cité et université de Reims, 1843
Montaigne, Michel de
  Journal de Voyage, 1895/1980
  Les Essais (annotations by Pierre Villey), 1929

Morley, Thomas
  A Plain and Easy Introduction to Practical Music, 1597/1952
Mulcaster, Richard
  Positions Concerning the Training Up of Children, 1581/1888 (ed RH Quick)
  The First Part of the Elementarie, 1582/1925 (ed ET Campagnac)
Naylor, Edward W
  Shakespeare and Music, 1896/1931
  An Elizabethan Virginal Book, 1904
  The Poets and Music, 1928
Neighbour, Oliver
  The Consort and Keyboard Music of William Byrd, 1978
Newman, Peter R
  Atlas of the English Civil War, 1985
Norden, John
  The Survey of Cornwall (Cornwall in 1610), 1728
O'Brian, Grant
  Ruckers: a harpsichord and virginal building tradition, 1987
Olivier, Eugène
  Médecine et santé dans le Pays de Vaud, des origines jusqu'à la fin du XVIIe siècle, 1962
Page, William
  'Tin Mining' (in *The Victoria history of the county of Cornwall*), 1906
Parker, Geoffrey
  The Thirty Years' War, 1984
  The Dutch Revolt, 1985
Paquier, Richard
  Histoire d'un village vaudois, 1972
Pinchbeck, Ivy, and Hewitt, Margaret
  Children in English Society, 1969
Platter, Thomas
  Tagebücher, 1984
Plunkett, Francis
  Heroum Speculum, 1655 (in *Catholic Record Society*, vol xxxii, 1952)
Polwhele, Richard
  The Civil and Military History of Cornwall, 1808
Price, David C
  Patrons and Musicians of the English Renaissance, 1982
Prockter, Adrian, and Taylor, Robert
  The A to Z of Elizabethan London, 1979
Pussot, Jehan
  Le journalier (1564–1625), circa 1850

Rowse, AL
   Richard Grenville of the 'Revenge', 1937
   Tudor Cornwall, 1941/1990
   The England of Elizabeth, 1950
   William Shakespeare: a biography, 1963
   The Elizabethan Renaissance, 1971 and 1972
   Eminent Elizabethans, 1983
   Court and Country, 1987
   The Little Land of Cornwall, 1986/1993
Schama, Simon
   The Embarrassment of Riches: an interpretation of Dutch culture in the Golden Age, 1987
Schoenbaum, Samuel
   William Shakespeare: a compact documentary life, 1978/1987
Schofield, B, and Dart, RT
   'Tregian's Anthology' (in *Music and Letters*, vol xxxii), 1951
Schofield, John
   The Building of London, 1993
Shakespeare, William
   Complete Works (the Alexander text), 1951
Sidney, Philip
   A History of the Gunpowder Plot, 1904
Simon, Joan
   Education and Society in Tudor England, 1966
Stone, Lawrence
   The Family, Sex and Marriage in England 1500–1800, 1977
Stourton Mowbray, CBJ
   History of the Noble House of Stourton, 1899
Stow, John
   A Survey of London, 1603/1972
   The Chronicles of London, 1635
Stoye, John
   English Travellers Abroad, 1989
Taylor, MT
   'Francis Tregian, His Family and Possessions' (in *Journal of the Royal Institution of Cornwall*), 1910
Thompson, Craig R
   Schools in Tudor England, 1958
Thomson, Peter
   Shakespeare's Professional Career, 1992

Tregian, Francis
The Fitzwilliam Virginal Book (ed Fuller-Maitland and Squire) 1899/1979
Tregian's Anthology (facsimiles of the originals, ed D'Accone), 1988

Treswell, Ralph, and Schofield, John
The London Surveys of Ralph Treswell (circa 1600), 1987

Trevelyan, George M
England under the Stuarts, 1904/1946
English Social History, 1944/1986

Trevor-Roper, Hugh
Catholics, Anglicans and Puritans, 1987

Trudgian, Helen
Histoire d'une famille anglaise au XVIe siècle: les Tregian, 1934

Underdown, David
Revel, Riot & Rebellion: popular politics and culture in England 1603–1660, 1989
Fire from Heaven, 1992

van den Borren, Charles
Les origines de la musique de clavier dans les Pays-Bas, 1913/1977
Les sources de la musique de clavier en Angleterre, 1912

Vuilleumier, Henri
Histoire de l'Eglise réformée, 4 vols, 1927–1933

Wedgwood, C Veronica
The Thirty Years War, 1938/1992

Willetts, Pamela
'Tregian's Part-Books' (in *The Musical Times*), 1963

Wilson, HB
The History of the Merchant Taylors' School, 1860

Wraight, John
The Swiss and the British, 1987

Wyatt, Thomas
The Complete Poems, 1557–1578/1978 (ed RA Rebholz)

Zumthor, Paul
La vie quotidienne en Hollande au temps de Rembrandt, 1959/1990

A DISCOGRAPHY

It would be futile to attempt a complete discography, for there are innumerable recordings of music from *Tregian's Ground*, some of which may no longer be available, while new ones are always appearing. By way of a soundtrack, I prefer to list some of the recordings of scores from Francis Tregian's manuscripts that I liked to listen to as I wrote.

William Byrd: Consort Music
   (The Consort of Musicke), LP, L'Oiseau-Lyre/Decca
William Byrd: My Ladye Nevells Booke
   (Complete, by Christopher Hogwood), CD (three), L'Oiseau-Lyre
William Byrd / Orlando Gibbons
   (Glenn Gould on the piano), LP, CBS
Dowland: The First Booke of Songes
   (The Consort of Musicke), CD, L'Oiseau-Lyre
'Draw on Sweet Night' English Madrigals
   (The Hilliard Ensemble), CD, CDC
Elizabethan Songs and Dances
   (Colin Tilney on the harpsichord), CD, Radio Canada
16th Century English Harpsichord and Virginal Music
   (Trevor Pinnock), LP, CRD
English Virginalists
   (Zuzana Růžičková), CD, Orfeo
Giles Farnaby
   (Pierre Hantaï), CD, Adda
Giles Farnaby: Virginal Music
   (Bradford Tracey), CD, FSM Adagio
Fitzwilliam Virginal Book (Excerpts)
   (Ton Koopman), CD, Capriccio
Gesualdo: Principe di Venosa
   (Madrigals Collegium Vocale Köln), CD, CBS
Lassus: Chansons et Moresche
   (Ensemble Clément Janequin), CD, Harmonia Mundi

Claudio Monteverde: Madrigals Book II
 (Collegium Vocale Köln), CD, CBS
Claudio Monteverdi: Terzo Libro dei Madrigali, 1592
 (The Consort of Musicke), CD, L'Oiseau-Lyre
Claudio Monteverdi: Quarto Libro dei Madrigali
 (The Consort of Musicke), CD, L'Oiseau-Lyre
Joyne Hands: Music of Thomas Morley
 (The Musicians of Swanne Alley), CD, VC
Music from the Time of Elizabeth I
 (The Academy of Ancient Music, Christopher Hogwood), CD, L'Oiseau-Lyre
Music for Virginal
 (Bradford Tracey), CD, FSM Adagio
O Mistress Mine: A Collection of English Lute Songs
 (Frederick Urrey / Ronn McFarlane), CD, Dorian
Peter Philips: Consort Music
 (The Parley of Instruments), CD, Hyperion
Jan P Sweelinck: Musique pour orgue
 (Roland Götz), CD, FCD
Shakespeare Songs
 (Deller Consort), CD, Harmonia Mundi
Francis Tregian's Collection
 (Martha Cook on the harpsichord), CD, Vanguard Classics
Watkins Ale: Music of the English Renaissance
 (Baltimore Consort), CD, Dorian

ACKNOWLEDGEMENTS

Before writing, I roamed Cornwall, then the south of England, the country of Vaud, France and Holland. I first heard of the piskies in a Cornish pub, of virginal-building in a dusty back room in Amsterdam and of the legendary lime tree of Echallens during a local storytelling evening. And so on. I should first, then, like to thank collectively the people of Cornwall, Vaud, Holland, France and London. I would moreover like to thank individually all those who helped me with their advice, hospitality, time and other kinds of support, both material and moral.

In London: Donald Adamson, Meg Henderson, Robert McCrum, Ann Saunders, Lady Gwen and Sir Roy Shaw, Michael Walsh and Dusty Wesker. In Birmingham: musicologist Nigel Fortune. In Cornwall: Ruth and Norman Jefferies of St Ewe, AL Rowse of St Austell and H Les Douch of Truro. In Reims: Mr and Mrs Patrick De Mouy. In Maintenon and Metz: Martha Cook. In Amsterdam: Patrick Ayrton, Titus Crijnen, Joël Katzman, Naomi Rubinstein, Wim Schut and Debra Solomon. In Switzerland: Roger Cuneo and Christiane Tornier of Geneva, Marianne Kuchler and Tiziana Mona of Zurich, Françoise and René Schnorf of Dommartin (close to Echallens).

Warmest thanks to all those who, with faultless patience, researched and found for me (or with me) texts that were exceedingly hard to track down, without which the writing of this book would not have been possible. I mean the librarians of the following institutions: Cantonal and University Library, Lausanne; Carnegie Library, Reims; Central Library (Zentralbibliothek), Zurich, with special thanks to the Maps and Music departments; British Library, London (Reading Room and Manuscripts collection); Catholic Central Library, Farnborough; Courtney Library (Henderson Archive), Truro; and Museumsgesellschaft, Zurich. Also Gérald Donnet, bookseller at the Librairie de la Louve in Lausanne, and May & May, music booksellers in Shaftesbury.

I also thank the management and staff of the museums who indulged my barrage of questions: Musical instruments collection of the Royal Conservatory of Brussels; Falmouth Art Gallery; Plantin-Moretus Museum, Antwerp; Rubens House, Antwerp; Amsterdam Museum; Carnavalet Museum (Musée historique de la ville de Paris); Le Vergeur Museum (Musée Hôtel Le Vergeur), Reims; Jura Museum of Art and History (Musée jurassien d'art et d'histoire), Delémont (Switzerland); Swiss National Museum, Zurich; Vleeshuis Museum (musical instruments), Antwerp; Museum of London; Victoria and Albert Museum, London.

With gratitude to François Cuneo for his essential IT support.

My thanks to Pro Helvetia, whose financial help enabled me to make numerous trips across Europe on the trail of Francis Tregian.

Should I have forgotten anyone, I request their forgiveness.

ANNE CUNEO

The translators gratefully acknowledge the valuable assistance received from Patrick Ayrton, Alan Brown, Christopher Clarke, Iain Fenlon, William van Geest, Christopher Hogwood, Joel Katzman, Anthony Sidey, Alice Siegel, Joseph Spooner, Mike Taylor.

We are especially grateful to the Looren Translation House (www.looren.net/) for their award of a Max Geilinger Grant with associated residency.

ROLAND GLASSER & LOUISE ROGERS LALAURIE

Dear readers,

We rely on subscriptions from people like you to tell these other stories –
the types of stories most publishers consider too risky to take on.

Our subscribers don't just make the books physically happen. They also
help us approach booksellers, because we can demonstrate that our books
already have readers and fans. And they give us the security to publish in
line with our values, which are collaborative, imaginative and 'shamelessly
literary'.

All of our subscribers:

—receive a first-edition copy of each of the books they subscribe to
—are thanked by name at the end of these books
—are warmly invited to contribute to our plans and choice of future books

BECOME A SUBSCRIBER, OR GIVE A SUBSCRIPTION TO A FRIEND

Visit andotherstories.org/subscribe to become part of an alternative approach
to publishing.

Subscriptions are:

£20 for two books per year
£35 for four books per year
£50 for six books per year

OTHER WAYS TO GET INVOLVED

If you'd like to know about upcoming events and reading groups (our
foreign-language reading groups help us choose books to publish, for
example) you can:

—join the mailing list at: andotherstories.org/join-us
—follow us on Twitter: @andothertweets
—join us on Facebook: facebook.com/AndOtherStoriesBooks
—follow our blog: Ampersand